Praise for the Silken Magic series:

"An alternate Renaissance Italy is the setting for this opulent tale of court intrigue and dark magics. This excellent first novel presents engaging characters in a well-realized world."

—*Locus*

"The sequel is as gripping as the predecessor, and the term richly textured is also applicable to this superior historical fantasy."

—*Booklist*

"An alternate Sicily is splendidly revealed, as seen through the eyes of new voice ElizaBeth Gilligan. Robust characterizations, multiple storylines and clever delivery of snippets create a satisfying tale."

—*RT Reviews*

"ElizaBeth Gilligan has created a fascinating realm that readers will want to revisit."

—Books n Bytes

"ElizaBeth Gilligan's first book deftly weaves fantasy, herbalism, history, romance and murder into a complex and intriguing pattern."

—Rambles Magazine

SOVEREIGN SILK

ELIZABETH GILLIGAN'S
SPELLBINDING FANTASY SERIES
FROM DAW BOOKS,
SILKEN MAGIC:

MAGIC'S SILKEN SNARE
THE SILKEN SHROUD
SOVEREIGN SILK

SOVEREIGN SILK

Silken Magic #3

ElizaBeth Gilligan

DAW BOOKS, INC.
DONALD A. WOLLHEIM, FOUNDER
375 Hudson Street, New York, NY 10014
ELIZABETH R. WOLLHEIM
SHEILA E. GILBERT
PUBLISHERS
www.dawbooks.com

Cover art by Matthew Stawicki.

Cover design by G-Force Design.

Map by Brook West.

DAW Book Collectors No. 1760.

Published by DAW Books, Inc.
375 Hudson Street, New York, NY 10014.

First Printing, June 2017
1 2 3 4 5 6 7 8 9

DAW TRADEMARK REGISTERED
U.S. PAT. AND TM. OFF. AND FOREIGN COUNTRIES
—MARCA REGISTRADA
HECHO EN U.S.A.

PRINTED IN THE U.S.A.

Every once in a while an author is lucky enough to meet their readers and develop a relationship with them; that has been my great fortune, and I dedicate this book to Bert Ricci, Carol Gray-Ricci, and Joey Shoji. I'd also like to dedicate this book to my longest-term fan, my brother, Dana Chris Murphy.

ACKNOWLEDGMENTS

I'd like to begin this novel with my humble thanks to my readers and my editor, Sheila Gilbert of DAW Books, all of whom waited too long for this book. My apologies. I plead health. For those of you new to the series, I say "Welcome" and refer you to the "What Has Gone Before . . ." in the opening of the story, which abbreviates the first two novels without diminishing your enjoyment of them should you decide to read them, which, of course, I hope you will.

Many people need to be thanked for their help in getting me writing again and first is, of course, my family, who nursed me through my two strokes and put up with me, then were ignored when the writing bug bit me again and I wrote six books of this size in fourteen months. I hope all of them will see the light of day.

Once I was writing again, fellow writers: Kevin Andrew Murphy, Patricia H. MacEwen, Lillian Csernica, Brook and Julia West, and dedicated reader/commentators Carole Newsome-Smith and Jenni Sherriff all lent me their time and various areas of expertise to make this the best book it could be before Sheila's guiding hand made it altogether a much better book.

And to my brother, Dana, who encouraged (nagged <G>) me to get back to my writing.

Introduction

THE Romani of this series are thoroughly fictionalized because, for one, those in our world have never found a homeland where they were free to establish themselves without social and political injustices to this very day. Over the years, they've been known as 'Little Egyptians' which became 'Egyptians' and then the popular 'Gypsies,' while they call themselves Romany (Latinized for my purposes to Romani), which often gets them confused with Romanians. For this reason, as they developed a written language in the late 20th century, they added a second r to become Rromani (or Rromanians, less frequently used). I don't use the second (Rr) in the novels because it was not used in the 17th century.

Even today, you'll find the Rromany working the old jobs of tinkers, makers of clothespins (a dying, if not already dead, profession), and purveyors of horses. Finding honest work, like the Romani of Tyrrhia, is especially hard since traditional education has been a low priority for previous generations, but more importantly since employers have been reluctant to give them honest work. So this culture, for centuries, has been excluded and demonized. Their children are still being taken from them by the establishment and the richness of their culture remains underappreciated. As they become more "sedentary" (the term for non-mobile Roma communities) as renters and, on occasion, land owners, they are becoming more "normalized"—they are losing their culture. Alas, "reality TV" has also found the Rromany. I hope that one finds a little more truth in my pages than on any of these television shows.

By the way, an interesting bit of info about the chapter epigraphs: *none* of the quotes are from 1684, the year this story begins, or after—an extra challenge I put on myself for the novel.

Another important note, at one point in the novel, Luciana uses the fact that she is nursing as a method of birth control. Just to be clear, this is *not* effective birth control, and in fact, Luciana learns this the hard way—but that's another book.

As a military brat attending well over a dozen schools and always being the outsider—until I went to Fort Knox and spent my high school years surrounded by fellow U.S. Army brats—I identified with the Romani and read voraciously about them. At Fort Knox, I made many many friends, one of them Lucia Fitzmorris (now Woods), and all those years ago Luciana was born. Seeking an outlet, she found it in "Vendetta in Silk," which later became *Magic's Silken Snare*.

I write about an average of fourteen hours a day, ten on Christmas, five on my anniversary. I love it. I can't not write. I also do other things: I participate in the Society for Creative Anachronism, I do fine needlework, I read voraciously (and some of that counts toward writing since I am a compulsive researcher). I manage a house with six cats, three dogs, and two large human males; one is Doug, my husband of thirty-four years, and the other is my son, who's looking to get married when he finds the right woman (intelligent with a good soul and fighting spirit)—and then there's the occasional project day with our daughter's daughters.

Basically, I live a very full, rich, and creative life with all sorts of regular adventures which find their way into my text. So thank you, readers, for enriching my life by giving me an audience to play out my dramas for, and I hope to educate while entertaining you!

ElizaBeth Gilligan

ElizaBeth Gilligan can be found on her web page (elizabethgilligan.net), on Facebook, and followed on Amazon's author page. She has also recently edited a collection of eccentric and excellent stories featuring intrigue around tea which can be found online as Alterna-Teas. *Happy reading, folks!!!*

"A State is not a mere society, having a common place, established for the prevention of mutual crime and for the sake of exchange . . . Political society exists for the sake of noble actions, and not of mere companionship."

—Aristotle

Tyrrhia
rome
naples
salerno
capri
ipari
lipan
citteaurorea
palazzo
volcano del porto
dragorione
d'orlando
stretto d'messina
gulf of
palermo
palermo
defaria
messina
reggio
d'calabra
fata
woods
niscemi
romani
caves &
orchards
modica
0
100
miles
©2016 Brook West

Preface

WHAT *has gone before . . .*

Alessandra, the *Araunya di Cayesmengro*, a Romani merchant princess, comes to court to find a husband and is persuaded by the White Queen, who is desperate to have more children, to help her cast a spell in secret for that purpose. The queen, however, limited by laws against spells being cast upon the royal family, extends the reaches of her spell to all Tyrrhia. In the ensuing court intrigues, Alessandra is murdered by Princess Bianca and those in league with her.

Luciana, elder sister of Alessandra, Duchessa di Drago and *Araunya di Cayesmengri* arrives at court to perform the funeral rites practiced by their Romani people. She discovers Alessandra's body gone, stolen by Cardinal delle Torre and Brother Tomasi who took the body and released her Romani spirit known as a *mulló*—half-ghost, half-demon—to use her in their magic. Luciana uncovers Princess Bianca's treachery in killing her sister and takes her revenge.

Alessandra's affianced, Maggiore Mandero di Montago, and his men of the Queen's Escalade and the priest, Gabera, go in search of Alessandra's stolen body, having only the young woman's shroud to tie her spirit to them. They uncover the magic used by Cardinal delle Torre who took Alessandra's body, releasing her Romani spirit to use her in their magic.

Ultimately, Mandero frees Alessandra's spirit and body and performs the funeral rites, himself disappearing into her burning *vardo* wagon. The maggiore's men arrest

Brother Tomasi who has worked in league with the cardinal, but find Cardinal delle Torre dead, killed by the spirits he had enslaved to work his magic. They return to the palazzo, without their maggiore, but with Brother Tomasi as their prisoner.

I

"Men in great places are thrice servants: servants of the sovereign or State, servants of fame, and servants of business."

—Francis Bacon

10 d'Novembre, 1684

WITH the skill of an accomplished swordsman, the White King dodged the crystal decanter hurled at his head. The missile shattered against the wall. Shards of glass and red wine flew everywhere, the ruinous results of the princess' ill-temper. Even now King Alban saw her looking for something else to fling at him.

Fighting the urge to lay hands on his long-estranged cousin, the king turned instead to her husband, the whippet-like man seated, insouciant, in one of the cane chairs. "Pierro! Control your wife!"

"I'm not subject to the laws of the harem anymore!" Princess Ortensia hissed, seizing the paperweight.

With a beleaguered sigh, Prince Pierro rose and caught his wife's sleeve. "Perhaps His Majesty will be more receptive to a less lethal argument, *mia bella*. Another time, we can only hope that he will be more sensitive to our cause."

Just outside the door, Strozzini, Alban's bodyguard, cleared his throat loudly. "Majesty, is all well?"

Alban looked at Ortensia who still seethed, but it was to her right hand that his attention was drawn. She held herself in that instinctively protective fashion of a woman bearing seed. Was it possible that she could be bearing the deMedici's child so soon? They'd married in *Agosto*, four months ago. Until this time, the princess' gowns had hidden her swelling middle, but now it was visible.

Did Pierro's fortune really run so well, or had the Turkish Sultan who held Ortensia for the past seventeen years returned her already pregnant with a sixth child by him?

In either case, clearly, this coming year was to be prime for Tyrrhia's population, which swelled portentously with the uncanny number of expectant mothers among the nobility. Alban's sources indicated that the swell included all that was Tyrrhian. Everywhere and in everything, Tyrrhia ripened and bore fruit well beyond normal expectations.

With his own beloved Idala in the very condition the princess now displayed, Alban compelled his own irritation to fade. As he knew from his wife's many pregnancies, women's emotions were at the mercy of their condition.

Ortensia shot the White King a venomous glare and pushed away from the desk. Alban knew this discussion would not be over until she had her way. She meant the *trono*, Tyrrhia's throne, to be hers.

Alban met the princess and her prince at the door, gracious as a steward, ushering them from his private offices. Strozzini stood to one side, allowing them access to the stairs. Alban watched Ortensia and Pierro descend, the bastarde deMedici prince overly solicitous of his stolen bride. The prince's pretty demonstrations sickened Alban. Pierro pretended at emotions other men, those Alban respected, genuinely felt for their wives.

Content that the interlopers were at last on their way, Alban dismissed his bodyguard and happily shut the heavy door. This time, he turned the key in the lock. As though summoned by the grating of the mechanism, a wooden panel in the far wall of his office slid to one side . . . with barely a whisper.

"If she's anything like her sister, Majesty, then you'll have even more trouble heaped upon your shoulders," observed Duca Sebastiani, the elder of the two men who entered from the King's War Room.

"I think we are beyond that speculative point, to be sure," Stefano, Duca di Drago, said, sighing tiredly. "I did not wish Princess Bianca dead, but I cannot say that I was not relieved when . . ."

Alban watched him fall abruptly silent, apparently remembering that even as a senior member of the Palantini, Sebastiani was not privy to all of the actual details about Bianca's death . . . or of Luciana's involvement. Though to what degree Stefano's wife was involved, probably even Stefano did not know and he, the king, knew even less.

Augusto Sebastiani nodded. "No need to hide your sentiments here. It would be a lie for anyone to deny that we had hoped the poison of their mother's insanity ended with Bianca's untimely death. Now, Majesty, the madness of your predecessor Queen Katerina is revisited upon Tyrrhia with the return of Ortensia . . . and who can know what was done to her during those years stolen by the Turks?"

Alban wiped a hand across his face. Though improving, the odd languor, which had sapped him these recent weeks, still troubled him. He stared, surprised, at the sight of blood, only then conscious of the sting caused by a shard from the decanter the princess had thrown at him.

"Majesty."

Alban looked up and saw that Stefano offered him a bit of embroidered linen. Despite being his brother-in-law and lifelong companion, Stefano never let his sense of formality slip—especially when in the company of others. It made their relationship easier; one Alban deeply appreciated. He accepted the kerchief and hesitated. "It will do ruinous things to this fine piece of needlework."

"But what purpose does a bit of cloth have, if not to serve at a moment's need?" Stefano replied. "Besides, we will be fortunate if all we lose because of that lady's vindictiveness is a bit of cloth and a gobbet of glass."

Alban smiled thankfully and dabbed at the wound, but his gaze fell upon the elder duca. "Sebastiani?"

"Yes, yes, he most definitely has the right of it," Sebastiani said, though his thoughts seemed miles away.

Alban followed the duca's gaze to the closed door through which the leech, deMedici, and Ortensia, his newfound bride, had gone.

Duca Sebastiani seemed suddenly aware of his lapse and shook his head.

"I would be most appreciative, Augusto," Alban said, using the familiarity of the elder man's proper name, "if you would share your thoughts."

"'Tis little more than the musings of an old man, Your Majesty, but it seems to me that the deMedici has the most inconvenient good fortune," Augusto said, reclaiming the spindle-backed chair and accompanying footstool that he had recently vacated upon hearing Ortensia's strident tones in the hall.

"Yes," Stefano said with a nod. He took the adjoining seat and reached down to assist the other duca in positioning his gouty foot. "What business was it that put him on the western roads where the Turks just *happened* to be releasing the princess—after nearly two decades when no ransom could save her?"

"I can't believe the deMedici bastarde would have raised a hand to defend her on his own," Alban grumbled. "So there comes one of the best men among the Queen's Escalade—a man my lady holds above reproach—and his party on the very same road at the very same hour. It's unnatural."

"And then, that he should so easily convince the princess to . . . to plight her troth with his?" Stefano added. "They are too cozy too soon, those two."

"Ah, yes, and as His Majesty says, a most *unnatural* good luck," Sebastiani observed.

The inflection in the deep timbre of the duca's voice was not lost on Alban, nor, he saw from the sudden guardedness of Stefano's normally open countenance, on his brother-in-law. But then, ever since his marriage to Luciana, the Romani merchant princess of all Tyrrhia's Gypsy Silk, Stefano had become close-mouthed when the subject of magic came up.

Apparently sensing the tension, for Sebastiani was no one's fool, the elder man pressed on quickly. "Am I an *imbecíle* for thinking that magic might be afoot? He came to court, last year, I'm told, with his own 'perfumer'! If he'll bring as recognized a proficient in salts and scents as a poisoner to this court, what other dark arts might he be willing to associate himself with? And then there was the cardinal who took up his cause. The *cardinal,* of all people!"

"He's a devout Catholic," Alban pointed out, almost

reflexively. "And not given to our Neoplatonic philosophies of other beliefs than his own."

"One would presume that he would be considered at least slightly less devout than a man of the cloth, a cardinal, by all means! I cannot suppose you have missed the rumors about His Eminence, Cardinal delle Torre? If word about court can be trusted at all, then you must know of the suspicious circumstances of his recently reported death," Sebastiani said.

Stefano cleared his throat. "We have yet to receive confirmation—"

"Too true, but—"

Alban raised a hand, bringing both men to complete silence. "I think that the word we have received from Maggiore diMontago's men can be taken as reliable fact."

"Then he was involved in this agency, *Magnus Inique*? These witch-hunters?" Sebastiani asked.

"I cannot help notice, Your Grace, but that you leap from hints of use of magic to this *Magnus Inique*," Stefano murmured.

"In point," Sebastiani remarked thoughtfully, "neither is a friend of the throne . . . in this instance." He added hastily.

Stefano fell silent, withdrawing. He crossed his arms, his expression almost unreadable, even to Alban who knew him so well.

"We don't know that the prince has truck with magic, just infernal good fortune," Alban said.

"But it would serve him well," Sebastiani argued. "He has never shown a particular kindness to your regency."

"One would expect him to be sympathetic with his wife," Stefano pointed out.

"DeMedici's *wives*, Your Grace," Alban said. "You must admit that something seems amiss. To marry again so quickly after Bianca died . . . barely out of the nuptials and not even to the bed!"

"By which argument, he has taken Princess Ortensia, Bianca's own *sister*!" Sebastiani said.

"And she *has* taken to his bed," Alban remarked. To the surprised look of his associates, he hurriedly explained. "She made a point of holding her belly in that guarded way women have when they bear seed. She shows signs of pregnancy that the cut of her gowns had previously hidden."

"A pregnancy . . . so soon?" Sebastiani coughed. "Barely four months have passed since they were wed! Could his fortune be *that* uncanny?"

"There is the possibility she *is* pregnant, but by the Turk who kept her in his harem, instead of deMedici," Alban said.

"We might only know by the date she presents this child," Stefano said quietly. "A woman who has borne more than one child is inclined to produce early in subsequent births . . . or so I've been told . . ."

Alban noted the flush of red staining his brother-in-law's cheeks. Embarrassment? He knew that Stefano had already hired a midwife for Luciana whose pregnancy was only about as far along as Idala's. "If a Turk, instead of her husband, has fathered Ortensia's child, we might be able to tell . . . but not every child betrays his parentage by his reflection."

"Forgive me," Sebastiani said, nodding first to Alban and then Stefano, "but we digress from my point. To be sure, it would suit deMedici to claim any child borne by the princess . . . and this, too, goes to my meaning. What chance their meeting on the beach that day? Further, that Ortensia would agree to marry him? Her sister's widower? And now, that she be pregnant? There is this matter of, as you say, Majesty, of deMedici's 'unnatural good fortune.'"

"And where do these points lead us, but around in a circle?" Stefano asked.

"It leads us back to magic, Your Grace," Sebastiani said.

"There is a reason that I sent deMedici from court," Alban said, uncomfortable for his friend at the constant talk of magic and the avoidance of mention of his Gypsy duchessa. "I hoped that being sent to the country would help to sever ties to his more nefarious alliances. I even refused to continue the elaborate allowance he expected from the coffers of Bianca's wealth. He had her bride price *and* a title that not even his father or legitimate brother can aspire to. Now, he has broken every sense of propriety by taking another wife so soon—never mind that she is the elder sister of his dead wife."

"We are agreed that no natural excuse could explain his good fortune, then?" Sebastiani pressed.

"There is still the possibility that he has connections that helped him in his timing," Alban said.

"But, of course, those connections have worked *know-*

ingly against the Crown and, as yet, are anonymous," Stefano said bleakly.

"I say magic is afoot, Majesty!" Sebastiani proclaimed. "And, reluctant as you or the Palantini might be to welcome him—even *before* he married Ortensia—he *is* a member of *la famiglia reale*."

"There is nothing I can do to change that. I saw the legal wedding to Bianca. Now Ortensia, another member of *la famiglia reale*, attests to a legal wedding by grace of law and Catholic supervision," Alban replied.

"But don't you see? There is his mistake!" Sebastiani exclaimed. "It was accepted that magic used in relation to *la famiglia reale* was ill-considered until your predecessor made it high treason."

"Yes, but what proof of magic is there?" Alban asked. He closed his eyes, trying to hide his wince. Against his enemies, it would be all too easy to pursue . . . given evidence, but he had more to consider than just this. He could not *prove* Pierro deMedici and his first bride used magic; but, then, there were others, friendlier to the crown, who had most definitely used it . . .

Alban noted that Stefano sat very still, his gaze upon his toes and his arms crossed firmly across his chest. Sebastiani was a good man, but he had no idea of the impossible situation in which he placed his king.

Padre Gabera studied the plump Dominican's back, turned from him in anger. He folded his hands inside the sleeves of his homespun brown cassock. "I offer you the sacraments, Brother; all you must do is confess."

"The cardinal is my confessor," the other man said.

"And he is dead. Consider where you are, where following the man has brought you!" Gabera said, waving to the dim, filthy surroundings of the dungeon. "Tomasi, save your eternal soul if not yourself!"

"I'll not confess. Leave me in peace!"

"Peace? Here?" Padre Gabera pressed. He reached out and touched the other man's shoulder. When Brother Tomasi shrugged off the physical contact, he sighed. "Is there anything I can bring you?"

"What would those men who arrested me let you do? Or the guards for that matter?" Brother Tomasi scoffed, his tone dismissive. "What would the Romani witches let you do?"

"No witch has say over you, Brother, and as to the maggiore's men, they are not evil. Indeed, they are not even misguided in being cautious with you. You served a man who used magic . . . against all that we believe in—"

"How do you know what I believe?" the short Dominican demanded. "You, like the others, think I served an evil man, that—"

"They know what they saw. You were in league with the cardinal! You helped the cardinal of your own free will, or did he control your mind? Make you his unwitting servant in the service of evil—"

"How do you know what the cardinal served? Was he not a Prince of the Holy Roman Church? And you doubt him, without evidence—"

"He held the body of a young woman to use in his spells!" Gabera protested.

"Those men . . . the vigilare who arrested me . . . they killed Cardinal delle Torre!" Brother Tomasi spat, finally whirling around to face him.

Gabera stood his ground, meeting the Dominican's wide, dark eyes, glinting with madness. "The cardinal was already dead . . . as the result of his nefarious magic. No mortal hand touched him while he lived. I saw that with my own eyes."

Tomasi presented him with his back again.

"I will return," Padre Gabera said reluctantly.

The Dominican Brother ignored him, striding over to the narrow little cot he used for a bed and began rummaging through the rags.

Gabera stuck his hand through the bars of the door and waved to the Palazzo Guard to let him out.

Tomasi turned in time to watch the priest leave. The man had been his daily companion since the death of delle Torre. The cardinal had promised him these would be trying times, that he relied upon him, Brother Tomasi . . . until his return. Tomasi spat into the straw. Beside the flame of delle Torre's compelling arguments, this Padre Gabera's persuasions were an unlit wick. Gabera possessed no foundation in the magic the Church could wield if pedants like Gabera did not hold them back or petty witches like the Romani did not toy with what belonged to the Church.

In amongst the rags, Tomasi found and gathered two silken white poppets made for him by the cardinal. The power of the White Throne was a serious threat to all the plans he and delle Torre discussed. According to the cardinal, the White King and Queen paid lip service to the Catholic Church but refused the magic power of the Church. They, instead, honored the traditions of the Neoplatonic State where the Jews and Muslims were equally recognized. They called magic blasphemy!

Tomasi sat with the poppets by the fire pit allowed him for warmth. It served pitifully to heat the dank dungeon. He laid the dolls out on his knees. One to represent the king and another his queen. Secreted within his robes, Tomasi pulled out the little bottle of anointing oil. There was little left, but he proceeded with delle Torre's directions and began to whisper Last Rites over the poppets. The cardinal claimed it would have an effect on the White King and Queen and, so far, Tomasi had no reason to doubt him.

Prince Pierro meandered the back hallway, toward the portico which overlooked the lawn, the Stretto d'Messina and the landing for the elevator which brought crates and trunks up from the ships to the palazzo. It was generally a peaceful setting for a reflective stroll, a quiet assignation even as it was less popular than the gardens or the maze. It also served as a discreet location to meet certain people in whose company one would generally prefer to not be seen. Of course, one had to take care, Pierro reflected, it would not do to be caught unaware or have another's secret meeting inconveniently timed to match yours.

Pierro yawned and leaned against the wall, stretching out his shoulder-high walking stick and flicking his lace cuffs into place. With casual ease, he glanced back the way he had come. Then, as though staring idly at the emerald knob of his cane, he studied the length of the bisecting corridor. He was alone. He stood up, rapping his staff on the marble floor, and went through the double gold and glass wrought doors to the lawn. He dropped down on the stone bench and waited.

A stiff breeze came off the *Stretto*, needling through his black Gypsy Silk suit and linen shirt. He smothered the chill, waiting. His ears perked at the sound of a man grunting and breathing hard coming from the edge of the platform. He quelled his instinct to go and look over. Either his appointment was here, or he was about to be privy to someone else's secret meeting. He schooled his expression into the equivalent of a hooded mask.

Momentarily, a dark head popped up over the cliff's edge beside the elevator and peered around. He spotted Pierro immediately and pulled himself the rest of the way up, darting nervous looks around the open lawn.

Pierro took one last look around the open lawn himself, focused on the shadowed hallways beyond the glinting glass, and waved the man forward. The swarthy man glanced below him and hurried up the rungs onto the plateau. He scrambled to his feet and, looking around cautiously, moved to Pierro's side.

"It was dangerous bringing me here," the man said.

"Nonsense, Boiko. You could pass as one of the damned Gypsies. Rest easy . . . but don't sit down. Everyone knows I don't willingly suffer their kind," Pierro said airily.

"All went well with your gaining custody of the princess, I presume? We didn't expect the soldiers. Were they your doing?" the man named Boiko asked, running a hand through his disheveled hair.

"A mere coincidence. I wouldn't have risked our arrangement. There was too much to gain," Pierro said.

"And you were able to court her?" Boiko asked.

Pierro looked at the Turk. "I won her within the week, but I have a question for you. She is pregnant. Is the child mine or Tardiq's?"

Boiko laughed. "Many blessings upon you. The sultan did not touch her for more than a year before he released her to you. Had she still held his interest, you would not have bargained for her so easily."

"Easily? Getting you the troop allotments for Tyrrhian coastal cities were far from *easy* to acquire," Pierro said. He scanned the area, removed a vellum map from his suit coat and extended it to the other man. "Keep that hidden, will you?"

"Oh, it'll not pass out of my hands until I place it in the hands of His Excellency, Sultan Tardiq," Boiko promised. "We'll be poised to attack on your signal. With Tyrrhia's forces tied up at home, we'll take the Peloponnesian front."

"Whether you take the front or no, is no concern of mine, but you'll tie up Tyrrhian forces. I'll time it just right. Now, begone with you before you're seen," Pierro said, waving his hand.

"Have a care how you speak to me. I am a captain of Tardiq's fleet and it'll be my knife at your throat if you fail to deliver," Boiko grumbled, balling his fist.

Pierro rose abruptly, to intrude into the other's space, but refusing to meet his eye as he deftly adjusted the front of his coat. "I am not afraid of you, Boiko. Take the correspondence and wait for my signal."

II

"O God! That one might read the book of fate, and see the revolution of the times . . ."

—William Shakespeare

21 d'Novembre, 1684

A COLD wind rattled through the branches of nearby trees and into Solaja Lendaro's weathered body, making the loose end of her shawl flap up against the back of her neck. She rose and turned into the wind, welcoming the needles of mist spraying into her face. Winter was on its way, riding on the waves of the Mediterranean. The northern and eastern coasts would be warmer for a time, protected by the Tyrrhian Sea and the harsh waters of the Stretto d'Messina. Winter moved in like the certainty of the waves on the shore, gradually sweeping its way across the Tyrrhian heartland to the mainland.

It was time for the clans and the *vitsi* to be on the move, the *Beluni* thought. A clan would stay to tend the groves of mulberry trees over the season. Unlike the traveling families, the sedentary of the clans did not receive an allotment of worms.

The rest of the clans would move inland. While they traveled, the old mothers and the witch-women, the *chovahani*, would tend the season's silk worms through daily rituals, readying them for the Guilds which would turn their homely little nuggets into thousands of yards of spun and woven magical cloth. Moving over the land of Tyrrhia would collect the power of the native soil, and, thereby, the blessings of the *Fata* which, with the Romani's own magic, created Gypsy Silk.

Solaja threw the dregs of her coffee onto the fire and gave the cup to Grasni. Age and position as *Beluni*, Queen of the Romani, merited the company of a student of the *chova*. Grasni had been Alessandra's maid and now filled the position as her apprentice well. Besides making a breakfast for her, the girl packed away the oddments of camp life.

The girl straightened suddenly, wiping her hands on her apron, and nodded respectfully. Solaja turned.

Bartolomeo, an elder in the *Kris*, climbed the hill toward them and was already well within hailing distance. She nodded. "*Meero-Kak*?"

The *Kris* elder noted Grasni's work at breaking camp. "I see that you anticipate us, *Beluni-Daiya*."

Solaja shrugged. "Winter nears, the horses are fat, and my feet itch . . . and I could not help but notice the *Kris* in conference. A mere reading of the signs, elder." She smiled inwardly that she should call him "elder." She had seen thirty winters before he was born and changed his *pannolini* when he was a babe, but being an elder was the recognition of a status within the greater *vitsis* and Bartolomeo's levelheadedness served all well on the *Kris*. The men's council needed as much of Barto's sensibility as they would pay heed to.

"*Daiya*?"

She ended her musings and gave Bartolomeo her full attention.

"We have been waiting for Petrus' return from Palermo, but we do not know when to expect him," Barto said.

"Nor I," she replied. "If I knew more about my son's whereabouts, the *Kris* would be just as familiar with news of his travels. My son knows how to follow the *patrins*. On the other hand, nothing shall be harmed if his family, or even the clan, were to wait for him . . . for a time."

Barto smoothed the ends of his full, tapering mustache. "Then let it be." He turned to go, but paused. "We ask that the *Daiyas* apportion the silkworms so that we can take to the road."

"They have already begun, *Kak*."

Barto nodded. "It is also time to cast for the best paths for the clans when we set to the road."

Solaja waved to Grasni who quickly ducked into the *vardo* and reappeared carrying a sheepskin scroll. Grasni unrolled the scroll and held it open for the elder to read.

"The *Daiyas* and I have read the cards, consulted the fairy folk and whistled to the wind," Solaja said. She tapped the skin with its ink-and-charcoal markings. "Autumn departs and winter is in the wind. As you can see, I've marked the paths I suggest the *vitsi* take."

Barto stiffened, but took the map and rerolled it. On another day, she might have been a little less . . . abrupt when turning the map over. The *Kris* hated their travels anticipated, even by their women. It spoke to the actual balance of decisions, and the men liked at least the appearance of power.

"The *Kris* will consult these suggestions, *Beluni-Daiya*, but *we* make the final decisions," he said.

"But of course," Solaja murmured, her tone quiet and acquiescent. Each year was the same. The *Kris* took the sheepskin with the markings made by herself, created from the consultation of the *Daiyas* of the various families and clans that made up the six Tyrrhian *vitsi*. The *Kris* would consult the map, make negligible changes and the Romani would begin their winter-long travels over the wide range of roads in all Tyrrhia, from heartland to mainland.

"And you, *Beluni*?" Barto asked respectfully.

Solaja's brows rose in silent query.

"Which of the *vitsi* will you travel with this year?"

Solaja shook her head. A sudden gust of wind whipped her hair free from the *diklo* she bundled it in, snapping her skirts up against her body and flapping merrily in the little buffets that followed. Needles of ocean mist pricked her roughened skin as she turned her face once more into the wind.

"I shall not be traveling with one of the *vitsi*, nor one of the smaller clans. This year I winter sedentary at the White Crown's Citteauroea. The *Araunya* nears the end of her pregnancy. The signs have told me that I will be needed . . . for her and for the Romani of Tyrrhia."

"She will produce your great-grandchild. Motherless herself, I can see that she would need you, but what if one of the *vitsi* or—" Barto protested.

Solaja turned her gaze squarely upon Barto. She had

been queen of the black-blooded Romani for more than forty years. She rarely enforced the power of that position, but now her jaw set and her eyes burned. The *Kris* could not—and would not—be allowed to interfere with her plans. "Then I say, *Meero-Kak* Barto, that I will be easy to find. Yes?"

The *Kris* elder, in the fullness of his years—still possessing the physique of youth and the position of father, grandfather, and a well-favored member of the *Kris*—was clearly unaccustomed to backing down. Yet he stepped back, his fingers tightening on the sheepskin. "As you say then, *Beluni*. If I may ask, when will you depart?"

"I will stay until the *vitsi* take to the road and leave the first *patrins*."

Barto nodded. "May the *Fata* bless you, *Beluni-Daiya*."

"And you." Solaja watched the elder leave. She did not like to press her position, especially upon members of the *Kris*, except, she realized with a smile, with Petrus, but then he was her only son, and neither of them acquiesced easily.

Now that Barto was gone, she returned to the innermost sanctum of her *vardo*. She closed the split doors and sighed, at peace. Everything was within easy reach in the compressed space of the wagon that contained a bed, a fold-down bench and table, and tiny cabinets and drawers throughout. Without even having to look while her eyes adjusted to the dark, Solaja pulled open a drawer at the base of the bed and removed a square of Gypsy Silk wrapped snugly around a deck of cards. Her reading earlier this morning had been particularly troublesome.

She folded the bench down, sat and pulled out the table, then laid out the Gypsy Silk. Having no particular query, Solaja fanned the cards and took several at random. She splayed the selected cards before her. The Tollgate spoke of travel, personal loss, and of upheaval, impediments to plans set. Four Queens—White, the *gadjé* Queen; Black, herself; Dark, the *Araunya*, Luciana; and Fair, she was the mystery. A fourth Queen, the card had stuck itself to the Death card, could only mean that there would be a Queen to replace one of the three existing.

With her age, Solaja easily reasoned the replacement would be for the position of *Beluni*. It made sense, after all. But what if her interpretation was wrong?

Childbirth was not safe, and there would be much trouble should something happen to the *Araunya*. What if she was to be replaced? More upheaval with the positions of the *Araunya* . . . Luciana already held the position of the two houses.

There was the White Queen as well. She, too, expected a child approximate to Luciana's lying-in cycle.

The Romani were a nation within the White Crown's land, their peace determined by the Council of Queens, managed on a daily level by the *Araunyas*—which was already made unsteady by having but a single woman hold both positions and she with child.

This White Queen had been a steady woman with an open mind and she, too, stood in peril. To lose this queen . . . especially considering that the queen who had preceded Idala almost undid the long-standing agreement of centuries that gave the Romani succor in Tyrrhia and, in turn, lined the pockets of Tyrrhian merchants and tradesmen . . . and the Throne.

Devil, it seemed was to be in the details of this meeting; upheaval was promised and Luciana was to finally bear a living child. The first child, a stillborn son, between her and her *gadjé* husband had ripped apart the couple and, potentially, the filial ties to the White Throne.

The *Beluni* sighed, rubbing a weary hand over her face. She could spend the day reading the portents: bones, scrying in the water bowl, consulting the *Fata* . . . and none of it would tell her much more than she knew now. Luciana, her only daughter's only living child, needed her, and the Romani and *gadjé* stood at a precipice that might lead to the destruction of the Council of Queens and the death of life as they now knew it.

III

"There is nothing more difficult to take in hand, more perilous to conduct, or more uncertain in its success, than to take the lead in the introduction of a new order to things."

—Niccolò Machiavelli

24 d' Novembre 1684

CONCENTRATING upon the hand-drawn map and directions, only the warning sound of a horse's flying hooves saved Cristoval a dunking in a nearby trough. As it was, he caught a nasty splinter on the side of his right hand from a poorly cared for *balcone* post.

Cristoval watched as the rider reined the white gelding in hard, hard enough that the horse went back on his haunches. By God's good grace, the animal contorted his body so that he did not snap one of his legs and only the rider landed face-first in the swamped street—a place Cristoval never wanted to be what with the city-dwellers' midden habits.

Cristoval reached the horse's side, capturing the reins even as its former rider slithered to his feet. Before the man could vent his anger on the animal, Cristoval maneuvered himself between horse and rider. He looped his right hand through the loose reins and tried calming the horse.

"You'll be kind enough to release my horse, *Signore*!" The rider stood, one hand edging toward his sword.

Cristoval stood his ground and, after a hostile moment

of silence, turned the reins over to the young brown lackey boy who stood beside the door to the establishment both men had just arrived at. "Have a care with God's own creature. Don't abuse the animal because you can't keep your seat."

"What—" the rider began with a roar that sent his horse skittering to the length of his tether.

"Brother diSotto!" A male voice snapped from behind Cristoval. While there could be no disguising the edge of anger in the soft timbre of his voice, it was also very recognizable. Cristoval's heart sank, but at least he had found the priest for whom he searched.

"Padre Caserta?" Cristoval asked, as he turned to greet the owner of the voice. In truth, however, it was less question than resignation. He was now thoroughly ensnared in Prince deMedici's private affairs, all because of a debt—one long ago well paid by service, to Cristoval's mind. The Duca Cosimo deMedici, a generous man, managed debtors as a function of his wealth and standing. His bastarde son milked every last bit of a man's soul for those debts given to him. Far from merely supporting the man as he established himself in Tyrrhian society, deMedici's bastarde son had managed miraculously to rise to a social position surpassing even his patron father.

His attention brought back to the moment, Cristoval saw that Caserta wore the clothes of a commoner—well-equipped, but nothing that spoke particularly of wealth or of the military, though he sported a baldric, pistola, and sword. He wore nothing of silk, nothing that would make him stand out and, certainly, nothing that defined him as a priest or the witch-hunting insurrectionist with whom Cristoval had become reluctantly involved through the calculating orchestration of the deMedici.

"Who is he, Caserta?" the one named diSotto demanded, one hand still clenching the hilt of his sword.

Caserta smiled beneficently at Don Cristoval Battista, but frowned as he turned to address the befouled rider. "He is our guest, diSotto, and what business brings you to me with such a . . ." here he paused to nod dismissively at the gathering audience, "noteworthy entrance?"

"I have *important* news, Padre—" diSotto said.

"News, hmm . . . and, gentlemen, may I ask both of you

to use a little more . . . discretion with our affiliations? Come inside, please. You can share your news and perhaps change into something else whilst a washerwoman has a go at your clothes. As to our guest, I bid you leave such matters to me. There is nothing that you will report that will not be told to him as messenger to our patron."

That, Cristoval realized, was an invitation, or at least all that he was likely to receive. After a reluctant pause, he followed the erstwhile priest and his messenger into *le Armi Dorata*, an establishment of questionable merit, certainly not a place that a gentleman would like to be seen in. Yet, despite its name and reputation, the front doors opened upon a salon with liveried servants. Two, precisely. By the color of their skin, Cristoval surmised they were young men of African heritage. Someone here apparently felt no compunctions about flouting Tyrrhia's antislavery laws and took advantage of the slave markets popular in other parts of the world. Of course, Cristoval realized, he made assumptions. The men could easily be free and getting what employment they could.

The salon itself was small. Light and shadow merged to maximum effect for privacy with three sets of heavy emerald velvet curtains that divided the areas to the left and right into discreet alcoves. One of the shadows apparently led to some sort of common room as the murmur of men's voices could just be heard, but not distinguished.

"We will be in our rooms," the priest said to the servants. "Send the laundress."

The liveried youths came forward silently; one pulled back a curtain to reveal a door to the left and stairs directly before them while the other young man took their coats. DiSotto refused, apparently choosing to keep his filthy coat for the laundress Caserta spoke of.

Cristoval ignored the insolent diSotto and quickly followed Caserta up the uncarpeted wooden stairs. At a landing, the stairway branched toward hallways deeper into the building. Caserta took the right and continued to a second-floor landing.

For an unimposing front, the establishment of *le Armi Dorata*—the Gilded Arms—proved to be surprisingly large, the building reaching higher and deeper into the street quarter than Cristoval might have expected.

Caserta led both men to a door at the end of the hall and bent to unlock it. Beyond, Cristoval found a sizable parlor furnished with a large table and chairs to one side and something akin to a sitting room with more chairs of various types and sturdiness gathered around a fireplace. From this room, four doors opened to bedrooms in a variety of states of orderliness.

DiSotto moved to the fireplace, sending disdainful glares in Cristoval's direction. Caserta took three goblets—he raised them to the light cast from the windows. With a frown, Caserta tipped the glassware out onto the tray and refilled each with a dark wine. He handed one to Cristoval, another to diSotto, and kept the third for himself.

"I cannot say that this offering is anything akin to the wine of your vineyard, Don Battista," Caserta said. "While we came virtually unannounced, you threw open your house. I have not forgotten your hospitality . . . or your new allegiance to our cause. You are sent by His Highness, Prince Pierro deMedici? Is there news?"

Cristoval swallowed his distaste at thought of his employer and sipped at the wine, raising the glass to his host perfunctorily. "He has shared little with me, but wished to—to—establish our connection. He intends that I should come weekly for exchanges."

"Ah," Caserta nodded. He motioned for Cristoval to sit in one of the rough spindle-backed chairs that bore little resemblance to those in the palazzo, even those that had been relegated to servants' quarters—where he now resided with his son and former housekeeper. "What news is there from the palazzo? Is it true the queen expects twins?"

"I am not privy to such information. I know only that she is seen very little these days. I chanced to encounter her in the gardens one afternoon and she is most definitely with child," Cristoval said. "If you will forgive the lack of delicacy . . . and taking my—Prince deMedici's words, he has likened her to a—a mare near her time."

Caserta blocked his face with his goblet momentarily, whether to hide his embarrassment at the coarseness or to hide a laugh, Cristoval could not be sure. Personally, he found such remarks incredibly distasteful, made all the worse that he spoke it of an indefensible woman who was his queen. The prince thought himself amusing and clever.

From where he sat, it seemed the prince took aim at easy targets while biding his time to make one feel yet more insignificant and powerless such as he had become . . . but Cristoval was in the beehive and no longer had any business criticizing the honey.

"How much longer do you want me to wait?" DiSotto's voice, coming from the other room, was curt, angry.

Manners, or a sense of survival, brought Cristoval to his feet.

DiSotto looked better cleaned up. He was the type of man that made young women giggle and blush when he entered the room. Nothing about the man put Cristoval at ease.

"You will excuse me for a moment, Don Batista?" Caserta asked. Rising, he set aside his goblet of wine and joined his surly comrade in the corner. It was impossible not to overhear their discussion, though diSotto put his back to Cristoval. The more Cristoval tried not to listen, the clearer the whispered words seemed to become.

"What do you mean you didn't deliver the message? The cardinal—"

"Is dead. I saw his corpse myself!" diSotto growled. "I went into the catacombs."

"This is no secret that cannot be shared with our guest. It will be known to all soon enough," Caserta said.

"Will it?" diSotto demanded. "Who else knows about the catacombs? Who else can report with confidence that he's dead? For all the royals and their followers know, he could have gone back to the Holy City—"

Cristoval rose, trying to quiet his mind, which latched one whispered detail to another. "*Scusi*, perhaps I should leave—"

DiSotto turned, shooting Cristoval an angry glare. "You see? He listens in!" He practically hissed at the priest.

Caserta looked from one man to the other. "*Basta*! Sit, diSotto and share your information with both of us."

"But—"

"He has sworn himself a member of *Magnus Inique*, just as you have," Caserta declared. He turned to Cristoval, "You are faithful to our cause—to suffer no witch, to purify Tyrrhia of its Neoplatonic philosophies and bringing it closer to the Church, are you not?"

Cristoval nodded. Yes, in a gathering of members of *Magnus Inique* arriving in his very own home without notice, without option, Cristoval had become a member of *Magnus Inique*.

"You see, diSotto? Come, let us do away with the pretense and allow me to return his favor as a good host," Caserta said. He returned to the fire and the arrangement of chairs. He held out the wine he had poured for diSotto, waving it at him insistently.

With obvious reluctance, diSotto took the wine and, eventually, the chair.

"Now, diSotto, your report," Caserta demanded.

DiSotto swallowed the vinegary wine as though it were water and set aside the empty goblet. "As I said, the cardinal is dead, his body found in the catacombs, the *secret* catacombs where he worked with that Gypsy witch's body."

"How did he die, could you tell?" Caserta asked, running his hands through his light brown hair dusted with gray.

"It was violent, but I could not be sure . . ."

"Magic, then?" Cristoval dared to suggest.

DiSotto never looked at him, but nodded his head in agreement. "There could have been no other way—aye, and to take that witch from him as well. There was sign, near the main entrance, of a large conflagration. I could not be sure, but what remained looked like one of those wagons of theirs."

"*Madre del Dio*!" Caserta swore. "We have lost many players in such a short period. There has been Princess Bianca and her man, the Conte di Vega, and the cardinal found it necessary for him to vacate the palazzo and lose his position."

"But there is Prince deMedici, and now Princess Ortensia," Cristoval said, feeling compelled to reassure the priest.

Caserta nodded. "But the cardinal . . . lost!" He sat back and sighed, then looked back to Cristoval. "Don Battista, have you heard word of the royals replacing the cardinal?"

"There has been no word that I have heard, nor that the prince has bid me tell you."

"Now it is a matter of whether the king will insist upon naming his ambassador to Rome— "

The door slammed open, and a man—Cristoval found

him vaguely familiar, possibly one of his earlier house guests—practically fell into the room. "It's Enzo again!"

Caserta leaped to his feet and darted from the room.

"If you're one of us, you might as well come and be useful," diSotto said, rising to follow Caserta, though not with the alacrity of the other.

Bewildered, Cristoval followed diSotto down the stairs, through a door to the landing, and into a *taverna* doing a rousing good business. The noise level exceeded that of the chickens at his farm with a fox in the pen, like a veritable wall pushing him back up the stairs.

All eyes in the large room focused on a big, burly man who raged at one side of the pub obviously fighting over a woman, who stood cornered behind him. The man barely looked up when Caserta called his name before he and the others tackled Enzo.

The young woman being brawled over was beautiful by any man's measure, but after first glance, it was easy to see that she was "a painted flower." Her gown was low cut, a brooch placed strategically to accent her charms, her hair worn long and loose but for a pin that pinched back the forelocks such as many of the young, common women did. She escaped the tussle of men by climbing over a spilled table and slipping into the shadows.

Enzo erupted from beneath Caserta and his cohorts, knocking over another table.

The young woman moved quickly to the wall nearest the newly distraught customers to reassure them their cups would be refilled and their dinner provided once again even as a scullery maid hurried out from behind the innkeep's bar and began to collect the shattered crockery and food.

Riveted by the fight on the other side of the room, Cristoval was unprepared when the battle suddenly turned in his direction. He barely ducked in time to avoid a wild blow from Enzo. Cristoval deflected Enzo's next blow with his right arm. He rose with a long-reaching left jab and a quick right uppercut to the jaw. His handiwork rocked the big man backward. Enzo stumbled and fell with sufficient force to overturn the next table, bringing it and its contents to the floor.

Caserta looked at Cristoval, clearly reassessing his skills.

Cristoval shook off the spark of adrenaline, straightening his suit coat and cuffs. He stepped aside as diSotto and two of his friends, half-carried and half-dragged Enzo up the stairs. In response to Caserta's questioning look, Cristoval said, "I'm only passing fair with a sword, ruinous at cards. My father felt I should be good at something in the manly arts."

"Indeed."

The painted flower made her way toward him. She was graceful, seeming to float across the room to his side. "Thank you, Signore!"

"*É niente*," Cristoval murmured, embarrassed by the woman's attention.

Still she persisted, her hands stealing around his arms not unlike ivy clinging to an edifice. "If there is some small service . . . some service at all that I might do for you—"

"No. *Grazie*," Cristoval said, trying to untwine himself from the woman who by now had snugged him into practically a full embrace. "Please, Signorina, I am—I'm moved by your charms—"

She released him with a knowing look quickly hidden behind the splay of her fan. "—but, alas, you were injured in the war?"

Cristoval smiled tightly. While he had not been to the wars, and it put his manhood into question, he took the excuse with a nod, allowing his smile to look faintly regretful.

By the time he had disentangled himself from the woman, he had noted that she was not the only painted flower attending to the customers' needs . . . and, thankfully, Caserta waited on the steps by the door to the landing. He—happily, this time—followed the priest's lead. On the landing, the door shut and leaving Cristoval alone, he paused.

"Are you surprised?" Caserta asked. "That we choose to room in such an establishment?"

Cristoval tried to fathom a polite answer, but his expression spoke for him.

"The truth of the matter is, this is the last sort of place *they* would look for us and, to be completely forthright, not all of us in *Magnus Inique* have taken a vow of chastity," Caserta replied with a toothy grin. "A place of this sort is always easy enough to find, no matter where you are. I thought it a stroke of genius myself."

“But of course,” Cristoval murmured, staying put and thereby resisting the priest’s silent prompting when taking the first few steps toward the second level of the establishment. “If there is no more news, I think I should be returning to the palazzo and . . . my—my patron, His Highness, Prince deMedici?”

IV

"Time, as he grows old, teaches all things."

—Aeschylus

10 d'Dicembre, 1684

PIERRO threw his goblet of wine at the fireplace. Magic! Poison! None of it seemed to have any effect! The king still thrived.

DeMedici reviewed his plans. He had been to see Brother Tomasi, and it had cost him a small fortune to ensure that his visit remained unreported by the Palazzo Guards. The little Dominican had shown him the poppets given him by the cardinal, shown him the spell he cast with the Last Rites over the little replacements for the White King and Queen. Perhaps if the magic were being worked by delle Torre himself instead of his little acolyte, it might have more effect, but the cardinal was long past his reach now that he was dead.

Pierro gnashed his teeth. He had no one to discuss his plans with. Cristoval was beneath him . . . and besides, he still had his doubts about the man. He was too reluctant. As for Ortensia, other than wanting the throne for herself, she was little like her sister Bianca. Perhaps the years in the seraglio had worn away her wit? Whatever! He did not trust his new wife with any of his plans. She might hesitate where Bianca had had no fear to tread the path of treason, or any other path that would take her to the throne.

Damned Exilli for being seen when he attempted to

assassinate Alban months ago! Now he was without his *perfumer* and was forced to make his own decoctions. He had little experience with the mixing of poisons; perhaps that was why the White King and Queen still lived? The obsequious Conte Urbano di Vega had had some skills with poison, but he was dead. And with Bianca dead as well, Pierro was left, an island unto himself with no connections other than *Magnus Inique* to help him in his plots.

"Your Highness? I heard something break. Should I—"

Pierro looked at the woman who had entered his study and broken his train of thought. Cristoval's housekeeper, Signora delVecchio. She had fallen silent at the black look he had given her. "Clean it up later," he snapped at her.

"But there might be a stain—" the woman began in protest. She ducked her gaze to the floor, avoiding Pierro's stare. She curtsied. "As you wish, Your Highness." She backed out of the threshold, closing the door after her.

Seizing pen and paper, Pierro sat down at his desk. He dipped the quill in the ink bottle and wrote quickly. *Magnus Inique* would have to be his solution; his other alternative would be exactly the wrong stroke. It would have to be the witch-hunters!

Luciana shuddered and made the sign against the evil eye. "I wish you would put that thing away," she said to the queen.

Idala shrugged. Her fingers toyed with the edges of a well-worn bandanna made of silk. In the center of the cloth lay the sign the fairy, by way of the Romani messenger, sent to them from the Black Queen weeks ago. Four birds—desiccated now—tangled in the misshapen root. To Luciana it was *marimé* even before the birds had begun to rot. The thing *was* positively unclean, and weeks of study had made it no less so.

The queen sighed and shrugged again. Her hand fell to her obscenely large belly. "It's just that I can't help thinking that this has something to do with the children I bear. Surely, if we put our heads together, we could discern its meaning. Why else would this message have been given to us?"

Luciana rubbed the spot where her own child kicked.

Thank heavens this child, unlike her first, thrived. Her time was coming, but the queen's was very near. Luciana could not help worry about Queen Idala, her friend and her husband's younger sister. The magic she wrought, lo these many months ago, was wearing heavily upon the queen, and the sign Idala would not leave alone only spoke ill news from what Luciana could see.

"We are not meant to know all things, Idala. Even when the *Fata* send us signs," Luciana said, setting aside her embroidery and moving to sit in the chair directly opposite the queen's chaise. Careful not to touch the bandanna, Luciana reached out and squeezed the queen's leg. "I think sometimes the *Fata* like to toy with our emotions."

"Punish me, don't you mean?" Idala said, her red-rimmed eyes tearing up once again. "It's because I cast magic when I had no business meddling in such things. Isn't that what you mean, Luciana?"

"I didn't say that," Luciana said, straightening in her chair, hand to heart. "It's just that you did not study the art like I did, like my sister did. . . . There are consequences to *all* forms of magic, and they must be taken into consideration when a spell is cast. Besides, you know as well as I that it is high treason to cast magic that affects *la famiglia reale*."

"But I didn't cast a spell on the royal family! I cast a spell upon the nation, upon you . . . not just myself," Idala said, dabbing at her eyes with her kerchief.

Luciana winced inwardly. What may have saved the queen from charges of treason was what had done her in magically. She glanced around the queen's salon, noting that for once they were truly alone in one another's company. Not even Giuletta, the queen's maid, or Kisaiya, her own attendant, accompanied them though she was sure both young women were but a shout away. Such was the privacy of the nobility. It rankled. She was accustomed to being alone at least on occasion, but as her time grew nearer, Stefano made it clear that she was not, under any circumstances, to be left alone.

"If this sign comes from the *Fata* . . . from the fairy folk, why can't you do something to make them tell you what it means?" Idala asked, pointing to the tangle on her lap, such as her pregnant belly allowed.

Luciana shook her head firmly. "You're asking me to cast magic, and Stefano has strictly forbidden it."

"But you say that your sister, Alessandra, is with the *Fata*. You've seen her spirit. Why can't you call upon her phantasm?" Idala asked.

"Her ghost is forbidden me, and what you ask for is magic, Idala. I would have to summon the *Fata*," Luciana explained.

"But it wouldn't really hurt you or the baby, would it?"

Luciana shook her head. "No. If my people quit casting when they were pregnant, nothing would get done; however, my husband does not want to risk this child."

Idala smirked, if somewhat sadly. "It's just like my brother to forbid you to do something you find so natural. He doesn't understand, does he?"

Again, Luciana shook her head.

"What if I commanded you?" Idala asked suddenly, leaning forward as far as she could.

"Idala!" Luciana gasped, her gaze swinging around the room rapidly to see if they had, after all, been overheard. "I can't believe you would suggest such a thing!"

"I didn't. Well, not exactly. I only mean . . ." Idala stifled a sigh and continued, "It's just that we have an opportunity to get some answers here. You wouldn't be casting magic on *la famiglia reale*. You'd be solving a riddle, possibly even saving . . . well, me." She wrung her hands in frustration, her face pinched and creased with worry lines. "I've been so worried. I'm afraid all the time and not just for me." Her hands dropped meaningfully to her belly. "*Please*, Luciana! If you thought it would hurt you, if I thought it would hurt you—I would not ask, but I have every confidence in you. If anyone can save me, if anyone can find answers, then it is you and only you."

Luciana chewed her lip and swiped at a lock of hair that had become loose, tucking it behind her ear. She took the queen's hands in hers, holding them together. "My grandmother comes in a few days, perhaps a couple of weeks at most. She could cast this for you."

Idala shook her hands free and laid back, turning her face away. "No! No, don't you see? I might not have a few days. The child . . . the children could come at any time!

Since when did you become the obedient wife? You've never been before. Why deny me over my brother's whim?"

Luciana's stomach lurched with indecision.

"No one has to know. I won't tell him and, besides, this could mean my life, the lives of my children, the future of the throne... You could be saving all of Tyrrhia!" The queen leaned forward again as she pleaded her case, snagging Luciana's hands in her own and practically crushing them with her frantic entreaty.

"There is the witch from the city, *Signora* Rui. She has helped us before. She could again," Luciana suggested.

The queen shook her head dismissively. "She is what you call *gadjé*. She and her magic are white like me, like my magic. I trust you and only you. I know you. Your magic is from the earth, blessed by the fairy folk. I want your magic, Luciana."

The two women stared at one another, studying one another's resolve.

"All right," Luciana said, her stomach roiling. She pulled her hands free and rubbed at her midriff as though it might ease her queasiness. "I'll do this thing. I'll summon the *Fata* so that they might answer your questions—"

Idala sighed, her shoulders sagging in relief. "I just have to know, Luciana. I have to know what's going to happen."

Luciana licked her lips. She studied her hands. "Idala, have you considered... you might not want to know?"

It was the queen's turn for her resolve to waiver. She took a deep, steadying breath and nodded. "Whatever is to come, I want to know. I want to be prepared. I need to know what to expect—whatever the outcome... *whatever*!"

"Then it shall be so," Luciana said.

With Giuletta sent on a fool's errand and Kisaiya at her side, Luciana took five candles—one black, one blue, one red, one yellow, and one white. As she lit the candles, she carefully placed them at designated locations around the table. She used salt to draw lines to connect each and close a circle. In the center of the circle, her black brazier—a sturdy little pot with ornate engravings on the sides—sat upon a dusky purple square of Gypsy Silk.

"If you are ready, then, Majesty, I will begin," Luciana said quietly, her tone solemn.

The queen nodded and leaned forward.

Sighing, Luciana motioned to Kisaiya, who took coal from the fireplace and placed it in the brazier. Luciana unfolded her leather pouch to expose within it a collection of jars, bags, and tiny bundles. She began to select bits and pieces of herbs—a dried yellow dandelion head and a bit of root; from another packet she retrieved several bay leaves and the leafy stems of Dittany of Crete—and crushed them in her hand, mixing them together as she did so. When they were thoroughly mashed together, Luciana sprinkled them over the coals. From a glass vial, she spilled three drops of tincture of wormwood.

Mindful of the candles, Luciana blew upon the coals as different dried herbs began to burn and smoke. With her right hand, she waved the smoke upward and began a silent prayer, to all fairy kind.

The smoke, thick and heavy, rose like a cloud. Wisps blew upward, tendrils feathering out.

"What's happening?" the queen asked, her voice a mere whisper.

Luciana warned her into silence with her left hand, continuing her prayers: her eyes closed, her head bowed. The child within rolled and kicked, but it was Idala who let out a squeak. The first sign that something was happening. Luciana looked up into the smoke.

Eddying in the herbal fog, a form began to take shape and gradually grow clear. It was as though a portal had opened and a man stepped through it and to the floor as though it were nothing more than taking a stair. His figure wavered briefly and then grew more solid. Without a word, he bowed to Queen Idala and then Luciana before offering his semi-solid hand to help her rise to a seat. It was like touching the surface of water, though warm and like a human hand.

The man—easily recognizable as Mandero, Alessandra's earthly lover, her spiritual husband, the missing maggiore—now stood before them. Some sort of shade or spirit, for he was no fairy of any kind Luciana knew.

"You have summoned me?" he said.

Luciana stared. Maggiore Mandero di Montago had

changed. He was thinner and even seemed somewhat taller. He no longer wore the eye patch over his left eye to hide the silver iris which had marked him as a Child of the Bloods, fairy-touched, in life. Both of his eyes now gleamed silver and sharp.

Luciana found her voice first—as was appropriate. "I called upon the fairy folk, the *Fata*, for their wisdom and guidance. Can you help us?"

Mandero bowed. "I will endeavor, but my knowledge is limited."

"How is it that you have come to my summons?" Luciana asked.

"I and my *adorata* live amongst the *Fata* now," Mandero said matter-of-factly.

"Live?" Luciana repeated, her voice a whisper.

"Since you've come . . . since you live among the fairy kindred, surely you know their mind?" Idala said, clasping desperately at his smoky form.

"For all that I have been accepted amongst their kind, to live with my beloved in the half-life of their world, it is a privilege I do not take lightly, for I would not be parted from Alessandra," Mandero said.

"With my sister?" Luciana repeated.

"She is *mulló* no longer—" he began.

"Luciana! He must help us! My time is limited," Idala pressed.

Luciana shook away thoughts of her sister, or the impossibility of Mandero answering her call and refocused her attention on the queen. There was time for her answers later.

"Can you tell us the meaning of this?" Luciana asked. She pointed to the bundle splayed upon the queen's lap.

Mandero looked at it, his lip curling. "It's *marimé*. Give it to me! You should not hold such filth!" He seized the bundle, threw it into the fireplace and relaxed only as the flames began to consume the oversized packet.

The queen cried out, "No! I need that!"

Mandero shook his head fiercely. "It was meant to be a message only! Not something to be harbored, held, or dwelled upon. Its meaning is clear, Your Majesty. It refers to your pregnancy and the children within your womb."

"But what does it mean?" the queen asked, near tears in

her agitation as she looked from Luciana to Mandero and back again.

The coal in the brazier popped and crackled. Mandero's form wavered. "My time is limited, my queen, but I will tell you what I can. Your magic created a cataclysm, coinciding with the magic of others whose intentions were not as pure as your own. At the time you cast your spell, you were already with child."

"I was? I did not dare hope . . . I've lost so many. It had been so long. I could not take the risk," Idala said.

"The *Fata* knew. Your time was due. You would have borne a daughter," Mandero said. He ran a hand over his face and through his smoky brown hair.

"Would have borne? But now?" Idala cried.

"Your spell doubled your pregnancy," Mandero said.

"Two? Two daughters?" Idala exclaimed, her hand rubbing her swollen belly with what looked like a cross between awe and a kind of mad greed.

"But there is more, Your Majesty," Luciana said as she watched Mandero's face.

Surprised, Idala looked up. "More?"

Mandero nodded and continued, "Aye, Your Majesty, because other forces were at work, a dying man sought rebirth in the royal womb, to be born to *la famiglia reale*. He used dark magic, the mandrake—a twisted root. He has found succor now with the twin sisters." Before Idala could react, he held up his hand, "There is still more. There will be a boy, as well as your girls. The son is the father of himself, but of the makings of a king and queen, of you, Majesty.

"There is one more spirit—a *mulló*—who, in seeking to prevent the cardinal's spell, was brought with him and found redemption. She has found a place amongst the children of this pregnancy, but she, too, while of your making, will be born of *two* royal families—of the White womb and of the Black bloodline."

Idala wrapped her arms around herself and lay back against the chaise. "Sweet *Jesu*! What have I done?" she whispered.

"A *mulló*?" Luciana gasped, shocked to her very foundation. "How is this possible? Redemption? And to be reborn?"

The coal popped and cracked again, sending up a little

shower of sparking cinders. Mandero's form became a shadow of the shade he had been.

"My time is short," he said. "The *mulló* became sister-kindred of your own sister, *Araunya*, of my wife, Alessandra. Their natures changed as they fought the cardinal who enslaved them both. This one is reborn by the cardinal's magic, in trying to prevent his rebirth."

Luciana looked at the queen who was lost in thought. Tears of mixed happiness streamed down her pale-skinned cheeks. Luciana turned to Mandero, "How will we tell which child is which?"

"You will know. The signs will be there," Mandero said. He faded slowly, as though he backed away, with a puff of dying smoke. "You will know."

"Will my children be evil, then?" Idala called after the fading spirit, desperation piercing the veil of her tears.

"Your children will have natures of their own. Where this is indeed a rebirth, its true nature is a mystery. They will each reveal the inclination of their souls over their lifetime," Mandero said, his voice now barely a whisper.

"Then how shall I raise them?" Idala asked, her voice hesitant.

"You will know each child, Majesty, but you will not raise them," Mandero said as the portal closed and he faded with the last of the smoke into nothingness.

The queen let out a little sob and turned her face into the champagne-colored chaise.

Luciana said a quick, quiet prayer to finish the spell, wet her fingertips, and snuffed out each of the candles. Then she motioned for Kisaiya to clean up the remnants and tools of the spell-casting before moving to the queen's settee. As she sat at the foot, Luciana laid a soothing hand on the other woman. "Idala," she said, "this is prophecy. Not everything he said will come to pass. We have free will. These are no guarantees, merely testaments of a projected future."

Idala turned, wiping her eyes. "No, Luciana, do not tell me pretty lies. I have known for some time—though I dared not face it—that I would not survive the birthing of these children. Once I knew that my spell-casting resulted in no natural pregnancy, I realized that there would be a price to pay for what I had done. My pregnancy is not just to that of these children in my womb, but in the wombs of all fertile

Tyrrhian women and beasts. You have said it yourself: magic comes at a price, and I am forfeit for the magic I cast."

"Not necessarily, my queen," Luciana murmured. "There might be—"

"No, my very dear sister, there is nothing that will spare me. I cry now, not for myself but for my husband, my family, and my guilt. I do not know how I could go on if I lost my beloved Alban . . . I know he loves me, and I fear for him and what may happen to the kingdom because of his grief. Just promise me that you will fight Ortensia and her bastarde prince and the coup they will try when I am gone." Idala's tears had faded, gone was the weakening queen and, in her place, was the queen of old—strong, fierce, and determined. She took a linen kerchief, deftly embroidered, and dabbed at her swollen red eyes. Her small chin jutted as she readjusted herself on the chaise, turning around to place her feet on the ground.

Luciana rose, getting out of her way, and taking the queen's elbow to steady her as the other woman cast aside the blanket that had covered her. "Majesty? What are you doing?"

"My time is near and I will be ready," Idala said. "For too long I have allowed myself to be coddled and tended to as though I were an old woman or an invalid. I am neither."

"It's true that you are no invalid, but too much activity will only hasten their time to deliver. I beg you to have caution," Luciana said.

The three women turned at the sound of a loud gasp coming from the doorway to the queen's sanctum. Giuletta had returned and even now hurried to the queen's side.

"Majesty, do you need anything? I shall bring it! The chamber pot? It's just yonder in the water closet," the queen's maid said, while casting a scathing look at Kisaiya and—slightly less so—at Luciana.

The queen shook off Giuletta's hands as the girl guided her back toward the chaise. "There are times when a woman must do for herself. You cannot carry, nor walk for me as I seek out my solar. I need air—fresh air—and the walk will do me good."

"There is a porter just beyond the door, ready to carry you wherever you wish to go, Majesty," Giuletta protested. "Besides, it's just rained and the air is too chilly. You'll catch your death of cold!"

"Nonsense," the queen declared. "The air will do me good. Fetch me a wrap if you wish, but I will do as I think best."

Giuletta grabbed the apple-green coverlet from the chaise and draped it around the queen's shoulders as her charge walked on unsteady feet toward the room closest to her garden.

Standing now as she was, the scarlet dress the queen wore seemed only to emphasize the enormity of her girth. Idala was a dainty woman, with fine bone structure and porcelain skin. Her light brown hair, normally luxurious with natural curls now hung limply about her shoulders. The bulk of her pregnancy seemed as though it must nearly double her regular weight, for it most assuredly was a heavy burden.

Luciana accepted her own shawl from Kisaiya and followed the queen and her still protesting maid.

Seeing that she was not going to convince the queen, Giuletta hurried ahead and brushed off the chair, pulling it well away from the table for the queen to sit.

Idala sank down, a faint, wan smile indicating her pleasure at the exercise and her exhaustion by it. She pointed to a chair for Luciana and turned to her handmaid. "Giuletta, I will take something to eat now, and if you summon the doctor, I'll be forced to replace you."

"Yes, Majesty," the young woman said, clearly displeased. She turned away worriedly when the queen suddenly burst into tears once more.

Idala was inconsolable. "He said I was not going to raise my children."

"But we can't know if any or all of the prophecy will come true," Luciana said. She looked helplessly at her own maid.

"I concur, Your Majesty," the soft-spoken Romani girl said. Hesitating, Kisaiya finally laid a consoling hand on the queen's quaking shoulders.

Tears welled in Luciana's eyes. She had not meant to make the queen's condition worse. She had *allowed* herself to be convinced, and why? To prove Stefano wrong, perhaps? Had her intentions been as honest as she thought now? Knowing, however, that her acquiescence had been an honest attempt to serve, Luciana's tears spilled over; within moments, Kisaiya was left trying to console both of them.

V

"Waste not fresh tears over old griefs."

—Alexander

"WHAT goes on here?"

Both crying women stiffened and turned at the sound of King Alban . . . and he was, without doubt, very angry. Beside him, he noted Stefano taking in the scene of what could only be half-cleared spell work and a wicker basket. He saw the recognition and sense of betrayal in Stefano's eyes as he then looked at his own wife.

The tears ran freely down Luciana's cheeks as she turned away, unable to meet her husband's gaze. Outside, the gathering thunderclouds let loose. The storm was reflected in his friend's expression.

"Lucia—" Stefano whispered, shaking his head.

"It was my fault, brother! I commanded her to," Idala said quickly, knuckling the tears from her eyes.

"But we agreed . . . ?" Stefano said to his wife, as though nothing else existed.

The hurt in her husband's eyes seemed to affect the *Araunya* like darts to her heart. She dropped her head and would not look at him, though she watched him from the corners of her eyes. Stefano reached out to the brazier, then turned to the fireplace and withdrew the half-burned bandanna with Alessandra's crest on it. The *Araunya* extended her arm as though to stop him, wincing when he touched it.

"*Marimé*!" The Duchessa *e Araunya* rose quickly, slapping her husband's arm so that he dropped the burned bit of cloth. Luciana grabbed a pitcher of water from the basin near Idala's water closet. With her free hand, she grabbed Stefano's sleeve at the wrist and, without notice or explanation, spit on him. "Living water!" she announced and then poured water from the ewer so that it flowed over his hand to the carpeted floor. "Running water. By these, I remove the stain upon you." She then spit on the hand that had held his arm and repeated the process on herself.

With Idala fully in his arms now, her head upon his shoulder, the king demanded, "I say again—what goes on here?" He looked pointedly at Luciana. He coughed at the smoke and smells coming from the fireplace, waving a free hand in front of his face.

Stefano closed on his wife's side, facing Alban and, before his wife could answer, said, "Majesty, perhaps this should be a more private audience."

Alban's attention turned to the atrium. Besides *il dottore* Bonta and the wraithlike chirurgeon, Sebastiani and also Idala's lady-in-waiting had joined the hysterical scene . . . as had a dozen more servants and courtiers.

"I agree." Disentangling himself from his wife's clutching arms, Alban said to the crowd, "Your concern for your queen is most appreciated. It would best suit, however, if you returned to your duties so that I might handle this *family* matter."

Not, Alban realized, that anyone could call this a strictly family matter with the attendance of not one, but two black-blooded Gypsies.

As the courtiers started to leave, some hesitated, looking to the *Araunya* and *then* him. Alban's face flashed with irritation.

"Majesty?"

Alban's attention returned to the entrance to his lady's receiving room where not one, but several members of the crowd had called out at once. Among them were Sebastiani, the Court Herald Estensi, the doctor, and his assistant. Alban shook his head but, reluctantly, waved Sebastiani to stay since he had been in recent conversation about crimes against the Crown. He suspected, sadly, that this conversation would be pertinent.

"But—" *il dottore* Bonta protested.

"If you are needed, you will be called," Stefano said, and his tone, though curt, at least sounded sympathetic.

At this point, Alban looked ready to scream for silence so that he could get an explanation for his wife's state of panic. Instead, he took a steadying breath and nodded to Estensi and his man, Strozzini. "You two will see that we are not disturbed."

The Court Herald bowed deeply. Strozzini nodded curtly and bowed. Together with Estensi, he ushered everyone else outside—except for one thin black figure who slipped around them with a dismissive wave.

"May I help you, Your Highness?" Alban asked through gritted teeth.

Prince Pierro deMedici produced a wizened, coy smile. "But, as you say, Your Majesty—*cousin*, this is a family matter and —"

"I am sure you are most curious and even wish to help," Alban allowed, "but you will understand that this is a most private matter."

Prince Pierro looked around the room at the Gypsy lady-in-waiting . . . and then to Stefano, Luciana, and the Duca Sebastiani. "Oh?"

"I will be advised and this is a subject for the more immediate family," Alban said, breaking free of Idala's grasp. "But it's unnecessary for me to explain this to you . . . and I am confident your own wife has her own demands on your time." For the second time in a matter of hours, Alban pointedly ushered the prince to a door and shut it tightly behind him.

"Wait!"

Luciana's voice was distinct from his wife's, most notably because it sounded strong and clear, no longer muffled from crying. He turned from the door to find her at his side.

"Where is Giuletta?" she asked.

"Pardon?" Alban said.

"Giuletta. The queen's lady-in-waiting. She came for you if I am not mistaken," Luciana said, reaching for the door.

"You are not . . . mistaken," Stefano admitted. "You stay with Their Majesties. I'll go . . . with your permission, Sire?"

Alban nodded. "Yes, yes, but return quickly. I want to get to the bottom of this business."

Anger twisted in Stefano's gut. How could she? How could Luciana have deliberately cast magic? He had argued with her, pleaded with her, and even outright forbade her use of magic. After they had lost Arturo, their firstborn, to stillbirth, how could she risk another by spell-casting?

He tried to contain his anger as he left his sister's suite and pushed through the crowd, searching the curious faces for the vaguely familiar one of the lady in question. As much as he wanted to question Luciana privately, he realized that was going to be impossible. Her use of magic had caused the scene in the queen's quarters. Ignoring the poisonous glare of Prince deMedici, Stefano finally spotted the young woman and caught her eye. "Your queen has need of you, Signorina."

The girl's cheeks turned scarlet. Dropping her gaze to the floor, she made her way back through the crowd and curtsied to him. "*Si*, Your Grace."

Stefano acknowledged the gathered courtiers briefly as he guided the young woman back to his sister's apartments. Strozzini opened the door for him. In the little antechamber, Stefano moved to stand between the lady and the queen's reception room. "Tell me, Signorina, why would you linger out there when you know you are going to be needed here?"

"I—" The girl bowed her head. "I am afraid of what Their Majesties will do."

Brows raised, Stefano presented the girl with his second handkerchief. "I am confident, Lady, that the king is a temperate man—"

"But not where his queen is involved and she, as you have seen, is in no fair frame of mind. I disobeyed her by summoning the king."

Stefano could not argue with that, though he, as Idala's brother and a husband himself, felt her decision had been perfectly appropriate. "Your abilities in observation, since accurate, will mean she will be even-handed." The girl's tears fell ever faster. Weepy women were not his customary habit to indulge, so thank heavens he had married a woman of a temper to not normally be so wet about the eyes. He sighed.

Though, thinking of Luciana, she was also of a temperament to do as she saw fit. "Well, be assured that the king is a fair-minded man. Come now, let's not try his patience further by making him wait longer." With that, he opened the door and swept the errant maid back to her Queen's side.

He felt no better when Idala and the girl were reunited and both began crying anew. He was almost to the end of his patience with the weeping when he looked at Luciana. Her eyes, a deep brown, were darker than normal. The two Romani—his wife and Kisaiya—stood together, as tight-lipped as ever. They would stand together, metaphorically as well. Duca Sebastiani stood frowning, looking from one woman to the next. If his frown were any deeper, it would have been an audible growl. Stefano sympathized.

He did a quick review of the room, besides the king and queen, Luciana, and the other duca, the two maids remained. So there were to be seven witnesses to whatever was to be said. Stefano wanted urgently to know how culpable his wife was in this business and whether he would be able to keep her out of trouble . . . at least with the Royal House. They would talk later. For now, in the immediate moment, something had to be done about the smell of whatever was burning in the fireplace.

He peered into the flames, coughing and wrinkling his nose. "What the devil is this?" he asked, pointing to the offensive remnants of what looked to be songbirds in the fire. Without a doubt the birds' burning feathers were the source of the smell. Covering his nose and mouth with his hand, he stoked the fire and pushed the birds back where the flames burned higher.

When no one spoke immediately, Stefano turned and looked at Luciana. "What *was* that? What were you doing with them?"

"They are a message . . . to Their Majesties," Kisaiya finally answered, moving to stand closer to her charge, Luciana.

"A message? Dead birds wrapped in Gypsy Silk . . . ?" Sebastiani ground out. "It's foul magic, I'd wager."

"In and of itself, no. It's *not* magic," Luciana responded angrily, her eyes sparkling with temper. "It was a *patrín* . . . a message in the fashion my people use to speak to one another when we are on the move."

Try as he might, Stefano's temper broke as he was caught between outright fury with his wife and worry about what it might have done to her and the child. "But what of this?" he asked, waving at the table where the vestiges of Luciana's magic use still remained.

Alban raised a silencing hand. "Patience! We are after facts and will hold judgment and criticism until the end. Sebastiani, I am sure that my wife, less distracted, would have long since offered you a seat to get you off of that foot . . . and I will assume that is the source of your tone for you would not wish to intimidate a witness before the Crown."

"Of course not, Your Majesty," Sebastiani said, plopping into the closest chair.

Idala, Stefano's queen and lovingly indulged younger sister, buried her face in her kerchief despite its being thoroughly sodden. Giuletta let out a fresh wail.

In a rare show of temper, the king snapped his fingers and pointed at Giuletta. "*You* will cease your nonsense!"

Immediately, the girl silenced her laments, whimpering as she bit down hard on her lip. Idala, too, made an effort to stop her tears, accepting Alban's proffered fresh kerchief with a tentative—and very wet—smile, which immediately disappeared into a solemn mask of self-control.

Guessing at what might be ahead; Stefano felt a twinge of pride at seeing something of the old Idala, a woman capable of intelligence and resolve, all of which had seemed to disappear in the recent months of this latest pregnancy.

Stefano turned to his wife. Luciana suddenly seemed to be the subject of everyone's immediate concern.

Torn, Stefano looked at her as Luciana straightened to her full height and boldly met the gazes of those around her. He could not help his reactions to her. Just her name warmed him, and knowing that she was his own . . . that she bore his child. . . . He did not like the deep circles beneath her eyes. She was beyond tired. What had the magic done to her? He could see that her own pregnancy weighed on her and, yet, Luciana made herself ever ready to his sister. He moved to her side. Whatever she was about to face, and no matter his anger, Luciana would not face them alone. He looked pointedly at his friend, the king.

"Now," Alban said, casting his gaze around the people

collected in the queen's parlor, "let us hear what all this business is about. Who shall begin?"

Though Alban asked the question of all and sundry, he focused on Luciana. Stefano felt a stir of protectiveness, an urge to defend his wife from whatever. Once a single stone was uncovered, other stones tended to follow and he knew—Alban and Idala knew—there were things Luciana had done that were best not discussed in front of Sebastiani lest a trial by the Palantini be formed and they would have her head. He knew nothing for certain and, frankly, had been happier not knowing what dealings Luciana had in the sudden and suspicious death of Princess Bianca less than a year ago. But should one incriminating word be said and, somehow, would find its way to Ortensia and Pierro, then neither he nor even Alban would be able to save the "Gypsy witch" . . . and, yes, he knew what the other courtiers said of her and her sister all the while wearing their magical Gypsy Silk with nary a thought.

Luciana, however embroiled in one suspense or another, was unfailingly truthful . . . in her own circuitous way. As she drew breath to speak, Stefano turned his back ever-so-briefly to the "*gadjé*" court and pressed a kiss to the edge of her ear, whispering, "Carefully, *mia cara*."

She swayed into him and, in more intimate surroundings, he would have gathered her all so willingly into his arms, carried her to her chamber and ravished her thoroughly from her smallest toe to her—Stefano stopped his thoughts there. The quickfire between them never waned and, knowing that his whispers burned a response from her, only made it harder for him to turn back and give his full attention to the proceedings. He noted Kisaiya's cautioning glare.

"These things *are* . . . ?" Stefano prompted Luciana, gesturing to the fireplace.

"More importantly, what purpose do they serve?" Sebastiani asked.

"They were a message sent by way of my people to . . . to me for the queen. It was a warning that an ill-minded sorcerer acted against the White Crown," she explained.

"And you know this how?" Sebastiani asked.

"How?" Luciana repeated as though his question made no sense. She shook her head impatiently. "I know the mind of the makers, the *Fata*, we call them—"

"Bah! Fairies are for children's tales," Sebastiani snapped, waving his hand dismissively.

Remarkably, it was Alban who countered Sebastiani's disbelief before Luciana could. "No, Alessandra, the *Araunya minore*, the *Araunya di Cayesmengro* said that this is part of the magic of the Gypsy Silk—"

Luciana and Kisaiya both hissed, the *Araunya* sending her attendant a quieting look. "My little sister shared more with you than she should, Majesty. I know that she did it in trust as the *Araunya di Cayesmengro*, but I am now *Araunya di Cayesmengri e Cayesmengro* and I ask that you tell no one else . . . No one that doesn't already know, that is." She nodded pointedly to the heavy-set, older duca sitting and nursing his foot.

"Now see here—!" Sebastiani began.

Alban raised his hands. "You, Duca Sebastiani, have been taken into a solemn, royal confidence and you shall treat all said before you as so. Do you understand?"

Stefano glanced over at his political comrade, meeting the man's gaze. "No good would come from trying to steal the Romani secrets. They alone have the power and the infrastructure to make Gypsy Silk. We dare not lose that trade to anyone. There are those among us who would try to take advantage—"

"Enough," Alban said. He helped his wife into her chaise lounge, sat on the end of it and took her feet into his lap. "We are here to discuss this bit of magic and the source of our wives' tears—if I am not mistaken."

Idala stuttered a whimpering sigh. She waved her hands. "It's no use now, Luciana. Tell them what they want to know."

"All of it?" Luciana whispered, paling beneath her dark complexion.

"Whatever they want to know. Tell them and no harm shall fall on your head, for you only did as I commanded. Yes, Alban?" the queen said. She turned her piercing green eyes on her sibling. "Stefano?"

"It shall be so," Alban agreed, looking expectantly at Luciana and Stefano.

Reluctantly, Stefano nodded. "It shall be as you say, my queen."

"The birds warn of multiple births, the black ones of . . .

something else," Luciana began, gratefully sinking into the chair her husband pulled 'round for her.

"Something else? What else?" the king asked.

Luciana rubbed her hands together thoughtfully. "In the course of time . . . about eight months ago . . . spells were cast and the queen bears ill-gotten seed."

Stefano gripped the back of his wife's chair. So much seemed clearer now. Idala's weakness this pregnancy . . . the sheer *size* of her. He smoothed his mustache into place. "And how do you know this, *mia cara*?"

"Spells?" Sebastiani gasped, looking from Luciana to the queen.

The queen sighed. "It's my fault and you should say it, Luciana. If I were not so desperate to be pregnant . . . to give you another child, Alban . . ."

The king laid a finger on his wife's lips, but the words were out.

"*You*! You, Your Majesty?" Sebastiani demanded, jumping up onto his good foot and immediately falling back down without the support of his left leg. "You cast magic on *la famiglia reale*?"

"No!" Luciana and the king burst out at once. The king motioned for Luciana to continue.

"Her Majesty, with the aid of my sister, cast a spell, but it was not on the royal family, rather on Tyrrhia itself so that it might prosper and . . . and . . ."

"Grow ever more fruitful," Idala supplied, resting her head against the back of the lounge. She was done with her secrets apparently.

Stefano stared at his sister, appalled. He spoke to her as a brother to a sister, forgetting for a briefest moment that she was also his queen. "Of all the harebrained things you've ever done, 'Dala! What were you thinking?"

The queen sighed. "I wasn't. At least not clearly. I kept after Alessandra, pestering her until she gave in." She looked at Luciana ruefully. "She—Alessandra—said you would not be pleased."

"There are many things my sister did that I was not pleased with, Majesty, the greatest of which was getting herself murdered by—" She bit off the words, but not soon enough.

"By whom, *Araunya*?" Duca Sebastiani asked. It was

clear he was not going to take her silence as an end to that discussion.

Stefano placed a hand on his wife's shoulder, fearing what she might say next.

"As Ortensia, Bianca was mad for the throne. She was . . . in league with certain people. I made it my business to find out," Luciana said. She patted Stefano's reassuring hand and continued. "Bianca conspired with the bishop—the cardinal—and Conte Urbano diVega and others for the White Throne, but of them I am sure. The conte tried to poison both me and my husband. Cardinal delle Torre . . . he cast the foul magic."

"The cardinal?" Sebastiani sputtered. "But he is—*was* a man of the cloth, of *the* Church. You must be mistaken. Did you play any part in his demise?"

Stefano breathed a little easier, knowing the answer to that question. "No. She was *here* with me, with *us*, when the cardinal met his end in Palermo."

"Of course, of course," Sebastiani muttered. One hairy gray feather of a brow raised and he looked at the king. "I have rather taken over this questioning. I'm sorry, Your Majesty."

"The truth has come out," Alban said, sighing.

Idala sniffed. "Not all of it."

The king, who had been preparing to rise, sat back down. "What more is there?"

"I have been so ill . . . and so curious. When Luciana—the *Araunya*—gave me the . . . the message, I could not hold my curiosity longer. I tried to, really I did. I was not going to endanger my pregnancy, but, you see, I *had* to know. So I asked Luciana," Idala said. "I asked her repeatedly. Finally, I had to command her assistance. It was necessary."

"Necessary!" Stefano scoffed. "You've done too much dabbling in magic, *piccolina*! You've no idea of the consequences and yet, even now, you meddle in things you should not, and know nothing about!"

"The Duca di Drago has the right of it, and now his wife is involved," Sebastiani said softly. "It's a serious matter. But there's more, isn't there?" He asked the question acutely, directing it at Luciana.

Stefano's wife nodded and hung her head. "I performed magic for the White Queen. I called upon the *Fata* to make clear their message." She paused, waiting for the other duca to protest again, but when he remained silent, staring at her, she began again. She looked to the king and queen and then to Stefano, pleading. "I had hoped, even though it was not right, they would send my sister as messenger . . . so I might see her *mulló* again."

"Her what? What?" Sebastiani interrupted, hand to his ear.

"Her *mulló*. My people, we do not just die when there has been murder—or other foulness committed. We become akin to vengeful ghosts . . . except worse," Luciana explained, shifting in her seat and glancing at her maid who stood silently nearby, head down. "They take blood to sustain themselves and torture the souls of the living. They are *marimé*, cursed."

"And you hoped *that* would appear before our queen?" Sebastiani asked incredulously.

Luciana looked away. "I am told she's no *mulló* now. She, unlike I, was fairy-touched, a Child of the Bloods as we call them and was taken to the Summerlands with the *Fata*. The maggiore was able to save my sister's body in time—we have one year from our deaths to be spared an eternal state as *mulló*—and saw that it and her *vardo* were burned," Luciana explained reasonably.

"The maggiore?" Sebastiani repeated.

Stefano looked at his friend impatiently. "The *Araunya di Cayesmengro*'s affianced. Maggiore di Montago?" He gently prodded his wife who nodded impatiently.

"The Escalade officer that's got himself missing?" Sebastiani asked, scratching his whiskerless chin.

"Oh, he isn't missing," Idala said firmly. When Sebastiani looked as if the queen had grown wings and feathers, she pointed to Luciana. "Ask her."

"He dwells among the *Fata* now," Luciana said.

"Oh, with your sister and all the other little fairies," Sebastiani retorted.

"Not all of the *Fata* are small, Your Grace, and I would not challenge them or one of them will play tricks on you," Luciana said stiffly, arching her brow. "I might even help."

"She threatened me! The Gypsy threatened me!" Sebastiani protested, pointing his finger at Luciana.

Stefano shook his head. Perhaps a trial was not so far off as he had hoped. As angry with her as he was, he could not lose Luciana. He tried to make peace. "You did challenge her, Your Grace, and she *is* the *Araunya*—of both houses now. And have care how you address my wife. She is of the Rom, of true black blood."

Alban waved his hands dismissively. To the older man, the king asked, "Is it a threat if you don't believe in them, Your Grace?"

Sebastiani looked between both men and then the queen and the *Araunya*. He puffed his lips, but otherwise fell silent.

For once, Luciana had accepted his assistance *and* his protection with nary a muttered breath, Stefano realized. Mayhap she was learning!

"It's just that . . . I would not contest our friendship, but even you must agree that what she says is preposterous," Sebastiani said to Stefano, shaking his head.

"What I talk of is magic, Your Grace, and if you do not believe in it, why do you wear Gypsy Silk as we speak?" Luciana said. "Doesn't it make you look younger? Perhaps . . . healthier than you truly are?"

Sebastiani looked at his clothes, then at her down his long nose and through one eye, clearly wondering how much she could truly see beneath the glamour of the silk.

Luciana shifted in her seat, and arched her back, rubbing it. "As I said, I summoned the *Fata*, seeking answers for Her Majesty, the White Queen. It was not a fairy, nor even my sister that came to us, but Maggiore di Montago—"

"How exactly did *he* come to be in the Summerlands?" Idala interrupted.

Luciana bowed her head and bit her lip. As Stefano knew, the details of the maggiore's demise had been reported to Luciana by Romani witnesses, but so far she had withheld the exact details of the maggiore's death from the queen. Now that the question was asked directly—and all eyes looked at her curiously—she would have to answer. She looked back up at him and then to her audience, with a slight smile forced to her lips. "He, I was told, ran into my sister's burning *vardo* and never came back out. His men searched the wreckage, but could find no evidence of either body . . . and then you saw him again today. He is happy. He is with his love."

"You *saw* him? I thought you did something simple, like

scrying, but this . . . this is big magic. Isn't it?" Stefano asked, tilting Luciana's face up to look into her eyes.

Luciana licked her lips—a sign that she was not telling the exact truth—and shrugged. "It was simple enough, really. The *Fata* were waiting to be summoned by someone. They sent the maggiore as their emissary."

Stefano decided to let her prevarication slip and motioned for her to continue. She looked back at her audience, focusing on the king.

"As I said, the maggiore came to us from the Summerlands—of the *Fata*'s magic, understand?" Luciana said to Stefano. To the king, she continued, "I used magic to summon him . . . to let them know that I wished to speak to them, the *Fata*.

"When he came, the maggiore spoke of a prophecy. Of the birds. There was one small white one, but split in two. You see, when . . . when my sister and the queen cast the spell, Idala was already pregnant. That child, by the grace of the spell, became two."

"Two?" the king repeated. "Twins?" In spite of himself, he sounded pleased. Stefano could not blame him for taking heart at the good fortune.

"And they are to be born healthy," Luciana added. "There were two black birds that looked as one. One was small, dwarfed by the other. The greater of the birds overwhelmed the other three in size, all in a tangled root of mandrake. This bespeaks great evil.

"The maggiore spoke not of two children, Majesty, but of four. You are to have a third daughter who is not of your bloodline, but of the black-blooded people . . . my people," Luciana said.

"Not of my bloodline?" the king repeated, looking at his wife in confusion.

"Hear her words and be patient, Alban," Idala urged.

"This child of the black blood is fairy-touched because she, like my sister and the maggiore, will be born of Tyrrhian *and* Romani blood. She will be reborn because of her great bravery, and you should be proud to call such a daughter your own," Luciana said.

Alban glanced between Stefano's wife and his own. He placed a hand on his wife's abdomen. "I swear it will be so. She will be of two people and the Royal House."

Luciana nodded her approval. "Now, what I must say is no great news as has come before, Your Majesty, for the other bird. There will be another and he, too, while of your making is not of your seed. He was the source of the evil spell that overtook the queen's and it was he who stole my sister's body from the crypt when all this began."

"He?" Sebastiani asked, his voice hushed, enthralled. "Who is this he you speak of?"

Luciana took a deep breath, sitting up a little straighter. Her chin jutted out. Stefano could see she was preparing for a fight. He knew the look. "The cardinal, of course."

"Of course? But magic—?" Sebastiani protested.

"Must I?" Stefano asked, stepping in lest his wife lose her temper and manage to get herself in deeper trouble than she was already. When the other duca fell silent again, he said, "I, too, can bear witness to the cardinal using magic. Black magic. The blackest. I saw it with mine own two eyes upon the cliff these many months ago before the mountebank made his final escape from the White King's court, thus avoiding justice in the murder of my sister-in-law, the *Araunya di Cayesmengro*."

Stefano felt Luciana's tension drain somewhat and guessed, in part, because he had not broken the law against speaking the name of the dead. It was an odd custom, but hers, and one he would respect.

Idala straightened her spine and dabbed at her eyes, once more regaining the regal bearing she had once had. "Duca Sebastiani, in my husband's counsel room you are permitted to speak freely and, while wishing to keep this freshness of presence, I must also be able to give some assurance to those who serve me that their word and good name will not be so frequently contested. Question, yes; but this scoffing attitude cannot be tolerated. If nothing else, it is not our Neoplatonic way."

Duca Sebastiani nodded and started to rise. When Idala signaled him to stay seated, he bowed from his chair instead. "Your graciousness is most appreciated, Majesty."

Idala nodded and turned back to Luciana, her gaze piercing with some hidden meaning. "We are done with this prophecy then, are we not? *This* was the source of our tears, Alban."

Silence ensued, for a moment. It could not last, of course, Stefano thought.

"Is there proof that you can offer?" Duca Sebastiani asked as he held up his hands in the sign of forbearance. "I speak not of proof for proof's sake, though that is always appreciated, but of the court because we have another man accused of crimes against the White Throne. He is said to be the cardinal's man."

Stefano squeezed Luciana's shoulders, willing her to choose her words carefully. "We have given the course of things . . ." She paused to lick her lips. "As I know it." She patted his hand, perhaps indicating his grip was too tight. He released her, but kept his hands resting on the back of the chair near her shoulders.

"According to the history given by Brother Tomasi, all has been confirmed," Stefano said. "If we are to take his word for it, this man was—"

"Held in thrall by the cardinal?" Luciana suggested.

Stefano nodded and shrugged at the same time. "We have but his word for it and your account which does not truly speak to it. The Escalade officers were convinced."

"As the cardinal's man, then, he committed magic against the State—be he 'in thrall' or no. He must be punished," Sebastiani growled, thumping his fist on the arm of his chair.

"One can be tricked into casting a spell," Luciana pointed out from her seat.

"How?" Stefano demanded, almost in unison with the king, queen, and Duca Sebastiani . . . only he regretted asking.

"There are many ways," Luciana said diffidently. "A prayer is nothing more than a spell."

"Heresy!" Sebastiani snapped, crossing himself.

"By my word, Your Grace," Alban growled, saving his wife from making whatever protest had come to her lips. To Luciana, he seemed to try to remove the anger from his voice. "You need to explain this so that *this* simple Catholic understands you." He touched his heart. "I study the Neoplatonic philosophies of spiritual freedom as most educated Tyrrhians do . . . but even this . . . it bends the mind in a manner that it does not want to be bent, *Araunya*."

Luciana nodded, biting her lip. Stefano leaned down,

preparing to speak to his wife again, but was interrupted by his sister.

"Do sit. Please forgive me for not having thought of it sooner," the queen said to Stefano and motioned for the two women to do likewise.

Beside him, the girl called Kisaiya sighed softly. From the girl's expression, it was clear she was not happy with the candor of her *Araunya* more so than relieved to be off her feet. Stefano bent near Luciana's ear. "I love you—witch or no—but not all share this fondness for you." He pressed a kiss to her temple.

"This audience seems to promise much," Alban said thoughtfully.

Luciana's hand slid up Stefano's arm, squeezing it briefly. It communicated volumes, most importantly of which was that she understood. "Were there another way, *mio caro* . . . there is so much at stake," she whispered back.

Alban cleared his throat and coughed . . . pointedly.

"Forgive me, Majesties, I was seeing to my wife's health," Stefano said, bowing. He sat upon the arm of her chair and took Luciana's hand. "You were explaining how a prayer was much like a spell," he reminded, keeping his tone light. He was eager to hear this explanation, for he had never thought of casting magic in this way . . . perhaps it would explain why she disagreed with him over the use of it and even outright disobeyed him.

"Mmm," Luciana said. "A prayer . . . it is an appeal to the Almighty, yes? Offerings of scents and oils, the breaking of the bread, you see?"

"Yes, yes, that is clear to all," Alban said, a curious edge creeping into his voice.

"Offering scents and oils of prescribed kind for Catholic ceremonies—or any other religion—is the same, even in what you call 'witchcraft.'" Luciana paused, her countenance taking on that expression of inexplicable awe. Blissful, Luciana continued, "What one calls a prayer, another might call a spell. You see?"

Sebastiani looked to the king and queen and folded his arms over his chest, clearly not convinced.

Luciana frowned, used to dealing with disbelievers. "Your Grace," she said, motioning to the elder duca. "You pray for your health. Appeal to the Almighty."

"God. I pray to God," Sebastiani replied, his jaw jutting.

"A name is a name. There are often many names for a single thing. So you pray for deliverance from your pain, yes? And yet that does not stop you from taking *il dottore* Bonta's poultices or his chirurgeon's bleedings."

"*He* helps those who help themselves," Sebastiani retorted.

"So you are a learned man. You understand the need to aid your prayers, and yet this is not heresy. In the Roman State to our north, it is heresy at various times to even read and study the Bible as you do here in Tyrrhia, being a learned man," Luciana pressed.

"Some people are closed-minded to the simple freedoms of a man's own thinking," Sebastiani said with a dismissive wave.

"And so, Your Grace, we are brought to our conundrum. To some people's mind a spell is no more than saying a prayer with offerings or behaviors meant to aid us in our endeavors," Luciana replied.

"By some people, you mean yourself," Sebastiani said, glancing toward the king and, reluctantly, the queen.

Stefano squeezed Luciana's hand in an attempt to warn her, but she would not have it and shook her hand free.

"Of course, Your Grace. I make no pretense of who and what I am, of *mi famiglia* connections," she said. "I am *Araunya di Cayesmengri e Cayesmengro*, sole representative of the Gypsy Silk traders—a luxury, we do not dissemble as being anything but magical and one that you, as noted in your garb, take full advantage of."

Stefano refrained from smiling at the blush of color in Sebastiani's face. It was a hard-won point.

"So, you mean to say, Your Grace, that by ease of . . . of, for lack of better terms, 'confusion,' someone can innocently be led down a path they might otherwise shun?" Alban asked.

Luciana gripped Stefano's hand. "If you must put it that way, then do so at your ease, but just as 'magic' and 'spells' can be meant for ill use, 'prayers' can also be offered with a selfish mind—that a troublesome enemy might be found at the bottom of the stair or that something meant in a goodly way be twisted by lies and illusions of doing good—"

"Such as the spell the cardinal used on Brother Tomasi . . . as he claims," Stefano said.

"And how is it that the maggiore actually came to be in the Summerlands, Luciana?" Idala asked, abruptly changing the turn of the conversation.

"You testified to me yourself that his love and devotion to my sister were unbending, and he had the black blood in him, too," Luciana said.

"He was vigilare, an Escalade officer; he foreswore his allegiance to his black-blooded brothers. He was on a mission for the queen. How could he—" Sebastiani began.

"And when a man takes a wife, by Tyrrhian law, he forsakes all others," Stefano said. "As your brother and *Colonello* in the Escalade, I am twice sworn to you, my queen, but . . ." He paused, kissing Luciana's hand. ". . . if something happened to her, I could not say that my reaction might be so very different from the maggiore's."

"But you speak of marriage—" Idala began. She stopped abruptly, looking up to her husband who had made some barely articulate noise.

"How long before we could ever have wed, did I swear myself to you? Did you ever take my word as less?" Alban asked.

"What needs of this?" Idala proclaimed, throwing up her hands. "Whatever means took him, he shall be missed, and I have not a reason for complaint of his service whilst he lived."

"Your Graces, *Araunya*, if you will pardon Us. My wife and I have much to speak of . . . perhaps we might have our lunches in private and we shall reconvene our discussion later this afternoon," the king said.

Sebastiani swung his foot off the stool and rose to his feet. As a youth, he must have been some lumbering giant, for in his elder years, he was no small man to be taken lightly, no matter his health. He was an admirable ally and a wicked foe.

Stefano pressed a smile to his lips, nodding to the king and queen. "Then we shall retire now, by Your Majesties' leave." When Alban nodded, he helped Luciana from her chair and all but rushed her and her maid into the corridor which was still busy with people. Some milled near the queen's apartment, but most had continued about their business of the day. He called out after Sebastiani, who stopped and waited for Stefano and Luciana to reach him.

"What say you to all this . . . this news, *compagno*?" Stefano asked him quietly, offering his hand to the older man in friendship.

The old man looked at his hand, hesitated, and finally took it. He looked at Luciana, nodded stiffly to her, and said, "Methinks there have been too many cooks in the queen's kitchen and all had best be wary of harder times ahead."

It was not the answer Stefano had hoped for, but the elder duca spoke with no real animosity, so he took him at his word and let the other man shuffle off.

VI

"Dignity consists not in possessing honors, but in the consciousness that we deserve them."

—Aristotle

ALBAN studied his wife over his plate. At first, he had eaten with gusto, his mind on the prophecy of four children to be born of this pregnancy, but then his mind had turned to the cost it would have to her, his queen. Looking very pale, she had only toyed with her food.

"Come, 'Dala, eat something," he pressed gently, reaching out to her.

Idala sighed and firmly pushed her plate away. "I'm not hungry."

"Perhaps some tea and ciabatta to settle your stomach, then?" Alban suggested.

She shook her head. "I am not ill and I am not hungry. I want for nothing." Idala took his hand. She forced a tremulous smile to her lips. "You have seen to that . . . that I want for nothing, I mean, and I thank you for it."

Feeling truly worried now, Alban pushed his own plate away, across the table. "Do we thank the bird for its song? No. There are no thanks you owe me, beloved."

The queen sighed, her gaze seemingly on the rain sliding down the windowpanes of her solar. She looked utterly sad and beyond his reach. Alban squeezed his wife's hand until she looked back at him.

"What troubles you so?" he asked. He lifted her hand and pressed a kiss to the inside of her palm.

Idala's hand tightened into a fist, as though holding that kiss so that it might never fade. She squeezed her eyes tight, perhaps fighting back the tears which she had shed so freely earlier in the day?

"Alban . . . there is more to what the maggiore said to me than has been told to you," Idala said.

He frowned. "Was Luciana keeping secrets from me? I'll—"

"You'll do nothing," Idala replied firmly, looking at him again . . . finally. Her green eyes swam with unshed tears. "I kept her silent on this. It is a matter that you and I alone shall address." She recaptured his hand and brushed a kiss across his knuckles.

"You are starting to worry me, 'Dala," Alban said. He twisted in his chair so that he faced her directly. "What troubles you so?"

"You know that I love you?" she asked.

His heart warmed, as it always did when she spoke those words, but something hung in the air between them. Something was being left unsaid. "I am humbled by your feelings. I love you, more than—"

She affectionately pressed her hand to his mouth so that he could not finish saying the words. "I *know*, Alban. You have made it clear to me every day since we first met and I . . . Alban, we must talk. Frankly."

Alban felt as though his heart were in his throat. Certainly, breathing seemed nigh on impossible. "What is it you haven't told me?"

She looked away then, her hand dropping from the side of his face to the table and then to her lap where she fretted with the handkerchief. "There was more to the prophecy, as I said." She seemed to gather herself together and thrust the kerchief onto the table beside her untouched plate. "Alban, you know the delivery of children is not safe, that women die in childbirth."

"We have the finest doctor—" Alban began, but stopped when she shook her head.

"A doctor! *Il dottore* Bonta may be the finest doctor in all Tyrrhia, but he has never given birth!" Idala said.

Alban tried to laugh, but only a strangled sound came from his lips. He took a deep breath. Idala was late in her pregnancy. It had been trying these past months. Her health had not been the best. Of course, she was frightened. He struggled, recognizing her fears and wanting to encourage her, but how?

"*Il dottore* Bonta has delivered many a child . . . all of ours—"

"And we have a single son to show for all of those attempts. He could not save our daughter. She was nine days old before . . ." She shook her head fiercely and rubbed her nose with the back of her hand.

"Then you shall have a midwife. All you must do is say what you want, *mi adorata*," Alban said. He reached for her and was surprised when she held him at bay. He sank back into his seat, looking at her.

"The maggiore . . . the spirit . . . the fairy, whatever you want to call him . . . he said that I will not raise my children, Alban, and I fear what that will do to you . . . to them," Idala said, hiccoughing as she struggled to hold back her tears.

Alban froze. He felt as though his world drained away. He could not face living without her! She knew it though he had not been able to speak the words. He shook his head. Of course, she could not die. She would not die! He had not realized he said the words, until she gave a short, bitter laugh.

"How can you know?"

"I—I won't permit it! The prophecy could mean anything. You have many duties, my treasure, *mia rarita*, that take you away from our children. We have a governess—this prophecy, if it is to be believed, could mean only that!" Alban protested, struggling to reassure her . . . and, truth be told, himself.

She shook her head. "That is not what the prophecy meant, Alban. You must prepare yourself."

There was no preparing for what she spoke of.

Idala! Try as he might, other than half-formed prayers, Alban could think of nothing else. Could it be only a few hours since they last spoke? He had no time to prepare. He should never have left her side. No matter what she had said to reassure him. Alban raced after the young woman who had summoned him and easily passed her. His brother-in-law kept pace and, somewhere behind, the gouty-footed Duca Sebastiani and other courtiers followed.

Alban almost knocked Bonta, *il dottore reale*, off his ridiculously heeled feet as he burst through the door and atrium. Sweeping past the half-toppled doctor, he found Idala on the champagne-colored chaise, propped with pillows and covered in a Gypsy Silk throw meant to disguise her malaise. Luciana, Stefano's wife sat at her side.

Brushing past Luciana, the king sank to his knees beside his queen, and took her gently into his arms, kissing her cheeks, forehead, and then her lips. "Are you sure it is time?"

His wife nodded, unable to speak through her gritted teeth as she experienced the pain of labor.

The king turned accusingly toward *il dottore*, "There is nothing you can do to stop it? Shouldn't she have more time?"

Il dottore gave a little cough, "*Sí*, Your Majesty. There is *nothing* I can do to stop the pain that brings the children. In a pregnancy of this magnitude, I find it amazing that she has lasted this long. Pregnancies with multiple children most oftentimes come early.

"Let us get her to her chambers and—" Bonta continued.

"I want a midwife . . . and Luciana!" Idala said, gasping.

"You know that I do not keep a midwife in my service. I have arranged for everything . . . even a wet nurse, Your Majesty!" Bonta said in soothing tones.

"I want a midwife!" the queen insisted, looking wildly from the doctor to her husband.

"There hasn't been time!" Alban murmured apologetically.

"I have a woman. Stefano has seen that she is well-paid to be ready for my call. There is no reason she cannot—" Luciana began.

"The midwife is not here, Majesty," *il dottore* Bonta said. "However, I am prepared to—"

Idala gave a cry, violently shaking her head.

Stefano turned to Luciana's servant and said, "Send for the woman! The queen wants a midwife! Tell her not to spare the horses!"

The girl nodded and ran from the room. Rodrigo

Strozzini, Alban's bodyguard, ran after her, no doubt to do whatever he could to assist.

"Hurry!" Idala insisted. She reached for Luciana. "I want you and the witch!"

Alban looked at his wife in surprise. "Witch?"

Luciana took a deep breath. "I will attend her. I've been trained."

"Make yourself useful, *dottore*. You will make sure the midwife reaches my queen in time," Alban snapped.

"But as *il dottore* for *la famiglia reale*, I am perfectly capable—"

"Her Majesty has made it clear that she wishes for a midwife and the midwife she shall have. Do not question me further!" Alban declared, turning on the doctor like a ferocious dog ready to attack. "Until she gets here, the duchessa *e Araunya* will serve, but stay close, *dottore*!"

Bonta stepped back several feet in surprise, but bowed and quickly made his way to the atrium where all the attending servants waited—except for Giuletta who had returned to Idala's side.

"Send for the witch at The Dragon's Hearth, as we discussed," Idala finally managed to say to Luciana.

Luciana darted a quick glance at her husband.

"Lucia—" he whispered, shaking his head.

The queen reached up, her arms encircling Alban's neck. "Take me to my bedchambers *now*, my love. My time is near."

Alban nodded and slid his arm underneath his wife as he had done so many times before. Once standing, he hiked her up a little, closer to his body and the warmth of his heart. Before heading to the stairs, he broke into the tableau between Luciana and Stefano, whose face now clearly read some sense of betrayal, but he had no time for it now. "*Araunya*, you are with me!"

As he carried Idala up the stairs, his mind was a whirl of distraction. All he could think of were the prophecies made and told him by his wife over their private lunch. He thought of Idala's sense of impending doom and the great fear that he might lose her. He forced such thoughts away.

All would be well. He would see to it . . . somehow. The *Araunya* was here to help. All would be well. He hoped. He prayed.

As he prepared to lay his wife on her bed, Alban glanced over his shoulder. Stefano came, aiding his wife as she climbed the stairs; behind them came Giuletta, clearly anxious to be at her mistress' side.

In the bedchamber, Luciana moved quickly to throw back the coverlets and reveal the linen-covered, downy mattress. Alban laid his precious Idala down and looked at Luciana expectantly. "Now what?"

"Now, Majesty, you must let me help your wife change into a night shift and make her more comfortable," Luciana said decisively as she reached for the fresh nightdress that lay over the back of a bedside chair.

"And what should I do?" Alban asked, vaguely aware of those standing just behind him. Trailing, at various levels on the stair, were the duchi—he had been consulting with them again in a second mad session to plan for the de-Medici and other State affairs—all milling about to be first with news. Alban beckoned Stefano and the girl into the room and firmly shut the door in the faces of the courtiers.

The *Araunya* drew his attention back to her, saying, "Now, My Liege, you have been through this before. Send for mulled wine so that the maid can make her a sustaining drink. I shall let you know as soon as the queen asks for you." She hesitated. "When the other women arrive—"

"They will be sent to you forthwith. Until then, do you have everything that you need?" Alban asked. He pressed a kiss to Idala's brow and reached reluctantly for the handle of the door he had only just snapped shut. He sighed, trying to gather his resolve. His wife had gone through five previous pregnancies: once producing the heir to his throne, Dario Gian, now five; another producing a little girl who lived for nine short days; and then there were the stillbirths. He had seen the toll these pregnancies had taken on his queen. Between that history and the prophecy she had shared with him, he was afraid. Idala was his wife, his very life . . . she must survive! Whatever would he do without her? "Perhaps there is something that I can do? Let me stay—"

Idala shook her head against the pillows, taking a deep, stuttering breath. "No, beloved. I shall see you soon . . . after."

Alban knelt by the bed, catching Idala's hand in his own.

"'Dala, nothing can happen to you—" He felt a hand on his shoulder, breaking his concentration on his wife, who looked away. He looked up and saw Stefano standing at his side.

"Come, *compagno*," Stefano said urgently. "This is women's business."

"Go!" Idala insisted, dropping the king's hand.

Reluctantly, Alban rose. He pressed another kiss to his wife's brow and then allowed himself to be shooed from the room. He closed Idala's chamber door behind him and Stefano.

With the door closed again, Luciana and Giuletta helped Idala change into a nightdress. Carefully brushing out the queen's hair, Luciana braided it and knotted a ribbon at the end of the long queue.

Over these last months, by magic, herbs, and wile, they had delayed the queen's delivery for as long as possible. Now the time had come.

Just as she finished the binding of the queen's hair, Idala let out a soft cry as the bloody water burst from between her legs. Giuletta brought a basket of rags, and Luciana helped the queen clean herself.

A scratch at the door heralded a servant—Kisaiya returning and bringing Luciana's bag of magical tools with her. Giuletta left through the servants' entrance and came back shortly bearing a goblet and large decanter of mulled wine. How long, Luciana wondered, would it take the midwife to arrive? The midwife Stefano had hired for her was the wife of Capitano della Guelfa, one of the maggiore's men, who lived nearby. It occurred to Luciana then that no one had sent for the witch whom she had consulted in recent weeks about the queen's pregnancy.

"Kisaiya, see to it that someone sent for the *gadjé* witch," Luciana said just as her attention was drawn back to Idala as the first serious contractions began. As they eased, Giuletta pressed the goblet of wine to the queen's lips.

Idala had barely swallowed when the next contraction began. Luciana knew it simply by reading the queen's face. Her pains were long and hard and too quick between.

Without a word, Luciana reached into her bag and pulled out her bundle of herbs. She added to the queen's goblet of wine a few of the most secret herbs of her people: flowers from Isis Loop and Bitter Grind. They would serve to slow Idala's labor, if just a little.

Since it was obvious even to her that it would not be long before the first child came, Luciana hoped that both the midwife and witch would arrive before the first of the children Idala was to bear this night. In the meantime, she had Kisaiya create a ring of protection around the queen with ivory candles.

Luciana watched the mantel clock like a hawk, wondering when relief would arrive as well as timing the queen's pains.

It had been more than an hour when the latch finally turned. Maria della Guelfa entered and came immediately to the queen's aid. Though little more than an hour, it had seemed to Luciana more like two. While Luciana had been trained in birthing, she was not skilled at it. She had only been present for the births of her own stillborn son and that of her sister, Alessandra, when their mother had died.

Luciana gladly made room for Donna della Guelfa to work her own type of magic. Now her only responsibility was to serve the queen's comfort as the first child—a girl, fair of skin and hair—arrived.

The *gadjé* witch, old Nunzia Rui, made her entrance moments before midwife della Guelfa delivered the second daughter—another fair child.

Giuletta tied a golden cord loosely around the girl's left ankle, just as she had tied a white cord around the ankle of her older sister. The maid placed the swaddled child in a cradle with her sister and then covered the girls with an embroidered coverlet.

Donna Rui, the old, hunchbacked proprietress of a little shop in the capital city, had been secretly in near-constant attendance upon the queen since Luciana had learned of the magical nature of Idala's pregnancy some months ago.

Nunzia Rui built an altar on a table at the foot of the queen's bed with supplies from her shop. Despite her great age, Donna Rui moved with an economy of motion. She did everything precisely and with intent.

Donna Maria della Guelfa was another matter. She was an

exceptionally tall and thickly built woman, who bustled about her work, humming cheerfully even during the grimmest moments of delivery. She flitted between charges, responsive to the needs of her patients. Though very experienced, this was her first time attending a noblewoman's—much less a royal—birthing. If she was nervous, Luciana saw no sign of it.

Sending for a midwife had caused a stir amongst the courtiers, what with *il dottore* Bonta serving at the deliveries of every previous child of Alban and Idala's. Luciana could only imagine the uproar if they had sent for a Romani midwife. While many of the court had grown accustomed to her own presence, Luciana realized another Romani would have been out of the question. It would cause trouble in the fragile balance of the court and the resident Palantini. Prejudices against the Romani still ran strong, even if buried deep.

Thankfully, Donna della Guelfa proved herself unflappable where magic was concerned. She neither protested nor asked questions about the work that Nunzia Rui did as she circled the bed with candles and herbs. Far from being disconcerted by the spell work, della Guelfa moved easily in and about Rui, working her own kind of magic.

Summoned by the gusty cries of the princesses, *il dottore* Bonta made a forced appearance and, while his attentions to the queen were refused, there were no protestations from anyone when he examined the twin girls. Afterward, he hovered briefly before being sent from the room by the queen, who was now in her seventh hour of hard labor. It was clear Idala was exhausted, wanting only to rest and be with her children, but if the prophecy were to be believed, there were yet two children to be born.

The third child, it turned out, was also a daughter, but she could not be confused as a twin to her sisters. Where the others were fair, she was dark. No curling blonde-brown hair for her, and her eyes were practically black compared to the blue eyes of the others. Her hair was almost inky except for a streak of silvery-white that grew from her right temple, which marked her as fairy-touched. She was the black-blooded princess prophesied and, impossibly, a Child of the Bloods.

Luciana was glad that so many women were in attendance when the dark girl was born, so no one could argue that a Gypsy had stolen a baby from the White Queen and switched it with one of their own. Still, Giuletta was moved to wash the dark newborn a second time, just in case the birthing fluids disguised her natural color. They did not. She tied a champagne-colored ribbon around the ankle of this girl and placed her in a second cradle.

After the girl's birth, all that passed from Idala was blood. Maria massaged the queen's abdomen. Luciana remembered the midwife's doing the same to her at the end of her delivery of Arturo. Could it really be over at last?

Maria felt the queen's abdomen, continuing to massage her to deflate her womb. Suddenly, she stopped and turned to the other women, "There is yet one more!"

Idala groaned, not so much from exhaustion as the other women thought, but because of the prophecy, Luciana realized. Like her, the queen had hoped to be spared the fourth child . . . the child of the cardinal's spirit.

For a moment, there was a buzz of excited conversation among the *gadjé* attendees. Luciana glanced at Kisaiya and bit her tongue. She met the queen's gaze and saw the fear in Idala's eyes. Luciana sat on the bed and smoothed Idala's brow, to calm her. By now, Idala was beyond exhaustion, her ability to push, or assist the midwife in any way, feeble at best.

Time passed. Giuletta and Kisaiya closed the curtains against the light as night surrendered to the dawn.

Donna della Guelfa gave each of the girls, in turn, to their mother to suckle, hoping that this would help the delivery to progress. Despite her periodic contractions, the queen took a bit of bread soaked in the mulled wine and time to count fingers and toes, stroking tiny curls of fuzzy hair and adoring her daughters. She paused only briefly before accepting her dark daughter whom she studied with great care.

"She . . . this *one* will be a living tie between our people, won't she?" Idala asked as she held the child up to her sister-in-law.

Luciana smiled softly and nodded, stroking the hair of the White Princess with black blood.

The idyllic scene ended suddenly, with an explosive gush of blood and cramps too intense to allow the queen to hold her daughter any longer.

Maria swiftly took the girl and gave her to the queen's maid before she bent to examine the progress. She placed a steadying hand on Idala's thigh, motioning for Luciana, in her place at the head of the bed, to hold the queen's hands.

Luciana quickly obeyed, unable to completely smother the fear she felt for Idala . . . and even for herself, wondering if her own delivery would be so complicated. It was impossible to know, to not think of it. She turned her thoughts from herself and concentrated then fully on the White Queen, hiding her wince that came because of the death grip Idala had on her hands.

After several minutes, Maria sharply called Kisaiya to her side. To give her credit, she tried to whisper so that the queen did not hear her, but it was to no avail. "Consult the Royal Physician! Have him prepare a simple to slow the bleeding!"

Luciana's young maid hurried from the room.

Donna Rui frowned after the girl and then at the queen. She bent and rummaged in her basket, bringing out a candelabra with a branch of black tapers that she placed on the bedside table and lit.

Late in her own pregnancy, Luciana shifted awkwardly out of the old woman's way. All was quiet for the moment.

The queen caught her sleeve, "Please, Luciana. Stay by my side!"

Luciana forced a soothing smile, then smoothed back wisps of the queen's drenched, light brown hair. "Of course, I won't leave you, sister."

Idala's eyes closed and her lips pinched tight. Her grip on Luciana's hands was almost crippling. As the queen's pain passed, she opened her eyes again. "I know that it is unfair . . ." She shook her head, ready tears welled. "It's my fault you're pregnant as well . . . I should never have toyed with magic!"

"Stefano and I played some part in the conception of our child," Luciana said, laughing gently. "We have discussed this, you and I, have we not? Do not worry yourself about such things . . . at least not for now."

"Let me worry over them, Luciana, and then I can put everything else out of my mind," Idala groaned.

"Come. Dry your tears. This will be over soon and you

will have four babes. Four, Idala! All of Tyrrhia will be celebrating," Luciana said.

Idala's tears returned with such force that they choked out of her. She jerked her hand free as she doubled with pain.

"It's here!" Donna della Guelfa exclaimed. "I can see its head!"

At that moment, Kisaiya arrived, shutting the door in *il dottore*'s face, leaving him in the antechamber the queen had restricted him to earlier. She passed Luciana a glass goblet with a murky tonic from the physician.

Even as Luciana pressed the glass to Idala's lips, Donna Maria shook her head. "Fetch the physician! There is too much blood," the midwife hissed through gritted teeth.

From behind the midwife, the old proprietress nodded.

Luciana took another quick look around the room. Candles were lit, a new ward had been set. A soothing mixture of herbs and spices burned in the brazier at the foot of the bed. There was little else Donna Rui could do now. Her arts, combined with the Luciana's, had brought these children this close to their appointed day.

Kisaiya quickly reopened the door and beckoned *il dottore* in, waving off someone else—possibly the king looking for news. The physician hurried into the room he had exited hours before after examining the twins. He assessed the queen's situation quickly and grabbed a freshly torn rag to staunch the flow of blood while, with a quiet, "*Permisso*!" reached for the babe. Between them, Maria massaging and pressing upon her abdomen, the queen summoned whatever last reserve she could find and the doctor eased the child into the world.

As the fourth child lay on the bed between Idala's feet, the attending stared in abject horror. The child, a son, was as tangled and twisted of limb as the mandrake root that had represented him in the prophetic bundle. It seemed impossible that the child could live, but he did. He mewled with life-giving breath.

"Sweet *Jesu*!" one of the women whispered—or was that all of them as one voice?

Weak, her head spinning, Idala stared in horror at the thing that had issued from her loins. Bile rose in her throat. She stared, trying to comprehend the bundle of life at her feet. The midwife and *il dottore* Bonta hurried to clean the boy—perhaps, with the removal of the afterbirth—the child would not seem so misshapen, so misbegotten.

Idala's head swam with the words of the prophecy. This son, her son, was the devil incarnate. She need only look into his eyes to see the cardinal again.

She reached behind her, her fingers digging into the feathered softness of a cushion. Her fingers tightened, a desperate plan forming even as she pulled the pillow to her side. When the doctor and midwife turned away, she seized the moment and planted her cushion over the child's face.

He was too weak to struggle against her, his cry—if there was one—was easily muffled. She could grind the cardinal back to hell where he belonged! She leaned into the pillow, feeling the twisted little thing wriggling beneath her hands.

So intent was she on her murder of evil incarnate, Idala was barely aware of the midwife's scream, of *il dottore* crying out or even of Luciana grabbing at her sleeves. Idala leaned in, intent on the slaughter of this golem child that had stolen its way into her womb, now born of her struggles.

Strong hands grabbed her around the torso and pulled her back, forcing her upon the pillows which had so recently given up one of their own for her murder plot. Luciana wrenched the cushion out of her clenching hands and midwife della Guelfa seized the boy from the bed.

Idala struggled against the restraining arms of *il dottore*, Luciana, and the two servants, fighting for her freedom and to finish the task not yet completed.

"You don't understand! He must die!" Idala cried out.

"Shhh!" Luciana urged, peeling back Giuletta's hand where she clamped it over the queen's nose and mouth.

Weak as a kitten, Idala fought to free her arms and legs.

"We need a sedative!" *il dottore* Bonta snapped at Giuletta.

"I don't need anything, but that child! Luciana! The prophecy!" Idala grunted out as she fought with the surprisingly strong doctor, Luciana, and Kisaiya.

"The boy will live," the midwife pronounced with a sigh, which only caused Idala to redouble her efforts to free herself from the grips of her friend and servants. Every time she freed a hand, someone else seized it.

Exhausted, Idala collapsed into her bedding. Nunzia Rui clumped her way to the left side of the bed where Luciana sat, still holding Idala's wrist and shoulder.

"Here's something that will soothe her," Nunzia said, handing a cup to Luciana.

Il dottore took it from Luciana and sniffed it. "What's in it?" he asked.

"A strong dose of rum, valerian root and hellfire berries," the old woman replied, unoffended by the younger man questioning her. When he hesitated, she gave his hand a push toward the restless queen. "In moderation . . . of course."

"Take this, Your Majesty," *il dottore* coaxed, pressing the cold pewter cup against her lips.

Idala wrestled again, turning her head away.

"'Dala, sister, take the drink," Luciana urged her.

Idala let her gaze lock with Luciana's warm brown eyes, concern etched in her expression. "I—I'll take it . . . just free my hands," she requested.

At the *Araunya's* signal, *il dottore* and the servants slowly released her. Luciana helped her into a sitting position.

The queen scanned the room, her gaze falling on the newborn still in Donna della Guelfa's comforting arms. The boy was being cosseted, she realized, in response to her attempt on his life. Was that how the cardinal succeeded? Any step against him seen as a cruel, unnecessary attack? In part, she knew it was true. She had watched it when the man lived . . . but he lived again now, as a child. Her child.

Luciana tipped the cup toward her, making Idala mindful of her promise to cooperate. The queen licked the lip of the vessel, tasting the syrupy goodness of honey, even as the scent of wild, New World rum seemed to burn in her nose. Idala swirled the drink, hoping to mix it better before taking a deep, swift swallow. She drew in her breath quickly. The rum burned the back of her throat, despite the sweetness of the honey. She coughed, spilling some of the concoction on her already sodden nightgown.

"Another, Majesty," *il dottore* Bonta urged.

Wrinkling her nose, Idala swirled the cup again and tried to concentrate on the other tastes in the cup than the overwhelming hit of rum. It was impossible to savor the musty taste of valerian root mashed and distilled in the rum, nor to find bitter tartness in the berries when the taste of the alcohol cut through her palate, threatening to send her into another fit of coughing.

With her head swimming, she let Bonta take the cup. Idala pointed to her final issue, the boy in Signora della Guelfa's arms. "Luciana, the prophecy was true." She crossed herself, letting the fingers of her right hand clutch the length of her braid which lay over that shoulder. When della Guelfa turned so that Idala could see the boy in her arms, he reminded her of the mandrake root, his spine and legs twisted. Only his arms looked something approaching normal and with his face contorted in tears it was obvious to see he had teeth, which was most definitely unnatural.

"Dear Lord, what have I done?" Idala stared at the infant, quaking in overwhelming fear. The baby, finally quiet, seemed to stare back at her with a malevolent gaze. "This child should never have been born," Idala pronounced. "Before anyone else sees him . . . can witness that he is alive, he must be . . . he must be put down. If none of you have the nerve, give him to me. I will not blame you."

Donna della Guelfa stared at her in horror, apparently unable to speak, though she held the infant boy closer to her own body protectively and looked around the room suspiciously.

Luciana took Idala by the shoulders and shook her until she was forced to meet her sister-in-law's gaze. "No, Majesty!" she said, "You cannot do that. This child—whatever else he may be—he is of *la famiglia reale* and as such is protected by the law, by the Crown."

Idala jerked her head, glancing wildly around the room. "But if he never lived—"

"The boy lives," *il dottore* Bonta said firmly.

Idala looked to the midwife who watched her in horror, then to the other women. All of them met her gaze in a solemn, steadfast manner that told her she could not protect her family and Tyrrhia by delivering them from the boy. Delivering them.

Idala's fingers tightened in the bedsheets. She was willing to *kill* the son of her own womb to protect her children . . . her other children . . . even Tyrrhia, but that was not to be, apparently. She stared vacantly at the child, at the cardinal who had won his bid. At an impasse, not knowing what—if anything—she could or should do now, the queen fell silent.

"Idala," Luciana said, shaking her again. Or did she repeat it? The inside of her head felt hollow. She was definitely feeling the effects of the drink Nunzia Rui had prepared. She blinked and looked into her sister-in-law's concerned face. "Do not lose hope now, Idala. No matter what the prophecy said, we cannot know the boy's true nature. Every child, no matter its circumstances at birth, must set its own path and has its own destiny. This is where the cardinal missed his calculations. He will not be, cannot be the same person he was before he was born again."

Donna Rui came close, leaning heavily on her cane. "The duchessa is correct, Majesty. You cannot take the child's life. You do not know what he will become."

Idala buried her face in the suffocating pillow and began to weep, deep wrenching sobs. "Oh, Luciana, what have I done?"

Luciana sat on the bed beside Idala and pulled her into her arms, gently rocking her and patting her back as though she were one of the infants now crying in their cradles. When she could cry no more and Idala's head felt almost detached from her hollow body, she sniffed and lay back.

Il dottore Bonta looked at her, leaning in close. His head seemed to swim in different directions when Idala tried to follow his movements. It made her dizzy. She put out a steadying hand and closed her eyes. "Let us make her ready for the king. He is most anxious to see her and the children," Bonta said.

Idala could not keep her eyes open as deft hands undressed and redressed her and rolled her this way and that while making the bed with clean sheets. All the world seemed to spin around her. She was aware of *il dottore* Bonta leaning close and lifting one eyelid.

"Madonna Majesty, can you roll to your side? Are you hungry?" he asked.

Idala obeyed his request, aware of his stuffing fresh rags in her nether parts to staunch some of the bleeding. Idala did not worry. Bleeding after childbirth was normal. She barely noticed his frown. "Majesty? Are you hungry?"

Idala blinked owlishly, realizing for the first time that she was famished. She nodded . . . slightly, anything else and her head might tip from her neck. "Please, I *am* hungry and probably so are the others."

Il dottore chuckled. "Good, Majesty, I'll send for a feast. After all, you have done the unthinkable. You've produced four new heirs! The king will be here momentarily!" the doctor said gently, patting Idala's hand. "Allow me to step outside and summon food for you and the ladies attending you. I will speak to the king personally. Yes?"

Idala breathed a stuttering sigh. Alban would know what to do. It occurred to her then that her husband did not eat when he was anxious and so, through the long night, had probably refused all food. "*Dottore*, make sure that there is well and truly a feast . . . suitable for me, my women, and my husband!"

Bonta chuckled. "You are correct, Majesty. Despite my urging, the king has taken nothing," Bonta said with a quick nod. "Do you hunger for anything in particular?"

"Meat, cheese and something sweet . . . I will eat anything prepared for me and, no doubt, everything," Idala said. She cast a glance at the babes who now began to settle once more and sighed.

"It will be as you say," *il dottore* said, bowing deeply. "I'll ask that the king give you a few moments to make ready . . . to brush your hair out and such."

A momentary sadness gripped Idala's heart. With a soft sigh, she said, "I fear no time allowed me will be enough to prepare to present these children to my husband."

It was clear from his expression the physician had no idea how to respond, so he simply bowed and made his exit. Once he was gone, Maria della Guelfa took charge again, sending Giuletta in search of a brush and hairpins while she focused her attentions on the infants. During the delivery, Maria had Idala suckle her newborns, advising that it kept the pains working to help deliver the next child. Now, as Idala settled back into her bed with the covers drawn up to her waist, Maria offered the new son to Idala.

"Will you suckle the child now, Majesty?" della Guelfa asked.

Idala turned her face away. As a mother, she ached for

the child, but she knew what he was . . . before he became a product of her womb and she could not condone that. "I do not even want to look at him," she said.

Out of the corner of her eye, Idala saw that the boy had freed his right arm from the swaddling and waved it in the air. His face was dark red, angry and shifting, as though fussy, but he elicited not a single sound.

"I've already arranged for more wet nurses," Maria said.

"So be it," Idala said, shuddering.

"As you say, Your Majesty," Maria replied putting the child back in the cradle with his dark sister.

"Normally there would be a shortage of wet nurses available, but with all the populace delivering *bambini* . . . I've delivered no less than ten children this week alone!" Maria said as she settled the child.

Inwardly, Idala winced at the reminder, however innocent, of the spell she had cast with Luciana's sister, Alessandra, the younger *Araunya*. She would have wallowed in guilt except there was the firm scratch at the door which opened unbidden.

Alban entered, brushed past Luciana and bent to kiss his wife. "How fare you, *mia adorata*?"

"I am well," the queen said. "We have twin daughters!"

"And another daughter," Luciana said, falling into the chair beside the bed. "And another son."

Idala put on a brave smile and nodded. "Yes, my love, we have three daughters. They're small, but beautiful."

"*E un miracolo*!" the king said, raining kisses upon the queen's upturned face. He glanced toward the cradles. "*Permisso*?"

Again, Idala nodded, looking eager for her husband's approval despite already having received such a hearty, happy response.

Alban strode around the bed and peered into the cradles happily until his gaze fell upon his new son. "What's wrong with the boy?" he asked, turning a concerned look on Maria and Nunzia.

"'Twas the magic ill-cast," the old proprietress said with a no-nonsense shrug. She came forward and tucked the twisted right leg of the baby back into his swaddling.

When the king glanced at his wife, Idala added hurriedly, "The cardinal . . . his spell was of the foulest magic."

"Aye, that is true," the old witch said, her tone philosophical.

"But we asked you to prevent such a thing," the king said.

Nunzia shook her white-haired head. "You hired me, Your Majesty, to counter ill magic and I have done so." She pointed to the cradle. "You have a son, such as he is, but all of your other children live, as does your wife. Perhaps this prophecy of yours has come to pass, perhaps not; yet despite their size, your children are hardy."

"Prophecy?" Maria murmured curiously.

"You are correct, Donna Rui," Alban said to the old witch. He glanced at the midwife and added, "We will speak no more of this, and I thank you for your service." He turned from the women and sat on the bed beside Idala. Gesturing to the children, the king said, "This was no easy feat, *mi amore*. No matter what has been said and done before, we have four new children. Estensi will record this day and your bravery. As your king, I give you thanks, *Madonna*, for you have served the Crown and the throne well. We are indebted to you. As your husband, I am humbled and live ever in your shining glory."

Idala laughed softly, feeling more than a little giddy as she kissed her husband. "I do all for you, who is my king, my husband, my companion, and my lover."

"I am a better man because of you," the king said, kissing Idala lightly. Without looking away from his wife's eyes, he said, "Duchessa di Drago . . . Luciana . . . you may summon your husband to see his nieces and nephew. Tell the Duca Sebastiani that he may announce the birth of my heirs."

"Thank you, Your Majesty," Luciana said.

Pierro looked up sharply at the sound of a scratching at his bedroom door. He set aside his book and glass of claret, then climbed off his bed. He opened the door and saw the woman outside in the small hall. Quickly, he pulled her inside the room and aimed a narrowed gaze at the floor beneath his wife's door. Sleeping. He smiled and slid his door softly shut.

"Did you wake anyone? Were you seen?" Pierro asked, pressing Renata to the wall. While he kissed her neck, one hand shoved up her skirts and the other fumbled with his breeches.

"No, no," Renata giggled, "No one saw me. Of course, I was careful."

Pierro nipped her breast through her light gown and reached to the apex of her bare legs. "I didn't expect to see you this morning. I thought you were in service this morning."

"I was!" she squealed as he entered her and pressed her into the wall.

He pressed a hand to cup her mouth and pulled her legs up around his hips. When he was through with her, he released her legs and let her slide back down his body, wiping himself off on her dress and slapping her bare ass.

She sighed and kissed him. "I was trying to tell you, Your Highness!"

"What news, *il mio*? Has the king fallen over in his dinner plate? Or the queen?" Pierro teased as he fastened his pants and moved to take a sip of his claret.

"Nothing like that, Your Highness!" Renata giggled, patting Pierro's as yet unshaven face. "I'm a little surprised to discover you awake quite this early in the morning."

Pierro sighed impatiently and took a drink of his claret. "So?"

"Oh! Forgive me . . . you distracted me, Your *cattivo* Highness. I shall have to punish you!" Renata wagged a finger.

Pierro caught her wrists with his free hands and folded hers in front of her. "You've punished me enough. What news have you brought me?"

Renata gave a moue and then sighed. "The queen has given birth."

"Why haven't I heard the bells announcing it yet?" Pierro demanded.

"Only some of the core Palantini know. She gave birth, as you said, to a litter," Renata giggled. "Three girls and a boy, but the boy is . . . I don't expect him to live long."

Outside in the religious ghetto, the bells began to peel. Pierro smirked and turned Renata around. "Out of here before the bells wake my wife. I'll give you coin later."

"I'm no *puttana*!" Renata complained as she swayed toward the door.

"Yes, you are, and we both know it, but the coin is more for the news. I wonder if the king and queen will reveal any of this," Pierro laughed, slapping her on her behind.

Idala lay as though sleeping. Alban stood with the midwife over the cradles. Stefano's first interest, however, was his own wife. Luciana looked exhausted, haggard and pale, but smiled slightly as she brought him into the room. It was not a full-hearted smile, though, and he knew something was not right when she looked first to Idala and then the second bassinet. Stefano kissed Luciana's cheek and nodded, before going to his sister's side.

Someone had seen to it that Idala was presentable; however, her cheeks were still puffy from pregnancy and her eyes red and swollen. Her lips pressed together in a grimace of pain. He started to turn away, to call for someone to bring her something to give her ease but realized someone would already have seen to it . . . his wife, if no one else.

Quietly, Stefano took Idala's hand and kissed it. "I am here, *piccolina*."

Idala's eyes sprang open wide. She managed a wavering smile.

Stefano knelt on one knee and kissed his sister's hand again. "I have been waiting . . . with the others." He jerked his head toward the outer door and the antechamber populated by the resident officers of the Palantini. Distantly, he heard the church bells begin, chiming the announcement of new heirs.

"Of course. Alban behaved horribly, didn't he?" she asked, whispering hoarsely.

"Certainly! You shall have to replace your carpet before the fireplace because your husband wore it threadbare with his pacing," Stefano teased.

She frowned and turned her head. "Luciana?"

"I am here," his wife said from just behind him. Stefano rose and made room for her at his sister's bedside, as much as he could with Idala hanging onto his hand.

When Luciana sat, the queen relaxed again. She took their hands together in hers. "I've begged your forgiveness many times . . . for the magic I used. Know this now . . . I have few regrets . . . for the meddling in your marriage and creating a magic that I did not understand. I wanted these children more than life itself . . ." She fell quiet as her eyes began drifting closed.

"Idala?" Luciana asked, squeezing the queen's hand.

Stefano looked from one woman to the other, his concern growing. His sister looked pale, depleted, but there was more to it. Luciana's expression was a mask of cool, collected gentleness as she smiled down at her sister-in-law. He motioned to the doctor just as Bonta entered the room. Glancing at the king, Stefano stood and moved toward *il dottore*. "What is wrong with my sister, the queen? Things do not appear as they should."

Il dottore glanced at the queen, edging closer to her. "No doubt she is weak from her efforts and from the hunger that comes afterward. Giving birth to one child . . . Your sister, our queen, is a remarkable woman, but she will need rest, so only a short visit, eh?"

"And the bleeding?" Luciana asked.

"Normal after a delivery . . . especially one of such . . . magnitude," *il dottore* reassured them.

Even as the physician spoke, there was a scratching at the door of the servants' hallway. Giuletta opened the door for no less than six porters bearing food and little cane stands for the heavily laden trays to rest upon. Behind them, came a slight woman almost as small and delicate of frame as Idala. She carried an infant swaddled and straddled to her back with a sling of homespun cloth. The wet nurse. The first of many for the Royal Nursery.

Il dottore took a plate and immediately piled it high with roast beef, cheeses, and selected fruits. He brought it over and laid it on the bed. "*Mangia*, *Madonna* Majesty! *Mangia*!"

Idala looked at the plate. Her eyes widened at the selection and amount she had been served. "Oh! I cannot eat this much," she protested.

"Then eat what you can, Majesty," the doctor said. He swiped at the love lock on his left temple and flicked the tail of hair hanging from his back in a nervous habit.

Clearly, the doctor was as concerned as he was, Stefano realized. Stefano looked to the king who now held his twin daughters. He watched Idala's expression brighten when she saw this.

"Have you seen them? The babies?" Idala asked.

Stefano shook his head.

"Then go, see them!" she said, stabbing a morsel of beef with her fork. "I *know* you must be hungry also, Luciana. Your baby needs nourishment as much as you do. We have all gone through so much, especially today. Let's not forfeit your well-being for lack of care." She looked pensive and set her fork down. "Stefano, I ask a great favor of you. I cannot bear to see him . . ." she nodded meaningfully toward the second baby bed. "I know he is Alban's child, but he is also an evil spirit got on me by the cardinal. Will you see what can be done for the boy?"

"For all of it, Majesty; he is of your blood and, therefore, my nephew. I swear to do what I can to see the boy set on the right path," Stefano promised.

He rose then and offered a hand to help his wife to her feet. He realized how weary she must be. He tried to read something in her face, in her eyes, but she looked away quickly and, instead, drew him toward the gently swinging cradles under the care of the king and midwife.

"This is Pietra Maria Albina," Alban said to Stefano as the friends stood side by side. The king pointed to one of the now sleeping twins. He nodded to the other still in his arms, "She is Rosalina Maria Idala." The king smiled happily even as the midwife took the girls from him. His smile faltered somewhat as he took Stefano to the second babies' bed, for vengeance lay in the cradle swinging on its chains. "Based upon the prophecy, this child, the girl, is as much of the black blood as she is of the white. I know that Chiara is a name used by both our people so I will name her Chiara Vanessa Esmeralda."

"And what of the boy?" Stefano asked, looking at the child, trying not to shudder when the midwife paused in reswaddling the boy so that all his deformities were visible. Besides the right arm that he insistently freed and kept raised as though in some unholy benediction, the boy's spine seemed as though it were corkscrewed and his face looked distorted.

Alban shook his head, gazing upon his new son. "I believe the prophecy and, in believing it . . . but still, despite the magic involved and to all the world, he *is* my son . . ." The king's voice trailed off briefly so that Stefano could not hear if he said more. Alban shook himself. "The deformities . . . had I not believed the prophecy . . . I would not consider them his fault and would treasure him as my own son, but magic *was* involved and the cardinal's magic has done this. . . . I will call him Massimo Giacomo Cosimo."

"Your father's name?" Stefano asked, surprised.

"Yes . . . it will give him something to live up to . . . perhaps," Alban said.

Stefano nodded. He could not help but wonder if the magic had truly caused the boy's deformities. Was it true? Was a prophecy to be believed? A prophecy by phantasm? And, if it were true, then the cardinal's magic was to blame for the boy's present condition. Magic. Magic his wife cast led to the prophecy from the maggiore. Unable to resist, his gaze fell to his wife's swollen belly. What if magic caused similar problems with her? With their child?

Stefano shook his head. He had little time for dwelling on his fears. There were powerful men waiting to hear what news could be given . . . and a royal family must be kept whole.

VII

"Where thou diest, will I die, and there will I be buried; the Lord do so to me, and more also, if aught but death part thee and me."

—Bible: Ruth 1: 16-17

12 d'Dicembre, 1684

THE hour was early, before the sun was fully up. The king loved a good, long ride in the early hours, before the day and duties began. He also enjoyed company. And so it was that Stefano found himself on the front steps of the palazzo waiting for the gouty-footed Duca Sebastiani to gradually make his way down the stairs to join the king, along with Lord Strozzini, the king's bodyguard.

The sprawling *palazzo di reale* lay perched upon land high above the turbulent waters of the Stretto d'Messina—a narrow corridor that served as the gathering point of mythical seas overrun by gods and their champions. The golden gem of Tyrrhian architecture served as the perennial residence of the White King, his family and, as happenstance may, ambassadors, courtiers, and the advisers of the Palantini who all lived in relative equanimity with varying alliances born, sworn, and—in accordance with the time and parties involved—foresworn.

Fog wound its tendrils around the statuary: the towering lions at either side of the great doors of the palazzo and the statue of the Visigoth King—whose treasure helped found this nation—mingled with the mist. Winter had only just begun its hold upon the kingdom, so the remnants of last night's snow dripped heavily from the roof, pooling and puddling upon the marble and cobblestone.

It was into this gray soup of a morn that Stefano, Duca di Drago, Colonello di Escalade and holder of assorted other honors and acknowledgments, had crossed the threshold of the palazzo to wait for his compatriots. The cold caught, freezing the breath half-drawn in his throat. He smothered a cough as the chill settled in his bones and chased away the last of the warmer memories of sleep curled into the rounded figure of his very pregnant wife. In relative high spirits, he dusted his hat—careful of the discreet black feather affixed to its band—on his leg and settled it on his head as they all set off in silence in the general direction of the stables.

He took care as he made his way, keeping a wary eye out on the path for the less able-bodied Duca Sebastiani. The cobblestone courtyard tended to be slick with thinly frozen ice covering the puddles remaining from the night before. Despite being near blind in the dense morning murk, the crunch of ice beneath his feet became that of gravel and confirmed that their course and his footing were true.

The muffled bellows of the Escalade Quartermaster rousting the men in the general billet further confirmed his location, as did the scent of the sea mingled with the dewy fragrance of the dormant citrus orchards on the stable side of the palazzo. All of it reminded Stefano of his early days in the queen's service—which began under the auspices of Her Majesty, Katerina Albertina Ricci e Novabianco partnered to Orsino, Alban's predecessor and uncle, parents of "the stolen princesses."

Here, near the Royal barracks where so much of his youth revolved, Stefano had first befriended Alban and, in time, introduced the young nobleman—with no reason to expect that the throne would one day be his—to his own younger sister, Idala.

Oddly, this was also where he had met Luciana, the woman who captivated his own heart. Away from her people and at court for the first time, her strange Romani customs isolated her from the other courtiers. Much about her served to set her apart from the rest of the women. Her darkly tawny, flawless skin and her long, luxuriant hair that took the hue of an inky, moonless night fascinated him. Her brown eyes, reflecting her perceptive intelligence, and the smile, which came so easily to her soft, curving lips, left him breathless and enraptured.

Stefano shuddered as the cold settled deeper into his bones. Pausing to put on his soft, russet, leather riding gloves, he waited for the stable boys to wipe the sleep from their eyes. The only voices he heard came from the barracks. Sighing contentedly, his nose caught the familiar scents of horses, hay, and saddle leather. On the other hand, it took no particular care for him to hear the horses since they tended to be loud beasts—in particular, Mercurio, the king's prize young bay Andalusian stallion given to him by the Spanish ambassador. Mercurio could be heard bugling his challenge to the other stallions housed in the vast stables. In the long rows of stalls and paddocks, more than one horse responded to Mercurio, and there came the resounding thuds of overexcited studs kicking at their various confinements as they sought to find not only the challenging stallion, but what mares in season he might be protecting.

Something about being around horses put Stefano at ease; these beasts were stabled there for both daily use and war. It was a love he shared with his *amorata*. He turned, hearing the king's stallion, but seeing him only in outline in the foggy conditions. His own mount, Fascino, a silver roan charger who carried Stefano from home to battlefield and back blended almost into nothingness in this gray morning.

As the men mounted, they were surprised by the arrival of Prince Pierro in the stable yard. "*Pardone,* Signores, but I thought I would join you this morning . . . If it is acceptable to His Majesty, of course." He bowed politely to the king and waved a flourishing half-bow to the other men. "Good morning, Your Graces." After a moment's long pause, he said with an arched brow, "and to you as well, Strozzini." He turned pointedly toward Alban. "Majesty?"

The king shifted uncomfortably in his saddle and then motioned to the other men, "As you can see, we're all ready to ride."

"Ah! But this is not a problem! My horse is already saddled," the deMedici said. He clapped his gloved hands, which summoned a groom leading a black destrier, prancing and lunging on the end of his lead. Pierro mounted the beast with little trouble, gathering the reins as he did so. Once seated, Pierro nodded and the boy released the lead rope, putting the horse completely at the prince's command. The horse danced under Pierro, shying and whinnying, which caused Mercurio to buck and kick at the new horse.

Stefano drew his horse to the side. While spirited, Fascino was well-trained and had seen the noisy fields of battle. Stefano patted his mount's neck and shifted him to stand beside Sebastiani and Strozzini's mounts.

It took a moment for the king to control his young horse, but when he did, he wheeled Mercurio about to face Pierro. He managed a small, if politic, smile. "Then *do* join us, Your Highness. I hope you're prepared for a long ride?"

The prince bowed in his saddle, "It shall be as you say, Majesty. I am gladdened that you were willing to let me join you. I hope this was not meant to be a private foray?"

Alban shrugged and gave his horse the heel, thereby concluding any further pretty speeches. They took off at a gallop, hooves clattering on the courtyard cobblestones which turned into dull thuds on the dirt road leading away from the palazzo between the orchard and the graveyard.

Stefano tried to push back his worries over Pierro joining them without notice or invitation. For some reason, he was glad that he wore his sword on his hip and that Strozzini was fully armed.

Strozzini, the king's long-time bodyguard, stood like a solid birch tree, slender but sturdy, and equal in height to his king. He wore the king's colors and a gentleman's wardrobe, with regimental cuffs. The deeply folded gold cuffs of his coat bore the decorative barbs that served as bolts for the bracer of scorpininis—pistola-gripped crossbows, a weapon particular to the Tyrrhian military forces—neatly tucked and ready for use in his belt. He wore a fawn-leather baldric which was studded with his insignia and draped to his left hip. Rather than the decorative dress swords favored by the courtiers, Strozzini carried a heavier, filigreed basket-hilt sword. He wore a hat with feathers—yet another mark of his skill. He was gray at the temples and his goatee, though he was only in his mid-forties, almost a decade older than his liege.

Stefano was glad of his presence. Even though Alban hated the necessity of the bodyguard, he understood his duty to tolerate it, but, an excellent swordsman himself, Stefano knew he still chaffed at the requirement.

When the horses had run full out for more than a couple of miles, the king slowed their pace and took to the field where a stream ran close to the road. Here, the king enjoyed the idyllic scenery and allowed his party to rest. All but Pierro and Sebastiani dismounted to walk their horses and allow them to cool off from their run.

Strozzini stood nearby. He walked over to Stefano while keeping an ever-wary eye on the king. "Her Grace? The *Araunya*? She is well?" he asked politely.

"She does not suffer these days lightly, I fear," Stefano said. He glanced around. "Why do you suppose that His Highness wanted to join us?"

Strozzini shook his head. "He is no military man and does not strike me as one who regularly rises early. I have given up trying to fathom his ways. His or his wife's. They want the Crown and nothing else matters . . . not even the good of Tyrrhia."

Stefano's mood soured. "It is his habit to arrive at inopportune times—like this morning, when we were just about to set off. I cannot imagine his intent to be anything relating to filial courtesy."

The bodyguard nodded. "Yes, but he was already *in* the stables. Why wait until the last moment to make his presence known and invite himself along on this ride? Why did he wish to ride with us *this* morning when he so clearly disdains our company?"

Stefano chewed his lower lip, his curiosity thoroughly piqued. "I don't trust him."

Strozzini shrugged, his expression made it obvious he was displeased and concerned. "And when has he ever given you reason to?"

Stefano watched the king lead Mercurio to the stream. The prince hovered near Alban, trotting in an ever-widening circle, posting in his saddle with his hands taut on the reins. His horse fought at the restraint, whinnying his complaints. Sebastiani allowed his spotted gelding to graze toward the stream. The older man seemed at home in the saddle and off his sore foot, relaxing and taking in the morning, patently ignoring deMedici's presence.

Stefano remounted Fascino, knowing that Alban would

soon be ready to ride again while Strozzini took his leave with a bow and also remounted. In that half-moment, there came an inarticulate cry and the king fell face-first into the water. Mercurio shied, and breaking away from the king, escaped from the field. Strozzini barely hesitated before digging in his heels and heading toward the fallen king. Stefano was right beside him and was the first off his horse, landing knee-deep in the frigid water.

Stefano and the bodyguard rolled the king over together to find a heavy crossbow bolt sticking out of his breast. To Strozzini, he yelled, "Find the murderer!" and began pulling the king to shore.

With a scorpinini in one hand and his sword in the other, Strozzini crossed the stream to the brush on the other side. Somewhere on the foggy other side of the stream came the crashing of branches and the sound of horses. Stefano, however, concentrated upon the king, gripping Alban beneath the arms and falling with him onto the shore. His hand went to the bolt, but stopped, remembering his field medicine training. He slapped the king's cheeks, and pressed on his stomach to expel the water he must have inhaled.

Alban coughed, choking and spitting out water as he captured Stefano's hand. "Stay! Friend," he gasped.

Friend? Stefano felt himself pale, knowing this was a bad sign.

The king's formality was gone as he gripped Stefano's hand. Alban's free hand went to the bolt in his chest and wrenched it out before Stefano could stop him.

Blood geysered briefly and then spread rapidly over the king's water-soaked coat. Duca Sebastiani and the prince landed on their knees on either side of the king and Stefano, the king's head in Stefano's lap. Sebastiani pressed a white silk kerchief into the king's wound.

"You shouldn't have done that," the old duca said to the king, worry and strain clear in his expression and voice.

"You are dying," Pierro said coldly, remaining physically aloof.

Stefano did not even spare him a glance. He was not worthy of his attention at the moment. "Get on your horse and summon the physician," Stefano told the prince.

Pierro huffed but stood, even as the sound of Strozzini splashing back through the stream met their ears.

Alban clutched at Stefano's hand, "There is no time for that. I am done."

"No, Majesty, there is yet time! There is—" Sebastiani argued.

"There is no time. Strozzini?" the king called weakly.

Strozzini fell upon his knees at the king's side. "Your Majesty, I have failed you utterly. The assassins have gotten away. I failed to protect you. I cannot even ask your forgiveness."

"You could not have known. Forgiveness is not needed. I charge you to protect my wife and children. The queen . . ." Alban paused, his hand went to his face. He shifted his head to look at Stefano, "I shall never see my beloved again, to gaze . . ." The king's chin jutted. He angled his gaze to Duca Sebastiani. "Augusto, deMedici, you bear witness to my final words. I . . . I . . ." His eyes closed.

"Majesty? *Brother*!" Stefano called, shaking Alban even as the spreading blood dripped upon the ground and soaked down, staining his clothes to well past the belt the king wore over his coat of gold Gypsy Silk.

The king opened his eyes wearily. "My time is short," he whispered. "This is such an effort." He gripped Stefano's hand spasmodically. "Stefano, you are my executor and I name you guardian of Dario Gian and . . . the others. You will guide my heir to manhood, to the Crown, as you did me. You will speak for him until his fifteenth birthday when he is old enough. . . . You will keep my children—"

"I will keep your children as if they were my own, Majesty," Stefano swore, gripping the king's hand tightly.

"Then," the king said, his voice wavering on faintness. ". . . my duty to the kingdom . . . is discharged. I have but one more duty and that is to my queen. Stefano, you will make sure she knows, that everyone knows that she . . . that she was queen of my heart from first sight. She has served me well and I can only hope that I—that I—" Alban fell silent.

Stefano shook the king's shoulder again, but the king did not respond. Sebastiani reached over and closed his eyes, bowing his head in grief.

"The crown belongs to my wife," deMedici said through gritted teeth.

"We have a plural throne. The Crown still rests upon the

queen, and she will serve," Stefano declared. He stared down at his friend. His king. Dead. But he could still serve him, by making his wishes for his kingdom and family come to fruition.

The prince rose, staring down at Stefano, his dislike evident. Instead of continuing his vent, deMedici announced sourly, "My horse is gone. How shall I return to the palazzo?"

Strozzini rose, whirling upon the prince. "You dare worry about—"

"Strozzini!" Stefano snapped before the bodyguard could speak his mind so that it could be used against him. "We have three horses. I'm sure that you will be accommodated in some fashion, Your Highness. The king's horse and yours will return to their stables. Someone will come for us."

"You expect us to wait here with . . . with the king's dead body?" Pierro demanded.

Stefano eased the king's head to the ground and rose to his own feet, dusting himself off uselessly covered as he was in mud, blood, and general wetness. "I expect nothing of you, Your Highness. Take Strozzini's horse. Sebastiani, you ride as leader."

"This will delay my chase of the assassins," Strozzini said, clearly torn between duties.

"They will leave their mark on the road. There's nothing for it," Stefano said angrily, darting a glance at Pierro.

The older man nodded and stood, limping to his horse. The deMedici hesitated a moment longer before taking Strozzini's horse.

To the bodyguard, Stefano said, "The king will *ride* my mount. I will not have him delivered to my sister like a sack of flour over the back of the saddle."

Strozzini nodded. "It shall be as you say, Your Grace."

Stefano walked down the checkerboard marble hall of Tyrrhia's palazzo, residence of the White King, his queen, their young family and, in times such as this, when peace within the country's borders was more than a popular fiction, a few citizens with petitions for the king were also present . . . all with their entourage. Everywhere, people whispered and tears ran freely, especially among the women. He turned to the duca who had fallen in behind him and Duca Sebastiani. "You will handle the populace, Sebastiani, and you . . ." Stefano searched for the unnamed and fell silent with loss.

"Raffia of Niscemi," the other man supplied. "What would you have me do, Excellency?"

"I am not a regent yet. Call me 'Your Grace' as you always have. My sister remains on the throne," Stefano said. "See to it that the Palantini-*grande* is summoned." He made a mental note that Portofino—Niscemi—stood on the side of the Crown rather than the would-be usurpers, Ortensia and Pierro. Now, he had the duty of telling his queen, his sister, that Alban was dead. She was not fully recovered from childbirth and he feared what this news would do to her.

He left the duchi and the rest of them behind. He was alone in this task. Hopefully, Luciana would not be long in joining him with Idala, but considering her condition and how exhausted she still was after the queen's ordeal, she had been sleeping in and might not yet know the news. The midwife, however, had been in constant attendance upon the queen since the new heirs were born . . . Some trouble, some complication, kept her at the queen's side. She could probably make a soothing tonic, while the Royal physician was away confirming the death of the king as was his sad duty.

Stefano stared out the corridor window, just outside the royal apartments. The sun pierced the horizon at the point where the dark waters of the Stretto d'Messina and deep blue sky met. Light filtered out from that point like the blood of the king spreading out about him. The sun shone through, glorious in its majesty, supreme in its raiment. To think that such glory acted as herald to the fall of a throne.

He leaned his forehead against the pane. News of Alban's death had been sent out through the couriers. While some Tyrrhians still lay content in their beds, confident of living by the rule of a just king; others, their mourning barely begun, feared the death of their queen would soon follow. But Stefano would not say that, would not speak of it, not even to Luciana.

Turning away from the window, Stefano scanned the weary faces of his counterparts. From the aging political lions, Sebastiani and di Candido, to Gianola, the newly made duca who still grieved over the loss of his own father. Young and old, these nine sleepy duchi made up less than half of the Greater House of the Palantini, but to them would fall the fetters and responsibilities of leadership. For all of them, this waiting outside of doors signaled the end of a reign and beginning of a new era.

The door to the queen's antechamber creaked. Each of the duca looked up from his distraction, eager for news of any sort; Stefano not the least of them. Giuletta waved Stefano in, her face pale and frightened. She had undoubtedly heard the news. What had she said to the queen, if anything?

"Have you spoken to the queen? Does she know?" he asked.

Giuletta shook her head. "She dozes, Your Grace. She just nursed the girls. Donna della Guelfa and Donna Rui are with her even now. I—I summoned them. I hope that was acceptable?" she said, her voice barely a whisper.

"You did right by your mistress. She will not take this news well. Have the witch prepare something for the queen's nerves," Stefano said.

"This way then, Your Grace . . . Your Excellency?"

Stefano fought to hide his unease. His king had recently died in his arms. Though he was guardian of Alban's children, and Idala would be leaning on him hard, he did not want to think of himself as regent nor even Regent Guardian. Such titles took time to accustom oneself to . . . such time as he could allow himself, he would. "My sister is yet queen. Do not address me so in front of her."

"As you say, then," Giuletta responded with another nod and a curtsy.

The queen's bedchamber was lit by the final glimmers of the last night's candles scattered around the room. The door to the portico stood ajar, letting in the bare light of dawn as well as fresh air. The room still smelled of blood mixed with the sharp tang of fresh, crushed herbs—rosemary and roses.

A young woman Stefano marginally recognized as Dario Gian's *governante* whisked by him with her charge, the Heir Apparent, curled sleepily into her shoulder. All around him, Stefano was aware of women in the shadows, quietly efficient and purposeful about whatever duties brought them there.

Stefano crossed the darkened room, suddenly aware that

he still wore the bloodied clothes from his ill-fated ride. He ducked his head beneath the fringes of the bed-curtains. Idala lay amongst her pillows with her eyes closed. She was wan, drained of the spark of life since giving birth. No one had admitted the queen's infirmity, but there were rumors, always rumors. Even the most dedicated and circumspect servant would have revealed something to her comrades in tending to the queen.

It was evident that in her headstrong folly to increase the size of her family, to provide a second heir, his sister had gotten herself killed. She seemed all but dead even now. He tried hard to focus above the foolishness of fear; maybe it would let him be angry instead of feeling the horrible emptiness, but all Stefano could picture in his mind's eye was Idala laughing and the sound of it fading into nothingness. He knew what this news was going to do to his sister. He felt like an executioner.

Idala smiled suddenly, sleepily and reached up, stretching. "Back so soon, my love?" She opened her eyes then saw him. She sat up, drawing the blankets a little higher, confusion as clear as her infirmity. "What are you doing here?" But even as she asked, she seemed to take in his bloodied clothes and perhaps all was clear in his expression for her hands balled into fists. "No! No! Where is my husband? Why are you here? Where—where is he?" she turned wildly in her bed and beckoned to one of the servants. "Send for the king! Send for my husband!"

Only then did the women cry openly, their tears muffled by their aprons.

Idala shook her head, beginning to quiver as tears welled up. "No ..." Tears began to fall with a sob that rent the room.

Stefano became suddenly aware of a small, wizened woman at his side pressing a goblet into his hand and pushing it toward the queen. "*Carina-piccola*, I'm so sorry. We did everything we could. We—I—"

The old woman pushed his elbow again, moving the goblet to the queen. Feeling like a dunderhead, Stefano said "Here, *carina*, take this. It will help." He offered her the goblet. When she did not take it, he tried to press it to her lips, but only succeeded in spilling it all over both of them.

After a time of tears, out of somewhere, somehow, Idala

found the strength to compose herself. She sat up straighter and wiped her eyes with the back of her hand. Her voice, when she spoke, quavered, and yet, there was a thin thread of strength, of resolve. "There is no doubt?"

"Absolutely none." Stefano sat on the bed next to his sister. "I held him as he died."

"How? How did this happen?" she asked, studying the edge of her lacy cuffs, avoiding the eyes of the other women.

"An assassin—" Stefano began.

"Assassin?" Idala repeated. She took a deep breath. "Was he caught?"

"No. Strozzini was but a few yards away. He searched the brush that led into the forest, but they got away. He has taken a squadron of the Escalade for a better search."

"How long has it been since . . ." For a moment, a brief second, the queen's strength quaked again. "You understand my question, *fratello*?"

"Yes, and it has been . . . perhaps an hour," Stefano replied.

"They will find nothing."

"You cannot know that," Stefano said. He wiped the wet goblet on his ruined frock coat and offered what was left to his sister. "Drink this. It will sustain you."

Idala took the amber glass goblet from him and drank obediently, then set it aside. She glanced at the other women now. Her expression hardened. "The Crown now rests solely on my head, does it not?"

"Yes, 'Dala, it does, but Alban made me guardian of the children—to serve as a father where he could not."

"But, Stefano, you will advise me and take my side?" Idala asked.

"Always, *carina*. I could do nothing else but serve you," he said.

"The Palantini has been called to court, correct? It will take at least a week for them to start to arrive. I will need to make myself ready."

"I did take the initiative and sent for them, but many will take longer than the usual week. Many of their wives are *incinta*, as you are aware," Stefano said.

"As I am *well* aware—I am to blame for so many—"

"You were not in their beds, sister. They share in that responsibility," Stefano replied.

"Everything but," Idala said with a sigh. "So I will have this day? At least *this* day, to grieve for my beloved?" Idala asked.

Stefano rose from the bed. "Heavy rests the Crown. I wish there were *more* time, but there is not."

"Have Alban's advisers ready. I will meet them on the morrow and, before the Palantini arrive, I will address the petitioners. Have Estensi prepare a list and whatever documents are necessary," Idala said.

Stefano saluted her with a courteous bow. He turned to leave but stopped when her hand caught his bloody sleeve.

"Did he . . . did he have words for me?" Idala asked.

While the tears were yet unshed, Stefano could see them filling her eyes and hear them in the catch of her voice. "But, of course, forgive me for not saying. He said . . ." Stefano hesitated, seeking the right words. How did one speak of a dying man's love to his wife? "He said that he loved you, dearly, and that you served him well as his queen, as his wife, in every way. He was proud that you were his wife. He said that you were the queen of his heart from the moment he saw you."

"Did he?" Idala whispered, laying back on the pillows. "Brother?"

"Yes?"

"Your wife is as blessed as I for having a man, a husband who loves her, but does she know it?"

Stefano's thought turned immediately to the small chest in which all the love letters he had written her during the war were held. He had never dared give them to her. What if he had been felled by the assassin today as well? "I shall heed your advice, 'Dala. As Alban's friend, I can tell you that he loved you beyond measure, and his love is paralleled only by the devotion I have for my own wife."

"You can never say the words enough. You can never show them enough and yet, Alban need not have said these words to you, for I knew his heart."

Stefano took a deep breath and sighed heavily. For as much as his sister and Alban loved one another, he and Alban had shared a brotherly love. He would never know another man like Alban Cosimo Abram di Mirandola e Novabianco.

As he turned once more to leave, an odd hollow cackle

filled the room, echoing through the chamber. Angrily, Stefano turned to the old woman, suspecting her, but she only stared back, her eyes round with fear. He looked to the other women, the midwives by the cribs, and saw new terror there, too. Idala had grown as white as the sheet pressed to her mouth. He followed Donna della Guelfa's gaze to the cradle which held the newborn son. He crossed the room in two steps, rounding the bed as he did so and stared into the crib. The dark daughter had begun to cry even as her sibling smiled with an odd, toothy grin.

"He has teeth? Did he just laugh?" Stefano demanded.

"Yes. I have never known such a thing before, for a child so small to laugh . . . and like that, but the teeth, some children are born with them," Donna della Guelfa said.

Stefano stared down into the cradle, watching the dark-haired daughter try to wriggle away from her brother as much as newborns could. The boy continued to stare up at him, his eyes mocking and old. Not in the way most infants seemed old and venerable, but in the way of an ancient evil. Stefano glanced around the room at the women. All of them, including Idala, the child's mother, was making the sign against the evil eye.

"Donna della Guelfa, I believe the queen has spoken of this before, but I think the boy needs to be kept in another room, away from the distress. Double whatever you're paying his wet nurse." Stefano reached into the crib and picked up the tawny-skinned girl. He held her, unspeaking, while the servants made good his order and, when it was done, he handed the child in his arms to the midwife. "Find a separate cradle for her. She should stay with her sisters."

Halfway down the stairs from Idala's apartment, Stefano was drawn to a stop by the sound of his name. "Your Grace! Duca di Drago!"

He turned to find the midwife not far behind him. He waited for the older woman to catch up to him. "How can I assist you?"

"It's not my place, but I must say this. The queen is not well. I do not see how she could do half the things she says she will do—at least, immediately. Women bleed after—after childbirth, but not like this and the royal physician himself has bled her twice to balance her humours for her childbed fever. It does not seem to be working," Donna della Guelfa said.

Stefano bit his lip. He had known his sister was not well, had known she was not up for the duties that lay before her, but she was queen unto death. "I thank you, good woman, but while her mind is clear, the queen must choose, and it's not so much a choice with us. It is the obligation of her station. I will do all that I am able to ease the burden."

The midwife sighed and shook her head, clearly unhappy with the answer he had given. After a pause, she said, "You already have helped her by removing that child. At first, I thought he was nothing more than disfigured by his birth as some children are. We . . . all of us . . . ignored her rejection of the child, even the king, thinking she might change her mind."

Stefano nodded. "But there is more?"

The woman tugged at the hair by her temple that had escaped from the cloth she used to bind up her hair. "Yes," she said. "Yes, but I cannot give you an example. I can only tell you the child is *wrong*. There is something not right about the boy. The evil eye has gazed fully upon him. I would swear it on my own son's life."

"But there is nothing you can say . . . not specifically . . . ?"

"Until he laughed, no. Not in all my years dealing with small children, and I have been at this for some twenty-five odd years. I have seen many things in my day. He, that boy, is neither the first disfigured child I have seen, nor would I even say that he was the first marked by evil, but he . . . he is not as he should be," Donna della Guelfa said. "For my part, I'm glad you had him moved from the room. I expect Her Majesty to improve now, but not nearly as quickly or as solidly as you and this kingdom need."

"I thank you, Donna, for your wisdom and I hope that you will not hesitate to share news with me again if your charges are to be better served by it, but there are some things I cannot do. You understand?" Stefano asked.

The woman nodded and turned to go, but stopped and came back. "Know, too, that I am not alone in my sentiment. Giuletta is terrified by the child and will not touch him unless bade to directly by the queen. Donna Rui . . . Donna Rui is an old woman and has seen more than I. You probably did not see her charms against evil about the queen's bed, but they hang in her curtains and in the canopy overhead; in all that, we all wear charms to protect us against evil. I'd thought us just being superstitious women, but mark my words, the child is not right. Ask Her Grace."

Stefano's brows rose in surprise. He quickly masked his expression. He knew that Luciana was superstitious—it was a part of her, part of her people, just like magic, just like her smile, just like the air she breathed. He did not, however, know that Luciana was that deeply afraid of the child. It was clear he needed to speak with his wife.

"I promise that I will speak to her this very day," Stefano said.

"Thank you, Your Grace," Donna della Guelfa said. "Much depends upon it, I fear."

Stefano found Luciana dressing for the day. Upon seeing him, she broke away from Kisaiya and came to him, taking his hands in hers. She stepped back to look at him, then shook her head sadly. Behind his wife, Stefano noted Kisaiya leaving the room and shutting the door to give them their privacy.

"I've heard the news. How can it be so?" Luciana asked, but it was not a question, merely a statement of surprise and shock. She held him as close as she could.

Her quick fingers found the buttons of his vest and the buckle of his belt. "Look at you! You're covered in blood! How can you think in these clothes?" Luciana asked. Her hair was mussed and one sleeve was loose from dressing. Apparently, Kisaiya had not finished tying the ribbons on her gown.

Stefano leaned into her, absorbing her comfort as though he were a sponge. He wanted to cry like a child and, even knowing she would not hold it against him, he could not. He felt, for the first time since Alban's last breath, connected to someone. He was not alone—unsheltered from the rain of grief pouring down on him. He had lost his boon companion. Alban and he had been friends for nearly twenty years and, except for the years at war on the Peloponnese front, they had never been far apart. The battles they had fought, the politics that they had wound their way through, the wives found. All of this had been together. Only Luciana could ease his pain.

He dropped his chin to capture her lips with his as he soaked up her comfort and felt the knot in his chest begin to loosen. She nestled closer, her long-fingered hands cradling his head as she kissed him back. He stepped back first, breaking the kiss and setting her aright.

For a moment, he let her undress him and then he slowly took over, gently moving her hands out of the way. He dropped his coat, vest, shirt, and boots in a pile on the floor of her bedchamber. He thought of his sister and the love she had lost and the love that he had found. He pulled Luciana back into his arms, ignoring her startled squeal, and kissed her, relishing the soft moan she gave instinctively as the flame of their mutual fire fanned. Her comforting arms wrapped around him and he found solace.

"What will this mean for us?" Luciana asked as she curled into him, her head snugged close to his heart and his arms wrapped around her shoulders. Her hair spilled loosely about them, like a mantle. "I know it's selfish to ask, to think of such things, but I cannot help it." She felt safe in his enveloping arms, protected from the cares of the world that existed beyond the doors of her bedchamber.

Stefano sighed and rubbed a weary hand over his face. "It means we shall not see Dragorione for some time. I am guardian to his children, adviser to his wife."

"Idala!" Luciana sat up rapidly, too rapidly. She braced herself against the wall of Stefano's chest and pushed away to sit upright when the spinning stopped. "How did she take the news?"

"Better than I could've hoped and worse than I feared," Stefano said. He captured her hand and kissed the knuckles before he, too, sat up.

"You're going to have to explain that," Luciana said, shaking her head in confusion.

"Why didn't you tell me about the boy?"

Luciana slowly pulled her hand away, reluctant to break contact, but this was well-traveled ground and more often than not led to an argument. "What was there to tell?" she asked.

"Don't be obtuse, *cara mia*, it does not become you," Stefano grumped, pulling her against him so that she was off-balance and forced to lean her gravid weight into him or fall.

"It's magic. I just helped Donna Rui make charms against the boy. What was there for me to say?" She leaned over him and rescued her camisole from the far edge of the bed. She slipped it over her head.

"I've never said that I don't believe in magic. The problem is that I do, and I see what it has done to Idala," Stefano said, taking her cue and swinging his legs off the mattress to the floor. "I just don't trust it."

"The problem is, you fear it," Luciana retorted.

"I don't—" Stefano stopped himself. "All right, I do fear it, but I think I have good reason." He raised his hands, waving them in front of her. "No, Luciana, no. I do not want this to turn into a fight. Especially about us, between us. Where magic is concerned, I am trying to learn to trust . . . at least, trust you."

Luciana sat back on her haunches on the bed, genuinely surprised. "You are? I mean, you *really* are?" She swallowed back her reservations. "What more do you want to know about the boy?"

"Until today, I had hoped this prophecy was the matter of stuff and nonsense, but I heard him laugh," Stefano said, shuddering. "We, first, must begin by starting to think of the boy as Massimo. He will be with us all of his lifetime and long after, just like the cardinal, apparently."

"So you really believe that?" Luciana asked, snapping her mouth shut so that she did not gape. "You truly understand that your sister—?"

"All of it. I have been forced to accept the obvious as fact."

Luciana stared at her husband for a long hard moment and then reached out and pinched him. Was this the same man she had married? The same man who had blamed her for their first child's stillbirth because of magic?

"Ow! What was that for?" Stefano complained, then shook his head. "Never mind. I know what that was for, I think. Now, tell me about Massimo."

"You have not been told this, but . . ." Luciana took a deep breath. "He—the cardinal—stole my sister's body because he enslaved *mullós* and used their magic. The dark daughter, *she* was one such *mulló*, but in fighting the cardinal, she freed herself to live again. I am told by Grasni—"

"Grasni?"

"My sister's attendant. She now studies the arts with my grandmother, the *Beluni*," Luciana said.

"When did you see her? I did not know you saw your people recently," Stefano said.

Luciana nodded. "They come to me from time to time with messages. It is part of my work as the *Araunya* of two houses and nothing I ever thought to concern you with, but this last time it was Grasni and Uncle Petrus. They came with Capitano della Guelfa."

"Della Guelfa?" Stefano repeated. He frowned, as he made all the connections. "The midwife's husband, di Montago's second, if I recall?"

Luciana nodded again. "Della Guelfa came to deliver di Montago's report . . . such as it was—"

"So the queen has known all along that he . . . that di Montago was dead?"

"Someone had to carry the *marimé* bundle to the queen and, I felt . . . I thought . . . I believed that she should hear his report from one of her own men. The vigilare are hers to command—"

"So you thought nothing of her not telling Alban or anyone else? Or of you telling me?" Stefano asked.

Luciana shrugged. "It is true that I am often in her confidence, but I do not know what she tells her husband or her other counselors. These are her secrets for her to share. She is queen, just as I am *Araunya*, after all." She could tell from his expression that he did not quite believe her. She let that pass without further comment. "It came out in our . . . session, the other day."

"Yes, but so much time and manpower—"

She placed a finger on his lips. "Such is not my affair. This boy, Massimo, as you say, he is another matter. He was made from *mulló* and other unclean magic. He is all that is bad about the Rom and bad about the *gadjé*. He is evil personified."

"You aren't saying he's the devil?"

Luciana shook her head. “A demon . . . something of a demon, yes . . . and no. He is *vampiro*, fiend, soul-sucker, phantasm, *espirito* . . . He is all these things at once and, yet, still nothing more than a boy. *Yet.*”

“You are sure?” he asked.

“How can I be sure of anything? I recognize it from the magic. I see it in his eyes. We all see it. He is unnatural in ways that have nothing to do with that disfigured body.”

“And Idala knows this?”

“She’s known since first she saw him. At first, even I hoped, but . . .” She shook her head. At mention of the queen, Luciana decided there was more that her husband should know. “She bleeds from birthing him. Neither the medicine of *il dottore* or Donna della Guelfa nor even the magic of Signora Rui—or me—have been able to staunch the flow. I fear for her, Stefan.”

She watched her husband dip his head. She knew from long practice that he was dealing with news he would otherwise have preferred not to face. She knew he would. He would come to terms with it, as he had with the king’s death; so, too, would he with his sister’s. Luciana felt the prick of tears as worry settled in. This was not a good day.

VIII

"It is the nature of desire not to be satisfied, and most men live only for the gratification of it."

—Aristotle

PIERRO paced the length of the reception room. The fire roared, blossoming with heat, but he would have none of it. His anger fed his body what heat it needed. The morning ride had been a success . . . of a sort. The king was dead. The attackers had time to get away. No tracker—not even a stinking Gypsy tracker—could follow their trail, even in the light snow and muddy road. All that and suffering to ride back on the plug the king's bodyguard rode . . . all for naught. In the halls of the palazzo, first to arrive, he had proclaimed the king's death and his wife's right to the throne. All ears had been for news of the king! Not even Duca LaCosta had seemed moved to press for Ortensia's throne because of news of the king.

Pierro pounded his fist in his hand, angry with himself. When should he have made the first claim for Ortensia's rights if not immediately? But her claims were ignored. His claims for her had been ignored. *He* had been ignored. It would not—could not—happen again!

"Husband? Is it true?"

Pierro froze. Lost in his own thoughts, he had not heard Ortensia come down the stairs from her chamber. He took a deep breath, schooling his features into an attentive mask. Pierro turned and went to his wife's side, bent, and kissed her hand.

"The king *is* dead," he said, not bothering to sound in the slightest sorrowful.

Ortensia smiled and clapped her hands. "Then I am queen now?" She wrapped her arms around herself and spun in place like a giddy schoolgirl.

Pierro gave her the moment, before capturing her hand. "You should be queen, but it seems there is yet Idala to consider."

"Idala?" Ortensia repeated, the joy leaving her puffy face.

Pregnancy was not kind to her, Pierro thought. She was a month farther along than they wanted anyone to know, having conceived, apparently, on their wedding night. Which would explain, of course, how she gave her Sultan Tardiq five children over the years. The woman . . . his wife . . . was positively a brood mare, and had she not been kidnapped and her life-course unalterably shifted, she would have served well as queen, except then he would not have been her husband and it would matter not a whit to him. Not that it mattered overly much to him now.

"Yes, there is the matter of the—" he began.

"Plural throne," Ortensia finished for him. Her hands ran through her hair, disorganizing its pretty arrangement. "But if she can sit the throne, why not I?"

Pierro guided her to the loveseat before the fire and sat beside her, taking her hands in his. "All is not lost. There is rumor that the queen is not well."

Ortensia looked at him thoughtfully. "And a child cannot inherit the throne now. The boy is too young. We will have my throne after all."

Pierro nodded. "Of course, the boy can't—Heir Apparent or no. He cannot sit the throne. There will be a void and we—I mean, you, of course, will fill it."

"But first the queen *must* die," Ortensia said. She shook her hands free and ran them over her hair again. "Perhaps, we could have a tonic made . . . for her . . . for her recovery?" She smiled artfully, her brows arching over her hazel eyes.

Pierro looked into the fire, tapping his lower lip. Once again he mourned the outing last spring and, the loss of his perfumer, none other than the infamous Exilli himself! He had paid too much money for the man's services and suffered the loss of too many schemes over that bungled attempt on the king.

Ortensia, he realized, had a point. Now if only they had a source for this tonic to come from . . . and then his mind settled on two resources, Renata and Don Cristoval Battista—his man.

Renata served the queen in her chambers, but not regularly. She might resist poisoning the queen, though she saw no harm in spying on her. Of course, she could be tricked. Then there was Cristoval, who had lost not one, but two wives to childbed fevers; his second wife had died even before producing the child. All this time, his housekeeper, the resourceful Signora delVecchio attended them. She would have a curative tonic that could be made innocently enough and carried—once doctored by himself—to the queen by Renata.

A vindictive glitter lit Ortensia's eyes. She was barely sane, Pierro thought. She was no coconspirator, to be sure, but with her came certain benefits . . . certain associations—one of which, if she knew . . . well, she did not have to know and he was determined to keep it from her, unless it served his purposes to reveal his part in her "escape" from the dread infidel.

IX

"Death be not proud, though some have called thee
Mighty and dreadful, for thou art not so;
For those whom thou thinkst thou dost overthrow,
Die not, poor Death, nor yet canst thou kill me."
—John Donne

13 d'Dicembre, 1684

LUCIANA watched *il dottore* Bonta hover solicitously over the queen.

"Majesty, are you sure you want to do this?" *il dottore* asked. He glanced self-consciously in Stefano's direction, no doubt trying to be circumspect. He lowered his voice, though Stefano could still hear him clearly. "Majesty, your bleeding has not subsided. Your humors are out of balance. You should stay in bed. There is no reason your counselors could not advise you here."

Idala sighed, closing her eyes. "I am experienced in childbirth, My Lord, and this is no different. I always bleed after delivery."

"Yes, but, Majesty, you have never delivered four children at once and the bleeding is excessive. Please! Listen to *il dottore* Bonta," the midwife urged from the far side of the bed. "Besides, there are the children to tend to."

"I am queen. I have obligations beyond my family. There are wet nurses and the *governante*—not to mention yourself—to take care of the children while I'm gone for a few hours," Idala said. "I will only be going as far as my solar, which is but down the stairs. I'll not be far away, and *il dottore* Bonta and the *Araunya* are welcome to attend me."

"But, Majesty, undue movement—" Bonta began.

"If my humours are misaligned, then I suggest you take care of it at once for I intend to fulfill my duty just as you will yours." Idala rolled up her sleeve and offered her right arm to the Royal Physician.

"I'll send for the barber, then," Bonta said in resignation.

"No, *dottore*, *you* will do it now. Just as you have done it three times in the last three days," Idala said firmly.

Muttering incoherently beneath his breath, the Royal Physician opened his kit bag and pulled out his barber tools. He pressed a hand to her fever-sweaty brow and shook his head.

While the doctor was busy, Luciana turned to Stefano. "Surely, there is something that you can do?"

"Do?" Stefano asked. He shook his head. He had already worn out his welcome on the subject when he argued that Idala take another day. At this point, he was going to make it as easy upon her to do her duty and stress her as little as possible. "She is determined and would hear none of it."

"Then try again," Luciana hissed at him. "It's important."

Stefano tugged at his blond-brown goatee in frustration. "And just as important that you do not stress yourself," he said. "What would you do in such circumstance?" He raised his hands. "I will try again."

"Thank you," Luciana breathed a sigh of relief and squeezed his hand.

Stefano watched the blood seep slowly down his sister's arm. "Idala—"

His sister looked up at him with a stern gaze. He could see the determination in her expression, even as he took in the hollow look of her face. She was not only pale, she seemed to have aged at least a dozen years since last he spoke with her yesterday. Her eyes were sunken and deeply shadowed. No amount of pretty powders could hide it from a discerning eye.

"Majesty, the affairs of State are in order . . . at least for now. It is customary to close the State for a week or more after the loss of a sovereign. No one would think the worst of you or Tyrrhia if—" Stefano urged, using his best politician's smile.

"*I* would think less of myself. My duty is to the State, my office and, more importantly, I will not leave room for the deMedicis to gain a toehold in the political arena," Idala said. "I have already acceded to your wishes and agreed to let you continue to carry me about as though I were some fragile doll. It makes me look weak. It makes Tyrrhia look weak. You are Regent Guardian. You are my only brother. You're my most prized adviser and I will not listen even to you in this matter. I won't disdain my office. Not for anyone. I do not relish leaving my children, but we must do what each must. Am I understood?" She looked from her brother to all those in attendance on her, wincing slightly when *il dottore* Bonta cinched a bandage closed over where he had let her blood.

Stefano chaffed at the limitations, but he understood her reasons. For a moment, she had sounded like their mother rather than his baby sister. Except for who she had married, she would never dare speak to him like this. She was, however, his queen. "It will be as you say, then, Majesty," he said with a deep and formal bow.

Luciana twitched his sleeve to get his attention. He refused to look at her, but said in a quiet whisper. "I have no choice. Be with me, instead of against me."

He almost showed his surprise openly when she said under her breath, "Yes, Stefano."

"I have bled you, Majesty, but your humors are dreadfully unbalanced. I've given you my best advice and I wish you would heed it." *Il dottore* bowed and stepped away from the bed.

"You are excused. You may attend me when I have returned this afternoon," the queen said firmly as she dropped her feet to the floor and raised up her arms for Stefano to take her.

Stefano hesitated one last time. Filial responsibilities followed after the royal ones. He bent, making sure that her arms were securely around his neck before he lifted her, light as a feather. He tried not to notice the deep red stain on the linens which had been beneath her, and carried her down to the solar. He hoped that the garden air would do her well.

He took the stairs slowly with Luciana's hand heavy on his shoulder. He felt extremely conscious of the two most important women in his life and the perilous balance they were all in. He settled Idala on her champagne-colored chaise and stepped back so that Giuletta and Luciana could arrange the queen's skirts.

Idala wore a black Gypsy Silk dress with a gold undergown, all of which helped to hide her malaise as well as mark her state of mourning. Someone had embroidered intricate gold medallions along the cuffs and hem. Giuletta draped a gold shawl around her shoulders—to protect her against the chill of the day—even though a fire was banked in a large iron brazier a few feet away. Luciana lay a blanket across her lap before starting to draw the wingback chair toward her.

Stefano quickly picked the chair up and set it beside the chaise so that Luciana could be close at hand to Idala's right. A small table with refreshments for both women stood between them.

"I am ready now," Idala said, smoothing the lap blanket.

"If at any time—" Luciana began, pausing at the solemn expression on the queen's face. "I am ready to serve you, Majesty."

"Thank you, Duchessa," Idala said with a firm nod, making it clear in which capacity Luciana was to witness the intimate affairs of State. She waved her hand. She was ready.

Estensi, the Court Herald, came first into the open patio. He bowed deeply. "Your Majesty, please let me express my sorrow at . . . allow me to express my sorrow. Your husband was a good and just king."

The queen accepted his words in silence, with a nod. For a moment, she looked like she fought back tears, then her resolve firmed into a mask of great dignity.

As the day progressed and the various Royal retainers filed in with reports, they also expressed their condolences. Estensi, Luciana, and Stefano remained in constant vigilance. The Court Herald remained at the queen's back, taking notes for future reference. Luciana plied Idala with food and drink so that she could keep up her strength.

Hour after hour passed and Stefano watched as the flower who was his sister began to wilt and droop. By the time her senior advisers, the elder statesmen of the Palantini arrived, she was clearly and distinctly ill. The men looked to Stefano for guidance as the queen seemed to melt before them.

While Sebastiani spoke, the young Duca di Candido turned to whisper to Stefano, "Should she be receiving? She does not look well. Perhaps another day?"

Stefano nodded, chewing his lower lip. Idala had done as she intended. The State remained constant. "So far she has refused to return to her room and insisted upon this audience. She is quite determined."

"What good is it if she kills herself?" di Candido asked. "If she will not hear it for herself, perhaps for your wife who attends her?"

Stefano smiled tightly. "If out of sympathy . . ." He nodded.

Duca Raffia, who had joined them, indicated his concurrence. "I know what my wife is like at present and she is not so far along as yours," he whispered. "Who would've thought, after all these years, my wife should produce a child? It is almost unheard of at her age, especially for a woman heretofore considered barren."

Stefano clapped both men on the shoulders and murmured, "You will excuse me?" He moved in a solicitous manner to his wife's side. While glancing pointedly at his sister, he dropped to one knee. "Are you well, my dear?"

The question had its effect even as Luciana frowned, confused momentarily. Idala turned to her, however, and said, "Forgive me, Your Grace. You have served me so well for so long. Perhaps it is time we rested." She smiled at Sebastiani who had stopped mid-sentence. "Tomorrow is another day, Your Grace. I'm sorry, but I know that I am anxious to see my young daughters."

"And your son, of course," Sebastiani said. "He *is* second in line for the throne."

Stefano considered leaning on the Duca's swollen foot.

"My son is well-tended. His every need is being met, but he . . . he is not well," Idala said sharply. She turned to Estensi. "The citizen petitioners? They can wait until tomorrow, yes?"

"*Assolutamente*!" the Court Herald responded with a quick bow. "So closes the court of her most Royal Majesty, Idala di Drago e Novabianco, Queen of all Tyrrhia, from the heartland to the continental lands and the outlying islands!"

Stefano bent and picked Idala up before she could

protest otherwise, careful to lift her so that the blanket which had been covering her lap and legs would cover any sign of bleeding the queen may have left. He was pleased, as he carried her up the stairs with Luciana at his heels that she did not protest.

"Luciana, forgive me please. I did not think of you today at all, sitting always at my side. Tomorrow, I will have—" Idala said, breathing heavily as Stefano laid her to rest on her bed.

"Tomorrow, Majesty, is another day. I'll attend you then as I did today—unless you would prefer someone else," Luciana said. She bent and removed the queen's shoes and then swung her legs so that Idala was in the bed.

Stefano hid a grimace. His attendance was mandatory, but Luciana could use the rest. He indicated that the doctor and midwife should attend the queen and pulled his wife out of their way. "Tomorrow *is* another day. We shall discuss what needs to be done in the morning."

Luciana shifted position, vaguely aware of a pain in her belly and down her back. She came wide awake with the second pain. She recognized the cramping immediately and reached out to shake Stefano's shoulder.

"Mmph?"

"Call for Maria," she said, feeling the onset of panic.

A little more awake, Stefano propped himself up on his elbow and wiped his eyes. "What? Who?"

Luciana struggled to be patient, but all was still fear, excitement, and frustration. "Della Guelfa. The midwife!"

Quite suddenly, Stefano was wide awake and sitting up. "Are you unwell? Or is it time?" he asked as he reached for his breeches.

"I think the time has come, but it is early yet," Luciana said, trying not to show him her fear and glad of the darkness of night still shadowing her features. "She sleeps in the servants' quarters above the queen's bed chamber."

Stefano tucked his nightshirt into his pants as he buttoned them closed and disappeared into the darkness. Several minutes later, a light bloomed as one of the oil lamps was lit and he reappeared at her side with Maria next to him.

"Do you think it's time? You shouldn't be so soon," Maria said, resting her hands on Luciana's belly.

"I know. I haven't had a chance to build my *bender* yet!" Luciana said, her worry apparently clear to the midwife. Luciana gasped as another pain hit her side.

"Your what?" the midwife asked, straightening.

"It's a tent her people use," Stefano answered. He looked at his wife and, in all seriousness, said, "I did not know you were serious about that. It's winter. Why would you want to give birth in a hut when you could have the luxuries of the palazzo and the padding of a feathered bed?"

Luciana sighed, grinding her teeth in frustration. "It's the custom of my people to give birth in the open air. It makes it easier for the spirit to find the child. Last time I did not do it and I've regretted it ever since." Her gaze sought his as they shared once more a moment of grief over the birth of their stillborn son which led to their five-year separation. She grieved not only for the child, but for the time she had lost.

"Then it shall be so. How do I build it?" Stefano asked.

Maria looked up from her examination of Luciana and interrupted. "You still have time to build your . . . your *bender*, Your Grace. The child is only making itself ready. It won't come tonight."

"Are you sure?" Stefano asked as he took Luciana's hand.

"I've done this many times, Your Grace," Maria della Guelfa said with a smile. She rubbed Luciana's left side and asked, "The pains are mostly on one side, *sí*?"

Luciana took time to think about it and at last nodded, "*Sí*, only one side. What do we do? Is there a problem?"

"You've been too much time with our queen, Your Grace. The child you bear will be fine, have no fear." Maria smiled and continued rubbing Luciana's side.

"But we *are* close . . . to the time, I mean?" Stefano asked.

"This child should come in three weeks, though it could be sooner. You spent too much time on your feet attending the queen," Maria explained. "If you asked, I am sure the queen would excuse you from further service."

"I am at the queen's side by my choosing. There are other ladies available to stand at attendance, but like me, many of them are also pregnant . . . or are too young or too old. She is my friend, and I am with her for mainly that reason. Besides, as *Araunya*, I am an adviser to Her Majesty on matters involving magic and, more importantly to me, my people," Luciana explained.

"Pardon me, but doesn't that make things . . . interesting what with the queen being your sister?"

Luciana glanced up at Stefano and licked her lips. "I am *Araunya di Cayesmengri e Cayesmengro*," she said. "My 'things' are always 'interesting,' as you put it. I serve Her Majesty, Queen Idala, but my first allegiance is to another queen, the black-blooded *Beluni*. For my people, I must walk two paths; for my love, I walk a third."

"But couldn't your paths be simpler if you just . . . walked a straight path?" Stefano asked.

Luciana laughed enigmatically. "Tell me, Regent Guardian, how straight your path has been of late."

Stefano sighed and sank down onto the side of the bed.

"It sounds confusing," the midwife said.

"It *is*!" both Stefano and Luciana said, almost in unison.

"Ah, well, I do thank you for your indulgence in explaining this to me, Your Grace," Signora della Guelfa said. She straightened, folding her hands in front of her. "My questions served another purpose, Your Graces. Now, *Madonna*, how are the pains?"

Luciana actually had to think before she answered. "They've passed."

"Oftentimes, a little distraction is all you need—"

A loud, energetic scratching at the servants' quarter door interrupted whatever else she was about to say. Stefano frowned, motioned them to silence, and crossed to the door. With his hand on the knob, he asked, "Who is it?"

Giuletta responded, her voice distinguishable, but her words were not.

Stefano opened the door. "Do you need something? Is it the queen?"

In tears, Giuletta only nodded mutely, then turned on her heels and ran back the way she had come.

"I must go right away," Maria said, edging past Stefano to the door.

Stefano nodded and opened the door wider. "As will I!"

"Me, too," Luciana said, reaching for her robe at the foot of the bed.

Stefano stepped back into the room, shaking his head. "No. You stay here. Rest. I will tell you what has happened in the morning." He departed, snapping the door closed behind him.

The floor was cold beneath Luciana's toes. She found slippers and quickly stuffed her feet into them, all the while wrestling herself into her robe. She opened the door to the hall, peered out and, finding it empty, closed the door behind her.

Stefano glowered at her as she finally caught up in Idala's bedchamber.

Upon entering the room, Luciana noted that Donna Rui had also been summoned from her bed. She looked worried and was lighting candles to ward the room. She glanced over at the babies. Two wet nurses were being well-employed at the moment, tending to the three girls, their expressions filled with fear.

"She's been like this—It came on very suddenly—She was nursing Rosalina—she simply went limp—she is so weak—" Giuletta stammered, edging away from the bed and back toward Stefano and the midwife.

Luciana pushed her way between Stefano and Maria, and went immediately to the queen's side. She took Stefano's sister's hand and knelt beside the bed.

Idala was cool to the touch. Her pulse seemed faint, her brow feverish. With her free hand, Luciana stroked the queen's face. "Idala! Idala!" she called softly. She was vaguely aware of Maria removing the covers to reveal the queen was blood-soaked. She felt Stefano behind her, felt him shifting nervously, torn between service and his sister's privacy. If nothing else, he remained to bear witness.

When the queen did not respond, Luciana glanced over her shoulder and reached out to pinch Idala's inner arm as hard as she could. She had seen this before, when her mother died. Pain would be the only way to make her stir from the death sleep she was falling into. It was easy to see in the queen's slack, hollow, expression; the deep, sunken eyes and the cold, lifeless pallor of her skin. All color—even the normally bright curls of her hair—seemed washed out of her. Her breathing was barely perceptible. Her jaw had grown slack.

In response to Luciana's second pinch, on her breast,

Idala suddenly took a deep breath and exhaled. Her eyes opened slowly and as though with great effort. Her gaze fell naturally, easily to Luciana. There was a reason why there was the expression "the ghost of a smile," Luciana realized, shuddering as the queen roused.

"I had thought to survive this, no matter the prophecy," Idala whispered. She licked her dry, cracked, and colorless lips. "Water."

Luciana moved aside for Stefano who quickly grabbed the goblet on the bedside table. She waited patiently while he propped his sister up and fed her the mulled wine that had been brought to sustain her.

Idala turned her face away after a couple of sips, sighing.

"Don't allow this prophecy to predict how you live, *piccolina.* You still have time, if you fight this," Stefano said and sank to the edge of his sister's bed, near her head.

Idala managed another hollow smile. She reached for his hand as though it were at some great distance instead of mere inches from her own. Stefano took her hand in his quickly.

"You must tell my children that . . . I wanted them more than anything. They are their father's legacy and my bequest to Tyrrhia. You, the two of you, will raise them to be . . ." Idala drifted off as though to sleep. After another long moment of silence, she began again. "They are for Tyrrhia. You understand? No matter where the Crown goes . . . I pray for Dario . . . whoever holds the Crown, these children are Tyrrhia. Vow that you will keep my trust." Her last words were stronger and held the wealth of a queen's command.

"We will," Luciana promised.

Over her head, Stefano spoke in quiet tones to the midwife. "Where is Giuletta? Have you sent her for the physician?"

"No," said the queen. "Let her stay. She has been my companion and I wish her to stay."

"I'll go," one of the attendants volunteered. "Here, give her this tonic. It might help revive her whilst I fetch *il dottore.*" She handed Luciana a small vial and left the room. Luciana barely noticed the young woman leave as she handed Stefano the vial.

"Luciana, I—I know you're an ambassador, but you're

my brother's wife as well . . . and my friend. For that reason, I beg of you to raise my girls . . . they will need a strong woman . . . of character. They must be more than royal ladies to be sold into profitable marriages. Promise me," Idala commanded between wheezing breaths.

"It will be so," Stefano and Luciana said.

"And, Stefano, you are to make a good marriage for Giuletta. She has been promised that," Idala said, licking her chapped lips. She faded, her eyes closing. For a minute, Luciana thought she had gone the way of her husband, but the queen was not done yet. "Stefano, I left papers in my desk. The last several days . . . I have prepared for just this moment. You will find my wishes about things. Some of little importance to anyone but me. As queen, I have one last duty left."

Luciana held her friend's hand tightly, keeping silent, knowing what a struggle these words were. Stefano emptied the vial into the queen's goblet and pressed it to her chapped lips. She drank thirstily.

"Is the physician here?" Idala asked. Her eyes still closed.

"No, Majesty. Is there anything I can do to make you more comfortable?" Maria asked. She hovered nearby, her fingers worrying the edges of the shawl she wore over her nightgown.

"No . . . I seek a witness. The Royal Physician is meant to witness Our final wishes," Idala said.

"Hush now," Stefano said, bending down. "There is still time. I will not lose you!"

Idala laughed, though it seemed more of a spasm than any sign of merriment. "You were always destined to lose me, brother, at one point or another. It was a matter of time and of who went first."

Luciana looked up at her husband and was startled to see tears coursing down his cheeks. He *really* was ill-prepared for this, she realized, even though he had been warned. Still holding Idala's left hand in hers, Luciana placed her other hand on his leg, rubbing in a small circle. Without looking away from his sister, Stefano placed a stilling hand over hers.

"Giuletta, I'm sorry, but you must send for Estensi as well. He will be close." Idala's eyes rolled from one side to the other as she looked from Stefano to the maid on the far side of the bed. "As queen, I have my final bequest and that is the throne. I would have witnesses here, but there is not much time."

Stefano bent and pressed a kiss on his sister's clammy forehead. A tear fell onto Idala's face. Stefano brushed it away with the hand that held his sister's. "You were always in such a hurry."

Idala smiled her hint of a smile. "Every time I close my eyes, I see death's veil. I am not afraid. I will be with my Alban, but I will miss you and the children. If anything, my use of magic has taught me that death is not final. I have not spoken of the boy . . . yet. I want him provided for, but he is not to see *the throne* . . . if I have to denounce him as my child, I will. You understand me?"

The door from the lower chamber all but burst open, serving as the only announcement Estensi was to have. "I am here, Majesty. How may I serve you?"

Idala sighed heavily. It was clear to Luciana that she was exhausted by her efforts. "Come, Estensi. Stand at the foot of my bed so that I can see you."

The Court Herald did as he was commanded, bowing deeply. He wore his nightshirt only, apparently allowing himself no time for the comfort of slippers or the modesty of a robe. "I am here to serve, Your Majesty. What would you ask of me?"

Even as he asked the question, the Royal Physician, Bonta, came bounding through the door from the servants' hall. He, too, was in his bedclothes, slipperless. He carried his medicine bag and came to stand on the far side of the bed with Giuletta who rejoined them now, breathless.

"Good. You are both here to witness . . . Stefano, wet my lips," Idala asked. Luciana released his hand long enough for Stefano to prop up the queen and give her another drink of mulled wine. "Be it known, Stefano di Drago is my Regent. He will guard the throne wisely until my children are of age. Dario Gian stands first in line. Massimo is to be sent away, to live in seclusion. His needs are to be provided for, but he is not to have the throne. Duca di Drago and his wife, ambassador to Tyrrhia's Black Throne, will be guardians of my children . . . the children are to be raised as they see fit. The girl, Chiara, is to be fostered by her . . . by the

Araunya and her people to one day be emissary to the Council of Queens and tie our thrones closer together . . . to make a stronger Tyrrhia."

Idala sighed. Her breathing became noticeably shallower. She did not even open her eyes when she asked, "Estensi . . . there are some other matters . . . that concern my affairs . . . my brother is to handle them as my final wishes. . . . I have left directions for him . . . As to the State, long live its Regent so that a Novabianco will once more take the throne." She breathed deeper, the breath escaping from her lips. "Is there anything . . . ? Any matter of State I have left undone?"

"No, Majesty," Estensi said.

"Then I am at peace," Idala said and let out another little sigh that was her last breath.

In his dungeon cell, Brother Tomasi heard the tolling of the great bells. He received his news by the bells—the pealing bells of new heirs to the throne, just days later the first of the death bells and, now, they rang again. The King and Queen of Tyrrhia were dead!

He performed a final utterance of the Extreme Unction and cast the poppets Cardinal delle Torre had given him into the feeble fire that could not keep the cold from his bones. Now he must wait!

X

"In adversity remember to keep an even mind."
—Horace

15 d'Dicembre, 1684

STEFANO stood dawn's watch alone over Alban and Idala who were laid out in State. Their bodies lay side by side, in coffins of glass and gold on catafalques in the central chapel of the Catholic Church. Baptism of the four new royals had been delayed until their blessings would not be overwhelmed by the presence of their parents' bodies.

Stefano took one last look at them . . . at Alban and Idala. They had been prettied up by the morticians and one could almost think they slept lightly, instead of lying in that final rest of the ages. Luciana had been unwilling or, perhaps truly unable, to witness them like this. He knew from the death of their son that Luciana shunned all dead things—except that which was prepared as food—as untouchable *marimé*. All the Romani were that way . . . which kept the black bloods from involvement in the duties for the dead. He shook off the idle thought.

Stefano had said his good-byes to the two still forms laying in their biers at the foot of the great altar, yet still he lingered. He prayed for Alban and Alban's strength and for his sister and her generosity. These were qualities he wanted to take away with him, take into the new world of politics he faced.

In a day's time, news of the dual loss had already reached

the populace of Tyrrhia—or, at least those in close vicinity of the palazzo. Couriers were sent to all points beyond, to notify the populace of the loss. The drive into the palázzo grounds was already filled with mourners, so many that the Palazzo Guards at the gate had quickly realized they were ill-prepared for the onslaught. The Escalade vigilare now manned the open roads.

Even as he said his good-byes, Stefano could hear mourners scratching at the doors of the sanctuary to get in. He nodded to the churchmen and departed by a back way used by the clergy.

Couriers were specifically sent to the duchi who formed the Palantini and the allies of the State, including the Black Queen, the *Beluni*. When a sufficient number of the duchi were present to form a quorum of the Palantini, they would validate Dario Gian as the Heir Apparent and Stefano and Luciana in their new roles as Regents during his and his siblings minor years—unless Pierro and Ortensia were able to convince them otherwise. Under normal circumstances, sending word for a gathering of the Palantini would be sufficient and a full fortnight of grieving would commence, shutting down all but the most necessary elements of the government.

The deMedicis had seen to it, however, that the accepted cycle was disrupted. Pierro, upon his return from the ill-fated ride with the king had pronounced his wife "queen," flying in the face of all known forms and laws that bound the country and Idala's expected role. She had spent a large part of her single day as Regent Queen squashing the hemorrhage caused by that attempt. The claim had been moot while she lived. With her death, the deMedicis renewed their claim to the throne, challenging the wills of both Alban and Idala.

Rather than risk encountering other mourners, Stefano circled through the "religious ghetto" on the palazzo grounds, looping through the nearly emptied Escalade barracks—with a full half of their local contingent away on courier duty—and from there, he swung by the stables. From the horse barns, it was easy enough for him to cross the familiar courtyard, past the ancient Visigoth's statue covered in a black shroud and to the palazzo itself. The Palazzo Guard at the front doors uncrossed their halberds and stood at rigid attention, their gold brocade coats and black baldrics in perfect order as they bobbed their white plumed-adorned helmeted heads toward Stefano.

He made his way to the Court Herald's office which sat on the first floor, directly beneath the king's offices. The Palazzo Steward, Ignacio Guglielmo, kept a small office adjoining Estensi's. Despite having a clutch of young assistants, the portly steward was usually flitting somewhere between stations in the back halls and grounds of his charged domain, the palazzo proper. Finding him during the day was nigh impossible, but mornings, he met with staff and then Estensi, the Court Herald. As he reached for Estensi's door, it was flung open and he found himself face-to-face with Princess Ortensia.

Despite her hair being somewhat askew, she was, as always, attired in the height of fashion in a dress of Gypsy Silk gold brocade. Her overgown gaped at the skirt more than normal, displaying a heavily embroidered and beaded white undergown and a distinctly gravid belly.

"Make way!" she snapped at him, her long cane smacking smartly against his ankles as she pushed past him.

Stefano stared after her wake as she strode down the hall driving courtiers and servants out of her path as she went. Nonplussed, he entered the office to discover Estensi and Ignacio in deep conversation over a stack of pamphlets left, wrapped in silken cord, sitting on a chair.

"What's all this?" Stefano asked, pointing to the papers.

Both men appeared harried when they looked up. Their expressions turned amiable upon seeing him. Estensi, however, was the one who answered Stefano's question.

"Her Royal Highness—"

"Her Highness, you mean. Whatever she says, she's *not* in line for the throne," Stefano corrected.

"Her *Royal* Highness," Estensi repeated, "has demanded that I and Guglielmo, here, make sure that every responding member of the Palantini get one of these."

"Responding?" Stefano repeated, looking toward the pamphlets with ever growing curiosity.

"The members who arrive at the palazzo," Ignacio growled, a furrowed frown etching his corpulent features. "At first, she expected us to send out another round of couriers!"

"She wanted more couriers sent out?" Stefano repeated, disbelieving.

"Of course, we pointed out that we could not have any more of the Escalade sent on such errands unless it were another emergency. It was only after I pointed out that I could not vouch for her own personal safety if we did this that we were able to convince her to let us give the pamphlets out to those members of the Palantini in residence and to the others as they arrived."

"What is it?"

Ignacio worked one free of the binding and handed it to him. "It is her treatise on why we should revert to Orsino's rule and that *she* be crowned, instead of having a Lord Regent—which we would have if the Heir Apparent, Dario Gian, is confirmed as His *Royal* Highness."

Stefano looked at the pamphlet in his hands and rubbed his forehead. He had known Ortensia would not wait, but to go as far as this?

"She kept the royal presses busy all through the night and left nary a soldibianco to cover the cost of extra wages!" Ignacio continued, his face turning several shades of red. "I've had to put them on three-quarter workdays for the rest of the month to make up the time—if they are to be of any use at all before the Palantini arrive! There are room assignments, menus, whatever else needs printing before the conference and all this on three-quarter time!"

Stefano patted the Steward's shoulder. "I'll see to it that others are more considerate. If Her Highness—or her husband—wish anything else printed, it should be brought to me. I'll see what I can do to stem her future prolific efforts."

"Until you are ratified, you have no standing against *her*," Estensi pointed out, jabbing his plumed pen in the direction Ortensia had taken.

"Yes. I know, but as soon as we have sufficient members of the Palantini here, I plan to call a council of the quorum and do something to slow her down. I'll not have her upsetting everyone in the Royal Nurseries and half the gentry of Tyrrhia," Stefano said.

Estensi coughed. "You think you can stop her or that son of an Italian *bisco* from causing more problems when they mean to see that you are never in power to interfere with them in the first place?"

"I will do what I am able. I have my ways," Stefano replied, unoffended by the Court Herald's doubt.

"That gives us over to the other problem we face," Ignacio said.

"He does not need to be troubled with that—" Estensi began.

"No. Trouble me. What may I do to serve?" Stefano invited.

Ignacio gulped and took a deep breath. "It has been many years since a full Grand Palantini was called and, well, the palazzo as large as it is, can only hold so many souls. Everyone will be coming with their servants and an entourage for each is to be expected. There will never be enough room!"

Stefano found himself surprised that the man, usually so unflappable, was as agitated as he was. "Then simply house the Palantini and their servants. The apartments have room for servants upstairs—"

"*That* was not the problem," Ignacio interrupted. He purpled slightly and bowed deeply. "Forgive me, Your Grace, but—I—actually, our concern was the Royal Apartments."

"The children are there," Estensi put in, rapping the Steward on the shoulder with his gloves.

"The children *are* there, but could they be moved to the suite with His Royal Highness, Prince Dario Gian? That would free the apartments to be used by . . ." Here Ignacio paused, looking discomfited.

"There is no one suitable for the Royal Apartments. The princess would take it as a foregone conclusion that her bid for the throne was more solid than we wish her to think it is—" Stefano said. He paused. "I'm assuming we are in agreement here, so forgive the . . . the . . ."

"Assumption?" Estensi said. "You're in good company, Your Grace. No one who has had to live with her wants to see her as Queen of Tyrrhia."

"Except her husband," Ignacio retorted.

"Except her husband," Stefano agreed. "Though she does have her sympathizers." Pierro's motivations, however, were too obvious to bear consideration and he returned his thoughts to the Royal Apartments. "There will be no one suitable but the infants to reside there—"

"For the time being. When you are made Lord Regent—"

"*If* I'm made Lord Regent," Stefano corrected the Steward. "Besides, I wouldn't take the Royal Apartments anyway. They will belong to Dario when he is of age. Until then, unless something else arises, it will house the infants' Nursery so that they do not disturb Dario," Stefano replied.

"Excellent," Estensi said with a nod.

Ignacio scratched his balding pate beneath his blond wig. "It solves many problems, but not where to put people, alas. That is *my* task, however, and not yours, Your Grace."

Stefano relaxed a little. "Then we are agreed?" When the other men nodded, he looked down at the pamphlet given to him earlier. He lifted it, noting its thickness. "I have reading to do . . . and quickly, I think."

Padre Gabera paced the dungeon cell, trying to find reason that would reach the intransigent Brother Tomasi. "I make no pretenses of being a cardinal. I am a lesser man called for lesser things. The new bishop has not yet arrived. None of us are of delle Torre's rank. When dealing with your immortal soul, can you really stand on rank and privilege, Brother?"

"I do no such thing," Tomasi argued, huffing up as he sat on his cot. "It is not a matter of pride, but the cardinal said *he* was my confessor and to him, alone, should I confess."

"But he is *dead*, Brother Tomasi! You cannot get absolution from a ghost, the ghost of a mere mortal! He is not our Christ! Nor can you take Holy Communion without the Sacrament of Confession!"

For the first time, Brother Tomasi looked troubled.

"Consider what you are charged with, Brother," Gabera pressed. "Not only was an *Araunya* murdered, but her body was drained of blood!"

"I had no part in her death. My soul is clean in the matter," Tomasi responded, folding his arms over his chest.

"What about stealing her from her grave?"

Tomasi eyed Gabera sullenly. "The Gypsy was a heathen. The Gypsies *are* heathen. We needed to save her soul. I was doing the Church's work!"

"And where does the Church or the sacred texts tell us

that to save a heathen soul, we must first drain her body o fluids?" Gabera asked, sickened at the thought of what h had been told this man committed.

"I have not been privileged to read the texts, and I trus the Church's wants will be told to me by my superiors, Brother Tomasi said, stuffing his hands under him and star ing at his feet.

"Superiors are but human vessels—"

"Through which God speaks to me," Brother Tomasi in terrupted. He rose and came to stand face-to-face wit Gabera. "Tell me you don't take orders from the Churc which uses, as you say, human vessels to relay those order Did you not take a vow of obedience? I did! I take my vow seriously."

"But can't you see that what you helped the cardinal d to the Romani women was beyond Church teachings? Gabera argued, running a hand through his blond, shor hair. "Give me your Confession, Brother, and take Commu nion. Be whole with God."

Tomasi seemed to hesitate. Gabera could read the con fusion and indecision in his expression in the shadowy ligh of day that shone into the prison through a single, miniscul window. The priest, Gabera, reached out to offer strengt and consolation even as Tomasi turned away again.

Gabera let his hand drop, forming into a fist of frustra tion. He was so close to winning back the man's soul. H could tell, the Brother was wavering in his teachings fron the cardinal. There was little he could do about the charge against him, no amount of Catholic Indulgences or Ha Marys would satisfy the Tyrrhian court that would judg him.

"What if—" Gabera began.

The metal cell door creaked open, banging against th stone wall behind the portal. "I'm sorry, Padre, but you time is done," the Palazzo Guard said, ducking his plume head as he entered the cell. When Gabera did not move t leave immediately, the guard said more sternly, "Padre."

Gabera sighed in consternation, looking at the guard. " am so close and there has never been a limit on my tim before."

"There are other, higher ranking visitors needing hi time," the guard insisted.

"I am to be judged now? Padre—" Brother Tomasi asked the guard, then reached for the priest.

"Padre." The guard remained solemn and insistent.

Gabera looked between the two men, torn by obligations in conflict with one another. "It would take just a little more time," Gabera pleaded.

The guard shook his head. "Perhaps tomorrow," he said. He pushed the door to bang, metal against stone, again. It spoke, quite loudly, of his earnestness.

"I'll return on the morrow, then," Gabera promised Brother Tomasi, who suddenly clung to his robe. He disentangled himself and pulled away from Brother Tomasi.

Starting on his way toward the light of day, Gabera was surprised not to hear the prison door clang shut immediately. Instead, over the sound of his footsteps echoing in the solid stone tunnel, he could hear Brother Tomasi's voice rise in a warm, relieved greeting as Gabera reached the outer door. Gabera hesitated, daring to look back, but the walk from cell to out of doors was just distant enough that he could only make out the fine dress of a courtier entering Tomasi's cell.

The priest pushed the outermost door open aided by a second Palazzo Guard. The fresh crispness of the winter air was a stark and welcome change to the dank miasma of the dungeons. Gabera breathed deeply of the cold fresh air, stuffed his hands into his cassock sleeves, and crossed the courtyard to the centermost place of worship in the palazzo religious ghetto, the Catholic Church. He circled to the back of the cathedral so that he did not have to disturb the Tyrrhian mourners, concentrating on the arguments he would make to Brother Tomasi in the morning. Tomorrow, he would accept nothing less than the little man's total capitulation to the sacraments of Confession and Communion.

Pierro nodded to the Palazzo Guard, one Corporal deGrassi by name, who had hidden him in the dungeon in a shadowy hallway of other cells leading beyond the guardroom. It was really none of Padre Gabera's business that it was he who visited the cardinal's assistant. He would discover in mere moments whether the little fool had admitted to Pierro's earlier visits, but first, there was another matter at hand . . .

DeMedici held out his gloved hand to deGrassi, confirming that the prison guard wore nothing on his hands. When the other man appeared honored by the friendly acknowledgment and extended his own hand to accept, Pierro clasped hands, clapping both of his gloved hands over the bare one and shaking firmly, allowing his hands to linger in a foppish manner. From the man's startled and slightly pained expression, Pierro guessed that his needle-ring had gouged the other man's hand just enough to prick him and graze his palm. It was all that was needed. In fact, it was more than he needed to do, but Pierro needed to be sure. While shaking the man's hand, Pierro pressed two soldibiancos, into the man's palm.

"Thank you so much for your discretion, Corporal deGrassi," Pierro said with a slow, casual air. "I appreciate remaining anonymous. Your prisoner is not exactly the most popular person at court these days, and I just hope that my visits can provide some Christian comfort in this, his darkest hour."

"But, of course, Your Highness," deGrassi said.

Pierro smiled and entered the cell. He hushed Tomasi's initial reaction with a raised hand and caught the door with his other as the guard would have closed him in with the prisoner. "Perchance, Corporal, what with your being so close, you might leave the door unlocked? I find myself agitated in close spaces."

The guard paused, confusion and a feverish brightness to his eyes. "It is not customary, but . . . perhaps, since it is you, Your Highness."

Pierro smiled his thanks and turned to Brother Tomasi, knowing that the contact poison on his gloves was already affecting the guard and that the man had but heartbeats to live. He slid the gloves from first one hand and then the other as he more fully entered the straw-littered chamber. The place smelled of feces, vermin and other unpleasantness. Pierro struggled not to gag. He folded his gloves over his belt, noting that the pale yellow kidskin palms were starting to show the stain of the contact poison he had used. He dropped the rings he had worn atop his gloved hands into the left pocket of his coat. He smiled beneficently at Brother Tomasi.

Despite the man's foul odor, the stains on his once black cassock and the desperation in the Brother's expression, Pierro forced himself to greet the man with a familiar embrace. He approached the cot to sit down and stopped. There was a limit to what he would do for this ruse.

Brother Tomasi sprang forward and swept aside his ratty blanket and the bits of straw that lay upon his cot. Pierro perched on the edge of the cleared area.

"Your Highness!" Brother Tomasi effused, clasping his fat hands together in front of him. "I am so honored that you would come to see me. I had thought that . . . well, with the time that has passed . . . well, it is so good to see you again."

Pierro forced a smile to his lips. His distaste, he did not bother to hide. "To keep a man of the Church in such a place as this!" Shaking his head, he clucked his tongue on the roof of his mouth. The conditions really were deplorable. "What sort of family did you come to the Church from?"

Brother Tomasi seemed surprised by the question. "My father was a merchant of some regard. Why do you ask?"

"Because it seems an awful sort of predicament you're in and that you should be treated better . . . at least that is my opinion," Pierro said smoothly. He reached into his coat and pulled out a leather-skinned flask. "Do they permit you a cup to drink from?"

Again, Brother Tomasi appeared confused momentarily. "Yes, certainly!" He went to the foot of the cot where he retrieved a pewter bowl and cup. After upending the cup to empty whatever dregs remained, the cardinal's disciple proffered it. "For your wine, Your Highness. I fear that I can offer you no better hospitality." His tongue darted out of his mouth, licking his lips as he eyed the wineskin.

"Oh, you mistake me, Brother Tomasi, the wine is for you. I could not bear the thought of your drinking nothing but water. I have brought you a sampling of a lovely Bordeaux that my father sent me. A very special wine and this," Pierro patted the skin, "is all for you, but we really must be quiet. Let us not draw the attention of the guard with this tribute."

Brother Tomasi's eyes widened as he nodded, eagerly offering his cup again.

Pierro uncorked the pouch and poured the prepared wine generously into the cup, then recorked his wineskin. "Drink, drink," he said.

"Oh, I could not drink before you, Your Highness," the Dominican Brother protested, partially spilling the wine as he pressed it back toward Pierro.

Pierro chuckled lightly. "I have not been denied wine for so long as you. Please, this is just for you."

"Just for me?" Brother Tomasi repeated looking hungrily at the pewter cup. He glanced over his shoulder toward the open door and where the guard stood just beyond.

Hearing the sounds of retching, Pierro knew the first poison was taking effect. "Hurry! While he deals with his stomach complaint," Pierro urged, hoping against hope that *he* would not have to drink the wine himself, but at his urging, the Brother sampled the wine, then quaffed the cup's contents.

Tomasi wiped his mouth with the back of his hand and held out the cup hesitantly.

Pierro smiled and refilled the mug. "So, have you made your Confession to Padre Gabera?" he asked in as neutral a tone as he could manage.

Tomasi drank from the cup and sighed, closing his eyes in pleasure even as he shook his head. "Gabera is a good man, but he is not the cardinal and I promised delle Torre." He put a hand to his head and sat down beside Pierro. "Forgive me, Your Highness, but I have been so long without wine and this . . . this is heady stuff."

"But, of course," Pierro said. He sidled over a bit, putting space between himself and the Dominican. Outside, the guard, deGrassi, coughed. Pierro directed his smile at his current quarry. "Would you like more?" He topped off the little man's cup. "So, you've told Gabera nothing?"

Brother Tomasi shook his head, then stopped, putting hand to head. "This wine of yours is good, but a little more . . ." He stopped mid-sentence and frowned up at the ceiling.

Pierro nudged the cup toward Brother Tomasi. The man drank automatically. By his estimations, Pierro judged the little man to have had more than enough of the concoction for it to have its intended effect, but why leave any behind? He filled the cup from the wineskin again. "Yes, it is, as you say, a heady wine, but you have been denied so long, perhaps it is having a greater effect on you? I did take the time to mull some herbs—healing herbs—in it. I had no idea what condition I would find you in. They might have been beating you for information, especially now that the king and queen are dead."

Tomasi nodded, then shook his head. "They have kept me here, but no one has questioned me . . . other than Padre Gabera, of course."

"About *Magnus Inique*?"

Tomasi set the cup on his knee and shook his head, dizzily. He gripped the wooden frame of the cot and braced himself, taking another deep swallow of his wine. "No one has asked me about that or anything much . . . I've only been questioned by the men who arrested me, and they asked about what the cardinal taught me, had me do . . ."

Listening carefully, Pierro could hear the guard stumbling about in the corridor, the sound of a wooden chair knocking against the stone wall. The guard retched again and could be heard gasping for air.

Brother Tomasi frowned, his muddied features contorting as he tried to form coherent thought. "Is something wrong with the guard? Do you think?"

"'Tis the conditions he lives in down here when he is guarding important prisoners such as yourself. He must be congested from the air down here. It's hard to breathe; it's a wonder you have no afflictions of the lung," Pierro said, wrinkling his nose at the foul odors which permeated the air.

"You have been most generous, Your Highness, first to think of me at all and then to—to smuggle your family vintage down here . . . to *me*, but I am no important prisoner. I am but a lowly acolyte of the cardinal, serving him as he bid me."

"You were integral to his plans—the Cardinal delle Torre, I mean—so of course you're important!" Pierro laughed lightheartedly. He found his mood lightening as time progressed. Though he looked pained and rubbed his stomach, the little Dominican Brother upended his cup to capture the last drops of wine.

"I?"

"Indeed, yes. The cardinal told me how heavily he relied upon your skills and discretion," Pierro encouraged and refilled the cup, feeling the wineskin nearly empty.

"He taught me more than I . . . more than most people would ever have thought to teach. He even taught me to read, so that I might follow his instructions closer," Tomasi confessed with a conspiratorial bump of his shoulder. He took a swallow of the wine and wiped his mouth. He grinned at the prince. "If I did not know better, Your Highness, I would say that I was in my cups."

Pierro chuckled again and squeezed the last of the wine into Tomasi's mug. Outside, in the passageway, the guard began a fit of coughing spasms that did not last. After the sounds of gagging and groaning, came the sure sound of a chair falling to the ground.

Brother Tomasi frowned. "Perhaps we should verify the guard is well? He does not sound it."

"What pains has he for you?" Pierro retorted.

"'Tis true," Tomasi said, slurping up the last of the wine. He giggled and leaned back against the wall. "But we are good Catholics even if he is not? Yes?"

Pierro sighed. "Has anyone else been down to visit you?"

Brother Tomasi closed his eyes and shook his head. He put his hand up to the crown of his pate. "I feel quite dizzy. I—I think I shall lie down a moment, while you look to the guard."

Pierro hesitated. He had more questions to ask the little Dominican, but once the man slept, he would never wake again. The brother had, however, answered the most important questions. He had not made Confession nor spoken to other interrogators during his stay. Apparently, everyone had been too busy with the queen's birthing of the heirs, Alban's death, followed by the death of the queen. All of it had worked in Pierro's favor, and now they would never speak to Brother Tomasi, for the man had already drifted into a fitful sleep, his breathing shallow and irregular. His inarticulate gasps came after moments of snoring that ended in a long period of silence.

Pierro rose and backed away, letting Tomasi slump limply on the cot. The man's face had turned even ruddier than before and a bit of blue tinged his lips. Pierro took the mug from the man's nerveless fingers and rinsed it in the bucket of water by the door. He dropped the cup and exited the cell.

The guard, deGrassi, lay on the floor near the table in the guardroom. A fire roared in the fireplace and dispersed an element of the dankness of the place. Pierro could hear other prisoners in other cells, but the little windows in their doors were closed and they could not see him. His first victim had fallen and knocked his chair over. Almost as an afterthought, the prince moved to the tunnel and looked to see if the outside guard had been alerted. From all appearances, he had not.

Pierro tossed the wineskin into the back of the fireplace where it burned hottest and turned up his nose at the smell of burning leather. He pulled his gloves from his belt and tossed them into the blaze as well rather than risk the poison seeping its way through . . . or unintentionally poisoning someone he did not want dead. He paused and reviewed his strategy. The rest of the plan required manual labor, something he wished he had brought Cristoval for, but it was one thing for him to bribe *his* way in to see the Dominican. There would have been questions if he had brought someone with him. Besides, he reckoned Cristoval did not have the stomach for poison, and he still did not quite trust the man. That left little else for him but to do the work himself.

Pierro set the chair upright, grabbed hold of the dead guard beneath his arms, and wrestled him up and into the chair. Grunting, he moved the chair closer to the little table and dropped his victim into it. DeGrassi immediately fell forward. Glancing down the tunnel again to be sure he was not being spied upon, Pierro took a moment to arrange the guard as though he were sleeping, head resting on arms and to cover the signs of retching with the loose straw that littered the hall from the cells. One last thing; he liberated deGrassi of the soldibiancos he had given him earlier and, while he was at it, his purse.

Satisfied, Pierro fed another couple of logs upon the fire, covering where the leather burned. Then he returned to Tomasi's cell. The brother still breathed, but his breath came shallow and the blue mottling around his lips had turned a bruised purplish color. Wishing for his gloves, Pierro reached over Tomasi and pulled his flea-infested blanket over the dying man. He cast a glance around the Dominican's cell and, seeing nothing that would give him away, departed, closing and locking the solid metal-and-wood door behind him. He took the key ring and returned it to deGrassi's belt.

Pierro dusted himself off, removing any remnants of straw or other telltale bits. He straightened his jacket and adjusted his cuffs. Now, the most hazardous step in his plan!

The guard, answering to the name Fieri, posted at the outer gate turned at Pierro's whistle as he neared the outer door. "Oh! Your Highness, come on through," he said, opening the lock that stood between Pierro and freedom.

The prince beckoned Fieri aside. Glancing over his shoulder, the guard came away from the door and into the passageway. "Is there something more, Your Highness?"

Pierro pulled two soldibiancos out of his pocket and held them out. Fieri reached for the gold coins, moving farther from his post at the door's edge. Pierro held them just out of reach of the other man. "It is imperative that no other knows of my visit here. You understand?"

The guard smiled and captured the prince's wrist to remove the soldibiancos from his hand. He pocketed the coins with a grin. "There is no one that I can think of who would *need* to know about your visit, Your Highness."

Pierro hid his snarl of impatience behind an aloof smile. "You'll see to it, then?"

"As much as I can, Your Highness. There are very few people that I would think merited this information," Fieri admitted. "But I can't imagine their having problems with Your Highness visiting the prisoner." He turned back toward the outer gate to the main courtyard, but paused. "Where is deGrassi? He should have escorted you back to this point. It's regulation."

"DeGrassi?" Pierro repeated.

"My fellow guard. Didn't you see him when you left Brother Tomasi's cell?"

Pierro paused, then nodded. "When I left, your fellow, deGrassi, was asleep at the table outside the acolyte's cell. I chose not to interrupt him and came on my own. I didn't realize there were any rules about such things."

Fieri muttered a foul oath about deGrassi's parentage.

"You'll need to wait until I've rounded him up," the Palazzo Guard said. "You *will* wait, won't you?"

"Not only that, I will accompany you back, Corporal."

"No need, Your Highness. I'll be but a moment," Fieri said, waving for him to stay where he was by the grated door which led to a circular staircase and then the freedom of the main courtyard.

Fieri started down the dungeon passageway, hand to the wall to guide him in the limited light.

Pierro followed him. "I prefer not to wait by the door and risk someone seeing me."

"As you wish, then," Fieri shrugged. He was making quick time down the hallway toward his dead compatriot.

Pierro reached up into the recesses of his left jacket sleeve and felt the coiled handle of the stiletto resting in its wrist brace beneath his clothes. He untethered the knot holding the long blade in place and drew it quietly.

As they neared the open guardroom, Fieri called out to his companion. Hearing no response, the guard uttered a more colorful curse upon deGrassi's sexual proclivities and took one of the slow-burning torches from its sconce on the wall to better light their way.

When Fieri and Pierro caught sight of Brother Tomasi's cell, they could also make out the table where deGrassi was just visible, apparently relaxing, head on arms, face to the table. For all the world, he looked as though he slept, except there was no rise and fall of the man's chest, a point he could not be sure if Fieri noticed. Before the remaining guard could take this clue in, Pierro freed his stiletto and waited for the right moment to strike. He rolled the handle of the dagger between the fingers of his right hand, keeping his hand to the side and slightly behind his back.

Fieri placed his torch into an open sconce and bent over deGrassi, shaking him. Instead of having the desired response of rousing, deGrassi's weight shifted and he and the chair toppled over.

"By the love of Mary, Jesus, and the Holy Spirit!" Fieri muttered. He kicked deGrassi's chair aside and rolled him over. "You know better than to sleep on the job—" Fieri stopped suddenly, taking in the yellowish cast to his skin. "I say—" Fieri began.

Pierro struck, hard and fast, driving the stiletto into the

base of Fieri's skull and upward until the point hit the bone at the top of Fieri's head. The guard slumped forward, falling upon deGrassi's limp body. With both hands on the hilt, Pierro twisted the stiletto, wiggling it around to cause the most damage. Fieri grunted as the air escaped his lungs. Pierro then drove the dagger deep, between the ribs, piercing a lung and his heart. Fieri, like deGrassi and Tomasi, was dead.

Pierro left the stiletto in Fieri's chest while he dug through the man's pockets. He finally found the coins he had paid the guard—four soldibiancos in all for Fieri—and relieved him of his thin purse, too. Last, deMedici lifted Fieri's keys to the dungeon.

He smiled. His plot was fulfilled and now he needed only to escape.

"Hey! Hey! You! Isn't it time for food?" one of the prisoners called from behind his cell door. Other prisoners started banging on their doors with their pewter cups.

That gave Pierro pause. The one thing he had not considered in his plan was when the guards changed post. The prisoners could die of hunger for all Pierro cared, but what if there was a station change before dinner? That meant he did not have much time. What would people think, considering the three dead bodies with only him to give an explanation? He knew what they would do; he would—at the very least—be questioned within an inch of his life. He did not like that thought. No, he must remove himself from this dungeon immediately.

Pierro moved quickly down the gloomy passageway, pausing at the outer door. He almost laughed exultantly. God must surely be on his side because, between the time he followed Fieri back and now, it had begun to rain. There was no sound of other guards coming. He opened the door slightly and climbed the broad circular steps toward the free world, peering out cautiously.

From his vantage point, deMedici could see that even some of the mourners waiting in line had left their places to get out of the foul weather, while others remained huddled, faces turned down. The rest of the courtyard was empty.

He looked down at his hands. In the left were the dungeon keys, and he should not be caught in possession of them. More importantly, however, he still gripped his bloody stiletto and blood had spattered onto his clothes.

The prince took a deep breath and considered his next steps. He had been a fool, thinking so shortsightedly of just getting rid of Tomasi . . . and then the guards who could reveal him. He had to think! Use his mind for more than a sausage box.

He slipped back into the dungeon and placed the keys in the inner locking mechanism. From there, Pierro crept up the winding stone stairs leading to the courtyard. He looked carefully to his right and left. No one looked or moved in his direction. If anyone saw him with the thin-bladed bloody dagger, hands and coat covered in blood, he would definitely be revealed. How to explain?

He retreated down the path, reached up over the wall, and plunged his dagger into the soil. He did this several times before being satisfied with the dirt cleaning the blade. He wiped the blood on his hands on his face and jammed the stiletto into his arm under his shirt.

With a hiss, he gritted his teeth. The pain of the sharp blade slicing through his own skin hurt like the devil. He slipped it carefully in its sheath. Blood ran down his sleeve and wrist. He had stuck himself quite well, and, for a moment, he was torn between cursing his ill-fated stab and giving thanks for his earlier decision not to poison the blade, figuring steel between the ribs of an unsuspecting man was enough.

He cursed himself for the fool he was. No plan was as easy as he thought it would be. He had had concerns only about what Brother Tomasi might reveal and had acted without thought. If he were an underling, he did not doubt his employer would put him out of his misery before he could cause any more damage. Then, desperation and an idea struck. He grinned to himself at its cleverness. Being bloodied was in his favor.

Gathering his thoughts, Pierro looked down at himself. He *was* good and bloodied from killing Fieri and wounding himself. His own blood dripped down his arm and left sleeve, making a darker stain as it soaked down his goldenrod-colored frock coat. He took a moment to think the entire plan through this time.

The deMedici stepped back into the dungeon passageway, freed his stiletto, and gouged a hole in his left sleeve, then, without further adó launched himself back into the dungeon. He dodged back down the passageway, groped around the guards' bodies for a knife, took a chair, and used the knife to carve "*Magnus Inique*" above the door of Tomasi's cell with the once fine blade. Pierro returned the blade to its homesheath, the chair to its place at the table and then began the next step of his charade.

He held his injured left arm close to his chest and took a deep breath. This was going to hurt. With deliberation, he knocked his head hard against the stone wall. It had hurt, but it was not enough. He took another breath, backed up and rammed himself, headfirst, into the wall hard enough to knock himself off his feet.

Pierro felt the head wound. He had broken the skin a little and developed a knot. It was serviceable. Satisfied, he staggered back down the passageway, up the circular steps and out into the courtyard.

"Murder! Murder!" he called as loudly as he could. He staggered to Alaric's fountain and dropped clumsily onto its edge. "Murder!"

The mourning pilgrims waiting by the Church huddled closer to one another. Some turned in open curiosity as the rain began to let up, but no one came to his aid until he looked up at the Palazzo.

The officers who guarded the front doors came to Pierro.

The first to reach him bowed and squatted before him. "Your Highness? Are you mortally wounded? Should I send for *il dottore*? Should I send someone for the princess?"

Pierro took the mostly blood-soaked kerchief from the left sleeve of his shirt. He dabbed the bloody bit of what was now, most assuredly, a rag over his face as though to clear the sweat from the exercise of his great battle, thereby exaggerating the look of his injuries. "I am well enough to make it to my apartment, I think," Pierro said. He eyed the second guard as that man approached.

"What happened, Your Highness?" the second man asked, casting a frowning glance around the courtyard. "You cry murder, but who has died?"

"You doubt me?" Pierro hotly challenged the man. He

rose unsteadily to his feet. Feigning weakness, he collapsed back down onto the fountain. He knew by now, he was a bloody mess. He put hand to head, squeezing his bloody kerchief so that blood ran from his scalp and down his face.

Both guards shook their heads, but it was the second, who, according to his insignia, was a sergeant, who spoke. "Of course not, Your Highness. We—I simply wanted to know what passed these few minutes before and where we should look to find the body."

Pierro glared up at the man. "I was caught in the rain and took cover in the trees overlooking the dungeon portal. As I stood there, I noted that a guard was not posted by the door in the usual fashion. As I came closer, a man burst out of the dungeon, accosted me and knocked me to the ground, stabbing me with his rapier. I must have been unconscious for a few seconds because of my head injury." He held his head, dabbing with his kerchief in such a way that more blood trickled from his hairline down the side of his face.

Both guards nodded grimly, arms crossed over their chests. The sergeant reached out a hand to help Pierro rise and said, "What else did you discover, Your Highness? Did you see which way the scoundrel went? A description? Anything that could help us would be most appreciated."

Pierro nodded and warmed to his theme. "Of course, when I came to my senses, I immediately went in to the dungeon. I found two guards dead on the floor and then I came for help. As to the murderer, he was dressed in black from head to toe and wore a hat—without plumes—and his face was covered by a gentleman's traveling mask and a kerchief."

The prince took the soldier's offered hand, clasping his wrist. When he started to rise, he leaned heavily on the other man and staggered to his feet. At this point, all that mattered was showmanship and selling his story to the gulls before him now and, he assumed, whichever courtiers wanted to hear the story from his own lips.

The sergeant took the brunt of Pierro's weight by shouldering deMedici's uninjured right arm. He started across the courtyard, but stopped at the steps. Turning to his second, he adjusted his stance and grabbed the prince by the back of his belt. "Vasili, send officers to see what happened in the dungeon and learn what they can and then return to your post."

The junior officer saluted, then turned on his heel.

"Come now," the sergeant said to Pierro. "Let us find someone who can get you to your rooms and summon *il dottore*."

The deMedici grimaced and sagged his way up the steps.

XI

"Truth is the highest thing man can keep."
—Geoffrey Chaucer

AT home, in the religious ghetto, Padre Gabera turned quiet, contemplative circles in his cell as he considered the ongoing reluctance of Brother Tomasi to confess his sins and accept Communion. After several moments, he sat down on the bed—little more than a pallet—and eased off his very worn sandals. He set his bare feet onto the granite floor and sighed contentedy as he stretched his toes.

It seemed forever since he was last home. He had seen so much, learned so much, been betrayed by a brother of the cloth and sheltered by heathens. Little of the last several months made sense if he thought of it as a whole, but to partake of a single memory and its context . . . the pain of the cardinal's new appointment and his and Tomasi's betrayal, not just of him, a single person, but all that they were supposed to hold holy. It had been the Judas Kiss anew with the Holy Father in Rome blissfully unaware. And how did one make such a report about a senior in the Church and expect to be believed?

The report to the Holy Father did fall to him; he was now senior here in the Catholic Church of the religious ghetto of the *Palazzo de Oro*, as ambassador of His Holiness to Tyrrhia.

"Aiyiyi!" Gabera muttered to himself. He had neither the training, the standing, the rank, the connections . . . not even the wardrobe to assume the role of even temporary ambassador.

Gabera allowed himself a long moment of—and there was nothing more to call it, he admitted to himself—self-pity, laying back on his bed.

After some time, Gabera knelt at the small altar in his room, crossed himself and began to pray, trying to sort out what the Almighty had put before him.

A scratch at the door distracted him from his contemplation. "Come," he said, climbing to his feet and rapidly finishing the proper ablutions.

"Forgive me, Padre," the acolyte at the door murmured, bowing deeply. Aris, a pimply-faced youth, held several scrolls and a sheaf of papers. "While everyone was gone . . . Padre, there is so much to be done. I've done my best but . . . I never realized . . ."

Padre Gabera was surprised, too, by the number of tally sheets, accountings, and the rest. He started to take the papers then merely stood back and motioned for Aris to put the papers on his bed, which the acolyte did with great alacrity.

There was no room on his tiny table for this onslaught of papers; the room itself was almost too small to receive it! Gabera started sorting through, learning more about the business of his tiny parish and church than he thought he already knew. He sorted the requests from the kitchen—there was not enough flour or money to make the communal bread—from the court invitations and then there were the missives from other parishes—most importantly, the letters from the office of His Holiness.

With the fall of the cardinal, the transfer away of another priest and his own travels, there had been no one and now . . . he was the *one*. Even the Tyrrhian diplomatic posts were to be handled, at least for the time being, by himself!

Suddenly the idea of day after day spent on the white jenny mule did not seem so uncomfortable when compared to the mass of papers to be addressed before he could lay his tired, sore body down.

There was nothing to be done but begin.

Stefano moved his pawn as he sat in the receiving room of their apartment. His man, Carlo, some thirty years his senior and his childhood tutor, studied the board.

"Your game is improving again, Master," Carlo observed, countering with the move of his own pawn.

Stefano made a self-deprecating noise. "I've lost my edge while at the front and given only lackadaisical attention to my game since. There are a hundred other things I should be doing!"

"Exercising your mind is preparation for the Palantini and your undoubted selection as Lord Regent," Carlo retorted. "At the moment, you have little else to do."

"But meanwhile my wife is contending with four newborns and expecting our own child at any time. I am a clod in the Royal Nursery and there are few things that I can do until we have a quorum of the Palantini on site."

"You allow yourself to be distracted, Your—" Carlo stopped mid-sentence and turned, curiously, toward the door to the hallway.

Just outside the apartment, came the sound of running feet followed by the rumble and roar of a collection of the curious. Stefano sighed. Who knew what mischief was happening and though he was not yet fully ranked as the Lord Regent, he was at least the appointed Regent. He rose from his chair and headed to the door.

"Master? Her Grace is resting. What should I—" Carlo murmured, nodding toward the upstairs bedroom.

Stefano wiped an agitated hand over his mouth and rubbed his fair mustache and beard. "Do what you can to keep her here. *Try* . . . but I don't expect you will succeed if she is roused by all this noise." He adjusted his frock coat and left by the door to the open corridor.

People—from courtier to servant—ran to Stefano's right. He sighed and began to move, pushing his way through the crowd until he reached the door to Their Highnesses' chambers where the crowd had come to a halt. Even more people milled outside the closed doors.

What new trouble had one or the other—or both—gotten themselves involved in and who was going to have to pay the tinker, he wondered. Stefano looked around him, spotted a Palazzo Guard, and waded his way through the crowd to him.

The guard saluted and stood at attention.

"What's happening?" Stefano asked, nodding toward the doors.

"*Permisso*?" the guard murmured, then leaned in conspiratorially. "The prince encountered a murderer in the dungeons."

"What business had he in the—Oh, never mind. I shall hear this from the horse's own mouth!" Stefano shook his head and then made his way back to the door. "Everyone back! What news there is, I'll send as soon as I can. For now, it would be best if you go about your own personal duties and give the prince his peace."

He turned back to the door and opened it just enough to squeeze through, then jammed it shut with the weight of his body. Silence suddenly reigned supreme in the room. Ortensia stood next to a divan glaring at him. On the couch, lay a semi-prostrate Pierro attended by *il dottore* Bonta. A third man, vaguely familiar to him, hovered in the rear, by the bookcases.

"What's the meaning of this intrusion, Your Grace?" Princess Ortensia demanded, moving protectively between the divan and Stefano.

Stefano bowed in his most courteous fashion. "Forgive me, Your Highness," he said, rising. "I heard that your husband had been attacked and came to see that he was well with my own eyes."

Ortensia stepped aside, allowing Stefano to approach. DeMedici whimpered like an unschooled lad, periodically taking hearty swigs of very expensive New World rum, while the doctor stitched up a long gouge to his left arm. Stefano looked at the wound knowingly, his eyes dropping to the bloodied floor where Pierro's ruined frock coat, and blouson lay. There lay also a twelve inch stiletto and sheath . . . the kind one secreted in a sleeve.

Stefano looked up from the sheath to see Ortensia watching him suspiciously. He smothered his smile, knowing full well that Pierro had stabbed himself. The wound was too common. Someone unfamiliar with arm sheaths or who moved too hastily made wounds such as these. He had seen it when he served in the Escalade and again in the Peloponnese.

Taking a nearby chair, Stefano sat it down by Pierro's

head and settled into it. "Will he survive his wounds?" he asked the doctor.

Bonta grunted and nodded in the affirmative, finishing off another stitch. He had several more to make.

"Do you mock me, Your Grace?" Pierro snapped and took another swig of the rum. He did not need more rum as he was, as Stefano immediately assessed, already well-beyond the point of drunkenness.

"Hardly! No," Stefano said. "I am not trying to make a fool of you. I came to hear what happened and how you came across this murderer? Who had he—I assume it was a he?—killed?"

Pierro moved the cold compress from his head, unobscuring his eyes. "From what I saw of him before he ran me through and threw me into the stone wall which knocked me unconscious, it was indeed a *he*!" He spoke with surprising clarity. The slurring of his voice was gone.

Stefano glanced at the bottle of rum held fast in deMedici's hands. Considering the long drinks he had been taking, the bottle remained surprisingly full. Stefano let his gaze flit away, and then make direct contact with Pierro's. "You are most fortunate this miscreant didn't kill you, Your Highness, being already a murderer."

Pierro's eyes narrowed and he managed a thin smile. "Yes, lucky, wasn't I, considering what he did to the Palazzo Guards?"

"I am most curious how he got *in*to the dungeons only to kill two men on duty," Stefano mused.

"And injure me!" Pierro reminded. "Ow!" he said to the doctor who made soothing noises.

"Many pardons, Your Highness!" *il dottore* said as he began putting away his tools. "I will have to go to my office to get all the supplies for a head plaster. Your head bumps are mild enough now, but they may cause you more trouble later."

"Never mind," Pierro snapped at Bonta. He sat up and shoved the bottle of rum into the cushions beside him. "All it does is mess my hair and never seems to serve any other purpose."

"But—" *il dottore* protested.

"You've heard my husband. There will be poultice, no plaster," Ortensia growled. Stefano found her aggressive defense of Pierro unsettling. Pretend what they might, this was no love marriage. It had happened too fast. Had something changed?

The Royal Physician bowed deeply, gathered his belongings in his kit bag, and departed quickly. Stefano watched him go.

"You'll excuse my forbearance of the plaster," Pierro said to Stefano, gesturing at the man by the bookcases to serve wine.

Stefano raised his hand and shook his head. "Nothing for me, Your Highness. I came only to see that you would survive."

"How kind of you," Pierro retorted. There was an edge of bitterness beneath his words. He looked at the hapless attendant. "Don't leave me entertaining company half-dressed, Cristoval!"

The other man scurried from the room, leaving Stefano, Ortensia, and Pierro alone. Stefano braced his ankle on his knee, feeling the weight of his own hidden blade in his boot. It put him a little more at ease since his sword was a practically useless dress weapon. He made up his mind to put up with the weight of a real sword from this point on.

Pierro rose and poured a glass of Bordeaux and drank, before turning to face Stefano fully.

Stefano could smell the sweet headiness of the wine, its fresh bouquet. "We don't get many French wines here in Tyrrhia."

Pierro shrugged, "My father, the duca . . ." Here, he paused to smile unpleasantly. "Yes, *my* father, the duca, sent it to me upon news of my second wedding. Would you care to have a couple of bottles for your collection?"

Thinking of all the additives deMedici might make to such bottles, Stefano shook his head. "I would not want to deplete your private stock, Your Highness."

Pierro shrugged. While he was a thin, wiry man, Stefano noted that he was muscular and, undoubtedly, much stronger than he looked. Most of his face had been wiped clean, leaving a ring of dirt and rusty-colored dried blood on the outer edges, down from his hairline, along the ear and down the side of his throat. ". . . so of course, you'll forgive my vanity with the plaster," Pierro was saying. "I wouldn't want bits of plaster in my hair to explain again and again to the officers of the Palantini. Do you understand my meaning, then?" Pierro asked, his nonchalance communicating clearly that it really did not matter what Stefano's response was.

Gathering Pierro's point from context: he wanted to appear at his best when the meeting of the Palantini finally came about, Stefano nodded and rose to his feet. "Would you like me to send your well-wishers away or will you see them *en masse* or one at a time? If you have any concern for your safety, let me know. We can double the watch of the Palazzo Guard to make sure that man does not return."

Pierro waved a dismissive hand. "I am a fine swordsman, Your Grace, and should we tangle again . . . when I am not caught off guard . . . *then* we will see who the master is."

"That's correct," Stefano murmured. "You were known to be quick with your blade in Venice . . . much sparring and dueling, I believe the word was."

Pierro flushed. "I see who has been reading the old briefs to the king. Rest assured, that nonsense is behind me now that I am married and expecting my heir."

"Ah, that we could leave all our odd bits of habit and inclination behind when we marry," Stefano said lightly. He rose and bowed deeply to the royal couple. He walked to the door, and, as he opened it, was called back.

"I'll be receiving no one, Your Grace, and your visit, however pretty, will not change my course," Pierro said.

Stefano did not turn, but laughed as he started opening the door again. "I would not think so, Your Highness. I would not think so."

He discovered the hall surprisingly sparse of onlookers. Bonta must have given the pertinent news and they had dispersed. Seeing no one in particular to address, Stefano shrugged and returned to his apartment to make the change in swords.

In his bedchamber across the hall from Luciana's, where they usually slept together, Stefano considered the three swords on his wall. The foil was too heavy a blade for everyday wear in the palazzo and much too obvious, clunky to be sure. With two fingers of his right hand, Stefano pulled free the heavier of his two rapiers. It was a compromise as the lighter blade was not much better than his dress sword.

Stefano hefted the blade, feeling its purpose almost like the beginning tones of a dance.

"What are you doing?"

The question broke Stefano out of his reverie as he realized he *had* taken a few steps. He turned to the door and saw Luciana watching him curiously like he had suddenly sprouted the ears of an ass and the antlers of a deer. He quickly hid his guilty expression in the business of changing the sword on his baldric. "Nothing, nothing, just reacquainting myself with this old girl," he said patting the blade. He leaned over and kissed his wife's cheek.

"Her?" Luciana responded lightly. "Should I be jealous?"

Stefano shook his head. "She was my only mistress when we were apart and there are times when . . . when I miss the feel of her at my hip."

Luciana made a moue and shook her head. "What else is troubling you?"

Stefano sighed. There would be no negotiating with her. "Come to the parlor and we will talk." Once he had her in the receiving room of the apartment, he ensconced her in a lounge and sat at her feet, which he placed upon his lap.

"So?" she prompted, smiling when he slid a slipper off her foot.

"Were you aware that we are three members of the duchi shy of having a quorum so that the Palantini can begin?" he asked. He slipped off her other shoe and massaged both her feet with his warm, dexterous hands.

"No, I was not aware," Luciana admitted as she studied her fingernails. She looked up quickly and caught him watching her. "We are ready for the inquiry, are we not? Why should it make you suddenly desirous of a handy sword?"

"With the meeting of the Palantini, we will probably become official Regents of Tyrrhia and there are those who wish it weren't so."

"That faction has always existed, but something has changed," she said in her quiet, perceptive way.

"I dally here when I probably have urgent business elsewhere," Stefano said. His hands fell still.

Luciana leaned back, snuggling in. "When you *know* you have urgent business, then you should go. Until then, you have a pregnant wife with the vapors."

Stefano sat up. "You have the—"

She shook her head, closing her eyes as she sighed. "It is

an excuse. If you are needed, they will come for you. So? Why do you wear your real sword?"

"Don't toy with me about your health," Stefano said angrily.

Luciana looked at him and sighed. "All will be right in the world and I in it for as long as I am meant to be. My grandmother says I am to have a long life and she predicts this child will be strong."

"Your grandmother said?" Stefano repeated. He dropped her feet back into his lap. "Other people make other predictions, and I don't want to take chances with you."

Luciana blew him a kiss. "You are my angel, Stefano. Now tell me what is happening that you take such precautions. Should I carry my sword as well?"

"No!" Stefano all but shouted at her. "No blades, no fighting. Promise me, or I won't tell you what is happening."

"I have my own sources in this great place. The very walls have ears," Luciana murmured.

"Lucia! Be solemn, for this *is* a serious matter! Earlier today two Palazzo Guards were murdered in the dungeons," Stefano said, repeating what he had overheard in the crowd on the way to see Pierro and Ortensia. "A masked man attacked Pierro and got away before anyone knew anything had happened."

"Was he killed?" Luciana asked sitting up.

"Who?" Stefano asked crossly.

"Pierro, of course!"

"No. As usual, he is fine. He says the man slashed his arm, knocked him down, stunning him, and made his escape," Stefano said.

"This is what happens when I listen to you and Kisaiya and take a rest! I miss all the excitement," Luciana grumbled. She pulled back her feet and found the flat-soled slippers which were about the only shoes she could still wear with any comfort. She put them on.

"You must rest. You haven't had your own baby, and you already tend to the special needs of four royal newborns and their elder brother who is just coming of an age for tutors," Stefano said.

"You're dooming me to a boring life," Luciana complained.

Stefano laughed. "Six children will hardly be boring!"

"You would tie me down with another six just to keep me isolated," Luciana accused, and though her words were light, there was the darkness of a brooding storm in her eyes.

"And safe," Stefano admitted. Before he could say more, there came a scratching, followed by pounding at the door. "Stay here. I'll answer the—"

"I have the door, Master," Carlo said, coming from seemingly nowhere. He opened it before Stefano could even rise from the chaise.

Luciana sat up straight and peered around Stefano's shoulder, trying to make out what was going on or who, for that matter, had interrupted them. She could not make out what was being said by the door and longed to get up and go, but her husband held her hand tightly—not so much that it would hurt, but close enough to restrain her.

After a brief consultation, Carlo bowed and motioned that one of the men should come into the room. The man, it turned out, was not so ordinary as their normal visitors. By his insignia and golden uniform, Luciana gathered that he was a very senior officer amongst the Palazzo Guards. He stood now before Luciana and Stefano, his attention directed upon her husband.

"Your Grace, Colonello Fieri of the Palazzo Guards. While you are not yet appointed Lord Regent, you are the king and queen's appointed regent, and for that reason I turn to you," he said glumly. He was an older man of middling size and weight. Beneath his dancing, white caterpillar eyebrows, he sported varicose veins that turned his bulbous nose somewhat purple. He wore a white wig with a tail down his back. He was far from a young man, but his movements were swift and sure. His hands rested, for the most part, at his sides. He wore a foil at his right. He was, apparently, a left-handed fighter.

"Please continue, Colonello," Stefano said. He remained sitting, but gently brushed Luciana's feet off his lap. A point of duty for this man *was* reporting to king or regent wherever he found them.

"I do not doubt that you have already heard of the deaths of my two men in the dungeons, but what you don't know is that one of them died with nary a mark on him and, when we checked, we found a prisoner dead also, still locked in his cell," the man said. "You should also know that one of the men was my son."

"I'm so sorry for your loss," Luciana said.

"As am I. This villain will see justice," Stefano said, rising to his feet.

"Begging your pardon, Your Grace, but this is a strange business. There are no marks on the other guard, deGrassi, and yet, by his expression, he did not pass pleasantly," Fieri said. "And the prisoner has nary a mark on him either."

Stefano rose. "I will come immediately, of course."

Luciana also rose. When Stefano looked at her, nodding toward the couch she had so recently reclined upon, Luciana shook her head. "If this is a 'strange business' as the colonello says, then who else can you consult? I know what has gone before, I am familiar with the ways of magic and skilled enough to out a poisoner like the infamous Exilli. Deny it if you can," she challenged him.

Stefano tugged at his short beard, staring down. "I don't want you in danger. I'll find someone else—"

"Like who? Signora Rui? Are you prepared to tell her everything I know? And as for poisoners . . . who do you know and would they even talk to you, admit their profession?" Luciana pressed softly. "I am your only expert, and I will be discreet."

Stefano shook his head in refusal, but he already saw her reason was without fault. He smoothed his mustache and beard before answering. "You will do as I say? You will obey me?" he asked, looking her straight in the eye.

She winced a little, looking back at him. He was serious. If she wanted to see what had happened for herself, then she must agree. "While I am not an obedient wallflower by nature and I bring thoughts of my own, for this instance, you have my complete commitment. I will *obey* you," Luciana promised.

"Colonello, do you have keys to the dungeon and cells with you?" Stefano asked.

Confused, old Fieri and Luciana stared at him, then the colonello came alive again. He took a large ring of keys from a notch on his belt, and handed them to Stefano who turned to Luciana.

"If there is any fighting, confusion, or possible danger, I will allow you to go with us only if you promise to keep these keys and lock yourself in a cell immediately until I say you may come out again," Stefano said, offering the key ring to Luciana.

She hesitated, rubbing her fingertips and not actually touching the ring in question. "What if—?"

"No, Luciana. These are my conditions; there will be no negotiations. Take them now or stay here," Stefano insisted.

Sighing heavily, Luciana took the keys. The ring was large enough so that she could wear it as a bracelet—heavy, but workable. Stefano eyed her a short bit longer then looked to the colonello.

"Lead on, Signore," Stefano said. He reached back and took Luciana's hand.

"Perhaps a mantle for Her Grace, Master?" Carlo suggested. He presented Luciana's short cloak, holding it open for her to slide into.

"Oh, I don't think—" Luciana began.

"Thank you, Carlo," Stefano interrupted, giving his wife a steely look.

Meeting Stefano's eyes as she spoke, "Thank you, Carlo," Luciana allowed the mantle to be placed over her shoulders and the hood drawn up while she buttoned the top button. She smiled prettily at Stefano when she was done, but he could still see the fire in her eyes. "Should I wear a traveling mask to disguise myself, too, Husband?"

Stefano smiled thinly at her, her sarcasm not lost on him. "No, *mi amore*, I think people could guess who you were even if you wore one. *Andíamo*!"

The colonello took the lead while his men fell in around them. He chose the front route, to the courtyard—where mourners still waited for a viewing of the dead king and queen even with dusk fast approaching—past the statue and fountain and to the far corner of the courtyard, near the stables. Colonello Fieri paused at a set of circular stone steps which wound down under the palazzo proper.

"Mind your step here, Your Graces. It can be slick after a rain," he said.

Stefano was surprised when Luciana did not resist his taking her elbow and leading her down the stairs. The great dungeon outer door stood open, with a guard on either side of it. They saluted the colonello and Stefano and bowed to Luciana before allowing them admittance.

Fresh torches had been lit along the passageway so they could see clearly. Stefano glanced at his wife and noted that she studied the ground, even kneeling for a closer look.

"What do you see?" Stefano asked.

"My people are trained to look for the *patrín*, the signs left on the ground," Luciana explained. She pointed to the floor, scattered with odd bits of straw and mud. "I see blood and a well-trampled walkway."

"My men. There must have been twenty or more of them through here from the time the alarm was raised. Can you tell anything from what you see?" Colonello Fieri asked.

Luciana shook her head, looking up at them from where she knelt. "Stone is hard to read at the best of times."

"Well, there's writing in the stone ahead that any literate can read. Come along," Fieri said. He reached a hand down to assist Stefano in helping Luciana to her feet.

Stefano noted she may have needed the assistance, but was still annoyed by it. He said nothing and, with her elbow firmly gripped so that she did not wander, he followed Fieri past cells on either side along the way. Fieri stopped at the guardroom, a mere widening in the passageway that narrowed again and angled on with additional cells.

Stefano released Luciana's arm. They stood in the company of several guardsmen all looking to the newcomers for direction. Fieri dismissed them with a small gesture.

Now that the room was cleared of the crush of warm bodies, it was easy to see the guardroom as a whole. A table to the right with four chairs. Blood had been spilled here, and recently. There was a fire in the hearth opposite the table which had settled to mostly embers. An iron pot, containing some type of gruel or soup, hung on its peg. The foul-smelling food must have been for the prisoners, Stefano surmised. There was little else of interest in the room: a small chest of drawers for basic medicinals and probably what little cooking supplies were needed here; a stool by the fireplace; firewood; and an oil lantern which had been set on the table.

Turning in place, Stefano looked at what was present and guessed at what was missing. The door to the nearest cell stood half open. It had housed only one prisoner. Someone, Stefano thought angrily to himself, he had had every intention of questioning. Now his waiting seemed foolish, but at the time, it had seemed best to wait until he was named Lord Regent and, thereby, had more power at his disposal to deal with this follower of the cardinal.

"The prisoner is dead as well?" Stefano asked.

Fieri nodded curtly. "The three all died differently, Your Grace. Someone knew his business with murder, never mind how he got into the dungeon and then escaped in the first place. And with only His Highness seeing him. We are most gratified to have a witness at all. He could have been killed."

Stefano held his tongue about the last of the colonello's words. He looked to his wife who had wandered first to the spill of blood near them, then to the fire and, oddly, she was sniffing it. "What are you doing, Luciana?" he asked.

Luciana turned. "I have barely left your side, *marito*. I am by the fire within easy reach," she responded defensively.

"Are you cold?" Stefano asked and reached for a piece of firewood.

"No, don't do that!" Luciana said sharply, warding him off. "I am not cold, but I smelled something more than that . . . gruel and the smoke of the fire." She took the fireplace poker and knelt. She jabbed at the remnants of the remaining log. It sent up a shower of sparks and fell forward in pieces.

Stefano moved quickly, placing himself between his wife and the rain of cinders, knocking her firmly on her backside.

Luciana spared him a glower. "I *have* been dealing with fires since I was a small child, Stefano. A cinder or two will do me no harm!"

He knew she was right and was embarrassed to have caused the scene. He needed to get better control of himself or they would both look like fools. "You are quite right," he murmured quietly. He offered her his hand and was gratified when she accepted his help in standing again, but Luciana's attention was already back on the fireplace.

"Someone has been burning something other than wood! I thought I caught the scent of leather!" Luciana exclaimed. She reached for the poker again, but it was already in Stefano's hand.

"My Lady wife, we must make clear between us what *is* and what is *not* obedience when you are told to stay by my side," Stefano growled softly at Luciana so that no one else could hear him. He prodded the coals around and began fishing out several bits of leather from the back of the fireplace.

"Obedience has never been my strong suit, and I note that I was within arm's reach of you, ever ready with the keys so that I can imprison myself," Luciana hissed back at him.

"What have you found there?" Colonello Fieri asked, approaching the narrow hearth where the scattered remnants of leather were laid out.

Luciana did not wait for permission or for the material to cool, but immediately began sorting the detritus. She pieced together what looked rather like the last vestiges of a pair of gloves and a portion of some sort of pouch. Luciana picked up the bit of pouch and sniffed.

"Until recently," she said, "this contained a very strong wine. Red, I would guess, from the stain."

"Red?" Stefano repeated. "It is cinders. How do you see color there?"

Luciana gave Stefano a long look which plainly bespoke her growing ire. "If you smell it, you will agree. I'm sure if I cleaned it in a water bucket, there would be the stain of deep red upon it." She held the leather scrap out to him.

Stefano sniffed it, his eyebrows raising in surprise. Despite the fire and smoke, there was the distinct smell of red wine . . . a Bordeaux. His thoughts went immediately to Pierro and his father's gift. He said nothing of his thoughts aloud, however. "You're right, *mi amore*. You have a good nose."

Luciana smiled slightly. "The rest looks to be the leavings of a pair of gloves, though why anyone would rid themselves of something as fine as these once were, I do not know!"

"Why did he not just take them with him when he escaped? And what purpose the red wine?" Fieri asked.

Stefano rose and helped his wife to stand. To one of the guards, he motioned to the scraps Luciana found and said, "Collect all of this and place it in a pouch."

"Where shall I deliver it, Your Grace?"

Hesitating, Stefano glanced at the colonello, who by rights should keep all evidence, but he wanted time to assess them more himself.

"For the time being, Your Grace, perhaps they should go to the safe room where I keep evidence? You have but to ask if you wish to see this or anything else," Fieri suggested helpfully.

"Thank you," Stefano said with a nod. As he spoke, something caught his eye. He turned more fully toward the prisoner's cell and the writing scratched into the stonework above it. "*Magnus Inique*. So now the group risks a foray into our arena? Perhaps these people are more than just mere witch-hunters?" He felt Luciana's hand slip into the crook of his arm as she moved closer to him. Surprised by her fear, Stefano patted her hand reassuringly. "What else is there to see?"

"The bodies," Luciana said softly, just loud enough to be heard.

"Oh, but these are dead men, Your Grace, . . . they are nothing a fair lady should see," Fieri said.

"I am Romani before I am a lady, as my husband will attest if pressed. Let me see the bodies."

Fieri shook his head, turning an appealing gaze to Stefano. Luciana squeezed his arm, just in case there might be any doubt of her thoughts in the matter.

Stefano took a deep breath and released it. "She'll be able to tell us more about the poison than anyone I know."

"Your wife? She is familiar with poison?" Colonello Fieri gasped, wide-eyed. He looked from Stefano to Luciana and then back again.

"It was part of my education," Luciana offered, apparently not in the least bothered by the colonello's wariness.

"And it has saved my life and King Alban's on more than one occasion, so please, where are the bodies?" Stefano said.

The colonello gulped, looking at Luciana in astonishment. "Then come this way. We have only moved them into another cell for the time being."

As they followed, Stefano took Luciana's hand still in the crook of his arm and leaned close to whisper. "If the sight sickens you or should you need to take a moment to collect your thoughts, there will be time enough . . . and you can change your mind if—"

"My only concern is that the bodies are *marimé*. I cannot

touch them, but I may have to inspect them carefully. Your help in this matter would be appreciated," Luciana said.

"They are in here," Fieri said, opening a cell they had passed on their way into the dungeons. "You there, Corporal, bring the lanterns. Their Graces will need light, and the rest of you, go on about your business. You'll get news when there is any to share."

As dungeon cells went, this chamber seemed suitable, Stefano thought. The straw was fresh, the privy buckets were empty, there were cots and blankets . . . all ready for occupants, except there already were. Three cots had been moved near a small fire pit which even now hosted a warming fire. The two guards were side by side and the prisoner on a farther cot. They lay on their backs, arms folded neatly over their hearts. Someone had been kind enough to place the Dominican Brother's rosary in his hands, prisoner or no.

"We're waiting for the priest, to—well—you know," Fieri said. "I'll be contacting the other man's family. As to Brother Tomasi, the only relation he had—that we are aware of—is the Church. In any case, here they are. What will you need, Your Grace?"

Stefano could feel Luciana steeling herself for the interval to come. She hugged his arm against her briefly, then slowly approached the foot of the cots.

"Which one is your son, Colonello?" Luciana asked.

The colonello stiffened, collecting his resolve. Without looking, he said quietly, "The bloody one, Your Grace."

Stefano followed Luciana closely. Death had captured a look of surprise on the man's face, or was it only because his mouth yawned wide as the morbid state took hold? Stefano moved closer and leaned over the body, careful not to obscure Luciana's sight or block the lantern light. Looking at the bodies gave Stefano a turn, and he shuddered. Too many deaths and all so young. It was akin to the battlefield in its madness.

He studied the wound in the younger Fieri's chest. A long, thin blade had done the job . . . an epee? But these tunnel quarters were tight, giving little room for swordplay, Stefano thought. He settled on a stiletto; it could fit the scenario perfectly. From the angle, he surmised that this man's attacker struck from behind . . . or perhaps the side. He pulled aside the man's clothes and examined the fleshy part of the wound. Young Fieri was already cooling to the touch. Stefano stood back up and looked to Luciana.

She shivered and asked, "Is this his only wound? It most surely was fatal . . . to the heart and lung, but was it just this single strike?"

The dead man's father breathed heavily. Stefano could see the pain etched by the flickering light of the lanterns on the man's face. "There was another attack, we think the first. To the back of his neck . . . the mountebank who did this didn't even give him a fighting chance."

Without asking, Stefano rolled the young man from his back to his side. "Here! Bring the light here!" he ordered the corporal with the lantern.

The youth came closer, shuffling forward. He was young, just probably past his majority . . . fifteen. Death of another so young frightened him. Stefano took the lad's hand and positioned it so the light exposed the back of the dead man's neck. He brushed aside young Fieri's ponytail all damp with blood and brain matter, exposing the wound. Stefano studied it with care. This, too, came as the result of a swift, sure hand, someone who knew his business with a stiletto and spared no mercy. Like the last, this wound would have been a death blow. The assailant had shown some form of sympathy with his second strike to the heart . . . unless he wanted to be absolutely sure the guardsman was dead. The latter seemed more likely to Stefano.

Luciana leaned over his shoulder and looked at the wound. When Stefano crouched out of her way, Luciana bent closer and sniffed. She shook her head and stood back. "There is no faster poison than the steel of a well-placed blade."

Stefano rose, his movement breaking the awkward silence which followed Luciana's statement. He gently rolled the first victim onto his back and placed young Fieri's hands over his heart as he had been before Stefano disturbed him.

The second guardsman showed no signs of blood, only a strange sallowness to his cheeks. Stefano looked at the man guessing at poisoning for there was no other sign of foul play.

"This here was deGrassi," the colonello said, as though formal introductions were still necessary.

Luciana shifted the young corporal holding the lantern and leaned down. She frowned, turning her head this way and that. To Stefano, she said, "Let me see the white of his eyes."

Stefano obliged her, tentatively touching deGrassi, half-expecting him to turn away when he parted the man's eyelids. Stefano held the young man's eyes open for a time before, Luciana indicated that he could stop. Self-consciously, he wiped his hands on his pants, watching her lean over deGrassi's face and smell his mouth. He noted Luciana's deep frown.

"There seems a slight yellowing about his eyes. He vomited soon before he died and there is the faintest hint of . . . no, it's too faint," Luciana murmured, shaking her head. She walked to the foot of deGrassi's cot and studied the length of him. "Is he dressed the way you found him or has someone prettied him up?"

"Prettied him up?" Fieri repeated. "What do you mean?"

"Has anyone adjusted his clothing? Was he perhaps bare-footed or wearing the gloves that are now tucked in his belt?" Luciana explained. Stefano could hear the strain of impatience edging her voice.

Colonello Fieri shook his head. "I'll ask the men to be sure, but protocol says they be laid out as we find them. If they are—are in nature's glory, why then, we cover them with a simple wrapper for modesty's sake."

"Why do you ask, Luciana?" Stefano asked. He took the lantern from the corporal and held it higher aloft.

"I am trying to determine how he was poisoned. I hazard he was not given something to eat," Luciana said.

"No, that would be unlikely and there are no marks of a struggle on this man. No bruises to his throat. This deGrassi did not fall in battle. Whoever came here planned this attack carefully, and odds are there was only one assailant," Stefano said.

"Fighting with one guard would surely have drawn the other," Fieri agreed. "The murderer couldn't afford a struggle with two men at once . . . even if he was good, there are too many chances."

"This deGrassi had to be killed quietly and quickly," Luciana said.

"And he would have been the first to die. Better to leave

an unwitting guard at the door so as not to risk drawing attention," Stefano said. He stretched the lantern from head to foot. "I've heard of poisons that strike a man dead just by the touch."

Luciana nodded.

"He would have greeted someone brought back here," Colonello Fieri said.

"His hands," Luciana exclaimed. She started to reach for the dead man's hands and immediately recoiled, holding her right hand to her as if she had been burned. "Touch him at the cuff, Stefano, and let me see his hands."

"Allow me," Fieri said. He reached down unceremoniously and took deGrassi's right wrist. "He would have greeted someone with this hand."

"I see nothing on the back of his hand. Let me see his palm," Luciana demanded, pulling the lantern closer still.

Stefano looked at deGrassi's palm and saw nothing of import. It was worn and roughened from service, nicks and scratches along the side and fingers. Luciana studied the palm for a brief time and then smiled fiercely.

"There! Do you see it? The pricking of the skin at the base of his fingers, near the little finger!" She pointed triumphantly at the smallest of pinpricks, barely reddened and then followed it along with her own finger hovering over the dead man's hand until the long, thin, scratch was clearly visible.

"But that could have been caused by anything," Fieri protested. "Look at my hands, if you wish it."

"Exactly. It looks like it could be anything, but odds are it was done deliberately, usually by a ring of a special design," Luciana replied.

"It doesn't matter if the ring was used or not, the man's hands were roughened. The poison must have gotten on the gloves. It's why the gloves were burned," Stefano said. "Our murderer didn't want to be caught with them."

Luciana nodded. "Let me sniff his hand."

Fieri looked at her oddly, but made room for her to do so.

"Do you smell it, Luciana?" Stefano asked, remembering an afternoon last spring when her sense of smell had caught a scent enough for her to make an antidote to a poison that would have killed Alban all those months ago.

His wife nodded. "Not so faint here. He must have put

his hand to his mouth, but I smell almonds. A poison with arsenic as its base."

Fieri sniffed. "I smell nothing."

Stefano motioned for Fieri to replace deGrassi's hand over his heart. "Apparently only the specially trained can smell it," he said, feeling proud of his wife.

The colonello swallowed hard at the "specially trained" and did as Stefano bid him. "So the little man, the Dominican Brother, he was poisoned with this as well?"

Luciana shook her head. "No. I think our murderer is a dabbler in these dark arts and likes to vary his—or her—game." She turned and looked at the ruddy-faced acolyte. "He swallowed his poison and it came in a pouch of wine. See how red his face has become and the spatter of blood on his lips and clothes. He, too, vomited . . . blood, before he died. I've seen this blend before . . . last spring. It was a mixture used by Exilli, the poisoner. It was nearly used on me and my husband. It isn't a pretty death, however quick. The final moments are quite . . . painful, I'm told."

"Her Grace knows her poisons," a voice near the door said, breaking into the silence that followed Luciana's description.

The corporal visibly jumped at the sound. Stefano—and Fieri, Stefano noted—put Luciana behind them as they all turned to look at the door.

Padre Gabera stood in the doorway to the cell, holding up his own lantern. He was looking sadly at Brother Tomasi and shaking his head. "He almost made his Confession and took the Eucharist today . . . if only I'd had a little more time." The man, perhaps five or ten years Stefano's senior, wore hair and beard shorn short and a gray cassock. "I'm sorry if I startled anyone."

"We thought we were alone," Luciana said, coming out from behind the two men.

"Not alone. There *are* men on watch," Fieri pointed out. To the priest, he motioned to the bundle in his hands and said, "You're here for Last Rites, Padre?"

The priest nodded and entered the cell. "I know the condition of Brother Tomasi's soul . . . are the others of the faith? Practicing as they should?"

"DeGrassi was a Jew. The rabbi will be here soon, too," Fieri said.

Gabera glanced over his shoulder. "Yes, I think I saw one of them coming from the synagogue. We will respect one another."

"You've been seeing this Brother Tomasi? Talking to him?" Stefano asked. Perhaps not all information was lost. "Did he make his Confession?"

Gabera shook his head. "I nearly convinced him this morning, but the guards . . . that one, the one you called deGrassi . . . made me leave because Tomasi had another visitor."

"Another visitor?" Stefano repeated, his curiosity piqued. "Did you know him? Speak to him? Or was it a woman?"

"A man, a courtier, is all that I can tell you. The guard kept him back in the shadows where I couldn't see him," Gabera said.

"But no one else had permission to see the prisoner!" Fieri said. He stood quivering for a moment and then sagged, shaking his head. "My own son! Pascal, what were you thinking!" The father suddenly raged at his son's corpse. He dropped to his knees and wept openly.

Stefano felt discomforted by the man's grief, his obvious sense of honor lost. He motioned for the corporal to leave and helped Luciana edge around Fieri. "Padre Gabera, I will be wanting to speak with you in the morning . . . and please, be careful. I leave you to your duties."

Outside the cell, Stefano breathed a sigh of relief, felt Luciana sigh beside him. "We've seen all there is to see now; let's get you out of this fetid air," he said to Luciana.

Luciana shook her head. "We should look in Brother Tomasi's cell. Probably, there will be nothing, but we should look."

Stefano shook his head firmly, taking her elbow. "You told me you would do as I said. The men have undoubtedly been through Brother Tomasi's cell already."

Balking like a stubborn mule, Luciana pulled toward the other cell. "They won't know what to look for. What is actually a ward may look like bits of straw to them. Please, Stefano. I can feel it. There is something in that cell, and we must find it and find it tonight!"

Stefano looked at her, considering. He was reluctant. What she described was magic and if it was, then it would be the cardinal's magic. He wanted her nowhere near it, around any magic for that matter, yet this was the reason he had brought her. He resigned himself to what must be done and released her arm.

"Go on then. I'll be with you . . . and I don't want you casting, especially if you might be anywhere near something from the cardinal. Understand?"

Luciana nodded her concession which seemed rather half-hearted to him since she was already heading in the direction of the cell. At the cell door, she paused and looked up at the name newly inscribed over the door. She looked frightened, but angry as well. She spat on the floor below the inscription before she went into the chamber. Stefano followed close behind. He had no love of *Magnus Inique*, but he was not about to spit as she had. As it was, the guards in the guardroom gave her a funny look. Stefano glowered at the men, who immediately went back to whatever business they were meant to be about.

Inside, Luciana proceeded slowly, her hands out as though running them along handrails. Her eyes were closed, but she walked purposefully. She stopped when she stood between the fire pit and the cot. She opened her eyes. Something sparked there in her gaze, a gleam of wildness, but of fire and ice, too. Stefano realized with a plummeting stomach that she was casting.

As she bent over the cot and then below it, he started to stop her for fear of rats or other vermin, but did not. Anger bit like acid in his mouth. Had she not *just* promised him? Perhaps she thought this magic so minor, he would not notice? He knew her ways, had seen her cast magic and he did not like it, especially with their babe so close to being born. She took too many risks! However, he feared interrupting her would only make the matter worse, so he held back.

Luciana pulled something from beneath the cot, something small and dirty that fit in the palm of her hand. She rose, her hands still outstretched, her eyes glazed with the wildness. As she passed through the moonbeam let in by the little window high in the wall, it almost looked as though her hands were sheathed in some form of white energy. It wafted from her hands like heat from the road on a hot summer's day. As she moved from the moonlight, it was harder to see the radiating energies, but having seen it once clearly, he could still make it out.

He turned in place, watching as she neared the fire pit. Before he could stop her, she reached into the bed of coals as though it were nothing more than her knitting basket and she was looking for scissors. Stefano closed the distance between them in a single step and wrapped his arms around her and lifted her physically away from the fire pit.

"Water! Water! Now! Someone, quick!" Stefano yelled, he knelt on the ground, pulling his wife down with him and, surprisingly, she did not struggle. She dropped whatever was in her hands and started to shake. The waves of energy Stefano had seen were fading now and her eyes were clouded with shock and pain. "You fool! You little fool! You promised me!" he hissed at her. When the guards came with a bucket of water, he shoved her hands roughly into it. She cried out and the energy was gone. To the guards, he said, "Fetch me *il dottore* Bonta! Post haste!"

Stefano rose, lifting Luciana in his arms and tipping the bucket of water. Luciana made a grab for the little bits she had collected and pressed them to her bosom. He carried her from the cell, the dungeon, through the courtyard and into the palazzo. *Il dottore* met them in the hallway and followed them into their apartment, making clucking noises and running to keep up with Stefano so that he might see what had happened.

XII

"The souls of emperors and cobblers are cast in the same mold . . . The same reason that makes us wrangle with a neighbor causes war betwixt princes."
—Michel Eyquiem, Seigneur de Montaigne

"OH, Your Grace, what have you done to yourself?" *il dottore* clucked at her as he sat beside her on the couch and looked at her sodden hands.

Luciana glanced up at Stefano, whose back was to her. From the set of his shoulders and the way he would not look at her, but instead stared into the fireplace, she knew he was beyond angry. She gave a quick little sigh and focused on first things first.

"She stuck her hands into the coals of a fire pit. Her hands have been dowsed with water. That is all the care she has received until now," Stefano said, his tone curt as he turned to address Bonta.

"Your Grace? Whatever were you thinking! Bring me water and rags," *il dottore* said, shaking his head.

Kisaiya brought a basin of water and the requested rags and set them on the cherrywood table before them. She looked meaningfully at Luciana's bosom and the tatters of whatever she had hidden there. She came behind the couch, took up Luciana's mantle, and offered her hands for the items. Luciana merely shook her head.

It was hard to concentrate upon *il dottore*. Her hands hurt, but she was more conscious of the siren song tempting her mind that came from her secreted treasures. She tried hard to focus on Bonta as he cleaned the ash and cinders from her hands, first the backs, then the palms and fingertips.

Bonta "tch'd" his way through his examination of her now carefully cleaned hands. He shook his head. "Your Grace, Duca di Drago, the coals could not have been as hot as you feared. She will have blisters here and there, but I expected more damage."

Luciana looked down at her hands. There were blisters already forming on the tips of most of the fingers of her right hand. The left hand had a burn that crossed her palm.

"I prescribe butter or olive oil. I prefer the latter," Bonta pronounced. He looked pointedly at Kisaiya who hovered near her mistress' side. "No needlework, Your Grace, until these are healed," he told Luciana. He turned to Stefano who had come to look at her hands. "It's not so very bad as you thought. Rest easy. I know this is a trying time for you with her time nearing, but all will be well."

"Thank you, *dottore*. We are most gratified by your speedy response," Stefano said. He pressed gold coins into the older man's hand. "You do not have to dress her wounds. I know that her lady has healer training."

Bonta looked like he would protest, but stopped, nodded with a smile, and rose. He knew when he was being dismissed. The older gentleman put his tools into his kit bag. He stopped as he headed to the door and turned back. "The wounds are minor, Your Grace, but if she develops a fever, then we will need to cool her bile with a bloodletting. My barber will be ready should you need him . . . or you may call upon me."

"Thank you, *dottore*," Stefano said.

The willowy-thin man bowed deeply, as though he were blown by a wind and had not the substance to withstand it. Carlo opened the door for him and closed it after. Stefano's man disappeared up the steps after Kisaiya, apparently going to aid her.

"How could you?" Stefano demanded, coming to stand directly in front of Luciana, his hands upon his hips. "After I specifically forbade you! After all that we have said about the use of magic while you are pregnant?"

"You asked me, you didn't forbid it," Luciana retorted sulkily. Her hands were beginning to truly hurt now, and she felt chilled despite the blaze in the fireplace.

"Luciana, you knew my meaning. You can't play the part of the simpleton with me."

"It was a subtle magic. I just reached out for what was magical in the cell and . . . it helped me find it. I didn't even think—"

"No! You didn't think! Have you felt the babe move since you cast this magic?" Stefano asked.

Luciana took a deep breath. At this point in her pregnancy, she usually felt more aware of the child than her own person and, now, concentrating upon it, the child did not like the secreted bits she had tucked into the bosom of her gown. Unlike the child, these bits of ill magic called to her as evil magic did ever since her battle with the cardinal. Careful of her fingers, she pulled the fragments from her dress and dropped them on the table. "Do you want to feel the child move yourself, or will you take my word that even now it feels like it dances upon my tender parts?"

"It moves?" Stefano said, sitting beside her. He hesitated and then reached out.

Luciana guided his hand to where the baby kicked hardest and sat back. Stefano fell quiet, his expression softening.

"Then the child is all right?" Stefano asked, sounding greatly relieved.

"I would never do anything to harm this child, Stefano. After Arturo . . . I take no chances."

"And yet you cast magic. I saw it on your hands, radiating from you," Stefano said, cross again as he sat back on the other end of the couch.

"That's what protected me—and our child—from being more severely hurt, Stefano. Look at my hands and tell me truthfully, did you expect so little damage?"

"*I* always speak to you truthfully," Stefano retorted hotly, but his ire eased somewhat. "No, your hands are not nearly as hurt as I feared, but what in God's good name would drive you to put your hands in a pit of coals?"

"There, on the table," Luciana said. She reached for the first bit and paused. "Would you mind?"

Stefano sighed and took up the three pieces. The first bit was woven from straw. A cross formed the middle of a twisted circle, with a five-pointed star bracing the cross in place. He looked up at Luciana who wrinkled her nose at it.

"What is it?" he asked.

"A ward meant for protection, but it is corrupted. It means little to us and served Brother Tomasi ill. Throw it in the fire, Stefano, and be done with it," Luciana said, pushing his hands toward the hearth.

"It is evidence. It must be kept," Stefano said. He set it back on the table and moved it as far from Luciana as he could. "And that?" He pointed to a bundle of once-white cloth.

Luciana shuddered. "It was in the fire pit. Tomasi had meant for it to burn."

Curious, Stefano picked up a bit of the cloth and discovered that the one bundle was actually two of knotted, dirty white cloth. He held both in his hand, noting how the fabric had been knotted to make two miniature dolls, both had a bit of gold thread encircling their heads. Their edges were burned, but the tight knotting had actually impeded the burning.

"What are they?" he asked.

"Poppets. They must have been to represent Alban and Idala. Tomasi worked some kind of magic upon them, affecting their well-being," Luciana explained. "Please, they've touched me already. I can hear the evil magic in them. It calls to me—neither I nor the child like it. Take it away. Please!"

"Master?" Carlo called from the stairs.

Luciana and Stefano turned to look at the duca's man holding a bottle of olive oil just out of reach of Kisaiya who stood on the stair above him, a small mortar and pestle in one hand and the other reaching for the oil.

"Come," Stefano bid, waving them both forward as he swept up the straw and cloth and put them in a drawer of his desk. "Is there some difficulty in following *il dottore*'s orders?"

Kisaiya, looking stubbornly at the other man, skipped down the steps and around Carlo, bringing her burden to Luciana's side. Carlo breathed the deep sigh of one whose patience had been long tested, and followed.

"Yes, Your Grace, your lady's lady insists upon using some mix of herbs and plants! I watched her squeeze the juices of one such plant until it was nothing into her vile mixture and she insists this is what the duchessa will use," Carlo said, eying Kisaiya irritably. "I say *il dottore* was quite specific."

"He was," Stefano said, giving Kisaiya a hard look.

"But this is the medicine our people have used forever," Kisaiya protested, edging even closer to Luciana.

"*Il dottore* was quite specific," Stefano repeated, looking from his man to Luciana.

She looked back at him, her chin tilting. It was obvious that there was to be another fight. Luciana ameliorated her expression and the angle of her jaw. "Stefano, *il dottore* did not prohibit the use of my family's remedy and they *are* my burns. Could we not use both?"

"Both?" Stefano said. "*Il dottore* Bonta—"

"Uses white medicine for *gadjé*. I am Romani. I am willing to accept his medicine in addition to my own," Luciana bargained.

Stefano looked at the bowl in Kisaiya's hands. "What's in it?"

Kisaiya glanced down at Luciana before answering him directly. "The juice of the aloe plant, a bit of comfrey . . . it will soothe the burns so my mistress can sleep." She looked at Carlo angrily, then down at her bowl and back up at Stefano. "I could add the olive oil, Your Grace. If that pleases you?"

Stefano sighed and looked down at his wife who worked very hard to look amiable. Whatever it was he read in her expression, Stefano sighed again and waved Carlo to Kisaiya. They would compromise.

16 d'Dicembre, 1684

Irritated by the gauze wrapping on her hands and, thus, her inability to do anything of consequence for herself, Luciana discarded it and eased her injured fingers into light Gypsy Silk gloves. She sat in her chair at her bureau and focused upon her hands. She wanted as much relief as could be afforded and for the gloves to not stand out, to instead blend and become part of her so that she could use her hands naturally. She sat and meditated upon them, feeling the fabric seem to soften and become like the second skin she would expect from doeskin gloves.

Luciana opened her eyes after several minutes and looked

down. These gloves were made of Gypsy Silk, the most expensive—even to her. The fabric seemed so sheer now, after absorbing the oils and juices of Kisaiya's salve. They were almost invisible on her hands. She reached out and touched one of her brooches on the dressing table. She felt the roughness of the metal filigree around the stone, but it was as though a gentle shield rested a hair's breadth between finger and jewel. The burns were still painful, but not as much. She breathed a sigh of relief and thanked her lucky stars that Stefano did not consider this, too, magic . . . though it was.

Stefano slept in his own room the night before and breakfasted without her, so she had not seen him yet, but she could hear him clearly in the downstairs receiving room now. She rose and examined herself in her floor-length mirror.

Despite her time being so near, Luciana felt she cut an attractive figure in her deep purple gown, with its matching undergown, all sewn round with embroidered peacock feathers. This morning, after dressing, Kisaiya had styled her hair using pins with the tips of more feathers from the peacock. It was smart and attractive looking, yet showed proper deference for the fact that she and almost everyone was in mourning.

She descended the stairs with care, Kisaiya walking just ahead of her. At the bottom, Kisaiya faded back against the wall, letting Luciana pass her.

Stefano stood at his desk, papers in hand. He looked up and watched her speculatively as she approached. "You look lovely this morning," he said and then in almost the same breath added, "Where are the dressings for your hands?"

Luciana held out her ringless hands—an oddity for her—and showed him the cleverness of her gloves. Stefano studied them and sniffed. "Gypsy Silk? They must have cost a fine fortune."

"But none of it yours," Luciana retorted. She immediately bit her lip. She did not want to fight. She wanted peace between them. They *needed* peace between them, and not just for their own sakes. She took a deep breath and tilted her chin so that she could fully meet the angry flame in his hazel eyes. She curtsied to him, dropping as low as her bulk allowed. "I dressed for you, *camómescro*. I had hoped you would be pleased."

Luciana watched the muscles in Stefano's jaw and neck

flex as he, too, attempted to control his own temper. "I could be nothing less than awed . . . and the gloves are . . . do they hurt your hands?"

"No," Luciana shook her head. "My hands feel much better."

"You slept late," Stefano observed setting the papers back down on his desk. He looked quickly pained and turned back to her, "That was not a criticism, just an observation."

"I slept a little late. It took me longer to dress and breakfast this morning. Understandably, what with fumbling with bandages, I chose to take my meal in my chambers," she said, hating the stiffness between them.

"Of course," Stefano nodded.

Silence fell, awkward and raw. Luciana glanced around and saw that Kisaiya had gone, apparently to other duties. They were alone. They were seldom alone, she thought, they should be enjoying this time. She searched for something to say as he turned back to the papers on his desk.

"Stefano—"

"Luciana—"

They had spoken at the same time and the awkward silence fell between them again. Luciana wished they could laugh it away. She motioned for him to speak first. He hesitated, then gestured to the couch.

"We must speak about things of an urgent nature, I'm afraid," Stefano said, guiding her to their mutual seat.

Luciana's natural curiosity quickened. "What about?"

"As of this morning, we have a quorum of the Palantini. We can meet to confirm our positions as Regents . . . but we must also address yesterday's murders and there are some things that you do not know," Stefano said. He smoothed his mustache and chewed on his upper lip.

He was nervous, Luciana realized. She sat up more attentively and, when he still did not speak, placed a hand on his leg.

He looked at her, earnestly. "I know who the murderer was—is, but I can't prove it . . . not to the level that would be acceptable to his station."

"Pierro," Luciana guessed.

Stefano's hand took hers and squeezed gently. She managed to not cry out. "Yes. It was he who raised the alarm about the murders. He was wounded. Minor, seemingly inconsequential injuries. I went to see him. I saw his wound . . . the wound he said was given him by the murderer. It was on his arm. A type of wound I recognized. When you use an arm-sheath for a stiletto and replace it in haste . . ."

"It makes that type of wound," Luciana concluded. Her first thoughts were for him having gone into the deMedici suite alone, but that was over, done. "You can't prove the wound happened that way, though."

Stefano nodded. "And he did have a head wound, but of little or no consequence. He refused treatment for it."

"Did you accuse him? Does he know you know?" Luciana asked.

Stefano shook his head. "Of course, I didn't accuse him. I pretended not even to be overly concerned with the wounds he claimed . . . other than in a mannerly nature, of course."

"But he knows," Luciana said, trying not to let the fear gripping her heart take control.

"He'll have guessed . . . and, if he hasn't, he will when we have the hearing of the evidence at the Palantini," Stefano admitted. He took her hands in his and then released them. "I'm sorry. Are you all right?"

"Yes, but what are you to do with Pierro? And Ortensia? Did she have a part in this?" Luciana asked.

Stefano shook his head. "We have no way of knowing, but the evidence will point to Pierro."

"And he will strike back," Luciana concluded.

"He may try. For this reason, you must be careful of your person. I have spoken to Capitano della Guelfa and his men. I have been too long without men-at-arms. Now that is resolved. He, or one of his men, will be your bodyguard from—"

"But, Stefano! Me?" Luciana protested, pulling away. "I can defend myself."

"In normal circumstances, yes, but you will give birth soon. There will be you and the child, and I simply don't know how far he will go to strike at me. I can't let him strike at me through you. I have already spoken with Lord Strozzini—" Stefano said.

"You mean, Alban's bodyguard?" Luciana interrupted.

Stefano nodded. "The very same. He will be with me

from now on . . . for our family's sake, for Tyrrhia's sake. I don't like it either, but we must think of the children and Tyrrhia first if we are to be Regents. Do you understand?"

"Surely, there is some other—"

He took her by the shoulders and shook her slightly. "Do you understand? *I* can't lose you. I would go mad."

"I thought I already made you mad," Luciana chided, her mind in a whirl of possibilities.

"Since the moment we met, but this is different. Think what Alban's death did to Idala and know she and I were kindred spirits, brother and sister, we give our hearts the same way. Completely. If not for me, if not for the baby or even your people, then for Tyrrhia, you must accept this. Am I understood?" Stefano insisted, shaking her again. "Promise me now. Promise me on whatever you hold most holy, but promise me!"

Luciana nodded. "I promise. What can we do about Pierro, though, besides surround ourselves with guards?"

"At the moment, even with the damning evidence, I fear there will be enough doubt to protect him. We—*I* must find more proof before we can act against him. I will try at the hearing, but I don't hold out much hope," Stefano admitted. "Now. You will need to see the babies before we convene the Palantini."

"When will that be?" Luciana asked.

"After the lunch hour. We begin at two. Will you be ready?"

"Of course."

Stefano pulled her to him and kissed her, then cradled her in his arms. "You *must* be safe. He could strike through any channel."

"And the same with you, Stefano. Pierro is nasty when crossed."

"Most people are."

"But he more than most," Luciana said. She took a deep breath and risked changing the subject. "My grandmother should arrive at any time. When she does, I will begin building my *bender*—when my other duties do not take me away, of course."

Stefano sighed and released her. "You really are quite determined in this?"

"I'm not risking another child, Stefano, not even to

please you. The spirit must find its way to the child as it is being born and this can be done only in the out of doors. It is my people's way. It is my heritage," Luciana insisted.

"But what of the cold? The comfort?"

Luciana laughed softly. "I shall be more comfortable than you might think. You've never been inside a *bender*. We have a fire, a vent in the top of the structure. I'll have every comfort *and* the confidence that my child will meet its soul when it is intended."

"*Gadjé* children have 'met their souls' in the indoors for generations," Stefano pressed.

"But I am not *gadjé*, and neither will our child be. This will be a Child of the Bloods . . . of both white and dark bloodlines and must be born according to custom."

"You are determined in this?"

Luciana caressed his cheek. "I'll not lose another child. I—I couldn't bear it."

"This will be safe?"

Luciana nodded. "The Romani are thousands strong, and very rarely is one of our children born indoors. Perhaps, in other countries, where the mother might have been arrested for being of the blood, but here . . . our children are born beneath the open sky. *Beano abri.*"

Stefano seemed to resign himself to her answer. "Speaking of children, though, you must visit your charges in the nursery."

"And I must interview tutors for Dario Gian, as well, but I will be at the meeting of the Palantini," Luciana promised.

"Until then," Stefano said.

She leaned in and gave him a kiss as she rose.

The Royal Nursery was working in quiet order under the auspices of Maria della Guelfa. One of the wet nurses tended Chiara while the child's twin sisters slept in their cradles.

After assuring herself that the girls were well, Luciana steeled herself and crossed the hallway to Alban's old chamber where Massimo was kept. She found the wet nurse dozing in her rocking chair while the prince and the wet nurse's boy slept in their separate cradles.

The wet nurse roused, apparently woken by the sound of the door latch. She rose quickly when she saw Luciana and performed an awkward curtsy.

Luciana waved her back to her seat. "I did not mean to disturb you. I was just looking in on . . . on Massimo," she said softly.

The young woman smiled. "Do you wish to hold him, Mistress . . . er . . . Your Grace?" She leaned toward Massimo's cradle.

"No! No, let's not disturb him when he's resting," Luciana said. Prince Massimo was swaddled up tight, his eyes closed in gentle slumber. At the moment, he looked for all the world like any other newborn. Luciana turned to the wet nurse. "I hope you will forgive me, My Lady, but I have forgotten your name."

"I don't think there was ever a time when we were introduced properly, Your Grace," the young woman whispered. "I am Bonita Boniface and this is my boy, Federico."

Luciana offered her hand to Bonita, "I am Duchessa Luciana di Drago and am *Araunya* of the Romani." She was surprised when Bonita kissed the back of her hand, rather than shaking it as Luciana had intended.

Luciana leaned back against the door to the bedchamber, oddly touched by the simple woman before her. "You have no problems with the boy . . . with Massimo?"

"The prince?" Bonita whispered and shook her head. "My youngest brother was . . . was not right at birth, either, so I have experience with the prince's oddities."

"And your boy? He isn't troubled by the prince?"

Bonita's nose wrinkled when she smiled, and she pushed a dark blonde lock of hair behind her ear. "My little Federico wants nothing more than to eat and sleep just now. He is only a week older than the prince and his sisters."

"Is there anything that you need to make your time more comfortable?" Luciana asked.

Bonita shook her head. "I have my sewing when I don't forget it and fall asleep with the babes."

Luciana nodded. "Then I will leave you to it. Should you change your mind and need something, ask Signora della Guelfa or me directly. Thank you for your service."

Bonita nodded and watched her as Luciana quietly opened the door and backed out of the room. In the hallway, as she turned, Luciana bumped into a man, his face obscured by the shadows of the ill-lit area. Luciana pushed the man hard and prepared to scream but was stopped by the man's voice.

"Your Grace, *Araunya*, it is I, della Guelfa. You left your suites before I could reach you. I am here under your husband's direction," he said.

Having met and spoken with the man a couple of times already, Luciana vaguely recognized his voice and what little of him she could make out. "You're here as my bodyguard?"

"At your service, Your Grace," della Guelfa said with as much of a bow as the tight space permitted.

"I was about to go to see Prince Dario Gian. There are three tutors there to be interviewed," Luciana said, feeling awkward this close to the man. She reached for the handrail and della Guelfa immediately took a few steps down the stairs ahead of her. Luciana hesitated. She was unaccustomed to strangers acting so familiarly and it unsettled her. "Have you seen your Signora?" Luciana asked.

"Briefly," della Guelfa responded, offering her his hand.

"You may visit her now, if you wish," Luciana volunteered, pointing to Idala's old bedroom.

The capitano shook his head. "My time is not my own, Your Grace. I go where you go. She and I both understand my duties. This new duty allows us more time together, so please do not worry on our behalf."

"Oh!" Luciana murmured.

He offered her his left hand, his right on the handrail of the stairs leading down into the royal receiving room.

Luciana shook her head. "I will be fine with the rail, Capitano."

"Please. We will be spending much time in one another's company . . . and as your husband's man-at-arms, I am technically no longer a capitano. Call me Marco, or della Guelfa if you prefer," he said.

Even in the near dark, Luciana could see the flash of Marco della Guelfa's ready grin. "Marco, then," Luciana agreed. She started to step down, and he pushed his hand toward her insistently.

"Take my hand, Your Grace. If you were to fall and hurt yourself or your child while on my watch, I would not forgive myself . . . and, more importantly, neither would His Grace," he said, offering his hand once more.

Luciana smiled at him nervously and took his hand, allowing him to lead her down the stairs. Once they reached the foot of the stairs, however, Marco shifted so that Luciana could take the lead.

Dario Gian, she found in his own nursery. In his common room, Luciana noted that the transition from play room to school room had already begun. The boy, himself, was out getting a riding lesson in the stable area. Marco assured her that one of his men, Maggiore di Montago's men, and now Stefano's, was with Prince Dario Gian as a regular bodyguard.

Of the three tutors applying to educate Dario Gian, Luciana selected two. The first, Signore Montagna, would school the young Prince in letters, numbers, and beginning philosophy while the second, Signore Rizzo, would begin lessons in geography, chess, and beginning politics. This would give the boy a well-rounded base for his other studies to prepare him for the duties he was destined to inherit when he was of age and became king. Dario Gian's bodyguard, deBonneta, would begin his lessons in swordplay and basic defense.

Satisfied that her duties to the children were taken care of, Luciana returned to her apartment, hoping to lunch with Stefano before the meeting of the Palantini. She found herself disappointed. Stefano took his meal with Estensi, the Court Herald; Guglielmo, the Palazzo Steward; and Colonello Fieri of the Palazzo Guards.

Kisaiya prepared Luciana a light lunch of cold chicken, prosciutto-wrapped dates—a particular treat she had been craving of late—and a variety of fresh fruit. Luciana ate in her bedchamber, then prepared for her afternoon with the Palantini.

XIII

"We must give lengthy deliberation to what must be decided once and for all."

—Publilius Syrus

STEFANO escorted Luciana to the Throne Room. He felt restive and anxious. Luciana said nothing, but he could tell from her uneasy glances that she was trying to find something to say. A few feet from their destination, he stopped and turned to his wife. "There is nothing that you can say, Luciana. I am anxious over this hearing and I expect trouble from the deMedicis." He kissed her forehead and started forward again while Strozzini and della Guelfa remained a discreet distance behind them.

Luciana held tight to his arm, not moving. "Surely there is something that I can do to help?"

Stefano sighed and scratched his beard. "If there were, I would tell you. Watch and listen today. Bide your time, and if the time seems right, speak your mind. Have care, though. The deMedicis will foul your meaning if they have a chance. Now come, the time is upon us."

Luciana nodded her assent and lifted her chin.

Despite being ten minutes to the hour, Stefano was briefly surprised to find that the Throne Room was already quite full. Courtiers ranking from duca to don filled the seats though the full quorum had not yet arrived.

Stefano led Luciana to the front of the room where he had arranged for a large, wing-backed chair from the king's study to be placed in front of the royal dais. He allowed a second chair to his left for Luciana and chairs to his right for Their Highnesses, the deMedicis. Guglielmo and Estensi had not failed him in setting this up.

As Regent, Stefano could have taken the king's throne and placed chairs for the deMedicis, but this would have allowed them the right to sit upon the royal dais. Alban had not allowed them upon the dais when he was king, and Stefano saw no reason to change that status now. He, however, could not bring himself to use the throne which was Alban and Dario Gian's to occupy. The new "row of chairs" decision was a strategic move that he hoped would discomfit Ortensia and Pierro. Anything to put them off their game.

As he handed Luciana to her seat and took his beside her, more of the duchi filtered in and found seats. Ortensia and Pierro were the last to arrive . . . at five past the appointed hour. It soured his stomach for everyone to rise, as the course of precedence, for the tardy Prince and Princess. Unlike him, Luciana and the rest of the court, who were all dressed in dark mourning clothes, Ortensia and Pierro wore matching white outfits of the finest Gypsy Silk. Their only acknowledgment to the state of grief was the black baldric and frog Pierro wore to carry his sword, and the bows Ortensia wore at her elbows, each attached with an ornate gold brooch. Their public display looked more like a statement of fashion than any show of grief.

Stefano kept his expression an impassive mask as he motioned to the chairs reserved for them. Beyond the flash of anger in Pierro's eyes, one could not tell the arrangement bothered him. His wife, however, stopped dead in her tracks at the head of the center aisle and her face grew icy cold with undisguised fury. Pierro reminded her of the audience with a touch to her hand and guided her to her seat, as usual, making a great show of his attentiveness.

In recent days, it had become increasingly obvious that Ortensia was, indeed, very much with child. According to the rumors, mostly passed through the servants, the sultan who had kept her these many years, had absented himself from her bed a good six months before her release. If this were true, the only conclusion could be that Pierro deMedici was the father of her unborn child which would, thereby, assure its legitimacy.

At a nod from Stefano, Estensi rose from his own

appointed chair—obviously something completely alien to his years of service with both Alban and his predecessor, Orsino. The Court Herald moved to the center of the room and stamped his rosewood staff three times. "I call to order the Royal Council of the Palantini. His Excellency, Duca di Drago, presides as appointed by his predecessors, our beloved king and queen, Alban and Idala."

"Today, and in recent days past, I have been collecting proxies of support from those unable to reach us by this appointed day," Estensi said to the crowd. "Six duchi and some fourteen contes and twelve dons have seen fit to give the appointed regent their proxies. Prince and Princess deMedici have received proxies from two duchi and a don."

Stefano glanced toward the deMedicis and nodded. Luciana captured his hand then. He glanced at her, seeing her concern. He shook his head and smiled to reassure her.

Estensi came toward him and bent down to speak. "Be aware that Ortensia and her husband have spent the last few days seeking support for their claim to the throne over you as appointed regent of the 'usurper king.'"

Stefano felt his face flush hot with his sudden rage. How dare they? Without Alban even placed in his tomb yet! Then he took a deep breath and released it slowly. "It is their right. They try to get us to act rashly at their terms, but we've heard the like before. Pray, do not let them induce you to reaction."

"Of course not," Estensi replied softly. "Are you prepared to go forward?"

Stefano nodded and the Court Herald stepped away.

"I hereby call into order this final court of King Alban and Queen Idala. We will begin by discussing any concerns about the appointed regent, Stefano di Drago, being named Lord Regent," Estensi said. He opened his mouth to continue speaking, but was interrupted.

"Excuse me, sirrah, but before we can discuss the appointment of a regent to stand for Alban until Dario Gian is of age, we must first consider my wife, Princess Ortensia's claim to the throne," Prince Pierro said. He then smiled coldly at Stefano.

"Point of order," Estensi replied. "You, as foreign-born royalty, never mind being a bastarde, and Tyrrhian-titled only by means of marriage with your spouse still alive, have no right to speak in the Palantini."

Pierro smiled a slow smile. "Princess Bianca is dead, leaving me a widower entitled to speak, but never minding that, my wife Ortensia has asked that I speak for her."

Estensi turned to the princess. "Is this so, Your Highness? You wish your husband to speak for you?"

"I do," Ortensia said stiffly. She reached inside her cuff and pulled a paper from it which she gave to Estensi.

The Court Herald took the paper grudgingly and perused it quickly. To Stefano, he said, "'Tis her proxy made out to him. He has legitimate claim to speak for her and the proxies made out to her."

Stefano took the paper from Estensi and looked it over. The letter was made out in her hand, signed and sealed. There was no arguing over the point, especially with her present to attest to its veracity. Luciana squeezed his hand, as though to give him courage. "All seems in order. If you truly wish to argue that Ortensia should inherit the throne, priority of claim goes to you, Signore," he said to Pierro.

Estensi addressed the duchi gathered. "While somewhat irregular, it *is* within Ortensia's privilege. There is a section of the law pertaining to it. Short of the king—and, alas, we have no king—or the Palantini refusing the proxy, then they are within their rights. Do I hear anyone calling for a vote on the matter or should Prince Pierro deMedici speak for his wife as they have indicated their intent?"

Luciana leaned over to Stefano. "This makes so little sense! Even I—were I not *Araunya* or the appointed Lady Guardian—could not vote and I am Tyrrhian-born and raised!"

"It is the law and we will abide by it," Stefano said. "I hear no protests, so let us begin. Herald, will you open the ceremonies, please?"

The Court Herald waved to the Palazzo Guards at the doors to close them, and then turned back to his larger audience, stamping his staff three times to make quiet fall in the room.

"By right of office, I, Don Benoni Estensi, call this gathering of the Palantini, Royal Council for all Tyrrhia, into session. I have recognized each member of the Lower and Upper Houses by virtue of family standing and right of peerage to be here present," the Court Herald announced. His booming voice rang clearly through the Throne Room.

Estensi read the list of names of those present, announced the registered proxies, and then, barring any business that was not already on the agenda, called the meeting open. He turned back to Pierro and Ortensia. "Do you still wish your husband to speak for you?"

"I so wish it," Ortensia conceded, nodding regally.

"Then, Your Highness, the floor is yours."

Pierro smoothed his mustache, adjusted his cuffs, and rose, rapping the floor with his silver-pointed cane. "My wife Ortensia, and your princess by King Orsino and Queen Katerina, claims by right of legitimate birth, and pursuing acts of God wherein she was kept imprisoned for sixteen years by the Turkish Sultan Tardiq, that she has been denied her honest position in Tyrrhia as your queen. She seeks means now to claim her throne.

"She is a grown woman who knows her mind and is capable of ruling as queen," Pierro announced, smiling coldly, "especially in preference to risking that Tyrrhia might look weak to outsiders and even some of the populace with a Lord Regent."

Duca Sebastiani slammed his fists and cane onto his knees. "There's been enough talk about this! To your wife, whom you say deserves her due, then let me salute your princess!" He paused to give a surly, hurried salute to Princess Ortensia from his seat which was just short of being flippant. "As to being a woman who knows and is capable of speaking her own mind, tell me why, then, are you voting and speaking for her instead of herself? If she cannot choose to vote in the Palantini amongst those who know and respect her, how, pray tell, is she supposed to rule? Furthermore, the Palantini, who knows her and you, *Signore*, for yourselves, has been moving to have the Lord and Lady Regents named. This discussion on inheriting from Orsino puts lie to his decision to name Alban Novabianco. *He*, after a very short and wise reign, left an Heir Apparent—"

"The boy is only five! You mean to have Tyrrhia guided all this time until he reaches his majority by Regents? It may be that this *is* a call for the Palantini at large and not just a small group that makes up the quorum—" Ortensia interrupted.

Duchessa Rossi rose to her feet, rapping with her knuckles on the wooden back of the chair in front of her. The rings on her fingers clattered against the polished wood. Her attire was impeccable, as always, and respectful of the recent deaths. "Excuse me, Your Highness, but custom has it that a decision once made by a mere quorum of the Palantini is . . . sacrosanct against all future appeals, and you have appointed your husband as your spokesman.

"You and I were schooled together, grew up and played together, and I missed you greatly when you and your sister were kidnapped by the Turks, and only Bianca was brought back. I'll vote now, Ortensia, and I have decided I don't believe you should have the throne."

"You, Martina?" Ortensia gasped. "But I thought you were my friend! You . . . You . . ."

"I am still your friend, but, you have been away from Tyrrhia for almost two decades, Ortensia! Nearly twenty years," the duchessa cut in. "Heaven, and perhaps a few others—not even I—know what happened to you in the Turkish seraglio and immediately upon your return—before you tried to notify anyone of your arrival—not even, God forgive you, your own father if he still held the throne—married! *You*, who were raised in privilege and educated in the responsibilities you owed Tyrrhia as one of *la famiglia reale*, for—if nothing else—an advantageous marriage, instead married your own recently widowed brother-in-law, also a member of *la famiglia reale*, who could have made another advantageous marriage for the State. You have thought only of yourself and what you want, not of king nor country and you would be queen instead of the Heir Apparent? You surely have some supporters in this group, but the Palantini, ultimately, will make a sound decision. Protest that some might, you will never be queen and, Prince Pierro," Duchessa Rossi smiled quite happily, "you, *Signore*, will never see the throne, not even as a Royal Companion of the Queen."

Before Pierro or Ortensia could speak, Stefano nodded to Duchessa Rossi. "Thank you, Your Grace, for your frank analysis of the situation and, unless someone can make further argument *other* than what has already been presented by Their Highnesses deMedici, let them speak now and then let us have the vote."

Martina Rossi nodded and took her seat once more, levelly meeting the gazes of the infuriated royal couple. A few of the gentry in the Palantini looked like they wished to make an argument, but Sebastiani stared them down.

Pierro fairly growled with his ire. "To you naysayers, why shouldn't I help my wife receive what she is due? Why shouldn't I seek more? I left my family and homeland for Tyrrhia and Bianca," Pierro snapped. "It was not my fault that the marriage was never consummated—"

"Except that you were then considered part of *la famiglia reale*, and both of you entered into an immoral marriage without the permission of the king. Some would say that your marriage itself is an alliance against Tyrrhia with the two of you bonding together, forswearing fortunate marriages that the Crown might have made to benefit Tyrrhia . . . and yourselves," Stefano argued.

"With the Crown having been and yourself being in what you assert to being a love match, surely you must understand two others falling in love?" Pierro countered, reaching down for Ortensia's hand.

"You claim a love match and yet you knew each other less than a week, some say less than a day, before you bound yourselves in a Catholic marriage. The Crown had every right to annul this marriage, but Alban let you have your way instead."

"And for this, Her Highness must forfeit her throne?" the deMedici demanded.

"Yes," Stefano said. He folded his arms over his chest and met the angry glares of both deMedicis evenly. "She chose a personal alliance over Tyrrhia, and this was the very reason her father chose Alban as his Heir and, in due course, Alban has chosen *his*. I will be nothing more than a placeholder for Prince Dario Gian."

Duca LaCosta rose, coughing loudly for attention. "Your Grace, you find yourself in the position that Orsino did. While it was argued before the *Palantini* that Her Highness Bianca was unfit to serve, no such ruling has been made of Her Highness Ortensia. Why, in this period of turmoil, must we live for the next ten years with a Lord Regent when we could have a queen of the Royal line?"

"Do you suggest, Your Grace, that Princess Ortensia take the throne only until Dario Gian is old enough to rule?

Or in his place—basically, sacrificing his claim to the throne because of his age at the time of his parents' death?" Stefano asked. He let his left hand drop to his hip, near his sword, the right he tucked behind him. It was a challenging stance. Deliberately so.

"I would not suggest that anyone *temporarily* take the throne," LaCosta said, shifting from one high-heeled foot to the other. He looked around the room for supporters, flushing when several gazes dropped to the floor or looked away. "Surely, someone agrees with me?"

Duca di Candido, sitting between his gravid wife and the Duchessa Rossi—one of the few women who held her title of her own accord—murmured something to them and took to his feet. "Far from agreeing with you, LaCosta, I think we should stay the course we have set. I beg Their Highnesses' forgiveness, for I would not normally voice this opinion, but Her Highness has been returned to us—for which I give thanks. However, she is, for all intents and purposes, a broken woman. Rather than saddle her with the duties of the Crown, I would suggest that she find happiness in her marriage and be allowed to retire to live out her days in whatever form of peace she can find."

"But I *want* the Crown!" Princess Ortensia said, getting out of her chair to stand beside her husband.

Sebastiani struggled from his chair with almost the same laborious grace as Ortensia. "For which I commend you, Your Highness. You were raised for duty and you expect to take on that duty now, but there is another solution at hand that is more than just to you and to Tyrrhia. All those who wish to recognize Her Highness' great sense of responsibility and duty, I say hail it now!"

The hail from the audience was resounding, echoing off the walls and into the corridors where the members of the populace and servants waited. It was a clear end to Ortensia's petition.

After waiting a few moments, Stefano pronounced to all, "Then let the vote be taken by the Court Herald as to whether the decisions of Kings Orsino and Alban as to their inheritors should stand or should we dismiss those decisions and let the deMedicis rule?"

"Those who wish Her Highness to remain as she is and not Queen of all Tyrrhia?" Estensi asked the audience.

There came an immediate stamping of feet. The Court Herald made a quick count and called, "And who stands with Her Highness, and wishes for her to take the throne?" Again came the stamping of feet and count by Estensi. When he was done, he compared counts and proxies before turning to *Her* Highness.

"By my count, we have forty-two members of the Palantini present—two more than was necessary for the quorum, plus thirty-five proxies. Your Highness," Estensi said gently, "you don't even have a third of the votes, much less half plus one to carry your motion."

Ortensia gathered her reticule and cane, said something to Pierro and, although he obviously disagreed, he immediately fell into step with his wife and headed for the door.

Feeling Luciana's hand touch his spurred Stefano to action. He rose and stepped toward the couple, in the direction of their irascible retreat. "Your Highnesses, your opinions are valued, and there will be important matters discussed here today. Please, won't you stay?"

Ortensia looked Stefano up and down and blew a rude noise from the side of her mouth. "You have no use for me, nor I, you. Move out of the way, if you please."

Stefano stepped back with a heavy sigh and bowed deeply to her as she made her exit, husband at heel, from the Throne Room. The Palazzo Guards on the inside of the room, hurriedly opened the door for her and when she and her spouse were safely clear, snapped the doors closed behind them.

Immediately, the crowd of mostly men began a low rumble of conversation as they conferred with one another. Stefano maintained a stoic mask, nodding cordially to anyone who made direct eye contact with him and meeting as many gazes as he could in quick, successive order as he stood in front of his chair. Estensi gestured for Stefano to speak. "We will welcome Her Highness or her husband back, if they wish to continue their obligations to the Palantini, but we are assembled today because the White King and his queen have fallen. There has been talk, much talk and speculation, over how the king and queen were taken from us, leaving their children orphans and, thereby, the *Araunya* and I as their appointed Lord Regent and Lady Guardian.

"For those of you not fully aware of the happenings of late. The king took a morning ride with several of us here.

He was felled by an assassin's bolt to the heart. Though the king's bodyguard searches valiantly, he has yet to learn anything about the assassin or who hired him."

"Isn't it just possible that it was a hunting accident?" Duca Gianola asked. An older man in his late fifties, Gianola wore what was the height of fashion a decade ago. He stood with the assistance of a cane and positioned himself so that he might be heard by the greatest cross-section of the room. "And as to the queen, she died from complications of childbirth. There is no great mystery in that."

At Stefano's signal, Lord Strozzini stepped from the back of the room and looked to Stefano for permission to speak. He nodded and the Royal Bodyguard spoke—his voice, though tinged with sadness, was strong and determined. "There were assassins, a party of two. We know this much from what sight I was able to make of them and the ground traces we found. The timing of the attack, when the king was alone for a few brief moments, that no one else came to injury despite his being in the company of a number of ranking officers of the court. Not even I, when I gave chase, was hurt, and the bolt used was too heavy for the hunting of anything but bear . . . or humans. The assassination was too well planned. Beyond that I *know* nothing more. I have leads, but they may come to nothing."

"Rather than continue that line of discussion now, I pray you have patience and allow us to reach that item on the agenda at its proper point in time," Stefano said.

Strozzini bowed curtly and stepped back. Stefano sat and motioned for Estensi to continue with the meeting.

"The next matter at hand is His Grace's swearing in as Lord Regent before the—"

Duchessa Rossi rose. "There is no question that you will serve us well, Your Excellency." She sat down and glanced around the room. She received a fast and heavy stamping of feet.

One brave soul stood in the face of the ringing endorsement and waited to be acknowledged. Eventually, the other members finally noticed him and stopped their noisemaking. Stefano recognized the man to be one Duca Silvieri who came from distant Barlete on the easternmost coast of continental Tyrrhia.

"While I am confident that His Grace, Duca di Drago, is

proud of the great bounds that have been taken in his family with the addition of the immediate *la famiglia reale*—all five orphans to be precise—and soon the addition of his own child, I cannot help but wonder why the young Duca Novabianco has not come forward to express his own wishes in guardianship."

Stefano took a deep breath and prayed for patience. "His Royal Highness, Duca Dario Gian Novabianco, is, as you say, very young. Being barely five, it will be difficult for him to understand the question you have just put forward and, since he is still grieving the loss of his parents, I think it would be cruel to ask him to make such a decision. Better to rely upon the wisdom and wishes of both his parents," Stefano said.

"Is this how it is to be for the next ten years? Or perhaps you will find reason for him to never be fit?" Silvieri suggested.

"Because we are in a consecrated Hall, seeing to the business the State has before it, I will assume that you did not question my loyalty or honesty, but asked a poorly worded yet heartfelt question," Stefano ground out. He could feel the heat rising up his neck and his ears burning from suppressed anger. "As it so happens, I prepared for this eventuality. The boy is very bright, but only five. It is the considered opinion of myself, Court Herald Estensi, *il dottore* Bonta, and the Duchi di Candido and Sebastiani, that the boy would not yet be able to participate fully in any part of these proceedings. The decision seemed apparent to us but if you wish to challenge that decision, our Heir Apparent can be sent for and be judged by the full Council as to his ability to contribute—no matter the scars left on the child's psyche. When he is ready to step up, then he will be crowned king and my job will be done.

"Have I answered your intended question yet, Your Grace?" Stefano asked, hoping the slight tremble in his voice and the flush of red in his face were the only signs of his anger.

"In part, yes. And, while I challenge you, Your Grace, I do not mean to deny your loyalty to the boy or his siblings but the truth of the matter is that there *are* other relations they have amongst the peerage," Duca Silvieri said.

"Indeed there are, but none so close to the children as my wife and I. The other immediate members of the famiies of his parents are all dead. Should the children be put n the care of people they do not even know? Certainly not known to the Heir Apparent? I think not," Stefano said, shaking his head firmly. "Besides, their parents delivered them into *our* care and no one else's."

The Court Herald looked around the room, staring through his pince-nez at the crowd. "Does anyone have something further to say before we ratify His Excellency?"

Were it night time instead of midafternoon, Stefano would have sworn he could hear the crickets in the garden beyond the windows. He looked around the room. Most here met his gaze evenly.

"Then the Lord Regent has been officially endowed with all the rights, privileges, and responsibilities of his new station," Estensi announced.

Duca Scala stood and bowed to the Lord Regent and then the others in the room. He had been sitting in a row of chairs back by the windows. "If you'll beg pardon, Your Excellency, while there has been no question of your service as Lord Regent and since this is the next item posted for the agenda, I must contest your wife being named Lady Guardian."

"What are your reasons, Your Grace?" Stefano asked, wanting desperately to take Luciana in his arms and protect her from this biting counter, but in this matter, he had to be at least somewhat impartial.

Duca Scala shuffled and fidgeted. "To be honest, Your Excellency, she is the *Araunya* and she is . . . she is . . ."

"Romani?" the *Beluni* completed for him.

Stefano blinked, surprised to hear her voice. He had not seen her enter the room and, until now, she had not spoken. He nodded a welcome to her and then looked over at Duca Scala.

"Well, yes. *They* are not like us. They have no education, no sense of responsibility to home and family that must be taught to the young royals," Duca Scala said, his tone diffident.

"We are no different than any *gadjé*," the Romani Queen said, staring the man down her long thin nose.

"*Beluni-Daiya*, I am quite content to speak for myself . . . and my people if necessary," Luciana said firmly, stepping forward so that she stood just in front of Stefano. "Signore . . . Your Grace?"

"He is Duca Filipo Scala, Duchessa *e Araunya*," Sebastiani supplied.

"Yes, that I am," the old duca confirmed, glowering at the back of Sebastiani's head. To Luciana, he said, "And you, *Araunya*, what are you going to do to me for daring to question your qualifications?"

"I will answer your questions. There will be no retribution from me or any of my people because we simply don't do that type of magic. The worst I might do is give you a fit of sneezing which is—" Luciana began.

Duca Scala and a couple other of the men immediately began sneezing and glowering at Luciana who laughed light-heartedly.

"Gentles, I promise you that the 'magic' used to cause your fits of sneezing was not of my doing, nor the *Beluni*'s. No, good sirs, you and you alone are author to this magic. I make a suggestion, and guilty consciences do the rest. If you sit and relax, I am confident your paroxysms will cease and let me tell you the answers to your questions named and unnamed."

The men looked sideways at one another, still occasionally sneezing and dabbing at their noses with their kerchiefs. Reluctantly, they sat down, and the sneezing stopped almost at once. Luciana smiled again and folded her hands in front of her, her countenance completely open. Stefano could only marvel at her courage in standing up to not only her inquisitor, but the nobles who had stood with him, even silencing her own grandmother. And she did all this with laughter.

"Now, it is true. I am of the black blood and I have duties to my people and our trade, but none of that precludes me from being a wife and mother. To be absolutely truthful, my mother married a *gadjé*, one of you. He is the Conte Patrin and he had me raised like his own daughter until my sister the *Araunya di Cayesmengro* was born, and then *we* were raised by him as his daughters. Our summers were spent with our mother's people, the black-blooded Romani. We learned the ways of the road and even some of the sedentary life. We were taught to love horses and bright colors and the folkways of our people. We learned about the silks and duty to our people on both sides. We have honor and obligations.

"The queen, as she was dying, gave me the responsibility of raising her children. If you need witnesses to this event, there is His Excellency, my husband, and the Court Herald right here. Others can be called to testify to the queen's desperate request. I accepted, and I have seen daily to the care of those children ever since. I was present at their birth and I, Duchessa di Drago *e Araunya di Cayesmengri e Cayesmengro*, took those children as a most sacred obligation. My being *Araunya* can only serve to protect them and widen their horizons a little about the people in their homeland." Luciana finished on a sigh and looked around the room at the gathering. "Is there more you would want to know?"

"Who truly has your fealty? Your people or the Crown?" Duca Anino asked. He, of all the Palantini, was the eldest still active at such gatherings, but more importantly he had placed his finger unerringly on the point of the problem.

Stefano chewed his lip, watching Luciana before him. She held very still. He prayed that she would not take too long to answer.

"A fair question, Your Grace. I am what I am. I am not ashamed of being Romani, but I married into *la famiglia reale* when I married His Grace, now His Excellency. He was the brother of the White Queen, and she, by relation of marriage and friendship, was my sister. I am now, first a mother of not just of the child to come, but of the five children of my *gadjé* sister. A mother must honor her children's needs before all, and should it ever come to a question between the two, I do not see that honoring one family must needs deny the other," Luciana replied with a gentle shrug.

Duca Anino leaned heavily on his cane, chin on his hands. After a moment, he nodded and looked at the *Beluni*. "What say you, *Madonna Grande*?"

"As my granddaughter has said, her priorities are her children . . . *the* children, and that is the way of our people. The children are gathered close and what goes to them is the first and best of the stew pot," the *Beluni* replied.

"Well, then," Augusto Sebastiani said with a heavy sigh. "It would seem that the Duchessa *e Araunya* has met all of my conditions. I say that she will be excellent in her new position; she has my 'Aye.' Does anyone second me?"

Along the vast length of the Throne Room, voices could

be heard raised in support, while still there were a couple of Nays.

Stefano moved Luciana to the side and took the lead position. "We have been seconded and, by my hearing, given at least a third and a fourth. The vote will be put before the Palantini," Stefano said.

Duca Scala rose to his feet again. "I think we might make our decision more freely if the Duchessa *e Araunya* was not present."

Stefano had half-formed the words of a response when Duchessa Rossi spoke. "Whatever safety you think that may give you, Filipo, then it is nothing more than a pretty pretense for your own mind. The Duchessa *e Araunya* will still have her grandmother and her husband—not to mention other allies—in the room to report whatever it is that you say. Better, is it not to have her present and be witness rather than risk having it misreported to her by accident or design from someone out to make mischief?"

"Then all of them should be put out of the room," Duca LaCosta suggested.

"I am just as much a member of this council as you, Your Grace. Why should my say not have as much weight as yours as it was meant to be?" the *Beluni* protested.

"Why? Because you aren't even one of us!" Scala snapped.

"Are you sure that you were educated as a child, or are you some fool that says whatever comes to mind without concern for the possible questions," the *Beluni* snapped. "Have you never heard of the Council of Queens wherein the Black and White Queens consult and negotiate for their peoples' common good? Something that guarantees my right to be here and speak my mind as openly and freely as anyone else in the Palantini? Or, are you so *ottuso* that—"

"*Beluni-Daiya*," Stefano interceded, "you are quite right about you and the *Araunya di Cayesmengri e Cayesmengro*, my duchessa, being part of the Palantini and having your say put on the balance sheet of the decision like every other member of this council. *Sí*, Scala? LaCosta? Tyrrhia is the one home the Romani have found that welcomes them and gives them their voice and, in turn, all Tyrrhia is made richer for it in the Gypsy Silk trade where no other country has even a hint of how to make it . . . and that includes even us, *gadjé*, of Tyrrhia."

"What does this word '*gadjé*' mean," young Duca Ugo Vivaldi—perhaps the youngest of all the gathered, having inherited his title, estates, and other responsibilities not much more than three months ago at the ripe old age of sixteen—asked.

Luciana leaned around her husband so that she could meet the gaze of the dark-haired youth. "'Tis no insult, Your Grace. Your people call us 'Gypsy' and we call others, especially, the white among you, '*gadjé*,' which means little more than 'white' and 'other.' The *Beluni* is the queen of our gathered people throughout Tyrrhia. It is a title no different than *Araunya*, or duca. You see?"

The lad smiled and nodded. "I understand now. Thank you and, as for me, I would second His Grace's decision to let the Romani women stay. They have as much right as anyone else in this Hall."

The stamping feet of most of the room's inhabitants signaled the general affirmation of the youth's new enlightenment. The boy's fair-skinned face turned beaming red at the attention and he sat down quickly, ducking his head.

To help ease the boy's embarrassment, Stefano cleared his throat twice, until he once more held the full attention of assemblage. "So. We take our moment of consideration and then we vote on whether my wife, as the queen clearly indicated was *her* choice, is suitable for the position as Royal Guardian." Here, Stefano gave the members of the Palantini a few moments of thought, before concluding with, "Well? Are there sufficient Ayes to carry the business of Royal Guardianship forward?" His words came out strong and purposeful, more of a command than a question, "Will the Ayes please signify your decision?"

The result of the stamping was enough to rattle the chandeliers overhead and sounded rather like the thundering hooves of a great many horses. There was a pocket of the room, along the wall and farthest from Stefano, that seemed relatively quiet, but he could not be sure. He raised his hand to hold the electors, when silence eventually fell, he took a deep breath, "Will those who vote Nay care to have further wishes known?"

At first, the reaction sounded just as loud, but faltered quickly. The chandelier above did not show even a small frisson of movement. Stefano took a quick look around the room, watching for those who voted Nay, knowing they would be his source of problems. In the back, Falluccaci used his cane as well as his feet—an illegal form of making a vote—LaCosta and Scala sat near one another also using their canes to help them vote. Calvino Anino, Silvieri, Calabria, and Rinaldi were amongst the last of the naysayers that he knew by name.

Estensi raised his hands. "The decision has been made. By a resounding vote of confidence. Luciana di Drago, Duchessa *e Araunya di Cayesmengri e Cayesmengro* is now Lady Guardian of *la famiglia reale-minore*."

There was a considerable number of stamping feet again, not as a vote, but as a celebration. Stefano kissed her hand and whispered for her ears only, "We're in the thick of it now, *camómescro*."

"Since there is clear approval for both and we have more than the quorum required, I suggest moving directly to coronation," Estensi said, looking back at Stefano as he spoke to the crowd.

"Coronation?" Luciana whispered. She was not alone in being surprised at that.

Estensi held up his hands, quieting the room. "I do not suggest we are actually going to crown them. Crowns are suitable for the intended king and queen only, but one can't very well say that we are chaining them!"

Stefano sat forward, intent on reassuring Luciana, but relaxed at Estensi's statement. The Duchi of the Palantini also seemed mollified, and quieted; some even laughed.

Hearing no further protest, Estensi went to a nearby table and opened two oaken boxes. From the boxes, the Court Herald took first a golden, jeweled chain—a thick, heavy thing—and then from the other box a second chain, lighter, slightly less jeweled, but nearly as heavy judging by the way Estensi's arm dipped under the weight. Setting his staff on the table, Estensi took the chains in either hand and held them up for the Palantini to see, then turned to Stefano and Luciana. He beckoned Stefano forward first. "Take a knee, Your Grace."

Stefano dropped to one knee, looking up at the Court Herald expectantly.

"Having been so named by King Alban and Queen Idala, and confirmed by the Palantini, do you, Duca Stefano di Drago, Colonello of the Escalade, accept the commission and mission of Lord Regent for all of Tyrrhia and surrounding islands and territories? Do you swear to hold trust with Alban and Idala, to raise their heirs to majority and, at that point, yield the throne to furthermore serve the kingdom as the Heir Apparent requests and otherwise turn your sole focus upon raising the younger children to their majority?" Estensi asked.

"I so swear," Stefano said, hand over his heart. He bent his head and felt the weight of his new offices rest heavy on his shoulders.

Estensi then motioned for Luciana to step forward, but stopped her from kneeling. "I think, considering your . . . your health at this time that placing a hand on your husband's shoulder will serve as sufficient, Your Grace."

Luciana rested her right hand on Stefano's shoulder and waited.

"Having been so named by Queen Idala and confirmed by the Palantini, do you, Duchessa Luciana di Drago, *Araunya* of both Gypsy Silk houses, accept the commission and mission of Lady Guardian for all of Tyrrhia's royal children, both the Heir and his siblings? Do you swear to hold trust with King Alban and Queen Idala, to raise their Heir to majority and, at that point, to serve the kingdom as the Heir requests and to otherwise turn your sole focus upon raising the younger children to their majority?" Estensi asked.

Luciana hesitated, glancing at her grandmother who pointedly turned away and stared at the colors in the stained-glass windows. Stefano felt his wife nod and then find her words. "I so swear."

He took her hand in his when she bent for the Court Herald to place the more delicate of the two chains around her neck.

"You may rise, Your Excellency, and stand with Her Excellency," Estensi said. When Stefano rose, the Court Herald continued. "You both understand that the weight of these chains of office, is like Tyrrhia and her children? Ever present and a continual reminder of the solemn oaths you have made here today?"

"We do," Stefano said confidently, his free right hand touching the collar newly placed around his neck. Luciana murmured her assent and nodded, glancing at her husband, her eyes round and wide from the enormity of their undertaking.

"Lord and Lady Regent, I present you to the Palantini, your Royal Council," Estensi concluded.

Duca Sebastiani and Duchessa Rossi were the first to stand, clapping and stamping. The rest of the occupants of the room rose, clapping. When the congratulatory salutes finally began to wane, Stefano escorted his wife back to her seat before turning to the gathering and motioning them to sit.

"Next comes something that I am loath to bring up and would not if I believed it fair for the council to be ignorant of the matter," Stefano said. "So I ask you to sit and listen, for I must tell you of a queen so desperate to do what was right for her country and king that she turned to folly," Stefano began and then—slowly, painfully—he retold the substance of his sister's story. He laid bare her crimes against the State in her use of magic that cut short her young life and set a course of madness resulting with the cardinal's rebirth through Queen Idala's twisted newborn son.

"You expect us to believe that the cardinal—" Falluccaci began, but was interrupted by old Duca Calvino Anino.

"Forget the cardinal for a moment! There are questions about the queen that must be asked first. Most particularly, how dare she cast magic against *la famiglia reale*! She must have known it was forbidden . . . a seditious act for which she deserves . . . deserved to see trial."

"Who helped her? She couldn't have done this on her own," Scala demanded, looking suspiciously at the Romani Queen and her granddaughter.

Luciana waved her hands to silence the hubbub that arose from Scala's question. She frowned at Stefano and, when the noise died down, said, "As you well know, I was in my husband's country estate, Dragorione, when the queen announced her pregnancy. I must confess, however, that my little sister, the *Araunya minore* served as the queen's aide in the casting of the spell so that it affected not just *la famiglia reale*, but the entire country . . . all of Tyrrhia was meant to grow more fertile and the land to profit, prosper, and grow. Have you not wondered how your wives became pregnant . . . well, became pregnant so easily and some at a great age? Or those who were previously considered barren?"

Duca Antonelli rose from his seat, "So you're saying that I can thank my new son off my wife—loved, but previously without children and at the great age of fifty-two—because of the queen's spell? And your sister's aid? Why would the queen do this? It nearly killed my Raquel! What were they thinking?"

The *Beluni* stood and stamped her staff for attention. She looked first at Antonelli and then the men in the rest of the room. "Are you not happy with your children? Some of you now have heirs of your own making instead of some brother or sister's child. Never mind if this child is your first or your tenth, do you not rejoice in them? Tell me you do not, and I'll have a clansman who'll gladly take your child and raise it as his own."

That stirred the pot, Stefano thought, before calling for silence. On his second call, the men finally fell into some reasonable proximity of quiet. "The *Beluni* was not serious. She only meant—"

"Oh, but I was," the *Beluni* interrupted. "We appreciate our children, even the new children of my clans based upon the spell of the White Queen and my dead granddaughter. Now, if this yammer is done, Your Excellency, I beg you to continue." She retook her chair, as graceful as a fairy, and as poised as any queen. She continued to scan the room as though seeking one who would take her up on her offer.

"Thank you for your point, *Beluni*," Stefano said. "And she does make the point, good gentles, that many of you are blessed now with children you might never have had."

"But that excuses neither the White Queen nor the *Araunya minore*," Scala pressed.

"Both the queen and my sister have died because of that spell! Is that not enough punishment?" Luciana asked. Her fingers worried the edges of her lace kerchief. Stefano had to take her hands in his so that he could keep her from destroying the pretty bit of linen. He had brought a set of them back from the Peloponnesian War. Out of a dozen, she was left now with only two.

"The queen didn't die of her spell, it was—" *il dottore* Bonta began.

"Oh, but she did! Unbeknownst by her, when she opened

herself up to the spell, she was already *incinta*, so one child became two. Within a short time of her casting the spell, the cardinal was fighting a mortal fight with an immortal foe, so he cast the spell to be risen once again, and the foe was dragged along in the swirling currents of the cardinal's magic," Luciana responded. "The birthing of four children is what killed her. She had that many children because of the spell she and my sister cast. Her spell made her vulnerable enough to receive the cardinal and his foe."

The men began arguing amongst themselves—many because they were having trouble believing, but it died down quickly when Antonelli, still standing, cleared his throat. "Tell me, *Araunya*, how did your sister die that she could be considered having been punished for her crimes, because it would affect the queen?"

"As some of you may remember about the *Araunya minore*, she was prone to taking up the cause of the suffering. She was convinced—in part, by the queen—that this was Queen Idala's cause and she took foolish steps to aid the White Queen in her pursuit of giving Alban another heir," Luciana explained.

She raised her right hand to regain the company's attention after they broke into bickering amongst themselves again. The uproar of the crowd did not dissipate even slightly until Estensi, the Court Herald, seeing Luciana's plight, stamped his staff and called for order.

When the nobles fell silent, and those that had stood in the course of their argument took their seats, Luciana began again. "You asked how my sister paid for her crimes, then let me speak to that. There was a conspiracy for the throne afoot."

Beside her, Stefano fidgeted in his seat. He had hoped they could avoid this topic and prayed fervently that Luciana did not wander too near her own crimes in the telling of this story.

"My sister discovered the accomplices and followed them. Her affianced was Maggiore Mandero di Montago of the Queen's Escalade, and she planned to tell him when he returned from his assignment— "

"And how do you know these things if you were at Dragorione?" Silvieri scoffed.

"She sent me letters regularly. Her last letter spoke of

this . . . it came in a delivery pouch along with Queen Idala's letter telling me that the *Araunya minore* was dead. In her last missive, she spoke of the traitorous alliance and her plan to see the maggiore at the earliest possible moment. She told me nothing of the conspirators for fear her letter might fall into the wrong hands or somehow put me in danger," Luciana said. "After receiving those letters, I decided to come to court, if for no other reason than to see our burial customs followed. Of course, I also could not allow the traitors to continue plotting against Tyrrhia nor her king and queen.

"My first order of business was to claim my sister's body and, though the queen was kind enough to bury her in a royal crypt, I discovered the body had been removed. A sorcerer had my sister's body extracted and taken to use to amplify his magic."

"Did you find the traitors? Who were they?" Sebastiani demanded. "Were they punished for their misdeeds?"

"There were three parties involved . . . as far as I *know* . . . Conte Urbano di Vega, the Cardinal delle Torre—who was then a bishop—and, alas, Princess Bianca."

"Not so!" Silvieri cried out, jumping to his feet.

"Careful, Duca Silvieri, or some among us may leap to the conclusion that the only way you could know for sure about the princess was by being involved in the confederacy yourself. Listen, and Her Grace will tell all," Estensi said. He turned to Luciana and nodded for her to continue.

"After discovering the intrigue for myself, it became easy for me to spy on them. I, personally, witnessed the three of them together on several occasions. Let us not forget that Bianca wanted the throne for herself . . . like her sister . . . I followed them one night going down into the oubliette, across the cavern bridge and from there to another hollowed-out room. I listened to them plotting to take the throne by foul means or force, and they seemed confident that they had the resources for either option.

"I also discovered, in the deepest ends of the great cavern, that it was Princess Bianca who ordered my sister's death and that the cardinal had my sister's body taken to use her like any other tool until her soul was spent. My sister did many things she shouldn't have, but she did so with a pure and open heart and a sincere belief in and love for Tyrrhia. She did not deserve to be . . ." Luciana paused to collect herself before going on. Stefano rested his hand on her arm. She was coming damn close to revealing her own crimes against the State. "Whatever her faults, my sister did not need to be abused in such a way. The cardinal escaped with the *Araunya minore*'s body. It was the maggiore and his men who discovered the cardinal's trail and, eventually, rescued my sister and performed the burial rituals, though the maggiore was lost in the resulting conflagration."

"I cannot help but notice that the three 'collaborators' are all dead now and, therefore, can't defend themselves. Conte di Vega died of some bile obstruction according to *il dottore* Bonta. The cardinal died at the hands of the maggiore—"

"No, neither the maggiore nor any of his men were responsible for the cardinal's death. My sister's *mulló* and that of another Roma he was violating rose up against him. It was the *mulló* of the second Roma who was dragged into the womb of the White Queen," Luciana insisted.

"We will get back to the children in a moment. Say I concede the point that the cardinal was some sort of sorcerer who enjoyed torturing the Romani—which I am not convinced of—by the way, why would he have reason to conspire against the Crown?" Silvieri asked.

"I can only surmise that he did it for the power and prestige he would gain when Bianca took the throne. He might have hoped to bring Tyrrhia solely under the Catholic religion . . . but these are only guesses. I did not know the man's heart, so I, honestly, cannot speak to it," Luciana replied, her tone barely hinting at her impatience.

Stefano realized that Silvieri was straying closer and closer in his questioning to Luciana's crimes.

"Then what of the Princess Bianca? You owed her a vendetta of blood. She, we know unequivocally, was poisoned, we know not how, but she was definitely poisoned. What say you to that, Your Grace?" Scala asked.

"Though I was not present, I have heard the results of the inquiry into Princess Bianca's death and, I'm afraid, that I agree with their findings," Luciana said, licking her lips nervously. "I believe she was poisoned, and I also believe that my sister's *mulló* came after her at the wedding. I saw that with my own eyes."

"You did?" Scala laughed. "I was at the wedding and saw no such thing."

"*Mullós* are particular to the Romani and so are seen by the Romani. There are exceptions, of course, a great sorcerer or someone attuned to death and the dying, will see it," the *Beluni* said. She paused. "I can assume, Your Grace, that you are neither a sorcerer nor an apprentice, nor are overly familiar with the dead and dying?"

"You can make that assumption, Madonna. I have no truck with witchcraft . . . unlike some of the others here," Scala said. He glanced around the room at the *Beluni*, then to the *Araunya* and, finally, to Stefano in an accusatory fashion. "I mark for the record that you have not replied about the Princess Bianca."

Stefano started to stand, but Luciana sidestepped in front of him so that he was forced to remain in his chair. He fumed against Scala and Silvieri. She glanced back at him, her eyes narrowed as she gave a slight shake of her head. Stefano understood. Luciana was going to risk it all. Even though a trial seemed ever closer, she wanted to answer these questions. She bit her bottom lip, then licked her lips before turning to face her accuser.

"I believe the princess was poisoned and that weakened her enough that my sister's *mulló* could strike back at her murderer, so Bianca's death was twofold. As to poisoning Her Highness, *I* did not poison her. I do note that Pierro deMedici brought a 'perfumer' with him to our court who turned out to be a notorious poisoner on the continent."

"You dare suggest that the prince had his own wife—barely married—murdered?" Scala gasped.

"I said nothing of the kind," Luciana said. "I merely mentioned a fact. The man—the perfumer—nearly killed my husband and me with envenomed glasses of wine, and not long after he was forced out of Tyrrhia altogether, it is believed he attempted to assassinate King Alban last spring. Perhaps he lashed out at his employer. I do not know," Luciana stated with a shrug.

Stefano was glad that she stood in front of him because he found it difficult to completely mask his surprise. He knew his wife well enough that she rarely, if ever, lied outright, though she was known by him to prevaricate, telling shades of truth. But how could she make such a bald-faced, outright lie in front of the Palantini? He would have to speak to her at his earliest possible convenience since lying to the Palantini when bearing witness was another way to bring about a trial. She would lose her position and standing in the Palantini and would be expelled from court—at the very least. He wiped a hand over his eyes, trying to quickly regain his composure and hoped no one noticed.

Luciana took the opportunity to sit down. Her hands were shaking slightly. Stefano, in the hubbub of others discussing Luciana's testimony, leaned closer to her. "I cannot believe you took the risk of lying to these men!"

"And women . . . there may be only three of us, but we *are* here," Luciana said, as easily as she might correct a child's grammar.

"Lucia!" Stefano hissed. "You know very well what I mean. You can't lie to this assembly without expecting consequences."

She turned in her chair to face him. "How exactly did I lie, Stefano?"

"How?" Stefano whispered in outrage. "You told them you didn't poison Bianca, for one."

Luciana turned her head and smiled at someone in the audience. "Well, in actuality, *I* didn't poison her. I merely provided the toxin to the Guild and someone—I know not who—administered it to her wedding dress."

"And what of suggesting that Pierro or his man did the deed?" Stefano asked.

"Merely a little misdirection. It was all perfectly plausible, and I did not say that he did, merely that he could have done it. Tell me that's not true," Luciana responded quietly, meeting her husband eye to eye. "I really have no compunction about causing the deMedicis' a little bit of trouble. They cause enough for everyone else. Besides, they'll never be able to prove—" Luciana stopped when Estensi came forward, clearing his throat.

"We should begin again, Your Excellency. I think our earlier topic has run its course and that we can safely move on to a discussion of the children," Estensi said. "Shall I start, then, Your Excellency?"

Stefano nodded his head as the Court Herald's back was being turned, he looked at his wife with a frown and shook his head. "I love you, Lucia, but we really must discuss this further." He rose at the sound of his name being called by Estensi.

"Now that that discussion is concluded, let us move on to the children," Stefano said. He pretended not to hear the grumbling among the faction of Ortensia's followers and pressed on. "There is the matter of young Massimo that needs the lion's share of this discourse, because he is the cardinal incarnate."

"You don't believe like your wife does, do you?" LaCosta protested. "You have always been an intellectual and above superstition."

"A superstitious mind is not likely to overlook the possibilities that are otherwise unexplainable," Gianola growled.

Duchessa Rossi put a steadying hand on the slightly older man's arm. She leaned toward him in a conspiratorial manner and whispered something which made the duca laugh, his rheumy brown eyes sparkling with humor. The middle-aged duca smiled and said, "Please, Your Excellency, pray continue. You have our attention."

"Very well, then," Stefano replied with a nod. "The youngest prince, Massimo, whom we believe to be the cardinal incarnate, will not—by decree of his parents—stand in line for the throne. There is something about the boy that is unnerving to even the most stalwart souls. It cannot be easily explained, but there is definitely something not right about him.

"I've been given the advice to kill the child instead of raising him here at the palazzo. We have his cradle in a different room from his sisters with a separate wet nurse dedicated to tending his needs," Stefano explained.

"Why is he not with the girls?" Duchessa Rossi asked. "I would think they would all be kept together at this age."

Luciana leaned forward in her chair, just enough for Stefano to see her face out of the corner of his eye. He nodded for her to continue as she now was the Lady Guardian and this was her area of knowledge. "The queen was upset by his presence—his uncanny laughter and misshapen form. She, Queen Idala, wanted nothing of or for the boy. The king insisted that the boy stay with his sisters for the few days after their birth . . . thinking that proximity might overcome her intense dislike for the boy, but it did not. Her first order as queen was to have Massimo taken to another room. In the king's chambers, the little prince can only upset his wet nurse. Even as a babe, he is a destructive force."

"You can't be serious!" Silvieri protested. "This is a small child being treated like evil incarnate."

Luciana looked up at Stefano, "Perhaps it is best to show them."

Stefano took a deep breath, studying his wife, and then looked around the room at the curious bystanders. Reluctantly, he nodded. "I will take only five, maybe six, to the child's room. We do not want to distress him overly. Who wants to see the young prince for themselves?"

Immediately, there was a show of hands. Most of the Palantini wanted to see the boy. Stefano shook his head, "There must be only six—at the very most. Choose your emissaries and meet me in the corridor five minutes after our meeting adjourns. Your Grace, Sebastiani, you have seen the boy on a number of occasions already. I ask that you sit out this time and testify to what you have seen before when we reconvene?"

Stefano bowed to Estensi, little more than a jerk of his head, and waved for the Court Herald to continue, which he did.

"And now, the question of His Majesty's circumstances before and after he was deceased. At the point of his death, His Royal Majesty, King Alban, appointed the Duca di Drago Regent Guardian of his children and adviser to his wife and queen, Idala. The usual witnesses were not available due to the conditions of his death, though the Royal Physician can testify that King Alban is dead," Estensi said, motioning to the man sitting amongst the audience.

Il dottore Bonta rose from his chair, adjusting his jacket nervously. "I testify before this gathering of the Royal Council of the Palantini that I have examined the body of His Majesty. I duly report his death by foul methods. A bolt, fired by crossbow or, possibly, even a scorpinini, found its way to his heart. King Alban is dead. His body has been laid out for viewing in the Catholic Church on the royal grounds.

"I further testify that Queen Idala passed from our grasp due to complications of childbirth. I cannot determine the truth of Her Excellency that magic was involved, but excess of childbirth ended her days. Queen Idala is dead. Her body rests beside her husband's." The little doctor bowed and returned to his seat looking flushed and uncomfortable.

"Are there testimonials to the circumstances of death?" Estensi asked.

Duca Sebastiani rose, hopping on his right foot—his left, looking worse than normal in its swaddling of bandages. He leaned heavily on a cane. "I bear witness to the death of King Alban. I was there when he fell."

Strozzini, standing behind Stefano's chair, came forward. "I bear witness to the murder of King Alban."

Stefano rose, nodding. "I bear witness."

After a long pause, Estensi coughed and looked pointedly at the deMedicis' empty seats. "I believe there was one more witness."

Apparently not wanting to give the lack of one testimony any room for substance, Sebastiani hoisted himself to his feet again. "I further bear witness to the ill circumstances, that the king was murdered by an assassin or assassins unknown. In his final words, His Majesty named Duca Stefano di Drago as Regent Guardian for his family and, furthermore, that His Highness Pierro deMedici was an unwelcome though *active* participant in the day's events." Duca Sebastiani turned, looking at the crowd. "I stand ready for questioning."

Strozzini nodded. "I, too, stand ready for questioning."

In that short time, Duca Sebastiani's face turned something nearing the color of eggplant while waiting for the questions he had invited. Stefano surmised his problem was his foot and the pain it caused him. He folded his hands behind his back. "I, too, bear witness and stand ready for questioning and, if I may suggest, in the matter of these proceedings that Duca Sebastiani take a seat until there is a question he might answer more directly than the rest of us?"

Estensi nodded immediately and waved for the older man to take his seat. Stefano, catching the appreciative look of Sebastiani, also noted the opening of the doors and

Pierro deMedici stealing back into the room. The Court Herald also noted Pierro's arrival and beckoned to the prince, who ventured boldly forward to take his seat.

Stefano stomached the man's prancing walk because, at least, now the fool could testify. "Prince Pierro, there has just been a call for witnesses of King Alban's death. Your absence was noted at the time, but now that you are here, perhaps you could witness before this assembly?"

Pierro demurred prettily.

Estensi glowered at the man. "Perhaps Prince deMedici does not understand that this is *not* a request, but a formal demand that, as a witness, he cannot deny . . . especially since he is *la famiglia reale*?"

Pierro contorted his mouth, but rose, leaning on his long, decorative cane. "Forgive me, I am still somewhat new to your customs." He smiled winningly at the audience and then, more somberly, said, "Then I, too, will stand as witness to the death of the king. I even concur that his death was caused by ill means. Other than that, I have nothing to say." He sat down, ignoring Estensi's thunderous look and the murmur of the courtiers.

Sebastiani stamped his cane, whether it was a comment upon the prince's behavior or not, Stefano could not be sure. One thing he did know, however, was that the prince did little for his cause by offending those around him.

The only response he received from His Highness was a brief, dismissive wave of his hand. Apparently, Pierro had already assessed Sebastiani's political leanings and did not seem to account for any further love that could be lost on that front.

A couple of hands from the Palantini raised and, when acknowledged by the Court Herald, Duca Raffia rose. "My question is to *all* who bore witness. . . . There has been no real sign, no hint who might have conspired against *the throne* and taken our king? Even now?"

A murmur of approval for the question rose from the audience and many raised hands fell. As the senior member of the court, Stefano motioned for Lord Strozzini to make his report. There was little to hide at this point.

Strozzini crossed his arms behind him and widened his stance somewhat. It was a military custom that Stefano recognized with ease. The king's bodyguard—and now, officially, his—chewed his upper lip, bowing his head before looking up and addressing those present. "His Majesty, King Alban, died in front of me, slain by the crossbow bolt of an assassin. Only a single arrow was shot, so there could only have been one assassin, but this does not mean there weren't others, waiting at the edges of the forest.

"After the king fell, I made my way through the stream and the narrow strip of woods on the other side where the bolt had come from and searched the area immediately and then, again, later with a contingent of the Escalade. I found a small encampment for two—possibly three—*manigaldo*. The campfire was still warm when first I visited the campsite—"

Stefano straightened his stance. "I was with him, as well as Duca Sebastiani, and Prince Pierro deMedici. Most of us had planned on taking the ride to one of the king's favorite places not far from the palazzo. Prince Pierro joined us at the last minute."

"Is that so?" Duca Gianola queried. He turned to Pierro deMedici. "And would this be the very day, reportedly, that you ran through the halls of the palazzo declaring your bride to be the new queen? And that was the way so many discovered the death of our king?"

Pierro smiled tightly and gravitated to his feet, rolling his pretty, shoulder-height cane's knob around in his palm. He paused for the affirmations from several members of the Palantini that Gianola had the right of it. Pierro adjusted the cravat at his throat with his left hand, his right still resting on the cane. He gave a pretentious little laugh, patting the cravat. "I must confess that my concern for my wife might have led me somewhat astray."

"Concern for your wife?" Augusto Sebastiani blurted out angrily, stamping his own cane on the floor. "You mean you were more concerned with her position in court and through her, yours, *Signore* deMedici."

"My wife is due her status of Heir Apparent, if not the throne," Pierro responded heatedly. Stefano noted the change in the deMedici position and it gave him no pleasure.

"But that has already been decided and we'll not revisit it," Estensi said. "Gentlemen, please! This *is* an information gathering process. Personal asides—"

"Could it have been Gypsies?" someone called out from the center of the room.

"Who said that?" Estensi demanded, stamping his staff on the floor for order when a rumble rose from the crowd. "Please stand when you question the witnesses!" When no one stood, the Court Herald sighed and turned toward Rodrigo Strozzini and Stefano. "Please continue, Lord Strozzini," he said and turned back to watch the attending, waiting for further outbursts, no doubt.

Luciana rose. "I am *Araunya di Cayesmengri e Cayesmengro*. I speak for the black-blooded brothers and sisters of Tyrrhia. *I* testify that no Romani of true black blood would strike at the White Crown. King Alban and Queen Idala were . . . loved . . . by my people, for their enlightenment and tolerance. If a black hand struck the king, then *I* will exact justice in the name of all Tyrrhia, including my kindred. I curse them!" She spat upon the floor. "I stand ready for questioning."

"That's not necessary at this time, Duchessa *e Araunya*, and now, Your Excellency," Estensi replied, glancing first at Stefano for approval. "The question clearly came from a source who dare not declare himself and is not educated in the way of your people."

"Thank you, Lord Estensi," Luciana said and sat back down in her chair, conscious of His Highness' dark look at her.

Lord Strozzini looked irked. "There were no sign of Gypsies—of the Romani. The camp was very simple. No indication of *vardos* or wagons or of the distinctive tents they build of any sort marked the ground or surrounding wood. Someone . . . some persons lay in wait and, eventually, escaped. I have, however, examined the bolt that struck our king. It bears the brand of a . . . a cult known as *Magnus Inique*. Surely no Gyp—no Rom would be party to this group."

"*Basta*! There is no such mark! Why do you choose to blame this group of the Church which some of us in the court know has nothing more to do with anything but faithful men living in opposition to the use of magic?" Prince Pierro, erupted from his chair to protest.

"*Magnus Inique*—'by hammer and fire'—is no friend of Tyrrhia . . . nor even you, Prince deMedici, for you, like so many others among us wear the Gypsy Silk," Strozzini retorted.

Pierro started to respond but was silenced by Estensi. Angrily, deMedici sat.

"Lord Strozzini has begun a full inquest into the king's death. Perhaps this marked bolt is nothing more than a bit of theatrics as you might have suggested," Estensi said, after stamping his staff for silence. "Pray, Lord Strozzini, as the king's bodyguard, you may continue."

Strozzini nodded, returning to his military stance. "Alas, there is little more that can be said . . . at least at this time. I and the vigilare search for new information, and anyone having it should come to me. I seek someone who can speak for *Magnus Inique*—a member, preferably—who might confirm what the group is, stands for, and whether they are involved or not." He chewed his upper lip—the edge of his mustache—and added. "I was present at the king's actual death and he, though dying, was of even mind, not intemperate from anger or fever. He, indeed, left the Duca di Drago as his Regent Guardian and spoke of his love for Tyrrhia and his wife before he passed from our presence."

"Thank you, Lord Strozzini. Are there any more questions from the gallery?" Estensi asked, watching those gathered for raised hands or some other signal that they wished to speak. When no one moved, the Court Herald stamped his staff. "Here closes the testimony concerning our king. We must now call for the witnesses to Her Royal Majesty, Queen Idala's death. Witnesses?"

Stefano waited for Strozzini to return to his post behind him and offered Luciana his hand. She stood at his side. Giuletta appeared from the back of the room, her voice breaking as she bore witness and stated that she was ready for questions.

"I note, for the record, that I, in my capacity as Court Herald, did officially witness the death of Her Majesty. Not present today are her babes-in-arms, their wet nurses, the midwife and the . . . the old woman as none of them are members of court. I also note that Giuletta Ferrigno, while not titled or a member of the Palantini, is of noble blood and was the queen's near constant companion. The Royal Physician, *il dottore* Bonta, was present as well. *Dottore*?"

The doctor rose from his chair again looking slightly

flustered. "The queen, Her Majesty, Queen Idala, was being treated for complications after the birth of the four new heirs. Her humors were badly out of balance . . . she was excessively sanguine . . . bleedings, feedings, and applications of cool compresses did not seem to assist her. In the end, while she had a fever, it was only slight, and she was of temperate mind and mood."

"Thank you, and can you testify to Her final words . . . at that time?" Estensi asked solemnly.

"She named the Duchessa *e Araunya* di Drago as Regent Guardian for her children. She spoke largely of her children . . . and Tyrrhia. She wanted the Duca di Drago, her brother, to stand as regent until the Heir Apparent is of age."

Discussion—bold and frank—of his sister's death tore at Stefano's gut which was a stew of conflict, yet he held his ground, ready to bear witness if it was called for.

"Does anyone require testimony to Queen Idala's passing?" Estensi asked. No one spoke, so he arched a brow at the deMedici. When Pierro did not even deign to meet the Court Herald's gaze, Estensi nodded and stamped his staff. "So be it. The agenda has been completed and so closes this final court of King Alban and Queen Idala. Our next formal meeting will be the first court of the Lord and Lady Regents, Stefano and Luciana, to be held on the morrow. I remind those here present, you must still decide among you who will represent the Palantini in the viewing of His Highness, Prince Massimo, and those appointees to appear in the corridor beyond these doors."

Stefano sagged momentarily against the back of his chair. He allowed himself the brief time to just relax, which he found impossible. He straightened, took his wife's hand, kissed her palm, and stood up. He could feel the almost oppressive weight of the chain reminding him of the solemnity of his new office. He touched the vast diamond in the centerpiece, allowing the chain to fall naturally. Luciana held out her hand to him. Taking it, he helped her from her chair. She smiled at him, her hand going to her own, thinner collar.

Behind him, Stefano heard Estensi stamp his staff and command, "All hail the Lord Regent and the Regent Guardian!"

The Duchi of the Palantini rose to their feet and cheered.

The noise of it echoed from the voices outside the Throne Room and in the corridors beyond as the Palazzo Guards threw open the doors.

Stefano, still holding Luciana's hand, turned to face the audience again. He felt exhausted from the meeting and yet the sense of power could not be denied. He bowed and held onto Luciana as she made an awkward curtsy. "Shall we go?" he asked as quietly as the unfolding events allowed.

Luciana nodded, apparently almost as eager as he felt to break free of the attention, yet knowing that he would not be disentangled of it or responsibility for the ten years it would take to bring up the Heir Apparent and five more years beyond that to finish raising Dario's new sisters and brother. Luciana leaned close to him, "Before the Palantini views Massimo, I must speak with my grandmother. It will be just a moment!" Then she darted away from him toward the back of the Throne Room to where the *Beluni* had been sitting.

XIV

"Slowly but surely withal moveth the might of the gods."

—Euripides

DONNA della Guelfa worried the edge of her apron, looking at the people gathered in the queen's old reception room. "We've just laid the girls down, *Araunya*," she said, a worried frown working its way across her face.

Estensi stepped from the pool of people and bowed slightly to the midwife. "*Pardone,* Signora, but to be accurate, the *Araunya* is now Lady Guardian and, therefore, addressed as 'Your Excellency.' "

Maria blinked and looked owlishly to Luciana for guidance.

"Never mind that just now. I understand, Maria," Luciana said, patting the other woman's ample arm. "But this could not be helped. These men and the duchessa just want to look at the babies."

Looking at the grim-faced nobles, Maria della Guelfa seemed even more agitated.

"You've heard the children's nurse. The girls have been put down for their midmorning nap. We don't want to disturb the children any more than necessary, so come along quietly and wait until we are downstairs again before we discuss anything that you have seen. Is that fair?" Luciana requested.

With some grumbling, the men agreed. Duchessa Rossi merely nodded her consent.

"Lead the way," Luciana bid Signora della Guelfa.

With a heavy sigh, the woman turned and led Luciana and Stefano up the stairs. Duchessa Rossi followed right behind them and was followed, in turn, by the *Duchi* Gianola, Antonelli, di Candido, LaCosta, and Silvieri.

In the queen's room, they seemed to be surprised not to find her bed, only seven cradles and three women sitting in a circle either knitting, doing needlework, or caring for their own young ones, chatting quietly among themselves. The women's talk died into a nervous silence when the nobles entered the room. Luciana waved them back into their seats when they would have risen to curtsy. Maria went to stand with the common women and watched the nobles like a hawk.

Luciana watched the gentlefolk file to the first crib. Only Duchessa Rossi acknowledged these women who kept the precious royals alive and she with a nod and a smile. Stefano moved to the head of the cradle between the twins. Luciana waited with the women while Stefano made the introductions in a soft voice. Quiet as he was, the deep timbre in Stefano's voice caused one of the wet nurse's children to stir in her simple cradle.

After duly inspecting the twins and making barely audible observations to one another, the gentles moved to the last royal crib and were surprised.

"Her hair is so dark, so thick compared to that of her sisters," LaCosta said. "Except for the white streak in her hair. Where did that come from?"

"She looks like she could be your daughter," Duchessa Rossi commented.

"Chiara is the child we told you was once a *mulló* and fought the cardinal. She was Romani and now reborn of a *gadjé*, she is half-caste. A Child of the Bloods, as we say. The white streak of hair marks her birth-right," Luciana explained.

"Then will your child have a streak in their hair as well?" Silvieri demanded, a little too loudly.

One of the princesses let out a soft cry and began to fuss. Maria moved quickly to the child's crib, unable or unwilling to hide her glower at Silvieri.

"Each child is marked differently," Luciana said, looking at Maria handing the princess to one of the wet nurses.

"How do we know you won't exchange the babies?" Silvieri asked.

Stefano took a deep breath. "Well, Signore, now that you have seen her, that would not be possible, would it? Of course, I will assume that you were asking a theoretical question and not impugning either my or my wife's honor and oaths which would make it a personal matter."

"If Her Excellency gives birth to a boy, then it'd be obvious the difference. If she births another girl . . . trust me, these fine young mothers would be able to tell the difference. And shame on you for even thinking—" Maria della Guelfa scolded the nobleman.

"That will be sufficient," Luciana said, gently nudging the midwife's shoulder. "You've made him understand."

"It's been testified to by His Excellency and the midwife who brought them into the world, Peppino," Duchessa Rossi said, keeping her voice low and soft. "I think we can believe them. The children will all be raised together as one brood. And, furthermore, I agree with the midwife. The wet nurses would note some particular difference between two girls."

"And *I* would know the difference," Stefano said. "I'll have seen both girls within moments of birth. To question if there might be an exchange of some sort is a direct question to my and my wife's honor . . . a point I'm willing to cross swords over."

Silvieri raised his hands in submission, shrugging. "I meant no harm."

"Don't worry, Your Grace, we know exactly what you meant," Luciana reassured him with a thin, angry smile. She nodded to Chiara who had begun to wriggle in her crib. "Shall we move to the hallway and then see Massimo?"

Before Silvieri or anyone else could protest, Luciana and Maria della Guelfa ushered them from the room and into the landing on the stair that connected Idala's bedroom to Alban's. Here, Stefano stopped rather abruptly and turned on Silvieri.

"There are only so many times a man may insult me or my family before I am forced to take action. Do I make myself understood, Duca Silvieri?" Stefano demanded, cornering the man in the small area. "I am a man of action, not just simple politics and this is no game that I play. I am *deadly* serious that those princesses be raised in the manner they should be so that they will be a credit to Tyrrhia. My child, too, will be instilled with the same lessons."

Silvieri, finding himself in the corner of the cubicle with Stefano's forearm across his throat, nodded. "Please forgive me. I have caused offense where none was intended."

"Then let us move on to the young prince, shall we?" Stefano said, scratching at the door briefly before turning the handle to Alban's bedroom door and leading the way in.

Bringing up the rear, Luciana was surprised when Duchessa Rossi leaned close to the still cornered Silvieri. "I wouldn't push the Lord Regent far. I understand he is a formidable swordsman and not a man to be lightly quarreled with."

Silvieri nodded, obviously shaken. He gestured for Luciana and Maria to go before him, but Luciana was firm that he should go first. "You have testimony to give. *We* know what we will find beyond the door."

The duca nodded and, slowly, hesitantly, made his way into the room. Luciana and Maria followed him in and closed the door behind themselves.

"And this child is kept separate from the others because—?" LaCosta asked, without even looking into the cradle.

"He disturbs the other babies and makes the women nervous. Only Bonita Boniface, here, has a way with the boy," Maria answered.

"He's merely an infant, what could he do—" Gianola asked, also avoiding looking in the crib.

A breeze swept up, seemingly from nowhere in particular, and began to swirl around the room, building to a storm-force mistral.

"Close the window!" Shielding her face, Duchessa Rossi called to the wet nurse, Bonita.

"It is closed, Signora," Bonita said. She came over to the crib and lifted Massimo up into her arms gently, holding him close. Only then did then wind die down and the room settle to some sort of normalcy. "The child wanted attention, that's all." She cooed to the infant and rocked him while also deftly checking his swaddling to see if it was dry. She clucked to the child and laid him back in the cradle, reaching for fresh swaddling.

"*He* did this? When he wanted attention?" Silvieri said, crossing himself automatically. The other members of the Palantini also crossed themselves and looked to Luciana for an explanation.

"He is a newborn and yet he already has a way with magic. When he is housed with the girls, he . . . is not happy and when he is not, then everyone is aware of it," Luciana explained. "The child has a laugh that will turn your hearts to stone. It is so cold, so—"

"But children this age don't laugh," Gianola protested. "I have ten . . . eleven children, and I never once have heard them laugh until they were a few months old. He is but a matter of a week. Perhaps you are all creating drama where there truly is none?"

Luciana shook her head firmly. "The drama is with the boy and with him only," she said. "He laughed as his mother lay dying; that is when we separated them. There is something evil about the boy and not just his misshapen body which is like the mandrake root the cardinal used to cast his spell."

"How would she know that?" Silvieri asked, nodding to Stefano.

"The Escalade officers who returned from the queen's assignment of finding the cardinal and bringing him to justice brought all of his spell-casting materials so that I could examine something of what he had done," Luciana replied. "He used mandrake root, all right, and this child looks as malformed as the root used for the spell. I will show you, if you wish."

Gianola shook his wintery white head. "That will be unnecessary. We can all see by looking at him that he is anything but normal."

"There is . . ." Duchessa Rossi began, then stopped. When prodded by di Candido, she sighed and said, "There is something familiar around the boy's face. I dare say he has a resemblance to the cardinal."

"Horsefeathers! He looks small, wrinkled, and red like any newborn. He's a scrawny thing, are you feeding him enough?" LaCosta asked the wet nurse.

"I give him his fill and press him to eat more, but he will not. I do not spare the child," Signora Boniface said.

"Do you need a second wet nurse, then?" LaCosta asked.

Bonita blushed. "I have enough supply for him and my son. I think you would have trouble finding another wet nurse who would take him on, Your Grace. There are strange goings on in this nursery."

"Aren't you frightened, then?" Duchessa Rossi asked as she folded back his blankets so that she could fully take in the distorted features of the child . . . from misshapen legs to twisted spine.

Wet nurse Bonita hesitated before answering, smoothing her apron into place and shifting the weight of her own son in his sling. "There are times, yes. He isn't a normal child. The wind he raises is . . ." She shook her head. "The laughter scares me, but he is . . . just a boy, is he not? In need of loving care? I give him that, and he seems to receive it in the manner offered, but there is no mistaking this prince for a normal child."

Luciana nodded her thanks to the wet nurse to keep her from dealing with any further questioning. "If you look, the boy's face is not unlike that of his—of his father."

"He looks nothing like King Alban Novabianco," di Candido said.

"Exactly! And King Alban was not his father! His father was the cardinal who cast the spell that brought him here, to us to contend with," Luciana pressed.

"If the girls are King Alban's, then he must be King Alban's, too," di Candido argued, clearly confused. "There can only be one father in humans, and, with their love match, I would not suggest that Queen Idala lay with another man."

Stefano shifted from foot to foot at the head of the crib, arms crossed over his chest, looking thunderous.

"What of Chiara?" Luciana asked. "Does she look more like King Alban or Queen Idala or myself? If one child can be from some other source, then so can he. Look at him. Look closely. In the face, does he not bear a resemblance to the cardinal?"

"I saw a familial connection," Duchessa Rossi agreed hesitantly. "It is just so hard to tell with a child as young as this, but, if my eyes do not deceive me, I think I see what you see."

"It is just so hard to believe that the cardinal—" Silvieri began, but stopped at the sound of a laugh . . . a knowing chuckle that came from the babe in question and slowly began to grow louder and stronger as within a moment the wind in the room began to swirl again.

Luciana opened the door without a word and quickly departed the room, followed just as quickly by the nobles as the laugh behind them became stronger and more diabolical. Stefano, the last to leave, snapped the door shut behind him.

"To the receiving room," Stefano said and led the retreat down to the first floor with Maria della Guelfa bringing up the rear. Even downstairs and beyond a closed door it was possible to hear the child's laughter . . . cynical laughter that caused shivers to run down Luciana's spine. The duchi seemed to be equally unnerved. In short order, the children from the queen's nursery began to fuss and cry while the laughter continued.

"Is it always like this?" Silvieri asked.

Luciana motioned up the stairs. "You are welcome to inspect the scene, Your Grace, but it isn't possible to coordinate children so small to cry on cue, and the wet nurses would rather the children be settled than upset."

Silvieri shook his head to the invitation to return upstairs.

"There will be no peace in this house while the boy remains, will there?" Duchessa Rossi asked.

"We've managed some measure of harmony since we separated the boy from the other children," Stefano admitted, "but it isn't enough."

"What do you suggest, then?" Gianola asked, flopping down into one of the nearby chairs.

Duchessa Rossi settled on the arm of another chair shaking her head. "We must come up with something fair to the boy. He is, after all, *la famiglia reale* no matter how he was conceived or the true nature of his being. That much we know."

"I have thought to take the boy away . . . where he could be raised in relative solitude and kept from hurting anyone," Stefano said.

"Apparently, you've been giving this much thought," Silvieri said. "I mean no offense, Your Excellency, only what I have said. Were this my problem, I would be giving it some deep thought myself."

"Will the five of you support me in sending the boy

away . . . to some place as yet undetermined? We will have to find caretakers for the boy, but he will be educated just as Dario Gian and his sisters. The only difference will be that his malignancy will be kept separate from the other children. It's possible that simply some time apart will be all that is needed . . ." Stefano faltered to a stop, held up his hands, and sighed. "We, who have witnessed the child, must come up with a plan."

"I'm surprised you excluded Augusto when you made this proposal," Silvieri observed, referring to Duca Sebastiani.

"It will be put before the Palantini and Sebastiani has already had his own experiences with the boy, but *we* are to be witness to the boy's disruptiveness, his perverse nature. It is important that we stand as one. This is why I was glad to see you, Silvieri, and you, LaCosta. We are not friends or cronies. No one will think I have swayed you by friendship," Stefano said.

Silvieri snorted. "No. No one would think we are friends."

"His Grace," LaCosta said, nodding to Silvieri, "speaks to my position as well."

"Now that that has been agreed, let us turn our attention to the boy, to Massimo. He endangers his siblings with his influence. He *is* . . . disruptive and not good for the other children. Are we agreed on that?" Stefano pressed.

Silvieri pursed his lips, staring off into the distance, then he looked at LaCosta. Stefano watched him. LaCosta seemed to be letting the decision be Silvieri's and neither man looked happy . . . no one was happy for that matter. The two men were of an age, both middling in stature and complexion. Silvieri's dark hair thinned at the top, an apparent reason for him to forgo the ever-fashionable love-locks, whereas LaCosta had an abundance of light red hair—wore love-locks at his temples, a bushy mustache, and short, full beard.

"There will be repercussions no matter what we decide to do. We have witnesses who will give testament that the queen declared Massimo is not to take the throne, but there will be dissension throughout his life about how he is raised and treated. You must be above reproach where it comes to his care and education. You understand?" Silvieri said.

"I understand," Stefano said, offering Silvieri his hand.

The other duca hesitated and then, finally, took Stefano's hand. They shook.

"Then we are all agreed?" Martina Rossi said, her words more a statement than a question. She looked to LaCosta who hesitated, scratching at his mustache, then finally nodded. "Gianola? Di Candido?"

"I don't want his influence on Prince Dario Gian, or the sisters," Gianola said. He stared down at his feet. "I am a farmer more than a statesman. Were that boy any one of my stock, I'd have smothered him, but he's not mine to do what is in my nature to do. He is *la famiglia reale*. I think this decision is best."

Di Candido blinked owlishly, shocked by the candidness of Gianola. Eventually, he, too, nodded his agreement.

XV

"A whole is that which has beginning, middle and end."

—Aristotle

AS Stefano led Luciana back to their suite, he worried about her. Lines of strain had marked her face ever since the "coronation," and the strain had only increased as the day progressed. In spite of it all, he was the one who had to hurry to keep up with her.

"We are returning to the suite, Luciana, why do you hurry so? We have no one else to greet or counsel or . . . the time is our own," Stefano said out of concern for her rush.

"There is the *Beluni*," she said over her shoulder as she reached the common door to their apartment. Luciana smiled at him and threw the door open.

"But she will be waiting. She will not be impatient, *mi amore*, and I am concerned that you hurry . . . so." Stefano found himself speaking to the air as Luciana had fairly flown through the receiving room and out onto their patio. Even now he could hear the creaking of the iron-gated door that led to the path beyond their suite. He sighed and closed the door, then followed his disappearing wife.

Before he reached the patio, he could hear the strains of music played by a fiddler of some merit. Luciana called them, he paused, trying to remember the bits of her native tongue, *boshmengro*. If there was a *boshmengro*, that meant that more Rom than Solaja Lendaro and her apprentice waited beyond the wall of hedge. Stefano braced himself as he followed through the gate.

Considering the spread of caravans into the lemon orchard beyond the path, the Romani were being relatively quiet. Stefano viewed the expanse of the camp and blew out a deep breath. There might be complaints . . . if nothing else than from the Palazzo Steward, Ignacio Guglielmo, concerned for the health of his orchard. There were at least ten *vardos* beside the *Beluni*'s and, oddly, Luciana's which were parked just on the other side of the path . . . and the *bender* tents. Stefano steeled himself to be greeted in the fulsome manner of Luciana's people and pushed his way through the door. His wife, he noted, was nowhere in sight.

The smell of cooking—stew pots and honey cakes—made his stomach growl. He glanced at the sky. Darkness had long since fallen, and he had barely touched his lunch. He sincerely hoped that Kisaiya had prepared some sort of meal before getting lost in the wild mix of colors, scents, people, and horses.

Stefano crossed the partially paved path, more of a road really, and entered the campsite between the two *benders* set up nearest. Between the tents, and the caravans of Luciana and the *Beluni*, he found a more isolated and elaborate campsite. Awnings had been set up and a large cook fire sat at the very center. The *boshmengro* he had heard before was deep in his music, the *bosh*, or fiddle, tucked beneath his chin while he puffed on a pipe. He sat, leaning against the trunk of a lemon tree. The pleasant smell of his tobacco mixed with the floral vibrancy of the lemon.

Kisaiya greeted him with a smile. She sported the bright colors and more casual dress of the Rom instead of the normal attire she wore for the court of the *gadjé*. She rose from the fire immediately and greeted him.

"Welcome to your lady's camp, *Lavengro*. I have prepared a stew and there is fresh bread," Kisaiya said.

"Where *is* my lady?" Stefano asked, turning in circles. A horse whinnied nearby, no doubt untied to any line or other restraints as the Romani horses were wont to roam free in the camp, never far from their *vardo*.

"In here!" came a muffled response and then the *bender* flap was tossed back and Luciana appeared, looking flushed and excited. Her grandmother followed immediately behind.

"When did all this happen?" Stefano asked, waving at the encampment at large.

"Don't be cross," Luciana said. She stood on the tips of her toes and brushed a kiss on his cheek. "Kisaiya has made us a stew. It's ready . . . or I can prepare a more— "

"The stew will be fine, I'm sure," Stefano said. "And I'm not cross, just . . . just surprised. There are so many. I expected only your grandmother and her—her *bender*."

"Don't be so sure of our stew, Your Excellency," the *Beluni* advised as she brushed past him. "You never know what's in it."

Rankled, Stefano turned to the old woman, "I've probably eaten far worse than anything you might provide when I was on the battlefield."

The *Beluni* smiled and shrugged as she ensconced herself in a small rocking chair by the fire. Luciana joined her grandmother, pausing before she settled in the slightly larger rocker next to the *Beluni*'s. "It's a fine present, '*Mam*. Stefano, did you see the rocker my grandmother commissioned from one of our craftsmen?" She started to rise, but stopped when Stefano waved her to stay seated.

"Your Gra-er-Excellency," Kisaiya said, offering Stefano a plate mounded with stewed meat, vegetables and barley, and a torn piece of bread.

Stefano accepted the plate and started to hand it to Luciana, but saw that in her quiet, efficient way, Kisaiya had already taken care of her mistress. He spotted a stool at Luciana's side and appropriated it. "We could eat at the table on the patio," Stefano suggested as he accepted a spoon from the young cook.

Luciana laughed merrily. It was a beautiful noise that he had not heard in recent weeks and was surprised how it lightened his own spirits.

"We can eat by the fire and sleep beneath the stars!" Luciana said.

Stefano glanced at the *bender* and remembered his unpleasant sleeping habits of a year or so ago in a cot constantly losing ground to the muddy conditions. "There's much to be said for a solid roof, good footing and a featherbed . . . especially of late."

"You aren't proposing that my granddaughter have *another* child in the *gadjé* fashion . . . under the roof, away from the air and the *Fata*, are you?" the *Beluni* asked contentiously.

Stefano glanced at the old woman. She was practically all the family Luciana had, as close to a mother-in-law as he had ever had, and, by the look of her by firelight, she was spoiling for a fight. "My wife knows my preferences, and that is all that matters," he replied and tasted the stew. It was wonderful . . . as long as he did not linger on the *Beluni*'s earlier words about not knowing what was in it.

"Come, *Beluni-Daiya*, the day has been quarrelsome enough and I would have peace between us all," Luciana chided.

"We all wish for many things. After losing one granddaughter this year, I am not eager to risk the other to childbed fevers and these busybody *dottori* . . . never mentioning, of course, the child whose spirit could be lost in that cavernous place," Solaja pressed, waving at the palazzo. "Better you give birth in a cave!"

Stefano set aside his half-eaten dinner, aware of the sudden stillness in the campsite. "There's much to be said for our ways. Our people have been studying the ways of healing—"

Solaja snorted. "Your people study, my people—*our* people—*do*! And is that what your sister would say?"

Solemnly, Stefano rose. "My sister gave birth to *four* children in one night, *Daiya*. 'Tis a wonder if even your people could have saved her, especially in light of her grief over losing her husband. They died but two days apart!" He was aware of Luciana tugging at his sleeve, pulling him back toward his seat. "This is not your child or your decision!"

Luciana rose, spilling her plate as she did so. She tucked her arm through Stefano's and pulled on him hard so that he was forced to sit down. She eyed them both, and Stefano could see her anger dancing in her eyes by the light of the fire.

"It is not to be decided by you, *Daiya*, or you, my husband! I will have my child in peace this time and if must be, I'll away with myself and Kisaiya and the two of us will bring this child into the world without either of you being happy!"

"The *vardo* is ready for you, *Araunya-Daiya*," Kisaiya said solemnly. "I can have the wagon hitched in five."

Stefano swallowed hard, realizing how serious his wife was. Solaja looked at him as though he had stolen her most prized possession—and, in a fashion, he had. Luciana was his, as close as it came to possessing a person in his mind's eye.

The Romani Queen's apprentice, who looked very vaguely familiar to him, leaned in between the old woman and her granddaughter to clear up the spilled dinner. "Do you wish more, *Araunya-Daiya*?" she asked softly.

Luciana shook her head. "It was delicious, but my appetite has turned." She leaned heavily on Stefano's shoulder as she moved in the narrow space between them. "I am for bed, if you have eaten, Kisaiya?"

The girl dutifully set her plate aside. "I have, *Daiya*."

Luciana looked hard at her grandmother and then Stefano before turning and, very deliberately, entering the *bender*. Kisaiya followed and whatever else was said by them was muffled by the layers of skins and canvas that made the *bender*.

"She embraces the *gadjé* too much because of you," the *Beluni* muttered.

Stefano did not know what to say to that, so he remained silent. His stomach, too, was turned by the argument. After a moment's thought, he said quietly, "I do what is best for my family, and, excepting those newborns in the nursery, she is the wealth of it. I have never . . ." He stopped, realizing that in many ways he *had* expected his wife to conform to his life. For all the years he was away, Luciana had perforce stayed and cared for the family estate, Dragorione. Now, she had been at court for the better part of a year, going home briefly, before being called back to Palazzo Auroea to tend his sister. In all that time, her time with her family had been in short visits when they came to her.

"Grasni, take His Excellency's plate. I think he is finished," Solaja said to her girl.

Hearing the girl's name, Stefano remembered in a quick slip of thought that this young woman had been attached to Alessandra and, had accompanied Maggiore di Montago on his quest for his Alessandra's body. He handed her his plate, nodding to her as she took it.

Rising, Stefano went to the *bender* and leaned down near the door flap. "Luciana? May I enter?" He heard a scurry of movement inside, then, after a pause, she called him in. Stefano ducked low as he entered the tent, surprised as he entered that he could stand to his full height, if he kept his head down.

He glanced around the interior of the structure, amazed to discover a small, warming fire which was vented in the center, between layers of branches and tarp. The *bender* smelled greatly of lemon and he knew then that it was a guarantee that he would have to face the Steward over the use of the lemon orchard. He turned his mind from that to the obvious sturdiness he could feel when his head brushed against the tight network of thin-limbed branches. The room was big, more so than he had imagined, and far warmer than the tent he had suffered in at the front. To his left, Luciana was already dressed in her nightgown and lay on her side on a low bed of animal furs, tarps, and a small feather mat. Kisaiya peeked at him from the covers of a second bed laid head to head with Luciana's. She quickly closed her eyes and turned toward the outer wall.

Stefano knelt at the edge of Luciana's bed, finding his knees far more cushioned than he expected. "Is there room for me?"

Saying nothing, Luciana reached over and folded the covers back for him. Stefano glanced at Kisaiya, then stripped himself of his coat, collar, shirt, shoes, and stockings, laying them in a neat pile before slipping under the covers beside his wife.

The bed was comfortable and, with the blankets pulled up, he was thoroughly cocooned. He shifted, finding a sleeping position in the bedding, which was a narrower fit than their bed indoors but much better for spooning with his wife. He kissed her cheek, then whispered into her ear, "I yield. The decision is yours." He felt her ease against him, no longer rigid. He smiled to the gentle sounds of people finding their own way about in the night, the bells jingling on their clothes. Somewhere, he was conscious of distant laughter and then the winnowing of the bow by a group of *boshmengros*.

17 d'Dicembre, 1684

Stefano stirred to the steady shaking of his shoulder. He blinked and yawned. He had been sleeping deeper than he thought possible. Outside, the wind off the *Stretto* blew against the tent which barely shifted. He was suddenly conscious of two things, Luciana leaning over him and a wetness about his knees.

"Stefan!" Luciana said his name sharply as he came wide awake. "You must go for Signora della Guelfa!"

He sat up, grabbing his shirt and moving out of the bed quickly. There was the shock of night's cold, even with the fire which Kisaiya was building up. She was dressed and left while he still shook the wool from his head. "It's time? Are you sure?"

Luciana nodded. "I'm surprised the flow of my waters did not wake you."

Stefano ran his hand through his hair, finding it askew. He never liked being seen in less than proper order. "Where is Kisaiya? I'll stay with you."

"No, she has gone to wake my grandmother and make the preparations. You must go," Luciana insisted. "Capitano della Guelfa is within call. Go!"

He leaned over, kissed her briefly, and darted out of the tent, immediately stepping on a stone. He shook off the stone piercing his foot, calling for Carlo to wake as he ran inside and up the stairs. He yelled once more for his man, leaning into the servants' stair that led to the third floor. He heard Carlo call back down as he threw open the door and ran for the midwife.

Stefano scratched, then without waiting, pounded on the servants' door to the nursery. He pushed on the door to open it just as someone on the inside flung the door wide. He nearly toppled through to land on the very woman he sought.

"Fool! You can't just—" Donna della Guelfa said sharply, then stopped as she recognized Stefano in the muted light. "Oh! Your Excellency! I did not realize it was you." She became even more serious. "You are here to fetch me? For your wife?"

Stefano nodded urgently. "Please! Her water has broken and she is in a tent—"

"In a tent? Whatever were you thinking . . . many pardons, Your Excellency," she said, pinching her mouth shut. Behind the midwife, one of the babies stirred in its crib and a wet nurse moved quickly to shush it.

"Come, now! My wife has need of you," Stefano urged, grabbing the well-padded arm of the midwife.

Donna della Guelfa shook off his hand. "We have more time than you seem to think, Your Excellency. Let me get my things, and I will be with you forthwith!"

"Hurry!" He watched her bustle back into the room and begin to gather things of a nature he could not tell. He tried to conquer his agitation and calm himself, to think of what came next.

So much was good in the world . . . had been good in the world and now their child was to be born soon. He would have an heir all his own, but what of the world the child would be born into? He thought of King Alban and Queen Idala's children, of the youngest prince yet to be dealt with. Conspiring assassins and sorcerers in the cloth of the Church he knew, all of it seemed to shatter his own foundations just when he must provide one . . . not just for this child to come, but for Alban's children and the children of all Tyrrhia. The thoughts staggered but could not distract him from his task. He seized Donna della Guelfa's fleshy arm the instant she returned to the door and pulled her along the back corridor.

Carlo stood waiting at the head of the stairs which led down to the receiving room and patio. He immediately followed after his master and the midwife while freeing her of her bundle of supplies. By the time they reached the *bender*, Donna della Guelfa was out of breath and gasping for air.

The *Beluni* came from Luciana's tent, looking serious. She looked at the gasping woman and waved to Grasni, her apprentice. "Fetch the woman some water with a little something in it." Solaja ignored Maria della Guelfa's motion to not bother and looked at Stefano. As his vision adjusted to the outside lampless night again, he saw perhaps more than she intended. In the dark of the midnight hours, it was impossible to read anything in her eyes.

"So, the mother and child have decided," the *Beluni* said, scratching the end of her nose.

Stefano took the cup from Grasni and pressed it into

della Guelfa's hands as he sought the right words. "*Beluni-Daiya*, I could just as easily go in the tent and carry Luciana—fighting me all the way—to her bedroom." He held up his hand to the old woman when she would have spoken. "I am willing . . . no. Let it be Luciana and the child who decide this rather than you and me."

Solaja Lendaro rubbed her nose again, her eyes narrowing up at him. She looked away, turning her back to Grasni and Kisaiya and the few other Romani who were gathering. "Much as I was delayed in taking care of the worm casings for the Gypsy Silk, it seems I have come just in time." She looked at Donna della Guelfa, studying her up and down. "Are you the midwife my granddaughter spoke of?"

Donna della Guelfa nodded and reclaimed her bag and bundle of supplies from Carlo. "I am ready. Where is she?"

The *Beluni* jerked her head toward the inside of the *bender* and pulled open the flap for her and Kisaiya to enter and then dropped it closed again. "*Fata* and God only know why she wants the *gadjé* midwife. She knows I've caught many a baby myself."

Stefano ran his hand through his hair. "It will be good to have so much experience on hand. I don't want what happened to—to my sister, to the queen—"

The *Beluni* placed a hand on his shoulder, then gave it a pat. "Have no fear, *meero-Rawn*. She is young, healthy, and there is only one child. Many generations of women in our family have had great success at delivering their own children." She chuckled briefly, then turned serious. "So long as you have the offerings for the *Fata* ready. This child is more than just of mixed blood, this is the child of an *Araunya*! They will take special note and the offerings must be made. Talk to Petrus."

Stefano sucked hard on the pipe Petrus had given him and coughed. He did not normally partake of the smoking habit. The pack of tobacco-and-herb mix was different from anything he had ever seen others use. For that matter, the mixture made him muzzy-headed, but perhaps that was the point? Luciana's Rom uncle had said it was a special blend, for fathers-in-waiting.

At least he was not alone, Stefano thought. Carlo had provided him with decent clothing, a plain coat and breeches. He stood at the gate ever ready, but not a part of the Romani party. Strozzini arrived in response to being summoned by the duty guard. He eyed the party of Romani just as warily as Carlo had. He found his ease among them, however, sitting near the campfire. The men of the Black Throne's council—the *Kris*—at least those within Luciana's clan, had gathered outside of her *bender* while Stefano had gone for the midwife.

Petrus had overseen the setting up of an offering, laid out on sheets of Gypsy Silk. The Roma came from the camp and brought gifts of honey, honey-wine, jars of cream, dried berries, bangles of gold and silver and honey cakes. All were left on the sheets of fabric. The Roma came and went with nary a word, melting back into the denser encampment in the orchard.

"What offering have you to make?" Uncle Petrus asked him.

Stefano looked at him. "Offering?" he repeated, feeling utterly unprepared.

Petrus looked at him and shook his head. "Hasn't the *Araunya* spoken to you about the offerings?"

"We . . . we have had so little time," Stefano said.

Petrus scratched his chin. He was ready for a morning shave. "You wear that fancy bit around your neck. Offer that. The *Fata* like shiny bobs."

Stefano's hand fell to the collar, the chain of his office and shook his head in refusal. "This is not mine to give. It belongs to the White Throne."

"On the road and thereabouts, we find things, you know, things that need looking after. Have you any of that? You're a rich man, so they say. Jewels? Gold? Spoils, *meero-Rawn*?" Petrus prompted, nudging him knowingly in the ribs.

Stefano thought instantly of his spoils of war. He hesitated. "Would they be . . . be offended by a jeweled dagger?"

Petrus took a long pull on his pipe and grinned. "Now, there's a start."

"Carlo, with me!" Stefano said, practically bowling the man over as he charged through the gate.

"What is it, Your Excellency? What do you need? Let

me—" Carlo asked, fast on Stefano's heels and traipsing up the stair with him.

"Where is my chest of drawers from the Peloponnese? Get me another pouch of coins!" Stefano demanded, turning in circles in his bedchamber. He opened the trunk he kept at the foot of his bed with some of his more prized possessions.

"Your Grace . . . I mean, Your Excellency! You can't! They're—" Carlo bit his tongue on the last of it. He tried more calmly, "How do you know this is no ruse to do you out of what is justly yours?"

Stefano did not even look up. Damn himself for it, the thought had occurred even to him! He took the top level of the trunk and put that to one side as he burrowed through the collection of things he had collected over the years. He turned to Carlo. "They had wine out there, didn't they?"

"No, Master, not the wine!" Carlo whimpered.

"The wine! At least two bottles! And the whiskey in the gold flask!" Stefano ordered. Carlo turned and left the room, clearly bereft.

"May I help, Your Excellency?"

Stefano started, unaware until now that Strozzini had followed them into private chambers. Rather than speak, Stefano shook free from a tangle of fabric a dagger of scimitar-styling taken off a Turkish officer. The jewels encrusting the dagger sparkled even in the pitch of night, cast by the few stars that glimmered through Stefano's window. "Take this!" He pressed the dagger into Strozzini's hands and turned back to rummaging. His fingers closed over the cold disk of a pocket watch. He pulled it free and handed it to Strozzini.

"But, Excellency, that is your finest dress watch!" Carlo protested, having apparently just returned from his errand.

"If it will guarantee this child lives, I'd give my very life. I've had little truck with the *Fata*, but my wife speaks of them in the highest regard, and on her word alone I base my gifts. Now come, both of you, and we will see if this will do!"

He skittered down the steps like a schoolboy, his arms filled with a bundle of baldrics once worn by his enemies, covered all over with bits of gold and other awards.

Stefano came back to Petrus breathless, looking anxiously toward the tent. "Has there been word?"

Petrus shook his head. "Too early yet, *chavo*."

Catching his breath, Stefano shook out the baldrics—seven or eight of them, if he remembered correctly. "Will these do?" While Petrus took the soldiers' belts, Stefano waved Carlo to put the wine on the sheets of Gypsy Silk. "That is like nectar . . . the finest I've tasted from other lands," he said pointing at the bottles. "And there are these . . ." He took the baubles from Strozzini and gave them to Petrus.

"You speak from deep desperation, *mi compagno*," Petrus said. He carried the offerings to the silk and laid them out. "This should please the *Fata*! Have no fear. They come to bless your child, not curse it."

Stefano took a deep breath and released it, trying to regain his equilibrium. He could not help but remember and think of the last time, at the birth of their firstborn, there had been no Romani presence. Luciana, young mother and wife that she was, had succumbed to his arguments to have a "modern," more *gadjé*—less heathen—birth. Furthermore, there had been no offerings left for the *Fata*. Luciana, though she loved him, blamed him for the death of their son, Arturo. He, too, had blamed her for her use of magic during the pregnancy, but, in truth, he had left her for the war front more out of shame than blame. Only the death of Luciana's sister, Alessandra, brought him back, and he could kick himself now for all the time wasted. His thoughts turned to his sister's words and he could have cursed for never having found the time to give Luciana the box of letters he had written for her during their time apart.

Time lingered on, passing tortuously slow. If Petrus, who had only recently rejoined his clan, or any of the other men tried to engage him in conversation, Stefano did not hear them. His focus, instead, was on the birthing. He strained his wits to make clear the muffled words within the tent. The waiting and not knowing had him on razor's edge—excitement for the child to come and fear for Luciana.

By the light of his pipe, Stefano looked for the time on his pocket watch only to discover that it had stopped near the midnight hour. Cursing himself for forgetting to find the key to wind it, he stuffed the timepiece into his coat pocket. He briefly considered returning to the salon—it was not so very far away—but he would not leave Luciana's side. Not this time.

It grew suddenly quiet. Stefano sensed the silence immediately and looked hopefully in the direction of the *bender*. "Luciana?" Fear curled in his gut when she did not answer. He could hear women whispering within—even faintly, and praises to all that was holy!—Luciana breathless and weary.

After another long, restless period, Solaja came from the brood *bender*, stretching her back this way and that. Holding up a hand to Stefano, Luciana's grandmother first spoke to her apprentice, Grasni, who had prepared whatever concoctions the Romani Queen or the midwife called for during the night.

Stefano took the pipe from his mouth, rather than shattering the stem between his clenched teeth, only to roll it absently in his hands. "Well?" he asked Luciana's grandmother, unable to wait any longer.

The old woman took a deep drink from a clay mug and handed it back to her student. "You are impatient, *meero-Rawn*. The lying in . . . we are no mares who drop their babes like foals. Nature has given us a harder path where things take longer."

"Is all well inside?" Stefano asked, nodding toward the *bender*.

Solaja hesitated, making room for her apprentice to return inside the *bender* with a goblet of one potion or another. She let the flap to the *bender* fall closed. "The baby is not turned as it is supposed to be, so it takes longer." She admitted this last quietly, facing Stefano.

He noted the worry in her expression and it was as though he—like Alban—had taken a bolt to the heart. "Will she—is she—"

Solaja patted his arm roughly while Petrus' hand fell upon his other reassuringly. "Don't be too quick to presume there will be bad news," the *Beluni* said. "Many a laying in started ill but came out right in the end. Now, let me return to my granddaughter and this great-grandchild about to be born."

Even with the reassurances, Stefano felt as though his knees were going to give out. Looking toward the tent, he wanted nothing more than to take Luciana in his arms and—

"None of that, *chavo*," Petrus's voice rumbled in his ear. "'Tis women's business and, in all her years, *mi mam's* lost less than five mothers and she's not going to lose the last of her matrilineal line on the most natural thing known to man and beast."

Inside the tent, Luciana groaned loudly.

"Pay the *boshmengro*," the Romani Queen called, "and set out the feast for the *Fata*, as I told you."

"And open the cupboards and drawers to encourage the baby's passage," Maria della Guelfa called from within. Grasni exited the tent, pulling the door flap securely closed after her.

"They'll keep *that* door closed now, y'see," Petrus explained, pointing to the portal of the *bender*. "They do that to keep the devil out. Now, *meero-Rawn*, have you any coin to pay the *boshmengro* so that he'll play his fiddle fine to herald the *bambino* into the world?"

Stefano nodded and pulled a purse from his coat pocket, which he took to the old man sitting underneath one of the lemon trees, dozing, fiddle in his lap. "Here," Stefano said, handing the pouch to the man. "Play my child into the world, like you've never played before and there'll be ten more soldibiancos for you."

"Ten?" the old fiddler blinked, then tucked the fiddle underneath his chin and began to play a merry tune. Stefano stayed to listen for a moment, watching Kisaiya and Grasni, the *Beluni's* apprentice, opening all the doors and drawers in the two *vardos*—Luciana's and her grandmother's. A bit of Romani magic and a bit of the *gadjé* magic—just like his child, Luciana's child.

Stefano turned on his heel and began to pace, worrying the earth beneath his feet near the *bender* tent's mouth, straining to hear something over the music, anything from inside. As it had been most of this long night, an odd sense of quiet reigned despite the continuous stream of light music from the highly motivated *boshmengro*, broken periodically by muffled cries and the hushed voices of the women attending his wife—her grandmother, the midwife, Grasni, and Kisaiya.

Despite being a seasoned field officer, Stefano could only stand as sentry, to wait hopefully for news . . . for the arrival of his family's future. He chaffed at the prolonged wait, anxious for something to do . . . for action! At the itch for action, Stefano's hand fell naturally for his sword . . . which, of course, he had not bothered to put on. Fool, he! But Rodrigo Strozzini remained present and the Palazzo Guard were a shout away. He stopped himself, recognizing the growing hysteria and loss of a sense for order in what was naturally nothing he could control. He was being a silly old woman . . . at least, that's what they would have said on the front. In his recent experience, he had discovered there was a distinct shortage of such wisewomen.

Someone nearby spoke. Stefano turned, his attention drawn from his station . . . and, as suddenly as he twisted round, he became acutely aware of another silence . . . this one eerie and unearthly that muted even the *boshmengro*. He felt an odd shifting around him, the way his senses warned him of magic. It did not come from the tent. His focus swept across the Romani encampment and finally to the road and field that separated them from the stables. He felt drawn to the strange sense of otherness that rolled forth in a miasma of gloamy fog. "What nature of thing is this?" he asked, reaching for the sword that was not there. Strozzini rose from his place by the fire again, hand on sword, following Stefano's gaze.

A cock crowed nearby . . . which was strange because it was not yet that time and those animals were not kept this side of the palazzo. Another cock crowed and now, Stefano realized, it came from the fog . . . which should have been rising from the Stretto behind him instead of in front of him as it was. As the fog rolled closer, Stefano began to make out shapes. His blood thrilled and his heart beat heavy. What came now?

A tiny light bloomed and faded nearby, then where there had been one, came two and more. One of the lights flitted across Stefano's vision and he was surprised to see what looked like a tiny person within the flame of light.

"*Candelas*? Fairies?" Stefano asked out loud, but as though he was questioning his sanity. Was he overwrought or had there been something more in the pipe than he realized?

"Aye, the *Fata* come for the arrival of your child," Petrus said, grinning around the stem of his pipe. "They come in full host for the *Araunya*'s child." Stefano bristled and

Petrus seemed to sense his mood, slapping Stefano's shoulder. "Aye, they come for the child, but not to take it. Nay, they come to greet your Child of the Bloods."

"La!" cried Solaja Lendaro, Queen of the black-blooded Romani. Stefano glanced away from the strangeness to find her beside him. Tears of happiness swelled the eyes of Luciana's grandmother. She clapped her hands, a sharp report blessed with the jangling of her bangled wrists, which broke the vacuum of breathless silence. "Lazlo! Make the *bosh* sing! Petrus, the candles!"

In response, Petrus left his side and the old fiddler changed the tune of his instrument from one of mere merriment to a gay pavanne, heralding the arrival of who? What?

The very first blush of morning, the sun's light—like a mother's kiss—pierced the black of night and, in that small yawning of space and time, came forth an eruption of life, a magical force that swept his breath away. From the fog, hopped small folk riding roosters like warhorses and all nature of other of their kin followed, some looming and fierce, others slender as twigs and earthen brown.

At once—in that moment where the cock takes his preparatory breath that marks the span of time when the dark of night is sealed and the light of day bursts forth—Stefano hurried to help Petrus set the last candles ablaze. The shimmer of tiny waxen suns, the conjuring of sacred fire, consumed its earthen-made bit of wick and wax, caught hold of the glamour of the Gypsy Silk and shone with the glimmering light of the moon captured upon earth's mortal soil. The magic of the Romani violin rose up, the essence of its soft melody joining with the first wisps of the dewy damp of morning. How had this small birthing camp come so alive in such a short time?

"What nature of thing is this?" Stefano whispered loudly, turning in place in the center of the silken moonlight. He was fully caught up in the magic of the moment, of knowing that the heralding was not just for the *Fata*, but for his child. With a full sense of knowing he returned to the *bender*. "It is time."

"And both of you have done well," the *Beluni* said, smiling upward as a chill wind brought a thunder of swirling, sweeping feathers and leaves dancing about their heads.

Stefano noted the midwife standing in the midst of another whorl of leaves, even more in bewildered amazement than he.

"And Luciana?" Stefano asked.

"She is resting now," Donna della Guelfa said.

"But . . ." Stefano began to protest, looking toward the *bender* and then, with dawning comprehension, back to the bundle wrapped in a gray shawl lying in Solaja's arms. Stefano's eyes widened as he took in the precious sight.

"Don't leave your arms to your sides, *meero-Rawn*," Solaja chided, glancing backward at the *bender* tent and the rapidly nearing *Fata*. "Take the child and prepare for those that come to bless her!"

"Her?" Stefano murmured. He had thought himself anxious for a son—a boy to carry on, but in his heart, he realized that it did not matter. Nothing and no one could replace or mend the grief caused by the death of little Arturo, he realized now . . . just as no one . . . no other child could replace the infant now in his arms.

"You are disappointed?" the *Beluni* asked, her eyes narrowed as she gazed up at him.

Stefano shook his head, right hand to heart. "Never, *Beluni-Daiya*."

The Romani Queen, his in-law of most eminent measure, harrumphed as she turned away. "I must prepare your wife."

Still awkward with the ways of his wife and her people after all these years, Stefano caught the old woman's arm, carefully balancing his daughter in the crook of his left. He realized, in a wayward thought that recent experience with his young nieces made him more comfortable holding his own newborn than he would have been otherwise. "Please . . . *mi amore*, my wife . . . she is well?"

"As well as one might expect," the *Beluni* replied, shrugging off his hand.

All too aware of his sister's death because of childbirth, Stefano held his daughter a little tighter than intended, resulting in the child twisting and mewling in protest.

"You can't hold a child like that!" Solaja groused, though her expression softened somewhat. "Give me a moment or two, and your wife will be ready to stand at your side when you present your offspring to *di gianes grado superiore* and their own company."

Stefano nodded, more eager to see his wife than the grand panoply of fairy folk beginning to gather round him. He glanced toward the assemblage of colorful fairies moving between the distant trees of the orchard again. Their pace had slowed—though their outriders, the small and outlandish warriors, astride their war birds—mostly roosters and hens smuggled from the pens of nearby farmers and, very occasionally, wild pheasants—the fierce *Fata* made their approach to and fro, clearing the path for the greater of their kind.

Shaking his head, Stefano scanned the laid-out feast—the offering—for the guests. Everything was in order.

Stefano moved toward the *Beluni*, intending to block her path into the tent where Luciana lay so that he might express . . . he was at a loss. What could he say? Every man proclaimed his daughter the most beautiful, or so he supposed. Certainly, he had more right than any other father to lay such a claim considering the beauty of the child's mother. Stefano stroked the shawl to one side, exposing a head full of black curls and, unusually deep, silver-violet eyes.

Looking into the child's eyes was like staring into the purpling black of the night sky, dashed ever so lightly with the glistening of stardust and moonbeams. Stefano felt like a philosopher trying to fathom the incalculable heavens. He could only marvel. He had never before studied a newborn's gaze—not even those of his sister's children. Despite the wealth of his experience of late and all the magic Stefano witnessed, none of it compared quite so magnificently and breathtakingly as the knowledge hinted at in his daughter's eyes. Her silver-purple eyes seemed to hold the wisdom of the ancients . . . perhaps they did.

The ancients! Stefano looked up, suddenly conscious of the presence of others and found he stared into the shadows of the deeply hooded face of the foremost of the *gianes*. Despite being hidden by her blood-red doeskin cloak and the omnipresent hood that covered her face, the leader of the *gianes*, the enchantress of the loom, chief among the mystical weavers, he knew she would speak for all fairy kind.

The fairy flicked aside one wing of the vast red leather cape, which covered her from head to back-turned feet. A long-fingered hand reached out and stroked his daughter's cheek. "Is this the child born of the high-born *gadjé* and of the Romani—our kindred folk?" she asked. Her words sounded like water running over rocks in a stream, gurgling and slightly indistinct.

Protectively, Stefano snuggled his daughter closer. Although he could not see the *Fata*'s face beneath her cowl, he felt the pressure of her eyes boring into him and, more importantly, his daughter—already grown most precious to him. "I recognize this child as my daughter and heir, through me, to both the di Drago name and all that that implies, including all those ducal properties, rights and privileges to inherit as is the custom," he said, tucking the gray stole closer around the babe. The baby arched, turning her face and rosy, bow-shaped mouth toward her father as her tiny fingers clutched and tangled in the knitted fabric of her great grandmother's gray shawl.

"Yes, but has she the black blood of the Romani in her veins?"

"Indeed," Luciana's voice raised behind him. "Madonna *Fata*, she has the blue-blood of the royal *gadjé* and the black blood of my own veins mixed within her."

Stefano turned, more relieved to see his *apprezzato caro* stepping out of the *bender* with her grandmother and her handmaid, Kisaiya, on either side of her.

Bowing hurriedly, Stefano stepped back from the *Fata* and offered his free arm to his wife, more than for the sake of courtesy and, perhaps, lending her his strength, but because it was the only seemly excuse he could find to touch her. In the moment, his heart felt as though it would burst from its mortal cage of ribs and sinew; Stefano wanted nothing more than to hold his beloved Luciana so that they might share in the miracle of their family. They were not alone, however—even the otherworldly fairy folk held less charm for him than his wife's nearness—and thus his embrace and kiss to Luciana's cheek were chaste.

He saw exhaustion in every move Luciana made . . . and her intent to hide it in the set of her chin. He noted that Kisaiya had attempted to put some order into the masses of his wife's long braid. However indecorous his wife and her maid thought it, Stefano loved that the bulk of Luciana's raven-black hair, loose from its braid, fell mostly free down her back. She wore her people's customary kerchief, tied at the back of her neck, which at least kept the stray hair out of her face even as the morning breeze off the Stretto gusted around them.

Stefano braced his wife against him and their daughter. Silently, he twined his fingers with Lucia's and, united, they bowed again before the delegate of all Tyrrhian fairies.

The leader of the *gianes*, with her face completely hidden by her blood-red omnipresent hood, nodded—or certainly, the top of the cowl dipped in a way that seemed vaguely approving.

For all of his upbringing, his years of study in diplomacy and protocol and his noteworthy career in the military . . . still Stefano stood tongue-tied, in a wordless tangle of awe and disbelief before these numinous creatures—his daughter and the fairy folk.

Stefano's logically trained mind struggled to reject what reason told him was impossible—in spite of the nursery stories of his youth, in spite of all that he had seen and, yes, even participated in this past year. Whatever the stories told him, his mind had not, so far, fully conceived of the *Fata*, but now, with his wife and newborn in arms, he took a deep breath and launched himself once more into the mystical madness of his wife's easy ken.

Before the assembled, Stefano spoke from his heart, bearing witness as much to Luciana's people—who had so reluctantly accepted him—as the beings gathered before him who questioned his paternity. Some of them, he had learned, thought his long absences of the past—before and after the birth of their stillborn son—were disavowals of his politically costly marriage. For Luciana's people and the magical folk with whom the Romani forged the Gypsy Silk that had steadied Tyrrhia's freedom more than once, Stefano proclaimed loud and clear for all to hear, "This woman, the *Araunya* of the Romani clans is my wife. Our child . . . our daughter is of the Lendaro clan and bears the name di Drago of the House di Drago and Dragorione."

The *Fata* shifted in their loose gathering, their gazes turned to the *gianes*, the weaver-fairy, who stood as their representative.

At last, the Old One laid bare her head, exposing her

nut-brown skin—several shades darker than that of Luciana and her grandmother—and slanted, moon-silver eyes.

For the first time, Stefano grew truly uneasy. Luciana and her grandmother had spoken of this naming custom as though it was little more than a christening. Only now did he begin to fully appreciate the depth and meaning of the Catholics' dedication of their children's lives and souls to the Church with their christening, or the brit for the Jews.

"'Tis the custom for the firstborn to be fairy-touched and fairy-blessed," the *gianes* said. "But your firstborn came early, and the fairy were not summoned. His stillborn death means now we can make certain allowances for those misfortunes. This child, then, takes the place of your firstborn? Yes?"

"She is our first," Stefano affirmed quickly. In his heart, he was not denying Arturo, but acknowledging his daughter's place. He turned to meet Luciana's gaze fully as he spoke and smiled at her in his most reassuring fashion.

"In accordance with tradition, your offerings are generous . . . libations of honey and wine and a feast fit for kings," the *gianes* continued.

Stefano glanced over his shoulder at the array of food and gifts. It was far from fine in his estimation—if it was to be considered an equal and fair price for his living daughter safe in his arms—it seemed, in the order of things, to be rather meager. Besides using the finest Gypsy Silk as dining linen and including an offering from the riches of his "spoils," the meal itself seemed quite simple.

Honey appeared frequently—in the wine, the mead, honey cakes, honeyed fruits and nuts—and then dried berries had been fattened in wine then mixed with cream. . . . The food was resplendent with richness in its own humble fare.

Stefano turned to face the fairy and saw that she held her arms out to receive the child. He hesitated. The woman was strange to him and, now reminded of the old nursery tales he could not forget, those that spoke of the fairy folk stealing small children and the double-edged blessings they gave.

Luciana kissed the brow of their infant daughter and lifted her from her father's protective arms. "Trust me, Stefano, all will be well. Please, do not offend them."

He released their precious and as yet unnamed babe reluctantly into her mother's arms, holding her long enough to place his own kiss upon her brow, as though it might warrant her some protection.

The *gianes* took the child from her mother, unfolding the gray shawl to expose the still-naked child to the dawn's light filtering through the branches of the trees. With one hand supporting the baby's neck and the other her back, the elder among the *Fata* said, "Then I welcome this Child of the Bloods. Let it be known to all that the mixed family lines mark her to be one of so very few that have come before in all the centuries past."

Luciana nodded as the fairywoman spoke, "Our daughter is inheritor in both the lines of the father and mother. Of an age and, at the behest of the *Beluni-Daiya*, she will claim the second of the *Araunya* titles from me."

The *gianes* lowered the child from the precarious heights she had held her in to quietly refold the anonymous gray shawl around her. The orchard filled the dawn with its crisp, citrus perfumes.

Solaja Lendaro, Queen of the Free Romani Clans and great-grandmother to the newborn, physically stepped into the void of silence between Stefano, Luciana, and the fairy folk. She stamped her foot fiercely upon the tree-knotted soil of the orchard path and added, "And no other—living or dead—may lay such a claim."

"No other?" the *gianes* murmured. She turned toward the center of the fairies' midst. "Come forth!"

The command issued bold and clear from the throat of the thin, angular fairy. Those others in the gathering of the *vitsi*, come together to celebrate the birth of the *Araunya*'s child, turned and paid full heed.

With the attention of all present, the *Madonna gianes* motioned to her companions. The various *Fata*—the childlike *lauru*, the stunning *sirena*, and other fairies whose names and kinds were long-lost with Stefano's other childhood memories—turned inward, as though to confer. Instead, they shifted so that they exposed to all what had previously been hidden within their inner circle. They pushed two of their company forward, expelling the silvery, shimmering things to early daylight and the easy sight of all gathered in the bower of the orange trees.

The silence—which passed in the space of taking a first look and then a second, to be sure what they saw—broke with the wordless commotion of a battalion in sudden retreat as the Romani broke ranks and fled into the orchard. The thick of the orchard echoed with the words "*mulló*!" and "*marimé*!"

How many of the gathered *vitsi* actually remained long enough to hear their *Beluni*'s command, "*Meklis*!" or simply chose to let their feet do their thinking, Stefano could not be sure. What had once been a merry gathering of a clan, feasting and bringing forth presents, now bore the semblance of a silent battlefield with only the battle-struck and the sainted souls who tended the dying remaining.

Beside him, Luciana expelled her breath distinctly. Stefano put out a reassuring hand, his gaze returned to the shawl-covered bundle once more. He itched for a sword while hazarding, as with most situations magical, it would do little good.

At last, the reaction of the Rom, including his beloved, and her taciturn elder, drew Stefano's full attention to the point where the women stared.

With an eye toward his daughter still in the *Madonnagianes*' arms, Stefano decided something must be done as any course of action was better than none. He did not bother trying to explain the unanswerable as he faced the couple, who looked for all the world like slivers of the fading moon as they stood before Stefano and women of his extended family.

Pulling his wife forward and to his side, and holding the *Beluni*'s arm, Stefano maneuvered something approximating a bow. He fumbled for the right words, counting each lengthening moment his daughter stayed beyond the scope of his protection.

Mindful not to use their names, Stefano acknowledged them. "*Piccolina*? Maggiore?" His greeting sounded more like a query than anything else, but how else did one address an in-law? Especially those dead—on the lady's behalf—almost a year? Stefano stole a quick look at his wife and then at her grandmother on the left.

By the half-light of early dawn, Stefano saw the *Beluni* wilt. Her lips pinched tight as she went deathly pale.

Whatever her age, her vitality escaped her in the space of a bone-withering breath. She suddenly looked very old. Every one of her years, and, perhaps, a decade more, rode her thin frame, dragging her almost to her knees.

Luciana, already visibly exhausted, rocked on her feet. Her hands clenched his right arm and shoulder as she edged closer to him.

For Stefano, Luciana and her grandmother's reaction served to ground him, to allow him to accept the reality of the visions before him, surrounded by their *Fata* host. Since his reconciliation with Luciana, he had begun to accept the unnatural and otherworldly better than the average man, though his instinct and his Catholic faith rebelled against the magical. As an educated and reasoning man, magic and its kindred were anathema. Strangely, he now faced the living dead and managed to keep at least some measure of his wits about him. He took a shuddering breath and pretended that it was every day he acknowledged the salute of a dead officer.

The maggiore took the arm of his own beloved, to escort the silver and shadows of his fairy-bride. The ghosts, *mullós*, showed a tenderness for one another, an acceptance of one another on an intimate level Stefano only found with his wife and, somehow, this made the hazy figures seem even more real, more sympathetic.

Alessandra, Child of the Bloods, fairy-blessed, paid him no mind. After an initial, frustrated glance at her grandmother, she turned her attention to her sister, her expression mirroring the pain of their separation. Parted by a mere few steps and hundreds of years of unshakable Romani beliefs, Alessa moved from the protective circle of her fairy-wed husband's arms and reached out an imploring hand.

Stefano felt the ache of Luciana's pain as she also reached for her sister, but both stopped before actually making contact. The grief in Luciana's expression struck Stefano deeply. Alessandra was like Luciana's own child; one that, due to death of the mother and the benign neglect of the father, she had raised.

Tears trailed down the *Beluni's* creased face. She, like Luciana, was heart-struck. Despite her open grief, the old woman still flinched away from Alessandra's outstretched hand, shaking her head. "*Marimé, chavi.*" The words uttered from her lips came out as a strangled cry.

Stefano's heart seemed to rise up in his throat. There stood, for all to see, the phantasmal forms of his *famiglia del marito* . . . Alessandra and her lover, or, more correctly, her posthumous husband, Maggiore Mandero di Montago, an Escalade officer who had served the White Queen. Stefano's problem, however, was how could he form a bridge between the living and the undead?

"You are beyond the grave, *piccolina*, at least to . . . us. What would you have your family do?" he asked, finally finding words. His voice broke the tension of the yawning moments of silence and unspoken angst.

Turning her steady gaze of longing from her sister, Alessandra looked at him then. "Do you think your eyes deceive you, *fratello*? Am I—is all this—but a dream? Or do you believe that I am truly in your presence, come to welcome my niece into the world?"

Stefano's mind raced over potential answers and none of them seemed the thing to say. He shook his head finally and said, "I have learned to trust in what I see, but trusting and *knowing* are two different matters at times like these."

"The words of a politician," Mandero observed knowingly.

A part deep within him protested the remark since Stefano still considered himself a man of action. "I cannot deny that, *Maggiore*. I am what I must be. My ties are to my wife and child, and to them you are both unclean," Stefano replied.

Luciana choked back a sob.

"Enough of this!" the lead *gianes* said. "The Children of the Bloods are blessed! They are a gift that is meant to heal the rift between Romani and the White. We have redeemed your *Araunya*, taken her to our breast, and preserved her lover, her husband. Let them be known to you as a part of us, a tie between the mortal and immortal!"

"This is *diviou*!" the *Beluni* cried, turning her back to Alessandra and the leader of the fairies.

"Madness, you say?" the *Fata* retorted. "It is madness to grieve over the immortal! They live beyond the curses of the mortal. *She* lives in us. Touch her and see if she is not real . . . as real as I who hold this precious babe of yours."

Stefano pulled Luciana's hand from his arm. He was not Romani. This fear of the evil undead *mulló* was not his. He did not believe in ghosts . . . but then, until a very short time ago, he had not given full credence to the actuality of the *Fata* either. There was no reason he could think of that would not allow him to span this gulf between sisters. He stepped forward, reaching out to Luciana's sister who came immediately toward him.

"No! Stefano, don't!" Luciana wailed, grabbing his arm and pulling him back with all of her might. She dashed the tears from her eyes. "As I love this child I have borne, so I love my sister, but our ways say that until the year has passed, your soul is not your own. Your presence is the trickery of evil!"

Alessandra's head dropped. "I wish no ill upon you, Luciana or *Mam-Daiya* . . . or any of the people who once claimed me as one of their own. I will test you no further," she said when she looked up again. The *mulló* stepped back, into the arms of her husband, and gazed longingly at the child still held by the *gianes*. "As to this child's claim of me and mine, I make no further claims upon the role of *Araunya di Cayesmengro*.

"Deny me as you have, I understand, but there is another child. I do not see her here. She was my sister-kindred in her former life; murdered and used up to near nothingness by the cardinal's bestial magic. We fought together to break him and end the suffering he caused. In her last moments, she was taken from all that she knew and drawn into his final, desperate spell. She, like he, should have been reborn in *la famiglia reale*. Where is she?"

Chills ran down Stefano's spine as he considered her words. Donna della Guelfa, who had all but become invisible during this drama, gave voice to his own realization.

"Sweet *Jesu*!" Donna della Guelfa whispered, dropping to her knees and crossing herself. "I thought this all superstition! If what I see before me is true, then the stories, the prophecy is true! The little prince was-is—"

Luciana touched the midwife. "The other child she speaks of is the dark princess. She refers to Chiara," she confirmed.

"Where is that child?" the *gianes* requested. "She is of the Bloods, too, even if she was born to two of the White

Thrones. Surely, there was a mark upon her to indicate her heritage?" The *gianes*' gracile face contorted into a deep frown that formed grooves in her otherwise beautiful face. She shook her head and her hair, which seemed both like long willow branches and green-brown feathers, scattered about her shoulders becoming caught in the folds of the red cloak.

"I—I know where she is," Donna della Guelfa breathed, her voice thin and thready with the mixture of awe and near-hysteria. She inched forward, as she spoke, closing the distance between Luciana and herself. "What do I do, Excellency?"

Luciana glanced up at Stefano before answering. "Go. Get the princess—and tell no one of this meeting!"

Maria della Guelfa dropped into a deep curtsy, smoothing her bloody, once-white apron. It was hard for Stefano to be sure who the curtsy was to . . . Luciana? The *gianes*? Or all of them at once?

"Go with her, Strozzini, and protect the princess. I am among friendly folk," Stefano bade his bodyguard, who, all this time, remained silent and at his place by the fire.

Strozzini followed the midwife without protest. What, Stefano wondered, must be going through the midwife's and bodyguard's minds right now? Would they be able to take it all in? Would they tell others what they had seen and heard this morning? Would anyone believe them if they did speak of it? Would anyone believe *him*, for that matter? Did he want others to know about this ceremony? Moreover, how, in all that he held holy, could Idala have *truly* given birth to a Child of the Bloods? His reasoning mind rebelled at the concepts, while another part of him accepted this, took it all in to digest later, neither believing nor disbelieving as he realized he was not just acting as a father or a guardian uncle. His actions this night might well bear on the future of all Tyrrhia.

"Thank you, *Daiya-gianes*, for thinking of Chiara when we did not. We don't have an offering for her," Luciana said.

Trepidation struck like an icy finger up Stefano's spine, all he could think of was that his daughter and, soon, a princess were to be brought before the *gianes*—leader of all Tyrrhian fey. Why had he not brought more?

"What you have provided will serve," the *gianes* replied

without even looking toward the feast and gifts lying just a few feet away. "It is written in the blood of our people, *Araunya*, that such children will be born marked and will be recognized by us as a special Child of the Bloods—born of the black and the white and blessed by our magical bloodline. This agreement ties all fairy and mortals further to the heart of the land where the deep magics lie. All that is good will find respite—just as your sister and her husband, since he, too, was a Child of the Bloods—have been taken into our hearts. The stain which marked their spirits from mortal and immortal toils has been lifted. They have been made whole again—as newborn babes."

"You speak again of the *mullós*?" the *Beluni* asked, finally turning to rejoin the dialogue. To be clear, she nodded to Alessandra and her husband. "For one year after their deaths, evil has its hold on their spirits. They may yet be turned. For one year, they are in transition to be finally good or evil. The *Fata* would have us believe that the transition has already been made.

"*Madonna-gianes*, I am yours, sworn and true, but the mark of the year must be honored. It guides our people in the ways of right and wrong. The spirit of my granddaughter and her husband can still be toyed with by the unscrupulous—as we saw with the cardinal—and, therefore, must be avoided until the year has passed."

Stefano listened, trying to fathom the intricacies of the Romani laws.

"We cannot accept this answer to our gifts," the *gianes* said, shaking her head.

"Gifts can be refused, *Madonna-Fata*," the *Beluni* snapped back with the heat of anger.

"And we can refuse to offer more . . . such as the blessings for these two girls," the fairy replied, lifting up the bundle containing Stefano and Luciana's newborn daughter and pointing to the gate where Maria della Guelfa and Strozzini had stopped. The midwife held the other child, the dark princess, the "sister-kindred."

"No!" the three Romani women all pleaded—the *Beluni*, Luciana, and even Alessandra.

"Please, it is not that we do not appreciate your gifts, it's just that . . . some will take time for acceptance and understanding," the *Beluni* reasoned.

Stefano guessed that the time the *Beluni* spoke of would fall somewhere in late *Aprile*, the anniversary of Alessandra's death.

The leader of the fairy folk seemed to have reached the same conclusion as Stefano. Her countenance appeared even more wooden than was her nature, a frown deepening the contours of her face. Before she could speak, however, Alessandra—or the spirit of her, Stefano did not know what to believe about her at this time—broke in to the conversation.

"*Madonna-gianes*, please! You *must* bless these girls. They are my niece and sister-kindred. Do not forsake them because of Romani traditions. Your gift will be honored!"

The fairy turned to look at Alessandra, contemplating. "As you are one of us, *Fata* now, I will hear your plea and not withhold our gifts, but—"

"She is *Fata*?" Luciana echoed in obvious surprise.

"She is of the fairy kind now?" the *Beluni* asked as though disbelieving her own ears.

The fairy nodded. "But you must still keep to the year of her death?"

The *Beluni* did not hesitate. "We must still honor the year, and when that time passes, I hope she," Solaja nodded in the direction of her dead granddaughter, but did not look directly at her. ". . . She will be welcome . . . as her husband now is because he passed directly into your world, his love for her surpassing even the hold of death."

"My grandmother will not be swayed, *gianes*," Alessandra said. Her voice came like a whisper through the trees, yet somehow distinct. "Let it be, the other child is here."

They all turned as the gate creaked open, held by Strozzini so that the midwife could exit the palazzo without disturbing her bundle in a silken blanket of olive green. Donna della Guelfa curtsied precariously and then brought her charge to Luciana who, in turn, passed the sleeping princess to the *gianes*.

Balancing a newborn in each long, leathery arm, the fairy looked at Luciana. "What shall you name your daughter, *Araunya*?"

Luciana glanced up at Stefano, her gaze questioning. Stefano nodded. It was the only encouragement he felt was appropriate at the moment. She gazed silently back up at him. Though she said not a word, Luciana's earthy, brown eyes spoke volumes. Throughout her pregnancy, she argued fiercely against naming their child after anyone in either family—especially if that family member's passing had been within Stefano's own lifetime lest they risk raising the dead and, thereby, drawing the curse of defilement upon the child and their small family. Of course, there were other, less important customs, but he could not remember them all. He knew, however, that there had been too much talk of *marimé* in the past hours, much less year; enough for him to be all too conscious of the fear-darkened glances between his wife and her grandmother. Again, he faced the warring customs of his heritage and Luciana's. The conundrums had driven them apart in the early days of their marriage and he was not about to have that happen again.

Time stretched. How many names had they considered and dismissed? Of course, he could not remember a single one they had settled upon, yet there had been several. Instead of taking offense at being the father and not being able to name the child himself, as was his own family's custom, Stefano resolved himself to having Luciana name the baby as she thought best.

"We shall call our daughter Divya Leonora Adorata, Child of the Bloods, fairy-blessed and *Araunya di Cayesmengro* upon her fifteenth birthday," she said.

"So it shall be! Divya Leonora Adorata, rise up and grow strong in the hearts of your people, for you are thrice blessed by the bloods and by the fairy who shall come to your aid upon your call." With this pronouncement, she kissed their daughter on her forehead and then on the lids of her eyes where her fairy-mark showed. After the kisses, she gently, carefully, returned the child to Luciana's waiting arms.

Stefano immediately wrapped his arm around Luciana's shoulders and arms, encompassing her and the baby, and, finally, relaxing now that Divya was in her mother's arms and now his again. Interest, however, was brief because he realized the *gianes* still held his niece. "What of Chiara?" he asked.

"Yes, the bastarde, orphaned princess," the *gianes* said. She smiled down at the child remaining in her arms, tucking away the edges of the blanket so that her face was more exposed.

"If she is a twice-orphaned princess, how can she be bastarde?" Stefano asked, thinking of Alban and Idala.

The *gianes* looked at him as though he were simple. Stefano forced himself to face up to the unexpressed impatience.

"Gypsy magic is her mother and the cardinal is her father. Your sister was merely a vessel which made her a princess, then she was, as you say, twice orphaned—first by her immortal parents and then by her earthly ones," the *gianes* said. She smiled down at the child and then looked up. "What is this girl's full name?"

"Her mortal father named her Chiara Vanessa Esmeralda di Drago e Novabianco," Stefano said.

"Hmmm," the leader of the *Fata* said, as she considered the name. "It's a good *gadjé* name, a strange name indeed for a girl destined to be *Beluni* one day."

"*Beluni*?" Solaja asked, clearly surprised, her tone challenging. "But what of my granddaughter? What about Luciana?"

"No, Grandmother, I have no wish to be *Beluni* in your place," Luciana said. "I am content raising my children—as they come along—and the children of the White Throne, as well as serving as *Araunya* of two houses—the *Cayesmengri e Cayesmengro*—until my daughter is of age. This child was clearly meant for something special."

The *gianes* smiled at Luciana. "You're very wise for a young woman. I hope those are your true feelings, because you are destined as *Araunya* to play an important role in the future of your clans and of Tyrrhia. You are needed where you currently serve."

"Then who is to follow me and only for such a short period?" the *Beluni* asked.

The fairy laughed. It sounded like the morning chorus of a dozen song birds, clear and unfettered by human emotion. "You are intended to serve a good many years yet and the girl will be young, but you will have helped to train her well."

"I do not see how the Palantini would permit such a thing—I mean, letting a Princess of *la famiglia reale* be raised by the Romani, by the Black Throne," Stefano said, trying to imagine such a thing. Even his supporters would complain about it!

"She must be old enough to speak her own mind before she leaves your care," the *gianes* said.

"But that is at least twenty years in the making and I am an old woman. I am tired and thought respite was near," Solaja said.

"You are not so tired as you think, old woman who is to be much older. Your guidance is too important. Your granddaughter and her children will need you for some while," the fairy explained. "In time, you will see the importance of this and understand your role."

The *Beluni* shook her head firmly. "The *Beluni* must be of the clans. She is—"

"You see her fairy mark? The streak in her hair? She is a fairy-touched child," Alessandra pleaded with her grandmother. "I beg of you to take her, for she was my sister-kindred when I was *mulló*, when I was tortured as she had been by the cardinal. She was of the clans then and she served her people well, even in death, her life cut unbelievably short by the machinations of a man who used her magic and did so most foully."

The *Beluni* sighed, looking at the child in the *gianes*' arms. Stefano could see her assessing and reassessing, taking note of her dark complexion. If neither of them had known better, and, if not for the streak of silvery white hair, it would have been easy to mistake her as a pure Gypsy child. "It shall be as you say, then," the *Beluni* finally and, somewhat reluctantly, agreed.

The *gianes* nodded. She kissed the child's forehead, the tip of her nose and the forelock of white hair and then, instead of returning her to the midwife, placed her in the *Beluni*'s arms. "You will spend more time with the *gadjé* than amongst your own people in times to come. Prepare for that, Solaja."

The *Beluni* did not immediately respond, her attention concentrated upon the child in her arms. She rocked the infant and played with her fingers until the child cooed and gurgled with delight. The babe seemed to have passed some test. The old woman nodded slowly at first and then more certainly. "I shall be the child's *Daiya*. I shall treat her as though she were sister to my great-granddaughter." She held the child a moment more, before beckoning to the midwife who came forward quickly to retrieve the tiny princess.

Dawn, a long time coming, broke through the darkness from the mist in a sudden blaze of glory. Stefano blinked. In that moment, they were all gone. The *Fata*, the feast, and the offerings vanished—leaving him alone with his wife, her family, the bodyguard, the midwife, and the princess in the nestled clearing made home with the *bender*.

XVI

"The gods visit the sins of the fathers upon the children."

—Euripides

19 d'Dicembre, 1684

CRISTOVAL cherished the short hours he was able to spend with his son, Ludovico. Every day, he could count on the breakfast hour to review lessons and discuss events of the day. Even Prince deMedici, who kept him busy, could not deny him that early hour . . . at least not usually.

The prince had turned Don Cristoval Battista, a land-owning lord of the king's Palantini, into little more than a servant and courier—though there were scant times he was actually permitted to pursue his own goal of finding himself a new wife with funds enough to bring the family home back to its rightful beauty and sufficient to raise his son properly.

"Papa! Papa!" the youngster cried, racing into the common room they shared with the servants in the deMedici suite.

Cristoval scooped the boy up. "And what has happened to make you so excited?" he asked, straightening the boy's clothes automatically as he set the child on the bench beside him.

"His Highness has told me that I am to attend his lady, the princess, at the truffle hunt today!" Ludovico announced, bouncing in his place on the bench so that the bowls on the table rattled. He took his porridge and poured honey on it until his father stayed his hand.

"And when were we to do your lessons? We have no other time—"

"His Highness said that I may catch up on my studies tomorrow . . . or the day after," the boy shrugged, wrinkling his nose.

Cristoval swallowed back his anger. Of course, the boy would avoid his studies, he did the same as any child, but . . . "You have been missing too many of your lessons and—"

"But, Papa, I am like you. You have duties, and now so do I!" Ludovico's eyes brimmed with tears. "I am growing up to be responsible, like you!"

How did you argue with that kind of reasoning? Cristoval thought. It was not the child's fault, but that of the man who practiced tearing them apart on a daily basis. "I *am* proud of you, *il mio figlio*. It's just that you are young and responsibilities such as . . ."

"Don Battista!"

The voice of Prince deMedici called up the stairs. "*Ragazzo*—boy! My lady waits upon you!"

Ludovico immediately rose, hurriedly stuffing another mouthful of porridge into his mouth.

"Stay! Sit! Eat like a person. You are not his dog!" Cristoval commanded his son.

Again the boy's eyes filled with tears, porridge seeping out of the corners of his mouth. "But—!"

"*I* shall go, if someone must," Cristoval declared, standing and setting aside his tea.

"And you have had less to eat!" *Signora* delVecchio pronounced. The *signora*, in the full order of things, had been the chatelaine of his house and general surveyor of all domestic staff he kept in and around his main properties and had been so since he was little more than a callow youth, himself. With the death of Ludovico's mother and then Cristoval's second wife, *Signora* delVecchio had been like mother and wife to the Battista men. The only good the deMedici prince had done them was to treat the woman and her staff as part of his acquisition when introduced to Cristoval who, due to his indebtedness to deMedici—the father, *il Duca* deMedici, rather than the illegitimate son—found himself unexpectedly in service to the *bastarde* prince.

Barely were the words out of the housekeeper's mouth than Don Battista, the younger, grabbed some bread and fled down the steps. Cristoval called to his son and threw him a plum as well before the ten-year-old disappeared down the stairs.

"Do me the favor of not undermining me in front of my son," Cristoval said to the woman, who immediately laughed good-naturedly.

"And when were you ever the good student? He's at court, Don Battista! He's gaining more practical experience these days than you could have taught him in a month!"

"Yes, that is what I fear," Cristoval said, stuffing a spoonful of porridge into his mouth. He chewed the pasty stuff and swallowed. He pushed the bowl away and picked an orange from a bowl in the center of the table. "The prince, he takes my son more and more. Some days, between our schedules, I do not even see him until I check him after the boy is asleep. This is not how a father—"

"If either of the Donna Battistas yet lived, this would be the same as it was with your father and you," *Signora* delVecchio said. She now sat on a chair by the fire with a bowl of the porridge for herself.

"If you are to be so free with your observations, as though you were family, you might as well share the same table," Cristoval said and tapped the bench Ludovico just vacated. He moved the boy's bowl and edged over to allow her room.

"No, I—"

"*Signora*—Rosalia, times have changed. Clearly, you are as much family, now, as my son. Come. Sit."

"When we return home—" she warned as she placed her bowl on the table.

"Then things will return to the old ways . . . perhaps. That will be then," Don Cristoval Battista said.

"Battista!"

The prince's voice carried up the stairs.

"He calls you . . . you will pardon, I hope, Don . . . but he calls you like his lap dog. The opportunities for young Ludovico are . . ." *Signora* delVecchio shook her head. "The things he might do for the boy are wonderful, Don, but you must speak to him of calling you like his dog!"

"Battista!"

Cristoval's cheeks burned that this woman, so much like kin to his family, should not only observe this, but somehow share in his humiliation. The sharing only deepened his embarrassment. He nodded abruptly to her and rose, crushing the orange in his hand. He dropped the pulped fruit into his porridge bowl, cleaned his hand on the rough linen napkin from his lap and answered the summons of his "master."

Maria della Guelfa tucked her skilled hands into her pockets and then out, worrying at the edges of her apron. It was an anxious habit she'd had since childhood.

Until a few weeks ago, she had been contented to be housewife to a gentleman farmer and military man. With him away often, it had kept her busy. Thankfully, they had a son turned into a youth. He was free where his father was not, and the two of them ran the farm with the help of hired hands; now her son was running the farm alone. With five generations of midwives before her, Maria carried on the tradition and was well-known for her skills.

Serving the village wives and those of his hired hands, the occasional desperate stranger or Romani, Maria was content providing this service to her community. She had never thought, not in all her lineage, not even in desperate dreams, that she might come to be known to or recommended to the White Queen of Tyrrhia, much less be summoned away from her comfortable farmhouse to serve her or her children. After no more than a couple of weeks at the palazzo, the others treated her like a fixture here.

No recommendation to a queen came lightly and without complications, for it seemed every married, recently widowed, or newly wed attendant to the White Throne was also pregnant and from simple farmer's wife and midwife to horses, cows, and the local women, she first served the White Queen, then the *Araunya* and now the courtiers! She was not to work completely alone, for she was to be assisted by the Royal Physician and Barber! The two men did not take kindly to her arrival since they had been accustomed to caring for the court's health by themselves for many a year!

But for reasons still not completely clear to her, her

friend—did a "friend" recommend you to such a position, for most surely this one had?—the chemist and apothecary who had provided Maria with the medicinal goods she needed but did not grow herself all these years; this woman, Donna Rui, now served beside her, though mostly concentrating her time on the newborn boy in another room in the suite. This new position included living at the palazzo so as to be at the beck and call of the White Queen's infants and in a place to make crucial decisions that would affect all of Tyrrhia and everything she held dear.

She had just moved herself from her beloved home to an apartment in the palazzo she shared with Donna Rui, her referring friend, and, on rare occasion, her own husband!

"Are you sure?"

Maria turned toward the voice. Donna Nunzia. "The *Araunya* needs the air. A truffle hunt where she gets outside and does nothing but lie upon a couch and watch? What difference, from the tent she insists on living in for the rest of the week?"

She turned at the sound of raised voices. As she spoke, so came the *Araunya*, the Regent Guardian, and her husband, the Lord Regent. The *Araunya* walked carefully, but with the Lord Regent oh so attentively at her side, toward the pavilion that had been raised for her that very morning at the edge of the small forest on the grounds of the palazzo.

When neither Regent recognized her, Maria moved into their path and stopped, forcing them to do likewise.

"Would you speak, Donna . . ." the Lord Regent looked up expectantly.

She started to speak, but *il dottore* coming from a wing of the palazzo interrupted her sourly. "If I may protest this—this tent you are living in with the child, never mind this jaunt—"

"You have protested," the *Araunya* said.

"Already," the Lord Regent, Duca di Drago, added, turning to Maria. "Donna della Guelfa? Please, speak freely."

Maria made a swift, unpracticed curtsy, teetering for a moment on the uneven ground. "With gratitude, Your Excellency. I think, mayhaps, that the *Araunya* has already exerted herself . . . sufficiently." She said no more than that, and the duca scooped his wife off her feet and onto the couched palanquin to be carried by four porters.

The *Araunya*'s color was high in her dusky face. Her face was quite pink, but she showed no signs of ill-humors and her mood was one of happy contentment.

"They listen to you as they should listen to me," *il dottore* said at her elbow. "Look at her color! Before the day is out, you will have her humors out of alignment, and I will have to order a bleeding to put them back to sorts!"

Maria shook her head. She had discovered almost immediately after her arrival that she had little, if no, patience for the rail-thin, middle-aged Royal Physician. Thankfully, any need to reply just now was peremptorily buried under the cacophony of dogs, large and small.

The *Araunya*'s lady in waiting came with two great, stalking, gray wire-haired hounds dancing on their ribbon leads.

"I hope that you do not plan to join the hunt," *il dottore* said to the *Araunya*.

The noble Romani woman smiled patiently and said, "I may . . . possibly." Anything else she might have said was lost in the noise of dogs and excited courtiers.

Almost in counterpoint to the *Araunya* came the Princess Ortensia and Prince deMedici with two small dogs who preferred to chew on their ribbons than keep pace with the young boy who carried their leads.

Beyond the prince and princess, like a great wave of cavalry, came the members of court. Not all the women were pregnant—thank the heavens above!—though in the past two days Maria had been introduced to yet one more and then another of those in the condition that required her attention. If it were Maria's choice, she would flee this "great honor" that had been bestowed upon her. As it was, she could not do the job alone. If the court wanted a midwife, best they find another to aid in the job!

Many of the ladies favored the palanquin in its many forms, from couches and chairs to the miniature carriages sometimes seen in the city. In fact, there were so many of the palanquins in use or close at hand, that Maria was confident some of them must be rented *from* the city as were the men carrying them.

Maria found herself lost in the gaiety and silliness of the moment. For each lady—littered or walking—came a servant of the palazzo or from some personal livery, following one of the oddest assortment of dogs.

"Donna Maria!"

Maria swung around, recognizing that, in her distraction, she had not heeded someone's call. The *Araunya* waved her closer.

"Come, Donna Maria, I've arranged for you here," the Regent Guardian said, motioning now to a chair covered with a throw and cushions. "I did not think that you would like to sit on the ground, but if I am wrong—"

Maria blushed, unused to the distraction the *Araunya* had devised and the expectations of court. She curtsied and took the appointed seat. Almost instinctively, she reassessed the *Araunya* who had given birth only two days before. Though her cheeks were still flushed, and she looked contented—to the point that she allowed her husband to fuss and bring her a platter of treats from the table set up behind the viewing area. The *Araunya* had taken a seat on a small divan, leaving yet another couch free for Princess Ortensia.

It was still so hard to believe that the princess had been returned from her years of capture and that in the short time since her homecoming she had already married the Prince deMedici . . . and, beyond all that, she was already heavily pregnant! Maria first found it necessary to believe she had truly returned before she could fully accept all the rest.

The princess took the couch to the *Araunya's* left, leaving Maria sitting between the princess and the Romani woman. The princess glowered at the *Araunya* and turned her head to watch the gathering of humans and dogs.

Maria took a deep breath and settled back in her chair. For once since her arrival, she was not actively pursuing one pregnant woman or another; she was being allowed to rest which gave her time to sort out the many things she was discovering about her world now that she was at court and saw the players at work.

Even with her husband, Marco, serving in the Queen's Escalade at court, she was finally realizing that the news she had gotten before would be weeks old and there was so much that went unreported. A petty tantrum by the princess could affect the country's affairs. It seemed so much of politics . . . and those things that would affect her life evolved from the affairs of the courtiers.

According to Nunzia Rui, the population at the palazzo had doubled since her own arrival. With word sent out to call the Palantini, the noble families were arriving daily from their distant homes. With the arrival of the young ladies attending their parents and families came the gentlemen—bounders and truly noble men alike—and their retinues.

All of these courtiers—the nobility, rather than the ambassadors—had been retired to their estates; many in grief for the dead Princess Bianca—Ortensia's younger sister—who had died under somewhat questionable circumstances at the reception to her own wedding, leaving Prince de-Medici a widower before he was ever a true husband. Maria shook her head. Perhaps that was how the prince and princess could now live with their new marriage, but then, she knew, marriages of State were never quite the same as those among the civilized folk at home.

Her attention was drawn back to the hunt as the sound of the dogs and their attendants grew even louder than before.

Played out in front of the royal pavilion, dogs and handlers wrestled for order. Because of the snapping and snarling and love-making of the dogs, order was not easily come by, and no royal decree would make it so. The *Araunya* seemed amused by the chaos.

The princess showed the first genuine emotion Maria thought she had seen from the woman when she jumped to her feet in very real concern for the dogs tethered to the youngest of all the handlers. It was precisely clear; the princess' concern was for the black and white and brown and white pups rather than the boy who was very young and trying desperately to sort out his charges.

A courtier, whom Maria had learned was named Estensi and was the Court Herald, somehow raised his voice above the chaos without actually yelling. Even the dogs seemed to take notice. As a result, within a very short time, sanity ruled. Or, rather, a measured sanity overtook the dogs and their assigned handlers. The Court Herald announced the rules of the hunt and off they went to gather their truffles, and other mushrooms which might be found so early in the season and the nuts fallen during winter from the various trees in this light edge of the forest.

Maria watched the *Araunya* sigh, apparently at ease,

while she continued to ignore the poisonous glares of the princess. Donna della Guelfa could not help but compare the two women. While the *Araunya* seemed serene, dressed simply in a dress of dark blue Gypsy Silk with a white undergown, the Princess deMedici wore the height of fashion—a light-leafy green dress and darker green undergown, all be-decked in starched lace, ribbons, and jeweled brooches.

"I see you gave birth," the princess observed, her tone sharp and more than a little shrewish.

"Two days ago," the *Araunya* said with a faint smile, her gaze never leaving the forest edge where some of the colorful members of court, their dogs, and the liveried attendants still scoured the ground for prize-winning delights. Somewhere, in the distance, a hound let out a hue and cry. Someone shouted excitedly.

At her feet, the *Araunya*'s great gray dogs whined and looked up at their mistress expectantly, their noses and paws quivering with excitement. She shushed the dogs and pulled her own feet up and under her.

"It's a great diversion . . . this," the princess said, nodding to the truffle hunters. "Though there would be greater luck if this were fall."

The *Araunya* nodded and shrugged. "The court would have been crazy with distraction if we were to wait until then. This is a harmless game that diverts the attention and provides the kitchen with much needed staples."

A long moment passed before the princess spoke again. "Rumor has it that you gave birth to a girl. I'm so sorry. I know His Excellency," she began, her tone hinting at sympathy, "must have been so disappointed."

"Not at all," the *Araunya* said with a merry laugh. "We are both content with our Divya."

"But the duca must've so wanted a boy . . . to carry on his name and hold the position of duca when he is gone," the princess said.

Luciana shrugged again and merely said, "There might yet be other children. If not, then Divya will inherit from her father just as Duchessa Rossi did, and let us not forget that my daughter will inherit from me, too."

"Ah, yes, the Gypsy ways," Princess deMedici snorted rudely.

"The Romani ways," the *Araunya* corrected, still without looking at the princess.

Maria bowed her head to hide her smile, inordinately pleased by the *Araunya*'s refusal to rise to the baiting of the princess who seemed rankled by the lack of attention from her intended victim.

"Well, I shall be having a boy," the princess predicted. She selected a dried date from a nearby platter. To the boy holding her dogs, she sniped, "Beware of their tethers, child! If you strangle one of my dogs, I shall—"

"You are so confident, then?" the *Araunya* interrupted, looking at the princess finally.

The princess nodded acerbically. "I gave the sultan four sons and only one daughter in my years of captivity. I know how a boy sits in the womb and this is, most definitely, a boy."

The *Araunya* frowned, her gaze sympathetic as it finally swung around to Princess Ortensia. "You were forced to leave your children behind?"

The princess shrugged defensively. "They were their father's children . . . never mine. *This* child, however, shall be mine own." She looked down at her belly and cradled it as if a child.

"I'm so sorry," the *Araunya* said, her voice full of sympathy.

"Why? I'm not!" the princess retorted. She sat back in her chair, resting her hands on the arm of the divan. Abruptly, the princess rose from her place. "Come, boy, we will join the hunt!"

"Ludovico, Your Highness, my name is Ludovico," the boy said, trotting after the princess.

The *Araunya*'s dogs whined softly, looking up at their mistress hopefully. Luciana shook her head at them, reaching down to pet the great beasts who immediately settled down. The dogs watched the woods, lifting their heads whenever there was a hue and cry when a dog was let loose.

After another hour, Kisaiya brought Divya to be nursed. The *Araunya* covered the child with a blanket which she brought up to her neck while she tended to her daughter's needs. When the baby finally slept, she cradled the girl in her arms, watching as the members of court, their servants, and dogs filtered back out of the forest one and two at a time. She thanked them each as they deposited their findings in a large basket at the front of the pavilion.

Cristoval made his weekly trip into Citteauroea to see the priest in charge of *Magnus Inique*. His horse seemed to know the way by this time, picking a path through the narrow, midden-filled streets of the outlying residences of the lower classes. Cristoval made his way into the merchant quarter. The streets here were cobbled, and the homes looked more well-kept. Most of the merchants used the bottom floors of their homes as shops. At last, he came to the city's center where were situated inns and booths holding merchandise.

The Gilded Arms, *le Armi Dorata*, was as it had been each time previous. A black youth came forward to take his horse even as Cristoval dismounted.

Keeping his mood nonchalant, Cristoval crossed the entryway and made his way up the stairs. At the priest's door, he could make out the sounds of laughter. He scratched as loud as he could on the door and was quickly greeted by Padre Caserta, who stood back and waved him inside.

Cristoval entered, immediately recognizing Enzo, the rampaging tavern brute from weeks before. Enzo looked at him, his hand going to his jaw.

"Ah, so here is the man who can knock the Great Enzo to his knees." Enzo stood up then and crossed over to Cristoval who took in the size of the giant mountain of a man standing before him.

"I meant no offense," Cristoval offered. The man had not looked so big under his compatriots when last they met in the taverna.

The well-muscled man only laughed and clapped Cristoval on the shoulder, making his knees quake. "Enzo is not so smart when he drinks. Come. You will have my chair! I have only returned from my sojourn." He guided Cristoval to a chair in front of the fireplace and sat him, rather forcefully—as one might a recalcitrant child—in the only empty chair in the room. "You see? Enzo bears no grudges!"

"Thank you," Cristoval murmured. When all present—diSotto, Caserta, Enzo, and four others whose names he did not know—looked at him expectantly, Cristoval reached into his inner vest pocket and pulled out the prince's letter for the priest. He handed it to Caserta.

The other man, dapper and thin in his street clothes, broke open the prince's seal and folded open the letter, reading the prince's flowing script with apparent ease. When he was done, Caserta lit the paper ablaze and cast it into the fireplace.

"It seems the *Araunya* has produced a female heir, and there is some talk of her using magic. She seems, alas, to be doing well after the birth!" Caserta said, watching the flames consume the letter. "She splits her time between the orphans and her own child."

"And King Alban's son is to inherit the throne? Despite the princess being ready to assume it?" one of the unnamed men asked.

"That is how it stands," Caserta said, "but there is some hope that that might yet change."

"That they made that Gypsy witch Royal Guardian . . ." diSotto ended his comment with an epithet not fit for polite company.

Cristoval tried to hide his offense, but the quick eyes of Caserta caught it.

"Men. Men. We all harbor hard feelings, but we are in the presence of a gentleman. Let's bear that in mind," Caserta said. He waved his hands in a settling motion.

The man who had spoken dipped his head in acknowledgment and uttered a quick apology to Cristoval who was more offended on the part of the party they spoke of than the words spoken, but such would not be a welcome admission. No, not in this group of men who felt that magic must be left in the hands of priests. As to the inheritance of the throne, Cristoval was quite happy that the power remained in the resourceful hands of the Duca di Drago and his Gypsy wife rather than the deMedicis. He had come to this conclusion over his time spent in close proximity with the prince and princess. They both were mad for power, and it showed in how they treated everyone around them, but he could not admit that here either. Somehow, Cristoval knew they would be less than pleased if he were to make such an observation.

"What other news of court?" diSotto asked.

Cristoval hesitated. He was usually not one for gossiping, but feeling he had to offer more, he said. "The prince was attacked in the dungeon, supposedly by *Magnus Inique* . . . Brother Tomasi and two guards were killed. The prince is well, as you have probably guessed from his letter. There is little more to report than which of the Palantini have arrived at court lately," he said with shrug.

"What of the assassination of the king? Do they speak of that?" Enzo asked, a grin upon his cheerful face.

Again, Cristoval was discomfited, this time by the lack of apparent sadness in the group, over the recent death of the king. "The court is in mourning. Lord Strozzini, the king's bodyguard, still searches for news of the assassin.

"And it is said that of the four children given birth to by the queen, two look like neither parent."

"The children are unimportant. Time will deal with them," Enzo laughed and prodded Cristoval's shoulder. "They did not, however, find Enzo that day, nor in the days since. They will never find Enzo!"

"You?" Cristoval said, shocked to his core. He did not like his enforced association with this group, and now he liked it even less.

"Yes," Enzo said proudly, with thumb to chest. "It was I, Enzo, who shot a single bolt from my crossbow and took down the Usurper King!"

Cristoval had dared to believe that the Royal Bodyguard had heard of the group *Magnus Inique* and confused their actions with the murder of the king. He knew better now. What was he to do about it? Instead, he forced a smile. "You must have good aim, then, to have felled the king with a single arrow."

"Ha!" Enzo laughed. "I did not serve in the *Armata* for five years and learn nothing!"

"You were in the *Armata*? The king's army?" Cristoval asked.

"*Sí*! Under King Orsino and . . . briefly under King Alban," Enzo said.

Cristoval nodded, feeling shaken, but hiding it as best he could. The rest of the conversation was a blur of men asking him questions about court, the health of the princess and of laughter, exultant as they were over Enzo's deed. Cristoval tried to keep a smile on his face, laughing when the other men did, but he noted Caserta watching him. He never felt so relieved as when he finally left the men of *Magnus Inique*, remounted his horse, and headed back to the palazzo.

Throughout the ride home, Don Cristoval Battista wondered what his course of action would be. The prince would be furious if he refused to come back to *Magnus Inique* and, yet, he had reached a point where he did not care. He and Ludovico, never mind Signora delVecchio, were not being treated fairly and, more importantly, he could not—nay, would not—associate with a pack of the king's murderers! By the time he reached the palazzo stables, he was certain of what *must* be done. He just didn't like it. Not at all.

Don Battista made his way through the corridors of the palazzo, stopping, briefly, at a large mirror to adjust his clothing. He used his riding gloves to dust himself off until, finally, he looked acceptable enough for an appointment with the Court Herald.

Don Battista felt thankful to find the Court Herald in his paper-stuffed office. The older man looked up from the book of numbers he was checking when Cristoval entered after a short knock.

"How may I help you, Don . . . ?" the Court Herald, Estensi, asked, snapping his fingers near his ear when he could not remember the other man's name. He smiled and pointed at Cristoval, "Baptiste, is it not?"

Cristoval was surprised that the man had gotten so close. "Battista, Signore."

The older man sighed, seemingly more at himself than Cristoval, dropped his quill into the book he had been reading, and slammed it shut. "How can I help you, Don Battista?"

Cristoval took a deep breath, "I need to arrange for different lodging."

The Herald looked nonplussed. "His Highness is not content with his rooms? He has one of the finest suites in the palazzo!"

"No, no, you misunderstand me," Cristoval rushed. "The suite will be for myself and my son . . . and a few retainers."

"Uh-huh," Estensi muttered, looking at Cristoval through narrowed eyes. "You understand there is little to offer you now that the Palantini has been called?"

Cristoval nodded and added quickly. "As don, I, too, am a member of the Palantini."

"Yes, yes, I know," Estensi growled. "I have not yet begun sorting housing for the dons. There will be so little room left after the duchi arrive."

"I will be happy with whatever corner you can find me and my people," Cristoval said very sincerely.

"Had a falling out with your master, did you?"

Cristoval cleared his throat. "His Highness is not my 'master' as you say. What debt I may have owed him is long since paid."

The Court Herald nodded. "According to Guglielmo, the Palazzo Steward, there are these rooms in the last eastern wing of the Palazzo Auroea." He jabbed his finger at the map of the palazzo on the wall beside his desk.

Cristoval leaned ever so carefully over the desk of papers, noting the exact placement of the rooms. There would be no courtyard and the rooms did, indeed, look small, but they were free of Their Highnesses and he was anxious to make ready. "That will be more than acceptable. Thank you, Signore!"

"Thank the next don who finds there is no room for him and his retinue. I suppose the prince and princess will be wanting new retainers to serve them?"

Cristoval nodded. "A cook and—"

Estensi reopened his book. "Yes, yes, I am familiar with what they will need . . . and they must have the very best, of course." He peered down at the figures on the page, took his quill, dabbed it in ink and started to write, stopping only when he realized Don Battista was not leaving. "Is there more?"

"Does Lord Strozzini have—" Cristoval hesitated, gulping nervously. "Is there an office that I might . . . ?" He tapered off under the Court Herald's withering stare.

"Lord Strozzini keeps no office. I can take a message for him. What is it?" Estensi asked.

"Might I have a bit of paper and a pen? To leave His Lordship a note?"

Estensi sighed, found paper beneath his book, and handed Cristoval his quill. Don Battista managed a tight smile and bent over the paper. He hesitated, choosing his words carefully. With slow deliberation, he wrote his message and, then reread what he had written. This would be his final act as a member of *Magnus Inique*. When he was content, he handed the feather pen back to the Court Herald. He blew on the script, careful that the ink was dried before he folded the paper. He looked up. "Might you have a bit of wax?"

Estensi appeared vaguely offended. "I would not read another man's letter."

"But still . . . this is, after all, a very private message," Cristoval pressed.

The Court Herald shrugged again and opened his drawer, pulling first a golden candle and then, finally, a half stick of red sealing wax and handed it to him.

Cristoval nodded his thanks, lit the candle of sealing wax on the little pot of burning oil, and dripped the thick, opaque wax onto the folded page. He rotated his signet ring so that it was fully face out and, with a deep breath, sealed it with his coat of arms. If anyone else found this . . . If the prince found out . . . He shuddered. "Please, Signore, hold this in the gravest confidence. It could mean my life . . . or that of my son."

The Court Herald's thick eyebrows rose, but he accepted the bit of correspondence and tucked it into his coat. "It so happens, Don, that I will be dining with Lord Strozzini this very evening, and I will see that he receives this personally."

"Thank you, Signore," Cristoval said with a courtly bow and then excused himself from the Herald, snapping the door closed behind him. Now, if only His Highness . . . if Their Highnesses were out on errands or some other chore, perhaps he and his servants could be cleared out of their current rooms without comment.

"What do you mean, you're leaving my employ?" the prince demanded as Signora delVecchio and Bucho, his porter, removed the last trunk with their belongings.

Cristoval frowned at his son who had let this particular cat out of the bag by making a very sincere and bereft report to His Highness at first opportunity. He could not fully chastise the boy . . . he showed loyalty after all, even if it were to the wrong man.

"I have hosted you and served you faithfully these many months and well paid back the loan from your father. I am a member of the Palantini, Your Highness, and have concerns of my own," Cristoval said.

"So you were going to leave me with nary a word?" Prince deMedici pressed.

Cristoval shrugged. "I arranged to have your needs met by palazzo staff."

"At least leave me the signora who cooks so well," the prince said. He adjusted the cuffs of his pretty new coat. The prince and princess spent a fortune on tailors and Gypsy Silk that would be ruinous to anyone else. It seemed every day that the prince sported new clothes. He had been . . . "kind" was not the right word, but perhaps insightful enough to see that Ludovico had a suit of new clothes for when he served the princess or the prince.

"I have arranged for you to have palazzo staff at your beck and call. Signora delVecchio has been with my family since she was a signorina and I cannot bear to lose her. She will, however, be gratified to learn that her meals pleased you," Cristoval said, glad that the housekeeper was already gone from the prince's rooms. He would not put it past the prince to try to hold the signora hostage.

"Then be gone, you useless bag of tricks," the princess snapped, waving him away with her kerchief in hand.

"But—" the prince protested.

"We don't need his kind here. Get rid of him and be done with it!" the princess snapped.

Prince deMedici pursed his lips. Clearly, he was spoiling for the fight, but he had to please his wife as well. "You are standing with the Palantini now. At least we can rely on your vote when the time comes?"

Cristoval took Ludovico's hand and bowed formally. It was the only answer he could safely give. Anything else would be a lie or meant further conspiracy with a plotter for the king's throne.

Ludovico lingered, holding back. "But, Papa—"

"Not now," Cristoval counseled his son and dragged him from the prince's rooms.

XVII

"The moral virtues, then, are produced in us neither by nature nor against nature. Nature, indeed, prepares in us the ground for their reception, but their complete formation is the product of habit."

—Aristotle

20 d'Dicembre, 1684

RECOVERED from the truffle hunt of the previous day, Luciana carried Divya, secured with a hammock-like swath of cloth that crossed over her shoulders and kept the baby tucked close, as she went down the hall. Stefano was quick to open the door to Idala's chambers for her.

In Luciana's absence for the past three days, Idala's rooms had finally been turned into a nursery as she had requested and Maria della Guelfa, on call to the court as popular midwife, had become head nurse. Donna Rui had returned to her home and business, though she apparently made a point of returning every couple of days, particularly to keep an eye on young Massimo.

Giuletta brought in a farthingale chair, padded with champagne-hued pillows, to the center of Idala's bedroom and set it down for Luciana while Kisaiya took Divya from her mother's reluctant arms. Once enthroned, Maria gestured to each of the wet nurses in turn who presented first the twins—Pietra and Rosalina—and then the dark Chiara. Each of the girls had grown substantially. They had been so tiny at birth. Pietra and Rosalina were fair compared to their sister's darker looks, but in all other ways they were the same. They were the pictures of health, despite their small size.

Luciana made a point of inspecting each girl—the condition of her skin, her tiny curls, her fingers and toes—before pronouncing each one perfect to the delight of Maria and their individual wet nurse. When she was done, Luciana steeled herself for the inevitable. "And Massimo?"

Just behind her, she felt Stefano grip her left shoulder. "I thought we might put him off until tomorrow," he said.

"Enough has been 'put off.' King Alban and Queen Idala have not been interred until the last possible member of the Palantini has arrived and there have been no sessions, no further discussion of the murders—" Luciana shook her head and glanced up at her husband. "He is my ward, my charge, just as his sisters are, and I would do no less by him than them."

"As his mother requested, we keep the children apart," Signora della Guelfa said, "and since we speak of children apart, there is the older prince, Prince Dario Gian. He has apparently been very eager to see his sisters and little brother. I thought, now that you were here, perhaps you would like to supervise his visit?"

The idea caught Luciana by surprise. It was not that she had not considered Dario Gian would want to spend time with his siblings, but rather she had been so focused on her own plans, she had forgotten all about it. As *Araunya*, she was obligated to bring her daughter before the clans and Guilds as soon as possible. The clans had already met young Divya, but she had yet to be presented to the Guilds and an appointment had been made for today. Several of the Guilds were gathering at the home and workshop of the Guildmistress of Citteauroea.

It was still early morning yet, there would still be time. Luciana nodded and said, "Yes, go ahead and bring Prince Dario Gian to meet his sisters now."

Giuletta raised a hand, "But, Your Grace, he will be having his breakfast now and after that is—"

Stefano interrupted her with a cough. "Perhaps we can review Massimo's nursery now while Dario Gian has his breakfast and he can come up afterward, before he begins the rest of his day."

Giuletta curtsied. "I will let his *governante* know at once."

So this was to be her life? Luciana thought. It was to revolve around children and fitting into their schedules rather than vice versa. It was not that she had made any great plans that could not be negotiated, but that she had not realized how easily her own plans could be waylaid.

Massimo's nursery lay across the small hallway in Alban's adjoining bedroom. Where Idala's room had been light and gay in color and its large bed removed to make room for the cradles, the opposite was true here. Alban's room tended toward the more muted colors of dark green and mahogany. The bed-curtains were drawn around the enormous bed, which occupied the greater part of the room. The windows were open, and the royal cradle sat in the center of the single green-and-gold rug in what was left of the room between the bed and large wardrobe. A carved oak chair had been moved close by, along with a small, gateleg table and candelabra. A smaller, less ornate cradle sat on the other side of Alban's bed. The wet nurse rose from the chair and hurried to tuck back the heavy curtains that hung over the window. Instantly, the babe in the cradle began to fuss.

The littlest prince's cry sounded eerie and muffled, wheezing and so like that of a carrion bird that it chilled Luciana to the bone. She turned to Kisaiya immediately and, loath though she was to be apart from Divya, she could not bring the innocent spirit of that child before this one. Unable to help herself or meet Stefano's gaze, Luciana made the sign against the evil eye before she could turn back into the room. The wet nurse and her child seemed to have grown accustomed to her new charge in recent days and did not seem likewise inclined to have to protect herself with such sigils . . . unless Donna Rui had given her something that she wore.

Luciana was thankful for the placid nature of the nurse, Bonita. Where his sisters were pink and fattening up, young Massimo remained bone thin and almost twisted over on himself. Despite the pin used to hold his swaddling in place, the infant's thrashing kept it from remaining together. There was nothing peaceful or charming about this child and nothing, short of horns, could have made his angry face seem more devilish. His right fist remained raised above his blanket as though ready to bless or banish.

Massimo's face, ruddy with angry tears, had a gray cast to it. More than just the sputum on his covers and the sheeting used by the wet nurse testified to his illness. Luciana steadied herself with a quiet prayer and reached out to lay a pacifying hand on the child's wriggling chest. He literally burned to the touch, causing her to recoil.

"Why was word not sent that the boy is ill?" Luciana asked.

The wet nurse shook her head as she curtsied. "Nay, Your Grace, the child is not ill . . . or rather no more than the day he was born. He does not thrive, but his body heat rarely changes. The young prince nurses well and often, even if he grows no fatter. The physician, *il dottore* Bonta, doesn't bleed the boy at all anymore," she testified.

To Luciana's mind and training, bleeding never made much sense, but to the White Throne and its people, bleeding was customary to balance the humours of the patient. "Surely *il dottore* does not think the boy well?"

"What can we do for him, then?" Stefano asked. He stroked his short beard as he studied the boy, a sure sign that Stefano was agitated and in thought.

Maria della Guelfa spoke as she came forward into the room. "There's little that can be done at this time. The child nears a point where he will turn—whether for the good or the ill—no one can be sure and nothing can be done to sway him one way or the other but to nurse him and keep him dry, as Bonita does. *Il dottore* Bonta concurs."

Luciana stared at the boy. She wanted to turn away, but was unable. Because of this she was watching when the small poppet was briefly exposed while the boy thrashed.

"What is this?" she asked, reaching into the cradle and burrowing beneath the boy's blankets until she found what she thought she had spotted. From the twist of blanket and limbs, Luciana pulled out a small doll. The little figurine had brown floss hair, a white gown, and a tiny gold crown. What was most distinctive about the doll, however, was that it looked like it had been crushed, very deliberately, underfoot.

"It's a sad little thing, isn't that?" Bonita, the wet nurse, said as she came forward to finger the dress of the poppet in Luciana's hand. "I found it . . . in the garden. It was such a sorry little toy. I thought perhaps Prince Dario Gian had had it and grown tired of it. It was buried most ways beneath a rock, with some of its stuffing all pulled out and the crown askew. It took some stitching to put it back to right. I thought the boy should have something of his mother. Was I out of place?"

"No, no, of course not," Stefano said hurriedly, but was stopped by Luciana.

"The problem with this toy is that it is no simple toy," Luciana said, pulling the dolly away from the young woman. "Your heart was in the right place, and I am well-minded that all of Idala's children should have something of hers. I go to town today and will have proper dolls for each of the children, Dario Gian included." Luciana was quick to silence with a pressed finger to the question half-formed on her husband's lips. "Thank you, my lady, for your care of the prince." With that she turned, motioning everyone else out of the room before her. "Prince Dario Gian should be joining us about now, I think, but I believe Massimo is not quite ready for visitors."

Despite being a more than adequate horsewoman, Luciana allowed herself to be convinced to ride in a carriage because of Divya. The *Beluni*, who joined them, chafed almost as much as she had over the stultified form of transport. To the minds of the Romani women—and that included the normally docile Kisaiya—the streets of the capital were too narrow for any vehicle to properly navigate.

Further complicating what should have been a quiet family outing, Luciana found that they were to be accompanied by Lord Strozzini and a small complement of Stefano's new men-at-arms so recently hired from the ranks of the Escalade. It seemed that despite being Lord Regent, or rather because he was Lord Regent, she and Stefano were going to be guarded at all times. Lord Strozzini was not to be argued with on the matter. Having lost one charge so recently, he was not about to lose another. To Luciana, it was a serious intrusion of the White Throne upon what was the business of the black-blooded peoples of Tyrrhia, even though she could understand their caution and, when she paused to consider the danger to Stefano, ultimately, she could not refuse the escort.

By the time they reached the city's center, their party had turned into a procession between the guardsmen and gawkers eager to see the Regent, his wife, and their new child. Not all onlookers were friendly, however. Even in the carriage, Luciana could feel the swell of hostility from the crowd, noted the pointing fingers, heard the whispers about the Gypsies and the black-blooded interlopers to the throne.

Luciana looked out at Stefano. He rode with his head high, a smile on his face, and a friendly wave in return to all those gathered. He turned to meet her gaze, and she saw that this smile was firmly placed, almost a discreet mask. Surely he must hear the undercurrents of what they were saying?

"Do you want me to take Divya?" Stefano asked. He slowed his horse to draw closer to the carriage window.

Luciana shook her head, folding Divya closer to her, close enough that the child squirmed in her arms. Stefano laughed, a genuine smile lighting his eyes as he nodded in front of them. Lord Strozzini led the party, using his horse to break through the crowded streets and make a path for them.

They had almost reached their destination when someone threw a clot of mud from the street, whizzing into the carriage past Luciana's face and nearly hitting the child. Someone in the crowd yelled out, "Gypsy whore!"

Luciana had time to gather the baby even closer, sheltering her from the splatter of rotted fruit thrown next. Someone else shouted, their words indistinct in the hubbub of the crowd, but one man stood out.

He was a big, brawny man who wore a sword and that was all Luciana cared about. Even as she reached out for Stefano, someone yelled, " . . . doesn't matter! Roundheel or witch, she's a Gypsy! She's a whore!"

"Stefano, no!" Luciana cried, sensing a trap. Stefano, however, was already off his horse with sword drawn.

One of the men-at-arms captured Stefano's horse, even as Strozzini wheeled about and slid from his mount with his hand on his sword as well.

"You insult my wife *and* my daughter! I give you leave to rethink your words!" Stefano yelled, brandishing his sword in the man's direction.

Luciana bit her hand to smother her cry of protest, knowing it would serve no purpose other than to distract her husband or the bodyguard at his side. When the man from the crowd drew his sword, three more men came forward bearing swords. She longed to be riding a horse so that she could drive the beast between the men. Without Divya in her arms, Luciana might have gotten out of the carriage to defend her own name, beside her husband, she was, after all, completely comfortable with a sword in her hand.

The first braggadocio crossed swords with Stefano, showing no hesitation. He was either full of wine or hatred; in either case he was absolutely fearless.

Another of the guards snagged the reins of the skittering carriage horses while the other three swung down off their own mounts and went to stand behind Stefano and Strozzini.

The three men facing Stefano and the bodyguard fanned out, swords at the ready, striking at whomever they could.

And then they were at it!

Stefano kept his rapier raised high and to the center, easily parrying the first two feinting attacks, first to his solar plexus and then to his head. He did not, however, take the bait of opening himself up when he lunged forward in return.

Stefano countered again and again, allowing the man and his comrades to press them back, into the center of the street and out of the crowd before he actually struck. With a feint and a slashing strike to his middle, Stefano attacked with full fury.

The braggadocio and his companions seemed surprised by Stefano's skill and hesitated before he struck again, circling crabwise toward Luciana and the guards trying to keep the horses from bolting.

Stefano leaped into the man's path, keeping him away from the coach. Both men launched at one another, their bodies meeting with force. The *bravo* was bigger and pressed his size, shoving Stefano back, sidestepping and dodging Strozzini's strike.

Luciana's husband dipped down and sidestepped,

dragging his foot so that he tripped the man, who fell into the street, landing on his face. He rolled over and righted himself in a blur of movement. Stefano, however, was already at his neck with his blade, ready to make a final blow.

"You owe my wife an apology," Stefano said, his sword poised to cut him from ear to ear.

The braggadocio smiled, or rather sneered, even as he let his sword drop. "She isn't Gypsy, then?"

Stefano ground his teeth. Luciana could see the muscles in face and neck working as he fought for self-control, keeping his gaze on the single man instead of the small war raging nearby him.

"My wife *is* of black-blooded Romani. Have more respect for the people whose trade fills our kingdom's coffers!" Stefano responded. He stepped on the other man's sword so that now the *bravo* could not retrieve it. He gave the man a push. "Be gone, before I arrest you for harassment of innocent citizens!"

One of the braggadocios shoved Stefano off-balance. The stranger laughed unpleasantly, touched his forelock, and backed his way into the throng before whistling, turning, and disappearing. At the sound of the whistle, the other three men, just apparently average citizens—except for their skill and obvious training with the sword—fell back and they, too, faded into the crowd.

When no one spoke above the general hushed babble of the populace gathered to witness the transpiring events, Stefano stepped back, allowing Strozzini to pick up the braggadocio's sword, while he crossed to the carriage.

"Are you well, *cara mia*?" he asked, standing on the coach step so that he could see his wife and daughter easily.

Luciana nodded and gave the bundle in her arms to her grandmother. She frowned, wiping a bit of blood from Stefano's face. He had not come through the battle unscathed. "It is I who should be asking you that question. Let's be on our way quickly. I am not eager to make more new *friends*."

Stefano chuckled, stilling her hand where she wiped at his blood. He kissed it. "I'll leave no insult to my wife—or my daughter—unanswered."

"But still it was very dangerous, Your Grace. The crowd could have turned and you are only one man," Strozzini said, handing him the reins to his gray horse, Fascino, with a proficient bow.

"I had you and the men. The threat was—" Stefano began.

"Was more real than you give it credit. Please. Just, please, think more carefully. You have more to consider than just me now," Luciana said.

Stefano frowned down at her from horseback. His only answer was to put heels to his horse, forcing Strozzini to hurry ahead so that he could cut a path.

Luciana looked at her grandmother. The old woman watched her speculatively and handed Divya back, saying nothing. Luciana glanced over at Kisaiya who sat back, her face hidden by the shadows of the carriage.

They reached the Guildhouse in a matter of minutes, drawing no further distractions from curious onlookers. Stefano came to the carriage, opened the door, and folded down the steps before reaching in for Luciana's hand. He patiently handed down the Romani Queen—the *Beluni*—and the handmaid.

Luciana paused, taking in the sight of the Guildhouse decorated from the curving stone banisters up the marble steps, the solid wooden door, and the upper windows. Everywhere, there were ribbons and bows of Gypsy Silk. From the upper-story windows hung a large banner of sky blue, bearing the sign of the traditional red *vardo* wheel overlaid with the symbol of a golden hand using needle and thread. Crowded about all the windows were Romani women—mostly young, though a few were anything but—pressing their excited faces to the glass to see the *Araunya*, her heir, and the *Beluni*.

The Guildmistress of the clothiers of Citteauroea whom Luciana recognized from previous visits, and what seemed a dozen of her apprentices, met them at the door to the Guildhouse, and eagerly welcomed them inside. In the humungous old house, the tone was completely welcoming. Four other Guildmistresses—of the weavers, the gardeners from the mulberry groves, the ladies of the worm, and other clothiers—stood arranged in a row behind them, each waiting their turn to greet the women of rank among the black-blooded people.

The apprentices present, ranging in age from roughly thirteen to eighteen, all hovered in the doorway to the salon where the hosting Guildmistress led Luciana with her babe in arms, the *Beluni*, and, of less interest, Stefano and Kisaiya. On another day, Luciana suspected that some of the older apprentices might have lingered near the door to catch the eye of one of the men-at-arms, but today all interest was on the baby as the girls and women angled for a better look.

The Guildmistress waved her fellows into the room and, with a stern nod to her apprentices, shut the door soundly. She guided Luciana to a large, wing-backed chair placed squarely in the center of the room.

Guildmistress Eleni had moved several bolts of Gypsy Silk to make room for her visitors. Mostly, the furniture seemed to serve the purpose of providing a shelf or table on which to display the rich, colorful fabrics. From experience, Luciana knew that this room served as a fitting room as well as the design room where the Guildmistress and her senior apprentices met with their clientele. Today, the room served as reception hall for honored guests.

Guildmistress Eleni served them each, including the other Guildmistresses, in turn from a decorative carafe and a platter of goblets set on the desk. The drink was a fruity elderberry wine she and her assistants put up each year. When the time was ripe and the occasion arose, the wine was brought out for special guests.

While Luciana tended to Divya's needs, Eleni and the Romani Queen spoke of matters of little consequence, pleasantries mostly, but all the while with an eye toward Luciana and her daughter. Stefano hovered protectively behind her chair, sipping his wine and peering out the window at the men waiting outside. She hoped having him here in the room would allow common sense to reign, occupying his time, so that he did not go seeking the troublemakers they had encountered earlier.

When Divya settled, Luciana finally turned her full attention to her grandmother and, more importantly, the Guildmistresses. She eased her daughter out of the sling and gently handed Divya to Eleni, slowly disentangling her forefinger from the child's fist. As the Guildmistress stood straight, the child in her arms, Luciana spoke.

"Mistress Eleni and mistresses of the Guilds, I have come for your blessing on my child. When she is old enough, she will be *Araunya di Cayesmengro*. She will be raised in the ways of our people even though she is half-caste."

The middle-aged woman smiled at Luciana and then down at her infant daughter. "May I receive this blessed child as I stand for all of the Guilds and mistresses of each?" She looked for and received the nodding assent of the other Guildmistresses.

The Guildmistress bent low to press a kiss to each of her cheeks and her forehead, cooing at the child. Divya gave a milk-bubble sigh and turned her widened eyes to Eleni. Luciana watched carefully as Eleni slipped one of her needle-chaffed fingers into Divya's tiny fist.

"Ah! Her eyes show her fairy mark! I have never seen such eyes as hers!" the Guildmistress murmured, showing her once again to the other women. She paced away from Luciana, down the long room, gently cradling the baby, playing with her fingers and touching her nose as she moved. "Such eyes as these were made for fine needle-work."

As she neared the far end of the room, the girls outside could be heard struggling for a better line of sight through the crack left open by the sliding doors—oohing and aahing between their edging for a better position. Eleni turned back to Luciana, motioning to the door. "May I?" she asked.

Luciana nodded, glancing at her grandmother who smiled approvingly.

Mistress Eleni never had to touch the door. It slid wide open as though of its own free will, no doubt under the hands of several eager apprentices. The girls swarmed and were immediately enraptured. From the way they clasped their hands and some stuffed them into their apron pockets, it was clear that they itched to touch the child. One of the youngest girls could not restrain herself and reached out to the tiny *Araunya*-to-be. Another of the older girls slapped her hand away, and Divya gurgled at the sound.

"*Permisso*?" Mistress Eleni asked as the girls pressed ever nearer.

Luciana knew that the girls were not likely to hurt the baby, but still her motherly instincts made her hesitate. Culture, however, won out and she nodded again. With whispers to be careful and a reluctant sigh when they had to pass the baby from one girl to the next, Divya was admired and adored by the sedentary Romani girls in training for a lifetime of sewing and crafting with the magic of the Gypsy Silk.

"We have been preparing for your daughter and have presents, if we may?" one of the other Guildmistresses said.

"But, of course," Luciana laughed, more than happy now that her daughter was safe in her arms again.

"The first gift is from the Guilds and all the young women who work with us," Mistress Eleni explained as she beckoned to the girls who hurriedly produced a small packet with a flourish. Mistress Eleni unfolded the plain paper wrapping to reveal a small, filigreed needle case strung on a long black ribbon. On the opposite end of the ribbon was a pair of shears in a matching sheath. "Her first chatelaine, with the case for her needles and her first snips for sewing. Your daughter, when she is of sufficient age, will be welcome in our sewing circles at any time."

"We are honored by your invitation, Guildmistress, and I would be pleased to have her learn the craft at your side." Luciana nodded for her grandmother to take the gift.

Mistress Eleni smiled in genuine pleasure. She held onto the case for a moment longer. "Inside the case, are Divya's first five needles. They are made of solid gold. They are the personal gifts of the Guildmistresses."

Luciana felt tears prick her eyes. Presents such as these must have cost the Guildmistresses dearly and were surely a sign of friendship as well as fealty. Thankfully, the girls saved her from having to speak as they quickly produced the next gift. It was a christening gown embroidered and heavily beaded from neck to hem in the arcane sigils of their people along with a matching cap. Also, per custom, it was covered with small white buttons that could one day be snipped off and sold as holy relics should she ever find herself in need.

"We made it ourselves," one of the older girls said.

"If you already have a christening gown, she could wear it at court," another of the girls hurried to say.

"It's a good and proper gown for the Christian blessing, so she will always have a bead or button to wear for good luck!"

"Or sell for—"

"She wouldn't need to sell blessed beads! She'll be the *Araunya*, silly!"

This discourse quickly diminished into a hubbub of girlish chatter. Seeing the Guildmistress' stern expression as she clapped her hands to bring order, Luciana struggled to smother her laughter. It was true. Divya was fortunate in that both her parents could provide her the solid financial future most of these girls had no hope of without the guild, yet they had seen to it, with their pocket money, to make sure little Divya would have "blessed beads."

When the girls finally came to order, Mistress Eleni cleared her throat and said, "We have also taken the liberty of making gowns for the little princesses and the prince. It—the gowns are made of finest Gypsy Silk as their mother would have ordered for them. We hoped that the Guild could give the gowns as a gift . . . if it would not be an insult if— You would know best, *Araunya*."

Luciana looked at the beautiful gowns and bonnets held up by four of the girls. The gowns were all of the same make—without beading—but deftly embroidered. The fine needlework distinguished each of the gowns in slightly different ways. They were all beautiful and would fit even the tiniest infants.

Luciana glanced up at Stefano and back at the hopeful expressions on the girls' faces. "Her Majesty would have been honored by such a gift, as I am in her stead," she responded.

"It is so sad . . . Is it true about the little prince . . . that he's not . . . well, as he should be?" one of the girls dared to ask.

"Margherita!" the Guildmistress said sharply, clapping her hands as she spoke.

Immediately, the girl blushed and backed up as though to hide amongst her peers, but they would have none of it and scattered away from her.

"It's natural for the girl to have questions, *Araunya-chavi*," the *Beluni* said softly. "Try as you might, there has been talk. Consider what you want people to know and then speak in trust." She spoke in the language of the black-blooded peoples, the language that the gentrified, city-dwelling Rom did not always know. Only the Guildmistresses could be confident of understanding, of hearing Luciana's grandmother. It was something for which Luciana was grateful.

Luciana felt Stefano's hand on her shoulder and knew without looking that he was asking for her forbearance, her caution. They had not discussed this eventuality, had not planned for this conversation, for the natural curiosity of the people shut away from the palazzo who only caught the occasional rumor. That this information was out . . . amongst the people . . . what else did they know? Did they think they know? Alas, this was neither the time nor place to begin an inquiry. She thought quickly. Whatever she said, she knew Stefano would not be happy, but there was nothing to be done for it. Even though the girl had been corrected, there was still an air of expectation in the room.

Luciana sighed. "The prince is . . . ill-formed. Probably a condition of the pregnancy. There is little hope that he will ever be normal in form and, thus, by the law of the land, he cannot be in line for the throne, like his brother, Prince Dario Gian."

"Or the sisters?" the girl, Margherita, asked.

"His sisters will be in line, but it is Prince Dario Gian who stands to take the throne," Luciana clarified.

"Is he ugly?" another girl queried.

"*Basta*! The *Araunya* is not here to answer your gossip! She comes for the blessing of her child. For us to see and know this child from the time of her birth, as the once and future *Araunya di Cayesmengro*, is enough!" Mistress Eleni said with another clap of her hands. "Off with you! To your work!"

The girls filed from the room, some of them curtsied in the way of the White Throne, others just bobbed their heads and turned to walk from the room in an orderly manner. The eldest girl waited to be last and then slid the door shut in its framework.

"Forgive me, *Araunya*, I thought I had taught my apprentices better than that. They should have little time for idle speculation," the Guildmistress said.

Behind her, Stefano squeezed and patted her shoulder, apparently accepting her decision to be honest.

"They are like everyone else, *Daiya*," Luciana said, using the address to a skilled and respected witch, for that was vhat the Guildmistresses must be to work the Gypsy Silk he way they did and then teach their students. It was not ften used to address her, though. "Your mind is free to vander when you sew and, if you have companions, then ou will talk."

"And since we are talking about such things, Guildmisress, I have a question for you," the *Beluni* said. "You, like ny great-granddaughter, here, are half-caste, are you not? Are you a Child of the Bloods? Are you blessed by the *ata*?"

Luciana sucked in her breath, surprised by the question. Only a queen or old woman could ask something so peronal and not expect offense. While it had been something uciana had been curious about over the years herself, she ad never spoken of it.

Eleni coughed slightly, reddening as she saw that everyne watched her. "You know that I could not be Guildmisress without being full of the black blood or a Child of the Bloods. I have a fairy mark . . . do you . . . do you wish to see t?" she asked, casting nervous eyes in Stefano's direction.

"No," Luciana said, even as her grandmother said, "Yes."

"Are you challenging me? My birthright?" Mistress Eleni asked, her voice rising as she spoke. It was obvious he was bordering on the point of tears.

"No, Mistress, I merely wished to have an old woman's uriosity satisfied since I see no obvious mark about you," uciana's grandmother said. While her words softened the low of her question, the question was still out. "It's just hat some are ashamed . . . they dye their hair, or in some vay, hide it."

"Very well, then," Eleni said. She quickly turned so that er back was to Stefano, and he could see little of what she howed to the other women as she raised her skirts to just he calf and put her left foot forward. She pointed forward, ot at her toe, but at her heel for her left foot was backward, ike the *gianes* fairies.

Luciana gasped in surprise, "But you walk so graceully!"

"Thank you, *Araunya*," Mistress Eleni murmured. "I was orn this way. I have the *gianes*' foot. I'm told by those who vould know best that I took no longer than the average hild to learn to walk. When I was very young, I studied the dance—when I was not sewing—and perhaps that is how learned the grace you speak of."

"You were very gracious in response to our curiosity and we thank you," Luciana said.

The Guildmistress smoothed her dress into place and shrugged, apparently comfortable with her "disfigurement" and the discussion of it. Undoubtedly, it had been noticed and commented on before. "If the information serves, then I am content to provide elucidation, especially if that helps your purpose in any way, *Araunya e Beluni*."

"Indeed," the *Beluni* said, "such information—while not directly beneficial—serves a purpose. While I do not and did not mean to accuse you of any falseness, to know your Mark, to have witnessed your Mark, provides a measure of assurance for us in these troubled times."

The Guildmistress blinked, as though surprised perhaps by the Gypsy Queen's candor and the measures she felt she must take. Eleni nodded and spread her hands in open acquiescence, "What other way may I serve you? I am, after all, your servant evermore."

Luciana glanced to the bay window. She could see only the tops of the men's heads and those of the horses. The men were growing restless. She stood. "Mistress Eleni, you have served us well and been an excellent hostess. I would ask no more of you this day. Thank you."

Mistress Eleni curtsied. "Yes, if there is anything else—*ever . . .*"

Taking the Guildmistress' hand, Luciana gave it a gentle squeeze and quickly bussed both her cheeks with light kisses. She turned and did the same to the other Guildmistresses. "I know who to turn to in my hour of need," Luciana promised them.

"May I?" one of the other Guildmistresses asked, nodding to the child wrapped in the cocoon of swaddling and sling once again. When Luciana lifted Divya up, the Guildmistress pressed a kiss to her forehead, sealing the bond newly formed.

XVIII

"Thus have the gods spun the thread for wretched mortals: that they live in grief while they themselves are without cares; for two jars stand on the floor of Zeus of the gifts which he gives, one of evils and another of blessings."

—Homer

1 d'Dicembre, 1684

STROZZINI prodded his horse into a faster pace. Six men of the Duca di Drago accompanied him on this er-and through the cold, sleeting rain. He slowed only when e reached Citteauroea and the narrow streets that made he outer quarter. He had read and reread Don Battista's etter to him, disbelieving. Even in an audience with the ordling, it seemed almost impossible to believe that he was o close to finding the assassins of King Alban! That his uery at court had led to this! To the whispered-about *Mag-us Inique*!

With him was Capitano della Guelfa, a man Strozzini new the White Queen had personally trusted. Della Guelfa was a man he knew some little bit himself, having een him around the palazzo and being familiar with his nce senior officer, Maggiore di Montago. Good men all. trozzini knew he could trust the capitano and his hand-icked men, and that was all that mattered for the moment.

Strozzini pulled his mount to a halt outside *le Armi Do-ata*, an inn and taverna with a questionable reputation, hardly the place he would have expected to find a priest and his cohorts, but was this not the best of hiding places, then? He dismounted and handed his reins to the youth coming out of the inn. He waited on the cobbled walkway just outside the doors for the other men to be ready. When they gathered near, he laid a finger to his lips.

"We must do this quickly and quietly. I want every one of them arrested. Batter them if you must, but I want these men alive!" Rodrigo Strozzini told them. With that, he turned and was met by two young boys in gaudy livery standing before a room of curtains.

"We are *vigilare*," Strozzini said. "We've come for one of your guests . . . a priest named Caserta."

The boys looked at each other silently. The taller one spoke first. "I don't know about a priest, but we had a man named Caserta. He left last night."

Strozzini felt his gut pitch. He was so close! "He was here with friends, was he not?"

The taller boy nodded and shrugged at the same time. "He seemed to be . . . but they all left last night."

"Do you know where they've gone?" Strozzini asked, pulling a soldibianco from his pocket. He held it up. "There's more where this comes from for information."

The boys eyed the gold coin with longing. This time the smaller boy spoke, reaching for the soldibianco, "They didn't say where they were going, Signore, but I know they were splitting up."

Strozzini held the coin just out of the boy's reach. "Where? Where were they going?"

"Don't know," the bigger boy said. "They didn't say . . . not near us anyway, but about half of 'em looked ready for a long ride."

"Half?" the capitano asked.

"*Sí!*" the boy said, holding out his hand expectantly. "There were nine or ten of 'em. Hard to be sure what with their comings and goings. Always on the move, they were."

Strozzini dropped the coin in the boy's hand. "Can you tell what any of them looked like?"

The boys looked at each other, shrugged, and snickered. The taller youth said, "They were men. We didn't pay much attention."

"There was one . . . big man," the smaller boy volunteered. "Taller than you and muscles, he had lots of those. Tore up the taverna more'n once."

Strozzini remembered the man who had faced down the Lord Regent in the street only yesterday. He had an uncomfortable feeling he had met one or more of the *Magnus Inique* only the day before. The braggadocios had been too coordinated in their movements for average rioters.

"Anything else?" he prompted, holding out another soldibianco. When the boys shook their heads, Strozzini flipped the smaller lad the coin. "If they come back . . . not a word to them and there's ten soldibiancos for the one who gets word to me through the *vigilare*. My name is Strozzini. Can you remember that?"

"For ten soldibiancos, I can remember anything," the smaller boy said with a wink. "My brother, too."

"Good!" Strozzini said. He hesitated, wondering if he really should trust the boys at their word. Instinct told him they would probably sell him their mother for ten soldibiancos. It was a remarkable sum.

"What do you want us to do now?" the capitano asked when they had recovered their horses.

"Now, I want you to search the city. I want news of these men. I'll take any of them. Search the tavernas, search the inns and get word to me. *I* want to be there when these men are arrested. I suspect them of the highest treason," Strozzini said. He remounted. "For now, I return to the palazzo. The Lord Regent is unprotected when I'm gone, and I'll not lose another sovereign under my protection!"

Stefano stared out the window, watching the gentle rain beat down upon the panes of glass. His hand moved to the collar that signified his position of Regent of all Tyrrhia yoked around his neck. It weighed heavily upon him; his charges to the children of his sister and her husband, his friend, were only complicated now by those duties owed to the kingdom. In all the years of their friendship, Stefano had never envied Alban's position as king, yet now the duties were his without the title. He could be more easily challenged and overridden than the king, but the expectations of him were essentially the same.

His life, he had already sworn in service to the Crown, but the onerous levels of the expectations . . . he found it as intimidating as fatherhood . . . and now he was father to the royal orphans as well as his own seed. He turned from the window, determined to shake off the ennui.

He stirred the papers on Alban's desk . . . on his desk. He had hoped for better news from the borderlands, be they enemies or cultivated alliances. Already the eyes of continental rulers and the Roman Church were watching and biding their time. Episodes of civil unrest had broken out, mostly caused by the witch-hunters who unofficially sought out and brought to "trial" men and women—mostly Romani.

Such episodes always erupted here and there, but the air of tolerance maintained by the balance of the two thrones was in jeopardy. Without the Black Throne, without the Romani, Tyrrhia would lose its major economic resource—the Gypsy Silk. Some of the *gadjé* thought they did not need the Rom for the Silk, expecting its natural magical qualities without anticipation of a magic-using witch to imbue the fabric . . . and it was not just one witch, but an entire network of magic cast from the sowing of the seeds and trees that fed the silk worms to the very sewing of the fabric. For its full effect, not just anyone could sew Gypsy Silk and, thus, the Black Throne had been able to curry more tolerance in other lands eager to have crafters of the fabric—tailors and seamstresses and the Guilds that supported them. All of it was a delicate network as fragile as the silk spun by a spider and he, as regent, was the new spider. He had no control of the actual web, but he must maintain its moorings.

Further problems troubled him as well as the Palantini. With Alban's death, even though the tribunal had already ruled, there were members of the *Armata* and Escalade who had thrown their allegiance to Ortensia . . . and the Church . . . or some other faction. Everywhere the underpinnings of what made Tyrrhia a rich and powerful nation seemed to be coming undone.

Tyrrhia was a philosopher-State, a virtual island in a sea of piety. On all borders, Tyrrhia met lands ruled as much by religion as the hand of a king. Prizing their independence of thought and freedom from the reigning religion, Tyrrhia—and, thereby its king and his counselors, the Palantini—could not ignore the differences between them and the rest of the known world, especially with the lands of the Holy Roman Catholic Church just to the north of continental Tyrrhia. Even the gathering of the Palantini usually began with prayers, though they honored the three major religions of Tyrrhia: Catholicism, Judaism, and the Muslim.

In the weeks since the deaths of the king and queen, the Palantini had begun to gather. The palazzo fairly burst at its seams as it attempted to host as many of the senior Palantini and their families as could be squeezed within the very gates. What members of the Palantini had not found residence in the palazzo were pressing their way into every inn, taverna, and open house to be found in and around the capital city. Thankfully, the Black Queen had opted to keep her *benders* and *vardos* as residence for herself and her entourage and his own household held the balance of the Black Throne with his wife serving as not just Regent Guardian, but also *Araunya* of both *Cayesmengri* and *Cayesmengro*—normally, one *Araunya* was charged with every tool that served to make their Silk and the other *Araunya* with every craftsman, thus encompassing the Silk Trade from the least unskilled laborer to the very needles used by the greatest of the Guildmistresses.

It was the largest gathering of the Palantini since Princess Bianca was set aside and then-Prince Alban stepped up to the White Throne and Stefano gauged this gathering was of greater importance than even then, for every Lord entitled to attend appeared to have arrived. The call to staff the Palazzo and various gathering houses had veritably put money in the pockets of anyone willing and able to work. How this temporary boom in the economy would affect the overall balance of things was yet to be seen.

To complicate matters further, Cousin Prunella had taken occupancy of Stefano's bedroom with her infant son. He was not looking forward to the return of her constantly shared opinions, but this was merely a nuisance.

Scratching sounded at the door and startled him from his reverie. "Come in," Stefano said.

The door opened and Estensi poked his head into the room. "Your Excellency, the new Bishop of Tyrrhia has arrived and wishes an audience. He is available now," the Court Herald said. He winced sympathetically.

"Better now than later. Send him up," Stefano said with a shrug. He took a seat behind the desk and quickly collected the papers that were strewn about. He was setting them facedown in a neat and orderly pile when the door swung wide. He rose, bowing.

"The Bishop Reginaldo Abruzzi!" Estensi announced and closed the door after the man entered the room.

Stefano motioned for the bishop to take one of the chairs opposite the desk.

The bishop entered and crossed to the far side of the desk. He held out his left hand and the ring to be kissed. Stefano shook his head and waved the gentleman toward the chairs again. The bishop, a man of mild olive complexion, frowned, clearly displeased. "I understood you to be a Catholic," he said.

"I am Tyrrhian first," Stefano replied in the most politic fashion he could muster. "In Tyrrhia, it is important for the leader of the people to remain as neutral as possible in matters of public affairs."

"And yet we are alone," the bishop pointed out, gesturing about the room.

"Yes, this is true, but tell me, Your Reverence, did you come to speak to Stefano di Drago or the Lord Regent of Tyrrhia?" Stefano asked politely.

The bishop frowned again. He was a middling man, more descriptive by the wardrobe of office he wore than by any personal features of note. He wore a cleric's garb, but richer than the average priest because his clothes were made of Gypsy Silk. Stefano wondered what element of glamour the man had focused upon and guessed that it was this air of holiness that exuded from him.

"I understand the king was openly Catholic . . . as was his queen," the bishop observed to no one in particular.

"And yet a king is not a regent, nor a regent a king, and there are certain precautions I must take," Stefano said, resuming his seat. "I am confident that you can understand my position."

"What position I do not understand is the christening of the children. I understand the newborns have not been christened in the way of their parents, despite their questionable health," the bishop said, sighing before he met Stefano with a pointed stare and arched blond brow.

"I'm not sure where you got your information, but the girls are all hale and hearty, and a little time set aside for your arrival could do no harm," Stefano replied.

"While I am gratified that you would indulge the Church so much as to wait for me," Bishop Abruzzi said, leaning forward to put his hands against the far side of the desk, "it is my duty to worry about the immortal souls of the princesses and the prince whose health, I am given to understand, is anything but 'hale and hearty.'"

Stefano ducked his head in acknowledgment. "While the prince may not be as sturdy as I would've liked, his health has seemed to remain secure, and no harm has been done by delaying his christening.

"Somehow a christening in the very church where their parents' body lay in state seemed, if nothing else, at odds with the purpose of the christening," Stefano said.

"If every child's christening were delayed because a parent lay in state, a goodly number of Christendom would not have received the sacrament within an appropriate amount of time. As it is, christening the children now, almost a month after their birth is highly questionable," the bishop responded tersely.

"Two weeks," Stefano corrected as he leaned back in his chair and smiled, opening his hands wide in an affable shrug. "If that is your counsel, Your Reverence, then I see nothing wrong in waiting to christen the children until they are old enough to choose for themselves and raise them in the fullness of Neoplatonic tradition. To let them to decide for themselves seems highly appropriate to me when they are older and I thank you for suggesting it."

The bishop regarded Stefano with a sour expression. "I suggested nothing of the kind! The children must be christened at once!"

"And when do you propose that this affair of State take place?" Stefano asked. He sat forward in his chair, leaning his elbows against the desk.

"The christening must be done immediately! With or without great ceremony!" the bishop demanded.

Stefano leaned back in his chair again, toying with his fingertips. "As it so happens, preparations have already begun for the christening of the children—my daughter included—"

"Your daughter? And how old is she?" the bishop asked diffidently.

"She is but a week younger than her cousins, Your Reverence. But who else do we include in this mass christening? There've been other children born in the palazzo since the birth of the heirs. Indeed, you will discover that a great boom has taken place in the populace, and not all of it is due to the gathering of the Palantini," Stefano said. "Indeed, unless you appoint someone to do this thing instead, you will find yourself quite busy overseeing the sacraments of all the little lordlings added to our population."

The bishop sat back, his brows raised. "Had I not been accosted in the corridor by so many anxious parents, I would guess that you were being facetious and not taking this matter seriously, Your Excellency. You *are* taking the matter seriously, I hope?"

"Oh, indeed! Indeed, I am, but I wanted you to be aware of the problems which faced me. Every mother will want her child to be blessed with the sacrament at the same time as the new heirs. So I have waited for you, and I leave it to your discretion how many children are to be christened with the cousins and when," Stefano said.

The bishop looked deeply uncomfortable. "Why not christen just the heirs and leave your daughter to your wife's discretion. She is Romani, I understand?"

Stefano leaned back in his chair, arms crossed. He was enjoying himself. "My wife is, as you say, Romani, yes, but she, too, is eager for our daughter to be blessed with a christening. Since the cousins will be raised as one family, as siblings, in fact, it makes no sense to exclude one, and if we were to omit one, there might be reason to eliminate another."

"Eliminate another?" the bishop exclaimed. "Do you mean one of the heirs?"

"Indeed, I do. You have not seen the boy, Massimo. The local priest who serves the palazzo parish was . . . shall we say—reticent?—when he saw the boy. He was quite alarmed," Stefano reported. "It was the actual reason why we waited for you. The children should be christened together or not at all—at least not until their majority."

The bishop rose, folding his arms into his clerical garb. "You've given this considerable thought, I see. You are quite determined that the cousins be christened together? The four of them?"

"Five, Your Reverence. Four siblings and the cousin. My wife is quite anxious to see our daughter blessed," Stefano said.

Again, Bishop Abruzzi's expression soured. "Then prepare the five. They shall receive the sacrament this afternoon! You will excuse me, Your Excellency, I have work to do and much to be prepared for."

"Ah! Before you leave, Your Reverence, there is the matter of the other children within the palazzo? What would you have me tell their parents?"

"Tell them their children will receive the sacrament on the Sabbath," the bishop replied, bowing.

Stefano rose and bowed also. "I will have the children prepared immediately!"

Stefano looked up from Divya in her new christening gown, surprised by the sound of childish prattle in a nursery full of infants. Prince Dario Gian stood in the doorway with his *governante* excitedly talking about the christening.

"Prince Dario Gian! You are looking fine, this morning," Stefano said, glancing at Luciana who was helping to dress Chiara.

"Yes, I've come to see the babies chrish'end," the boy announced. "Donna Flavia says that I must come."

Luciana left Chiara to the wet nurse and the *Beluni* and joined them. She gave a stern look at the *governante* and knelt in front of her nephew. "Wouldn't you rather be doing something else?" she asked.

Dario Gian, looking for all the world like his mother's son, nodded. "Church is boring," he said.

"It can be, yes," Stefano agreed, sitting down so that he was closer to the boy's eye level.

The young prince leaned away from Donna Flavia and whispered loudly, "Signore Montagna was reading to me from a book, but Donna Flavia said that must wait for another day."

"Would you like it if I could convince Donna Flavia to

let Signore Montagna read more of the book to you?" Luciana asked.

The boy looked up at his *governante* and then nodded quickly.

Stefano nodded and looked up into the bright angry eyes of the *governante.* "Signora, I think that a child sitting through a single christening would be a trial, but five? No, let him return to his tutor."

"But—" Donna Flavia began.

"A child his age would not understand the significance of the moment, and there will be enough children there with all four of his siblings and our daughter being christened," Luciana said, her voice forceful but pleasant.

"As you wish, Your Excellency," Donna Flavia replied, clearly unhappy with the decision being made.

"Can I play with the babies later, though?" Dario Gian asked.

Luciana laughed, "They are still too small to play, Prince Dario, but you can come visit them before bedtime if you wish."

The boy nodded again, smiling. "Come, Donna Flavia. Signore Montagna was reading to me about . . ." His words trailed off as he took his *governante's* hand and pulled her back down the stairs toward his own suite.

Luciana breathed a heavy sigh of relief and closed the door behind the child.

"But shouldn't the prince be present for the christenings?" Donna della Guelfa asked, her voice showing her surprise.

"In normal times, yes, perhaps, but with him . . ." Luciana nodded toward Massimo's nursery. "We think it better to save the prince from any unseemly . . . effects. In fact, we want all the girls baptized first and then they are to be taken from the church immediately."

Donna della Guelfa nodded and turned to her charges.

"I think this best," Stefano said quietly. He brushed a kiss against her temple. "We have no idea what to expect."

"Actually, I have more than an idea," Luciana grumbled and left his side.

Crossing to the church, Stefano shivered in spite of himself, not from the cold of the drizzly day, but rather thinking of the monstrosity of this child, Massimo, that was to be finally brought into a church. He felt the anxiety of it all roil in his stomach. What would happen when *he* was brought to the church? If he believed in the signs and stories, what would become of the man who would not let death defeat him?

Stefano shivered again. That bastarde was supposed to have met his maker, but he had detoured through evil magic. What would happen now in this simple church? He silently wished he could have kept the girls . . . *his* girl, Divya, from this, but what better way to fill the private royal chapel with the Romani who might help combat a soul gone awry?

The bishop clearly did not favor Stefano's choice of audience—half the room was given over to the Romani and, the other half to selected members of the Palantini. Padre Gabera standing at the bishop's side, also understood the making of Massimo.

Padre Gabera crossed himself and averted his eyes from the boy. Stefano silently vowed to do what he could to keep Gabera in the palazzo chapel where he could provide counsel. He neither liked nor trusted Bishop Abruzzi.

They were in the small chapel rather than the great cathedral hall. The room was small, close even, with all assembled. Tapers burned in seven stepped iron stands that curved to the halfway point on either side of the apse. In place of the normal altar, a platform had been erected for its recent purpose of holding the bodies of the White King and Queen. Now, however, it held four wriggling girls and an unusually still boy-child.

Even with the candles, the room was gloomily dark and yet warm enough that the babies did not fuss.

The funerary dais had been made for larger bodies than the infants. The children lying there now were tiny in stark contrast to their earthly parents who had been laid out less than a week before.

Crowded around the children, the wet nurses served in the place of the dead mother. Stefano and his *Araunya* stood to serve as godparents—except for their own infant. For her, the old *Beluni* stood, her head covered with a shawl in all proper form.

As each of the twin princesses was blessed and handed to her godfather, Stefano held the girl to be kissed by

Luciana, their godmother, and then passed to the wet nurse in charge of her. Members of the Palantini seemed to mutter over the rush to take the princesses from the church, but when Chiara was christened, a number of the Palantini gasped when Stefano was named her godfather and the Romani Queen, Solaja Lendaro, was named godmother.

Throughout the ceremony, instead of having his mind on his prayers, Stefano concentrated on Padre Gabera who had been the priest who had spied upon *Magnus Inique*—the witch-hunters' league—and narrowly escaped with his life. Gabera fell under the protection of Maggiore di Montago, Alessandra's now husband in the afterlife, and had witnessed the final results of the fight with the bishop's predecessor, Cardinal delle Torre, who not only stood behind *Magnus Inique*, but had authored more than one plot against the Tyrrhian throne, with pretenses of it being in God's name.

After the princesses, Gabera took up Divya and handed her to the bishop already in the midst of his prayers of sacrament.

For a moment, Bishop Abruzzi looked as though he would protest the order of precedence but then proceeded, prayers half-said.

Divya's christening completed, Luciana's grandmother gathered her great-granddaughter and godchild, and the wet nurse of her other godchild, Princess Chiara, and pulled them to one side of the room, away from the blessings of the last child, Massimo.

Gabera, finally and with obvious reluctance, took the boy from Stefano's hands. Massimo squirmed. Gabera cast a terrified glance at Stefano—after all, he, too, had seen a Prince of the Church cast spells.

Bishop Abruzzi scowled at Gabera's reticence, no doubt accounting the man's reluctance to the boy's disfigurements. As the bishop began his words of dedication, Stefano took note of the sudden darkness almost of night outside. The world seemed to stop, on bated breath as the bishop began the words of solemn prayers to the Lord, binding the child to God. Even as he said those words, the heavens ripped wide. The darkness was seared in half with a dagger of lightning which seemed to stab at the very chapel where all were congregated. The heavens opened to a sudden and harsh blinding rain. Another lightning bolt crackled its way from the sky, shattering first darkness and then ears with the following rumble of thunder.

The child, Massimo, let out an odd cackle of laughter. Stefano's chest hurt as though his heart had stopped in its cage, only beginning to thud back into natural rhythm when the boy and the bishop—like everyone else in the room—fell silent. Padre Gabera cringed.

Bishop Abruzzi asked for the godfather and godmother. Stefano and Luciana spoke their words, seemingly oblivious to the thunderstorm or that the candles guttered or that an unnatural cold swept through the room so that everyone's breath could be seen as it escaped their lips. Around the small chapel, those in attendance grew restless. The bishop looked up, his attention drawn by the strangeness around him. A woman screamed as another bolt of lightning struck, as though at the *Cattedrale* itself, followed immediately by a resounding clap of thunder.

The room crackled with energy not of the Church and the door to the chapel began to rattle as though tugged at by someone. Bishop Abruzzi folded Massimo close to his breast even as the child let out another hideous cackle.

The windowpanes began to jiggle in their frames as though someone knocked at the windows—except no one was there—as though unable to enter in the usual fashion. When the door began to vibrate again, louder than before, several of the Palantini glanced toward it and huddled closer to one another. Power and cold swirled about the room, snuffing out candles lit on the steps to the altar.

One of the oil lamps in the apse was extinguished as though by an unseen hand. Even the bishop seemed aware of the magic swirling around the room. Stefano gave silent thanks that Abruzzi clutched the prince closer instead of handing him to Stefano as godfather. In other days, Stefano would have been angry with himself for his superstitious reaction, but he had seen and heard too much in recent times not to pay heed to the feeling like an icy spider crawling up his spine. He grabbed Luciana to him and, thoughtlessly, joined her in her whispered prayer . . .

". . . and, yea, though I walk through the Valley of the Shadow of Death, I shall fear no evil . . ."

A harsh wind swept through the room. Another crash of

thunder and lightning, the energy crackling on people when they moved against one another. The door began to vibrate, jiggling in its jamb as though it were being set upon by fiends. With a cracking sound, the door to the chapel splintered. The rest of the candles were snuffed out, casting the room into utter blackness. Windowpanes cracked in their frames. A howling wind snapped through the church, buffeting and tearing at those gathered as though with unseen fingers. Another bolt of lightning shattered the blackness outside and its flash lit the chapel again, the rumble of thunder shaking the entire *Cattedrale*. Then, there was silence again. Stefano's heart pounded painfully in his chest as he peeked at the door through half-closed eyes.

As though released from their prayers, the *gadjé* in the room rapidly crowded through the chapel door, emptying the room except for the priests, Massimo, Stefano, and the Romani.

Bishop Abruzzi looked down at the suddenly squirming child in his arms, his eyes growing wide and round as he took in the strange red glow beginning to form around the boy.

The Romani left their pews and crowded forward, pushing close. Someone called, "Finish the sacrament, *Rashi*!" Stefano found himself pushed up against the altar with Luciana. There was no room to move and Massimo was an arm's reach away. His eyes glowed demon-dark.

"Finish the words, Padre!" Luciana urged. "In his last life, he twisted Church magic, don't let him do it now!"

"In his last life—" Bishop Abruzzi began to protest, then he looked at the boy in his arms. He held him over the baptismal font. "May the powers of darkness, which the divine Redeemer had vanquished by his cross, retire before thee—What will this child be known to the Lord by?"

"Massimo Giaccomo Cosimo Novabianco!" Stefano yelled over the whirlwind that had risen in the room.

"May the powers of darkness, which the divine Redeemer had vanquished by his cross, retire before thee, that thou mayest see to what hope, and to what an exceeding glorious inheritance among the saints, thou art called Massimo Giaccomo Cosimo Novabianco," Bishop Abruzzi pronounced. "Let us pray!

"Almighty, everlasting God, Father of our Lord Jesus Christ, look graciously down upon this child, whom thou has called to the grace of regeneration by the Holy Ghost; banish all darkness from *his* heart, and vouchsafe unto *him* the Holy Spirit of thy Son, who liveth and reigneth with thee and the same Holy Spirit evermore. Amen."

Outside lightning flashed again, thunder rumbled, and the entirety of the Cattedrale seemed ready to come down around their very ears. Bishop Abruzzi dashed the thrashing Massimo into the baptismal font.

With a suddenness that rocked people on their feet, the wind ceased. Even the ungodly presence seemed to fade. Stefano sagged with relief as Bishop Abruzzi handed the soaking baby to him.

Stefano looked down at Massimo and, for the first time, saw the inquisitiveness of a child. Outside, the sky brightened and the rain slowed to a natural light patter against the broken panes of the chapel windows.

Everyone began looking at each other, straining forward to look at the child. Stefano handed the child to his wife and let her turn for the others to see.

"This . . . this was no normal christening," Bishop Abruzzi said, looking faint, confused, and exhausted.

"No," Stefano said. "This was no normal christening."

Rather than stay for the sermon or to wish the children well, the room was notably empty. The Romani were filing out of the chapel.

Still shaking, Stefano did his best to hide it and urged Luciana to pass the child to Grasni who stood in for Massimo's regular wet nurse. He was glad now that Luciana had bid the young woman stay in the nursery, to wait and help settle the children as they returned, glad that the woman who cared for Massimo had not witnessed this christening.

Abruzzi and Gabera genuflected when Grasni passed with Massimo in her arms. "Could it have been a ghost, then? Or some malevolent spirit? Here? In the protection of the Lord's house?" Abruzzi asked.

Luciana nodded. "I think it was."

"But how?" Abruzzi demanded, moving along the back of a pew.

"It could only have been brought in . . . by its vessel," Luciana replied, taking momentary solace in Stefano's arms. "The cardinal may well have been defeated today. He lost his grip on the boy with the power of the Christian naming."

"You mean the prince?" Abruzzi whispered in abject horror. He turned, squinting into every narrow corner. "I thought babes could not be ghosts. I thought the living could not be . . ."

"This spirit usually takes consciousness of complex thought to create such an embittered soul," Luciana said, glancing around the room. "Where is Divya?"

"With your grandmother," Stefano said. Was she well? he wondered. And what of the other girls?

Luciana patted his arm. "The *Beluni-Daiya* would not let anything happen and, if all were not well, we would know it," she said.

"This prince was definitely no mere babe," Gabera said.

Stefano put his arm around Luciana rubbing heat back into her arms. The sense of bitter cold had faded. The state of violence was gone. "Perhaps the ceremony gave the spirit its power?"

"The ceremony cleansed the soul of the *boy* and rededicated him with his new name to the service of God. I *think* his body has been reclaimed," Luciana whispered.

"Cleansed," Abruzzi said.

"We will have to watch him, but I think . . . I am confident the cardinal was defeated here today with the power of the Church," Luciana said.

"The power of the Church," Abruzzi repeated. He started to shake his head and then said, "What do you believe, Your Excellency?"

"I believe the Church has won a war it didn't know it was fighting," Luciana replied. She turned to her husband and looked up at him. "What do *you* believe?"

Stefano paused. He knew what he believed now, but did it bear the light of day? Did he dare speak it? He glanced at Luciana watching him, willing him. "I believe a spell was cast and that it affected Massimo, that his basic nature was not the innocence of an infant, like his sisters, but that of an older, more experienced consciousness, capable of great evil, controlled this child. I think . . . I hope . . . I pray this monstrosity no longer controls Massimo," Stefano said.

The bishop, a middle-aged man, an educated man, had quite obviously not considered anything like this before . . . even when told to him by Padre Gabera. "I think, perhaps, that I shall have to take a greater interest in the education and raising of this child . . . and his sisters."

"All of the children will benefit from a solid education and I thank you for your concern," Stefano said formally. He placed a hand on Padre Gabera's shoulder. "You are new to the palazzo and Tyrrhian society, Your Reverence. I recommend Padre Gabera's good counsel to you in the strongest of terms."

The bishop glanced notably at Stefano's hand on Gabera.

"I hope," Abruzzi said, "that further services will be better attended and that the parishioners might . . . linger a little longer than they did today."

"It is my hope also," Stefano said, walking toward the door with his right hand on the small of Luciana's back.

Stefano opened the outer door, standing so that his body took the worst of the buffeting from the wind. "Where would the *Beluni* have taken Divya?" Watching her face as she considered his question, he marveled again at her exotic beauty. Her face was still fuller than normal—from pregnancy, he guessed—but it suited her, softening the edge of her jawline and smoothing the planes of her face. The buffeting wind and rain rosied her cheeks and the tip of her nose which he could not resist kissing.

Luciana, startled from her pondering, looked up at him with a smile. "This is no place for demonstrations of that sort!" she chided, though there was laughter in her voice.

Stefano responded by tipping her head back and kissing her on the mouth and ending with yet another peck to her nose. "You, Madam, are my wife, which makes it suitable for me to kiss you where and when I please. Now let's go and collect our daughter and get out of the weather, so that the two of you can sit close by a fire."

Luciana shivered. "I could use some warming after today's events. I hope that you will join us by the fire so that we may discuss young Massimo. His fate concerns me."

"Yes, today's events trouble me, too, but let us discuss this further somewhere warm and where none of us will take a chill," he said. With that, Stefano gripped Luciana's right arm firmly and steered her out of the alcove and into the drizzle, using his own body as best he could to protect her from the wind and rain.

"I think my grandmother will still have Divya . . ." Luciana said, gasping for breath when struck by a forceful gust of wind. ". . . and probably Chiara. She is most likely in our suite or her *vardo* with the girls."

Stefano nodded, and they plowed onward, facing into the heavy winds that sent the drizzling rain into them like needles of ice. They hurried out of the churchyard, bodyguards on either side, pausing only briefly in the archway that framed the gate that separated the palazzo grounds from this residence of the religious ghetto. They crossed the cobbled courtyard, skirting the fountain and statue of Alaric on their way into the giant structure which was to be their home, now and for the foreseeable future, and that was currently home to the dozens of noble families gathered for the Palantini.

Inside the palazzo, they were greeted by porters who took Luciana's shawl and Stefano's coat before they went in search of his daughter to make the family whole again. His family. It struck him again then, with a sudden wave of grief, that Luciana and their daughter were all that was left of his family now that Alban and Idala were gone. But then he reminded himself of the children who had come in from the storm ahead of them—his nieces and nephews. His family was not so small as he had been thinking. He recollected that for all practical purposes those cousins of Divya were now like his own children, and he must begin thinking of them that way for the sake of them all.

They turned left at the Throne Room into the Clock Walk. Hearing the noise of voices in the room, Stefano stopped, raised a hand, and pushed the doors to the chamber wide. Inside, he—with Luciana still at his side—found several of the duchi collected. Many had attended the christenings. Seeing them, the nobles fell into a stuttered silence.

Duchessa Rossi was of that indeterminate age somewhere between her mid-thirties and possibly forties. She was the first to acknowledge them with more than silence. She was also notable in that she was one of the rare noblewomen who took her position on the Grand Palantini with great diligence and as more than an opportunity to make a fashion statement—although she was always impeccably well-dressed.

"Your Excellency! *Araunya*! We were just discussing the

baptisms. May I take this opportunity to congratulate you on the christening of your daughter?"

"Thank you," Stefano said, glancing around the room. There were seven or perhaps nine people gathered together, of which, he only recognized the ever-present Duca Sebastiani and his wife; Duca Raffia of Niscemi; Duca Scala and his bride; Duca Gianola; and Duca Baldovino. The others' faces he knew, but not their names.

Luciana bobbed her head to the other woman. "I am gratified by your kindness, Your Grace."

"Surely, there must be some significant reason for this impromptu assembly . . . and in the Throne Room?" Stefano asked, curious.

"The Great Hall is being prepared for the Palantini and there seemed no other place for a convenient rallying point," Duca Sebastiani said, hobbling forward while leaning on a cane to ease his foot. "We had hoped that you would join us and . . . well, here you are!"

"If you thought any of us meant to usurp your position as Lord Regent, Your Excellency, then you are mistaken," Duchessa Martina Rossi said. "We are . . . concerned . . . or rather some of us are concerned about . . . about your new nephew."

Stefano stiffened, reminding himself that these people were not his enemies—at least he knew many of them not to be. He had surprised the nobles, no need to complicate matters with ill-thought-out reactions. He reached down, took Luciana's hand, and gave it a squeeze. He needed to take the correct action before he ruffled feathers and turned this session into one of actual ill will. He bowed to Duchessa Rossi, took her right hand, and kissed it as was appropriate for a married man.

"Your Grace," he said, "it is always good to find you in good health. You are well-known for your equilibrium, and I believe I saw you in the chapel this afternoon. Tell me, what is your perspective on the matter before us?"

Skilled in the social graces, the duchessa glanced to the floor in a show of demureness. "I believe I'm not alone in finding young Massimo something of an oddity. He laughs like a madman at the strangest of times . . . such as at the death of his mother. . . . Some see more in the storm we have just had . . . Well, the timing disturbs many and, then, there is the matter of the sudden, uncanny cold within the chapel itself. Several among us feel it was . . . unnatural."

"Many? Several?" Stefano asked, scanning the crowd of nobility.

There were nods from some, while others refused to make eye contact. One of the duchi, a much older man, pressed forward. "Is it true that he has teeth?"

"It is," Stefano said carefully. He had been prepared to speak of this matter, but he had thought that the discussion would include only Luciana and himself, and perhaps her grandmother, the *Beluni*. This was a different conversation altogether; he would have to tread cautiously to protect Massimo and to keep his allies. With the Palantini reaching its current numbers, he would need as many friendly faces in the gathering as he could garner.

Beside him, Luciana licked her lips. She had a debt to this child, too, to be sure he was raised in security and to one day become part of polite society. He knew, at least, that she hoped that if she were careful, the cardinal would not be able to take complete control over Massimo's soul. "There is nothing outright unnatural that he should have teeth or that his christening should be . . . such an event."

"'Tis unnatural, I say, for a child to be born all twisted and toothy like he is and live. There has even been talk of magic. What have you to say to that?" Duca Baldovino demanded.

A fair-haired man who had gone prematurely white, Baldovino was not quite as old as Duca Sebastiani. His florid features were compressed into a frown. He was an educated man, but known to be suspicious of signs and ill portents . . . some of which made Luciana laugh. It had taken years for him to treat the *Araunyas* with more than an overabundance of caution for fear one of them might cast a spell upon him. Only their frequent interaction at court allowed Gianola to treat Luciana, if not as a friend, certainly as a potential ally. More importantly, Gianola seemed to be listening to the rumors that ran rampant in the palazzo—especially those rumblings of superstition. There was a hush from the group after Baldovino's brutally honest question. They waited.

Stefano felt like he had just been forced to drink some vile potion. Certainly he had a bad taste in his mouth. "The child is just that, a child," he said. He could not help but look at Duca Sebastiani accusingly. The old man shook his head in a barely perceptible manner. Good. Sebastiani had not talked, not broken the oath of silence. Stefano wiped his mouth and tugged at his beard. "Some of these matters were brought up here in the Palantini. Can we not hold this discussion for one more day? Nothing will change from now until then."

"Not one more day, Your Excellency," Duca Sebastiani said. "This is the week of Yule. We have our duties to our families and the Church."

But Baldovino, like a pit bull with a piece of meat, seized upon the moment. "What subjects will we discuss? How do we know nothing will change? It seems change is all about court."

Stefano sifted through the duca's words and found an answer he could live with. "Of course, change is all around us, it is as it has always been and will be ever more. It's true that more has happened in times of late than usual, but we're in a time of calm now. The storm is outside—for the moment—and does not need to be brought indoors until absolutely necessary."

"What is it that you're keeping from us? Don't we have a right to know?" Duca Gianola asked.

"I am trying to keep nothing from you. All will be discussed when the Palantini meets. There is too much to . . . explain. We will debate all of these matters until there is a resolution or course of action you are satisfied with. Preferably, you and the rest of the Palantini will have both," Stefano said.

Duca Sebastiani stepped forward, wincing as he bumped his foot against one of the chairs. "You are a friend of the throne and to me, di Drago. I will give you this time you seek to prepare for it . . . time enough for reason—"

"And excuses!" Gianola barked out.

Sebastiani cast a withering glance over his shoulder. "Time enough for reason to take place for all of us. Time enough for real questions to be fully formed and shadowy details to take their rightful place in the light of day," the old man said. "This man, here," he nodded to Gianola, "is grieving over the loss of his wife, so that is to be enough for one day."

"For a week?" Baldovino said. "We must wait that long?"

"It was the Palantini who requested Yule week, Your Grace, and I believe you were among those who tendered the suggestion," said Sebastiani.

"I thank you," Stefano said to Sebastiani. He nodded to one of the nobles now departing from the Throne Room and returned his focus to Baldovino and Sebastiani.

"Make no mistake, Your Excellency. You have gotten out of nothing, for tomorrow, people will expect answers and it will not just be the few of us. I will demand answers," Baldovino said. He turned to leave, but paused, "And do not be mistaken, my friend, I have seen some of the answers with my own two eyes, and I will have more questions than have been asked of you today."

Outside the door, Gianola had allowed himself to be stopped for the condolences of his peers. Baldovino left, and the crowd around Gianola dispersed. Stefano and Luciana were left alone with Duca Sebastiani and Duchessa Rossi who closed their ranks, shaking her head. "I was not here at court when the king died, nor the queen for that matter. Too much has happened. Too many strange things have occurred for people to *not* have questions, but that man . . . Baldovino? . . . will demand answers. Please, I beg of you, do not make the mistake of turning an ally into an enemy as you nearly did this afternoon. He is that . . . an ally, I mean. . . . At least for now. I hope that you may also count me as a friend."

"*Then*, let us four friends go our separate ways until we meet again," Sebastiani said, gratified when the group dispersed.

Pierro pressed his thumb into the black wax seal and took a soldibianco from his pocket. He handed the packet and coin to the ruffian waiting beside his table. He did not like the look of the man, but Caserta had sworn he was trustworthy and quick about his work. "Don't get caught. I've given you your directions, and you'll be looking for a man named Boiko. No stops. It is imperative this message gets there tomorrow. Can you do that?"

The ruffian scratched his unshaven cheek and looked at the gold coin in his hand. "It's short notice. I had plans tonight . . . with my lady— "

"Two soldis and you can meet with her when you get back, have a fine dinner . . . that's enough to buy her a new dress and still have plenty left over for yourself," Pierro coaxed as he held up another gold coin.

The man laughed and snatched the coin from Pierro's fingers. "I spend my time trying to get her out of her clothes, but I'll take the extra soldi as promise that it will get there by tomorrow night."

"Tomorrow morning," Pierro insisted.

"Tomorrow by noon," the courier said, tucking the packet into his coat pocket.

"Your life may depend upon it," Pierro said tightly.

The other man sketched a bow and left the room Pierro had paid for in an out of the way taverna just on the far reaches of town where he was less likely to be seen. Despite having an impatient bride waiting for him in the palazzo, Pierro poured himself another goblet of wine and waited for nightfall when he could make a more discreet departure. He eyed the light coming through the curtained window. He would have to wait some time. He tugged the bell pull for service. There was no reason he could not be entertained while he waited.

XIX

"Do not trust all men, but trust men of worth; the former course is silly, the latter a mark of prudence."
—Democritus

29 d'Dicembre, 1684

STEFANO rose early. He had been waiting for this day for a week. The Yule festivities had been dampened enough by taking place in the palazzo and away from home. Princess Ortensia, however, had organized a Yule Ball which nearly everyone in the palazzo attended. The gaiety and socializing seemed to fill a need to share and be with others. There were panoramas and little plays put on by the various duchi all to the splendor of the occasion. At last, all of Yule was over and the Palantini would meet again. They would discuss the murders of King Alban, Brother Tomasi, and the Palazzo Guards—Fieri and deGrassi. The subject of the White Queen casting magic on *la famiglia reale* by using it on herself would have to be discussed again, but not at such length.

Luciana rolled over on the bed and propped her head up, yawning. "It's barely dawn, *mi amore*. What has you awake and dressing at this hour?"

"I told you the Palantini meets today," Stefano said. "Prunella even gave me her proxy. Why she discomfited herself and her son to come to court when she was not intending to attend the meetings amazes me."

Luciana shrugged her shoulders. "Your cousin wants to

find a new husband and a father for her boy. What amazes you about that?"

"It doesn't surprise you that Prunella is already seeking a new husband when her first has been in the grave not even a year?"

Luciana shook her head, her hair a riot of curls. "Her match was never one of love, but of practicality. She now runs a large estate and wants a man to help her. Your dear cousin has always been one to be practical."

Stefano sat back on the bed with stockings in hand. "It doesn't bother you at all?"

Luciana shifted so that her body rested against his. "She is not me. Were I to lose my husband, there would be the practical to consider, but I think I would wait longer."

"You think?" Stefano mocked, faking offense.

She laughed outright and merrily. "Yes, that is what I *think* I would do."

Stefano bent and kissed his wife.

"Perhaps I would wait a few years, now that I think on it a little longer," she said. Growing more serious, she nodded, "Yes, I think I might spend my life without a husband at all if you were to go before me."

Turning to put his stockings on, he sighed, "Let's not discuss this any further. It is enough to know that you would mourn my passing if such were the case."

"So, why do you rise so early, *adorato*?" Luciana asked. "Even I, who is expected to attend to the children prior to the meeting, was not planning to rise for another couple of hours."

"To see your wards, eh?"

"And my daughter. My milk still flows and last night was her first night in the company of her cousins. While I've enjoyed the sleep, I must admit to being more wakeful than not with her outside of my immediate supervision."

Stefano pulled his other stocking on and gave her a hard look. "If she is with us or with her cousins in the nursery, she is still under your supervision. You are the Lady Regent Guardian, and besides, there is one of my men always on duty with a Palazzo Guard. Two men that would be perfectly capable of defending her with their lives."

"Oh, aye, I know that, but . . . such was the case with Brother Tomasi, and consider his and his guards' fate."

"Would you be happier if I made arrangements to double the protection around *la famiglia reale*?" Stefano asked.

Luciana shook her head. "No. Whatever the number of the guard and however you have them staged, someone determined could find a way around or through them. We've seen that. Are you sure that Divya should stay in the nursery . . . with her cousins? I know that it was my idea, but I have doubts. You need your rest before these big gatherings, but perhaps I— "

"You should stay where you are, Lucia, and if the child's fussing gave me that much trouble sleeping, I could always sleep on the divan in the reception room— "

"That would be most unseemly, and I wouldn't hear of you doing any such thing . . . unless you wish to embarrass me?" Luciana protested.

"Fine, then such will be the case," Stefano promised, "but better for you that your charges are in one place."

"Two places. You forget Dario Gian is in his own rooms and he does not require so much attention."

"Would you have Dario Gian moved to the nursery?" Stefano asked.

Luciana shook her head again. "No, he is too old for a nursery. Besides, he has his *scola* now. The tutors—if not Dario—would find all of it too distracting."

"Then he stays where he is," Stefano agreed, stepping into his shoes.

"So you still have not said why you rise so early."

Stefano waved his hands in a dismissive gesture. "I do not know. I'm all keyed up for the Palantini meeting, I would guess— "

A scratching sound came from the other side of the door, followed immediately by the sound of knocking.

Stefano's brows rose. "Whoever it is apparently requires an audience without delay." He rose and approached the door, pausing to look at her before answering the persistent knocking. "Cover yourself, my lady. We have visitors."

Luciana lay back on the bed and pulled the blankets close to her chin. Stefano winked at her and opened the door. Estensi, only half-dressed and breathless, stood outside the room. The Court Herald glanced over his shoulder, apparently to be sure he was alone. When he saw that he was, he rushed into the room unbidden and slammed the door closed behind him.

"What meaning do you have—" Stefano began.

"Forgive me, Your Excellency, but this is of great importance. I have only now just received word from a messenger," Estensi said, gulping for air. "Messina has been sacked by the Turks!"

Stefano's mind raced at the news. Messina was a coastal town in the heartland of Tyrrhia, on the coast by the mouth of the *Stretto* bearing its name. It was a distance away, but one that could be covered in a day's riding hard. The Turks were attacking close to hand!

"What of the ship that protects the *Stretto*?" Stefano asked.

"That is how I got my news," Estensi said. "Or rather, from the sailors. The ship was nearing the eastern mouth of the *Stretto*, on its regular course between points East and West. They saw the Turks and their ships and the city burning. They were well outnumbered so they raised the alarm rather than intervene. The capitano of that ship is raising the fleet. They are preparing as we speak."

Stefano glanced to his wife, who now sat up with the blankets still drawn to her chin. "The Palantini cannot meet today. Have someone saddle my horse and bring him around to the doors, I must go to the *Armata*, myself. They were sure the city was sacked?"

"Or in the process of being. The capitano's messenger was not very specific," Estensi said.

"Then you have your orders for now," Stefano said, opening the door for the other man. When the Court Herald was gone, he looked at Luciana again. "We are under attack. The Tyrrhian homeland is under siege."

"That hasn't happened since Orsino's reign, when his daughters were kidnapped," Luciana said. "Of course, you must go at once. I'll have Carlo pack your things."

"If all goes well, it will be a day or two before I return," Stefano said, "but have him pack for a fortnight." He opened the door again, stopping this time, and came back to kiss her. "Have the Palazzo Guards watch for a plume of red smoke, it may be your only warning that the Turks are moving down the coast to Citteauroea. Consider taking the children inland, definitely by the time you see smoke."

"I know what to do," Luciana promised him. She clutched the shoulders of his frock coat, giving him a shake. "And have care! You have too many reasons to return."

"So it will be." Stefano departed after Estensi, through the servants' level door.

Pierro stretched and yawned. Two hours of rest after his hard ride did not seem enough, but there were matters to deal with. Important matters. He rose and put his clothes in order, just in time to open the door to Capitano Boiko.

The man, dressed in European commoner's clothing, looked like a Gypsy. He was an irascible sort, a man of action and cunning who hated his role as go-between. Behind him, Pierro saw that Boiko had three men of his own who were crowded into the small common room with Caserta.

"I presume you are rested enough, *Yurttas*? I have been kept waiting," Boiko growled.

"My man has barely just wakened me," Pierro said. "Caserta, you should have woken me when the capitano arrived."

The *Magnus Inique* priest nodded his head in acknowledgment, taking the blame even though he had been told that Pierro would take two hours' rest before he would speak to the Turkish capitano. Pierro stepped back so that Boiko could enter the bedchamber. The Turk brushed past him, and Pierro closed the door abruptly, cutting the other men off from their conversation.

"Well?" Pierro asked, motioning for the Turk to take one of the chairs.

Boiko sat and immediately rose again and began to pace. "Our ships attacked Messina at midnight and our soldiers took the shoreline within an hour of that. As you *suggested*, we started pillaging in the areas you pointed us to so that we could get our ransom of Gypsy Silk. Now, tell me why we must limit our attack to Messina? Wouldn't an attack farther along the coast—south or west—be advisable?"

Pierro sat in the comfortable, overstuffed chair and put his feet up on a nearby stool. He yawned. "What did Tardiq say?"

"My sultan says to do as you bid. I have done it, but I question—"

"Your sultan and I have made plans, plans that will see me to the Tyrrhian throne. If he is pleased with my strategies, what right do you have to question me directly?" Pierro responded.

"I do not question my sultan. I question you *for* His Excellency, the sultan," the capitano said, obviously vexed.

Pierro looked at the man as he sank into a more comfortable position amid the cushions of his seat. He sighed. "This plan of ours hinges upon my plans for the taking of *all* Tyrrhia. Yes, it would be satisfying to crush the capital city, but then what will I have to work with once the throne is mine? I seek to unsettle the newly named Lord Regent . . . *and* his Gypsy wife, the Regent Guardian . . . then take their place."

"You would rule with Tardiq's concubine at your side?" the general scoffed, laughing harshly.

"If it gets me what I want. Besides it will only have to be for a time and then it will be a simple matter to have her fall ill or even to have an accident, if Tardiq is sure that he has had his fill of red-haired Tyrrhian women."

The capitano waved his hand in dismissal. "If His Majesty weren't tired of her, he would never have given her up to you."

"Then I keep her for whatever time that it appeals to me."

"So, you want no further attacks on Tyrrhia? Heartland or continental for the time being?"

"For now. I'll get word to you through a special courier should I need another attack to seal his fate," Pierro replied, tapping his lower lip with his steepled fingertips. "Yes, that is what we must do. No doubt, my Lord Regent has responded in some fashion. He is or will be in Messina soon, and there is the possibility that he might send ships looking for yours and the others, so I would be away from here soonest."

Boiko rubbed his stomach. "If you don't give Sultan Tardiq what you've bargained for, I shall take great pleasure in exacting his revenge."

Pierro smiled, dropping his hands. "Then I must deliver what I've promised, mustn't I? Messina is only the beginning."

By noon and without pomp and circumstance, the *Armata* departed. Two ships moved to the westernmost end of the Stretto to protect their rear flank while thirteen ships of the local fleet turned eastward. Luciana knew, without being told, that Stefano was heading into the east. He had taken only two of his men-at-arms and half of the resident Escalade, leaving the rest to guard *la famiglia reale* with the equally impatient Palazzo Guards and remainder of the Escalade chaffing to join the fight. Luciana watched from cliff-side as Stefano's ship, safely tucked in the center of the *Armata*, departed in all due haste. Stefano and the others would join the battle this afternoon—earlier if the Turks had been brazen enough to continue into the Stretto.

Most of the Palantini and some of their wives had come to see the *Armata* set sail. Luciana glanced sidelong at Princess Ortensia who looked agitated. The prince was nowhere to be seen.

"Stefano will stop them," Luciana said with as much conviction as she could rouse. "Tardiq won't get his hands on you again."

Ortensia turned from watching the last ship sail out of view, her eyes narrowed and dark. "Will he? Will your husband truly protect *me*? No matter how determined the sultan gets? No. Tardiq *always* gets what he wants, *always*. If he meant to reach the palazzo, he wouldn't have stopped to take Messina."

Luciana shuddered and crossed her arms over her chest. How could Ortensia take her ease with such knowledge? Had Stefano considered this possibility? Would Stefano even return to her and the baby? She took a deep breath and took comfort in the knowledge that Stefano was a seasoned veteran and could take care of himself on the battlefield.

"So, Your Highness, Prince Pierro has joined our Lord Regent at battle?" Sebastiani asked, drawing Luciana's hand through the crook of his arm. He offered his arm to Ortensia as well. "I'd 've never thought it of him."

Ortensia looked at Sebastiani's proffered arm as though it were a dead snake. She started back with the rest of the

Palantini, but looked at Sebastiani and Luciana with eyes so dark they looked black.

"Your husband, Your Highness?" Luciana prodded when the princess was unforthcoming.

"I don't know where he is. He left yesterday toward evening time to attend to some business somewhere else on this god-forsaken island. It is not unusual for him to do so," Ortensia finally answered. She turned away and put distance between them.

"If she doesn't think Tardiq is after her again, why is she so angry?" Luciana asked Sebastiani.

The older man shrugged. "Perhaps she is not so confident as she would have us believe and discovering that the man is sacking parts of Tyrrhia while her husband is away can only be more discomforting especially when she is expecting."

Luciana nodded and did not speak again, not wanting to speculate further with her and the Palantini so close. At the back doors of the palazzo, she broke away from Sebastiani and headed for the nursery, trying to think of something other than her husband dying in battle. Try as she might to set aside her own worries about Stefano and to focus upon the children who were now her charges, Luciana found herself at odds. It felt strange to be mothering someone else's children when she was such a new mother herself, and it set off a weird dichotomy between ambassador for the black-blooded people, yet surrogate mother to the heirs to the White Throne. What would happen to her and Divya if Stefano never returned? She doubted even the friendliest members of the Palantini would make her Regent, but would she remain Regent Guardian? Would Ortensia finally claim the throne?

Luciana stopped outside the door to Idala's suite, now the nursery. The babes would sense her mood and respond to it, as would the wet nurses. She collected her wits and forced a smile to her lips. These would be interesting times.

Stefano searched the horizon. From the forecastle of his ship, he could see as far as the Mediterranean Sea and only distant sails. Could it be possible that Sultan Tardiq of the

Turks had only done a strafing maneuver on Tyrrhia? Or had this been a trick to lure him and the *Armata* from the palazzo?

A cheer went up from the men on the various ships when there was no sight of the Turkish war ships.

"What now, Your Excellency?"

He turned to find the capitano of the ship waiting for an answer. Over the man's shoulder, Stefano could see the city of Messina, Jewel by the Sea. In some parts of the city, fires set by the Turks still raged; other sections were blackened from flames that had already moved through, but, thankfully, there were still other areas . . . farther back on the hillside that remained untouched. From that part of the city, the rebuilding would begin. He looked back at the capitano in his blue and gold uniform.

"Send four ships to circumnavigate the heartland to be sure the Turks haven't tricked us. They are to stop in Palermo, gather more ships, and make them aware of the Turks' attack. Send six ships after the Turks, and the rest of us will settle on Messina's shore and do what we can to help," Stefano told him.

The capitano saluted and made his way to the gangway and his signalman who immediately began signaling to the other ships. Surprisingly, it took only a short time for the signalman to convey Stefano's wishes and the ships to bring their sails back up. It took the better part of an hour to find a place to land the remaining vessels since the dock and the ships at pier had all been destroyed.

Stefano led Fascino off the ship. Once on land, he mounted and surveyed his company as they gathered on the shore. He had ten men who were mounted, the rest of the soldiers—Escalade and men of the *Armata*—totaled near one hundred. He waited for the men to fall into formation before he addressed them.

"We are here to help the besieged. Any man caught looting will be shot, the single exception to this is if a mount is found. A horse or mule may be taken in the name of assisting others, but it is to be returned! To the fires first, so that we can stop them before they spread further. With me!" Stefano turned Fascino around and charged into the broken city.

XX

"All truths are easy to understand once they are discovered; the point is to discover them."

—Galileo Galilei

2 d'Gennaio, 1685

PRUNELLA sniffed and blinked at her cousin Stefano. "The *Araunya* goes to the Palantini? When she has a nursing baby?"

Luciana stifled a sigh and pushed aside the last of her breakfast. "I have duties that must be performed, Contessa diVega. I supervise the Heir and his siblings, and as ambassador to my people, I must attend the gathering of the Palantini."

"*I* have duties to the Palantini myself," Prunella said with another sniff. From the folds of her son's blankets, she produced a slightly damp piece of vellum, complete with seal, and handed it to Stefano. "This is my proxy, to you, of course, dear Cousin. I would have you vote in my stead." She smiled and turned back to Luciana, "You see? So easily handled. It would take you five minutes."

Luciana tucked her clenching hands into the folds of her skirt, glancing at her remarkably restrained grandmother. "Unfortunately, my duties are not so easily set aside. I must answer to and for my people. I also speak for the Gypsy Silk trade."

"But your grandmother is here to do that," Prunella said sourly.

"I speak for the black-blooded people as a whole, my granddaughter speaks for the half-blooded and those who run the trade," the *Beluni* said. "Were this another time or place, she, too, would be allowed the pleasures of motherhood over the tasks of service."

"As Regent Guardian, she must speak for the Heir and the infant children as well as worry about and represent the trade of Gypsy Silk," Stefano said, taking a moment to review the paper Prunella had given him. "I thank you for your vote of trust, Cousin. If you are ready, ladies?" Stefano murmured.

"As to the Palantini meeting, I am more concerned for His Excellency who only returned late last night. Have you had enough sleep or did you sleep at all?" Luciana said eying her husband.

"I have rested, *camómescro*, or was it in someone else's arms you thought you slept last night?" Stefano teased "Now, Cousin, we must leave you." He rose, offering an arm in turn to his wife and then the *Beluni*.

Once outside their apartment, the *Beluni* sighed heavily "How do you put up with that onerous creature?"

Stefano bit back a smile, but Luciana laughed aloud When she controlled herself, she replied, "'That creature' as you say is our cousin—mine by marriage. She has her times and places when she can be quite helpful, and for those reasons we see fit to indulge her. When she is at her most troublesome, I find a reason to escape. Thankfully, my duties require frequent absences. Besides, she is still newly widowed and she managed to come for the gathering of the Palantini."

"Which, I note again, she is not attending," the *Beluni* remarked to no one in particular.

"Ah, but more importantly, she has given me her vote," Stefano pointed out, waving the paper he held in his right hand.

They quieted as the hall grew more full, those entitled heading into the Great Hall where Queen Idala had once thrown her grand balls. As Stefano cut their way through the gathering horde of nobility, the *Beluni* abruptly dropped his left arm and waved for Grasni to catch up to her. When Stefano looked at her, confused by her action, she whispered loud enough for Luciana and Stefano to hear.

"We may be family, Your Excellency, but it does neither of us good to remind certain people," the *Beluni* nodded, and smiled at one of the mortal enemies of the Romani as though he were an old friend. Passing him, she smiled more broadly and winked at Luciana. She took her apprentice Grasni's arm and leaned heavily upon her as though her aging body was having trouble standing independent of aid. "Shall we *dukker* on, Grasni?"

"I trust there will be fair *dukkerin'* today, *Beluni-Daiya*," the girl said, as they disappeared into the crowd.

"*Dukker*?" Stefano asked his wife as she drew him to a halt.

Luciana licked her lips and smiled. "It's . . . a form of mischief-making that my people use to make money . . . or such things." She stood on tiptoe and kissed him. "Before court, I must see the children and make sure that all is well. I promise not to be gone long."

Leaving Stefano to cut his way through the crowd and into the Hall alone, Luciana darted through the mass of people and into Idala's apartments. She surveyed the changed room. The receiving room had been turned into a work and sleep area for all of the women attending the infants. The solar was decorated with drying swaddling. Could it truly be less than a month since the king was shot and Idala breathed her last?

Luciana shook off the creeping depression that came in moments of grief. She had to at least appear happy for the babes who sensed the moods of the women tending them and reflected it. The last few days, while Stefano and his men dealt with the attack on Messina, the women had worried about war and what it would mean for them, causing the babies to become fractious. Hopefully, the women's mood was more settled now that Stefano and many of his men were returned.

As was her practice, she paused in the nursery to examine each child before crossing to the suite Massimo still shared with his wet nurse and her son Federico. Luciana scratched at the door and waited for Bonita to speak up. She entered at the wet nurse's summons.

The room was as she had seen it before: all mahogany and dark green with accents of cream and gold. Massimo lay in his cradle in the center of the room and beside him was Bonita and her son's cruder cradle. The wet nurse sat in a rocking chair, using her gentle motion to lull the boys in their cradles.

"I have just fed and changed them," Bonita volunteered.

Luciana nodded her appreciation and went to peer into Massimo's bed. "How has he been since he was christened?"

"He has been well, as far as I can tell. He is more settled, and you can see that he now puts on weight like his sisters," Signora Bonita Boniface said with a smile.

"Well . . . I cannot stay. I must feed my daughter and attend the council meeting," Luciana said, fading back toward the door.

"I've noticed that you do not hold him like you do his sisters. He has had no further spells," Signora Boniface said.

"None? Since the christening?"

Bonita shook her head. "None."

Luciana left the young woman to her charge and her son and returned to the nursery for Divya. It was an interesting concept, that Luciana considered while nursing Divya, to think that Massimo had been more like a normal baby since his christening. Would that be all there would be to conquering the cardinal? A simple christening?

"Well, where is this boy?"

Luciana looked up from the sleeping Divya who had just finished nursing. The *Beluni* was looking around the nursery, bringing all the business of the nurses and della Guelfa to a halt. This morning would be Luciana's only quiet time with her baby, and she had not wanted the affairs of State to interfere, at least not here. As though sensing her mother's tension, Divya began to fuss. Kisaiya, ever at Luciana's side, came forward and took the child. She spirited Divya away before the *Beluni* could get her answer.

Luciana rose, putting her bodice in place. She took a deep, calming breath before turning back to her grandmother. "How did you get into the nursery, *Mami*? These rooms are guarded at all times."

The *Beluni* shrugged eloquently. "He is still there at the door, guarding."

"But how did you get past him? You are supposed to be escorted up here by my husband or myself."

"Grasni has her charms, being young and beautiful," the

old woman said with a devilish smile and a wag of her eyebrows.

"You tricked your way in! Do you know what Stefano will do to that man for Grasni's *dukkerin'*?" Luciana threw up her hands and moved away.

"The reason was important. I need to know what that child is. Is he that *benglo* . . . that little devil or just an infant?"

All motion around the nursery halted as everyone turned to look at Luciana's grandmother.

"Please, go on with your duties, ladies. Come, *Mami*, we will talk on these things elsewhere," Luciana said, taking her grandmother's wrist and leading her into the hallway between bedrooms. "You cannot talk this way in front of them. They're frightened enough!"

"They should know what they deal with!" the *Beluni* spat back.

"I will show you the boy, so that you can look on him yourself and, after that, we will go to the meeting," Luciana whispered heatedly.

The *Beluni* nodded. "So be it!"

Luciana scratched at the door to the room set aside for Massimo and let herself in, closing the door firmly in her grandmother's face. "Bonita, perhaps you could take Federico to the solar for some sun? It's a pretty day out and he spends so much time cooped up in this room."

Bonita hesitated, looking up at Luciana with concern, but she bent and lifted her son out of his cradle. She edged by the *Beluni* and made her way down the stair in the direction of the queen's solar.

The *Beluni* entered the room once Luciana opened the door for her. She went immediately to the royal cradle and looked down at Massimo, her eyes studious as the boy kicked free of his swaddling. Massimo, however, did not cry; he met the *Beluni*'s gaze with his intense dark eyes.

"He is the cardinal arisen from the innocent loins of my sister by marriage. It is he who killed her, tearing at her insides until she bled to death. As a child, he is unnatural. His sisters—and even Dario Gian—are still afraid of him. He is not . . . He's not normal. We have put him away . . . away from the others who might be traumatized by the boy," Luciana said.

"If you are guardians of the other four children, then you should strangle the child where he lies and be done with his evil," the *Beluni* replied. She stamped her cane in such a way that the bangles on her arms fell to her wrists with a clatter like the sound of a dozen bells.

Luciana sighed and buried her face in her hands as she sank to the chair so recently occupied by the wet nurse. "We are his guardians, *Beluni.* If we were to kill the boy, the Palantini could have our heads and the next likely guardians would be the Prince and Princess deMedici, whom we have all agreed are simply unsuitable as either guardians for the children or the kingdom."

"Yes, well, there is *that,*" the old woman agreed sourly. She reached into the crib, as though to straighten his swaddling. "Is there no way the child could simply die in his crib? It happens and with a little arrangement . . ."

Luciana grabbed her hand in the cradle. "There will be *no* arrangements! The Palantini must decide. The Rom will be blamed if there are mysterious circumstances and there will be a Royal Inquest."

"But—"

"Enough now. There is too much to do. Swear that you will leave Prince Massimo to his people!"

The *Beluni* was clearly unhappy, but after several long, tense seconds, nodded her agreement.

XXI

"If it were not for injustice, men would not know justice."

—Heraclitus

LUCIANA and her grandmother slipped into the Great Hall as the rabbi finished the final prayer of the three holy men in attendance.

Stefano looked at Luciana sternly and then to the *Beluni*. How had the *Beluni* gotten access to the nursery? He was sure that was where both women had come from. Luciana produced a faint, apologetic smile as she slid into the chair beside him.

Stefano rose immediately after the prayer ended. "To our religious leaders, I offer you thanks and welcome. While you are here, you may recommend courses of action to us, but you cannot vote. Do you understand?"

The imam and rabbi nodded. Bishop Abruzzi motioned his acquiescence as he crossed his arms over his chest.

"I had planned to speak of many things this day, but first we must address the attack on Messina," Stefano said. The room grew immediately silent. All eyes turned in his direction, waiting. "We lost half the city. It was caught unaware by no less than four Turkish warships. The Turks had already set sail after their looting and murderous rampage. Six of our warships followed in pursuit, four others are circumnavigating the heartland and then continental Tyrrhia to be sure there will not be another attack . . . at least not soon."

"You are so sure that the six warships will be enough?" Prince Pierro asked sardonically. "This is why—"

"That is why more of our ships joined the pursuit last night," Stefano said, trying hard not to let the prince agitate him. "Our ships can outmaneuver the Turkish fleet. We'll chase down the dogs until we are sure they will not come again so willingly."

"You believe," Prince Pierro said, looking at his wife adoringly. "But if they've come for my Ortensia, they can't have her. I demand more protection for my wife to be sure some land incursion won't attack and retake her!"

"The Turks remaining on home soil have been routed," Stefano said.

"But can you be sure that you found all of them?" Duca Silvieri asked, rising to his feet.

Stefano stared down at his hand on the tabletop. He looked up, first at Silvieri and then Ortensia who was paler than usual. "That is why I am ordering a doubling of her personal guard . . . and for you, Prince Pierro, as well."

For the briefest second, the deMedici looked apoplectic. Very quickly, the reaction was hidden and Prince Pierro took his wife's hand, leaning forward. "I have no need of extra guards; it is my bride I am concerned for."

"If they are after one deMedici in Tyrrhia, they may as well be after *all* of the deMedicis . . . including your unborn heir, Your Highness," Stefano pointed out mildly. At this time, he had his doubts about the prince, could put nothing past him . . . but had he *any* part in recent events? All Stefano had was suspicions.

"If Ortensia were queen, she would have all of the Escalade protecting her!" deMedici cried, stamping his foot.

There were a few more stamps in the room, more than had made themselves known in the Throne Room. Stefano waited for the stamping in agreement to pass. It was only natural that more of Ortensia's sympathizers would be heard now, as there was almost a full gathering of the Palantini present now.

Stefano did not let Ortensia's supporters bother him. "The guard *will* be from the Escalade, but they have more to do than protect one family. They have joined the fight against the Turks, some have even asked for reassignment to the Peloponnese. Right now, a major force of them is already in Messina and others will soon join them. If you feel this is not enough protection, Your Highness, you are free to do as I have done and hire your own men-at-arms."

"You still have Lord Strozzini," the prince argued.

Lord Strozzini stepped forward, "With your pardon, Excellency, but it is the State's business to protect the State's leaders. If at no other time than when we are still mourning a slaughtered king, this should be obvious to all!" He bowed to Stefano and returned quickly to his appointed position behind the Regent and his wife.

A low rumble of voices broke out amongst the peers of the realm as they consulted with one another. After a short time of consulting with fellow sympathizers, Duca Silvieri rose again.

"Your Excellency, since the attack was so close and the princess is . . . in the family way . . . we ask that you treble the number of guards around the deMedicis," he requested.

Without hesitation, Stefano raised his hand and slapped the table. "Done!"

His agreement was followed by high-charged noise as Silvieri's confederates congratulated him. The noise, in fact, drowned out Pierro deMedici's protestations which only pleased Stefano all the more.

After a long pause, Estensi stamped his staff to bring order to the room. "Are there further questions about the Turkish attack or Messina?" Several partisans looked amongst themselves before shaking their collective heads. "Then we move onto the formal agenda, which begins with the queen's use of magic."

"Which queen?" the *Beluni* asked.

"The White Queen, of course!" Duca Anino said, rising. He looked around the room. "Is there anyone here who doubts the White Queen, the beloved Idala, cast this magic? And that it saw to her undoing?"

Again came the rumble of voices, pitched between quiet discussion and even a call or two across the table.

Duca Anino rose again. "I argue that as the 'mother' of *la famiglia reale*, the queen—the White Queen—in future, and no matter her intent, shall not be forgiven *any* spell. I argue the law should become more explicit. *La famiglia reale* should be banned from *all* use of magic for fear of expulsion or death."

Luciana jumped to her feet. "That, Your Grace, seems unreasonably harsh! Idala's thoughts were of her family. She sought to better Tyrrhia, not to harm it."

"Nonetheless, in future no other person in *la famiglia reale* is to cast magic. Furthermore, the law should reflect that anyone helping any member of *la famiglia reale* break the law shall suffer as that member of the family does—expulsion or death," Duca Anino insisted.

"What if that person is ordered to help? Can they truly deny *la famiglia reale*'s rightful position to command obedience?" Luciana argued, shaking off Stefano's hand.

Stefano rose and put his back to the Palantini as he faced Luciana. "Sit down. You are too close to this and your arguments might be your undoing!" he whispered. For a moment, Luciana looked as though she were going to fight him, but she took a calming breath and then a second. She sat, looking patently unhappy.

"My granddaughter is *beano abri*! She was born a Romani before she ever took up your ways. For her to do her duty to her people and the Gypsy Silk trade, she must be allowed to cast magic," the *Beluni* argued strenuously, coming to her feet with a stamp of her own staff.

Anino shook his head firmly, "I have trouble with even the Regent Guardian casting spells, but . . . in the name of peace and economy, the Regent Guardian, Luciana di Drago, is excused from this proposal . . . as long as she is not casting directly upon *la famiglia reale*. From now on, there should be no excuse for magic in our *la famiglia reale* excluding those duties related in one way or another to the production of Gypsy Silk. Lord Regent, I ask that you put this to a vote."

"Do we hear a second?" Estensi asked, looking around the long table and to the tables gathered to either side of it.

Duca Raimondo diCalabria, one of the princess' puppets, raised his hand. "I'll second Anino's motion."

Duca Teodorre Gianola stood from behind one of the outlying tables. "I'll carry the motion, Estensi."

"Then we are to vote," Estensi said.

Stefano rose uneasily from his chair at the head of the main table. "This law will apply from this time forward?"

"We cannot punish either queen or the *Araunya minore* for what they have already done as both women are dead.

We speak to the future, Your Excellency," Duca Silvieri said.

"Is this law against casting all forms of magic, such as charms and healing potions?" the *Beluni* asked solemnly.

"Charms are nothing. They can be purchased on any street corner in the capital city. And as to healing potions, this is the purview of *il dottore reale*," Anino said. "Or does anyone argue against me?"

"But what if *il dottore reale* is not present or otherwise unavailable?" Stefano asked. "Another . . . a Samaritan might offer a healing potion to ease pain or prolong life until *il dottore reale* can be reached. What of this situation?"

Anino's face registered the internal war; after a long pause, he bowed his head. "The exception could be made."

Immediately an uproar of those present broke out, with some people arguing for and others against the exception. Stefano waited for quiet. "What if I could have saved the king with a healing potion or a spell? Should our king be denied life-saving, or preserving, measures solely for the reason that he is the leader of *la famiglia reale*?"

"No. No. Under this argument, I cannot help but agree with the Lord Regent," Anino admitted. "Life-preserving potions were not what we discussing. We spoke of outright magic. It is the devil's business—"

"It is the business of *beng* to distort all good men and women's intentions," the *Beluni* argued.

"And without magic, there is one less way for the devil—or whatever you called him—to distort purpose and turn our royalty into hapless servants," Sebastiani countered.

"Do you wish for me to call a vote?" Estensi asked.

The proposed law had enough support for a vote. Stefano reluctantly nodded.

Estensi turned back to the room. "Duca Anino's proposal is put to the vote. Let those for the new law against magic used in *la famiglia reale*, now be heard."

The response was resounding. Estensi raised his hands. "Let those against the law now be heard."

The answer was a disheartening few stamps of the feet, echoing in the chamber.

Stefano rose to his feet again and surveyed the room. "The new law will go into effect when we have the wording exacted. I suggest the Duchi Anino and Sebastiani, but we will need a third to write the proposed language."

Immediately, hands went up all around the room. Stefano considered Luciana's grandmother long and hard and then the sea of other candidates. Finally, his gaze settled on Ortensia deMedici. "What about you, Highness Ortensia? You can speak for *la famiglia reale* and be the third to balance out any votes put forth?"

Ortensia swung her gaze from the needlework in her hands to Stefano. "Me?"

"Yes. I thought you might have strong feelings on this and it gives you an opportunity to form the new law," Stefano said. She had wanted the throne. Let her get a sense of what it was like before she made another attempt at it.

Princess Ortensia rose from her chair at the opposite end of the great table. "I accept!" She ignored her husband trying to speak to her, shaking off his hand when he would have pulled her back into her chair. "We meet in my chambers an hour before dinnertime—if this meeting has concluded by then." She sat and stared at Stefano, as though daring him to rescind his offer.

"The Black Queen, the *Beluni*, and I will consult this committee, but we withhold our votes unless requested . . . or I think it notably worth casting *our* votes. If *I* vote, the *Beluni* will also vote, so that there is always an uneven number," Stefano added. He bowed to Ortensia and then Sebastiani and Anino before taking his place in his chair beside Luciana.

"I could have taken my grandmother's place," Luciana whispered harshly.

Stefano took her hand in his and turned a loving smile upon his wife. "You could have, but then the focus would be on *you*, not the new law. No, your grandmother will serve just fine."

"But what if she is called to our people?"

He shrugged. "We will cross that bridge when we come to it, but for now, *mi amore*, you are to stay out of these discussions. Besides, it isn't as though you had nothing else to do . . . what with the care of five royals and our own daughter to pursue and the care of an entire trade so important to Tyrrhia."

Luciana bit her lip and bowed her head so that Stefano

had trouble making out her expression. Even without being able to see it, Stefano knew she was angry. For the moment, he was willing to accept that.

"The next matter, Your Excellency?" Estensi asked.

Stefano took a deep breath and somehow managed a relaxed smile.

Estensi turned to the gathered, stamping his staff. "Our next matter for the agenda is to discuss Cardinal delle Torre and some recent . . . events. Your Excellency?"

Stefano stood and surveyed the angry yet curious faces of the assembled body. "There are those among us who think my wife and I persecute Cardinal delle Torre's memory unfairly," he announced. "I intended to turn to this assembly for judgment of the body proof of the cardinal's perfidy."

Cries of protest and outrage erupted immediately. Stefano let the Palantini members' protests roll over him, until the arguments died down. He looked to Bishop Abruzzi, noting the man's face was florid with anger. Stefano motioned to the Palazzo Guards standing by the door. "I'd meant to bring before you, Brother Tomasi of the Dominican order who served the cardinal."

"Why not bring the accused?" Duca Garibaldi Falluccaci demanded.

"Brother Tomasi cannot testify. Many of you may remember his murder in the palazzo dungeon last month. Not only did we lose him, but two Palazzo Guards were slain in the course of protecting our most special 'guest.' Tomasi was poisoned in his cell, but I can offer two witnesses." Stefano motioned for the men to enter. First came Colonello Fieri and then Padre Gabera.

"What is the meaning of this? Padre Gabera has not sought my leave to testify before anyone," Bishop Abruzzi cried, rising from his seat.

"This is Tyrrhia, Your Reverence," Stefano said, smoothly. "In Tyrrhia, *anyone* may be called for testimony before the Palantini. Signore, while your displeasure has been noted, the padre will speak."

"From Confession? Every legitimate State acknowledges the privacy of the confessional!" Bishop Abruzzi declared.

"If I may?" Gabera asked Stefano, motioning to the outraged Bishop. Stefano nodded, so Padre Gabera addressed his senior. "Brother Tomasi told me many things, but none a Confession, not even a secular Confession. He died without taking any of the sacraments of Confession or Communion nor even Last Rites before he died."

The bishop sat down, eying Stefano and the priest with anger. When Abruzzi offered no further arguments, an uneasy silence fell in the room. Stefano looked around, pointedly meeting the gazes of anyone who dared meet his eyes. He stopped at Bishop Abruzzi.

"This man was of the Church! Brother Tomasi, whoever he was, should have been kept in the *Cattedrale*," Bishop Abruzzi argued.

"You *wouldn't* have wanted to protect him, Your Reverence," Gabera warned. "He has been in league with—"

"Enough! You do not have permission to speak, Gabera. We will discuss this in my chambers—" the bishop raged.

"Bishop Abruzzi, you are here to witness and to pray. You are not a member of the Palantini, and your presence is not necessary for us to continue. On the other hand, the padre *must* testify," Stefano replied, his tone affable, as he leaned forward with the table as his brace. "You are welcome to be seated—silently—and hear his testimony. It will give you all the explanation you need."

"If I'm not satisfied?" Abruzzi asked, stiffening up.

"*Then* we'll have a disagreement. Tomasi's crimes were committed against our country," Stefano replied. "And We consider it an offense against the best interests of Tyrrhia if you act against Padre Gabera for doing his duty."

When the bishop fell silent once more, Stefano turned to face the colonello and the priest. "So speak to the Palantini, Padre."

The cleric, a tall, slender man in a gray cassock with closely cropped gray-brown hair and beard, nodded and addressed the Palantini. "I am Padre Romero Gabera. I served under the cardinal at the Cattedrale. I became aware that all was not as it should be. I decided to look into these matters, and because of this I was forced to join a militant group called *Magnus Inique*. Eventually, I escaped the group and was rescued by Maggiore di Montago and his men as they traveled in search of the cardinal because he, with Brother Tomasi, had stolen the *Araunya minore*'s body. They recovered her body, in the possession of

Cardinal delle Torre, and captured Brother Tomasi," Gabera said.

"Did you witness the death of Cardinal delle Torre?" Stefano asked.

Padre Gabera shook his head. "I was with the maggiore's men atop the tunnels where the cardinal and the *Araunya minore* were found. Brother Tomasi was found hiding nearby."

"What condition was the body of the cardinal in when he was taken from these tunnels?" Duca Giacomini asked.

Padre Gabera shifted on his sandaled feet, rubbing the back of his neck. "He had the appearance of someone who had been strangled. He was found gripping a mandrake root and other things to do with magic."

"What was done with the cardinal's body?" Duca diCalabria asked.

"The maggiore had us burn it rather than bring it all the way from Palermo to the capital—by then the decay would have set in," Gabera replied.

"And you did not listen to his protests? What of the right of Inquest?" Giacomini pressed.

"It was the decision made at the time, considering the sins of the cardinal, and the fact that he would have decayed before we would be able to return. He did not deserve better," Gabera reported.

"Tell them what they did to my sister," Luciana urged. Only her eyes gave away her sense of defilement and loss.

"I know, from seeing the body and from Brother Tomasi that the *Araunya minore*, a woman not yet twenty, was murdered—poisoned. The White King and Queen had her interred. Tomasi claimed the cardinal ordered him to steal the body and bring her to a secluded cave beneath the palazzo. There, Tomasi and the cardinal drained her of blood and embalmed her in an arcane process, then took her with them when they left at about the time of Princess Bianca's death."

"And this was done for what purpose?" the Duca diCalabria demanded.

Gabera wiped at his brow with his sleeve, glancing down once more at Luciana. His voice, when he spoke, was surprisingly firm and confident. "Tomasi said it was so the cardinal could syphon her magical powers and that he saw delle Torre use her spirit a number of times."

"It is not possible!" Abruzzi stood and shouted. "This is sacrilege! Do you have any proof, or do you regularly take the word of a madman?"

"Bishop Abruzzi," Stefano snapped and motioned for him to take his seat again.

"As it so happens, Your Reverence," Luciana intervened. "*I* saw my sister's body. The *cardinal* took her despite my efforts to save her."

"You do not have to just take the *Araunya*'s word. This much testimony, Tomasi confirmed to the maggiore's men," Gabera argued.

"Yes, and they are all now safely hired as the Lord Regent's men-at-arms," Prince Pierro observed out loud, to no one in particular.

Gabera looked at Stefano, his eyes widening in anxiety.

Stefano rose, sighing. "I did not realize the prince paid attention to the inner workings of my household. I knew the maggiore and his men, which is why I selected them to guard my wife and *la famiglia reale* with the assistance of Palazzo Guards. But I did not hire *all* the maggiore's men. . . . There is a young man, Corporal deConde, whom I felt was too early in his career. If you wish confirmation, I'll send for him. Pray continue, Padre Gabera." Stefano sat down again.

"I do not forget that Tomasi was a Brother of the Church, but his sins were so great, I have trouble addressing him as such. The same with delle Torre," Padre Gabera continued. "Tomasi said delle Torre had him run errands: gathering odds and ends, even at apothecaries who carried unusual and unnatural paraphernalia. Delle Torre had him do other things more involved with 'advancing the cause against the wicked' as Tomasi explained. He further claimed that it never occurred to him that he should not do exactly as he was told."

"He had God's gift of free will," Luciana pointed out.

Around the room, there were gasps of surprise, even some of denial. Stefano glanced over at Luciana, knowing how hard this testimony must be for her. He moved to stand behind his wife, taking hold of her shoulders so that he might keep her from breaking into the testimony again, keep her from quaking as the words were said of what was done to Alessandra.

"Tomasi told me delle Torre even forced him to drink

the young *Araunya's* blood. He claimed to have only taken a sip and was sick, but delle Torre said the drinking of blood was to tie them to her body spiritually."

Luciana pressed the handkerchief she had earlier been rending, to her mouth as her shoulders shook. Reactions in the gallery came mostly in the form of gasps of dismay and shock.

"They took refuge where they could until they reached Palermo and the caverns of the dead. Something in the magic went wrong about the time the maggiore caught up with them there. Tomasi says that he ran, leaving delle Torre with his two Gypsy bodies. The maggiore and I caught Tomasi and brought him back. By then, delle Torre was dead and the *vardo* of the *Araunya minore* was burning. The maggiore ran inside the *vardo*. He yelled something about coming back out, but never did and I saw . . . I saw there was nothing left in the coals but ash," Padre Gabera concluded.

Stefano could feel Luciana's body go rigid with outrage beneath his hands. He tightened his grip, softly, enough to maintain control but not hurt her. "Is that all?" he prompted.

"Isn't it enough?" Sebastiani asked, the sound of his voice coming out in a soft, low, rumble that somehow seemed to echo throughout the Great Hall.

Padre Gabera shook his head. "No. There's more. I tried throughout our return trip and while he was in the dungeon to convince Tomasi to make his Confession, but he swore he took an oath delle Torre would be his only Confessor. I came close to changing his mind, but we were interrupted by the Palazzo Guard who said Tomasi had another, higher ranking visitor, that I could return on the morrow. For Tomasi, there was no tomorrow."

"Is there anything that you can tell us about the other visitor?" Stefano asked.

Gabera hesitated. "It is not that I do not wish to help you, Lord Regent, but I caught only a glimpse of who must have most assuredly been the murderer. I know only that it was a man, dressed in the fancy clothes of a courtier."

"Thank you, and now this is Colonello Dominic Fieri of the Palazzo Guard," Stefano said, waving to the older man waiting beside Padre Gabera. "His son was one of those killed. He investigated the events in the dungeon. Colonello, report."

"There's little we know. My son . . ." the older man's voice cracked, but he continued to recount the events in the dungeon, concluding with Pierro's cry of "Murder."

"Yes," Stefano said, fighting to keep the irony from his voice. "We owe a debt of gratitude to His Highness."

The members of the Palantini turned to look expectantly at Prince Pierro. Someone clapped and was joined by the rest of the assembled . . . except for Stefano, Luciana, and Estensi.

Prince deMedici rose, bowing and murmuring disclaimers about the seriousness of his wounds. Ortensia glowed with pride.

Stefano gave the deMedicis their moment. "There is more the colonello has to share with us, so please, Prince deMedici, know that your *sacrifice* has been noted. Colonello Fieri?" Stefano said, taking his seat once more.

"The only explanation we have for our men to let someone enter, anonymously, to visit prisoner Tomasi—who was only to be seen by Padre Gabera—was that they were given coin, but the Judas price was reclaimed. While casting no aspersions, I wonder how the prince was able to access the dungeons," the colonello concluded, looking pointedly at Prince deMedici.

The prince rose from his chair. "I was caught in the rain. I found no guard by the dungeon door and the door unlocked. I knew this could not be right, so I went to find out what was happening . . . that is when I encountered the . . . the assassin who, for some reason, was content to knock me senseless and to make his escape."

"And did you recognize him?" the colonello asked, before Stefano could even find the words himself.

DeMedici shook his head. "His face was completely covered."

"And, yet, Padre Gabera says that he was dressed as a gentleman," Estensi countered.

"Gentlemen wear masks all of the time," Prince Pierro said, with an elegant shrug.

"Only a single set of footprints tracked in the rain," the colonello argued.

Prince Pierro flushed angrily, rising to stand before his elevated chair. "Do you accuse me, Colonello?" he demanded.

The colonello took a long moment to shake his head. "I only report what was found, Your Highness."

"Your son and fellow guard must have accepted bribes to let someone other than Padre Gabera in to see Brother Tomasi," Pierro countered.

"I know," the colonello admitted, his cheeks flushing red with shame. "The Lord Regent and his wife, the *Araunya*, came to witness the evidence. It was the *Araunya* who discovered the scratch on deGrassi's hand and surmised that he died of some contact poison and that Brother Tomasi had swallowed his—"

"*Venefica*!" Duca Anino choked out. "The Regent Guardian is a *venefica*!"

Luciana rose. "I am familiar with the ways of poisoning. It was taught me as part of my healing tradition. I have never claimed I was not familiar with poison, but my knowledge has been used for good.

"Prince Pierro deMedici brought a perfumer to court who turned out to be an infamous poisoner. This man, Exilli by name, attempted to assassinate the king just this last summer. By my training, I recognized the poison and was able to give King Alban the antidote in time to save his life."

"Is this true?" Anino demanded of first Stefano and then the room at large.

Sebastiani stood up. "It *is* true. It's one of the times when I witnessed the poisoning of King Alban by poisoned dart by the poisoner Exilli who was, at least once, in the employ of Pierro deMedici. The king fell immediately and was very shortly incoherent. I was with His and Her Majesties when the *Araunya* was brought in to do whatever she could. I note that he did not die that summer, but rather this winter when he could not survive the shaft to his heart. Let us hear what the Regent Guardian has to say about what was in the dungeon before we allow our superstitious minds to convict her, eh?"

Luciana rose as Sebastiani reclaimed his seat. She carefully reported her findings of poison and the burnt remnants in the fireplace. At Stefano's prompting, she went on to describe finding the poppets in Tomasi's cell. "By the look of them, and the fact that he tried to burn them, I would say that Tomasi was working some kind of spell to hurry Their Majesties' deaths." Finished with her testimony, she sat down. She studied her hands in her lap, still covered by the sheer Gypsy Silk gloves.

"I thought it was the cardinal who performed the perfidy of spells," Duca Anino observed.

"Apparently, it had been, but when the cardinal saw the potential end of his plans, he trained Tomasi," Stefano said. To Fieri, he nodded and motioned to the table.

Colonello Fieri took a white bundle from his pouch and set it on the table, letting it fall open. Inside the white bundle lay the two dirty, scorched, crudely shaped dolls. Touching the fabric surrounding the dolls only, Stefano shoved the bundle down the table.

"Have a look," Stefano invited. "Convince me that these dolls do not represent King Alban and Queen Idala."

The duchi crowded around the table, pulling the fabric of the bundle, and thereby the dolls, this way and that. The undertone of their conversation was unintelligible. The expressions on the faces of the duchi, however, said it all. Many were terrified while some seemed also angry. After several minutes of examination, the material was left to lie in the center of the main table.

"You found this *in* Brother Tomasi's cell?" Bishop Abruzzi asked, coming from his seat at the back of the hall to look at the two characterized dolls. "Where?"

Stefano folded his arms over his chest and tried not to look defensive. "They were in the fire pit. We found them in the ashes where they should have burned, but did not."

The bishop looked from Stefano to Luciana speculatively, but did not question or contradict what the Lord Regent had said. He looked closer at the poppets, then picked one up. He turned it this way, then that, finally sniffing at the doll before setting it back down with its mate. "I suspect from where the points of oil were placed," the bishop said diffidently, "that Brother Tomasi was merely giving the king and queen Last Rites by proxy. No evil done there, except that he probably had to use the oil from his dinners to perform the ceremony. Gabera, did you ever see these *bambola* in the possession of Brother Tomasi?"

The priest shook his head. "But then Tomasi was very private, especially about that which involved the cardinal."

"*Brother* Tomasi, Gabera. He was our brother," Abruzzi softly rebuked the priest.

"No brother of mine—in the Church or out—would be so sacrilegious as to toy with *bambola* representative of our king and queen," Gabera replied, standing straight and looking the bishop squarely in the eye. "I have seen them . . . the *bambola*. If you are right and he was saying Last Rites over them, then he did not do it a single time . . . and how could he have known that the king and queen were to die?"

Abruzzi sighed and shrugged. "I cannot know the workings of the mind of a madman."

"But the evidence is there that something untoward was happening in that cell between Tomasi and the *bambola*," Stefano said. "Please tell me, Bishop, what is the religious significance of giving Last Rites to somebody in good health?"

Abruzzi frowned. "I have never heard of such a thing." He returned to his chair.

Stefano moved away from his seat, from Luciana, and stalked the length of the extended table, to the point where the *bambola* lay. He leaned between a conte and a duca. "So, we have it here. Proof that the cardinal and Brother Tomasi were casting magic of a sort that did not fit with their charged duties as churchmen.

"I can have the other witness brought forth, for further questioning, but is it truly necessary?"

"This *Magnus Inique* writ above the . . . above Tomasi's door. Was it truly someone from them or is that to mislead? How does one know?" one of the duchi asked. "And how does this murder have anything to do with King Alban's death?"

"Other than being the same group, I don't think the murders are related," Stefano said. "I think Brother Tomasi was murdered because he knew too much about the cardinal and, probably, the group itself."

"Has anything more been discovered about this group?" Duchessa Rossi asked.

Stefano nodded to Lord Strozzini who stepped forward. "We cannot be certain that either the cardinal or Brother Tomasi were involved with these men. They were last reported to be in Citteauroea, but had moved on before I could detain them for questioning."

"How interesting that they are always eluding you, Lord Strozzini," Prince Pierro said, his expression challenging.

Stefano placed a restraining hand on the Royal Bodyguard. The action also served to remind him that they were not yet ready to charge the prince with anything. Pierro deMedici had been corresponding with *Magnus Inique*, that much they knew from Don Battista, but they were waiting to present their evidence until they had more than the don's word and Pierro's questionably injured arm. It would take more than this to take down a prince . . . or a deMedici, for that matter.

Duca Gianola interrupted the yawning divide of silence, with a question. "What do Last Rites said over dolls do?"

"The dolls were used in what we call sympathetic magic," the *Beluni* answered. "Effectively, what was said over the dolls, was said over the people they represented." She shifted in her chair, finally rising, leaning hard on her staff. "The effect of such a spell would only hasten the subjects' deaths."

"*Impossibile*!" the bishop cried. "None would use Last Rites in such a fashion. You say he sought to hurry their deaths!"

"We are saying exactly that," Stefano insisted. "I note, despite all the attention either the king or queen was given, there was no saving them, because they were already slowly dying under this final spell of the cardinal's and Tomasi's."

"Effectively, they turned to God for assistance, to give their evil spell strength. Tomasi continued even after the cardinal was dead," Gabera said. "His service made him ill, Your Reverence. It ate away at his foundations, and he had a part to play in his own sickness."

"Surely, you can find mercy in your soul for one of your Church brethren?" Abruzzi said.

"I truly did not consider him one of the Church's anymore. His prayers were secretive, he would not confess his sins, and he did not take Communion while I knew him." Padre Gabera folded his hands into his cassock sleeves and met the bishop's gaze squarely. There was neither apology nor sympathy in his expression.

"You weigh your brother's sins heavily, Padre Gabera," the bishop said harshly.

"He's not the only one, Eminence," Duca Silvieri said. He turned to the bishop, away from the dolls. "Is it true what they said? That giving the Extreme Unction . . . Last

Rites to the *bambola* would hasten the death of our king and queen?"

The bishop opened and closed his mouth wordlessly, growing more and more defensive as others turned to look at him. "How would I know?" he finally burst out. "I have no business with magic or its kin."

"Would *you* give the Last Rites to a perfectly healthy person?" Stefano asked.

"No, but—" The bishop floundered for words, then shook his head. "No."

"And you most certainly wouldn't give it to a doll," Gabera added.

"So this man played a part in the deaths of our king and queen," Lord Strozzini stated. "He was a traitor."

"He was not Tyrrhian and could not be forced to abide by your laws," the bishop argued, pushing between Capitano della Guelfa and Father Gabera. "As ambassador of the Holy Roman Church, he fell under my aegis and should have been kept in the Cattedrale d'Alaric."

"Tell me, Most Reverend, would you be so quick to protect him if he played a part in the death of your emperor, the Pope?" Sebastiani asked. A general consensus in support of the question ran through the crowd of nobles. Sebastiani leaned forward, "How would you feel about the matter if *our* ambassador's man played some part in your Pope's death?"

"I—I don't know," the bishop admitted.

Luciana looked at Padre Gabera and asked, her voice rough with emotion. "I have one more question. You said Brother Tomasi spoke of two gypsies. One was my sister. Who was the other?"

"Tomasi did not say, *Araunya*; the cardinal, I have surmised, already had her when Tomasi came into his direct service," the cleric shrugged helplessly. "Her body, despite the unnatural embalming, had withered to little more than a skeleton—which we also burned."

"And for what purpose did the cardinal have them?" the *Beluni* asked the priest.

"For their magic . . . they 'renewed' him, Tomasi said. I don't know what he did to them. It is all unspeakable to me."

"Where did he get the body of the other woman?" Sebastiani asked.

"I don't know the when, where, or how, but Tomasi hinted that she was supplied to him by the witch-hunters," Gabera replied.

"Witch-hunters?" Lord Strozzini asked from behind Stefano and Luciana. When Stefano motioned him forward, Rodrigo Strozzini moved quickly. "Who were these witch-hunters? Were they *Magnus Inique*? Do you know any of their names?"

The priest shook his head. "Names were seldom mentioned. The only one I remember was *Magnus Inique*—Hammer and Fire—by which they've been claiming to drive all of the witches out of Tyrrhia."

"This *Magnus Inique* claims they're fighting evil when the witch-hunters kill and burn innocent travelers and sedentary Romani who've done no evil to anyone!" the *Beluni* choked out, her anger and grief clear.

"So far, Madonna, we're only getting word about the witch-hunters as rumor," Strozzini replied.

Stefano nodded to Strozzini and then said to the *Beluni*. "We have heard of a couple of random attacks, *Beluni-Daiya*. Have there been more than those few reported?"

"Few? If you would call twenty-eight families at last count 'few,' then yes, only a few. The lonely women count as more, the ones without husbands or sons to protect them. Midwives and weavers of the Gypsy Silk, all murdered for their 'corruption,' according to the notices left," the *Beluni* said. "*O beng te poggar le loro men*!" She spat again.

"What did she say?" the bishop demanded, making the sign of the cross.

"She wished the devil would break their necks," Luciana said. "It's no curse, only a heartfelt wish."

"What more do you know of *Magnus Inique*, Padre?" Strozzini asked. "You must have learned something?"

"Very little. They're a brotherhood of sorts and the cardinal—he seemed to be high in the order of things based on what I learned from Tomasi."

"Was there one above him?" Stefano asked.

Padre Gabera rubbed his nose and hesitated before finally speaking. "There was little direct talk of the group. Tomasi seemed to think there were none higher within the brotherhood, but . . . I know he was very respectful of . . ." He stopped, hesitating again.

"Of whom?" Stefano pressed.

"Of the Princess Bianca, but that may simply have been because they—the cardinal and Princess Bianca—were friends . . . it might have nothing to do with the brotherhood or the use of magic except that Tomasi spoke of delivering charms and potions to her and a couple of other courtiers . . . but I don't know their names," Padre Gabera said, shaking his head.

"Lies! My sister's name is despoiled by this hearsay!" Ortensia cried out. She rose and lunged down the length of the table at Padre Gabera.

The Colonello of the Palazzo Guards stepped forward and captured the princess' arms. "Your Highness," Colonello Fieri said, wrestling with the enraged woman. "Your Highness! I do not wish to hurt you, but you cannot attack a witness!"

"But he lies about my sister!" she cried, collapsing onto the floor in tears.

"*Pardone*, Your Highness, I did not mean to offend or cast unwarranted aspersions upon your sister, but I must answer the questions put to me. I know these things from months of talking to him. It's possible that I misunderstood, but Tomasi seemed very sure your sister Bianca was somehow involved with the cardinal's doings," Padre Gabera said in soft tones that did nothing to comfort the enraged royal.

Pierro came down the length of the table and gently helped his wife up and into his arms. "Come, come," he murmured as he guided her very purposefully from the room.

"Are there any further questions for the padre?" Stefano asked, looking around the gallery at the assembled duchi.

"I have another," Luciana said. "What claims did Tomasi make about the cardinal?"

Gabera shifted uncomfortably. "Part of the reason I had so much trouble getting him to Confess, to take Communion, was because he believed the cardinal was or would be alive in some fashion . . . in some other body than the cardinal once occupied. It's all very confusing and laced, I suspect, with lies and exaggeration."

Stefano looked pointedly at Duchi Gianola, di Candido, LaCosta, Silvieri, and Rossi in turn. He met their eyes, each and every one of them, before he said, "Do we have any further questions?"

When no one spoke, he turned to where Capitano della Guelfa stood behind Luciana. "Capitano, do you have anything you wish to add to the testimony?" Stefano asked.

"Nothing that has not already been said, Your Excellency." The capitano shook his head. He wore his dress blue-and-gold uniform, his hair tied back in a small bow.

Padre Gabera looked worried and avoided eye contact with Bishop Abruzzi. Rather than exacerbate the problems that clearly already existed, Stefano did not question Gabera again directly.

"We should take our seats. Is there anything anyone else would like to say on this matter?" Stefano asked. He made a point of sitting and getting Luciana to retake her chair. He looked up, more than a little annoyed that the bishop remained standing nearby. "Are there any among you who doubt the cardinal and Tomasi traversed a dark path of magic and politics?"

No one spoke.

"Now, we speak to the matter of the children for whom the *Araunya* is Regent Guardian. Duchessa Rossi, would you care to make a summary statement of your visit to the youngest members of *la famiglia reale*?"

Duchessa Rossi rose from her chair, looking at her hands resting on the edge of the large table for a moment. "I have seen the four newborn *bambini*. With a single exception, they are all healthy and will represent their parents and the kingdom well. There are two twin girls, Pietra and Rosalina. There is another girl-child, but she shows all the signs of being half-Romani, a Child of the Bloods as the Romani call it. She, Chiara, is marked with a streak of white hair."

Here, the assembly broke into mayhem, arguing and discussing this revelation amongst themselves. Stefano leaned forward to get their attention again, but the Duchessa shook her head at him, so he sat back, letting her handle the announcement as she saw fit. After several long moments of pandemonium, she knocked on the wood of the table and cleared her throat. One by one, she had the assemblage's attention again.

"I believe, the Child of the Bloods—a half-Romani child—was born of the queen because of the spells she and the cardinal cast. Chiara is probably the spirit of the second Gypsy that Padre Gabera spoke of. As I understand the reasoning behind the magic, she was dragged into the queen's pregnancy with the cardinal who cast a spell to be reborn into *la famiglia reale* . . . and he is the fourth child, Massimo," Duchessa Rossi announced.

Again, havoc reigned as voices rose in argument and derision. Duca Silvieri stood, slamming his hands on the table for attention.

"God and most of you know I have my sympathies elsewhere, but from all evidence, what Her Grace, Martina Rossi, said was the absolute truth. Tomasi's testimony via Padre Gabera confirmed it for me. I absolutely believe what she says is the truth," Silvieri said.

Gianola, di Candido and LaCosta also rose, confirming to all what the Duchessa had said was accurate. Sebastiani stood then, leaning heavily on the table, "Like it or not, magic was involved in the queen's last pregnancy and there are two who do not truly belong to *la famiglia reale*. I have this evidence from the queen's own lips," Sebastiani admitted and was immediately inundated with questions and accusations.

Stefano rose. "Enough!" he said roughly. He strode around the room, looking at anyone who would meet his eyes. "You chose these five to be witnesses for you, and a sixth has stood up to confirm what they said. Well, I, too, tell you this is the truth as I understand it.

"The Child of the Bloods, Princess Chiara, offers no threat to her siblings and will be raised with them and as they are, but the boy, Massimo, he is not right with the world. For all that I hold dear, I believe—or believed—him to be the cardinal incarnate, and I think that *he* is who Brother Tomasi spoke of when he said the cardinal was still alive. The question before us is what to do with Massimo *now*. He disrupts the nursery. The christening which many of you witnessed . . . it might not have been enough. Something must be done. Many of you witnessed the christening!"

"What would you have us do?" Duca Raffia asked. "We can't kill the boy. He is, after all, *la famiglia reale*."

"I propose the boy be raised by caretakers, tutors, and be given whatever else he needs," Stefano replied. He returned to the head of the table. "It seems to be the only humane and safe thing to do."

"Who will supervise his care?" Raffia asked.

"I will," Stefano said, "and the Regent Guardian. We must give him a secure place to live and learn, but he must be away from court and away from temptation. This way Massimo has a chance to redeem himself in this lifetime."

"If he were not *la famiglia reale*—" Gianola began.

"But he *is*, and that ends the discussion," Stefano said firmly. "Are we agreed? Estensi, I want the decision on record."

"We must give our 'Yea' by a raise of hands," Estensi announced. "To your seats where I can see you better."

With some grumbling, the Palantini members scattered back to their chairs and the election to remove Massimo from court was made with few dissents.

XXII

"You cannot have a proud and chivalrous spirit if your conduct is mean and paltry; for whatever a man's actions are, such must be his spirit."

—Demosthenes

PIERRO deMedici leaned against the tree of his saddle and loosened the reins on his big black stallion so that the animal could graze. He kept an eye on both ends of the road, not sure from which direction his assignation would come, and watching out for random travelers who might see him when he did not particularly wish to be seen. As was the custom of nobility, for the sake of his anonymity, he wore a traveler's mask, but his horse was distinctive. Had he been thinking of it when he left the stables, he would have taken one of the humbler beasts, but he did so enjoy riding Calypso. . . .

He had had a devil of a time escaping his assigned bodyguards, but elude them he had. Pierro heard the sounds of horses approaching from the rear, which meant the riders had gone off the road some while back and looped around to catch him unaware. He wheeled Calypso around, a scorpinini in his hand, ready to shoot should the necessity present itself.

Padre Caserta, the man on the left, on a light chestnut gelding, was recognizable to Pierro in spite of the traveler's mask he wore. DiSotto, on the right, riding a dark bay mare, wore no such mask.

Pierro uncocked his scorpinini and tucked it back into his belt with his backup as he turned his stallion around so that he could watch the road.

"I was wondering if you would show or not," he said, flicking Calypso's reins loose for the horse to graze again. He shifted ably as the horse pawed the ground cover for fresher shoots of grass.

"Word came late. It took us a while to be sure we weren't followed," Caserta said. "What news have you brought us?"

"The Duca di Drago is now solidly supported as Lord Regent and his wife is Regent Guardian. Ortensia's position as queen has been quashed," Pierro reported sourly. "The attack on Messina did not work as we planned."

"Permanently?" Caserta asked. "Your wife, I mean."

"In theory," Pierro replied. "But if something happened to His Excellency, of course the question would have to be revisited."

"We should lie low for a time, I think," Caserta said, edging his golden gelding forward so that he and the deMedici were side by side. "Was I right about Battista? Did he defect from our cause?"

"I'm not sure," Pierro said thoughtfully. "He certainly cleared his things from my apartment and stands on his own again. I would say, to be safe, that we must count him against us. His withdrawal from my household came at a significant time for us. I had plans . . ."

"As did I," Caserta admitted. "But something in his manner that afternoon put me on guard. That's why we left the inn that very night. DiSotto's been watching the inn. He thinks there have been men asking after us, but those boys in the front have been vague. We can't know for sure."

"You could have warned me sooner," Pierro snapped at the plain-clothed priest. "I could have been better prepared. I might even have rallied the situation—"

"We sent you news as soon as we could," diSotto said from behind them.

Pierro cast a glance over his shoulder at the mercenary who worked for their cause. He looked back at Caserta meaningfully. "News has a narrow window of being worthwhile or even news. After a point, it's dead information. You aren't paid for dead information, Caserta." Over his shoulder, Pierro added, "Nor you. I would have expected one of you to make it to the palazzo before Battista with such news."

"Next time—"

"There will be no surprises, or there will be consequences," Pierro interrupted the priest.

"What else happened in the Palantini?" Caserta asked.

"Her Highness made me look the fool. She won't do it again," deMedici promised.

"The woman must be brought to heel," Caserta said.

"I have my ways of knowing what happens after I've left the meeting, I just wasn't able to have my say in matters," Pierro growled. He squinted into the sun, noting the heavily laden carriage lumbering in their direction and, eventually, to the palazzo. Another late arrival for the Palantini, he surmised. "Let us get off the road before someone sees us."

The deMedici gathered his reins and pulled his horse around, giving him the heel into the wintery forest. They would have to go deeper into the wood than in full springtime or summer when the foliage would provide cover. He rode deep into the wood, enjoying the ride when Calypso jumped over fallen trees and narrow brooks, casting winter leaves behind him as he ran. Pierro pulled the stallion up at a small clearing away from anything but the stream.

It took several minutes for Caserta and diSotto to catch up. Their horses were winded in the cold air, whereas Calypso frisked in the open area, tugging for control of the reins.

"So . . . we were discussing the Palantini and what happened," Caserta said, reopening their discussion.

"What *is* happening. When I left the palazzo, it was still in session," Pierro replied.

"Still? Is it common for them to go all day?" diSotto asked.

"Yes, still, and I have no idea what is common for the Palantini as this was my first general assembly and, as I said, I did not get to stay," Pierro said, barely containing his temper. "With di Drago Lord Regent and his wife Regent Guardian, both of them are trouble for us. If we could get our hands on the children, away from that Gypsy *stronza* . . ."

"Perhaps, if we struck hard enough at the Romani witches, it would draw her out of the palazzo?" Caserta suggested.

Pierro tapped his lip with his forefinger. "It's a good idea, Caserta. Strike hard at her witches, and let's see if that draws her out."

"Then I will get the word to the outriders," Caserta said.

"The sooner, the better," Pierro agreed. "And meeting with you will become trickier as the Lord Regent has increased my bodyguards. I'll have to elude them every time I come to you.

"So let us plan a bit more before we part."

XXIII

"Whatever ignorance men show, from none disdainful turn; for every one doth something know, which you have yet to learn."

—Romani saying

RETURNING from the makeshift nursery, Luciana found her husband sitting on the side of the bed, still in shirt and pantaloons; head and his chain of office in his hands. Luciana sat next to him.

"What is it *camómescro*? The day is done and won," she said.

He did not immediately answer her, but sighed and sat back, dropping his chain on the bedside table. "The day is done, yes, but won? I am not so sure. There were deep concerns about you because of . . . well . . . your race and the whole subject of witchcraft."

"You handled it well. You served as a good and proper Regent today."

"Today? I was a disaster. As much as I prepared, I was still unprepared for the vehemence. I let you talk. I did not take your side as I should—" Stefano protested.

"Really? I remember differently," Luciana said as she smiled wickedly and kissed his cheek. "Besides, *mio adorato*, you've always said my memory was better than yours."

Stefano laughed softly and pulled her down onto the bed, resting on his right elbow so that he could lean over her. "I would tickle you until you cried 'Mercy' if your corset would let me!"

Luciana chuckled and reached up to buss him on the cheek, but Stefano turned and captured her lips. He laid her back on the bed and deepened the kiss, his left hand roving over her body. He stopped suddenly.

"You *are* a witch! Seducing me out of my pensiveness, but mull on this I must or I'll never be a good Regent!" Stefano murmured, dropping another kiss on the crest between her breasts, just visible above the neckline of her deep green dress and black undergown. He sat back up, kicked off his heeled shoes, and turned so that he sat cross-legged on the bed.

"Careful, or I may cast a spell on you," Luciana said.

"Ha! You did that years ago, and I've never lost its effect."

"So you say now, but just last year you were—"

"None of that foolishness. We—*I* was overpowered by my grief and . . . and being too headstrong for my own good. Let us not speak of it, please? The five years apart were too much for me to bear," Stefano said.

"I've never asked you, but while you were . . . away . . ."

"Were there other women?" he finished for her.

Luciana nodded, dreading the answer because she knew he would tell her the truth.

"No. Never. I loved you even then and could not consider another woman," Stefano said. He clapped fingers to palm. "Which reminds me . . . I have something for you, but you must wait until later for me to give it to you."

Driven by her curiosity, Luciana said, "Give it to me now! I don't want to wait . . . it might be months before you remember to give it to me!" Her eyes narrowed when she saw the guilty look on her husband's face. "Has it been months? Already?"

"Yes, I meant to give them . . . it to you before, but the time never seemed right. Come, *mi amore*, give me a little more time so that I can work this problem through. It is important to a nation of men, women, and children that I perform my offices well these next ten years until a certain five-year-old reaches his appropriate birthday."

Luciana sighed heavily and lay back down, turning her face away from him. "You were speaking of not defending me, but you were wrong. You did speak up, only I took charge of my situation and spoke freely—heaven only knows if it helped or hurt me."

"Us," Stefano corrected. He captured her hand in his and caressed it. "Come, do not be angry with me."

She turned her head back so that she faced him. "I'm not . . . angry, just . . . frustrated. What is it that you have to give me that you could not for all these months, but now is the time to tell me and not the time to give it to me?"

"Promise me you'll at least wait to open it," Stefano said, rising from the bed. He went to his trunk of clothes, rummaged for a while and finally rose with a small chest made of cherry wood. He very carefully presented it to her.

She noticed, at once, that there was a lock on the box and so did not even try to open it. Luciana simply held out her hand and waited.

With a heavy sigh, he removed the thin gold chain he always wore—ever since he had returned from the war—from under his shirt and handed it to her.

In that moment, she was ready to hurl the box back at him. How many nights had she toyed with that necklace and fob—some nights even when he was awake—and never known it was meant for her! Instead, Luciana forced a smile to her lips while her fingers closed around the tiny key dangling from the chain and used it to unlock the box. He folded his hands behind his back and began to pace while she rummaged through the box. It was all papers. Bits and pieces in some places, the back of a strategic map on another and all bearing his distinctive handwriting.

"What is this?" she asked, mystified.

"Letters . . . written to you. I did not send them, because . . ." Stefano shrugged diffidently. "There was a time . . . at the war and after that I did not . . ."

"When you did not what?" Luciana prodded.

"When I did not think you would treat my heart as kindly as you do now." He said the words in a rush.

Luciana felt tears forming and willed them back, blinking to keep from shedding them. Her heart felt sundered by his very words. When she felt in control of her emotions again, she spoke, "I have *always* held you and the gift of your heart most precious, even in the blackest days of my depression over the loss of Arturo. That is why I did not beg you to return to me those years. I hoped you were merely grieving, as was I . . . and that you would return when you were ready. But you weren't when you came back, were you? You weren't ready to return. Your first question was about what I was up to, if I recall correctly."

Stefano winced. "Clearly, *mi amore*, you have a better memory than I . . . and, as I recall now, my words were to those general effect, yes."

"So you weren't ready to return to me, but came home because you thought I might be in some trouble at court."

"Which you were, if I recall," Stefano said.

"You win no points from me there . . . even if you were helpful at the time!"

"Then I have no point at all, but to ask you to read the letters . . . or just one, they are of one subject, but I was afraid to send them, hence the cursory letters about the estate."

Luciana selected one of the scraps and unfolded it to read,

"May 8th, 1682

My heart burns for you like the flame that lights my soul and makes my breath warm."

She looked up at him then, not bothering to stop the tears that came unbidden. "All the while . . . while you were away from me?"

"Yes, and I did not send them because I was a coward. Now you know the true man at his very core. What say you now, wife?"

She launched herself at him, twining her fingers through his hair as she kissed him long and deep. He responded as though a drowning man seeking air. His hands roamed—as they were wont to do—finding their way to the small of her back where her dress was tied closed. He pulled at the braided ribbon until he felt the knot give way to his plundering hands. It was only then that he pulled his mouth from hers. They both panted with excitement and desire.

He groaned and took her wrists in his hands, forcibly breaking the lock they had had around his neck, and stepped back. "No! We must talk . . . if nothing else matters, then we must speak of Massimo before I . . . before we . . . are distracted."

It was Luciana's turn to sigh heavily and sit back on her heels. She actually hurt, being separated from him . . . oh, how she ached! "Then let us be done with the subject and let our hands do the reading of the text that is between us!"

Stefano took a step back, hands raised. "This is important, Lucia. Do not tempt me right now!"

Luciana crossed her hands in front of her, in plain view of her wary husband. Her mind was consumed with but a single thought and it had nothing to do with young Massimo. "Say what you will, Stefano. My ears are yours to command," she said.

Stefano still did not trust her . . . or maybe it was himself, or perhaps both of them. Instead of returning to the bed, he took up the pink, upholstered chair from beside her dressing table, set it down opposite her, and sat in it. Just far enough that they were unable to touch.

"You would speak to me of Massimo," Luciana reminded him when he sat silent for a long moment.

"When I proposed sending Massimo away today, I must confess that I had not thought it through. Which estate do I send him to? Who can be trusted with his upbringing? None of this, had I thought about. Only after speaking so forthrightly on the matter, did any of this occur to me. Who—if anyone—do I tell?"

"You would tell me, of course," Luciana said, watching his expression. She saw doubt in his eyes before he tipped his face downward so that she could not see it. "Stefano, you *would* tell me."

"I don't know what inducements they might use . . ." he said, looking up as he spoke.

"There is nothing that could convince me—" Luciana began, her voice deadly even.

"What if they threatened me? Or Divya?" Stefano asked.

"I would trust you to take care of yourself until I could rescue you," Luciana said. "As to Divya, she is a Child of the Bloods. All fairy kind are sworn by their blessing to come to her aid if ever she were in true peril."

"They didn't protect the maggiore when he faced the mortal fire," Stefano said.

"Oh, but they did, even though the peril was caused by his own conscious intent, they did not make him suffer the burns of a thousand deaths," Luciana replied with absolute conviction.

"Then I will trust your word on this, for you know the *Fata* better than I."

"Thank you . . . for believing me, and I promise to raise all the girls to understand the importance of thinking for themselves and to rescue themselves instead of waiting to be rescued. We will have drills if we must, but our daughter and those children of Idala and Alban will know how to defend themselves capably," Luciana promised.

"There will be some things I can teach the children?" Stefano asked, with the hint of laughter in his voice.

"Of course, you will teach all of them to lead their people and be sure of their honor lest we have another Bianca or Ortensia." Before Stefano could reply, she suddenly held up a hand, pressing a finger to her lips. "You will teach them to lead by example and by will . . ." she continued speaking as she rose from the bed and crept toward the door leading to the landing she shared with Stefano's room, now Prunella's and her son's. Without notice, Luciana threw the door open wide, exposing Prunella, son in arms, leaning intently into the door which, once moved, caused her to stumble into the room.

"Cousin!" Luciana said, as though happy to discover Prunella listening in to their conversation. "Are you ill? The boy?"

Prunella straightened up, her spine stiffening into rigidity as she did so, and sniffed. "Little Urbano was fretful, and I was walking with him. Nothing to concern yourself about."

Luciana nodded knowingly. "You might consider walking him around your room or taking him downstairs. The landing is precarious. You might fall down the stairs, possibly kill you both."

The tip of Prunella's tongue peeked out between her lips as though she were actively biting her tongue. After a moment, she nodded, "You are quite right, *Cousin.* I shall be more careful in the future. Thank you for your kind consideration. As you can see, my son has fallen asleep now, and I shall return to my bed."

Luciana nodded and waited for her cousin-by-marriage

to absent herself from the landing. Prunella did so with hurried economy of motion. When Luciana heard the key in Prunella's door turn, she left the door wide open and returned to her seat opposite Stefano.

He nodded toward the door. "Do you truly think it's safe to do that?"

"Of course. This way we will know if Prunella returns. If one of our retainers comes down, they know well to announce themselves," Luciana said.

"How did you know she was there, by the way?" Stefano asked.

Luciana waved her hand. "I heard her sniff. I hate that." She shook her head, her distaste clear. "But we were talking of Massimo and your confusion in placing him."

Stefano nodded and lowered his voice. "We were. Do you think it's safe to speak with the open door?"

"Of course, if she listens it will be through a closed door, a stretch of hallway and the better part of a room dividing us. If you prefer to talk later, I will understand," Luciana said saucily, shrugging out of her overdress and reaching for her corset strings.

"Hold, woman!" Stefano said with a laugh, inching his chair farther away.

"I'll hold, but don't move farther away, please! You'll make it harder to . . . hear you."

Glancing at the doorway, Stefano stood and moved the chair closer to his wife. "So I am at a complete loss regarding Massimo. My gut tells me that I must tell someone . . . more than even you, but who do I tell? If I choose just sympathizers with the throne, the other duchi will feel remaindered, and then more quarreling will break out. I feel like a child of five struggling over my first mathematics problem. There are so many ways to do this wrong, and he is a child of *la famiglia reale* whether he ever rules or not!"

"You've already selected a privy council when you chose who to take to see Massimo. Add Duca Sebastiani to the council if you wish. Perhaps they can suggest someone to raise the boy?" Luciana suggested.

"I hesitate to take the subject before a committee, especially a mixed one," Stefano said. He braced his elbows on his knees and leaned closer to Luciana. "I have a very strange request for you, Luciana . . ."

"Yes?" she prompted, her voice and expression clearly showing her reluctance. When he did not respond, but only stared at the carpet, she went so far as to prod him verbally. "Go on." Luciana was careful not to touch Stefano . . . not when he fell quiet like this. His mind was too wrapped up in other concerns.

Stefano sighed and looked her straight in the eye. "I want you to . . . to do your magic, by use of your scrying or the cards to help me decide who I must choose to raise Massimo. If you will do this for me, I would take your advice with me to the privy council you have suggested for I think you offer wise consultation . . . or, at least, your leanings incline with mine own."

She slumped against the footboard at the end of her bed and stared at him long and hard. "This is not some test . . . to see if I will go against your express wishes?"

He shook his head firmly. "No test. I ask you truly."

"Truly?" Luciana repeated, considering this option which she would never have expected in a thousand lifetimes. It was an opportunity for her to use her magic in a way that would help him and he was asking for it, for her to do this thing for him. She slowly nodded her head. "I will do this divination for you, *camómescro*, because you ask it of me. It is difficult for me to not use all of my skills, when I know that they could be useful. I will do this in the morning, when my mind is fresh with the new day."

Stefano dropped a kiss on her forehead. "Before I go to the privy council?"

"Yes. Of course," she agreed.

"I know this is a very different path than the one I've taken previously, but since Divya's birth, I have realized how much magic is a part of you . . . and her. It is like denying you the use of your legs and has been unfair of me," Stefano apologized.

Luciana reached over and claimed his right hand. She held it to her heart. "I knew that one day you would understand. It's just that I have been so patient, and it seemed like this time would never come."

Stefano rose and kissed her on the mouth, for one sweet moment, letting it deepen and then he broke away. "I know you have been patient. I still have misgivings . . . after the officers of the Palantini gave you so much trouble over your . . . your skills, but I understand denying you your magic is like denying me you and I've done that already." He crossed to the door and closed it, smiling at her conspiratorially. "There are some things that I don't mind scandalmongers overhearing if they are so daring as to listen at the door. You have taken steps to see that you don't get pregnant?"

Luciana smiled, opening her arms in welcome. "I am still nursing Divya, so I can't get pregnant yet. But soon, I'll start to take a special tisane my people make."

3 d'Febbraio, 1685

Stefano sat on the bed and watched his wife pull out a carved and lined box from her small table under the window. She glanced up at him, perhaps to see if he still approved, still wanted her to commit this act of magic. He nodded his assent firmly, hiding his instinctive hesitation. He was not like her, had not been raised with the ready use of magic. He still had misgivings, none that he would admit or demonstrate to her in any way. She was his wife and this was her nature. He could bear to change neither condition.

Luciana opened the box and cautiously removed the bit of Gypsy Silk, which she carefully unwrapped to expose her cards. She gently shuffled them and offered them to Stefano. "Cut the cards, thinking of your concerns."

Stefano hesitated a moment and then accepted the cards. Their edges were worn soft from use, the finish on the back still slightly slick. He concentrated as much as he could on the problem facing him, of Massimo, of the boy's overall well-being. He then cut the cards with his right hand, breaking the deck into three parts and then re-ordering them. He smoothed the cards into place and handed them back to Luciana.

She closed her eyes, cards in hands, tipping her face toward the warmth of the morning sun filtering in through the windowpanes. She whispered, as though to the room at large, in Romani, "*Mukalis man av abrí.*" She opened her eyes and began sorting cards. One down, a second across it, and, following, two rows graduating by one each to form a sort of pyramid.

"What does—"

Luciana held up a silencing hand, carefully adjusting each card so that it lay in perfect order. She set the unused cards to one side and looked at him. "You were asking?"

"First, what does what you said mean?" Stefano asked.

"*Mukalis man av abrí*? It means 'Let it come out.' Are you ready for the reading of the cards now?" she said.

Stefano closed his mouth tight, unwilling to further risk interrupting whatever flow of magic existed between her and the cards. He motioned with his hand for her to proceed.

She flipped the first card and he sucked in his breath at the sight of the Devil drawn on the card. She looked at him, slightly impatient. "It does not mean what you think, Stefan, have patience. It is indeed, *Beng*, the Devil, but he is the jester, the laborer who brings stability. He is you."

"Me?" Stefano repeated, surprised.

"Yes," Luciana said. She turned over the card turned side-ways on top of it. It was the Prince of Swords.

This time, Stefano stilled his reaction and waited. "This is who you fear and fear for, but he—Massimo—will surprise you. He will be intuitive, magic will always be a part of who this child will be, but not the way it was . . . before . . . but he will also be inventive, a critical thinker . . . for good if he is raised right."

"If he is raised right," Stefano repeated, he dropped back onto the bed, covering his eyes. "If he is raised right . . . that is the whole of the question, is it not?"

"Indeed, Stefano, that is the question and the answer. The boy should study chess from early on. To improve his mind and his wits." She turned the first card in the second row. "The Five of Wands. He will face trial and defeat . . . both physically and spiritually. This is not a happy card for Massimo or the person . . . or people who raise him."

Stefano sat back up and watched her as she first turned and then ran her fingers over the second card in the row. A crowned woman sat astride a colorful *vardo* wheel. He waited.

"The *Araunya* of Wheels," she said at last. "The Princess of Wheels is *enceinte* . . . expecting . . . or she was recently. I have no interpretation for that other than this might foretell of Massimo's mother-to-be. It is definitely not your sister, though the card shows her with light hair, this far into the reading this is a 'what will be' card rather than the past."

"Are you sure?" Stefano asked, contemplative.

Luciana sighed heavily. "Of course not! It's divination magic. It comes from my understanding of the cards and the clues in them. Trust me or don't, Stefano, but no more interruptions if you want me to continue."

"*Excusi*," Stefano said and motioned back to the cards.

His wife waited, as though she expected him to speak again. When he did not, she turned the first of the three cards in the next row. "*Puri-Daiya* of Wheels . . . she is the Queen of Wheels . . . she is the physical feeder . . . she tends to Massimo's most basic needs. Could it be? Two Wheels so close together in the reading. I must think on this before I say more. There is much to consider here."

With difficulty, Stefano kept silent and waited for his wife to continue rather than sit and contemplate the cards. Within a few seconds, Luciana reached for the middle card in the third row and slowly turned it over. She sucked in her breath.

"The *Beluni* or the Empress, a second major card with two royalty cards of the same suit and another royalty card in Swords. Interesting to have so much royalty when we speak of royalty by birth.

"This card, however, is not referring to some type of queen in the usual way. This card means that we speak of the divinity in women and that is motherhood, the caregiver, or the one who nourishes. I think I know who this refers to. I know who is meant to be Massimo's guardian!" Luciana said with a sudden smile. "Despite the Empress, she is *not* royalty by birth, marriage or in any other way other than she is meant to be the mother of a Prince of Tyrrhia. Though Massimo is not intended to inherit the throne, he will always be a Prince of Tyrrhia. She is the person who already mothers the boy, this prince, and sees that he is fed and his needs tended to!"

"One of the nursery women?" Stefano asked, then bit his lips closed. He raised both hands in apology.

"Not *one*, but, rather, a specific One. There is only one

woman who is not so suspicious of Massimo that she has trouble with him and that is Bonita. She already has a son practically the same age as Massimo. They could be raised together. Sharing tutors and lessons. Massimo will grow up understanding what it is to have his health, if not perfect, like the other boy." Luciana smiled again and nodded. "Yes, this is who is meant to parent Massimo through the troubling years ahead. I know it deep in my heart. It is only a matter of what her husband will say."

Stefano kept silent this time, bobbing his head in a slow-burning approval.

Luciana reached up and patted his knee, then refocused on the cards. She reached for the third card in the row, the final card and, with great care, turned it over, smoothing it into place in the pyramid. "The Nine of Wheels . . . interesting. This could refer to the father's influence . . . Bonita's husband, I mean. It speaks of growth and amplification of the physical form, a positive influence.

"It is also a third Wheel card . . . three will come with the bargain . . . an entire family. What say you, husband?"

Stefano remained quiet for another moment of clear contemplation. "I think you have come up with an ideal solution. Massimo, though a prince, will be raised by commoners who will be more family to him than his brother or sisters. When it is time, he can have access to court . . . it makes the most sense to me. There will be little political influence in his life. This is good."

"When will you speak to her, then? Before or after your privy council?" Luciana asked.

At this point, Stefano raised a cautioning hand. "I think, as Lord Regent I might intimidate her, get her to agree if she is not fully confident of the move in her own mind. She is familiar with you and you are the Regent Guardian of the children. You speak to her and if she agrees, come to the king's—my office and give me the news while I speak of these things with the privy council."

"If that is what you feel is just and right, then I will comply. Some of these women are used to serving royalty. By now, the others are becoming accustomed. I don't think you would intimidate anyone, but if this is your decision, then I will carry out this mission on my own," she agreed. She gathered up her cards, shuffled the played cards into the mix of the unused, covered them with the bit of Gypsy Silk and put them back into the box and then the cabinet.

"The reading is done, then?" Stefano asked.

"It is done, and I see no need for further magic," Luciana said. She dusted her hands and rose unassisted by Stefano's proffered hand. She shook out her skirts so that they fell properly and sat at her dressing table, where she began applying touches of rouge to her cheeks and lips. She was conscious of Stefano watching her. Her lips done, she looked at him through the mirror. "What? Have I displeased you in some fashion?"

Stefano shook his head. "No . . . I was just thinking that you didn't need to paint yourself. You are beautiful without it."

Luciana smiled at him through the mirror. "So you say, *mi amore*, but not everyone loves the sight of me and a little extra color hides my misgivings."

"Do you have misgivings about what I have asked you to do?" he asked.

Luciana shook her head emphatically. "No, Bonita will hear me out fairly. You have your reasons to hesitate speaking to her yourself, so it makes sense that I approach her."

The small cuckoo clock which rested on the wall between the bed and the window, cuckooed its song of time. Ten o'clock. "Stefano? What time was your privy council meeting to be? Wasn't it for ten? It is that time now."

Stefano looked up at the clock and winced. He scooted off the bed, slipped into his heeled shoes and reached for his jacket.

"Don't forget your chain of office," Luciana said as he reached for the door to the servant's hallway.

He released the door and gathered the chain from his bedside table. He slung it over his head and came to her side. Stefano leaned down and kissed her cheek. "Thank you, *camómescro*," he said, then turned and hurried on his way, pulling on his white-and-gold brocade jacket as he left.

Luciana watched the door snap shut after him and sighed, rubbing her eyes. She still felt the lethargic aftereffects of working magic, even relatively simple divination magic. She felt the nagging onset of one of her headaches, sighing again. She could not, of course, admit to Stefano that sometimes magic was the source of her headaches or that would end the pleasant rapport they were developing over magic. She only hoped that Divya did not have the same reaction, or she would never get their daughter properly trained to be an *Araunya*!

With her day in mind, Luciana applied the makeup with deft skill. All she needed was help finishing her hair and Kisaiya would be with her soon enough, in fact, was this not her maid now? She turned, expecting to see someone hovering near her in the room, but it was empty. Luciana rose and opened the door to the landing, only to find that hall also empty. Shaking her head, she closed the door and turned back toward the dressing table. She stopped.

Filtering through on dust motes, standing in her room stood Alessandra. Alone.

Luciana skirted the bed and came to stand in front of her sister. "Do you come to me as a *mulló*? As you have before?"

Alessandra shook her head. "I am *Fata* now, sister. I *live* the life of the immortal fairy. The *Madonna-gianes* told you that when Divya was born." In the light of day, she did not appear so sparkling gray and silver, but rather as the woman as she was meant to be. Her clothes were simple—a covering shift of green Gypsy Silk and a bodice of patched leather bits—and stunning. Her hair flowed like locks of flax set out in the sun. Her eyes glinted, warm and brown. She was barefoot, wearing bangles, bracelets, and tassels of bells.

Luciana looked at her, sore of heart. She reached out and almost touched Alessandra's hair. Once she, like Chiara, had a streak of white running down the center of her head. Now it blended with the light color of the rest of her hair.

"I am she, Luciana! I live again through the kindness of the *Fata*. Mandero is mine and with me, there is but one thing I do not have and that is my sister's loving acceptance."

Fearing the supernatural form and hating herself for it, Luciana backed away. "You have my love, *piccolina*, but you are still *mulló* to me."

"No! This is no trick of a demon to befuddle you. I stand here, in your presence, made whole. Mandero united my body and soul before he took his own life," Alessandra pleaded.

"You come to me uncalled for," Luciana countered.

"All the more reason for you to believe me. *Mullós* travel with their bodies . . . or some other part. I come to you of my own free will."

"*Mullós* don't have free will, they are dead."

"Exactly!" Alessandra said, taking a step toward her, her bells and bangles chiming as she moved.

Luciana backed up again and bumped against the wall. "Sister, this is madness!"

"Why? Because of tradition? You believe tradition over me? Over the *Fata*—who were very offended by the way that you did not accept their gift," Alessandra said, stopping before Luciana.

"This can't be real," Luciana whispered. She shook her head, eyes closed, sure that when she opened them the figment of her imagination would be gone. She was not.

"Touch me, Lucia. Touch my hand and tell me you do not feel the flesh of another living being there," Alessandra tempted.

"You're *marimé*!" Luciana protested, folding her hands behind her back.

Alessandra shook her head sadly. "I will not force you, sister-mine. Part of why I live, of why Mandero lives is because of the spell I cast with the White Queen."

"I thought you said you lived because of the *Fata*?"

"I did say that. I do, for without the *Fata*, a living form could not have been mine. Touch me, Luciana, see that I am real. There will be no *marimé*," Alessandra coaxed. "If there is, wash it off as you have the filth of the signs we sent to Idala to warn her."

"You were trying to warn her?" Luciana asked. "She is dead."

Alessandra bowed her head. "We know. We felt her passing and the gap that was left without her . . . and so too we felt the passing of the king before that. They were good and true people.

"Lucia, you know you were more mother than sister to me. Yes?"

Luciana bit her lower lip, but nodded.

"I hold your Divya in the highest esteem. She and the child to come . . . for there will be another . . . they are like my siblings and yet, you also are my beloved sister. On all that, I hold holy and I say to you now, by the breath they take—"

"No! Don't curse my daughter!" Luciana ground out, coming forward quickly, striking out without thought, only instinct. She stopped where she stood, amazed that her hand had slapped against skin, that Alessandra's cheek reddened where she had slapped. Luciana stepped back again, confused, cradling her left hand. It stung where she had slapped her sister. "By God and *Fata*!" she whispered.

Alessandra gave a throaty laugh . . . when had she developed that mature chuckle instead of her girlish giggles? Luciana could not help but wonder.

"Sister, that is what I have been trying to tell you. I *am Fata*! I live!" Alessandra said.

"This cannot be!" Luciana whispered, clutching her left hand. She could feel her own skin as it came into contact with her hand, could feel the subtle roughness of the sheer Gypsy Silk gloves and, yet, they felt as real to her as Alessandra had.

"I am not *mulló*. I haven't been for months now. I would not approach you while Divya was still in your belly for fear of causing you harm, but you are a mother now and free of the concern of corrupting your unborn child."

Still disbelieving her own senses Luciana reached out and touched her sister's arm. It felt as real as Stefano had felt to her before he left for the day. "This is contrary to our laws, our understanding."

"Not everything is or can be understandable by the living, and laws do not cover every situation. You must parse your way through and make the decisions best as you can." Alessandra broke away, stepping back so that Luciana could move freely. "The magic is changing, Sister. The house of the White King will know magic and you must help them find their way . . . as you will Divya and Chiara, my sister-kindred."

"The White? But this has never happened before!" Luciana exclaimed.

"As I said, magic is changing. The *Fata* want us to share

our magic with them . . . and it is because of the spell I helped Idala cast," Alessandra explained.

"But the White Throne . . . they cannot cast magic! It is against their own law!"

"Some of it is, but not all. You must see to it that they have the most range they can . . . and, the spell with Idala, she—I—I feared what she might add to the spell, so I set it to last for one year and one day."

"Oh, Alessandra, you ask so much! I am but one woman—"

"With many crowns," Alessandra laughed. She opened her arms and said, "Luciana, come to me now. Embrace me as your sister rather than leave harshness between us."

Luciana moved forward slowly. Her sister had not turned into the monster she feared, had not attacked her, even when she had struck out. She took a deep breath and stepped into her sister's embrace and was surrounded by Alessa's arms, body to body, taking in the smell of the wild wood, feeling the soft straight flaxen hair. Her hands, however, felt like they touched soft furs . . . Alessandra's bodice . . . but it wasn't. Even as Luciana stepped back, she could still feel the softness, but also the crackle of magic like she had not felt since Massimo's christening. She looked down at her hands.

"Take off your gloves, sister-mine," Alessandra prompted.

Warily, Luciana stripped off the gloves and found fresh, unscarred skin where once there had been burns.

"I did not mean to do this without asking your permission," Alessandra admitted. "I am a healer now . . . of somewhat limited capabilities, but I can heal wounds such as yours."

"Thank you," Luciana finally said, gazing at her hands in wonder. She took her sister back into her arms and hugged her close. How she missed her fire and her humor! Luciana leaned into Alessandra, stroking her hair in wonderment. Could it truly be that she was holding her sister? That she was not *marimé*? That she was no longer *mulló*? It somehow did not seem possible.

"Come, Luciana, our time is short and there are things that I must tell you," Alessandra finally said, taking Luciana's shoulders and pushing her back. "The blessing of the trees takes place soon. Because of the division between the *Beluni-mami* and the *Fata*, at Divya's birth, *you* must do the magic, if it is to work this year."

"I?" Luciana repeated. "But . . . it's winter and Divya is so young. Couldn't I wait until spring?"

"Spring comes in weeks, not days. If the *Beluni* casts the magic, it will not work. Only you can save this year's crop. By recognizing me . . . accepting me . . . you are blessed by the *Fata*, and your earth magic will work. You will need to gather women around you. The *Beluni* will resist you and, there is one other thing . . . I must be recognized by as many of our people as possible and before the 14th of April when I fell. Those who wait will have to make peace with the *Fata* before their magic will work as it always has. Do you understand?"

Luciana looked at her sister seriously. "The *Fata* are truly angered, aren't they? Oh, dear!"

"The fairy folk are offended . . . which is worse . . . and in these changing times," Alessa shook her head sadly.

"*Piccolina—*"

"Alessandra. Say my name, it is part of the peacemaking with the *Fata*."

Luciana bit her lips, licked them and looked down at her hands. So far, the Romani traditions where her sister was concerned seemed to have no effect. "Alessa."

Her sister smiled, then grew serious again. "How long will it take you to get to Modica and the mulberry orchards?"

"I must tell the Guildmistresses. They must have a chance to use their magic if the Gypsy Silk is to stand the test. The babes are so young, though . . . " Luciana hesitated.

"It must be soon. Before month's end. Do you understand, Lucia?" Alessandra demanded.

"Dear God!"

Luciana and Alessandra turned to face a very pale Kisaiya holding onto the door frame.

"What have you done, *Araunya*?" Kisaiya whispered.

Luciana glanced at the closed door to Prunella's room. "Come in and close the door!"

"No." Kisaiya was firm, shaking her head as she backed away.

"Kisaiya, you know me. You know that I keep the faith

and follow the traditions of our people . . ." Luciana reasoned. Distantly, she could hear Prunella singing to Umberto the Second. "Come, *chavi*! I am your *Daiya* and have much more experience than you. Into the room before that *dorida* comes upon us!"

Long years of training brought Kisaiya into the room, snapping the door shut behind her. She came no further.

"*Chavi*, come and greet my sister the *Fata*," Luciana said.

Kisaiya hung back, shaking her head. "She is *mulló*!"

Luciana hissed a sigh. "It will be like this with the other women, too."

"You are persuasive, Lucia," Alessandra encouraged.

Luciana released her sister's hand and rose to cross to Kisaiya, who skirted just out of her reach. "Look at my hands, Kisaiya. I will not touch you, but I ask you just to look. The silk is off."

The girl hung back for a moment, then slowly came forward to look at Luciana's hands. "They are healed, *Araunya-Daiya*, but how? Not even the Gypsy Silk heals this quickly."

"No, but my sister does. This is one of her gifts as a *Fata*! What are the tests to ward against evil? The first lesson!"

Kisaiya hesitated again, searching her mistress' gaze for signs of madness. "Sea salt."

"You know where I keep it. Get some!" Luciana commanded.

Staying as close to the walls as she could, Kisaiya moved around the room until she knelt by the little cupboard near the window. She quickly brought out the pouch that held the salt and offered it to her mistress with two fingers, lest Luciana touch her.

"Sprinkle salt over my sister and see what happens to her. If she is evil, her power will fade . . . she will fade," Luciana commanded.

Kisaiya took a handful of the salt from the pouch and threw it at Alessandra who only blinked her eyes when the salt caught her in the face. Luciana's maid dropped the bag and covered herself, as though expecting retaliation. She looked up when neither Alessandra nor Luciana reacted. "Living water?"

Alessandra held out her hand. "Go ahead."

Kisaiya spit into Alessandra's hand, "Living water!" she proclaimed loudly and, grabbing the ewer from its bowl, poured a stream of clean water over Alessandra's hand and arms. "Running water!" The girl watched, expecting something to happen. When nothing did, she looked at her mistress in confusion.

"She is of the *Fata* now. She has been redeemed. She lives again as the immortals do," Luciana said. "The *Madonna-gianes* told us this when Divya was born, do you remember?"

Her maid nodded, "But this is impossible—"

"It is *supposed* to be impossible! You have seen and done magic and have seen the full entourage of the *Fata* and have felt their power and you speak of impossible? The fairy kind has been good to us, but the *Beluni* insulted them. We must get word to the Guildmistresses and hie ourselves to Modica before month's end. Will you help me?" Luciana asked.

"In the winter? With the children?" Kisaiya balked.

"With the children," Alessandra confirmed.

Kisaiya still shrank away from her. Luciana reached out and took her sister's hand in her own. "You see? I am able to touch her. Were she *mulló*, she could touch me, but I could not her."

A long sigh shuddered out of the young woman who stood staring at the sisters. "And what will we tell the *Beluni*?"

"Let me worry about that. For now, nothing. You are not to mention this to *anyone*, do you understand?" Luciana commanded.

"It shall be as you say," her maid agreed, still a little wide-eyed from shock.

"I must go," Alessandra announced abruptly.

"Will I see you again, Alessa?" Luciana asked, ignoring the gasp of surprise coming from her maid.

Alessa shook her silvery-white head. "Not until you have summoned me at the camp of the *vitsi*."

"Be well and know that you are in my heart," Luciana said.

"As you are in mine," her sister said and moved back to the window and the sunshine streaming into the room.

Luciana watched, but saw only a dazzle of sunlight splintering off the beams bathing the bedroom. Like that, Alessa was gone and she was left with only Kisaiya's presence.

When she could bear to look away, she turned and took her place at the dressing table. "If we are to be in Modica before month's end and the Guildmistresses are to be there, then there is much to prepare. I will write a letter. Copy it and send word through the pigeons. Hopefully, they will meet us there."

"As you say, *Daiya*," Kisaiya whispered. "Should I do your hair while you write your note?"

XXIV

"God creates men, but they choose each other."
—Niccolò Machiavelli

STEFANO stood in front of the mirror on the back of the door to Alban's old office. He adjusted his jacket so that it fell properly, then the baldric of blue and gold that kept his sword on his left hip, and finally the chain of office which sat atop shirt, jacket, and baldric. When he was sure that everything was in its respective place, he opened the door and called down to the Court Herald. "Estensi, there should be some of the duchi waiting to see me. You may send them up," Stefano called. After hearing Estensi's assent, he went over to the desk and sat down, waiting for his visitors.

Sebastiani, never one to let his infirmities slow him down overly, came through the door first, stepping back to hold open the door for Duchessa Rossi and the others: Antonelli, di Candido, Gianola, LaCosta, and Silvieri.

Antonelli pulled out the first chair in front of the desk for the duchessa. Stefano watched her notice the nearby footstool.

"I believe this is Duca Sebastiani's chair," she said with a gentle smile as she stepped to her left one more chair and allowed Antonelli to assist her into that chair.

"Thank you, Your Grace," Sebastiani said as he settled into his normal chair and propped his foot up on the little peg-legged footstool.

Silvieri took the chair to the duchessa's left, forcing Antonelli and the others to pull chairs from around the room and sit in a second row. It was clear that Antonelli was displeased with the arrangement. He found a wing-backed chair and edged it between Silvieri and the duchessa, sitting down partway in the front row, but more behind. LaCosta and di Candido did much the same, wedging their chairs into a portion of the front row. Gianola, however, chose to stand behind Duchessa Rossi, leaning into the back of her chair.

Stefano closed his eyes briefly, wondering if the chair arrangements were going to typify the behavior of this privy council. He let go of the idea and forced himself to stay in a good humor.

"So," Stefano began, drawing the attention of the gathered duchi, "this is to be considered a privy council. We have equal representation in points of view. Gianola, Antonelli, and di Candido consider themselves impartial and so they will have deciding say if a decision cannot be made."

"What is the purpose of this privy council, Lord Regent?" the duchessa asked.

Stefano considered her. She was wearing a black-and-blue brocade overgown, with a midnight-blue undergown. Patterns were delicately stitched along her cuffs and, he assumed, her hemline. Gold buttons fastened the overgown over her breasts and down to her sternum, leaving the rest of her overgown open and swinging back to display her undergown to perfection. She wore her chestnut hair tied up in a tidy bun, eschewing the rather silly fichu, which Idala had made popular in the heartland of Tyrrhia. In place of the beribboned bonnet, she wore a small hat of the same brocade as her overdress, adorned with flowers and a short peacock's feather. Her appearance was stylish and, yet, subdued as was appropriate for mourning a pair of monarchs. Stefano shook his head, refocusing on her question.

"This council is intended to aid in my decisions for Prince Massimo's future. Our discussions will be kept quiet—it is not for the Palantini or other public at large to know for the sake of Massimo and the kingdom. There is only one other person who will be made aware of the discussions we have regarding Massimo's future, and she is my wife. As Regent Guardian, she is entitled to know. At times, she will join us to partake in our exchanges, but for the most part her position is to fulfill our decisions, to insure what we have planned comes to fruition," Stefano said. "Do any here have any trouble with my plan as I've explained it?"

He looked at the duchi, one by one, reading their expressions as they eventually all consented. LaCosta and Silvieri showed distinct reluctance. It was LaCosta who gave voice to his doubts.

"Does this mean Princess Ortensia and her husband as well?"

"*O sí! Altro che!*" Stefano said, confirming the man's concerns. "They, while currently angry with the Palantini at large, are definitely to be considered members of the Palantini always! For their sakes and that of the boy, we must not talk beyond these doors about the subject. *Sí*?"

All nodded, even the dissenters.

"So why do we gather at this time?" Sebastiani asked. "You've already convinced these others that as is with the wishes of the late White King and Queen, Massimo is not to be king, should something befall Prince Dario Gian or his sisters."

"Affirmative," Stefano said, glancing at the expressions of defeat or reluctance on the part of the gathered Duchi. He looked at Sebastiani. "Do you have problems with this decision?"

Sebastiani flapped his hands, waving off the question. "I have agreed since the queen told us the nature of his birth . . . or shall I call it, rebirth?"

"Then we're all agreed?" Stefano asked. The duchi all nodded their heads. "Good. We can move on. I think Massimo is restorable if he is given the right opportunities. Toward that end, we must select a set of proper parents—"

"That leaves me out as I have no spouse," Duchessa Rossi sighed . . . whether from relief or disappointment, Stefano could not be sure.

"I have decided that all in the privy council are either too old to see him to his majority in good stead and, as the case with most of you, your wives are expecting, or just had a child of their own. It is too much to ask," Stefano said.

"But I could take him," Fario di Candido protested. "My wife and I are young and Orsina is only newly pregnant."

"So you would take on a broken child?" Stefano asked. He shook his head firmly. "No. It is too much to ask of anyone to do that. I will not ask it. Besides, are you willing to move to one of the Novabianco estates for the next fifteen years and put aside your own properties? No, I think not."

"If this is a privy council, and we are not to tell the other members of the Palantini, have you found someone who would be able to raise a prince?" Augusto Sebastiani asked.

"This will remain a privy council, as I said at the start. There will be a couple that we will tell just enough for them to raise the prince. The Regent Guardian and I have already selected someone, but we will not discuss them just yet. I want to focus on the estate where we will be sending the boy and his foster parents," Stefano said.

He could see that none of them were exactly happy with his decision, but none protested, so he moved on to the next matter, reaching into the bin behind him and sorting through until he found the map that authenticated the various borders of the estates of the landed nobility. He stood and unfurled the map across the desk, planted a paperweight and a goblet on either side of the map. Stefano motioned for the duchi to gather closer around.

"King Alban held three estates. The Novabianco estate, the first and grandest, near Lipari. The second Novabianco estate, large and imposing, rests near Barcelona, and finally, his mother's estate, deFaria di Grotta rests between Palermo and Bagheria, near enough to the Tyrrhenian Sea that it provides good air and occasion to swim."

"Swim? The boy will never even walk," Sebastiani burst out.

"But swim, he might," Stefano said. "In either case, this makes it possible for excursions to the coast easy enough so that deFaria di Grotta does not seem so small. I think it ideal."

"It has the added benefit of not being a Novabianco estate, but the old deFaria one of the king's mother. No one would think to go there," Duchessa Rossi pointed out, nodding. "I concur."

"The duchessa makes an excellent point," old Sebastiani said. "I, too, concur."

"*Si*, I, also agree with the duchessa," the white-haired Duca Gianola said.

Guidi LaCosta nodded. "The arguments are sound. To protect the boy and the populace, I think the deFaria estate is best."

Silvieri sighed unhappily but waved his hand, indicating that he agreed with the others' arguments, or, at least, would not fight them. Antonelli and di Candido, Stefano's two remaining neutral parties, considered the map.

"It *would* keep him well away from court," di Candido finally said.

Antonelli's expression remained sour, but, at last, he, too nodded his consent.

"So we are in agreement, then? The deFaria estate will be Massimo's new home," Stefano said, smiling. He shoved aside the paperweight and goblet, rerolled the map, and returned it to the bin of maps. "Now I shall send for wine and we will drink on this first agreement until my wife finally arrives."

"What kind of upbringing will the boy have? And tutors?" Sebastiani asked.

Luciana got to the main nursery much later than she had intended and went straight to Divya's cradle where she found her daughter wide awake and starting to fuss. She checked the swaddling and found it still clean. She gave her daughter her knuckle and, immediately, Divya seized on it and began to suck.

"We have not fed her in the past three hours, my lady, so she should be hungry," Donna della Guelfa said, coming up beside her.

"Oh, she is indeed," Luciana laughed, lifting her daughter from the cradle and taking one of the several rockers in the room. Without modesty, she exposed one of her turgid breasts, covered by undergown and overgown and began the blessed release of feeding her daughter.

It took nearly an hour. When she was done, Luciana allowed Donna della Guelfa to take Divya to change her now soiled swaddling. She sat back, rocking as she observed the tides of activity in the nursery for a few moments, but time was passing and she had business.

Luciana eased into Massimo's room, praying she did not disturb the child. For once, he appeared to be sleeping and, in her chair near the cradles sat Bonita Boniface, also napping. Mindful of the sleeping children, Luciana crept to the wet nurse's side and laid a gentle hand on her shoulder.

Bonita startled awake and would have spoken but for the finger Luciana laid across her lips. Luciana beckoned her from the room, backing her way to the door and out onto the landing between the king's and queen's old rooms.

The wet nurse bobbed an unpracticed curtsy and looked at Luciana expectantly.

Luciana nodded. She had left the doors to the two nursery rooms open slightly. With presence of mind, she closed the doors. "Signora Boniface, what does your husband do?"

"My husband?" the wet nurse repeated, blinking owlishly. "He worked the forge in a smithy's shop until a little more than a year ago. He was injured and . . . well, since then, he does odd jobs where he can find them, which was why this opportunity came at such an opportune time. I've been setting aside my wages and—"

Luciana raised a quieting hand. "It has been decided that Massimo will be raised away from his siblings. He will need caretakers . . . foster parents, if you will. Would your husband be willing to take him on . . . in the condition he is in? To raise the boy as if he were his own?" Luciana asked. "Would you?"

"I have no problems with Massimo," Bonita said, looking thoughtful. "I think my husband would be willing to do that . . . if there were an allowance given us for his upkeep, but do you really intend to raise the little one as a commoner?"

"No, you misunderstand me, Signora Boniface," Luciana said.

"I have been Bonita to you for the last couple of weeks; do not let that change now, Your Excellency," the wet nurse urged.

"Bonita, then. No. The boy is not to be raised as a commoner. He will be moved to an estate in secret and raised there as a member of *la famigilia reale.* Your boy will also benefit from the tutors and such sent for the upbringing of Massimo. They are to be raised as brothers. Your family will want for nothing. You will supervise the estate . . . or your husband will, while you tend to the boys' needs. A monthly stipend would be allotted for the care and upkeep of the boys and the estate. All we ask, in return, is that Massimo be raised as though your own son and that your lives will be secluded and quiet," Luciana hurried to explain. "Will your husband be willing to do this?"

"My Eduardo will see this as heaven-sent, Your Excellency. When do you want us to leave?" Bonita whispered, her eyes shining with hope and excitement.

"I want you to send for Eduardo today. He will meet the boy and make his commitment. From there, we would have you moved soon, within the month," Luciana replied.

"A month? But we will have to pack . . . to gather our things . . ." Bonita hesitated.

"Your husband can take what is necessary. If you own your own home, then lease it to another family. Or, we will see that it is leased. Take only what you must. All other things will be provided for you—wardrobes, basic necessities, and there will be a staff to actually care for the estate and prepare your meals. You will concentrate your time and energy on the boys. Your husband can learn estate management and do that in his spare time," Luciana said.

"Then let me send for my Eduardo," Bonita said, turning as Massimo began to fuss.

Luciana let her go, pleased with her decision. She sent for a messenger to come to Bonita and hurried to Stefano's office.

Stefano raised his glass in toast to the privy council and together they drank deeply of the Tyrrhian red wine. It was only as he set his goblet of glass down that he heard the insistent scratching at the door. "Who is there?" he called, refilling his goblet and several of the others as well.

"It is I, Luciana!"

Smiling at her timing, Stefano turned the key in the door and opened it for his wife. "Success?" he asked her.

Luciana nodded. "At least partial. I've spoken to Bonita and she is willing. She thinks her husband would also be willing," she said. "Have you decided where to send them?"

Nodding, Stefano poured a fresh goblet of the red wine and handed it to her. "We decided on the deFaria estate, near Palermo. We are all agreed."

"Then my news will speed along the matter," Luciana

said, sipping her wine. She smiled at Duchessa Rossi and then Duca Sebastiani. To the other duchi, she bobbed her head. "Stefano, how long do you think it will take for the estate to be made ready? Staffed and the house aired, and such?"

He frowned thinking. "I'll send palazzo staff if I must, but it should take no more than a few weeks."

"The palazzo staff is already taxed, Lord Regent," Duchessa Rossi pointed out. "With the Palantini in residence and taking up nearby homes, all of Citteauroea and even as far as Messina are being robbed of their support staff . . . at least they were. I would guess anyone of Messina has requested to return home."

"I'll send word to the estate manager immediately, then," Stefano began. "If anything, there should be extra staff in western Tyrrhia with all of the nobility here. We will, of course, swear them to secrecy and once recruited, they will stay at the estate."

Before anyone could respond, there came another sound of scratching on the outer door. Stefano looked curiously around the room at the gathered duchi. "Who else knows we meet here?"

"Only Estensi," Sebastiani replied, glancing down the row of faces to his left.

"Estensi?" Stefano called.

"Aye, Your Excellency," Estensi called from the other side of the door.

"Then come in," Stefano said.

The door creaked open and Estensi popped his head into the room. "I bring news of Princess Ortensia. I am told she is giving birth to Pierro's heir as we speak. I thought you should know."

"Yes, thank you, Estensi," Stefano murmured.

"Many pardons for the interruptions," Estensi said, starting to back out of the doorway.

"Keep us apprised," Stefano said with a wave of his hand.

"This 'Bonita' you mentioned, *Araunya*, the one you have selected to be Massimo's new foster mother. I do not think I know of her," Duchessa Rossi said.

"Nor I," Sebastiani concurred.

Before another could confess to not knowing the woman

tending to Massimo, Luciana interrupted. "I think you all have misunderstood. She is not of the Palantini. I don't expect any of you *know* her, but all of you have met her. She is the wet nurse who currently tends to Massimo's needs."

Silvieri frowned darkly, "A commoner? You would entrust the raising of a prince to a commoner? Better to let Princess Ortensia and her husband raise the boy. They will soon have a child and this baby will only have a month difference. The princess has, after all, raised five children for the Turkish bastarde who kept her all these many years."

"And I note, for the record," Duchessa Rossi argued, "that she left her Turkish prison without bringing with her a single child, not even a girl-child. I know she reputedly gave birth to five children, but that does not mean she was allowed to raise them. For all we know, this child, too, is another Turkish bastarde gotten on her before she left. She is two months short of the due date she set forth."

"This child is a product of her legal marriage to Prince deMedici!" Silvieri protested. LaCosta nodded his head fiercely.

"Bah!" Sebastiani retorted, waving a dismissive hand. "Have either of you been privy to her bedroom habits these past ten months? You cannot be sure that she isn't carrying another *il Turche* bastarde."

"It is not uncommon for a woman who has given birth to so many children to have their later children come early," Luciana pointed out.

Stefano gave his wife a look. She was the last person he expected to have defending either deMedici.

"It's true!" Luciana defended herself. "It's a known fact."

"It was true of my Balbina. She gave birth to our latest son, a fourth child, more than a month early," Gianola said, in confirmation of Luciana's statement.

"My wife's second and third came early, too," Sebastiani admitted. He glanced in the direction of Duchessa Rossi.

"Don't ask me! I've had no children and have never married. I would not know," she said, with a small, self-derisive laugh.

"It could be either. We won't know until we see the child," Stefano said. "But we were discussing the viability of a set of commoners to parent a Prince of Tyrrhia. To those comments made earlier, I say who better to raise this re-risen cardinal with pretensions to the throne?"

"Bonita is already raising Massimo with her son. He knows her like no other woman and is likely to have an affinity for her. On her part, she has taken to the previously near-demonic boy with ease," Luciana added.

"You both are so convinced?" Rossi asked, sipping her wine.

"Of course, or we would not have put it before you," Stefano said, while Luciana nodded. He added, "The woman understands the importance of her charge without fixating on him in some way. I have seen her with him. It makes more sense than expanding this privy council or setting up rivalry in the Palantini as to who will raise the prince."

"Oh, I hadn't even thought of that. Yes, you are quite right. Giving the prince to anyone in the Palantini will only cause dissension. Whomever we chose could be at risk of political ostracism or outright threats . . . attempts on their lives. If a noble family took him in, the secrecy of Massimo's location would not be as protected, either," di Candido said, reasoning his way through the decision.

"Exactly my thoughts," Stefano said.

"Divisiveness in the Palantini cannot be tolerated," Gianola said, setting his empty goblet on the desk.

Sebastiani sighed, "We already have divisiveness in the Palantine council over and with the princess and her deMedici husband!"

"Not just over the new deMedicis! There are other matters our council struggles with, but I agree that one more reason could cause the Palantini to split loyalties in such a way that things may never be set aright again," Duca LaCosta said.

"Then we are agreed? If this couple will take on Massimo, then they are our choice as guardians?" Stefano asked.

"What do you know of these people, besides that they are commoners and this Bonita is good with the boy? Our Prince of Tyrrhia, no matter our questions about the nature of his being gotten on our Queen Idala, will still be a prince," Silvieri growled.

"All of the women serving in the Royal Nursery were

investigated for their character and social standing in the community by the Queen's Escalade . . . long before Idala gave birth. The queen had the Escalade find as many as twenty women who would be giving birth within weeks of when she thought she might have her children. I know, personally, that the queen handpicked Bonita, and it was I and the midwife and Nunzia Rui who asked her to take on Massimo which she did without hesitation for his deformities or strange nature. What more can I say?" Luciana said, shrugging.

"And this Nunzia Rui . . . she was . . . ?" Duca Antonelli prompted.

"She was the white witch that Queen Idala chose to oversee the birth of her children . . . once she understood the nature of her babies," Duchessa Rossi replied. She looked to Luciana for confirmation of her answer.

Luciana, Stefano noticed, licked her lips and held her breath when she confirmed the duchessa's guess with a nod of her own. Whatever happened with Nunzia Rui, he suspected his wife of not telling the complete truth. He did not expose Luciana's potential for deception, but kept it to himself . . . at least, for now. He would ask her about it later, when they were alone.

"All this talk of magic . . . it makes my skin crawl," Gianola said, shivering. He quaffed the last of his wine and poured himself more from the bottle Estensi brought them earlier. He frowned deeper when the bottle produced only a small splash of wine. He put both goblet and bottle back on the desk and retook his position behind Rossi's chair.

Sebastiani looked meaningfully at Luciana, who shook her head. Stefano guessed that Sebastiani had been recommending an education in prayers to Gianola such as he had received some weeks earlier. Luciana had refused. He glanced around the room and decided she was probably right to do so, too many ears, too many dissenting perspectives.

"When will we know about Bonita's husband?" Stefano asked his wife, hoping for good news.

"Hopefully sometime today," Luciana replied. "I will notify you as soon as I hear word."

"Good. That leaves one more matter for us to discuss," Stefano said, returning to his side of the desk and sitting down. The others also sat again, leaving Luciana and

Gianola standing. Luciana pushed aside some papers and perched on the edge of the desk so that she was facing the Fuchi. "We are going to need to meet on a fairly regular basis, and that means I will need at least most of you to take up semi-permanent residence in the palazzo, so that you can be easily called upon."

"I am usually here instead of my estate," Duchessa Rossi said, glancing at Sebastiani.

The oldest man on the council nodded. "As am I," Sebastiani agreed.

Fario di Candido frowned. "I suppose my wife would like spending more time here, with her friends. I'd intended to raise our child at the estate. My mother still lives there . . . but I suppose we could split time between the palazzo and the estate since we live near Piccolo di Salerno."

LaCosta sighed heavily, as though it would be a trial for him to live near his precious Princess Ortensia. "We will stay here. Silvieri?"

Peppino Silvieri shook his head. "We live a little over an hour away by horse. Give me a day's notice and I am here." Whether this was directed at him or LaCosta, Stefano could not be sure; either way, he made note of it.

"We live just west of the capital city. We are here in the religious ghetto every Saturday and Sunday. It will be of little consequence for me to come to the palazzo should you need me," Duca Gianola said.

That left Duca Renzo Antonelli. He shrugged and waved his hands, "That leaves me and my Raquel . . . we have other children, but they are nearly grown. We can bring them here, if we must, besides Raquel is the oldest recorded to fall pregnant . . . at least among the Palantini. I'll not want to move her until after she gives birth . . . if then."

"Thank you," Stefano said. "That leaves most of you here at the palazzo for most of the year and only two others not far away. I think we will have the overall mindset of the group represented at most any time I may need you."

Duchessa Rossi rose, stretching a little. "Then we are done?" she asked.

"We are," Stefano confirmed. "There should only be a matter of a few details once we begin moving Massimo to the deFaria estate, and those matters I can attend to without consultation."

"But if you should need us—" Sebastiani began.

"I'll know where to find you," Stefano completed for him.

With that, the duchi filed from the office, leaving Luciana and Stefano alone.

"That went well," Luciana said, sliding off the desk and moving to stand closer to him, her right hand falling to his left shoulder.

"Better in many ways than I had hoped," Stefano agreed easing back in the chair. He looked up at Luciana and noted her attention seemed far away. "Are you wondering how Ortensia fares?"

She grinned at him and nodded. "This will be her first freeborn child. She claims the baby will be a boy."

Stefano shrugged. "She would know if anyone would, I guess."

"Shall I go and wish her well for us, for you?" Luciana asked.

Stefano snaked his left arm around his bride and gave her a gentle squeeze. "Do as you think best . . . you usually do anyway."

"And I make no apologies for it either, though I do try to take your opinions high in my regard when considering," Luciana said. She dropped a kiss on his head and danced out from within the circle of his arms. "I shall tell Ortensia and Pierro that you wish them . . . their family well."

XXV

"Don't limit a child to your own learning, for he was born in another time."

—Rabbinical saying

4 d'Febbraio, 1685

"WHERE is she? Where is the Regent Guardian?" Luciana heard a female voice demand in a supercilious tone. She looked up from her consultation with Bonita who was in the process of feeding Massimo. The boy broke away from the breast and started fussing. Luciana rose from where she knelt by Federico Boniface's cradle, excused herself and headed into the Royal Nursery from whence the voice had come, closing Alban's bedroom door as she did so.

Ortensia and Pierro stood in the middle of the nursery, their expressions unrelenting. In her arms, the princess held her newborn son. When she saw Luciana entering the room, she crossed over to her, not quite able to manage her normal bone-jarring pace since she'd only given birth yesterday afternoon.

"Ortensia?" Luciana murmured her surprise. She nodded to Pierro.

"I have decided that since you have the 'Royal Nursery' that you could raise this royal as well," Ortensia declared, thrusting the boy at her.

Luciana managed to get and keep hold of the baby as he fell from his mother's arms. She looked down at his dark head and juggled him into a more supported position in her arms. She looked back at the princess already halfway out the door. "Wait!" she called, trying not to notice the wet nurses and midwife staring at her and the princess . . . and her husband in disbelief.

Ortensia turned back, her hand on the door. "What?"

"But surely you can't mean to leave your son here? With me?" Luciana protested.

The princess recrossed the room, staring down at the newborn in the Regent Guardian's protective arms. For a moment, she looked like she might reconsider. Instead, she folded her arms over her breasts. "I most certainly mean to. He looks like my other children. He is *il Turche* and I won't raise him. It's all I can do to look at him!"

Luciana looked down at the infant and then to Pierro. "He could just as easily be your husband's. The prince is dark-featured, too. It doesn't mean he is as you say he is."

Pierro looked at the boy. "It doesn't matter. The boy is royalty by at least one of us. Keep him. He deserves the same opportunities as these princesses."

"But these children have come to me because their parents have died. You are both well and living," Luciana protested.

"Whatever the reason they are in your charge, my *son*—we have named him Luca Giorgio—will have the same education and connections as his cousins," Pierro retorted.

"But they are hardly cousins. They are . . . what? Four generations apart?" Luciana said and held out the boy to Pierro.

"If he *is* my son, I want him to have every advantage. If he isn't—as my wife thinks—I want nothing more to do with him, so keep him, Your Grace," Pierro stated matter-of-factly.

"And you won't relent either?" Luciana asked the princess.

"My position is that of my husband's. If the boy belongs to him, then we owe this child 'every advantage' and that is best served here. If the boy is *il Turche* . . . I've already given that *figlio di puttana* more than any kidnapping, raping monster deserves and will not raise his child for even one full day. Keep the boy and do what you can with him."

With that, the princess turned away. Pierro placed a hand at the small of her back and ushered her quickly from the room. Neither gave a single backward glance. Luciana snapped her open mouth shut and turned to the other women of the nursery who were also staring open-mouthed.

"Donna Maria, I think we'll have need of another wet nurse," she said, gathering her wits as best she could.

"Are you sure, Your Grace?" Maria asked. "Perhaps she'll want the boy back tomorrow?"

"You heard them. I think they are sincere, but I will try them again on the morrow. In either case, we will need a wet nurse for him, I'm sure," Luciana said with a heavy sigh of resignation. She glanced at the door leading to Queen Idala's reception room where they had exited and shook her head. "Please, find a cradle for the boy."

"Some women are taken with melancholy after the birth of their children, perhaps it is so with the princess," Maria suggested.

Luciana shook her head. "Whatever is to happen, the boy badly needs a changing, a cradle, and a wet nurse." Unlike the princess, she turned the child over to his new caretaker with caution.

It was early evening before Luciana found time for herself. Everything had been a crisis today after the arrival of Luca. Massimo fussed most of the day, except notably when Eduardo, Bonita's husband, arrived to meet him and confirm his willingness to take on the boy and the estate at deFaria. The new wet nurse, a very young and new mother, arrived late in the day despite having been sent for before the morning's ten o'clock. Finding yet another cradle for the prince's wet nurse's daughter had been more than a trial and, in the end, they had been forced to send for her home cradle. Knowing more children were due to be born in the upcoming days, weeks and months, Luciana had commissioned two of the three palazzo furniture makers to start building more cradles.

While Eduardo was still in the palazzo, Stefano had broken away from his other chores to meet him, Bonita, and their son Federico. Stefano took his time with the family, talking about his plans for them, the deFaria estate, and life near Palermo. He also arranged to send a palazzo estate manager to their house and someone to help Eduardo pack his family's things so that they could leave for the midwestern coast.

With everything now settled, Luciana considered her options: there was the small trunk which held Stefano's love letters that she had barely had the time to peruse, and there was always something to be done in the nursery. Her body ached from exhaustion, but she could not sleep. Her letters to the Guildmistresses had been written earlier and, no doubt, were already being attached to the ankles of messenger pigeons and sent on their way as she considered what to do next. She rubbed her eyes and yawned. So much to be done before the end of the month! There was also the matter of a deathbed promise to Idala and one that, with a little extra attention, would see them free of Cousin Prunella as well.

Luciana went downstairs warily, hoping that Prunella was off and about other business this evening. Wherever she was, Luciana was pleased to discover the receiving room empty. She crossed to the marbled oak desk which Stefano used when he was not in the office. She sorted through the papers, looking for the list of the Palantini and Stefano's notes.

"May I help you, Your Excellency?"

Luciana startled and turned to find Carlo, Stefano's man, at her elbow. "No, Carlo, I'm just looking for something, and I thought it might be here."

Carlo's expression was unreadable as he straightened the papers on the desk. "What are you looking for? I might be able to assist you."

Luciana hesitated and finally blurted, "Stefano keeps a sort of ledger of the Palantini . . ."

"That holds the Lord Regent's private notes, Your Excellency," Carlo said, his fingers curling around just the ledger she had been looking for.

"My husband has shared it with me before. I've even made some of the notes in it," Luciana said, holding out her hands.

It was Carlo's turn to hesitate.

"I've come searching for it so that I can free him of some of his responsibilities that he has not had time to even consider," Luciana continued, leaving her hands out to receive the small ledger book. "If he's left it here in the receiving room of our suite, he cannot be too concerned over what he has said because he knows his cousin, Contessa Prunella diVega, is something of a snoop. Let me have it and I'll tell him I found it myself."

Carlo reluctantly handed the book over. "I will tell my master that I found it for you, Your Excellency. I know that he . . . trusts you with many of these matters."

"Thank you," Luciana said, folding the book to her bosom and returning upstairs to her room. From the rank and file of the Palantini, she hoped to find a suitable husband for Giuletta and, if she were lucky, one for Prunella as well. She closed her bedroom door and sat on the bed. Giuletta should be relatively easy to find a husband for, but Prunella would no doubt insist she have a new husband equal to or of superior rank to Conte Urbano diVega . . . one of Luciana's archenemies until his death by poison of the sort he intended to force upon her. She had taken an opportunity to pour it into his inkwell, knowing of his odd habit of sucking on his pen nibs. No one, to this day, knew the part she played in the man's death. Since she could think of no one that would be served by the information, she kept it to herself.

Luciana cast such thoughts aside as she sank onto her bed and opened the list of Palantini members. She scanned through the book, looking at the random notes about each. Duca Calvino Anino was the first name she came upon. He was widowed, but also the eldest of all the Palantini members. Prunella would not find him father material for her son and she hated the thought of plighting Giuletta who, other than being something of a silly nit on occasion, was a perfectly nice girl.

Stefano's notes, she discovered ranged from the prolific, to little more than a name and space to put further information. Thinking to add to his notes, Luciana got up and collected the plume and ink from her dressing table and set it on the bedside table. She made notes as she came to names she recognized. Stefano had noted a little of everything in many places: the age and spouse, political leaning, if they stood for the State or Ortensia and, in some places, both were noted, but not often. It was not until she came across the name of one Duca Giorgio Cirello that she paused. Despite being a duca, he possessed very little land of his own and his coffers were . . . abysmal. At 24, he had only received his title and debts within the year. Apparently, he inherited his father's obligations with his title. It was a shame, really, she thought as she recalled the young man. He was quite the pleasant sort. Luciana gave him more consideration. With his debts, he would be looking for a way to pay them before he could find a wife . . . unless the wife came with a fortune of her own and would accept the man on his own terms.

Luciana's thoughts turned to Prunella. She was only a single year older than the duca and already possessed an heir, but what treatment would she give a new husband in search of a landed bride? Prunella, she thought, would gladly share some of diVega's land, especially if it meant she could be a duchessa like her friend the erstwhile Duchessa Orsina di Candido. It would not be a marriage made in heaven, but however the connections were made, Luciana was fairly certain Prunella would accept.

She found a bit of vellum in a side drawer and penned an invitation to the usually private di Drago family dinner. When Luciana was finished with the letter, she set it aside and returned to the book.

Giuletta needed a good marriage. Idala had promised a handsome dowry for the girl—just turned twenty, if she remembered aright. Giuletta was the seventh daughter of a minor member of the nobility, however, and would not insist upon a duca for a husband.

Luciana perused the volume, page by page, with growing disheartenment . . . until her gaze fell upon Don Cristoval Battista. He had strikes against him since he had worked for the deMedicis, but it spoke well of him when she noted that not only had the don left their employment with little or no notice, but he'd stayed to participate in the Palantini, had apparently in some way aided Stefano, and had come to Citteauroea in search of a wife. She smiled. The man was land rich but cash poor, perfect for Giuletta's circumstances. She quickly penned a second note, advising Stefano. She set the notes on Stefano's pillow so that he could approve the plans and slipped back down the stair to put his ledger back in its place. She was just turning away from the desk when Stefano joined her in the receiving room, dismissing Strozzini for the night.

Stefano shrugged out of his frock coat and kicked off his

shoes, which Carlo immediately retrieved and then disappeared to afford them privacy. "So, my dear, what have you done today?"

"As you know, I spent most of the day with the children. I met Eduardo . . . as did you. What do you think of them? Will they suit our designs?" Luciana asked. She came and joined him on the couch, drawing up her legs so that she could curl into him.

Stefano relaxed, letting his head fall back against the couch. "I think your assessment was a good one. They are both down to earth and the signora has experience with children deformed at birth. Massimo will get thorough attention, but also learn patience when he is with their son. Thankfully, they both read and can do their sums, but I think a tutor to help them would not go amiss."

"To improve their skills before the boys come of age," Luciana nodded. It was not ordinary to find fully literate commoners. Their example would directly affect Massimo, however, and the raising of the boy.

"You haven't told me why Massimo must be moved by the end of the month. I thought soon, surely, but this fast? You must have a reason."

Luciana glanced around the room. She had already been surprised by Carlo twice this day: first, when he protected Stefano's papers, and, just recently, when he had appeared out of apparent nowhere to retrieve Stefano's coat and shoes. "Perhaps we should talk in our chambers? We have no idea when Prunella might return from whatever task has taken her away . . . perhaps the grand dinner?"

Stefano sighed, stretching. It was clear that he was not anxious to move. After another long stretch, he rolled to his feet and held out a hand for Luciana. Together, they climbed the stairs and closed the door on the rest of the people in their world. He spied the papers on his pillow straight away and reached for them.

Luciana slipped to the bed and removed the letters. "These are for later, when I have discussed other things with you."

Stefano frowned but nodded his acquiescence as he dropped into the chair set up against the papered walls and under the cuckoo clock. "So tell me . . . make your report," he prompted.

Luciana could tell by his voice that he was almost too exhausted to care. She sat across from him, on the foot of the bed. She leaned against the bed post. "I thought they were well chosen and Eduardo can learn a new trade now that he cannot work with the smithies. It suits them all well. Massimo listens to Bonita as he listens to no other. Their baby does not seem bothered by him and, according to Bonita, there have been no more spells since the christening."

"Then that is settled. They move to the deFaria estate . . . but why must it be so soon?" Stefano asked. "He is quiet enough to not bother the other babes."

"Who knows when that will change, Stefano. We must get him away as soon as possible!" Luciana urged.

Stefano sat straighter. "There is more to this move than you are telling me."

Luciana licked her lips, a sure sign she was anxious and prepared to equivocate. "This morning, Alessandra came to me."

"Alessandra? You've used her name!"

"I am convinced now that she is of the *Fata* as we were told on the night of Divya's birth. Stefano, I *touched* her! I felt her with my own hands . . . and look what she was able to do!"

Luciana held out her hands, palms up.

Stefano leaned forward and examined her hands, turning them over. "She healed your burns? Or could it have been the Gypsy Silk gloves you've been wearing?"

"The gloves helped, but it was Alessandra who cured them," Luciana said. "Stefano, we are in trouble. Because of how the *Beluni* and I reacted to Alessandra when they tried to give us this great gift, our magic to create the Gypsy Silk might not work."

"What does that mean?" Stefano asked, alarmed.

"What we would make will be silk, but not Gypsy Silk as we know it. It's possible that if we wait for the actual anniversary of Alessandra's death, that there will be no more Gypsy Silk . . . possibly forever!"

Stefano gaped at her a moment and then snapped his mouth shut. "What can be done? What *must* be done?"

"Alessandra must be reconciled with the *Beluni* and our people," Luciana said. "I know my *Mami*, Stefan, she will not budge on this matter unless someone . . . I . . . find a way to get through to her. I must tend to the first watering of the trees myself and get as many of our people to act with me as possible. I must be in Modica by month's end."

"We don't know if it's safe. Turks could have landed near Modica," Stefano reasoned.

"I know that we will have no more Gypsy Silk if we do not go. We can't afford to live without the Silk," Luciana said. "Stefano, this task she has set me will not be easy. Even I was hard to convince. Now I must persuade my people. How does one do that? I tried to help Kisaiya understand, yet I think she still believes I'm more than a little mad myself!"

"How was Alessandra able to convince you?"

Luciana looked up, into his gaze. "She started to swear on the lives of Divya and Chiara, and I lashed out and struck her. A *mulló* can attack and touch me, but I would be unable to touch the *mulló* myself. With Kisaiya, I've taught her to protect herself with wards against evil using salt, and then there is the Running and Living Water test. If Alessandra was still *mulló*, it would have burned her, but it didn't."

Luciana looked intensely at Stefano. "Do you see? She is neither *mulló* nor *marimé*. Alessandra comes to me as a whole being. I could *feel* her, Stefano, as easily as I can feel you now!"

"And this is enough for you?" Stefano asked. He shook his head. "I'll learn to trust you more with . . . this magic. You must take Divya with you . . . to Modica?"

Luciana nodded, chewing her lip. "And Chiara. They must be exposed to the Romani way of life as soon as possible. It will be a trying enough education for them when we will live most of our lives in the palazzo."

"I cannot go with you . . . to Modica," Stefano said. "There is still too much happening here and throughout the kingdom that requires my immediate attention, but I won't have you traveling the roads of Tyrrhia—even the heartland—unescorted."

Luciana nodded and shrugged. "I assumed that Capitano della Guelfa would be joining us."

"More than just he. There must be a royal bodyguard and several men who will see to it that you and the babes are safe."

Luciana wrinkled her nose at the idea of being joined by more than a single guard. "Is there any other—"

"No! I'll have della Guelfa be ready when you are prepared to go. He'll take what men of his I can spare," Stefano said firmly.

"My people know the capitano's men through the maggiore, but we are not accustomed to escorts of this sort and it will only make a difficult time more so," Luciana urged.

Stefano looked at her pointedly. "You are taking a Princess of the Realm and *our* daughter with you. Have the men camp a bit away from you, whatever. You will have what I consider a proper escort."

"Perhaps we can discuss this later, when . . ."

"When I will insist upon an even larger unit of men," Stefano said. "Consider, if you will, your grandmother delaying the acknowledgment of Alessandra. What might she have done differently to escape the problems you face?"

At last, Luciana nodded. "I will take the escort . . . but those from the Escalade, can you at least look for half-caste Romani among the men?"

"I'll do what I'm able, Luciana," Stefano promised. He eyed the papers tucked behind her back. "Now, tell me what those are."

"As Carlo will tell you, I went and got your ledger where you keep your notes about the Palantini," Luciana said.

"For what purpose?" Stefano asked, his expression not quite pleased.

"Your sister made the request that you find a husband for Giuletta. While the favor was not asked of us, there is also the matter of Prunella finding a husband.

"For Prunella, who is now a contessa, and would not accept anyone less than her current station, I found Duca Giorgio Cirello. He is cash- and land poor, but has a title Prunella would want," Luciana said.

"He's of an age with her?" Stefano asked.

Luciana nodded. "And then, for Giuletta, I found Don Cristoval Battista who has land and a title, but could sorely need the influence and dowry she can offer him.

"I thought we might get things started by bringing the separate parties to share in our dinner," Luciana concluded. She began pulling pins from her hair, letting down the mass of black tresses until she shook them free to fall down her back to her waist.

"But listen, I have some news," Luciana laughed as she folded back the blankets on her side of the bed. She climbed in, pulling the covers back up to her chin and curling into Stefano's nightdress-covered chest as she wriggled into a comfortable position.

"And what news is this?" Stefano prompted. His hand stroked down the length of her hair, tangling it a little as he reached the bottom.

"I was concerned about the length of time that Queen Idala's spell would be active. You can imagine how dangerous it would be if women kept having babies one after another. We would grow old before our time and Tyrrhia's population would explode."

Stefano pulled his left arm up and under his head. "I can see that this would be problematic . . ."

"The older men are especially worried about their wives," Luciana observed. "But Alessandra . . . oh, to say her name again! . . . she says that she tied a timeline into her spells. A year and a day. She was murdered within days of doing the spell with Queen Idala, so that means the effects of the spell should be over by the anniversary of her death."

"That *is* good news," Stefano agreed. "Until then, nurse Divya yourself—"

"It occurred to me that with the effects of the spell still rampant that even nursing might not be enough to keep me from becoming pregnant again, so I will begin the tisane tomorrow and hope that that magic is sufficient to counter Queen Idala and Alessandra's spell."

"Just please don't tell me I cannot even touch you . . . for a month!" Stefano groaned, dropping a soft kiss on her forehead.

"I would not deny myself," Luciana retorted. "So what have you spent the day doing?"

"Preparing the deFaria estate for Massimo. I sent word to hire a full staff for the residence of the family and the prince. I have also ordered new clothes to be made for the boys and the Bonifaces, so that they look proper enough to raise a prince," Stefano said. "I've arranged for two wagons and a coach to take them to Palermo where, if they must, they can wait for the estate to be made ready. I will send them with an escort as well. The two of you can travel west and part ways on the road to Palermo, with you heading south."

"Oh, had you heard about what happened in the nursery today?" Luciana asked, propping herself up on her elbow so that she could look at him properly.

Stefano shook his head, his eyes focused on her every expression.

"Ortensia and Pierro showed up with their son and turned him over to me! We had to send for another wet nurse and then to her house for a cradle for her child."

"What? Why would Ortensia and Pierro do that?"

"Ortensia called the boy, '*il Turche*.' Said he looked like the children she bore the sultan and wouldn't raise him a day," Luciana said, shivering at the idea of giving up her child. She took full advantage of the nursery for Divya, but she had not abandoned their daughter.

"What did Pierro say?" Stefano asked.

"Oh, he was at Ortensia's side the whole time. He said that if the boy—Luca—was a Turk, then he wouldn't raise him either, but if he *was* his son, then he wanted him to have every advantage and he would only get that in the Royal Nursery."

"He actually gave up his son?" Stefano repeated in disbelief, sitting up.

Luciana nodded.

XXVI

"When the quality of a person is unclear, look to their friends."

—Tyrrhian proverb

5 d'Febbraio, 1685

LUCIANA enjoyed a private moment on the patio with Divya nestled in a large basket bassinet which lay tucked beneath the edge of the table after her morning feeding. She had begun taking her daughter out of doors more often, and it occurred to her as she lingered in the sun that she should be taking Chiara with Divya. That would mean, however, that she would require the aid of her wet nurse and she would not be able to spend these stolen moments alone. She must, she realized, think of the needs of the girls first and sighed.

The squeaking of the outer gate heralded an arrival. Placing a protective hand on the bassinet, Luciana looked up and saw Prunella returning from she knew not where. In fact, that Prunella had actually left the apartments, and without her son, was news to Luciana.

Her husband's cousin hugged herself and stamped her feet in excitement. "May I sit?" she asked.

The surprises continued for Luciana. Ever since she had caught Prunella eavesdropping, the other woman had not had two words for her. She nodded and waved to a chair next to her, which her cousin promptly sat in.

"You'll never guess who I found at Mass today!" Prunella exclaimed.

Ah, Mass! This made sense. Prunella tended to be a very devout Catholic.

She grabbed Luciana's hand in her excitement. "Orsina! I found Orsina! She had been here when last I was here searching for a husband. She, too, was looking to wed and she found a young duca. She is now pregnant and expects her first child soon. She's staying to have her child at the palazzo, and then she will return to his estate with her new husband . . . and the child, of course!"

"It's so good that you found your friend," Luciana said, smiling.

"Yes, but she'll be gone within a month, possibly a week more," Prunella replied and sighed with disappointment.

"Perhaps you can visit her at her husband's estate?"

Prunella shook her head. "She is still newly married and will have a new son or daughter to concentrate her energies on. I wouldn't want to intrude."

Luciana bit her tongue so that she would not be unkind in making the observation that Prunella had no trouble interrupting Stefano and her. She looked down at her hands which toyed with a now shredded sprig of rosemary. She dropped the bit of greenery and swept it off the table. "You remember that we are dining with Duca Cirello this evening?"

"I haven't forgotten, but does Cousin Stefano truly believe he would he be suitable for me? My father was a farmer. Of course, his property is not nearly so large and developed as mine at the diVega estate," she said. "We needn't rush into anything since the estate manager is accustomed to managing on his own. Conte diVega was good at many things, but being a farmer was not one of them." She smiled sadly again and sighed. "He married me so quickly and took me to Reggio di Calabria. We consummated our marriage . . . and then he was gone, back to court, leaving me to spend the summer alone. He was dead before he even learned that he was to be a father.

"My sisters joined me there . . . for visits, in the hopes of making a profitable marriage. They will come again, of course. It's just so lonely," she concluded.

"Then the duca may well prove to be the answer to your prayers," Luciana said.

Prunella scoffed. "You think? He's a young man. Why would he want to marry a new mother?"

"He knows you have a child from your first marriage and though he is a year younger than you, he *is* interested in marriage or he wouldn't be coming to dinner. What you must decide—hopefully, before this evening—is would you consider marriage to him?"

Prunella shrugged. "I will not say 'no' to what I doubt will even happen, but I cannot approve it either. This is pure speculation." She pushed away from the table and stood. "I am going back to my room. My little Urbano will wake soon and will want to be cared for."

Luciana nodded silently and watched her leave. She rose, scooping up Divya in her basket bassinet, and headed upstairs. She had chores in the nursery to address.

Stefano did not look up from his papers when he called out for his visitor to come in to the office. He signed an administrative order and let gold sealing wax dribble onto the paper preparatory to his applying the great seal of State. After applying the seal, he put it back into the drawer where it belonged and looked up, surprised to discover Luciana sitting in the chair he thought of as Sebastiani's. In the weeks since he taken the office of Lord Regent and she Regent Guardian, they had developed a rhythm. For one thing, Luciana did not normally interrupt him during the day unless he sought her out.

"Well, a pleasant surprise!" he exclaimed, rising from his desk to come to her side and give her a kiss. "To what do I owe this visit?"

"To whom . . . your cousin, Prunella," Luciana said, tilting her head so that he could kiss her more easily.

"What has she done now?" Stefano returned to his chair and shuffled the papers in front of him.

"Nothing, per se," she admitted. "We talked and she is anxious about this dinner with Duca Cirello this evening."

Stefano looked at her down the length of his nose. "Even if she refuses him, I won't help you kill her—if for no other reason than you do not need to be responsible for another child. You already have charge of seven."

Luciana drooped noticeably at the mention of the number of her charges instead of laughing. He knew she had hoped to have only two, perhaps three children at most. She shook off her ennui and refocused on the subject at hand. "I do not want charge of another child and, forgiving your insinuation that I might cause Prunella harm, I want to speak to you about her most seriously.

"Prunella is not happy—"

"As though anyone could not help but notice that," Stefano said smartly.

Luciana licked her lips, drawing his attention away from the papers in front of him. She required his full attention when she began a conversation with the telltale gesture. "She was reunited with her friend Orsina . . . or should I say, Her Grace, Duchessa Orsina di Candido?"

"Di Candido? I had not realized," Stefano observed, recalling that di Candido was on his privy council. "So, Prunella *is* happy now? Thank God!"

"She is happy, to a degree," Luciana said. "After the di Candido's baby is born—apparently within a matter of a week or two—they will stay for a short time before they return to their estate. So she is happy and yet sad at the same time."

"She will be happier when they are of the same rank again," Stefano said pointedly, wiping the scowl from his face. "In my last conversation with di Candido on this very matter, he and his wife will be staying at court for some time and their visits to their home estate will, of necessity, be short and relatively infrequent."

"This liaison with Cirello could easily make a happy political marriage," Luciana said. "Unfortunately, it also means that Prunella's father will be sending you his other four daughters to match for him."

Stefano nodded. "We will deal with one cousin at a time. Thank you for making the arrangements for these two marriages." He had not been attending to the needs of his cousin nor keeping his promise to Idala about seeing to Giuletta's marriage. Luciana had made reasonable matches. It would surely result with his having the duca's support in the Palantini and privy council. Alas, this was not the only matter he was faced with. There were too many good propositions made to him recently and all demanded his immediate attention. Sighing, he admitted as much to Luciana.

"Then let me make way so that you can attend to your business, but I am going to give Estensi the appointed hour of our dinner so that he'll make sure you're there," Luciana said as she rose to leave him.

Stefano stopped her with a raised hand. "At the moment, before Massimo leaves, I am detailing the future of the children. I want it very clear to the Bonifaces that they are not raising a potential heir to the Tyrrhian throne. Since Massimo is not to inherit the throne under any circumstances according to Idala's papers, it must be stipulated who *is* to inherit if something should—God forbid—happen to Dario Gian. As Regent Guardian, I need your signature as well."

"Who backs Dario Gian?" Luciana asked, accepting the document.

"His next eldest sister, Pietra."

"Pietra, one of the twins? You verified with Donna della Guelfa which girl was eldest, of course," Luciana murmured. She looked over the papers which further specified that should Pietra be unable to serve, then Rosalina; if she were unable to serve, then Chiara; and if not her, then the Lord Regent would be elevated to king. "Ortensia will protest you being named from regent to king . . . and have you considered that if Chiara took the throne, then the girl would inherit the reins of two kingdoms?"

"No, I had not considered that. What do you think should happen? Should we indicate my stepping up instead of her?" Stefano asked.

"It would be better than Chiara being charged with leading the Black and the White Thrones at the same time. The interests can be so divergent at times and each faction deserves its own leader," Luciana said. "Besides, the Council of Queens demands two women and for the next ten years you represent the White Throne."

Stefano sighed. "I will redraft this then and present it to the privy council on the morrow. When it is approved by them, I'll present it to you for signature."

"What do you plan to do with Ortensia and Pierro? They will be back after the throne should it come to you," Luciana said.

"The Palantini-at-large and the Palantini in residence dealt with the question twice. Neither Ortensia nor Pierro can inherit."

"Then perhaps this should be specified as well?" Luciana suggested.

"I will provide for it. There will be those in the privy council unhappy, though," Stefano agreed.

"And others who will be happy," Luciana replied, going to the door. "I'll be leaving for my people's mulberry orchards no later than the seventeenth. The children will be a month old then, and that gives me time to see that Alessandra and the Romani are reconciled before her anniversary date."

Stefano sighed. "You will take Divya?"

"And Chiara. Send Capitano della Guelfa and his men to protect us if you wish. My people have become accustomed to them," Luciana replied. "And, if you must send more, have them *beano abri*—born the way of a Romani."

"Children of the Bloods, you mean? From the Escalade? The maggiore was exceptional. I doubt I could find more."

"That, then, I leave for you to reconcile. There will be magic used and these men cannot react," Luciana warned.

"I will discuss this matter with the privy council. They should know sooner rather than later what is destined for the girl."

"As you think best," Luciana agreed.

"Dario Gian is five. He will be six in May. He should begin his tutoring toward being king, and it shall be thus for the girls, as well," Stefano announced. "You've already set tutors for him in chess, mathematics, fencing, and politics."

"And language," Luciana nodded. "The maestros have already begun to meet with him. They report him to be an able student."

XXVII

"To him that you tell your secret, you resign your liberty."

—Romani proverb

13 d'Febbraio, 1685

PIERRO watched the packing curiously. Two carts had come fully laden to the palazzo grounds by the time he had returned from his ride—with bodyguards. He was finding their presence tiresome and difficult to manage. He had not talked to Caserta in weeks. It was true that the bodyguards were his to command and that they guarded his royal personage, but he had no doubts that anything he did that was the slightest bit untoward would get to the Lord Regent.

But the packing of two more carts held his attention at the moment. He stood in a narrow alcove, watching the activity through a window, rather like a schoolboy watching the out of doors instead of doing his school work. Of course, all information being important, Pierro took the time to watch, ignoring the three bodyguards who waited on the other side of the curtain.

Was it possibly true? Did they intend to move Massimo as they had discussed in the Palantine council? Pierro's jaw ached from gnashing his teeth. Where would they take the boy? He had no way of alerting Caserta and his men without also risking alerting the Lord Regent . . . and then he thought of Renata or one of the other servants he had cultivated. No, Renata would serve. She was happy with him at the moment. He had actually taken her to his bed last night after Ortensia had retired. Yes, Renata would go to Citteauroea for him.

After a time, he came out of the alcove and strode down the hall to his suite. He was loath to be there, in the suite, for Ortensia's mood swings would drive any sane man to drink! He must find a way to reach Caserta. There was much they could do with a Prince of the Realm and, if he were who he was supposed to be, raising up the cardinal in their own fashion, bespoke of greatness. To be the power behind the throne was almost better than having the throne itself. He would have to find a way to get word to Caserta!

14 d'Febbraio, 1685

Luciana instantly awoke to Kisaiya's gentle shake. She nodded to her maid and then rolled over to wake Stefano. He was already awake. "Have you slept at all?"

"A little," Stefano admitted, rising from the bed.

They dressed quickly. Luciana wore her Romani clothes and, therefore, could dress herself unaided. Stefano wore common clothes, no Gypsy Silk. He carried his chain of office in a pouch at his side. Luciana wore hers, but covered it with other necklaces of gold and silver.

It was long before dawn when the group of them crept from the palazzo and onto their horses or carriages. The *Beluni* was waiting with her people and the carts which had been packed earlier in the day. Luciana checked the hitch of her horses, adjusting a bridle here and a lead there, then swung up into the driver's seat. She looked back into her *vardo*. Three women stared back at her owlishly. In the arms of two, were babies Divya and Chiara. Kisaiya, not responsible for a child, lay on a mat on the floor. The two wet nurses lay end to end on the narrow *vardo* bed each with their child and royal charges tucked close.

Traveling with children was slow going, Luciana found. Or, at least, with Massimo and the gadjé. Though they started out near midnight, they were only just beyond the western gates of Citteauroea by dawn.

Stefano rode Fascino beside Luciana's seat on the *vardo*, his eye ever turned over his shoulder. By nightfall, they found a taverna by the side of the road. They were near Avenocce, a good twenty miles from Citteauroea. The Rom set up their *benders* and created a merry campsite by the road. Stefano took the gadjé travelers—the Bonifaces, Massimo and Federico and the various drivers of the carts to the taverna. They occupied all the rooms and still had people sleeping in the common room. The innkeeper, at least, was happy.

Luciana waited in her *bender* for Stefano to join her. Divya was lying on the bedding nearby, sleeping. The two wet nurses, Melora and Caprice, were in the taverna with Chiara, and Kisaiya was in her bed already fallen into an exhausted slumber.

Stefano pulled back the door covering and slipped inside. He sat on the bedding and pulled off his boots. "I've set guards, though with your people's camp, it was probably unnecessary," he said, slipping between the covers Luciana held open for him.

"Stefano, we must speak of tomorrow," Luciana whispered.

He nodded. "We didn't make much ground today, but tomorrow, they will be more accustomed—"

"Tomorrow, they will be tired, aching, and fractious," Luciana replied. "They will travel about the same distance if they are pushed."

Stefano sighed, nodding. "This is why I did not want to move Massimo so soon."

"It has nothing to do with the boy. *Gadjés* are not used to traveling. Were it just our people, Stefano, we would have covered almost twice the distance headed in the right direction," Luciana said.

"You have to travel west anyway," Stefano said, taking Luciana into his arms and working his way into a comfortable position.

"Tomorrow, we will come to a crossroads. One will lead west, to Palermo and deFaria, and the other will lead south, toward Modica. We must part ways there," Luciana said. "I must reach the *vitsi* campsite by the end of the month. I cannot travel all the way with Massimo, and still reach my destination on time."

"But you are the Regent Guardian and I cannot be away from the palazzo so long as this trip will take," Stefano argued softly, lest he wake Kisaiya.

"We should have left sooner," Luciana groused.

"Perhaps, but the babes are all so young, and Massimo has special needs. We cannot overstress the boy."

Luciana sighed. Stefano spoke truth. "What if we travel ahead of the laden carts? In carriages, though uncomfortable, we can press faster. The carts will simply have to follow and catch up to us in deFaria."

"But what if they are waylaid by highwaymen?"

"Then leave some of the guard with them if you think that they must. Have them wear their colors and fly the standard. They will be apart from us and hopefully not draw so much attention," Luciana said.

"So it will be done," Stefano said, his voice giving evidence of his misgivings. "Strozzini and I will part ways with you tomorrow around noon. We estimate that we can get back to the palazzo—being on horseback—in a day's time so we will only have been away three . . . perhaps three and a half days," Stefano said.

"And the Palantini? What will you tell them?" Luciana asked.

"What I have already told them. Strozzini and I are seeking more word on *Magnus Inique*," Stefano replied. He sighed and stretched as he found a comfortable position.

"But you will have nothing to report," Luciana protested.

"There are men . . . trusted men who seek out *Magnus Inique* in various parts of the heartland. We will have their reports to build on."

"So you will lie?" Luciana asked, her voice guarded.

Stefano shook his head then kissed the top of hers. "We will not lie. We will report on the findings and proceed from there. Already, many of the Palantini, tired of the cramped quarters, are returning to their homes."

"Will I return to marriage banns for Giuletta and Prunella?" Luciana asked.

"I will do all that I am able, short of holding the grooms at gunpoint to see that the marriages will go forth. I think Giuletta and Don Battista will marry, if for no other reason than he needs her dowry, but I've been assured he treated his first two wives very well. It should be a good match for her."

"And Prunella?"

"With Palantini members beginning to vacate the palazzo, I will be able to have Guglielmo find her own suite soon. The negotiations with the duca are proceeding. He is cautious, never having married before," Stefano said.

"I feel almost guilty with that match. Duca Cirello shows signs of being a very nice man and one sympathetic to our side of the political arena," Luciana murmured.

"Luciana, we start early in the morning. Get your rest," Stefano bade her.

15 d'Febbraio, 1685

Stefano left the cavalcade the next day with Strozzini securely at his side. Luciana took her *vardo* to the lead position and increased the pace of the travelers. The Escalade guards kept easy pace on horseback as they surrounded the conglomeration of *vardos* and two carriages. By the time they stopped for the evening they had reached Cefalu and the end of the Palermo Bay. Tomorrow, they would reach the deFaria estate and Massimo's new home.

As they had the night before, Luciana found a roadside tavern that could take the gadjé passengers, but the Rom were forced to make their camp some distance away on a hilltop in a field not far from the road. She insisted that della Guelfa and his men stay in the tavern, for their comfort, and to protect the princess. She knew she had her own people who would look after her and Divya. Besides, the *gadjé* did not always care for the Romani food.

After the parties separated, the young women for the *vitsi* made dinner: *hetchi-witchi* and greens with bread to sop up the juices. They ate and laughed. Della Guelfa and one of his men came to the camp to see that all was settled and safe before Luciana finally was able to retire for the night.

It seemed to Luciana that she had barely drifted off to sleep when the alarm was raised. She forced herself awake, leaving Divya snuggled into the bedding and blankets when she slipped from the *bender* to see who raised the alarm and why.

At the far end of the Romani camp, a *bender* was on fire and dark shapes moved with torches. Somewhere, she heard the clash of metal. Someone gave a guttural cry even as nearby, a woman screamed. Luciana turned to go back into her tent for her sword when she was caught unaware by someone taking a fistful of her hair and dragging her away from the *bender*.

Luciana struggled to break the hold on her and stopped as a cold steel blade was put to her throat. "Go ahead, witch! Give me reason to slit your throat." Unarmed, she quit fighting and allowed herself to be forced to the bonfire in the center of the camp. She spotted her uncle, Petrus, and another man lying near the fire, unmoving. They had been the main watch, all she had thought the Rom needed, before sending della Guelfa and his men back to the taverna to get a good night's sleep. She could have kicked herself. The man holding her shoved her to the ground. She was joined, in quick order, by the *Beluni*, Grasni, and a couple of other women. Five women in all. Luciana prayed Kisaiya stayed where she was and that they did not burn all the *benders*.

Luciana gathered herself together and stood, belligerently meeting the eyes of the man who had thrown her down. "What's the meaning of this attack on peaceful people?" She could hear men fighting.

The man laughed and then punched Luciana in the face, knocking her to the ground. His comrades—or those nearby—were six burly men.

Luciana touched her bloodied lip and swelling cheek, and then slowly picked herself back up. "Why do you attack us? We have harmed no one. Taken nothing."

"You are witches and your men adulators. I'd tell you to say your prayers, but that would be pointless, wouldn't it?" the man said with a harsh laugh. He punched her again in the face, knocking her down again. She saw stars blinding her and felt her eye already puffing up. "Now, have the sense to stay down, girl."

"So it's easier for you to control us?" Luciana asked. She could not see out of her right eye, and her teeth ached.

"No, you're easy enough to deal with, but we don't want you casting no spells at us," one of the other men said.

Luciana scuttled a few feet back, toward her grandmother who showed signs of being hit as well. "Are you with *Magnus Inique*?"

The men looked at her and then between themselves. The first man came forward and kicked her in the hip. "You have no right to say our name! Keep silent, d'ya hear?"

"*Brutto cretino*!" One of the other men hissed at Luciana's attacker. Being called an idiot did little for the first man's humor as he grabbed Luciana's arm and twisted it behind her back, nearly, if not actually, pulling the arm from the socket.

"Don't call me that. Pay attention to the women! We have to make sure they don't say anything!" the *lottatore* snapped at the other man.

"Are you afraid I might say something like this?" Luciana hissed. She raised her free arm toward the fire, "*Fata*! I call upon thee as a true believer! Send us a protector!"

The man holding her shook Luciana hard enough that her teeth rattled in her head and she could barely see anything but the glow of the bonfire and stars all around. He pushed her back to the ground and kicked her again and again.

"Look!" one of the men screamed, pointing.

Her attacker laid off and turned to look at the bonfire. Luciana could barely make out what happened next. The fire leaped up high and in the fading brightness a man's form could be made out. It was Maggiore di Montago, sword in hand. He stepped from the center of the blaze unharmed and turned in a half-circle, taking measure of the men facing him. Two ran away, and when Luciana's attacker would have stepped forward to fight, she swung her legs hard and brought him down.

More of the men spread out throughout the camp heard the men by the bonfire screaming in terror. Within moments, more men left what they had been doing to the Romani and came to see what the excitement was about. There were easily a dozen of them.

Mandero, the maggiore, seemed to be made all of flame as he stepped out of the fire pit. He slit one man's gullet before the man even had a chance to scream. His blade seemed to move as rapidly as wildfire, consuming everything in its path. He waded into the men, slashing and cutting through them like a hot knife through butter.

Luciana crawled to her grandmother's side, and the two of them helped each other to their feet. In bare seconds, it seemed that the only *aggressore* left living were the ones who had run away.

Mandero turned and looked at her. "I was sent by the *Fata*, believer, but your men will tend you now." He pointed to where the Escalade vigilare were running up the hill toward them.

Luciana nodded. "You have served us well, Maggiore."

Saying nothing more, Mandero once more entered the flames of the fire and was consumed.

"How did you do that?" the *Beluni* asked, blinking at Luciana.

"I believed the *Fata* and was rewarded," Luciana said quietly. Her ribs ached where the man, now dead, had kicked her.

"But I believe—" the *Beluni* began, clearly confused. She was interrupted by della Guelfa.

"Oh, Your Excellency! If your husband could see you now, I would most surely die by his hand," della Guelfa said, picking up Luciana and carrying her to a toppled fireside stool. He righted the stool with his foot and set Luciana down there. He turned to his men, yelling directions.

When all seemed to be settling down, Marco della Guelfa knelt by Luciana's side. Luciana watched over his shoulder as Grasni assisted the *Beluni* back toward her *vardo*. "Where is the baby? Kisaiya will know," Luciana demanded.

Immediately, a call went up for Kisaiya. It seemed to take forever to find her. When the vigilare finally found Kisaiya, she was huddled in a ditch with Divya. She was reassured and brought to Luciana who immediately took her child into her arms. She allowed herself the time to fully take in that the tiny girl was safe, then looked up. "The princess? How is she?"

"She is with Melora in the tavern."

"Good! Thank you, Kisaiya! You thought first of my

baby and that was the right thing to do. The babes must be protected at all cost," Luciana said.

Kisaiya looked at her mistress, shaking her head. "Oh, *Araunya-Daiya*, you are a sight! What did that man do to you?"

Luciana shrugged, watching the Escalade men take the bodies away. She was happy to see Uncle Petrus and his companion rouse and that already someone was bringing forth a quickly mulled wine. She accepted a cup gladly. She found it difficult drinking from the cup, however. Her lip was split, and her teeth felt like they would barely stay in her head.

"Were they *Magnus Inique*?" della Guelfa asked, kneeling at Luciana's side.

"They said so."

"How were these men killed?" he asked.

"By blazing sword," Luciana replied.

"Then my eyes did not deceive me. The maggiore was here, but all in flames. Is it possible?" della Guelfa asked, doubting himself.

"You saw what you saw. It is up to you to decide if your eyes have deceived you," Luciana said with a shrug. "But be assured, my eyes told me the same, as apparently these dead men learned as well."

"Shall I take Divya now?" Kisaiya asked.

Luciana shook her head. It was too hard to say anything else, and she was simply glad to feel Divya's heartbeat so close to her own.

"Get something to help clean these wounds," della Guelfa bade the girl. "You were lucky, Your Excellency, and if your husband lets me remain your bodyguard, I will not be sent away again. No matter how compelling your argument!"

Luciana smiled, but that hurt her bruised lips and cheek. She licked her lips, took a sip of the wine, and asked, "Is everyone well?"

Della Guelfa rose. "I'll go and find out. I think your people were lucky."

"Yes, we were lucky they intended to burn us instead of merely beating us," Luciana replied darkly.

"I *am* sorry, Your Excellency," della Guelfa said.

Luciana nodded and waved for him to go.

Kisaiya returned first, carrying her own *putsi* bag. She lay the medicine bag down and wet a rag from the wineskin she carried with her. Gently, she worked on Luciana's face, and the other open wounds.

Della Guelfa returned as Kisaiya was putting a healing ointment on Luciana's wounds. "Well?" Luciana asked.

"There are the wounded, Your Excellency, but you seem to have taken the worst of it. They stole a horse, but that won't matter since I intend to ride on your *vardo* from now on," della Guelfa said, summing up the situation.

"Everyone should get some rest," Luciana said, taking Kisaiya's hand and putting it away from her face. Divya had started to fuss and needed looking after. "We leave in the morning."

"Morning? But it is just a couple of hours away. We should stay here for—" della Guelfa protested.

"We leave in the morning. You can stay or go, as you please, Capitano."

Della Guelfa eyed her, as though debating if it was worth arguing about. He seemed to decide it was not and helped her up and to her *bender*.

XXVIII

"For a good cause, wrongdoing is virtuous."
—Publilius Syrus

17 d'Febbraio, 1685

LUCIANA cuddled Divya close as she stepped out of the *bender*. She was no longer tired, but her body ached and eating had been difficult these last few days. She pulled the strap of cloth over her shoulders and nestled Divya into it so that her hands were free. She turned in a slow circle, taking in her wild home, the mulberry groves stretching out into the valley, the caverns, the Fairy Wood beyond, the west end of the valley with their scattered caravans, and horses everywhere she looked. Apparently, the word she sent out by carrier pigeons had reached more than just the Guildmistresses.

"Kisaiya?" she called softly into the tent. The wet nurses were still sleeping, as were their children and Chiara.

Her maid rustled through the blankets and bedding and came out. "Yes, *Araunya*?"

"Get Chiara and our kits. We have work to do."

Kisaiya's misgivings shone on her face. "Are you sure you want to do this?"

"I am apart from my husband and here early for the express purpose of bringing Alessandra home as soon as I can," Luciana said, holding back the heavy homespun door for her maid.

The maid flinched at the use of the dead *Araunya*'s

name, though her reflexive action had lessened. For her and the rest of the Romani, using the name of the dead came at the year-end celebration of the death, when the dead could be safely acknowledged without calling them back to their lives and, thereby, toward something they could not have again. It would frustrate the *mulló*, tempt them and slowly turn them into the evil undead. It was *marimé* for Luciana to even speak her sister's name so soon . . . except for the magic of the *Fata* who had saved the dead *Araunya*: the *Araunya* who had started to turn to the dark side.

Kisaiya ducked back into the *bender*, gathering the bags and baby the *Araunya-Daiya* had called for.

Della Guelfa threw back his quilt and sat up on his bedroll by the fire. "Where are you going so early, Your Excellency?"

"Just to the other side of the valley. I stay within my people's home," Luciana said.

Marco della Guelfa yawned and stretched, rising. "Where you go, I go." He bent to fold up his bedding.

"But you can't come . . . to where I'm going!" Luciana protested in a harsh whisper.

"Why not?" Marco asked, placing his sleeping things beside the tent so that they were tucked out of the way.

"Because she means to go to the *Daiya's* Cavern, and men are not allowed there," Kisaiya replied quietly. She exited the tent with Chiara balanced against her shoulder and the bags in her other hand.

Della Guelfa relieved her of the bags. "If you'll forgive me, Your Excellency, you look like you barely survived a brawl. I told you I won't leave you again."

"There is a place . . . a shelf, where you can sit and be able to see her and anyone else who might try to enter the sacred space," Kisaiya suggested. She grinned at Luciana. "Mind you, *I* wouldn't choose to sit there, but if you are determined . . ."

"I am," della Guelfa said.

Luciana gave Kisaiya a chiding look. "There is only one way in and out of this cavern. You are welcome to sit by the steps and wait for us."

"There is no way for me to secure the cavern, is there?"

Luciana shook her head. "I truly take no risk here."

"This is one place the witch-hunters would love to

raid," della Guelfa observed, turning to take in his surroundings.

"Where is the *Beluni*? Will she be joining us?" Kisaiya asked.

Again, Luciana shook her head. She climbed into her *vardo* and retrieved a staff from just inside the door. She used the staff to brace herself on the slippery, grassy hillside. "The *Beluni* . . . does not know . . . yet."

The maid caught Luciana by the arm, half-turning her back. "Your grandmother does not even know what you plan? You are asking for trouble."

"According to my husband and grandmother, I'm always in the thick of *curépen*. Why should I change now?" Luciana said with a grin.

"Do you really have no misgivings, *Araunya*? You throw yourself in the face of all the traditions of our people! They will never accept this," Kisaiya warned, hurrying after her mistress who strode confidently toward the largest of the caverns.

"Aye, I do. I risk this for the love of my sister and my people. I believe in the *Fata* and what they have done for her and her husband. Kisaiya, why can't you understand? They *live*. They are *not* dead," Luciana replied, shaking her head fiercely as she soldiered on through the dewy and still foggy morning.

"*Araunya-Daiya*, I believe. I've seen not just your sister, but her husband. What they have done would be impossible for a *mulló* . . . well, perhaps not the maggiore. A *mulló* could have done that, or something like that," Kisaiya said. "It's just the others. They won't know what to believe."

"The problem before me, Kisaiya, is that they *think* they know what to believe. It is my job to convince them otherwise."

The caverns and valley of Modica were close enough to the sea that if she stopped and listened hard Luciana could hear the seabirds, just miles away. As though bidden, a seagull swooped and turned in the wind, flapping its way to the ground. It came boldly up to her, looking for food. Luciana waved her shawl to send the seagull back to its mates . . . the ones that hovered and nested near the caverns.

As Luciana crossed the field, one of the other women at

a morning fire pit sang out a greeting and waved. Luciana returned the salute and kept on her way, aware of her unhappy maid following close behind.

"Perhaps you should at least prepare the *Beluni*?"

"I will consult her when the time is right. Now is a time of action. You are with me as my apprentice. Unless you wish to surrender your position?" Luciana asked, turning back. The girl had lived a lifetime of being taught to avoid the dead and all things pertaining to it—could she change now? She watched her maid look away.

"I have served you faithfully for seven years now, *Araunya*. I serve you still, but if you wish to rid yourself of me, then—"

"That is *not* what I was saying at all," Luciana protested. "You have done well by me and I, in turn, hope I've done well by you . . . training you as I am supposed to in the ways and uses of magic. This past year, your education has been more about the *gadjé* than of magic, so I am offering you a way to avoid this duty I would ask of you. Even in the ways of the *chovahani*, there are times you will have to face death. You must be strong and deal with it bravely lest it consume you."

"In the way it consumed the cardinal?"

"No. The cardinal's sin was not cowardice. It was greed. Greed so overwhelming it destroyed his spiritual teachings and led him to incredible depths of depravity. The cardinal sought to build his power by summoning the dead and trying to harness them to his bidding," Luciana said, sliding in the grass. Della Guelfa hurried forward to help her, even as she righted herself. "This conversation must seem very strange to you, Capitano."

"This past year has been . . . an education, Your Excellency," he said noncommittally.

"But aren't you doing the same thing as the cardinal?" Kisaiya asked, returning them to their previous conversation.

Luciana shook her head firmly. "What I do is very different. Alessandra, my sister, is dead to this world of the mortals, yet she lives on in another world as an immortal *Fata*. I do not summon the dead and I do not mean to harness her in any fashion, only bring her back to her people in the manner she deserves, not as the honored dead, but as a living being."

"But if she died . . ." Kisaiya dropped her gaze to the ground, slowly shaking her own head. "This is so very hard to understand, *Araunya-Daiya*."

"Think of my sister as having passed through a magical door made by the *Fata*. When they could not save her as a Child of the Bloods, then the *Fata* needed to retrieve her. It is as simple as that," Luciana said. "What is crucial is that we get our people to understand that the *Fata have* saved her, or we risk offending them more, enough that they will not honor our earth magic, causing us to lose the ability to make the Gypsy Silk, and with the Gypsy Silk lost, then endangering our people as a whole. Even here in Tyrrhia, as the attack on our caravan testifies, the Romani are still not safe from persecution. Should we face another diaspora, where would we go?"

Luciana reached the steps carved into the chipped stone that led down into the cavern where the *Daiyas* performed their magic. She paused here and pointed to the open mouth of the shelf favored by the bats. "You can go no farther, Capitano."

"Let me at least carry the bags to—"

Shaking her head, Luciana took one of the bags from Marco and Kisaiya took the other. "Wait here, or over yonder where you can see us, but you may not come down the steps."

Obviously disgruntled, the capitano went in search of a safe spot to sit on the shelf. Luciana made her way down the steps, looking at the floor as she walked. Bats frequented this cave, but where the *Daiyas* worked their magics, there was a shelf that protected them from the bat droppings, with sufficient natural openings that the smoke from the fires safely chimneyed upward, through the same paths the bats flew.

She stepped over the little stream that ran through the open doorway, her feet crunching on the crumbling stone. Kisaiya hopped over it.

Luciana found the great open space dimly lit by a single torch. She took the torch down from its stanchion and used it to light eight others, making it much easier to see. Kisaiya carried Chiara to the side of the chamber and, nestling her in blankets and her own cloak, settled the child down. When the child was secure, she automatically took up a broom and began sweeping the floor, dusting away the occasional bat droppings and what was left of the last circle from the previous casting done by the *Daiyas*. Cleaning was the beginning of any spell work. Tending the tools, was, of course, done immediately after.

Inside her cocoon, Divya stirred and fussed at her mother's constant movement, forcing Luciana to stop and make a bed for her with her shawl and cloak next to where Kisaiya had done the same for Chiara. Luciana shivered a little without her coverings, but dove into the work to be done with a fervor her bruised body protested. She gathered wood from the bin the women kept full and began piling it in the depths of the empty welling on the floor.

No coals burned from the night before. She piled the fresh wood to one side and set about the business of lighting a new fire. While Luciana worked on the fire, Kisaiya gathered the accumulation of her own efforts onto a sheet and began ferrying it up, into the compost pile above and beyond the cavern. The Romani gardeners used the dropping-enriched compost to nourish their groves of mulberry and the gardens which supplied vegetables to their people.

The grove gardeners, unlike most of the Romani of Tyrrhia, led fully sedentary lives; living in permanent shelters built into the network of caves that honeycombed the rocky hillside which protected the valley from the sea. To them, also, were left the duties of sowing seeds and tending their vegetable gardens. The ebb and flow of the valley was symmetry in motion, life ever-revolving, a part of the cycle of the magic between the *Fata* and the Romani in the making of Gypsy Silk. Now the cycle was endangered.

Without Gypsy Silk, her people would be nothing more to the *gadjé* than the miscreants and witches they were seen as throughout the continent. Luciana let her mind drift over these thoughts as she built up the tender into a small, warming fire. This is what she had brought Chiara and Divya to experience for their first time, so that it would be as much a part of them as it was of herself and others like her, the *Beluni* and Kisaiya.

With the fire feeding greedily on the branches, Luciana turned to the kits that the capitano had carried from their encampment on the north side of the valley. She found the block of chalk and began marking the circle on the floor.

"Oh, *Araunya-Daiya*, it's you!"

Luciana and Kisaiya looked up from their work. They had been quietly joined by Grasni, Alessandra's maid and now the *Beluni's* apprentice. Luciana sat back on her heels and wiped her brow, knowing, self-consciously, that she was without doubt smudging coal and chalk dust on her face.

"Yes. You remember Kisaiya?"

Grasni looked to the other woman of about the same age as herself and gave her a friendly smile. "Yes, I remember you." She nodded to the maid and turned back to Luciana, "The *Beluni* . . . your grandmother saw the smoke and wanted to know what was happening down here."

Luciana waved to the circle she had been drawing on the stone, fully encompassing the fire pit. "I am preparing for tonight."

"Tonight?" Grasni repeated, tilting her head to the side. "I did not know there was a ceremony tonight. Your grandmother was unaware of it, as well. Or has she forgotten?"

"No. I have not broached it with her yet."

"Why not do it now?" the *Beluni* suggested, coming up from behind Grasni. "You know you have a *gadjé* up top watching you, don't you?"

"*Beluni-Daiya*, you did not need to—" Grasni began.

The old woman, Luciana's grandmother, waved her to silence. "Of course not, *chovahani*," she said, patting her apprentice's shoulder as she came around her. "What are you preparing for so industriously, Luciana? And is that my great-granddaughter over there?" She skirted the circle Luciana was drawing and went to the babies where she squatted down and smiled. "You brought Chiara as well!"

"Yes, I thought the more she was around magic . . . it will be difficult for her with the *gadjé* laws and her being *la famiglia reale*, but I aim to educate her well," Luciana said.

"Good. Good," the *Beluni* nodded. She sank to the ground, setting her own staff aside as she drew Divya and Chiara into her lap. "So . . . what *are* you doing?"

"*Curépen*," Kisaiya whispered under her breath.

Trouble. It seemed the time was upon her, Luciana

realized. She took a deep breath, glad that the babies were snuggled in the *Beluni*'s lap which, thereby, provided her a measure of protection from the old woman's wrath. "I am setting up for the celebration."

"What celebration?" the *Beluni* asked, shaking her head while making faces at the babies.

"I—I thought we might *celebrate* Alessandra's return early," Luciana replied. She took another deep breath, warming to her subject.

The *Beluni* looked at her in shock, even as she freed her flowing gray locks from the baby's fingers. "You have uttered the name of the dead! How dare you? And in front of two impressionable—Luciana, you know you cannot speak her name! Cleanse yourself!"

"I have no need to cleanse myself," Luciana said firmly, standing to stare at her grandmother. "You heard the *Fata*. My sister lives, and what should I call her by but her name?"

"Her anniversary is still two months away. You've heard my decision on this matter, as have the *Fata*!" her grandmother snapped angrily. She waved Grasni and Kisaiya over to take the baby girls. Once she was free of them, she worked herself up to stand, somewhat painfully. "Have you gone mad?"

"No!" Luciana shouted. The babies immediately started to cry, so she lowered her tone. "*Mami*, you must accept the gift of the *Fata*. We are in danger of losing *all* our earth magic because you have offended them. There will be no more Gypsy Silk!"

"There has been Gypsy Silk for twelve generations before me. It comes from our treaty with the *Fata* when we found our home here in Tyrrhia. We tie the people—all the people—to the land with the Silk!"

"Indeed, we do!" Luciana agreed. She took another, quick, deep breath. "But the *Fata* have extended their gifts to us. Alessandra is alive."

"Again, you spoke her na—What do you mean she's alive? I've seen her *mulló*!"

"No, you have seen her immortal *Fata* body. Alessandra is alive now in the realm of the fairy kind. Just as the *Madonna-gianes* told us! Between their magic and the love of the maggiore, she was brought back . . . to life," Luciana said. "She is immortal now. You saw her husband respond to my call these few nights ago. The *Fata* sent him to *me* because I believe they have made my sister whole again. Oh, she will not and cannot live among us as if she lived like you or I, but she *is* alive!"

The old woman shook her head, looking as though Luciana had suddenly grown addle-pated. "Your sister is gone, *chavi*. She can never return to us."

Luciana nodded. "No, she can't . . . except in the manner of the *Fata*. She *is Fata*, now."

"She's not— " the *Beluni* began.

"You do not believe the *Fata*. You have broken faith with them, but she *is Fata* now!" Luciana insisted. "When we call upon her tonight, I can prove it!"

It had been a frustrating day so far. Luciana looked up the hillside at her grandmother's encampment resentfully. The sound of feet drew her gaze back to her own fire. She smiled sadly at Mistress Eleni, Guildmistress of the main Citteauroea chapter.

"*Araunya*?" the woman said, dropping a quick curtsy. Curtsies were a *gadjé* invention and not considered necessary in the Romani encampments. "Is what they say true?"

Luciana bit her tongue on her first harsh reply. The woman had always been kind to her, and her tone now was sympathetic. She looked down at Divya, snug in her lap, toying with her fingers. "Depends on what they're saying. If they say I have gone *diviou*, then, no. They aren't speaking the truth."

"They said you spoke the *Araunya minore*'s name . . . aloud," the Guildmistress said. "If I may?" She gestured to one of the stools Kisaiya had set out.

Luciana nodded. "Please. Sit. Join me. You're the only one besides Kisaiya and the *gadjés* willing to have anything to do with me at the moment." She glanced up the hill again, where her grandmother consulted with the other *Daiyas*—mothers and wisewomen, all.

"You've been crying, *Araunya*," Eleni prompted.

"I'm *so* angry! I thought if I explained it that she would understand, but she won't listen to reason!" Luciana lashed out and immediately raised her hand in apology.

"You, of all people, know the ways of the Romani, *Araunya*. Your . . . sister is gone . . . until the celebration two months from now." The Guildmistress spoke softly, gently.

Luciana looked up at her. "I don't care what you've been told, Mistress Eleni, I have not lost my wits. I am not *diviou*!"

Kisaiya lay a comforting hand on Luciana's wrist. "She's not, you know," the maid said. "It's just this problem with the *mulló* and *marimé*."

"Tell me," Eleni encouraged.

Tired and frustrated, Luciana sighed heavily. She made her argument again. "I *know* this, Mistress Eleni. I have *touched* my sister. She is as corporeal as any of the *Fata* I have ever met. Her husband came to me when I called for protection stating that I believed in the *Fata*!"

"But they are the fey. They live between worlds, *Araunya*, so they are part of this world and yet, not," Eleni pointed out. "They aren't always of the flesh as you and I are."

"No, but they can be. When they choose. You have experienced them . . . you must have or you could not be a Guildmistress. You have had training. Perhaps not as much as I . . . or the *Daiyas*, but you have seen them," Luciana pressed.

Eleni nodded. "They are wondrous beings, but why would they make the *Araunya minore* one of them?"

"She, like you, was a Child of the Bloods, but she—I will say her name!—Alessandra—they failed to save from an untimely death. They were not able to keep their promise. The cardinal and Bianca used a fast-acting poison, and magic to cover their vile work. The *Fata* did not know until it was too late. Alessandra was owed. My sister gave of herself, continuing her sworn duty to defend the *Fata*'s way even after her death," Luciana said. She noted that Eleni struggled not to flinch and make the sign against the evil eye each time Alessandra's name was spoken, but it was an ingrained habit. "You see? She has not been summoned and I've spoken her name all day. Where is her *mulló*? Where is her rage?"

Eleni glanced around her and slowly nodded. She even looked skyward. It was a fair and sunny day, without the hint of storm cloud or clue to unnatural influences. "I hear what you say, *Araunya*, and you are right. There should be some sign of her, but perhaps, because it is so close to the end of her year . . . ?"

"All the more reason for her spirit to be nearby, waiting to be called back from the everlasting," Kisaiya said.

Luciana looked at her maid and sighed. Finally! Someone really believed her . . . or was beginning to.

"But how? How is it possible for . . . the *Araunya minore*'s *mulló* to have become *Fata*?" Eleni asked.

Luciana shook her head. "I think it was in the reuniting of her spirit and her flesh and the maggiore's love for her. The cardinal also worked much magic over her and the *chova* was strong in her. At the pyre, too, the maggiore sacrificed himself for his love of her. The *Fata* did nothing to protect him either, but I think that decision . . . that sacrifice was all that the *Fata* needed to be moved to help them both in a way they have never done before. The *Madonna-gianes* said as much when she came to bless Divya and Chiara.

"We have been visited by both Alessandra and Mandero di Montago. You heard of the attack upon us on our way here, surely? Not all saw, but enough did, when I summoned the *Fata* to help us by swearing that I believed. I don't think they would have sent the maggiore if I hadn't stated my belief in them."

"It's true," Kisaiya offered. "I've seen him with my own two eyes thrice now."

"Both of them are with the *Fata*?" Eleni asked, her voice rising to almost a squeak.

"Both were Children of the Bloods and their deaths untimely, surrounded by magic. The maggiore gave his *life* to be with Alessandra in death . . . but he is among the *Fata* as well. Kisaiya, you saw them at Divya's birth!"

Kisaiya nodded. "I did. Both of them appeared the same . . . glowing silver in the night."

"But it is more important than my word over another's. The *Fata* are angry. They feel we have denied them, that we do not welcome their gifts of ever-loving life. They have said they will take away the magic that makes the Gypsy Silk!" Luciana pressed.

"Take away the Gypsy Silk? But if they did that, then—we cannot let this happen! What would we do? Where would our people go to begin again when the *gadjé* of

Tyrrhia deny us because they don't have their Silk? What will Tyrrhia do? Succumb to the Church?" Mistress Eleni gasped. She took a deep calming breath and reached out to touch Luciana's hands. "I have given you my sworn oath, *Araunya-Daiya.* I am yours . . . as are the other Guildmistresses. I will speak to them and then *we* will speak to the *Daiyas.*"

Guildmistress Eleni looked up the hill, her firm jawline setting. "We *will* be heard, *Araunya.*"

Luciana handed Divya to Kisaiya and rose, embracing the Guildmistress. The other woman startled back, surprised by the rush of affection, but after a brief hesitation, she returned the hug. Smiling shyly, she swept another curtsy and left the encampment.

"*Curépen*, in a large dose, *Araunya*. Are you ready for this?" Kisaiya asked.

Luciana took her daughter back. "I am ready. Have Melora see to Chiara. Make sure they are well." She felt the thrum of her blood beginning to sing in her veins. She never wanted to fight the *Beluni*, but if that was what needed to be, then that was what it would be!

"What do you mean, you believe her?" the *Beluni* demanded of Eleni and the other Guildmistresses around her. "She has gone *diviou* from her time amongst the *gadjé* or perhaps from childbirth . . . it happens like this sometimes, but she cannot be—"

"*We believe her, Beluni-Daiya*, and we owe her our fealty," Eleni interrupted.

"You owe *me* your allegiance," the *Beluni* snapped angrily.

"No," Luciana said, cresting the hill in time for the confrontation. "The Romani are your people, Grandmother. The Guildmistresses are the Gypsy Silk trade and they owe their loyalty to *me* . . . and the other *Araunya*, Divya, when she is old enough.

"To protect your people, *Beluni-Daiya*, you must accept Alessandra and her maggiore *now*! Save face with the *Fata* by doing this!"

The *Daiyas* almost as one body made the sign against

the evil eye, looking away from Luciana to the other body of women on the other side of the cook fire.

"Most of us are Children of the Bloods. Look at us, *Beluni-Daiya*, and you will see. The *Araunya* is our mother and we have—in turn—spoken with her. I now speak for us all, and we are of one mind about this," Eleni said, standing firm. "*We* will be acknowledging Alessandra into our company once more, be she *Araunya*, or no."

"You challenge *me*?" the *Beluni* gasped, looking to Luciana.

"You challenged the *Fata*, the source of our magic which is the source of our fortune which is the source of our protection from persecution!" She hesitated, chewing her lip. "I do not seek to be *Beluni*, but for the sake of the tribes . . . for even the Silk. I challenge you to acknowledge and celebrate. I bring with me my woman, Kisaiya, who will testify that she believes me and the *Fata*. Alessandra and her husband, Mandero, whom *you* married, are one with the *Fata*. We would not bring evil into this site. None of us would."

The women collected behind the *Beluni* openly gasped and some spat and crossed themselves, over Luciana's use of her sister's and her husband's name.

"Don't you see?" Luciana continued, this time searching the faces of the *Daiyas*, all women she knew well and respected. "The old road . . . it is good and true, but sometimes . . . as the time passes, there is a new road . . . a fork—"

"An unworn road isn't safe," her grandmother responded.

"But sometimes it offers riches, and is not so dangerous as you thought," Luciana said.

"There are some roads you cannot take," one of the *Daiyas* offered. She turned to the Guildmistresses. "You do not understand, being sedentary . . . in the cities . . . among the *gadjé*, but the route we live by . . . the traditions have not failed us in more generations than there are of you here."

"Enough, Bella," Solaja said. She folded her arms across her breasts and looked straight on at Luciana. "This is between my granddaughter and myself. She—"

"I, what? Am *diviou*? No, honored *Beluni-Daiya*, I have not lost hold of my senses. You saw Alessandra at Divya's birth. You saw Alessandra, and then we refused her. You saw Mandero that night, protecting us when we had no other beside us," Luciana said. She turned to the *Daiyas* and spoke to them as one body. "I have said her name twenty times, if not more, this very day. Where is she? Her *mulló* has not rained down any evil upon us. The horses and children are fat, the men are at the *Kris*, keeping their own council. They will follow you, and I fear—"

"*We* fear," Eleni broke in. Several of the Guildmistresses spoke, too.

Luciana nodded to them and continued. "We fear that you would lead us away from the spirit of the *Fata* in your dogged hold to tradition. Not all tradition is wrong, we make no such claim, but not all that are dead in our lives are *mullós*. Not *this* one . . . these two. You speak his name freely enough."

"Mandero sacrificed himself to the flames to be with . . . your sister. He is not undead," the *Beluni* said flatly.

"But if you think that, believe that he can be retrieved from the world of the *mulló*, why not Alessandra?"

"Alessandra Patrini di Montago, *Araunya di Cayesmengro*," Eleni said. She held out her arms and looked up at the sky, before turning back to the *Daiyas*. "You see? I remain unharmed. I say . . . *we* say that the *Araunya* should be given leeway to begin the celebration. We are gathered."

"It is not done!" the *Beluni* insisted.

"Then celebrate in two months' time, but let her come among you acknowledged as an immortal. You fear for me, but I fear for us all. I will summon my sister this night. If you say we cannot use the great cavern, we say fine, but summon her we will!" Luciana said.

"Better she does it here where we are strongest and best able to defend ourselves," another of the *Daiyas* offered from the midst of the *Beluni*'s group.

Solaja Lendaro rounded on her women, hair flying, hands raised, but then she stopped. She looked at them and nodded silently. "Use the cavern," she finally said, her back to Luciana. "See yourselves damned, but use the cavern . . . if you must."

"Perhaps the Fairy Wood is best," one of the Guildmistresses suggested. "She . . . Al—Alessandra will be strongest there."

"All the more reason to use the cavern," the *Beluni*

countered, turning back on them. "Go. We will follow to do what may be done to save your silly souls. We will take charge of the babies."

Luciana hesitated. She knew her grandmother would do nothing to harm Divya, but still . . .

"Do not take the girls into that magic. Hasn't Chiara seen enough magic for now, for her soul? And Divya is so young," the *Beluni* urged.

Luciana slowly nodded. With one long last look at the *bender* tent down below, she took a deep breath and began the silent march to the cavern, with the Guildmistresses trailing behind her. All around her at the grand site, she could feel the eyes of her people upon them. She could also hear their whispers . . . or some of their whispers.

The Guildmistresses stood up to the *Beluni* for her, but brave as they had been, they were afraid now. Luciana stopped at the top of the steps and smiled sadly at the women in her wake. "I know you are afraid. You have been bold . . . very bold and very brave. I would not blame you if not a single one of you came into the cavern with me. That includes you, Kisaiya, and you, Eleni. I—did not mean to—"

"Don't lose faith now, *Araunya*," Kisaiya said. "I believe you and I shall be at your side. I *saw* your sister. She was no frightening thing, but as beautiful as the day I met her . . . the *Araunya minore* . . . *Daiya* Alessandra."

Mistress Eleni glanced back at her Guildswomen. "I, for one, meant what I said."

Luciana took a cleansing breath and nodded again. "Then, those that wish it, come with me . . . I shall be too busy with my sister, with Alessandra, to see who is there or not . . . and I will not ask later." She turned and took the steps carefully, her shoes echoing on the stone. She heard footsteps behind her, not so many as she had hoped, but more than she had reason to expect. She lifted her skirts and hopped over the rivulet that crossed the doorway, unimpeded by Divya this time.

The tools of magic, their kits, still lay on the floor where Luciana had left them that very morning. Of the torches, two still had the nub of a fire in them; the others were either put out or had gone out. The fire in the welled-stone pit was long out. The pile of firewood still sat, waiting to be burned.

She rubbed her hands against the apron she wore over her belled skirts and reached for the nearest torch.

Kisaiya's hand reached the brand before hers. "I'll get it, *Araunya-Daiya*," she said.

Luciana tried hard not to look at the doorway, but could not help stealing a glance in that direction. Mistress Eleni was helping Kisaiya gather the used torches and replace them with newer ones from a chest pushed up against the cavern wall. Some of the other Guildmistresses entered—two old, henlike women entered with surprising hesitation and another, young woman not much past the flowering of her maidenhood joined them, while the rest hung back near the door, slowly edging into the chamber.

One of the older women went to the larder of wood and tinder, gathered supplies, and brought them to the fire pit, starting a new blaze. From there, Luciana concentrated on what lay before her. She had missed most of the day to make her preparations. There was no honeyed wine nor humble cake here to receive Alessandra, but the purpose would be served. The block of chalk had broken when the *Beluni* had taken hold of her earlier that day. As she picked up one of the shards, the young Guildmistress' hand brushed hers.

"Just a simple circle," Luciana said quietly and began again where she had left off that morning, conscious of the other woman drawing the circle from the other side . . . and more of the Guildmistresses filtering into the cavern. She concentrated, focusing on the beginning prayers. Instead of whispering them under her breath as she normally did, she began to sing the words of old, the words of summoning. What women knew the words joined in. Even some of the *Daiyas* on the hill lent their voices.

The singing felt good, and she could feel the sense of urgency rising in her, like water filling a cup and slowly spilling over. Magical power began to buzz through the room like a great whip. It felt like an ecstatic shift that buffeted her body and swelled around her. Luciana opened her bag of salt and took a handful to ward her circle, and she was joined by the others.

Several spread the rushes of sweet grass, not quite dried. Another woman set candles at the proper stations around the circle. Someone . . . Kisaiya? . . . began handing her herbs and flowers from the bundles on the floor to pass into the fire at appropriate intervals in the song. By the time the flames in the fire pit leaped up, consuming the dried greenery, bursting in flying cinders and sparks, the smoke made Luciana's throat tighten, but the magic swirled all around giving her new energy.

At the bloom of cinders, the smoking fire created a backdrop against which an eerie silver light puddled within the circle. Beside it, a second puddle of blue-silver also began to form.

Above Luciana and her women, at the cave's great mouth, came a sudden raucous noise of voices and movement. Luciana, fighting the urge to cough, kept singing, kept her eyes on the growing pool. Somewhere behind her, women faltered and coughed, but Luciana kept singing.

The puddles filled and swirled and began to take slow form in the hazy fog. As the puddles grew, they stretched for the roof, rising to human height and an opalescent light glowed at where their hearts must be.

Even half-formed, Luciana knew which was her sister. She called "Alessandra!" swallowing back her cough.

All around her grew quiet. At the cave's mouth above, the noise stilled and gave way to the subtle sounds of nature's night. Crickets sang their nocturnal love songs, seeming to grow in volume as the women within the cavern fell silent.

The two numinous forms became complete and separate. Alessandra and Mandero stood before them. They looked as real and vibrant as they had in mortal life. A slight breeze whirled about the room, as though some great hand swept away the vestiges of smoke. The fire simmered into a normal blaze, barely visible through the two people.

Alessandra stood beside her maggiore, her hand on his arm. She wore the simple dress of the Romani, faint hints of bright color in her skirt and top flared in the fire's light. She took a step away from her husband. Wordlessly, she reached out.

Luciana stepped to the salted edge of the circle, barely having the presence of mind to avoid the candle. Alessandra met her midway and the two embraced.

Tears of thankfulness rolled down Luciana's cheeks as she felt her sister's arms close around her, felt her sister's hair as she buried her face in Alessandra's neck. More even than last time, Luciana physically experienced her sister's body against hers as they embraced.

An audible gasp rose from many throats from within the chamber and outside at the vent as well.

As they broke apart, Alessandra seemed to notice the women behind Luciana. "Who?" Dawning realization reflected in Alessandra's otherworldly eyes. "You have kept your word! You summon me and you have brought others. Where is Grandmother? *Mami*?"

Luciana took her sister's hand and drew her fully from inside the warded circle. "I did not wait," she said. "You must be brought back into the arms of your people . . . in your new form . . . in your new life."

Alessandra gleamed, a smile cresting her lips. "I did not think you could do this. I thought I would always be denied . . ." She looked around at the women surrounding her. "You are so brave . . . so—"

"Is this truly possible?" an old woman's voice exclaimed.

Turning with her sister, Luciana saw their grandmother, Solaja Lendaro, *Beluni* of the Tyrrhian Romani, had actually come into the chamber. The Guildswomen stepped aside as the *Beluni* came closer.

"You are beyond the ward. I saw it set. A *mulló* would be held!" the *Beluni* continued. She walked a full circle around the pair of her granddaughters . . . one in normal form, the other seeming a colorfully captured moonbeam.

"I walked freely before you the night of my niece's birth, as well," Alessandra reminded them both. She held her hands out to her grandmother, but the *Beluni* stayed just out of reach as though still disbelieving what stood before her.

"She is your gift, *Beluni-Daiya*," Mandero said, also stepping free of the circle drawn in chalk and salt, lit from within and without.

An owl cried out, shattering the stillness of the night. The *Beluni* crossed herself as they all looked into the sky.

Darting above the heads of those watching—more than just della Guelfa and the *Daiyas* now—a white owl flitted through the vent and into the cavern's chamber.

"The harbinger of death!" Someone from above shouted.

The great, snowy owl landed between the sisters and

their grandmother in a flurry of feathers and a swirl of red cloak as it twisted its shape into that of the *Madonna-gianes*. The fairy stood, shaking her scarlet covering, which looked almost like a ruffling of feathers that settled.

"*Fata*!" One of the Guildmistresses called out.

The fairy woman stalked from her landing spot, her gaze flying about the room and up into the crowd that continued to gather overlooking them. "Did you not hear the man? *She* is your gift. A wielding of supreme magic summoned her from the very brink of what you know as hell. A magic that took the gathered strength of our entire force, that has never been cast before . . . and where are the gifts? Where are the riches of your people? Where *are* your people?" the *Gianes* demanded. She blew out her breath in a show of disappointment, perhaps even of disgust.

"There were . . . distractions," Luciana offered, glancing at her grandmother.

"There were distractions," the *Gianes* repeated, shaking her head. White feathers came loose from beneath her brown corded hair and scattered to the floor. She looked up at the crowd of Romani gathered at the large vent of the cavern. "You hide! You hide from the glory of the *Fata* united with one of the Children of the Bloods! Don't you see she is the very honor of our three peoples: the *Fata*, the Romani and the *gadjé*, as you call the children of Tyrrhia?"

The throng shifted as people shuffled about. Some of the Guildmistresses collected in a tight knot at the back of the room began to move forward. This fight today had started with them, over this very spirit . . . this very woman. Some of the *Daiyas* filtered down into the craggy stone cavity.

"Alessandra is one of our own now. Does anyone dare deny it?" the *Gianes* demanded, focusing her hard, birdlike gaze upon the *Beluni* . . . hunter examining the prey.

Solaja Lendaro looked away from the fairy's gaze and ended up staring into Alessandra's eyes.

"Can you truly deny me again, *Mami*?" Luciana's sister asked. "Can you deny the spark of life you see in my eyes? The beat of my heart?" Alessandra captured one of her grandmother's hands and pressed it to her breast, ignoring the *Beluni*'s initial resistance.

The *Beluni* flinched. People gasped in horror. When nothing happened, the *vitsi* elder who was their queen, slowly came out of her cringe, until at last she stood face-to-face with her once-dead granddaughter. "You live?"

A great murmur rose from the people watching and all was confusion until the *Beluni* stood full upright, her back straight, her face up and boldly meeting her granddaughter's eyes. "You live!"

The murmur grew to a roar as people talked among themselves and exclaimed over what they were seeing. The *Beluni* turned then to the grand fairy and bowed.

"There *are* gifts," she said. "They are not here, but up . . . yonder. The food and drink, we lack. We were not yet prepared."

"There are the *boshmengros*?" Alessandra asked. She looked from the *Madonna-gianes* to her grandmother and up to the people watching from above.

"Yes, little one, there are the *boshmengros*!" a deep male voice called down. From the audience, Uncle Petrus came forward. He raised his injured hand, snapping his fingers. "Summon the *boshmengros*!"

Distantly, came the sweet sound of a fiddle being struck to life and then another and another.

Alessandra smiled broadly. "Ah! I have missed that! Come, husband. Come dance with me."

"First, greet your grandmother," the *Fata* insisted.

The *Beluni* looked from the fairy to her granddaughter made new again then she looked at the granddaughter who had made it possible. Weeping, the *Beluni* drew both of her granddaughters into an embrace and when they broke apart, she held both granddaughters' hands and held them up to the people above.

XXIX

"It is in the character of very few men to honor without envy a friend who has prospered."
—Aeschylus, *Agamemnon*

24 d'Febbraio, 1685

PIERRO reclined on the chaise in the receiving room of the suite he shared with his wife. He was making a study of looking relaxed while reading. Internally, however, he chaffed at the ever-present guards . . . two inside, another pair at the outer door in the hallway, and another pair standing outside in their patio area. Between his bodyguards and Ortensia's, he felt imprisoned! He needed to get away if for no other reason than his sanity, though he did have pressing issues that he needed to address with Caserta.

What *Magnus Inique* was doing was not enough. He could not believe the ill luck they had had! The Regent Guardian had been in their hands, yet somehow she had escaped! He wanted, nay, needed to know how she had managed to escape when she had been in the weaker position. The coded correspondence simply did not tell him all that he wanted to know. What training were new recruits getting, if any, to have let a woman with two newborns and a couple of family men escape them? How strong was the network? As for the Turks, it was impossible to send word to them even if he relayed the message through Caserta. Di Drago had militarized the entire coast of the heartland and sent regular sorties around the boot of the continental territories. His options were narrowing. He turned the page of his book and continued to ignore the bodyguards.

Ortensia came down the stairs and stopped in front of him. "Well?" she said.

Pierro looked up, at a loss for words. Ortensia clearly expected him to notice something, but for all the world, she looked much the same to him as she had this morning. "What a charming picture you make," he said in his sweetest voice as he set aside his book and moved his feet from the bottom of the chaise so that she could sit if she wished.

"Then you like my new riding clothes?" she asked, turning first one way and then the other.

Her body still showed the puffiness left over from her recent pregnancy, but she had hidden it fairly well beneath a dress of goldenrod Gypsy Silk, with white undergown and embroidery throughout the garment.

"You look wonderful, *mi amore*," Pierro said, rising to his feet to capture her hand and kiss it. "Are you going riding now?"

"Yes, I've been in seclusion long enough. I want the open air," Ortensia said. She made a face. "I am riding with Duchessa Rossi. Perhaps some time alone with Martina might convince her to change her mind about her position denying me the throne. What say you to that?"

Pierro had any number of things he would have liked to say to her, one being that this avenue was most likely pointless. Decisions had been reached and were not likely to be revisited, but if it pleased Ortensia to talk a little treason, he saw no reason he should stop her. "Be careful that you do not outshine her too much, my dear. She is a clothes horse of the first order."

Ortensia chuckled and tapped his cheek with her fan. "Aren't we as well, my treasure?" She sighed and looked around the room. "Well, if I'm off to ride, I'll need my bodyguards," she announced.

One of the Palazzo Guards by the inner door nodded and bowed. "I shall alert the other two men, Your Highness, and send someone for your mount."

"Be quick about it, then," Ortensia said. She dropped her fan on the nearest table and poured two glasses of wine. She sipped from one and handed the other to her husband.

Before the man could go, however, Pierro called him

back. “I’ll be staying in this afternoon and have a palazzo full of guards. I want my wife protected. The lot of you should go.”

“All of us, Your Highness? But the Lord Regent—”

“Is not being guarded by you. The Turks have struck close to us in Messina. I dare not let anything happen to my bride on what should only be an innocent ride. All of you are to escort her,” Pierro said. He ended the discussion by turning to Ortensia and addressing her. “Where do you plan to ride, my dove?”

Ortensia chuckled suggestively and came to stand with him. She touched her glass goblet to his. “I thought north and along the coastal road to Valencia and back. It won’t be as crowded with Palantini entourage and such there.”

Pierro nodded. “It’s a fair ride. Be sure to be home for dinner, *mi minuta*, so that I will have the pleasure of your company at the dinner and ball this evening. . . . And all the more reason for you to take the full company of bodyguards. The Turks could be anywhere!”

Ortensia’s expression soured somewhat, but she shook it off. “Let’s not talk of those beastly men! Though I appreciate your concern, *marito*, what of you? You would have no protection if all the guards came with me!”

“But I am content to stay here and there is a palazzo full of guards and the Escalade barracks but feet away. I shall be shall be fine!” Pierro reassured her in his most doting manner. “Please! Take the whole contingent—unless you believe that someone must stay to guard me against paper cuts?”

Ortensia laughed. Their senior bodyguard indicated that they were ready. Ortensia put down her goblet and retrieved her fan. She used the fan to stroke Pierro’s cheek and then they were gone.

Pierro rejoiced. That had been all too easy! Ortensia should go riding more often, he decided.

“What do you seek that I or one of our people cannot do for you?” Rodrigo Strozzini asked. “Going into the streets of Citteauroea is dangerous.”

Stefano looked across his desk at his bodyguard. “There

are some things that I wish to see and hear for myself. I've heard rumors of civil unrest, but is it truly unrest or fear in reaction to losing a king and queen, then having a major city attacked all within a couple of weeks' time?"

"But what can you expect to find in a single day's sortie?" Rodrigo protested.

"First, it will not be a sortie. I intend to take you and that will be sufficient. It would be more an outing than even an adventure if you must call it something. I have sat for two months, listening to the council of nobles and receiving reports from various stations of the Escalade. Today, *I* want to see and hear the people themselves.

"I want to buy a new primer for His Royal Highness, perhaps a gift for my wife, and these things cannot be done by someone else. I want to barter for my trade and hear what the common man thinks," Stefano said.

"No merchant will barter with you, Your Excellency. You can set your own prices and the merchant will gain from having sold goods to the Lord Regent," Rodrigo pointed out.

"Do they have to know I am Lord Regent? Can't I simply be Duca di Drago for the afternoon?" Stefano retorted, gathering his riding gloves and sidestepping the lord who now insisted on protecting him. "My wife has returned after two weeks away. She has seen misadventure, and I wish to find something that pleases her."

"Perhaps a bit of silk?" Strozzini suggested, planting himself *casually* in the doorway.

Stefano stopped and looked at Strozzini. "You seem to have forgotten that my wife is *the Araunya* of both houses of Gypsy Silk. She has no trouble acquiring silk of any type or color. As to the merchants and people knowing me . . . my visage is on no coin or emblem, and I have but this chain to set me apart. It is easily removed."

The bodyguard sighed, aware of his blunder. "I could have merchants come to you with their wares—"

"I cannot have a corner table in an alehouse where I can listen to the talk brought to me and as to them knowing me by my chain, I leave it behind. Now, the question is whether you will join me or if I go alone?"

"I will have someone prepare our horses," Rodrigo conceded.

"And I will be with you shortly. I must speak with Estensi and then the afternoon is ours!" Stefano said.

"Perhaps one of the other men-at-arms could join us, to hold the horses while you shop," Strozzini suggested.

"I think they still have hitching posts in the city, Rodrigo. Too many accompanying us would interfere with my plans." Stefano stopped when he took in Strozzini's expression. The man would follow him wherever he went. "Come, we are men of the world. Our lives are not restricted to the palazzo as much as was Alban's. Put yourself at peace. I will wear my best sword."

Strozzini hesitated a moment longer, looking as though he desperately wished to argue the point. He seemed to realize further arguments would be useless. He bowed and departed, no doubt to send for the horses.

Stefano pushed himself away from the desk, his thoughts turning to Luciana who had returned to her duties as Regent Guardian for the Royal Nursery, supervising the raising of a prince, three princesses and the deMedici child, as well as their own daughter. According to his beloved, Alessandra had done much to heal her wounds from the beating she had taken, but the bruises spoke volumes, and it made his blood run cold. He had every intent of buying her some little present to please her, but he also meant to learn more about *Magnus Inique* today. He was confident that Strozzini did all that he was able, but Stefano could not be satisfied leaving the matter in another man's hands. His wife, while traveling a Tyrrhian road and breaking no laws, had been set upon and this was simply not acceptable!

He stuffed his traveling mask into a pocket of his coat, folded his riding gloves over his belt, and removed the chain of his office which he placed in a drawer and locked. He glanced around the office. It had been weeks since he had stepped out of this place.

It occurred to him as he gathered some papers for Estensi that Don Battista, the nobleman who had first dared speak of *Magnus Inique* and even told of Pierro deMedici's consorting with known members, might be a handy person to have on this ride. He stopped and considered the thought for a time, then decided not. Battista was already in an unenviably vulnerable position, and it was important to keep him alive and safe so that he could testify when the time came. Besides that, Battista was marrying Giuletta in the morning and would have too many other concerns to concentrate his time or energies on espionage.

Estensi was absent from his office, so Stefano placed the papers for him in the center of his desk and headed outside, putting on his riding mask as he left the palazzo. The mask was meant to lend a certain amount of anonymity while he was out of the palazzo, but Strozzini cut a tall, lean, and fairly distinguishable figure. Stefano would be lucky if he were not recognized simply because of the royal bodyguard. At the doors of the palazzo, attending guards bowed deeply to him. Strozzini was already mounted on a dun gelding and held the reins to his own iron-metal dappled horse, Fascino.

Stefano mounted easily and took a moment to relish the feel of a horse moving beneath him again. He started off to Citteauroea at a gallop, passing through the gate at the end of the palazzo drive with a shout to the palazzo guards who manned it. A good distance down the road to the capital city and in sight of another rider, Stefano pulled up Fascino and let Strozzini catch up to him.

Squinting forward, the bodyguard covered his eyes with his hand and sighed. "Isn't that the prince up ahead?" he asked Stefano.

"I think it is, and, if I'm not mistaken, he has stopped his horse . . . more interestingly, where are his bodyguards?" Stefano said, making a great show of studying his boot.

Strozzini stiffened in the saddle, pulled one of his scorpininis, loaded it, and rested it on the saddle fork in front of him. "I know he joined us that morning to make sure the king died," he said.

"Ah, but you have no proof and there is the crux."

Lord Strozzini bowed his head. "He's dangerous. He'd have you dead if he could."

"Perhaps, but I'm not willing to oblige him, so let's not put him at our backs, shall we?" Stefano said, pasting a pleasant look on his face as they caught up with the prince. "What, ho! Is that you, Your Highness?"

Strozzini scowled, slowing his horse so that he rode a little behind the higher-ranking noblemen.

Pierro deMedici slowed his mount until Stefano caught up as he rode toward the city. "What takes you to the *citta* this fine day?" he asked in a pleasant, though distant voice.

He moved his horse farther toward the side of the road when his mount took a snapping bite at Fascino.

Stefano watched the prince's horse mouth at the bit, shake his head, arch his neck, and strain against the reins. Pierro was going to ruin the horse's mouth and then it would be good for nothing but stud which was a fine enough thing for an Arabian, he guessed. "Just looking for something for my *amorata*," Stefano said with a lackadaisical shrug. He glanced over his shoulder and saw that Strozzini rode an arm's reach and half a length behind. "What takes you to Citteauroea, deMedici? And without your guards?"

"I no longer have the services of the don, so, alas, I must perform my own errands," the prince said with a laugh, "and the guards are with my wife. This was a last-minute decision to leave the palazzo. I think if we ride in one another's company with Lord Strozzini at our backs, that we should be safe."

"Surely one of the servants— " Stefano began, trying to keep his tone light.

"Would not do. They are always getting lost or misdirecting my correspondence, even losing it on two occasions," Pierro concluded. They rode in silence for several moments. Stefano glanced back at Lord Strozzini who remained ever vigilant. "It would be easier to see your bodyguard if he just rode alongside us." The prince's tone was cuttingly acerbic.

Stefano motioned for Strozzini to move up beside them. He noted that Lord Strozzini kept maneuvering room between them, so that he had plenty of room to break away if Stefano felt the need to escape. Apparently, thinking of such things was both effective and commonplace for the bodyguard who was clearly taking few chances in the company of Prince deMedici.

"I see you have employed the king's bodyguard . . . much good *he* did King Alban or Queen Idala," Pierro observed.

"A man is worthy of his work," Stefano replied. "And an assassin hidden in the shrubs on the far side of a river is easy to miss."

"I *am* the Royal Bodyguard," Lord Strozzini said, somehow remaining calm despite the insult.

"If your mission is to protect the Royals, then you should be tending to my bride . . . if I would have you," Pierro said.

"My *mission*, as you call it, is to protect the leader of Tyrrhia. *Princess* Ortensia is not queen."

"No. No, she's not," Pierro said meaningfully, looking over at Stefano who rode between them. "So have you had any luck finding this group of yours, Strozzini?"

"*Magnus Inique*," Strozzini replied, somehow keeping his voice indifferent in the face of Pierro's goading. "They share your sentiments, I understand."

"Do they?" deMedici asked lightly. "And what sentiments are those? And, indeed, how would you know? You haven't found even one to question, have you?"

"I have been taking advantage of speaking to the Palantini while they are in residence," Strozzini continued.

"It doesn't seem to have taken you far toward making an arrest," deMedici observed.

It was all Stefano could do not to drive Fascino into deMedici's horse. It would give the prince something more to do than toy with the bodyguard. Instead, he edged his steed into a ground-eating trot, forcing the other men to hurry to keep up.

Strozzini, however, seemed unwilling to let the subject go. Once caught up, he moved a little past Stefano and looked back at deMedici who kept to the Lord Regent's side. "I've gotten further along than you might think," he said. "You'd be surprised what so many of the Palantini know."

"I'd be surprised if they knew anything considering how they treated Ortensia and myself," Pierro retorted. He waved ahead. "And we've reached the city. I must leave you now to run my errands!" With that, Pierro gave his black stallion a kick of the heel and they jetted forward, into the narrow streets of the city.

Lord Strozzini stopped his horse and stared angrily after the prince.

"Go ahead and follow him," Stefano urged, drawing up his gray at the side of Strozzini's golden-brown-and-black mount.

The bodyguard shook his head. "I'll not leave your side. We know that the prince is in the city and he may double back."

Stefano controlled his urge to sigh. "Then let us give him a few minutes, and *we* will see where he is going."

Strozzini considered. "We could find an Escalade vigilare and he could take over . . ."

Stefano shook his head. "Now *I* am curious where he's going. Let's be off before he finds some way to dodge us!"

They found it easy to follow the skittering black steed of the prince. It drew attention to him wherever the deMedici tried to go. After some time wrestling unsuccessfully with his horse, he just continued on his way. When he turned a corner, though, Pierro would stop to see if he was being followed. Stefano and Strozzini passed him casually on a side road, then doubled back onto Pierro's trail.

Stefano made sure to hang back or, periodically, send Lord Strozzini up ahead alone so that he looked like a single rider rather than part of a pair, which irritated the bodyguard each time he had to leave Stefano's side.

The prince made his way through side streets, never going to the city center, but skirting it, until they reached the southwestern corner of Citteauroea. When he had assured himself once again that he was not being followed, deMedici dismounted and led his horse up to a taverna. He hitched his stallion alone, to a free post away from the other patrons' horses.

Stefano dismounted and tossed Fascino's reins to Strozzini as he made his way into the darkened taverna. From his travels and by his nose, he guessed the establishment concentrated on food from Greece. He removed his traveling mask and slipped into the common room, his eyes adjusting to the muted light. A server passed by bearing a tray with bowls of *pastitsio* and *souvlaki* confirming Stefano's guess.

"There," Strozzini said, nodding his head in the direction of the back, least-lit, table.

Stefano followed his gaze and spotted Prince Pierro sitting with a table full of commoners. He sucked in his breath, recognizing one of the men. It was the idiot who had confronted him in the street when he brought Luciana to the city weeks ago. He grabbed Strozzini's arm and ducked down at a nearby table, waving off a helpful server who came in their direction.

"Let's go! I think he saw us," Stefano said. Staying low he made his way into the bright light of the city street. "Where are the horses?"

Strozzini glanced over his shoulder, back toward the taverna they had ducked out of, and pointed to their horses tied to a post across the street. They mounted and hurried on their way, looking back for sign of the prince in the doorway of the taverna.

Stefano guided his horse toward the city center, confident that the bodyguard would be close behind. He dismounted again and let Fascino trail behind him. Lord Strozzini caught up to him quickly, being the taller man and able to see through the crowds more easily.

"Did you see who he was with?"

The bodyguard nodded, looking unsure. "He was with commoners—"

"No," Stefano said, stopping and facing Strozzini. "He was with the man from the crowd that attacked us when we came last with Luciana."

Rodrigo frowned, then suddenly turned it into a nod. "I recognize him now. Shall we get the vigilare and go back?"

"Will he even be there?" Stefano asked with a shrug. "Let us just leave with the knowledge of what the prince is doing. He is in league with at least one man who had no hesitation to attack me—"

"*After* you became Lord Regent," Rodrigo said. "I've not been able to stop all the plotting at the palazzo because I haven't stopped the prince."

Stefano grabbed the other man's arm. "Don't listen to the taunts of fools."

Strozzini's jaw tightened, but he nodded as though listening. "The prince, however, is no man to be taken lightly."

"Quite obviously," Stefano agreed. "I would not give deMedici the upper hand by showing our distrust. Let him suspect. It's his nature to do that in any case, but let us not give him cause to know."

"'Tis a good path you choose, Your Excellency," Strozzini said and took another look over his shoulder. "If anyone follows us, then it is one of the ones we do not recognize. We do not seem to have anyone behind us. Do you still need to hear the people, or do you have a good sense now of who riles them?"

Stefano released his pent-up breath. "No need to sit in a dark corner of an alehouse now, but let me find my gifts and then we can return to the palazzo. We can talk to the merchants and gauge the people's happiness by them and we can keep an eye out for spies."

Reaching the city square, Stefano began pausing to look

at the knickknacks and pretty things to be found on the handcarts, booths, and storefronts of the vendors. He found a perfume he liked, then discarded it. Luciana made her own scents when she used them. At a handcart, Stefano found a jeweler with cameos of various fashions. He selected a few, paid, and moved on, dropping the brooches into his pocket. For his part, Rodrigo stayed vigilant, never looking bored or impatient while Stefano shopped. Stefano found a bookseller and bought several volumes, some for Luciana, some for himself, and a couple of primers for Prince Dario. While the vendor wrapped the books, Stefano turned to Strozzini.

"I am going to the old witch's shop next . . . to pick up some supplies for my wife. You can go for the Escalade while I'm there. If you leave now, I should be just done with my purchases and—"

"Your Excellency," the bodyguard said in a loud whisper, just enough to be heard over the other shoppers and vendors, "I told you I would not leave your side. We will visit the vigilare together to get an escort home. I'm sorry to take your time with such endeavors, but it is now more important than ever that I—"

"Have made your point," Stefano said after waving the other man to silence. "It's this way."

They found several horses already at the first post in front of Nunzia Rui's store, The Dragon's Hearth. Stefano used the second post and tied up Fascino. He was about to tell the bodyguard to wait with the horses when they heard a scream from within the shop. Rodrigo vaulted from his saddle—without tying up his gelding—and raced Stefano through the doors, sword drawn and at the ready.

Stefano followed Strozzini into the store and jerked him out of the way just in time to avoid being hit by falling jars and boxes from the apothecary shelves by the door. He ducked a thrown piece of glassware and jumped back into the room, skidding across the slats of the shelf, driving his left shoulder into the man who had just attacked them. He felt a hand on his back as he stood, so he shoved his elbow back in the vicinity of what he hoped was the other man's ribs. Stefano winced when he heard Strozzini groan.

"It's me!" the bodyguard called. "No one else on your back."

"Thanks," Stefano said, dodging a hasty sword swipe in

his direction. He sidestepped and dragged his foot so that he tripped the man now heading in Strozzini's direction. "Heads up!"

Jumping to avoid the low swing by the next swordsman, Stefano knocked the man's knife strike out of reach. He noted the man coming down the stairs along the back wall of the shop and heard the thunder of feet as someone ran across the floor above him. "Two more!" he yelled over his shoulder. "One on the stairs, the other on the floor above!"

He dodged another blow from the swordsman and caught the first man down the stairs, sticking him clean through as he jumped over the witch's counter. Stefano took a second too long to make sure the man from the stair would fall, and lashed out belatedly with his rapier catching his opponent's sword just in time to knock the other man's blade into his shoulder instead of his heart. He grunted and struck out with his knife hand. He caught his opponent in the jaw, the blade dragging along the lower part of his face.

His opponent reeled away, grabbing his jaw and pulling his sword free of Stefano as he moved. The man on the floor clutched at Stefano's ankle. Stefano kicked the hand away and stuck the man again with his rapier, piercing him through the heart. A part of him regretted the death, but the swordsman in him could not let him dwell on it. His scarred opponent was back and at him.

Stefano parried with his rapier, knocking the other man's rapier from his hand, and lashed out with his knife, narrowly missing him as the braggadocio dove for his sword. He managed to kick the rapier away before the other man could reach it. The fourth man reached the bottom of the stairs and came roaring at him. This fourth was the big man Stefano had faced before and only recently seen in congress with Pierro. He was better with the sword than either man Stefano had already faced.

Not liking his back to the big man, Stefano danced away and backed up to the shelves against the wall, unfortunately giving his first opponent a chance to arm himself by grabbing his rapier from where it had skittered under the fallen shelf and struggling to his feet.

Stefano was obliged to dodge the first man's flashing blade and parry the big man's downward strike with knife and rapier. The bigger man was a brute, driving down with his blade until Stefano felt his knees start to give. He also heard a muzzle blast. The jar next to his head erupted into shatters, raining dried herbs throughout the area.

The big man coughed and sneezed, backing away from Stefano so that he could not be reached. "Where were you?" the man yelled at the man beyond the door.

Before the gunman could answer, Strozzini kicked the door behind him shut . . . unfortunately, it was a half-door, leaving the man free to bludgeon Strozzini with his weapon. The bodyguard slumped to the ground.

"I was around the corner," the gunman replied.

"Get your sword and get in here!" the big man ordered.

"Strozzini!" Stefano yelled, hoping against hope that the bodyguard was only stunned.

The gunman, a much younger man than the other four, waded into the store with the confidence of life-everlasting blowing hot wind in his sails. Strozzini stirred but did not rise, forcing Stefano to reconsider his options. Instead of striking, he climbed onto the counter and swung by a plain chandelier over to the other side.

The old witch lay crumpled in a broken heap on the floor. A woman screamed as she came into the store behind the gunman, turned, and ran away. Stefano noticed another woman crouched underneath the stairs, hands over her bonneted head. Everywhere around his feet were glass-and-clay shards, making his footing difficult. Why had the others not seemed to struggle to keep their ground, but come wading into things with nary a problem?

The *bravo* Strozzini had battled threw open the hinged counter and shoved his way into the back of the shop.

"Get out here and help me if you want to live!" Stefano yelled at the woman under the stair.

"We intend to let her live!" the man behind the counter said. He glanced down toward the woman, waving his sword to keep Stefano away as he spoke, "*If* she doesn't help you."

"I'm not helping!" the woman protested.

"But *I* am!" Rodrigo staggered to his feet and took on the young man who was nearest him. Stefano was never so glad to see a man standing in his life . . . which, truth be told, centered around these last humbling few minutes. Strozzini let out a cry as a sword pierced his right side—from out of doors. Unbelievably, a sixth man had joined the fray. Strozzini twisted, dragging the other man's blade free of his wound, and shoved the man in the face to push him back out the door. He slammed the upper door shut and put his back up against the corner.

The big man grinned. He jumped to the counter and lashed out with his rapier.

Stefano jumped back, putting the underside of the stairs to his back. He glanced down at the woman. "Don't help me, but whatever you do, don't help them!"

The young woman held up her hands in complete resignation.

"What would you do about it even if you lived long enough?" the big braggadocio laughed, jumping down to the floor from the counter. Glass and clay crunched beneath the weight of him.

Stefano considered his options. Strozzini was struggling to deal with the two men by the door, leaving two men for him on each side of the counter. The big man was closest. He lashed out to the left upper quadrant of his assailant and swung wide to strike at Strozzini's original opponent with his knife. He succeeded in striking the man, slashing across the man's chest with a raking cut that would have caused a lesser man to back away.

The giant's next strike grazed Stefano's hairline as he ducked out of the way and his left hand swiped at him. Stefano danced back and took a hit in the head from the stairs when he rose up too quickly. The wooden stairs echoed with the knock to his head. Stefano narrowly parried Strozzini's first opponent with his knife. The rapier caught his wrist and slid up his arm. He could hear the tearing of cloth and felt the sting of a cut up to his elbow.

Stefano dove at the counter, knocking back the muttering braggadocio when he, too, would have clambered over the counter, but it left his back open to the two men behind him. He took a jaw-cracking punch to the face from the closer man, which blocked the way of Strozzini's man.

Staggering back, Stefano caught the stairs overhead with his wounded arm, his knife hand. Reflexively, he threw his knife without thinking. He almost got struck when the big man lunged at him again, because he was staring in amazement at the knife which had sunk its way into the other man's throat. That trick had never worked the way he intended! How it had worked this time, Stefano put down to sheer luck.

The big man was fast for his size. He snatched the fallen man's sword into his left hand, having to shake it loose from the dying man's grasping fingers. He hefted the sword, so that he was now armed with the two rapiers.

Stefano looked at his remaining opponent, grinning as though in some sort of fiendish delight. He struck out with a thrusting blow to the big man's midriff. The other man easily parried, but skidded in his footwork on the uneven floor.

Stefano took advantage of the time element given him. He grabbed the upper balustrade and swung himself up and over it. He instantly regretted it. The stairs and upper balustrade were littered with layers of women's clothing. While the big man regained his footing and one of the other men came through the counter, he took the moment to kick the center of the stairs clear, stuffing the wardrobe onto either side. By the time the big man stepped up two stairs, leaning in with a momentum-driven stab at his midsection, Stefano was ready with a sliding parry that drove down the man's sword up his arm and into his shoulder.

The big man winced and dropped back a step. Stefano pressed his advantage, following his opponent down. He lunged, twisting his sword so that the tip of the blade sidestruck the big man's parry and drove home, sliding neatly under the big man's right arm and into his chest by way of his armpit. This time, Stefano's opponent let out a guttural groan and jumped back from the stairwell altogether. From the run of blood, it looked like a mortal wound, but Stefano knew better than to trust that.

Keeping to the stair, Stefano sprang forward—he, two steps from the ground floor—finally finding himself at face level with his big opponent. He used a sky-blue, velvet overgown as a feinting tool, swiping away the big man's swords with the dress and slashing at the man's throat.

The big *bravo* dodged the blow to his throat, then leaned forward to strike at Stefano's legs. Frustrated, Stefano threw the dress at the big man's head and succeeded in tangling him in the lengths of cloth. He gripped the hilt of his rapier and drove the basket-hilt as hard as he could muster into the big man's jaw. He stared in amazement as his opponent rocked on his feet and dropped to the floor like a stone. Apparently, it was better to be lucky in this fight than just good.

He yelped in surprise, jumping away, when he felt a pain in his ankle. Stefano looked down and found that the second man behind the counter had stabbed him through the stairs. Reflexively, he stepped down on the man's blade.

This opponent cried for help, trying and failing to completely withdraw his sword from beneath Stefano's weight. Stefano pulled the rapier from beneath his foot when his opponent quit tugging. He stabbed the floor with his sword and reached for the hilt. With a sword in each hand, Stefano slashed the air, testing the new blade's worth. He grinned and turned to face his opponent, noting that Strozzini had just dispatched his second *braggadocio*, but in the confusion it seemed the young gunman had seized the opportunity to escape. Hopefully, he would be found before he could bring further trouble upon them.

Stefano limped down the stair, catching the unarmed man as he reached for one of the big man's swords. With his blades crossing at the last man's neck, Stefano shook his head. "I would rather you didn't."

The last man seemed to debate his alternatives and slowly, raised his empty hands. "I surrender. Don't kill me!"

"Wise choice," Strozzini said, prodding the man in his back.

"Hold!"

With blades still poised to strike, Stefano looked toward the door and Strozzini turned to face the newcomers. Stefano relaxed at the sight of the vigilare in dress Escalade uniforms, their swords drawn.

"I am Colonello of the Escalade *e* Duca di Drago, Lord Regent of Tyrrhia. Arrest this man and detain the one on the floor there before he wakes up!" Stefano commanded. He looked over at the old witch, Nunzia Rui. "And send for a chirurgeon. We have a fallen woman who might be served by—"

"It's no use," came a trembling, feminine voice from beneath the stair. "She is gone . . . and I will have to truly learn the business now."

Stefano lowered his swords, staring in amazement at the

stairs where the woman huddled. This woman was some kind of relation to the old witch and, at this time, with the crone laying but feet away, she worried about the business she was inheriting?

Without the swords at his throat, the unarmed man moved desperately toward the window.

"I don't think you should consider that," Strozzini said, pressing his sword against the man's spine through his jacket. He turned to glance in the direction of the Escalade guards. "Are you going to arrest this man or continue staring at him while he makes his escape?"

The officer amongst the vigilare nodded and one of his men broke away from the contingent bearing shackles.

The big man on the floor groaned and stirred.

"He will not be as easy to detain if you don't get him locked up before he's fully awake," Stefano warned.

The officer nodded again, then pointed at two more men and Stefano and Strozzini.

Without hesitation, Stefano dropped the swords and raised his hands. "You'll find that neither my companion nor I will give you any trouble, just *please* don't shackle us."

"It's procedure, Signore. While I appreciate your—" the lieutenant began.

"I *am* who I claim," Stefano said. He nodded to the other man. "This is Lord Rodrigo Strozzini, my bodyguard . . . the *Royal* bodyguard."

"Do you have credentials? Identification of some sort?" the officer asked, looking hopeful.

"No, what need I of those?" Stefano asked, feeling very foolish for not having any. "You, Signore, are young in your career so you do not recognize me from my service in the Escalade. Do not risk your career by arresting the Lord Regent."

"He might not do anything to you, but *I'd* see to it that you were harassed out of the service," Strozzini said. "Ask the woman. We came late to this . . . this party. We were trying to give aid to the proprietress and, well, things got rather messy."

The officer turned three shades of red. "I do not like to be threatened—"

"Then ask the woman, dammit!" Strozzini said impatiently.

The woman came out from under the stairs, her bonnet and dress askew, looking the worse for wear. She knuckled her eyes. "I don't know who they are," she declared.

Stefano sighed and bowed his head.

"What's your name, Signorina?" the officer asked. He clambered over the fallen shelves and met her at the counter where he offered her his handkerchief.

"I—I am Emilia Rui. The old woman . . ." Emilia buried her face in the borrowed handkerchief. "The proprietress was my aunt. I am her only living relative."

"Is what these men have said true? Did they come late to . . . this destruction?" the officer asked kindly.

"All I know is that these men," she took the time to wave at the men on the floor, "came into the store and began breaking things and upending our wardrobes. These two," she nodded to Stefano and Strozzini, "came in late, but others fighting with the first men came in after them as well."

"Wait!" the officer said, laying a placating hand on her shoulder. "These others who came late . . . whose part did they take in the fight?"

Emilia shook her head, tendrils of her hair escaped from the fichu she wore on her head. "There were swords everywhere, so I ducked beneath the stairs. I don't know for sure."

The last standing opponent pinched his mouth shut tight.

"I was rough with her when defending her. I did not want her attacking me in the confusion. It wasn't particularly kind of me to make her feel threatened, but so did these other men," Stefano said.

"These 'others' . . . the ones who are dead and cannot speak?" the officer asked.

Stefano sighed. "You have two men to question. We did not—and would not—have killed them. We think they have something to do with *Magnus Inique* and might know something about the assassination of King Alban."

"And you would *not* have killed them?" the officer asked archly.

"Well, they would be held for trial by the Palantini, which is in session as we speak," Stefano said.

"Pshaw," the Escalade officer snorted. "Everyone within fifty miles is well aware that the Palantini is in session. Try again."

Stefano closed his eyes in frustration. "Send for your officer-in-charge. Hopefully, he will recognize me . . . and if not him, then do you know the Duca Gianola who lives on the outskirts of town?"

The officer nodded. He turned to his last man and said, "Get the maggiore from the barracks and send for the duca. We'll settle this one way or another."

"Thank you," Stefano said and sat on the stairs. His body was beginning to ache from his various wounds. Strozzini came to his side. "Are you well, Your Excellency? You are quite bloodied."

"Thank you," Stefano told the bodyguard. "I don't have any idea what I would have done without you. Are you hurt?"

"Only a couple of flesh wounds, Your Excellency," Strozzini said dismissively.

Stefano took a look at his man, for he now was truly *his*. He owed Rodrigo his life. If he had tried to take on six men—with one of them being a gunman—he most assuredly would have been taken, if by nothing else but sheer numbers. He shuddered to think of it. Surely, these men would have no reason to let him live, once he was held captive, and with Pierro's influence he counted their resources as all lethal.

The bodyguard had a bleeding wound to his left side. A cut on his right cheek had ceased to bleed overly much and his suit coat was full of well-placed pricks about his torso and hips.

"You should see a chirurgeon, yourself," Stefano commented.

"Only after you have consulted with *il dottore* Bonta. Then I will confer with my physician," Strozzini assured him, folding his arms over his chest.

"Lieutenant d'Este, what is this all about?" the commanding bark of an older man demanded.

Stefano closed his eyes and buried his face in his hands.

"What is it, Your Excellency?" Rodrigo asked, leaning urgently in his direction.

"If I'm not mistaken, I recognize that voice . . . and we were *never* friends—" Stefano said. The officer came into the store, sidestepping the broken shelves and pottery. Immediately, Stefano rose, throwing his arms open as though welcoming a boon companion. "Egidio? Is that you? After all these years?"

The maggiore looked immediately confused and stepped back. He gave a tight smile and waved Stefano off. "My uniform, Your Excellency. You understand?"

Stefano dismissed the other man's retreat with a friendly smile.

"Your Excellency? Then what he said was true?" the lieutenant asked in a dazed voice.

"Well, it would depend upon what His Excellency said, wouldn't it?" the maggiore grimaced a halfhearted smile at him.

"He claimed to be the Lord Regent... I mean, he doesn't look like a churchman to me," the lieutenant babbled.

The maggiore bobbed a bow to Stefano and addressed his subordinate officer. "Of course, His Grace is no churchman—"

"His Grace or His Excellency?" the lieutenant asked, obviously confused.

"Both, actually," Stefano said to the young officer. He offered the man his hand in friendship.

Instead of shaking his hand, the younger man, d'Este, bowed low. "Please forgive me for not knowing... for not recognizing you, Your Excellency."

Stefano shook his head. "You are very correct. You did not... could not... recognize a man you had never seen or known before. Think nothing further of it."

"You are very forgiving, Your Excellency," Strozzini said sternly, indicating clearly by his tone that he would not have been.

"It's not as if my face is, nor is it likely to be on *soldibiancos*... nor a drawing of me put up with the other warrants and faces you've seen," Stefano retorted, focusing his energies on the maggiore and his lieutenant.

The maggiore, Egidio, seemed to brighten a little at the idea of a drawing of him being on the Watch List posting at the barracks. "Perhaps there should be a drawing of you in the various barracks around Tyrrhia. That way you could travel without worrying about being mistaken for someone else."

Stefano shook his head. "No. My face would be too familiar to officers... and their men. There would undoubtedly be mistakes, and I would find myself detained everywhere I went."

"That *would* be unfortunate," Lieutenant d'Este agreed.

The maggiore's hopeful expression soured rapidly, then he focused on the business at hand. He was, after all, a senior member of the Escalade.

"I need to press upon you further," Stefano said. He felt dizzy and his shoulder felt like it was on fire. "I must take these men back to the palazzo with me. I'll need the lieutenant to come there tomorrow to testify before the Palantini . . . and one more thing. I'll need a contingent of men to escort us back home. I have reason to believe that we may be attacked again on the way and, as you can see, I and my man, here, are rather the worse for wear."

"Do you need a chirurgeon—"

"What, ho? I say, what the devil am I doing to be brought here and, no, young man, I will not step inside this place where witches are known to frequent!" protested a familiar voice. "Your Excellency? What are you doing—Are you well?"

Stefano looked down at his rather ragged appearance. "I'm sorry, Your Grace. I asked that you be a witness on my behalf that I am, indeed, the Lord Regent."

"Good heavens! Of course, he's the Lord Regent," Duca Gianola declared. "Get him a chirurgeon . . . and a barber to bleed him . . . and . . ."

Stefano raised his hand. "In the meanwhile, Your Grace, since sending for you, the maggiore here was good enough to identify me. We served together for a time in the Escalade. I, of course, have retired from service, but the maggiore has dedicated his lifework to the Escalade."

"So I am not needed?" Gianola asked, looking at the two men who had rushed him from his home.

"You were needed, until the maggiore identified me, but you would have already been on your way here. I apologize for the inconvenience," Stefano said.

"You," the duca pointed at the man who had been trying to get him to enter the store, "will get my horse . . . and, Maggiore, you *will*, at the very least, get the Lord Regent *un dottore* in the next few minutes before he falls on his face. It will be on your head if he has trouble reaching his wife in short order."

Stefano winced at the thought of what his wife would, or could do to the maggiore and himself when she saw the wounds on his body. He rubbed his forehead. "Yes, perhaps you *should* call on a chirurgeon," he finally agreed, already regretting it even knowing that Luciana would expect him to seek medical attention before he came home to her. "And I mentioned the contingent to assist us to the palazzo?"

"It is being taken care of as we speak, Your Excellency," the maggiore said, waving one of the men away from the body and toward the door. "My man will, of course, be on his way and at a hurry to the nearest *dottore* he can find."

Outside, at least one of the prisoners began causing trouble with the guard who stood watch over him. Careful of not losing his footing on the shards of glassware and pottery, Stefano limped around the broken shelving and out the door. Finding both culprits arguing with their guard, he looked at each man narrowly.

"Do you *want* to arrive at the palazzo for judgment slung over the back of a horse like a sack of flour?" he asked.

The *bravo* with the cut jaw looked away. The big man met his gaze with a hostile glare. "You only caught me because you bashed me unconscious," the big man said.

Stefano grinned. "It doesn't matter what state you were in. You were taken, and you'll die before you get a chance to escape judgment if I have to kill you myself."

"You couldn't," the big man taunted.

"I might surprise you, *viscido*," Stefano retorted. "Don't tempt me . . . or my man, if you wish to live . . . at least long enough for the trial before the Palantini."

"You cannot put me on trial! I demand to be taken to the Bishop of Citteauroea," the man with the cut jaw said.

"Eh, Caserta, what about me?" the big man asked his cohort.

"Now you've given him my name. Fool!" the one referred to as Caserta snapped.

"Fine," the braggadocio retorted. He looked from Caserta to Stefano. "He wants the bishop because he's a priest!"

"Fool!" Caserta repeated and kicked his accomplice in the shin.

The big man responded to the attack by ramming his head into the other prisoner's face. Caserta yowled in pain, his nose broken by the head bash and the gash Stefano had given to his jawline started to bleed again. The prisoner was a mess of gushing blood and curses upon "Enzo."

The big man, Enzo, allowed himself to be pulled away from his partner in crime, making rude gestures at the "priest," if this Enzo were telling the truth. It would also explain why Caserta thought the bishop might be able or willing to protect him.

"Vigilare, shackle their feet and get someone to help you with them," Stefano ordered.

"Yes, Signore!" the young sergeant agreed. He called to one of his fellows to assist him.

Stefano nodded while looking down at his aching ankle. He was lucky today, indeed. Caserta had narrowly missed hamstringing him and that would never have healed properly. He limped back into the store, skirting the shelves and carefully made his way back to the stairs, bringing a watchful Strozzini with him.

"Sit, Rodrigo," Stefano bade, noticing the blood pools on the bodyguard's jacket had only gotten larger. When Strozzini started to refuse, he simply intimated a stair and pointedly took another one.

Sitting felt much better than standing. He started to bury his face in his hands but noticed the maggiore approaching, so he sat up.

"Your Excellency, *il dottore* should be here momentarily. I must return to the guard post to order a fresh unit to accompany you back to the palazzo. The post is only a short distance away, so it should take no time at all for the men to join you," the maggiore said, bowing.

"Thank you," Stefano said with a deep nod.

The maggiore turned on his heel and made his way out of the store. He swept the shards of glass and pottery out of the way with his foot as he went.

Il dottore arrived on the heels of the maggiore's exit. A corpulent man in his late fifties or early sixties, *il dottore* had Lieutenant d'Este point him to where he was most wanted. Of course, the young officer indicated Stefano was to be first.

Stefano started to protest that Strozzini's side wound was more dire than any of his injuries, but stopped when the bodyguard shook his head, looking away. Clearly, there was no way Strozzini would tolerate attention to himself when the Lord Regent was injured in any way. There were times when he hated being Regent and this was one of them. As a senior officer, he was more accustomed to seeing that the least of his men were taken care of before he entertained a *dottore* or chirurgeon himself.

"You should come back to my home. I have a plaster already mixed—" *il dottore* began.

Stefano shook his head. "Just see to it that the bleeding has stopped and then attend my man here."

"But the best way to tend—"

"We will consult the *il dottore reale* when we reach the palazzo. I intend to get us there before dark and it is a good ride from here, the day is already late," Stefano countermanded.

"But—"

"*Il dottore* Bonta will want to inspect His Excellency's wounds himself anyway and would only pry up a perfectly good plaster to examine it," Strozzini said amiably. "Please, *dottore*, just do as the Lord Regent has bid you."

"The Lord Regent?" the doctor breathed looking at Stefano with new eyes. He turned to the lieutenant who hovered nearby. The young man nodded urgently, giving the doctor a slight push in Stefano's direction.

Stefano, however, was more aware of Signora Rui's small body being lifted onto a litter. He excused himself and got up to see the old woman's body. He asked the guards to pause as he looked Rui over. Now that she lay on her back, with her face in full view, Stefano saw what the other Rui woman had apparently seen. The entire right side of Nunzia's face had been caved in with what appeared to be a single blow. At least her end had come quickly, he thought as he waved the guards on with their sorrowful duties. He returned to *il dottore*'s attentions.

The sky was already darkening when the old doctor finished with them and tended to the wounds of the prisoners. Anxious to be home, Stefano mounted Fascino while Strozzini was reunited with his horse, found wandering a street over. Their prisoners, Stefano had mounted sidesaddle on the military saddles of the horses brought for them. It would be an uncomfortable ride for the men, but Stefano did not particularly care.

"Lieutenant d'Este, see that you are at the palazzo by nine in the morning. The Palantini gathers about then," Stefano reminded the young man as he gathered Fascino's reins.

"I'll be there," the lieutenant promised with a salute and a bow.

Stefano sighed. Such was the duty of privilege to accept the acknowledgments. He wondered, as he started off, how Alban had endured it all the years, because his instinct, like Stefano's, was to defer the overly formal salutes even though they had both been raised to expect them. Perhaps it was their shared time in the military service of the Queen's Escalade? Whatever it was, he would have to adjust. It was part of the job he had been forced to assume.

He watched the roadside as he led the party back to the palazzo. Thinking of Luciana, he touched the pocket where he had placed the cameos and was frustrated to find a large rip. Stefano patted about the inside of what was left of the pocket and discovered two cameos remained. The others were gone, lost somewhere during the fight or jangled out of the pocket on the ride home. He stopped Fascino and dug around, looking in the other pocket of his jacket to see if they would be safe there. He discovered another rip in his second pocket and turned to put them in his saddle sack with the books, only stopping when he saw movement in the field short of the woods that bordered much of the road.

"Hold!" Stefano called out, dropping the cameos in the bag. "I see movement there, in the field." He pointed to what he now saw was a black, saddled horse. Pierro's stallion?

A vigilare broke away from their group and rode out to the stallion which would have reared away, but something or someone on the ground held the reins securely. As the Escalade guard dismounted, Stefano recognized Pierro as he began to sit up, holding his head. The prince rose swiftly and leaned against his mount for support.

A head injury, yet he rose quickly, Stefano thought.

As though signaled, men broke from the forest on either side of Stefano and the party on the road.

"It's a trap!" Strozzini yelled. He slapped Stefano's horse hard on the rear, causing Fascino to bolt.

Stefano wrangled Fascino under control within a

hundred yards and wheeled back on the road to see his party arming themselves as a dozen or so men on either side closed in. He ducked automatically at the sound of cracking pistola fire. He felt the burn of hot shot hitting his left side. Fascino let out a loud cry, rearing. The horse had been hit, too. One of the young vigilare fell from his mount as it bolted for home.

Pulling a scorpinini from a tether on his saddle, Stefano—reins in his teeth—brought it up, braced the large pistola-sized crossbow against his stomach, and pulled back the strings. He took a bolt from its quiver position at the points on his left sleeve and loaded the steel-levered scorpinini. He gave Fascino the heel, and his mount sprang forward into the fray.

Stefano took as careful aim as he could from horseback and shot. The man he had took aim at, in process of reloading his wheel-lock pistola, took the bolt in the throat rather than in the chest, but in either case, he fell from his horse. The dropped pistola hit the ground and fired off its shot, startling several horses.

Dropping the scorpinini to the ground, Stefano pulled his sword and closed the last bit of distance. Without compunction, he struck the first two men he encountered from the back. This was no battle of honor, but one of life and death, and many of his men were still very young and green and had not faced such a battle before.

One of the men Stefano slashed, arched his back and cried out as he fell from his horse. The other turned from attacking Strozzini and focused his attention on him instead. The bodyguard's sword flashed in the moonlight and pierced the man from behind. The sword tip punctured its victim all the way through, coming out of the right side of his chest. When the man fell forward, it jerked the sword from Strozzini's hand, leaving him defenseless.

"Here!" Stefano called to Rodrigo as he tossed his sword to him.

Strozzini caught the sword by the blade, no doubt glad that he wore riding gloves. Stefano winced as he saw one man take advantage of the bodyguard's distraction and slash his exposed left arm.

Stefano noted the two men shoving through the mass of men and horseflesh, heading in his direction. He leaned low in his saddle and grabbed Strozzini's blade by the hilt and jerked it free of the fallen man's back. He came back in time to block the first man's downward strike. The other man brought his horse up close, preparing to attack. Stefano urged Fascino forward and squeezed his knees tight. The warhorse moved forward, then kicked out with his back hooves—as he had been trained. The second man's horse snorted and sidestepped, forcing the rider to delay his attack.

Stefano wheeled Fascino around and charged into the second man's dark bay which reared and skittered away, neatly avoiding the first man's attack. Charging back into the first man, Stefano stopped Fascino and signaled him to rear while he lashed out with his own sword. He caught the first *bravo* across the back of the shoulders, then brought his sword up around the man's neck and pinked his jawline. He followed hard after the man when he tried to escape into the field.

Stefano drove his sword into the man, piercing his chest and, from his reaction, likely taking a lung. The man used his sword as a crop, slapping his mount in the hindquarters with his sword. His horse bucked him off and ran away, leaving the man lying in the grassy field.

Stefano turned in time to hang off the side of his saddle to avoid being struck by the second man, parrying away the tip of the man's blade. He thrashed back only to have his blow parried. He lunged, launching himself off Fascino's back, and taking the other man, rolling, out of his saddle.

He landed on his wounded shoulder and felt the packing fall out. His sword flew from his hand. With the knife from his belt, and, while his opponent was still trying to shake off the stun from his fall, Stefano rolled atop the other man and drove the blade deep into his chest, twice in quick succession. The man went limp under him.

Whistling to Fascino, Stefano recovered his sword from the grass and heard the prisoner called Caserta shouting orders at their party of attackers and singling him out. He heard Strozzini yell for someone to quiet the prisoner. The bodyguard then broke away from the fight he had been in to place himself and his horse between Stefano and the three *bravi* answering Caserta's orders.

Stefano felt the familiar burn of hot lead hitting his left, already wounded, shoulder, but lower. The power of the bullets was enough to knock him off his feet at Fascino's side.

"Your Excellency!" Strozzini cried out.

"I'm fine!" Stefano replied and staggered to his feet again. He picked up his sword. With his knife between his teeth, Stefano found his left arm practically useless when he first tried to mount Fascino. Adjusting his sword in his right hand, Stefano tried a one-handed mount. It was difficult, but he managed . . . just . . . to get into the saddle.

Strozzini stopped the men sent to attack him, using his horse as a moving barrier. Stefano crowded in at Strozzini's left side, parrying a blow meant for the bodyguard. Behind the blackguard he was now facing, he saw one of the guards break from the fighting mass on the road and gallop toward the palazzo . . . hopefully for relief. Pierro got on his horse and struggled to control it. When he got his black brute managed, he gave it the heel and shot down the road after the guardsman.

Hopefully, Pierro would not catch the young rider before the guardsman reached the palazzo. Stefano could give it no more mind, focusing, instead, on the *attaccabrighe* in front of him. Stefano urged Fascino forward and clashed swords with his opponent. The man facing him took out his knife, took it in his left hand, and moved forward. Stefano watched for the feint, striking down his next sword strike with a forceful parry that nearly took the man's sword from his hand. Concentrating his energy on the sword kept Stefano open for the dagger strike which caught him in the left upper arm. Stefano could not help but cry out in pain when his opponent twisted the knife hard. When Stefano did, he dropped his dagger from between his teeth and left himself open to the man driving his own blade deeper.

Leaving his knife blade in place, Stefano's opponent brought his rapier to play, stabbing toward his heart. Stefano blocked the strike and in doing so accidentally struck the other man's horse in the withers just in front of the saddle. The horse reared high and tumbled backward. The horse lay on the ground, snorting in terror, breathing hard. The horse also lay on top of his rider, pinning him by the right leg to the ground.

Stefano pulled the dagger from his arm and cast it aside

so that his pinned opponent could not reach it. He guided Fascino forward, driving him into the next horseman and freeing Strozzini of another opponent. The other horse was easily muscled aside by Fascino—a horse trained in close-up battles with weapons flashing in the air, the report of gunfire, and attack in such circumstances. Stefano urged Fascino to approach from the side so that his left arm was away from his new opponent, and struck the other man while he was being forced to contend with his horse. He slashed his blade across the man's neck, kicking the horse in its left side. He need not have bothered goading the horse, his rider fell from the far side, knocking into the remaining horse and man.

The last man they were facing, paused momentarily, realizing he faced two horsemen alone. Without a word, he dropped his sword and held up his hands, releasing the reins. Strozzini reached out, took the reins up and over the other horse's head and led the horse back toward the road and where the battle seemed to be raging on.

Stefano turned at the sound of horses' pounding hooves. A company of Escalade rode in. He could hear the pinging of scorpininis singing through the night. Two men from the attackers fell, leaving just three men. One tried for the forest, but was chased into the darkness by three—or was it four?—Escalade vigilare. The two men remaining dropped their swords and lifted their hands in surrender. They were shackled in quick order. An Escalade officer broke from the other vigilare and came toward Stefano and Strozzini.

The officer bowed deep in the saddle to Stefano. "Your Excellency, I trust you are well?"

"He's taken some hits and at least one pistola shot," Strozzini reported.

Unable to make out the ranking insignia on the man's uniform, Stefano decided not to use an honorific. "And he's been wounded . . . and I, daresay, that some of the men from Citteauroea have been wounded as well. I propose that we get to the palazzo as quickly as we can in case someone has been given a potentially lethal blow," he said.

The horse that had been lying on Stefano's first opponent rolled to his feet, causing the man to cry out in pain as the saddle gouged into his flesh. "I advise you not to try and get up, or the officer here will put an end to you," he told the man lying in the grass. The new prisoner placed his hands upon his head in surrender.

The officer turned in his saddle and whistled. One of the *vigilare* broke away from the crowd of men in the road. "Shackle him and turn him over a saddle. His leg might be broken."

"Yes, Capitano," the vigilare said, sliding off his horse.

In the distance, on the other side of the field, Escalade men rode out of the forest. Some of them "whooped," which Stefano knew from his years in the service meant they had detained a prisoner. He found himself relaxing. There were a total of six hostages now, by his count, hopefully enough to sort out what was happening with this group of men, because, considering Caserta had been yelling orders to them, it was likely they were all of one group . . . *Magnus Inique*.

Stefano guided Fascino to the road, followed by Strozzini and the newly identified capitano. On the road, the vigilare were in the process of sorting through the bodies, looking for their dead and wounded.

"Come, let us get you to the palazzo," the capitano said.

"Bring the prisoners with us. Turn them over the saddles, one and all, so no more trickery can be done by them," Stefano ordered.

"I'll need four men to accompany us," the capitano said to the vigilare, some continuing to check bodies while others dealt with the detainees.

"Hey, this one is alive, but he's calling for a priest!" one of the men going through bodies called out.

"He's a priest," the big man said, pointing at Caserta.

"Shut up, you idiot," Caserta snapped.

"He needs a priest. You're his priest, his confessor. Do what God called you to do," the big man named Enzo yelled back at Caserta.

Complaining bitterly, Caserta slid off his horse. "I can do nothing while I am shackled like this."

When his hands were freed, he patted his coat. "My holy oil has fallen out. I can't give the Extreme Unction."

The injured man held out his arm to Caserta.

"Give the Last Rites, or so help me . . . !" Enzo swore, grabbing at the priest from where he was, now upended over the saddle of his horse.

"Hah!" the priest spat, stumbling just out of reach of Enzo.

One of the vigilare grabbed Caserta by the collar of his coat and thrust him at the man laying in the road. The priest landed on his knees at the man's side. Under the weight of the vigilare watching him, he proceeded to give the unidentified man the Last Rites as he was clearly being ordered to do. His fellow prisoners watched his every movement.

When he was done, his hands were reshackled and he shuffled to his horse and tried to mount the best way that he could with his feet shackled like his hands. One of the capitano's men pushed him roughly over the saddle and took his horse's reins. The uniformed man gathered the reins of Enzo's horse and the man's horse that had fallen on his rider earlier, mounted, and rode up to the capitano. Behind him, another three men broke away from inspecting the bodies and each took the reins of one of the prisoners' horses and mounted their own.

The palazzo, it turned out, was a shorter distance than Stefano predicted. Light shone from the great windows, streaming out into the night. On the front steps, Luciana and many members of the Palantini stood waiting and watching.

Stefano tried to slide from Fascino's back to land on his good leg, but crumpled when he hit the ground. Embarrassed, he waved off Strozzini and Luciana who came to his aid. Using Fascino's stirrup, Stefano dragged himself up and limped over the few feet to Luciana's side.

He buried his face in Luciana's neck and held her for a long moment. His wife apparently used the time to assess Stefano's condition. She put her arm around his lower back, away from his wound and braced him to make it up the stairs and into Palazzo Auroea.

Strozzini came to his side as he made his way down the long Clock Walk and into the royal sitting room just to the right of the Throne Room. Stefano turned on the bodyguard. "You, Signore, will see *il dottore* immediately!"

Quietly, Strozzini made his appeal. "At least let me see you seated."

Stefano glowered at the bodyguard and moved into the sitting room. He pushed Luciana away, crossed the short distance to the couch, and sank down in relief. He was careful not to stain the fabric-covered settee with blood from the wound across the back of his shoulders.

"*Scusi!*"

He looked up and saw *il dottore* Bonta and a Capitano of the Escalade pushing their way through the crowd of curious onlookers.

"Your Excellency, what have you been doing?" Bonta cried, eying the bloody mess that were Stefano's clothes.

"Getting outnumbered . . . badly," Stefano retorted. He looked at Rodrigo Strozzini. "Weren't you going somewhere?"

Strozzini appeared frustrated, but he bowed and excused himself. The crowd was kind enough to make way for him.

"Please," Stefano said, wincing as *il dottore* eased off his coat with Luciana's assistance. "Go about your business. The Palantini will meet on the morrow to judge prisoners."

"Do you want them in the dungeons or—" the capitano began.

Stefano recognized the capitano's voice from earlier. He waved a hand. "Put them in the dungeons and make sure that the priest is kept alone in a separate cell."

"Do you mean a Church cell or the dungeon?"

"I'm not giving him to the bishop. I doubt we would ever see him again," Stefano replied. "While you're about your business, I want you to arrest Prince Pierro deMedici and bring him to me."

That stopped the capitano in his tracks. The officer turned back, "You mean Princess Ortensia's husband?"

"I do. Send him to the cells for tonight. If nothing else, it will do him some good to contemplate his options," Stefano said.

"I really must protest."

Stefano looked up and saw Duca Silvieri. He always sided with the princess . . . and her husband. "Your Grace, I have done with protests of any sort today. I have more than sufficient reason to believe that Prince Pierro was actually involved in the death of our King Alban."

"Impossible!" the duca practically shouted.

Il dottore looked up from his examination of Stefano's wounds, looking down his pointed nose at Duca Silvieri with displeasure.

"Please do not argue with my husband further," Luciana said.

"If for no other reason, he left us on the road to be killed and did nothing about it," Stefano said.

The capitano bowed and made his exit.

"But wait!" Silvieri protested. He turned back to Stefano. "You are making a mistake. The prince was probably coming to get aid."

"Amusing thought," Stefano said. "It is one night, Silvieri. He'll hardly rot. Besides, you have yet to hear all of the story and—ow!" He glared at Bonta who was inspecting the pistola shots to his left, upper arm and leg.

"I'm sorry, Your Grace, but the Lord Regent needs to be taken to his chambers where I can better tend him," Bonta said. "I'll ring for the *portierre*, so you must all leave immediately." He yanked on the bell pull and ushered the duchi from the room, ignoring Stefano's protests that he was fine.

Two brawny porters answered the ring and looked at Bonta, Luciana and, finally, Stefano.

"He was mistaken. We don't need you," Stefano said abruptly, waving them off.

Luciana grabbed the closest man's sleeve. "Ignore the Lord Regent. He has been injured today and is ill-tempered. I need you to pick him up and take him to our apartments." Stefano tried to wave them off, glaring now at his wife who also ignored him. "Are you going to cooperate, *camómescro*?"

Stefano looked at her sourly and started to rise. She pushed him back into the couch and turned back to the *portierre*.

"You will need to take the entire couch, I'm afraid. With him in it . . . and roll him about if you must to keep him in," Luciana commanded, clapping her hands impatiently when the servants looked at her to see if she were completely serious. "Gentlemen, if you please!"

Without further word or paying heed to anything Stefano said, the men picked up the couch and rolled him back into it.

XXX

"Double, double toil and trouble . . ."
—William Shakespeare

25 d'Febbraio, 1685

"I DON'T need the chair. I'll walk!" Stefano protested, looking angrily at the palanquin brought for him.

Luciana looked at him. It was not a kind visage she offered, but one of impatience. "*Il dottore* Bonta has ordered bed rest and yet you insist on going to the Great Hall where the Palantini meets. You cannot walk. This is your only choice . . . that or we let Estensi and me preside over the trial . . . or we could simply wait a week or more until *il dottore* and I think you should be walking again. You've been stabbed in the ankle and shot in the thigh of the same leg. Only a bloody fool would insist on walking when it is so obvious that he cannot. It won't send a strong message to the Palantini, if that's what you're concerned about," Luciana argued, clearly unembarrassed to chastise him in front of Palazzo staff. "If you want, your men-at-arms can carry you. That is the only concession I'm going to make!"

Stefano felt the hot rush of blood to his face and ears. It was bad enough that she and Carlo had insisted on helping him dress, and now this. "Luciana, you go too far," he said.

"I've made no scenes in front of the duchi. You've been wounded, and I would have you follow *il dottore*'s advice for once," Luciana replied. "If we leave now, you can be in your chair before the majority of the Palantini arrive for this trial, or you can have them witness you falling in the hall. I think only of you."

Stefano gave her a narrow look. She was playing on his ego and it was working. "All right! My men-at-arms will attend me."

"Excellent!" Luciana said with a smile. "They are waiting on the stair."

Before he could comment, she opened the door for Duarte, Giordano, della Guelfa, and Strozzini. "Duarte and Giordano, you may carry the palanquin."

The men touched their forelocks as they bowed to her and Stefano before taking up the poles on either side of Stefano's chair and began immediately maneuvering the chair out of the door and down the stairs. It was an awkward and sometimes clumsy proposition that the men finally managed while Luciana kept a firm hand on his shoulder to keep Stefano from getting too impatient and rising from the conveyance.

"What are you doing here, Strozzini? Of the two of us, you belong in a bed somewhere," Stefano growled.

Strozzini smiled pleasantly. "As you can see, I am still ambulatory and *il dottore* saw no reason for me not to attend the trial, especially as I am witness to not one, but two attempts on your life yesterday."

"Since we will be together, *camómescro*, there is no reason that Capitano della Guelfa cannot serve as protector of us both," Luciana added from beside him.

Stefano kept his head up, greeting people as he passed them in the hall, trying to pretend that the chair he was being carried in made no difference, but to a man of action, such as himself, it was a humiliation. There was only so far he was willing to have this charade carried out.

They reached the Throne Room with few encounters; few of the duchi were already in the room, so Stefano was spared that embarrassment. With della Guelfa's assistance, he hobbled the few feet to his chair before the thrones.

"Move that chair to the Great Hall, somewhere out of the way," Stefano told his men.

While they were gone, Sebastiani arrived also on a palanquin. Stefano studied his *compagni* carefully to see if it was truly the man's health that had demanded the conveyance, or if he were trying to make Stefano's position less embarrassing. He had not reached a conclusion when the greater body of the Palantini arrived and began taking their seats.

Stefano looked around the room. Everyone sat close to their compatriots and curiosity seemed the norm. Their number was not so great as it had been in weeks since, as the duchi had begun returning to their homes, but there were still—at last count—twenty-four of the duchi left staying at the palazzo and at least five more that lived close enough to be able to attend such summarily called courts.

"Estensi," Stefano said, "you may retrieve the prisoners."

The Court Herald bowed and would have left the room, except that Bishop Abruzzi rose to block his path. "Your *Excellency*," Abruzzi acknowledged in a tight voice, "I wish to protest these proceedings—"

Stefano waved him to silence. "Nothing has yet happened for you to protest, Your Reverence. I'm confident that when the time arises, you will be most eloquent."

Abruzzi stood to his full height, using the glamor of his Gypsy Silk robes to enhance his presence—or so Stefano did not doubt. "At least, let us begin with a prayer?"

"There can be no communal prayer because the rabbi and imam are not present today and our trials are based on logic, honor, and testimony rather than faith," Stefano replied. "Estensi, please!"

Abruzzi stormed from the room, pushing Estensi to one side as he departed. Stefano waited for the Court Herald to leave before addressing the audience. "While Estensi is gone, let me acquaint you with the details—"

"Did you truly arrest Prince deMedici last night? Put him in the dungeons?" Silvieri asked.

"Yes," Stefano replied.

"Unconscionable!" This came from the cluster of the Palantini members centered around Silvieri.

"Unconscionable?" Stefano repeated. From the way his face colored, Luciana knew he was angry. "I said and did nothing about deMedici after the king was slaughtered before me. DeMedici joined us unexpectedly for that ride, and his presence was always questionable to me . . . especially after—"

Strozzini cleared his throat, drawing everyone's attention to the arrival of Princess Ortensia. She was dressed in her usual best, a gown of salmon Gypsy Silk over a matching gown of gold. Despite the care taken in dressing, there were smudges of makeup on her face, and the walk toward the chair Stefano had granted her was anything but decorous. Silvieri jumped from his seat and went to offer her assistance only to be pushed aside. She finally reached her chair and stared around the room at everyone watching her. "Well? This is a trial, isn't it? I have a right to be here, too!"

"But of course you do," Stefano said as gently as he could. He tapped Luciana's hand, quickly motioning to the princess.

Luciana, in turn, beckoned della Guelfa over and sent for *il dottore*.

"You were saying, Lord Regent," Ortensia prompted.

Stefano looked at her, wishing there were something that he could do to make the scene about to play out easier on her. Better to be quick and sure, he decided. He turned back to the Palantini and continued, "Especially afterward, when he took the king's death as an opportunity to pronounce his wife queen by way of telling everyone that King Alban was gone! For those of you who would protest the prince's innocence by way of ill-considered timing, allow me to continue.

"Yesterday, we encountered the prince on the road to Citteauroea and rode with him a good portion of the way there. When he excused himself, Lord Strozzini and I took the opportunity to follow him as his behavior seemed suspicious. Prince deMedici was found in a taverna with the very self-same men who attacked us on the road in *Gennaio* and, later, in the day, in a shop and again on the road back to the palazzo yesterday. If nothing else, he must speak to this," Stefano said.

"Because of the company he kept, you dared to arrest a royal?" the princess exclaimed.

Stefano turned to look at her. "It was . . . is more than just the company he kept at a taverna. There are also his actions which we will go into later. I had expected your protest earlier . . . perhaps last night."

"I was with my husband, in the dungeons, last night!" Ortensia snapped angrily.

Silvieri who had not yet vacated the princess' side, bent and whispered into her ear.

Ortensia looked slightly more mollified, but closed her arms over her chest in a protective position. Silvieri moved to the front of the room, bowed, and returned to his seat.

The doors in the back of the room opened, heralding Estensi's return. "Shall I bring them *all* in?"

"Bring in the prince first. He deserves to be attended to before the others . . . if for no other reason than he is of *la famiglia reale*," Princess Ortensia demanded.

Stefano looked anxiously at the princess. "Are you sure you want to stay? Are you prepared to accept his fate?" Stefano asked.

"As decided by you? I didn't say that," the princess said.

Stefano's only reply was to shrug and look to Estensi at the door. "Bring deMedici in."

Estensi's head bobbed, and he disappeared through the doors. A moment later, he returned with the prince, thrusting him into the room ahead of himself.

From Pierro deMedici's expression, done up as he was in two sets of shackles, it was clear the man was furious. His words, when spoken, were full of vitriol. "How *dare* you make me spend the night in the dungeon!? As if I were just anybody . . ."

Ortensia rose and moved to stand with her husband, the deMedici bastarde. She did not speak further, but her eyes shot fire at Stefano as she looped her right arm through his chains to stand locked in place with him.

"How dare *I*?" Stefano repeated. He sat forward and stared boldly back at Pierro. "You are the one to be questioned! Why did you join us that morning when King Alban was killed? That of all mornings and, then, without due notice?"

"I stand trial for a breach of etiquette? I was trying to—to—" Pierro sputtered. He caught his breath and continued. "I knew my company is an—an acquired taste, shall we say. I was trying to get some time with His Majesty and, perhaps, to win him over."

"To you or to your wife's cause?" Sebastiani asked.

"If you must know, yes. I thought he might be more willing to consider her cause, if we were on friendlier terms. If for no other reason than I hoped for a more filial relationship with the man," Pierro said.

"You thought he would step down as your king and give

the crown to you and Ortensia?" Stefano gasped. He adjusted the sling on his left arm. "Do you really believe he . . . or any other king would step aside for you?"

"It was a hope . . . perhaps, eventually, when he truly understood my wife's position."

"I think the king, more than adequately, understood her position," Duca diCalabria said.

Luciana glanced at this duca in surprise for he had never hidden his dedication to Princess deMedici and her causes. Pierro arched his brow at diCalabria, but said nothing. The duca returned to relative anonymity in the center of the Palantini.

"And what of yesterday? When Lord Strozzini and I saw you at a roadhouse in the company of the men we later were forced to fight and detain?" Stefano asked.

Pierro studied his feet briefly. When he looked up, he was smiling slightly. "Had I known you were there, Your Excellency, I would most assuredly have invited you to join us, but I did not know and you did not make *your* presence known." He made his last sentence sound almost like an accusation, but Stefano did not rise to the bait.

"Your Excellency, under further questioning, these men have admitted to representing *Magnus Inique*! Furthermore, I have separate testimony confirming this," Strozzini said.

Pierro glared into the mass of nobility.

"*Magnus Inique* . . . you have testimony, too, that they were responsible for King Alban's death," Duchessa Rossi said. "Is that not so?"

Strozzini nodded.

"And, if that weren't enough, according to Escalade reports I've read, there were also the deaths of seventeen accused witches," Sebastiani added.

"Twenty-eight, according to the *Beluni*, and I myself was nearly put to death by members of *Magnus Inique*," Luciana burst out.

"Twenty-nine," Stefano said quietly as he the thought of the old woman who had helped Idala in her time of need coming to such a violent end. "Obviously, these are only those deaths that have been reported. I am sure there are more of you, your people."

"Twenty-nine women?" Gianola said, shuddering. "But witches by accusation."

"You may call them witches, I call them wisewomen who knew the craft of herbs and teas and were sometimes the only *dottore* or midwife in the region or at least for many miles," Luciana argued. Stefano reached out, gently took her arm, and pulled her back in her chair.

"Who gave you this testimony that the prince was party to this group, and how were they familiar with *Magnus Inique*?" Silvieri asked.

"Fair question," Stefano said. He looked to Strozzini.

Strozzini looked into the sea of faces in the Palantini. "Don?"

From the back row of the duchi, a short, angular man rose self-consciously with his eyes cast down to the ground rather than look at Pierro or Ortensia or even Stefano. He made his way down into the center area.

"You can bear witness to anything related to this?" Stefano asked. The don did not immediately answer; he looked to Strozzini.

"Don Battista, now is the time for your knowledge to come to light," Strozzini said.

The don nodded, finally glancing at Pierro. "For a time after his first wife's death . . . Prince . . . the deMedici came to stay with me at my estate near Dragorione where he, perforce, introduced me to *Magnus Inique* and made me a member of same."

"You toad!" Pierro spat at him, unable to reach Don Battista for the strong hand of a Palazzo Guard on his shoulder and the princess' grip on his arm.

The don continued when the prince was quieted. "He demoted me to the status of a mere servant and forced me to carry messages to Padre Caserta of *Magnus Inique* where I met many more of the men. I heard Enzo, who was a member of *Magnus Inique* headed by Caserta, boasting he had shot the king. He said this in a group that included myself and Caserta, whom he knew to be in the prince's employ. I knew I could no longer participate, so I left the employ of the prince and delivered written testimony to the Royal Bodyguard. I cannot think of any more I could witness to, but ask me questions, if you will."

"Did the prince seem to be aware of the missions of *Magnus Inique*?" Stefano asked.

"Yes. I took his regular messages to the padre as a part

of his directions," Cristoval Battista said. "He seemed to have charge of them when they were in my home months ago."

"So he has been consulting with *Magnus Inique* for some time—before the king was slain?" Stefano prompted.

"At least, six months ago at my home," Don Cristoval Battista affirmed.

"Do you know why he joined the king's party that fateful morning?" Stefano asked.

Cristoval shook his head. "No. I've no knowledge of this, but then I never read the letters to the padre since they were always sealed when I took them and no one ever shared the contents."

"What have you to say to this?" Stefano asked Pierro.

Stefano watched the prince turn several shades of red—almost purple. He raged, Stefano thought, and the princess, he noted, never looked at her husband but rather doggedly clung onto his arm. At the moment, he felt sorry for the princess . . . until she spoke.

"On this alone you charge my husband? Based on this, you threw him into a cell? You should be ashamed of yourself, Duca di Drago!" the princess seethed with anger.

"The Duca di Drago, as you call him, is your regent, Your Highness," Estensi retorted. "And there is also the matter of your husband being seen with those in charge of *Magnus Inique* just yesterday, according to the word of the Lord Regent and his bodyguard."

"It proves nothing," Pierro said through gritted teeth.

"It proves you had congress before and after the king's death," Stefano responded evenly. "Evidence has shown you to be in close ties with the witch-hunters and by the law of the land, that is enough to charge and convict you of any number of additional complaints, never mind your probable involvement in the king's murder!

"Then there were the murders of Brother Tomasi and the two Palazzo Guards, Fieri and deGrassi. I saw your wounds that day. The wound on your arm was very like the kind you would get if you were to miss the sheath of your stiletto when putting it away. No one else saw this strange attacker you spoke of . . . no one was reported wearing black and running from the dungeons. And you had reason to keep Brother Tomasi quiet, since he was the cardinal's man and the cardinal conspired with you and Bianca. Remember, deMedici? It was you who brought the famed poisoner Exilli to our shores and before *he* made his escape, he attempted murder of the king. It all ties together.

"Then there is the question of how you knew to be on the road when Princess Ortensia was released by the Turks. In all of Tyrrhia . . . on that particular day and hour. I found that suspicious. How were you able to do that, I wonder?" Stefano asked.

"You would convict me further on happenstance?" Pierro drawled coolly. "You are just angry that I found her and married her!"

Stefano shook his head. He turned to the attending Palazzo Guard and said, "Take him back to his rooms and post enough guards to be sure he stays there."

A collective sigh escaped from within the assemblage of the Palantini when the prince, scowling at all in the room, was led up the aisle toward the back of the room. Stefano could not be sure if it were in sympathy for deMedici or relief that the confrontation was over.

The Palazzo Guard tugged the prince's free right arm, to no avail. A second Palazzo Guard came up and disentangled the princess from Pierro and gave the prince a light push toward the door. Pierro turned his hostility on the guards, but finally moved. Ortensia trailed after her husband looking like a broken doll. The guards positioned at the door closed it behind the deMedicis and their escort with a snap.

"What are you going to do with him?" Silvieri contested.

Stefano shook his head. "To be absolutely forthright, I'm not sure. In part, it depends upon what his confederates have to say. He was involved in some fashion with King Alban's death and the attacks on me and my family. Those three incidents alone are sufficient for me to have his head, but I am not so inclined, even though the king was a relative and meant much to me."

" 'Not so inclined'!" Duca Antonelli repeated. "He is royalty, for pity's sake, and the princess has already lost so much. You would take her husband from her, too?"

"That is where my sympathy lies. With the princess, that is. As to being royalty, Pierro is an Italian bastarde who married *into* the royal family of Tyrrhia," Stefano said.

"Twice!" Antonelli argued.

"He is little better than the *Turche*! He stole her away from the Turks, to be sure, for she had not reached home before she was already married and her life plighted to his!" Sebastiani argued.

"You are the Lord Regent's puppet, Sebastiani," Silvieri sneered.

"But it doesn't change the fact that Pierro must have had some way of knowing when and where the Turks were leaving Ortensia. As they tell it, he was present when she was found. What else might that mean? Could he have some sort of relation with the *Turche*? And if he did, what, if anything, did he have to do with the attack on Messina? He *was* absent when the attack happened."

A devastated silence followed Sebastiani's last question; even Silvieri and Gianola sat down.

Stefano let the silence wash over the crowd for a long moment before he spoke again. "We are all aware of the prince's faults and the only good he serves is for the princess' happiness, but still there are members of this gathering who support him.

"Please. Let us concentrate on what lies before us. Let's talk to the other prisoners and see what *they* have to offer us before any of us decide about the serious charges against the prince," Stefano told the group.

Luciana leaned over to him. "Are you able to continue? You've grown pale."

Stefano rubbed his beard and pinched his lips as he looked at the floor. "We must get through this today. We cannot let these charges continue to drag on uninvestigated."

"Then let us pursue the matter in haste. You should be abed. Here, drink this. It will sustain you," Luciana said, handing him a goblet of red wine.

"Estensi, the other prisoners, please," Stefano said. He sniffed the wine, then set it aside, as he turned attentively toward Estensi and the open door in the back of the room.

Six men were brought forward with a Palazzo Guard on either side of each one.

"We have here the arrested from yesterday, Your Excellency and Honored Palantini members," Estensi said. "Who attacked you first?"

"When I took my family into the city, the big man there, Enzo, I heard him called, and two other men attacked us in the street. Yesterday, it was Enzo and Padre Caserta and four others who attacked us in Donna Rui's shop," Stefano replied.

"You know them by name, Your Excellency?" Estensi asked, looking surprised that his regent knew any of the prisoners' names.

"I listened when they had altercations between themselves," Stefano said.

The Court Herald smiled and nodded. He looked the men over, many with dark bruises forming upon their faces and bloodstains on their clothing.

"Were your wounds tended to?" Stefano asked the two men brought forward.

Sullenly, the smaller, more average-sized man closed his mouth tight and looked away, to some unknown point above Stefano's head. The big man shrugged. "Aye, Enzo saw *il dottore*, and I was fed as well. I'll not complain of my treatment if I get to keep my head."

"Shut up, fool," Caserta growled.

Stefano held up a hand. "No! We will not start this again today!"

Caserta looked down at his feet, his stitched jaw tightening shut.

"Why do you think we'll take your head?" Stefano asked Enzo.

"For many reasons." The big man replied as though he were casually sharing a drink with a comrade.

"Please elaborate," Duchessa Rossi requested from the front row of the duchi.

Enzo gave her an admiring once over from head to foot. The duchessa merely met his gaze and waited. After a brief hesitation, he smacked his lips, then rubbed them. "You want Enzo to . . . to clarify? Yes?" She nodded. He took a deep breath and answered her directly. "Because Enzo has fought at these men's sides for the past two years and participated in the witch-hunting, and more . . . Enzo was responsible for the bolt that slew the White King and then for attacking what Enzo is told is now the Lord Regent. That should be enough."

Stefano hazarded that most people did not hear all of his confession because of the outbursts coming from the duchi when he admitted to killing the king. He clapped loudly to draw the attention of the duchi. When they turned, Stefano said, "Do you wish to continue with this trial or talk among yourselves?"

He waited, letting the silence fill the room again . . . except for the rattle of the prisoners' chains as they shifted.

"Do you freely admit to killing the king?" Stefano asked.

"Enzo does . . . in the hopes that what Enzo says may serve to keep his head one with his body," the big man replied. "I hope that the information will be sufficient to warrant some form of amnesty."

"Amnesty? You killed our king, and you want amnesty?" Sebastiani said, his voice fairly cracking with disbelief.

Enzo nodded and shrugged. "I've told my compatriots to speak up to save their hides by confessing all, but this one ordered the men into silence." He jerked his head toward Padre Caserta.

"Is this so?" Stefano asked the priest.

The one called Caserta only stared down at his boots.

"I would guess it so," Stefano said. "Tell me, Enzo. What are the names of the other men?"

Enzo turned. He pointed to another large man—not as big as himself—"This is Elmo diSotto. He comes with experience from the *Armata*, like me. The others are Constantine, Giovanni, and Giraldo." He pointed at each man as he spoke.

"Will none of you speak to your deeds, or does Enzo continue to speak for you?" Stefano asked them. In response, diSotto, Constantine, and Giovanni copied Padre Caserta and stared at their respective toes, but Giraldo stepped out of line.

"I'll speak of what I've done. Until now, I meant to hold my tongue, but Enzo seems to have the right of it," the youth said. "I have spent most of my time in *Magnus Inique* attending to the witch-hunters in the deepest parts of the heartland of Tyrrhia. I was brought to Citteauroea just last week. Yesterday, I was ordered to lie in wait and attack the riders the prince identified on the road. I did not realize it was you, Lord Regent. Forgive me, please!"

"We will get to that. How did the prince signal you that I was the one on the road to be attacked?" Stefano queried. He relaxed a little as he spoke, taking another drink from his goblet.

Giraldo shook his head. "DiSotto was leading the band that attacked on the road. Only he and one other man, leading the second band hiding on the other side of the forest knew the signal. That man I do not see here. Perhaps he escaped?"

Strozzini interrupted with a polite cough. "All the other men are dead," he told Stefano.

The young witch-hunter glanced at diSotto in surprise. Apparently, in the confusion, he had not realized his side had lost so many men.

"What did you do before that?" Sebastiani asked.

Giraldo blushed and hid his face briefly under the fall of his long hair. "I was with the witch-hunters in the interior of the heartland. I couldn't kill the women they said were witches, though. I didn't have the stomach for it. All I could think of was my grandmother! I mostly held the horses and tried not to hear the women's cries when they burned." He shook his head, tears springing to his blue eyes.

"You're no better than an old woman, boy," the one Enzo identified as diSotto said harshly.

"Perhaps he is also worth saving," Luciana said. "You could not harden the boy in all the time with you because you were not worthy of his respect. It takes no great honor or show of strength to tie old women to a stake in the center of town and burn them."

DiSotto sneered at Luciana. "You are a witch, *stronza*, and would have died by our hands eventually."

"Perhaps." Luciana smiled. "But now you are captured."

"And if I weren't, I'd see you dead!" diSotto hissed at her.

"Enzo, how many more of the witch-hunters of *Magnus Inique* are there?" Stefano asked.

"Maybe forty-five . . . perhaps as many as fifty, if the group has been recruiting, but they'll have problems because the padre here isn't going to be able to induct them into the 'sacred trust,'" he scoffed at the priest.

"And what is your count of witches' burned?" Stefano pressed.

Giraldo looked to Enzo. "We've killed thirty-seven old witch women," Enzo admitted freely and without much in the way of remorse.

"Including the old woman from yesterday?" Luciana asked.

Caserta smiled slightly. "So she was dead, eh?"

"That's what happens when you crush an old woman's skull," Stefano said.

The padre only smiled and returned to looking at his shoes.

"The priest here, he was in charge of your little mob?" Stefano asked, pointing to Caserta.

The padre looked up then and scowled angrily at Giraldo and Enzo . . . to no avail, as they both nodded in confirmation.

"What happened with the king?" Sebastiani asked. "Who ordered that?"

Enzo yanked his head in the direction of the padre. "He said that it needed doing, but we think he got his orders from somewhere else, the prince—where he got most his directions. DiSotto and Enzo went since we were both in the *Armata*. Enzo was the better shot, so it was I, Enzo, who shot the crossbow bolt at the unsuspecting king. The prince's presence served to confirm it was the royal party. Enzo had seen the king before this, recognized him by sight. DiSotto waited with the horses. When the bodyguard made the road, searching for us or our tracks, we had reached the woods again and hid while he looked for us."

"So at one time you were what? Almost at arm's length from me?" Strozzini asked.

"Aye, but you were alone and wouldn't 've captured us," diSotto said from the rear of the party of prisoners. "I wanted to kill you," he added, "but Enzo said we might not escape if we did."

"No," Strozzini said sadly. "I was in too much of a hurry to return to my king."

"You did not fail him, Strozzini," Stefano murmured. "So, the deMedici bastarde was involved in the planning of the king's death."

"That was Caserta's plot with the prince. He thought it a good way to transfer the kingdom to the princess," Enzo said.

Giraldo shook his head. "I know nothing of this. I was deep in the heartland when the king died. I joined *Magnus Inique* after our king was killed. I thought it a way of fighting back against those disloyal to the crown. I'd no idea that the group was responsible, else *I* would've turned them in."

"Coward!" diSotto hissed at the youth.

Giraldo responded with a swift elbow to the gut of the older man, then rammed his shackles into diSotto's mouth. "I'd have killed you myself . . . in your sleep, if need be, because you were part of the assassination of my king!"

"Enough of this!" Estensi commanded, nodding to the guards responsible for the men. They parted the prisoners forcibly.

"I have heard enough from the boy," Stefano said. "Take him back to his cell for now."

"But, Signore . . . Your . . . Your Excellency, please! I've only been a member of the group for a matter of weeks—I—" Giraldo called as the Palazzo Guards pulled him from the room.

"What are you going to do with him?" Luciana whispered, watching as the door closed on the youth.

"I would plead for the boy's clemency," Duca Ugo Vivaldi said, standing.

"I will take it in full measure that you all are curious, but I will not answer while we have other prisoners to judge," Stefano replied. He looked at the big man who had been confessing to all and sundry without hesitation. "What are your other sins—"

Without warning, the Bishop of Aurorea, Abruzzi, returned to the room, coming up the center aisle so that he stood among the prisoners. He looked at the men in shackles and then stared down, arms akimbo, at Stefano. "One of these men is supposed to be a priest. I, as your diplomatic representative from the Pope, ask for clemency! In fact, he should be turned over to me immediately!"

"You were invited into this inquest, Your Excellency," Stefano replied, trying to keep a leash on his anger. "To all my understanding, I do have a priest before me."

"It is my place to judge the priest and determine if he should be punished," Bishop Abruzzi announced. He glared at Stefano angrily, sparing a glance for the other duchi around the room.

"You will have your chance . . . *after* this court is through," Stefano said. "The charge is high treason in the murder of King Alban and my attempted murder on three occasions."

"Three?" the bishop hissed.

Enzo laughed, "You done yourself in, Padre. You had us

attack him in the streets of Citteauroea when he came to the capital on business not so very long ago, then again when he broke into our occupation of the store yesterday and then, Enzo believes he heard you shouting orders at our men on the road last night as well. The men wouldn't have attacked without the prearranged signal."

"The prince again?" Sebastiani asked.

Enzo laughed. "You don't think that priss would lay in the grass otherwise, do you?"

"If he fell?" Duca Anino suggested.

"He would have sprung up immediately," Enzo laughed again.

"Would you please be quiet? I'm trying to barter for my man—" Bishop Abruzzi snapped at Enzo. He turned to Stefano. "What *did* happen to you?"

Luciana looked up at the bishop angrily. "Your man was in charge of having my husband attacked twice yesterday or didn't you hear that?"

"Hyperbole," the bishop dismissed with a wave of his hands.

"Non!" Enzo chuckled. "He was witnessed giving orders to his men—the other prisoners—yesterday. Both times. Enzo knows because Enzo was there!"

"Who is this Enzo you keep talking about?" the Bishop demanded.

The big man frowned sourly at the bishop. "*I* am Enzo."

"You, Bishop Abruzzi, may stay if you can keep quiet," Stefano said. He looked to Estensi. "Have the Escalade officers join us, Court Herald."

"Why—" the bishop began, sputtering with indignation.

"Because there are too many witnesses to your man's culpability, and I must needs hear them all. You might as well hear them, too," Stefano said, looking up when three men in dress Escalade uniform filed into the room. "Are you all witness to the depravity of these men here?"

The three men bowed: the lieutenant from the store; the capitano from the rescuing Escalade; and a third man, a sergeant, with minor injuries.

"Tell your stories, men, in order, if you please," Stefano said softly.

The lieutenant stepped forward after giving the prisoners the evil eye. "I am Lieutenant d'Este in the Escalade and serve in the city proper. I was witness to these two men and four others having been in a fight with the Lord Regent and his man, Strozzini." Here, he paused and pointed out the padre and Enzo. "I did not see the fight, but I witnessed the aftermath and heard the detainees speak of their fight."

The sergeant stepped forth, bowing to Stefano and then the duchi. "I was with the contingent that escorted you to the palazzo, Your Excellency. They killed all but three of us. That's six dead at my count. I heard the one you call the priest yelling orders and trying to escape. He only stopped because of the young man returning with too many reinforcements for him to be able to fight."

"The young man," Stefano said to the sergeant, "he is well?"

The sergeant nodded. "Well enough. He was shot by one of the surviving prisoners, I know not which."

"Thank you, Sergeant," Stefano said.

The capitano came forward next. He bowed to Stefano. "If I may be so bold, how fare you today, Your Excellency?"

Stefano waved off the question, then seemed to think better of it. "I will live, Capitano. Thank you for asking. Now, tell us your tale."

The capitano nodded. "My men and I were manning the gate when the vigilare came for us. We, of course, followed procedure and came to your immediate aid. No lives were lost in my company in detaining the prisoners, and we recovered the bodies of twenty-six attackers. The Escalade force with you, for being so green in the service of our queen, acquitted themselves well. We had the one man of the opposing force who wished to be blessed by this . . . this priest, here," he pointed to Caserta, his face registering his disgust, "with Last Rites, but he was . . . reluctant to comply."

"He wouldn't 've given it, left to him," Enzo said and spat on Caserta's shoes. "Take that to your precious bishop, Padre."

The bishop looked askance at Caserta. "Not everyone is due the Last Rites . . . if he'd failed to Confess, or was not of the faith—"

"Pshua," diSotto said in revolt, "Caserta was his Confessor, and the man Confessed if he spent the night with a whore."

"Mind your tongue! There are ladies present!" Duca Gianola declared from across the room. "And as to the

Extreme Unction in Tyrrhia, it is given to anyone who Confesses and asks for it!"

"We are in basic agreement," the bishop said, "but that is between me and the priest . . . not a matter for this . . . this tribunal!"

"It speaks to his character," Stefano replied. "I would hesitate to lay claim to such a man as he has evidenced himself to be . . . especially after the cardinal."

Gianola genuflected reflexively.

"You can't judge—" the bishop began, heatedly.

"I adjudicate anyone who comes before me with charges of killing our king and ordering the murders of thirty-eight known citizens," Stefano said, peremptorily. "Does anyone have further questions of these men?"

When no one spoke, Stefano waved his hand. "Guards, return them to their cells while we decide what to do with them. Bishop Abruzzi, if you wish to consult with your man, I give you the liberty to—"

"*You* give *me* the liberty?" Abruzzi repeated, aghast.

"Enough!" Stefano bellowed. "Yes, as Regent, *I* give you liberty to speak to admitted conspirators against the Throne. I give them the advantage of going to God with their Confessions taken and the Last Rites given, sacraments King Alban and these women were denied . . . unless Caserta wants to confess to giving these 'witches' their due? Considering how reluctant he was to give his own man the final sacrament rather than expose himself as a priest, I somehow doubt he or any of his men arranged this. Now, begone before I change my mind. I'm leaning less toward that mercy the longer you delay!"

Choking on his outrage, the bishop stormed from the room. The Palazzo Guards caught the door before it could slam and quietly closed it.

Stefano rubbed his face and took a brief moment to control himself. He waved to Estensi to continue.

The Court Herald bowed and turned toward the convened Palantini. He stamped his staff. "We have reached the stage of judgment. What say you to this offered testimony, good gentles?"

"Execute them all!" Sebastiani declared.

Shouts of assent came from many of the duchi, though there were those who disagreed.

"Let the dissenters speak!" Stefano said, waving his free right hand for silence.

"You cannot kill a royal!" Duca Falluncci said. "You cannot judge him the same as you would a commoner."

"No, the weight of his crime, if anything is heavier," Stefano said. "To my mind, he is no royal. He was born on the wrong side of the blanket, is foreign born, and married into his title. He has murdered and connived."

"Begin by removing those titles he may possess from Tyrrhia and let him stand as his station in his homeland. He is a commoner by rights. Our only consideration is that the Duca deMedici has acknowledged him at all," Duca Giacomini responded.

"No! Just removing his titles is enough of a punishment for one such as he, and that will be punishment as well to Ortensia who has done nothing out of order," Duca Anino protested.

"Just removing his titles is not enough," Silvieri said quietly.

"Nor do we know if Ortensia has done 'nothing out of order,' as you presume, Duca Anino," Stefano pointed out evenly. "For all we know, she may . . . Where is the don who spoke before us? Don?"

"Battista, Your Excellency," the man said from the corner he had managed to escape to. "What would you have of me?"

"I would know if you have any evidence against the princess," Stefano replied. There was a murmur of approval from the duchi for the query.

Battista made a movement that Stefano could not make out. "Speak up. Your voice must be heard."

"The princess was not involved as I know it. There were no letters from her to the padre, nor him to her that I am aware of. Within the realm of my knowledge, the princess is not guilty of involving herself in her husband's affairs, whether he claims they were for her benefit or not," Battista witnessed. "The princess wanted the throne, but she— "

"Of course, she wanted the throne!" Silvieri snapped. "She believes it is her birthright. Denied the throne, I don't think she was then willing to cause civil unrest to meet her ends."

Old Anino agreed and so did LaCosta.

"Then we will take no charges to her. She will be badly

shaken to lose her husband, though," Stefano said. He breathed a heavy sigh. "Are all agreed that we remove the deMedici's title?"

Reluctantly, even the princess' faction of the duchi agreed.

"Then he returns to the rank of privileged commoner, a bastarde son of a neighboring kingdom's merchant prince. Does he die by the sword or by the method I choose for his confederates?" Stefano asked.

Uproar in the Palantini reigned until the rapping of Estensi's staff brought them to silence. Stefano had half-expected the wooden staff to shatter under the pounding the Court Herald gave it.

"I give you these two options only. He conspired to kill King Alban. That is treason in this country which he adopted. Treason is punished by death here—as in most other countries. I, at least, offer him a gentler method to die by," Stefano said. "I am willing to let you decide."

Sebastiani was forced to rise from his chair to partake in the conversation that followed among the Palantini members.

"Drink more of your wine and quit wrestling about if you don't want to reopen your wounds," Luciana whispered to him.

Stefano sighed and rearranged the sling on his left arm. He sat back and eased his leg forward. "There, I am more relaxed. Now give me peace, woman! I want to be up and on my own feet. This sitting here is a position of weakness."

"It's not weakness to be recovering from two bullet wounds, and I lost count of how many cuts you took from the blade. Rest yourself—"

"Like Strozzini is?" Stefano growled, temperamentally.

"Strozzini has not been shot in the leg and shoulder," Luciana replied. She offered him more wine. "It has healing herbs. Drink!"

Stefano took the goblet and drained it before handing it back to his wife. "No more, for now."

Ultimately, Duca Gianola spoke for the Palantini. "There are some who disagree with the notion of sentencing the prince to death."

"Point taken under advisement," Stefano replied, waiting.

The graying duca cast a glance over his shoulder, fidgeting with his coat. When he turned back to Stefano, he spoke with surprising resolve. "The sword for the prince. It is the death chosen for royalty. Though he is not royalty as proclaimed already, his wife, the princess will be comforted by this form of execution."

"Comforted?" Luciana whispered.

"I hardly think she will be *comforted* by losing her husband in any form of execution, especially a public one which is what is called for," Duchessa Rossi observed.

Gianola shrugged dismissively. Duchessa Rossi flushed with anger, but said nothing.

"And for the others?" Stefano said. "I recommend burning at the stake."

"But we haven't burned anyone at the stake since . . . since . . . well, before my father's time," white-haired Anino protested.

"That's true, but then with these witch-hunters, according to their own reports, their common practice of murder was by burning at the stake. It seems on point to return the favor," Stefano said.

"'Tis no favor, execution by the flames of a thousand deaths," Luciana said, shivering in spite of herself.

"What of the witnesses?" Sebastiani asked.

"What of them? The boy is a separate matter, entirely, but Enzo deliberately planned and took part in the murder of King Alban," Stefano said.

"But his testimony helped make it possible to recognize all that Pierro did. He was, at least apparently honest because his comrades were not pleased with all that he disclosed," Duchessa Rossi pointed out.

"And then there's the matter of the priest," Gianola said. He shook his head. "I don't advise the burning of the padre."

"He more than most because, probably, it was he who chose the method of death for the so-called witches. Tyrrhia fought wars to keep the Spanish Inquisition from our shores in generations gone by, and now he scuttles it like a crab over our borders. No, *he* more than most." Stefano stood firm on the matter.

"What about the cardinal?" Gianola pressed.

"What of him?" Sebastiani asked.

"The cardinal and he are both Catholic priests. What

if . . . what if the padre knows some of the cardinal's magic?" Gianola asked.

"Not likely," Stefano said shaking his head. "No, it is unlikely, but to be safe, he can wear a leather gag that will keep him from speaking magic and his hands will be bound so that there is no way for him to use magic by gesticulation."

"You seem to know very much about magic, Your Excellency," Gianola observed, his tone anxious.

"Look who he is married to, Your Grace," Duchessa Rossi said, then added quickly to Luciana, "and by this I mean no offense, Regent Guardian, but you have made no secret of your use of magic to the distress of some others here present."

"I cannot fault truth," Luciana replied equanimically. She reached over and stayed her husband's hand with her own when he started to scratch at his wounded shoulder. Without speaking, she thrust his goblet into Stefano's hand.

"But what benefit does the one calling himself Enzo get for his testimony?" Duca Raffia asked. "It seems he brought some of the others into our reach by his free speaking."

"Fine," Stefano said. "We will spare him from death by flames. He'll feel the fires, most assuredly, but I will have a marksman standing by who will end his suffering before the others. Would that satisfy you, Your Grace?"

Raffia rubbed a hand along the back of his neck and finally nodded in agreement.

"And what of the boy?" Duchessa Rossi asked softly, but loud enough to be heard.

"He will be exiled to the Dutch Netherlands, never to step foot on his native soil again," Stefano said. "He will be escorted to a Dutch ship. His passage will be paid for and he will be given a bit of money to start a new life. It is a harsh, but forgiving punishment."

With a final decision reached, the Palantini broke up and departed, gravely speaking to other members as they shuffled from the room.

"Don Battista, please wait! Excuse me," Stefano said to the others.

Cristoval Battista stopped and waited, hands behind his back. Strozzini stood by the door, waiting until the last of the duchi had been ushered from the room.

When everyone else was gone, Stefano stood, ignoring his wife's hiss of frustration.

"Rodrigo, Don Battista was fundamental to your placing the *Magnus Inique* as conspirators against King Alban, yes?"

"*Sí*," Strozzini agreed with a slight bow. "It was his note that laid bare the entire operation of the witch-hunters and gave me the first hint that Pierro deMedici might be involved. He—Don Cristoval Battista—did this at great risk to himself, his son, and his staff. He requested and was moved from the deMedici's state rooms immediately."

"So you were at some risk?" Stefano murmured thoughtfully. "And you have just married Giuletta—Queen Idala's personal maid, as well. You had much to protect."

"I have been blessed with two wives previously. My first wife died when my son was born and my second when she tried to give birth to my second son. They were both taken from me," Don Cristoval explained. He chewed his lower lip and dared go on. "I am doubly blessed to have found such a treasure for a new wife while here."

Stefano nodded. "What you did was very dangerous, Don, I give you my thanks. She came with but a small dowry being the youngest of seven daughters, but there are benefits to working with *la famiglia reale* as you two have done. There will be a consideration paid to both of you that should help you along your way, and if I may somehow return the favor . . . ask," Stefano said.

Don Battista bowed. "Thank you, Your Excellency."

When the don left, Luciana turned to Stefano. "Now, *camómescro*, will you let me put you to bed as *il dottore* suggests?"

"Of course not."

XXXI

"Better no law than laws not enforced."

—Italian proverb

26 d'Febbraio, 1685

"YOU really intend to do this today?" Luciana asked as she helped Stefano with his green-and-gold Gypsy Silk brocade frock coat. Carlo stood to one side looking like he had eaten a lemon. Stefano ignored him. He was letting her help him dress because it was *some* distraction from her fussing over his wounds. He had suffered worse and with less ministrations in the Peloponnese!

"It should have been done yesterday," Stefano said.

Carlo stepped in quickly with his master's baldric and sword, displacing Luciana, as he put the baldric over Stefano's shoulder and looped the rapier into the frog at his left hip.

"I haven't had this many people insisting on dressing me since I was a tot!" Stefano growled, grabbing the chain of office from the bedside table and pulling it on over his head.

Luciana shoved Carlo aside with a withering look and adjusted his chain. "Have them make a bed for you in the *infermeria* if you insist on being this difficult."

Stefano captured her hands and kissed them. "I do not have the luxury of resting while I heal, *camómescro*. I am Lord Regent, not some run-of-the-mill duca who could afford to disappear for days. The country depends on me, whether I like it or not."

Luciana sighed. "Yes, I know, and I must review Dario Gian's progress with his tutors, but still, there is a palanquin all ready for you to use—"

"Woman, I let you have your way with that yesterday and felt the bloody fool. I will use the crutch that *il dottore* has provided."

"Grudgingly provided," Luciana retorted. "So, you will go to the *infermeria* first?"

"Yes, the men should see that I appreciate their sacrifices," Stefano said.

"And then, the . . . executions?" Luciana asked.

Stefano nodded.

Luciana rolled her eyes. "If you're going to hold Ortensia guiltless in Pierro's crimes, then you must take all due care of her. Have *il dottore* sedate her with a good tea and then watch over her. Her life may be on your head."

"I spoke of that to *il dottore* Bonta this very morning. Her spells of madness have been deleterious to her and everyone in the palazzo," Stefano said softly. He hated to think of how this was affecting the princess, but there was nothing more that he could do. He certainly could not excuse deMedici for his crimes, not and keep his own head. "You will not be at the executions?"

Luciana shook her head, shuddering. "I cannot. Carlo, I expect you to stay with His Excellency today in case he needs anything."

Carlo nodded.

"At least," Luciana said, "Ortensia's child is safe."

"See to it," Stefano bade her.

A measure of crossness flitted across Luciana's features. "I have, as yet, to let those children suffer for the conditions of their parents. Divya is in the nursery to remind people of my constant presence there. As soon as you are off, I am gone as well."

"Then let us begin the day!" Stefano sighed, taking the crutch from Carlo.

"You are a difficult man to serve," Strozzini sighed. "Can you not just trust me?"

"I *do* trust you otherwise I'd have long replaced you . . .

or at least dismissed you. I have my men-at-arms. I was not eager to replace the ones I had. I took them to the Peloponnesian front with me. Two died in recovering me from Turkish captors, and the others I left to continue the fight at the front. They were of a mind to, anyway. I've been back barely a year and have replaced them at your behest from one of the smartest units the Escalade had to offer."

"It serves a purpose. You are the Lord Regent and you should have a staff of your own capable of defense, should the need arise. You and the family should always be protected," Strozzini said.

"They are. I've blasted the capitano . . . della Guelfa for letting his guard slip on Luciana when they were on the road," Stefano growled.

"I hope he was suitably embarrassed?" Rodrigo asked as they made their way toward the barracks with Carlo just behind them.

"He was, but I cannot punish him too harshly. He was working on orders from my wife, and she does not always think of her health before she decides what is best to be done, even if she did protect herself by summoning the maggiore," Stefano said. "I would have liked to have seen that. She says he rose from the fire and attacked a dozen men. Only one escaped by stealing a horse.

"So, tell me, Rodrigo, why do you attend me when you should be nursing your wounds? I have other men to stand as my bodyguard . . . at your insistence," Stefano asked.

"This day is important and my wounds are . . . merely troublesome," Strozzini replied. "You must have the Royal Bodyguard at your side today. Later . . . there will be others with us, in case there is unrest."

"You've arranged it all, then, have you? And tomorrow you rest?"

"The arrangement has been made. There will be no lapse in your protection, Your Excellency," Strozzini remarked. "You chastise me and do not take good enough care of your own wounds. What did Bonta say when you told him you were making this trip?"

Stefano laughed. "He said nothing because I did not tell him. I'll have to listen to his fussing at me tonight, but at least I will have served my purpose this day and ended this awful waiting."

"Indeed," Rodrigo agreed.

"Come, let's find the vigilare as you have arranged and get ourselves back." Stefano set the pace, hampered by the crutch and noting that Strozzini did not seem eager to rush him as they covered the ground to the Escalade barracks.

"They are already ready, Your Excellency," Strozzini said.

"Good. Then they will be prepared when I am," Stefano retorted. With a disgruntled sigh, he pulled the crutch under his right arm and hobbled in the direction of the Escalade barracks.

A posted guard bowed to him when Stefano reached them. "May I assist you, Your Excellency?" the man asked while pushing the doors open wide.

"*Infirmiera*?" Stefano said, then waved his hand. "Same place it's always been?"

"*Sí*, Your Excellency," the guard replied, pointing down one of the halls that yawned open from the entryway.

Stefano thanked him and returned to once familiar halls. He hesitated only momentarily when he reached what he thought was the right door. Inside, he found the room filled in orderly fashion with cots on both sides. Men occupied the first five beds at the head of the room, near the man wearing the bloodstained apron who apparently tended to them.

Seeing Stefano, the apron-covered man bowed, causing the heads of the men in the *infirmiera* to turn as well. They started to struggle up into sitting positions.

Stefano waved his hand. "Please, stay resting. *Il dottore*?"

"*Il infirmiere*," the nurse corrected him, bowing again.

"Please. Stop that," Stefano said, catching the man by the shoulder. "Where are the men who were wounded on the road?"

"Most of them received only minor wounds or such that they have already returned to duty, Your Excellency," the nurse said. "Guido here malingers, and Fidelo, Filippo, and Armando will be ready for duty again in a week . . . perhaps a little more." He spoke with an open smile, then frowned, apparently thinking better of joking in front of the Lord Regent. "Guido will return to duty in the next few days . . . this other Lorenz is here because of *another* incident and are *non importanza*."

"They are all important, Signore. They serve in the Queen's Escalade. Just because we have no queen, does not mean that they are less important to me than the *Armata*," Stefano said.

With Strozzini hugging his side—which Stefano thought unnecessary in the Escalade garrison, but did not argue—he spoke first to the youth named Guido and the others before addressing the last man, Lorenz.

When Stefano finished his visit, he found himself swaying slightly.

"You have spent too much time on your feet, Your Excellency," *il infirmiere* said, coming to his side. "You have gone pale."

Stefano shook off the nurse's ministrations. "I am fine. Thank you for your service." He hobbled off, out of the *infermeria*, out of the building, and leaned against a hitching post.

"You *are* failing," Strozzini murmured attentively. "You are not well. Let me summon—"

"Get me a horse. I must stand for the executions . . . but if I cannot stand, then I will sit . . . astride," Stefano countered, finally willing to admit, at least to himself, that the light-headedness was not passing. Bonta had predicted these spells because of the seriousness of his wounds and his loss of blood that day. Whatever it was, Stefano wanted only to sink back into his bed, not that he would admit it to anyone—not to Bonta nor even Rodrigo; not that he would willingly return to his bed, not when there was too much to do.

Strozzini reappeared quickly. "They are readying your horse."

"Fascino?" Stefano asked. The aging gelding had a nice seat on him, like a familiar and comfortable chair. "But he was wounded?"

"Yes, but the stable manager says that he can serve this light duty without causing him trouble," the bodyguard replied. "Unless, of course, you want to ride one of the Escalade mounts . . . or my horse."

"You will be on your horse, Rodrigo, and the other mounts are a little green . . . and I will not ride any other horse if I can safely use Fascino," Stefano replied. He pushed off from the hitching post and started to cross the short distance to the stables, but Strozzini caught his arm.

"They will bring our mounts to us, Your Excellency," Rodrigo said.

Carlo lingered nearby, watching for his master. He came immediately to Stefano's side. "How may I attend you, Your Excellency?" he asked, fretting. "Would you take some of the medicinal wine?"

Stefano started to refuse, then feeling the dizziness and weakness of his body, nodded instead and took the wine-skin from his man. He took a long pull from the bag and then handed it to Strozzini with a no nonsense look. The bodyguard drank and returned the flask to Carlo.

Fascino whickered, welcoming him when he was brought from the stables. Stefano rubbed the horse's head and then took a look at his mount, looking over legs, withers, and, finally, the hip where he had caught the buckshot. The wound was, indeed superficial. Without asking, Carlo offered Stefano a hand up into the saddle.

Rodrigo mounted his big steed with not quite the speed and elegance he normally had.

"Your horse . . . he doesn't look of Italian or Romani heritage. Where did you find him?" Stefano asked.

"A cross with a Belgian horse and some questionable stock. The breeder didn't want him, so I took him," Strozzini said, patting the black-striped withers of his mount. "He's been good to me."

The time was upon them, Stefano realized as he listened to the pealing of the church bells marking the noon hour. It was time for the first of the executions. Pierro deMedici. His life, like the others, could not be spared. The law demanded consequence and the people would expect it. This, of all times, was not a time for internal unrest in Tyrrhia because of an excess of leniency.

Stefano guided Fascino into a steady walk. They rounded the palazzo only to discover a crowd gathered—nobles and retainers; man, mother, and child—some laughing and calling to their friends. He shook his head, angry. Someone catcalled, another whistled as Pierro was led out of the palazzo and to the station raised beside Alaric's statue.

"No!" Stefano yelled and prodded Fascino into the midst of them. "No! Do you hear me?"

The throng of people turned, one head at a time; even Pierro looked at him. The deMedici, shackled and disheveled, his eyes red and swollen, stared daggers at Stefano from where he stood at the top of the dais steps, held by two of the Palazzo Guards.

Stefano stopped at the executioner's dais and turned Fascino around to face the mob. He scanned the crowd, his gaze wrenching suddenly in the direction of a woman and the small child in front of her. Heir Apparent, Prince Dario Gian stood before him with his *governante*, right in the very front. He shook his head again, trying to control his blinding anger. Beneath him, Fascino began to prance, sensing his owner's mood, and paw out at the people.

"This is no entertainment and certainly no place for children! Take them inside, at once. A man's life stands at stake for his crimes against the State, against our people. We are meting out justice here. This is not an invitation to casual gawkers, but a serious business of enforcing our laws that bind and guide us into a single, unified nation. Take the children away!" Stefano clapped his hands when no one moved immediately, instead staring at him as though star struck. The noise caused Fascino to rear up on his hindquarters and truly paw the air with his great hooves.

People moved back, away from the warhorse and began to disperse . . . at least, some of them. Servants and ladies-in-waiting began hurrying the children from the midst of the throng. Stefano noted that Dario Gian's governess remained where she stood, with the young prince.

Stefano calmed the horse and closed the distance to the woman who watched over the prince. "I mean you to go."

"Me?" she repeated, looking around her, her hands clutching the five-year-old's shoulders reflexively.

"You and the boy."

"But he is to be king. He must understand justice and the need to hand it out," the woman replied.

"He will understand justice because he will receive it. He will understand punishment because there will be times he will receive that. He will learn nothing by having a man's head land at his feet!" Stefano snapped. "Now, take the Royal Prince and go inside, where *he* belongs!"

For half a breath, it looked like the *governante* would argue, but she did not. She bowed her head, picked up the small boy—who suddenly had a lot of questions—and took him away via the back entrance into the palazzo.

Stefano turned Fascino again and backed him into the

crowd, to take his place at the center of the stage, but far enough back, hopefully, to be out of the way of the viscera that would fly.

Strozzini moved his horse to stand beside Stefano's gray warhorse. The bodyguard nodded to him silently.

Looking down at his hands, Stefano gathered his wits together, shoving away the bitter taste of anger that still rose in his throat. He heard Pierro's shackles rattle and scrape against the wooden station as he was moved to the center. For another moment, he paused. This justice was not to be enforced with anger, but a sure hand. It was something he wished there were another answer to, but . . . no . . . this was what was expected, accepted. Taking a deep breath, Stefano looked up into Pierro's sullen gaze.

"Do you have any final words?" he asked.

The deMedici stiffened and tilted his head up. "I *am* the Prince deMedici, rightful Prince of Tyrrhia. What you do to me . . . to my wife . . . there are no words for that, *Your Excellency*!" he spat.

Stefano nodded, breathing deeply. "And you have nothing else to say? You do not wish to speak to your crimes, or more of your wife or son?"

"What crimes I committed were seen by your eyes, di Drago. I'd 've gladly split you in two had I the opportunity. As to my wife, take her back, such as she is, and marry her off now. To the boy, I—" Here, deMedici faltered. Tears welled in his eyes. "For his sake, I denounce him. He is now, and forever more, *il Turche*!"

Without being bidden by the executioner, Pierro jerked away from his guards and knelt himself before the stump. "If you must strike, strike true, strike now!" he commanded.

The executioner looked to Stefano, then raised his blade and struck a single blow with the great sword. For a minute, there came a sudden and deep silence over the people. Blood sprayed out, showering the black-robed executioner and those at the front of the crowd. Pierro deMedici's head rolled from the wooden stump and into the basket beside it. The body sagged to one side and spasmed before becoming still. Life flowed forth, in a silent red river, spilling over the station and between the boards. In the end, there was silence.

Fascino stamped, snorted, and champed at the bit. The accumulated noises were not so very different from a battle scene with the sound of the much larger crowd congregated from Citteauroea.

The prisoners were led out of a cart, two of them screaming, another crying. A lone man remained tied to the inside of the cart, sobbing as he watched the others taken. It was the youth, Giraldo.

Stefano had dispatched vigilare throughout the mass of people, searching for children and other young folk who were ordered to be sent home. Some obeyed; others hid in the tall grasses on the far side of the now cleared field. There were too many children, too many adults to make sure it stayed safe for Stefano to enforce his decision on the crowd without bringing out a full force of the Escalade, and that would only enrage the people.

Strozzini kept to Stefano's back as he guided Fascino through the throng of people, toward the five prisoners now standing in a line. The young man in the cart had fallen quiet; his eyes huge as he watched the proceedings.

"These men will burn for the sake of justice," Stefano finally said to the gathered nobility, merchants, and commoners. "They have been duly convicted of the death of our King Alban and the deaths of people . . . women, like you—Tyrrhians who did not fit their belief of what a Tyrrhian should be. They will die as they sentenced many of our people to die.

"There is no avenging Alban, our king, but there is justice, and it should be swiftly carried out. That is why we are gathered today—for the sake of justice—to see that one and all follow the same laws, the same freedoms of thought and religion that unite us against others who would oppress us and force their beliefs upon us.

"There is no vengeance, no joy in my heart to see what must be carried out here today. Search your own hearts, follow the laws, and let it be known that such crimes will not be tolerated by anyone!" Stefano cried, unleashing the booming voice he used to address his troops on the battlefield. He watched as some people looked away, but many others nodded. He wheeled Fascino toward the palazzo, toward the cart next to which the bishop sat upon his own horse, watching him, ignoring the man in the cart and the guards who protected him. "There is one other man who was also charged. He is young and foolish. In reaction to the loss of King Alban, he searched out vengeance, yet instead, tied his lot with the very men he sought to avenge himself and this country against. He, we have decided, will be spared, but he will be sent from our land for evermore. Speak to me the meaning of the law!"

The mob called out. "Justice!" rose on most of their lips, variants of it on others. Stefano nodded, encouraging the call until the crowd spoke as one. "Justice."

Stefano waved them to be still and turned to the bishop. "Your Reverence, please attend these men for the last time."

Abruzzi rode up on his white horse, pausing beside Stefano and the ever-present Strozzini. "You know how to stir a crowd. With this, there are no last appeals," the bishop growled.

"Their last appeals were made and refused," Stefano said, keeping the returning anger tamped down. "Serve them or deny them, Bishop, but the prisoners will receive their mercy from you . . . if you give it."

"They'll have their Last Rites," Abruzzi said and trotted off. He dismounted before the prisoners, threw his reins to one of the vigilare, and pulled his prayer book from beneath his deep purple cassock.

Stefano and Strozzini took their place in the crowd, the bodyguard watchful of everyone around them. When the bishop was done with his prayers for the first prisoner . . . the priest, Caserta . . . he moved on to the next. Stefano nodded to the guards behind him.

Despite his crimes, the Escalade guards were as easy with Caserta as he allowed them to be. The priest struggled a bit, or perhaps he merely lost his footing as he climbed to the post and was tied to it.

As the prayers were said over each man, Enzo, being next and getting one of the forward posts was led to his final station. Once tied and shackled, each man's guards turned to the business of adding thatching to the pile around their feet. The prisoners would die from the smoke ere the fire reached them.

Stefano studied his hands again, the leather straps, which were Fascino's reins, held tight. He said a silent prayer for the souls of the men and made the sign of the cross.

"Funny to find you at prayer, Your Excellency," Abruzzi's sharp voice cut in onto Stefano's concentration.

"I was just praying for them myself, Bishop," Stefano replied, trying to stay unruffled by the man's cutting demeanor.

"The least you could do is release the priest to me. I'll send him to Rome. He'll never be seen or heard from again," Abruzzi bargained.

A couple of men turned and hissed at the bishop when they overheard the suggestion.

"You see?" Stefano said. He blew his breath out heavily between his pinched lips. "There is nothing more to be done. He was the leader of these men. He must die."

"*You* set this in motion. You'll pay for this! The Church won't stand for this kind of treatment of its people!" Abruzzi said.

"You aren't threatening the Lord Regent, are you, Your Reverence?" Strozzini asked, his hand resting lightly on his sword.

Stefano laid hand on his bodyguard's arm. "At ease, soldier," he said. "Bishop, it is time 'to render unto Caesar what is his' as the Church teaches us. Just to be clear, Your Reverence, are you saying that the Church condones the murdering of kings now? Or is the Church, through its priests, orchestrating the murders themselves? Really, you have made it quite clear it is one or the other by your heated protestations. Once you clarify this for me, I will gladly so inform the other heads of State of the Christian nations so that they may better protect themselves."

Abruzzi fell silent, scowling daggers as hot as any Pierro cast in his direction that afternoon. He made the signs of the cross on his chest and face in exaggerated deliberation, then turned his horse so that he was next to Strozzini.

Stefano signaled to the executioner, who got off his seat on the cart holding the young prisoner and picked up one of the brands from the small bonfire to the right of the field and the posts.

With slow deliberation, the official moved from one pyre after another, lighting each in several places so that the fire would burn evenly, and, therefore, be more mercifully swift. Stefano worked hard to keep his expression dispassionate, but could not help thinking of Alban who had fallen so unnecessarily. It had been a useless, stupid crime committed against a nation since the Palantini would never have approved of Ortensia and Pierro ruling even without Stefano's influence.

When the fire leaped up skyward, fully engulfing each man on their separate pyres, their cries drowned out the buzz of talk in the throng of people witnessing their deaths. The smell of burning fabric, flesh, and hair began to fill the air. The heat of the flames bathed the faces of the people.

Stefano twisted in his saddle, spying the officer in the tree closest to the road. He had made early arrangements for a sharp shooter to be hidden, to make the mercy shots. Stefano nodded to the man, who immediately fired his crossbow. It was possible to know Enzo was dead only by the lack of his voice crying out his misery. Stefano nodded again. The officer braced himself against the tree trunk and reloaded his large crossbow.

One by one, the men's voices fell silent. The smoke stung the eye and the smell gripped the nostrils of those who attended. Somewhere, someone retched. The mob began to filter back to their homes and businesses, be it in the city or at the palazzo.

Stefano and Strozzini left the bishop staring at the pyre built around the priest.

XXXII

"If we had no winter, the spring would not be so pleasant: if we did not sometimes taste of adversity, prosperity would not be so welcome."

—Anne Bradstreet

12 d'Marzo, 1685

STEFANO stood in the nursery. These babies were all healthy and growing . . . even "*il Turche*," the deMedicis' son. Luciana sat with Divya in her arms, and the baby tracked him as he moved around the nursery. Dario Gian sat on the floor playing with a ball, and his three sisters laughed as the bright yellow-and-red wooden toy rolled into them. All was well in the nursery. The children thrived.

It was difficult not to think of the other prince, of Massimo. Just back from visiting him in deFaria, Stefano remembered the twisted boy lying out on a blanket with his foster-brother. Federico Boniface, the foster, was as healthy and thriving as the children here, but Massimo remained small and weak, his development significantly delayed.

Stefano said nothing, but bent and kissed Luciana and Divya before departing. He had been subdued ever since the executions. He made his way from the nursery through the halls to his office, Strozzini strolling behind him, casual and relaxed.

"You seem depressed, Your Excellency," Rodrigo commented at the top of the stair. "Is all well?"

"Well enough," Stefano said, motioning for Strozzini to join him in the office rather than stand at post outside his door. More often, these days, Rodrigo was growing to be more than his constant companion. He was becoming a friend.

Stefano sat at the desk and scattered the neat stack of papers Estensi had left for him. He sorted them again, scanning their contents as he did so. There came a scratching at the door.

Strozzini rose and opened the door, stepping back for Estensi. The Court Herald entered the room and bowed to Stefano.

"Your Excellency, there are duchi who wish to meet with you," he said. His expression was a closed book. Stefano could read nothing there.

"Who are these duchi and on what matter do they wish to address me?" Stefano asked.

"They are Duca Calvino Anino, Duca Augusto Sebastiani, and . . . Her Highness, Princess Ortensia Novabianco," Estensi said. "They are waiting downstairs. In my office. They would speak to you now."

"Novabianco?" Stefano repeated, sitting very still. "The princess has repudiated her marriage to deMedici?"

"It would seem so, Your Excellency. She was very specific," Estensi replied.

"Show them up," Stefano ordered, motioning to Strozzini to take a seat at the back of the room.

"As you wish," Estensi said and disappeared out the door and down the stairs.

"This should be interesting," Stefano commented to Strozzini. He stood up at the sound of Sebastiani struggling up the stairs and two other sets of footsteps.

Ortensia entered the room first. She wore a subdued gray gown and undergown adorned with embroidery, but few other embellishments. Her hair had been pulled back and put into a rather severe bun and snood. It seemed she used rouge and powder, but there was little of it.

Stefano bowed over her hand and guided her to a chair, leaving Sebastiani's favorite chair and footstool open for him.

Sebastiani entered, leaning heavily on a cane, and collapsed, breathless, in his chair beside the princess. Duca Anino came last and, despite being the oldest of all the duchi, seemed fit and steady, his eyes sharp and clear.

"We have come to discuss the wording of the new law regarding magic and *la famiglia reale*," Anino announced, taking a seat and sparing a quick glance at Strozzini.

Stefano nodded and slowly took his seat behind the desk. "You have considered this carefully, I presume?"

"Of course!" Anino snapped.

Ortensia remained stone-faced, not rising to the opportunity to retort. She briefly met his eyes, but quickly looked away. She folded her hands in her lap and then gripped the arms of the chair she sat in. "The wording is very simple and straightforward."

"Go on," Sebastiani urged her.

Ortensia took a paper from her cuff and unfolded it. She shoved it across the desk for Stefano to read.

"The law will state that 'any member of *la famiglia reale* using magic automatically concedes his or her claim to the throne. Magic involved in the birth or conception of a member of *la famiglia reale* makes them ineligible for the throne,'" Ortensia said.

"This will be in addition to the existing law that forbids casting magic on *la famiglia reale*," Sebastiani added gruffly.

Stefano took the paper in his hand and read the wording written down in a neat, firm hand. It was very explicit. He wet his lips, forming a question.

"This means, Your Excellency," Duca Anino said, "that Dario Gian stands first in line for the throne."

"Of course," Stefano said, "but what about his sisters?"

"It applies to the brother as well," Sebastiani said.

"So this means that Chiara, born of a Romani spirit is—" Stefano began.

"Ineligible for the White Throne. The Romani can do what they like with her . . . keeping in mind that she *is la famiglia reale*," Anino added. "They will be teaching her magic and there's talk they'll make her Queen of the Gypsies one day. That is to them to decide. She cannot and will not take the White Throne *ever*."

"That leaves Pietra and Rosalina," Stefano said.

Ortensia shook her head. When she spoke, her tone was soft and even. "Rosalina, according to the story you told us, was a doubling of an existing pregnancy. Though she is a twin, only Pietra, as firstborn, can inherit the throne should something happen to His Royal Highness."

"So Pietra is second-in-line for the throne, and that makes you third-in-line, Ortensia?" Stefano asked.

Ortensia shook her head, a tendril of her red hair escaping the snood she wore. She took another paper from her other sleeve. "By this paper, I formally, regretfully, withdraw. I will not inherit . . . but my son, Luca, the one everyone calls '*il Turche*,' he will be third in line, and if he cannot serve, then a new line must be found to inherit. The Novabianco line will end with him."

Stefano's mind raced over the possibilities. "That could mean civil war!" Stefano said.

"But you will be there to stand in the breach, di Drago . . . if you live so long," Anino said.

La Fine

Appendix

Abruzzi, Bishop: (Character—Italian) The bishop who replaced delle Torre at the Cattedrale d'Alaric.
adorata: (Italian) beloved
d'Agosto: (Italian) the month of August.
Alaric: (Goth) Name of infamous Visigoth king who sacked Rome twice. Departing after his second sacking (in 410 AD), Alaric is said to have died on his ship (412 AD). Myth has it that his men docked in Messina, diverted a river and buried Alaric and his treasure, rediverting the river before their departure. Tyrrhian history states that this treasure was found and used by certain Italian nobles to separate their duchies from mainland Italy and to side with Sicilian nobles, forming the homeland of Tyrrhia and the wealth of the kingdom.
Alban Cosimo Abram di Mirandola e Novabianco: (Character—Tyrrhian) King of Tyrrhia and Jerusalem, Duca di Citteauroea (*Regis di Tyrrhia e Geruslemme, Duca di Citteauroea*), a.k.a. "The White King." A nephew of King Orsinio Novabianco.
Alessandra Zingara Nofria Patrini e di Montago: (Character—Tyrrhian Romani) *Araunya di Cayesmengro* before her death. Sister of Luciana Mizella Elena Patrini e di Drago, *Duchessa di Drago, Araunya di Cayesmengri*. Died April 14, 1684 at the age of 20.
Anino, Duca: (Character—Tyrrhian) Eldest member of the Palantini, prone to suspicion.
Araunya: (Romanes) Title for a Romani noblewoman of the rank of merchant princess.
attaccabrighe: (Italian) Troublemaker.

bambola: (Italian) doll
Battista, Don Cristoval: (Character—Tyrrhian) Petty lord living near Sciacca, Tyrrhia, sympathetic to the Catholics.
Battista, Ludovico: (Character—Tyrrhian) Young son of Don Cristoval Battista.
basta: (Italian) Enough, done, sufficient.
bastarde: (Italian) Bastard.
beano abri: (Romanes) "I was born out of doors, like a gypsy." This is a common greeting to identify oneself as part of the community.
Beluni: (Romanes) Honorific title given to the Queen of the Gypsies, Solaja Lendaro
bender: (Romanes) A dome-shaped tent set up at a Romani encampment for roomier housing. Made of branches and tarps.
beng: (Romanes) Devil.
Bianca Estella Renata Novabianco: (Character—Tyrrhian) Daughter of King Orsinio Ricci e Novabianco, sister to Ortensia Elettra Rosaria Novabianco.
Bishop Abruzzi: (Character—Italian) Replaces cardinal.
Boiko, General: (Character—Turkish) Allied to Pierro de-Medici and Turkish Sultan Tardiq.
Bonta, il dottore Dionisio: (Character—Tyrrhian) Royal Physician.
bosh: (Romanes) Fiddle, violin.
boshmengro: (Romanes) Romani Fiddler.
bravi: (Italian) Ruffians. (Plural of *bravo*.)
bravo: (Italian) Ruffian.
bricconcello: (Italian) Villain, rascal.
camómescro: (Romanes) Beloved.
candelas: (Italian) Fairies of light, will-o'-wisps
Capitano: (Italian) Captain (military title)
Cardinal Pius Enrico delle Torre: (Character—Italian) Bishop of Tyrrhia as assigned by the Catholic church. Served as the Church's representative in Tyrrhia. Killed by *mullós* Alessandra and "sister-kindred."
Caserta, Padre: (Character—Italian) Leader of the priests belonging to *Magnus Inique*. A Roman Catholic Father. Inducted Cristoval Battista into the order.
Cattedrale d' Alaric: (Italian) Cathedral of Alaric within palazzo grounds.
Cayesmengri: (Romanes) Silk thing, made of silk. In this

case, referring to the land where the mulberry and oak trees which feed the silk worms and all things related to Tyrrhian Gypsy Silk trade (such as looms, needles, etc.).

Cayesmengro: (Romanes) Silk fellow, referring to both the silk worms and the Tyrrhian Gypsy Silk Guild members and artisans.

chavi: (Romanes) Girl, girl-child; an expression of affection to a junior female.

chavo: (Romanes) Boy, youth, young man; an expression of affection to a junior male.

chova: (Romanes) Magic.

chovahani: (Romanes) Sorceress, witch. Female student of the occult or mystical arts. Also plural of chovahano.

chovahano: (Romanes) Sorcerer, male wizard. Male student of the occult or mystical arts.

Citteauroea: (Tyrrhian) City of Gold. Capital city of Tyrrhia.

Colonello: (Italian) Colonel (military title)

Colonello Fieri: (Character—Tyrrhian) A Senior Palazzo Guard, father of guardsman Fieri who was murdered, in charge of solving the mystery of the deaths in the dungeon.

compagni: (Italian) Brothers in arms, comrades.

Corpo d'Armata: (Tyrrhian) The Tyrrhian army and navy commanded by the king.

Conte: (Italian) Nobleman with the title of count.

Contessa: (Italian) Noblewoman with the title of countess.

Daiya: (Romanes) Honorific title given to senior females to whom a Romani owes a debt of allegiance, usually also learned in the ways of Romani magic.

Dario Gian Novabianco: (Character—Tyrrhian) His Royal Highness, Crown Prince, eldest son of Idala and Alban. At the time of the events, he's a bare five-year-old.

deBonneta, Ennio: (Character—Tyrrhian) One of Mandero's personal unit. Hired as Stefano di Drago's man-at-arms and is Dario Gian's personal bodyguard.

dela Chola, Vico: (Character—Tyrrhian) One of Mandero's personal unit. Hired as Stefano di Drago's man-at-arms.

delle Tello, Tazio: (Character—Tyrrhian) One of Mandero's personal unit. Hired as Stefano di Drago's man-at-arms.

delle Torre: (Character—Italian) The cardinal (see cardinal).

delVecchio, Rosalia: (Character—Tyrrhian) Don Battista's

housekeeper and governess to his son, Ludovico. She is their *governante*.

della Guelfa, Capitano Marco: (Character—Tyrrhian) One of Mandero's personal unit, his second in command. Wife is Maria. Hired as Stefano di Drago's man-at-arms and assigned to Luciana as bodyguard.

della Guelfa, Maria: (Character—Tyrrhian) Capitano della Guelfa's wife, midwife and royal nurse.

diCalabria, Duca: (Character—Tyrrhian) Senior member of the Palantini

di Candido, Duca: (Character—Tyrrhian) Senior member of the Palantini

diklo: (Romanes) Kerchief worn by men (around the neck) and women (over their hair).

Divya Leonora Adorata di Drago: (Character—Tyrrhian) Daughter of Stefano and Luciana di Drago.

Drago: (Tyrrhian) Italian for dragon, Tyrrhian family name. Family crest and the hereditary name of the duca. Currently held by Stefano di Luna, Duca di Drago, Colonello dagli Escalade e con di Palantini.

Dragorione: (Tyrrhian) Foremost of the Drago estates.

drom: (Romanes) road

Duarte, Piramo: (Character—Tyrrhian) One of Mandero's personal unit. Hired by Stefano di Drago as man-at-arms.

Duca: (Italian) Nobleman with the title of duke.

Duchessa: (Italian) Noblewoman with the title of duchess.

Duchi: (Tyrrhian) Plural form of duca, also refers to nobles in general.

dukkerin': (Romanes) Fortune-telling of various sorts, also involves a little of the "con."

Escalade: (Tyrrhian) This is a fighting unit making up the queen's personal guard which also acts as a type of police force. This is an armed, assault force at the command of the king via the Queen of Tyrrhia, able to move on short notice. Standard equipment are rapiers and a set of small, hand-held crossbows called scorpininis (latchet crossbows).

Estensi, Don Benoni: (Character—Tyrrhian) Royal Court Herald.

Exilli: (Character—Italian) Came to court as a "perfumer" for Pierro deMedici which is a polite way of saying he is a poisoner. The character comes from history and was renowned throughout the European countries as a skilled poisoner.

Fata: (Italian) The Fairy, the Fairy folk. Considered by some to be a representation of goddesses.

figlio: (Italian) son.

focaccia: (Italian) Bread. A flat, rounded bread.

gadjé: (Romanes) Caucasian; not of Romani descent. (Plural is also *gadjé*.)

Gabera, Romero: (Character—Tyrrhian) Roman Catholic priest rescued by Maggiore di Montago and set up in the Cattedrale d'Alaric.

Giordano, Dego: (Character—Tyrrhian) One of Mandero's personal unit. Hired by Stefano di Drago as a man-at-arms.

Generale: (Italian) General. Military title.

gianes: (Italian) Fairies with backward feet. They are the spinners and weavers who taught the Romani women and created what later became Gypsy Silk. Leader of the *Fata* is the *Madonna-gianes*.

Gianola, Duca: (Character—Tyrrhian) An older member of the Palantini, tends toward superstitious.

governante: (Italian) governess

Grasni Nevi: (Character—Tyrrhian Romani) Once Alessandra Patrini's personal maid and servant, now apprenticed to the *Beluni* Solaja Lendaro.

Her Excellency: Honorific used to refer to a noblewoman of the rank of Regent or Regent Guardian.

Her Grace: Honorific used to refer to a noblewoman of the rank of duchessa.

Her Highness: Honorific used to refer to a noblewoman of the rank of princess.

His Excellency: Honorific used to refer to a nobleman of the rank of Regent or Regent Guardian.

His Grace: Honorific used to refer to a nobleman of the rank of duca.

His Highness: Honorific used to refer to a nobleman of the rank of prince.

Her Majesty: Honorific used to refer to a noblewoman of the rank of queen.

His Majesty: Honorific used to refer to a nobleman of the rank of king.

Hetchi-witchi: (Romanes) A delicacy of hedge hog cooked in clay.

Idala Rabiah Damaris di Drago e Novabianco: (Character—Tyrrhian) Queen of Tyrrhia and Jerusalem, Duchessa di Citteauroea. Wife of Alban Cosimo Abram di Mirandola e Novabianco, King of Tyrrhia, Duca di Citteauroea, and sister to Stefano di Luna, Duca di Drago.

Kris: (Romanes) The male council of elders that oversee the various clans, *vitsi*, *kumpanias*, etc.

kumpania: (Romanes) Clans, owing allegiance to one another.

la famiglia reale: (Italian) the Royal Family

la sirena di mare: (Italian) mermaid (See *sirena*)

Levant: (French) The land around the eastern Mediterranean especially Syria and Lebanon.

Luciana Mizella Elena Patrini e di Drago: (Character—Tyrrhian Romani) Duchessa di Drago, *Araunya di Cayesmengri* (*e Cayesmengro*). Wife of Stefano di Luna, Duca di Drago, Colonello dagli Escalade e con di Palantini; sister of Alessandra Zingara Nofria Patrini e di Montago; granddaughter of Solaja Lendaro, *Beluni* of the Tyrrhian Romani; stepdaughter of Conte Baiamonte Patrini e Davizzi.

d'Messina: (Italian) Of Messina, referencing the city of Messina in Tyrrhia (Sicily) anchoring land mass of one point of the Stretto d'Messina.

Maggiore: (Italian) military title/rank of major.

Magnus Ignique: (Latin) Hammer and Fire . . . religious order and cult.

mam: (Romanes) mother

mami: (Romanes) grandmother

Mandero Ercole di Montago: (Character—Tyrrhian Romani) Half-caste maggiore in the Queen's Escalade, husband of Alessandra. His mother came from the Bliardi Clan.

manigaldo: (Italian) ruffian

marimé: (Romanes) Impure or defiled.

Meero-Kak: (Romanes) Honorific for senior male, a Clan Chief.

Meklis: (Romanes) Hold! Wait! Hold your tongue!

minore: (Italian) smaller, lesser, younger

Montagna, Matteo: (Character—Tyrrhian) Instructor for Dario Gian.

mulló: (Romanes) Ghost, spirit, undead, wraith. In Romani tradition, the *mulló* can only be one of their blood (in other words a *gadjé* might be a ghost, but not a *mulló*) and its nature is one of impurity—no matter how good the person had been before their death—and is similar in many ways to a cross between a vampire, succubi, and ghost.

Neoplatonic: (Greek) Of or relating to Neoplatonism. The revival and transformation of Platonic philosophy. Its ideas are a synthesis of Greek thought and of certain trends in Oriental mysticism and were adopted by medieval mystics and by humanists of the Italian Renaissance Neoplatonists. Its central doctrines are Emanation, the belief that the human spirit can participate in the divine, and the belief in the transcendent One, which is beyond all knowledge and all being. It has been adopted by Tyrrhia as the national philosophy and adapted to encourage/tolerate a variety of religious practices as a search toward the transcendent One.

Ordineri: (Italian) Commander(s), military commander(s).

Ortensia Elettra Rosaria Novabianco e deMedici: (Character—Tyrrhian) Daughter of King Orsinio Ricci e Novabianco, sister to Bianca Estella Renata Novabianco. Second wife of Prince Pierro deMedici.

palazzo: (Italian) Palace.

patrín: (Romanes) Hidden, coded road "sign" the Romani leave for one another to indicate the best path or leave messages for one another.

pen: (Romanes) A term of affection or endearment, used as a suffix.

Petrus Lendaro: (Character—Romani) Clan chief, the *Beluni*'s son and uncle to Luciana and Alessandra.

Prunella Allegra Carafa e diVega: (Character—Tyrrhian) The contessa is maternal cousin to both Idala and Duca Stefano diLuna e di Drago. Bespelled, she ran off and married the conte who was shortly thereafter murdered, leaving her with land, in a very healthy financial situation, and a son, Urbano II. She disapproves of Luciana's lifestyle but is actually quite devoted to Stefano.

putsi: (Romanes) The proverbial "bag of tricks." A small pouch or bag carried by a Rom. The *putsi* normally contains items regularly used, as well as (or in a separate *putsi*) components and tokens of spiritual meaning. A *chovahano* always carries one, but especially when planning to work magic.

Reggio d'Calabria: (Italian/Tyrrhian) Southernmost Tyrrhian city on the Italian Peninsula.
Regina: (Italian) Queen.
Rizzo, Timoteo: (Character—Tyrrhian) Instructor for Dario Gian.
Rom: (Romanes) Adult (usually) male Gypsy.
Roma: (Romanes) Adult (usually) female Gypsy.
Romanes: Language of the Romani or relating to the gypsies.
Romani: Of or relating to the Gypsies.
Romero Gabera: (Character—Tyrrhian) Roman Catholic priest rescued by Maggiore di Montago's men and set up in Cattedrale d'Alaric.
Rossi, Duchessa Martina: (Character—Tyrrhian) Friend of the Crown and Regents politically. Being an only child, she inherited her father's title upon his death and is currently the only person of this rank to hold her title on her own rather than through marriage.
Sanzio, Rabbi Davizzo: (Character—Tyrrhian) Rabbi serving the palazzo *reale*
scorpinini: (Tyrrhian) A small, hand-held crossbow or latchet capable of being loaded easily and firing 30 to 40 lbs.
scrying: A method of divining the future via crystal ball, bowl of water, or other reflective surface.
Sebastiani, Duca: (Character—Tyrrhian) Senior noble and member of the Palantini.
Sergente: (Italian) Sergeant (military title)
Silvieri, Duca: (Character—Tyrrhian) Palantini member who supports the Princess Ortensia's claim to the throne.
Signore: (Italian) Sir, Mister.
Signora: (Italian) Honorific for a married woman.
sirena: (Italian) mermaid
sirena di mare: (Italian) mermaid (See *sirena, la sirena*)
Solaja Lendaro: (Character—Romani) *Beluni* of the Romani
spadaccino: (Italian) A sword wielding bully, swordsman.
Stefano Eneco Isaia di Drago: (Character—Tyrrhian) Duca di Drago, Colonello dagli Escalade e con di Palantini, husband of Luciana. Is a Colonel-in-Reserve in the Queen's Escalade and is the queen's older brother. A member of the Palantini. Major landholder with estates in central Tyrrhia and Salerno and several commercial

enterprises such as Banco di Drago, silk merchandising, horse breeding, and training, farming, etc.

strega: (Italian) Witch woman.

stregina: (Italian) Little witch.

stretto: (Italian) Strait, narrow body of water connecting two larger bodies of water.

Stretto d'Messina: (Italian/Tyrrhian) The Strait of Messina, the channel of rough water between the Italian Peninsula and Tyrrhia (Sicily) connecting the Tyrrhian and Ionian Seas in the Mediterranean. Part of the Levant.

stronza: (Italian) Bitch (as in the curse); strong-minded, uncontrollable woman.

Strozzini, Lord Roderigo: (Character—Tyrrhian) Bodyguard of the White King and, later, Stefano.

taverna: (Italian) Tavern, restaurant, inn.

Tyrrhia: (Italian) The country occupying the island opposite the Italian mainland coast (Sicily) and the southern tip of the Italian peninsula.

Tyrrhian: (Italian) Of Tyrrhia.

vardo: (Romanes) The wagons of the Romani which serve as their traveling homes.

venefica: (Italian) Witch who uses poison

vigilare: (Italian/Tyrrhian) Inspector, junior officer of the Escalade serving in a police-like capacity.

vitsa: (Romanes) Clan/family. Extended family unit. (Plural is *vitsi*.)

Your Excellency: Honorific used when addressing the Regent or Regent Guardian.

Your Grace: Honorific used when addressing a nobleman or noblewoman of the rank of duca or duchessa.

Your Highness: Honorific used when addressing a nobleman or noblewoman of the rank of prince or princess.

Your Majesty: Honorific used when addressing a nobleman of the rank of king or queen.

yurttas: (Turkish) Companion, compatriot

S.L. Farrell

The Nessantico Cycle

"[Farrell's] best yet, a delicious melange of politics, war, sorcery, and religion in a richly imagined world."
—George R. R. Martin,
#1 *New York Times* bestselling author

"Readers who appreciate intricate world building, intrigue, and action will immerse themselves effortlessly in this rich and complex story."
—*Publishers Weekly*

A MAGIC OF TWILIGHT
978-0-7564-0536-6

A MAGIC OF NIGHTFALL
978-0-7564-0599-1

A MAGIC OF DAWN
978-0-7564-0646-2

Tanya Huff

"The Gales are an amazing family, the aunts will strike fear into your heart, and the characters Allie meets are both charming and terrifying."

—#1 *New York Times* bestselling author
Charlaine Harris

"Thoughtful and leisurely, this fresh urban fantasy from Canadian author Huff features an ensemble cast of nuanced characters in Calgary, Alberta.... Fantasy buffs will find plenty of humor, thrills and original mythology to chew on, along with refreshingly three-dimensional women in an original, fully realized world." —*Publishers Weekly*

The Enchantment Emporium
978-0-7564-0605-9

The Wild Ways
978-0-7564-0763-6

The Future Falls
978-0-7564-0754-4

Joshua Palmatier

Shattering the Ley

"Palmatier brilliantly shatters genre conventions. . . . An innovative fantasy novel with a very modern feel. . . . For readers who are willing to tackle a more challenging fantasy, without clear heroes and obvious conflicts, Shattering the Ley is an excellent read." —SFRevu

"Shattering the Ley, the terrific new fantasy from Joshua Palmatier, is built of equal parts innocence, politics, and treachery. It features a highly original magic system, and may well be the only fantasy ever written where some of the most exciting scenes take place in a power plant. I couldn't put it down." —S. C. Butler, author of *Reiffen's Choice*

ISBN: 978-0-7564-0991-3

And don't miss the *Throne of Amenkor* trilogy!

THE SKEWED THRONE	978-0-7564-0382-9
THE CRACKED THRONE	978-0-7564-0447-5
THE VACANT THRONE	978-0-7564-0531-1

MICHELLE WEST
The House War

"Fans will be delighted with this return to the vivid and detailed universe of the *Sacred Hunt* and the *Sun Sword* series.... In a richly woven world, West pulls no punches as she hooks readers in with her bold and descriptive narrative."
—*Quill & Quire*

THE HIDDEN CITY	978-0-7564-0540-3
CITY OF NIGHT	978-0-7564-0644-8
HOUSE NAME	978-0-7564-0703-2
SKIRMISH	978-0-7564-0777-3
BATTLE	978-0-7564-0851-0
ORACLE	978-0-7564-1010-0

And don't miss *The Sun Sword*:

THE BROKEN CROWN	978-0-88677-740-1
THE UNCROWNED KING	978-0-88677-801-9
THE SHINING COURT	978-0-88677-837-8
SEA OF SORROWS	978-0-88677-978-8
THE RIVEN SHIELD	978-0-7564-0146-7
THE SUN SWORD	978-0-7564-0170-2

Plus, available August '16 in a new omnibus edition:
THE SACRED HUNT DUOLOGY 978-0-7564-1172-5
(*Hunter's Oath* / *Hunter's Death*)

Kari Sperring

Living with Ghosts

978-0-7564-0675-2

Finalist for the Crawford Award for First Novel

A Tiptree Award Honor Book

Locus Recommended First Novel

"This is an enthralling fantasy that contains horror elements interwoven into the story line. This reviewer predicts Kari Sperring will have quite a future as a renowned fantasist."
—*Midwest Book Review*

"A satisfying blend of well-developed characters and intriguing worldbuilding. The richly realized Renaissance style city is a perfect backdrop for the blend of ghostly magic and intrigue. The characters are wonderfully flawed, complex and multi-dimensional. Highly recommended!"
—*Patricia Bray, author of The Sword of Change Trilogy*

And now available:

The Grass King's Concubine

978-0-7564-0755-1

To Order Call: 1-800-788-6262
www.dawbooks.com

DAW 206